William Hazlitt, Michel de Montaigne

Works of Michael de Montaigne

Vol. I

William Hazlitt, Michel de Montaigne

Works of Michael de Montaigne
Vol. I

ISBN/EAN: 9783744700542

Printed in Europe, USA, Canada, Australia, Japan

Cover: Foto ©Andreas Hilbeck / pixelio.de

More available books at **www.hansebooks.com**

WORKS

OF

MICHAEL DE MONTAIGNE.

COMPRISING

HIS ESSAYS, JOURNEY INTO ITALY, AND LET-
TERS, WITH NOTES FROM ALL THE COM-
MENTATORS, BIOGRAPHICAL AND BIB-
LIOGRAPHICAL NOTICES, ETC.

By W. HAZLITT.

A NEW AND CAREFULLY REVISED EDITION,

EDITED BY

O. W. WIGHT.

Viresque acquirit eundo.

IN FOUR VOLUMES.
VOL. I.

NEW YORK
HURD AND HOUGHTON, 401 BROADWAY
BOSTON: WILLIAM VEAZIE
MDCCCLXIV

EDITOR'S ADVERTISEMENT.

THIS edition of Montaigne's Works is a reproduction, with changes in form, with corrections, and important additions, of Mr. William Hazlitt's edition, published by Templeman, in London.

The first three volumes contain the Essays; the fourth, and last, contains the Journey into Italy, and the Letters.

The Essays are preceded (at the beginning of vol. i.) by Mr. Hazlitt's Preface, and his Life of Montaigne. They are followed (at the end of vol. iii.) by an Appendix, and an Index to the Quotations.

The Appendix consists of two parts: A bibliographical notice of the various editions of Montaigne's Essays, and an account of the portraits of Montaigne. The notice of the various editions of the Essays is as complete as even a professional bibliographer could desire.

The Journey and the Letters (vol. iv.) are preceded by an Abridgment of Mr. Bayle St. John's recent Biography of Montaigne. They are followed by an Appendix and a very full Analytical Index to all the volumes.

The Abridgment of Mr. St. John's Biography will be found to contain all the facts concerning the Essayist, recently brought to light in France by Dr. Payen, M. Grün, and others. We have abridged the work considerably more than one half, but have aimed to omit nothing directly pertaining to Montaigne. We beg to recommend its perusal as a preparation for the Essays.

a

The final Appendix contains references to the principal opinions that have been passed upon Montaigne and his works. From the more important of these opinions copious extracts have been given. It is, we believe, the completest list of works to be consulted with reference to Montaigne, anywhere to be found.

The changes in form, then, consist in the distribution of the matter of Mr. Hazlitt's prolegomena into the two Appendices. We have omitted portions of his longer quotations—especially of those in foreign languages,—and have added much that is new.

As to the corrections, aided by our intelligent printers, we have verified the quotations in the Essays, not only by recurring to the best French editions, but also to the originals. In this important regard, we sincerely believe that our edition is the most accurate hitherto published, whether in French or English.

The completion—already indicated—of the bibliographical and critical notices, the Abridgment of Mr. St. John's Biography, and several letters more recently discovered, and published in no previous English edition of Montaigne's Works, constitute the additions we have made to the edition of Mr. Hazlitt.

The Indices have been prepared with unusual care. The typography speaks for itself. We hope the lovers of the wise old Gascon Essayist will find in this edition all they could desire, and to them we cordially dedicate it.

O. W. WIGHT.

February, 1859.

CONTENTS OF VOLUME I.

CONTENTS.

PREFACE.

THE first English translation of the Essays of Montaigne was executed by John Florio, Italian and French tutor to Prince Henry, son of James I., and is entitled: "The Essaies, or Morall, Politike, and Militarie Discourses of Lord Michael de Montaigne, Knight of the Noble Order of St. Michael, &c." It was first published in 1603, and was reprinted in 1613, and again in 1632. The form is a single volume folio, and it is dedicated, " To the most Royal and Renowned Majestie of the High-borne Princess Anna of Denmark, by the Grace of God, Queene of England, Scotland, France, and Ireland, &c." The Essays are prefaced by a copy of verses, in Italian, addressed to the same princess ; a preface to the reader, and some complimentary verses to " his deare brother and friende, Mr. John Florio," from " Samuel Daniel, one of the Gentlemen Extraordinary of her Majestie's most Royal Privie Chamber." There is also an engraved title-page, of the most ornate description.

The translation by Charles Cotton appeared somewhere about the year 1680, but I have not been able to ascertain the exact date. It is dedicated in the following terms :—

" *To the Right Honourable* GEORGE, *Marquiss, Earl, and Viscount Halifax, Baron of Eland, Lord Privy Seal, and one of his Majesty's most Honourable Privy Council.*

" My Lord,—If I have set down the only opportunity I ever had of kissing your lordship's hands amongst the happy encounters of my life, and take this occasion, so many years after, to tell you so, your lordship will not, I hope, think yourself injured by such a declaration from a man that honours you; nor condemn my ambition, when I publish to the world that I am not altogether unknown to you. Your lordship, peradventure, may have forgot a conversation so little worthy your remembrance; but the memory of your lordship's obliging fashion to me all that time, can never die with me; and though my acknowledgment arrives thus late at you, I have never left it at home when I went abroad into the best company. My lord, I cannot, I would not flatter you, I do not think your lordship capable of being flattered, neither am I inclined to do it to those that are; but I cannot forbear to say that I then received such an impression of your virtue and noble nature, as will stay with me for ever. This will either excuse the liberty I presume to take in this dedication, or, at least, make it no wonder; and I am so confident in your lordship's generosity, that I assure myself you will not deny your protection to a man whose greatest public crime is that of an ill writer. A better book (if there be a better of the kind—in the original I mean) had been a present more fitly suited to your lordship's quality and merit, and to my devotion. I could hardly wish it such; but as it is, I lay it at your lordship's feet, together with, my lord, your lordship's most humble and most obedient servant,

"CHARLES COTTON."

The dedication is followed by this letter from Lord Halifax :—

This for CHARLES COTTON, *Esq., at his House at Berisford.—To be left at Ashburne in Derbyshire.*

"Sir,—I have too long delayed my thanks to you for giving me such an obliging evidence of your remembrance; that alone would have been a welcome present, but when joined with the book in the world I am best entertained with, it raiseth a strong desire in me to be better known, where I am sure to be so much pleased. I have till now thought wit could not be translated, and do still retain so much of that opinion, that I believe it impossible, except by one whose genius cometh up to that of the author. You have the original strength of his thought, that it almost tempts a man to believe the transmigration of souls, and that his, being used to hills, is come to the moor-lands, to reward us here in England, for doing him more right than his country will afford him. He hath, by your means, mended his first edition. To transplant and make him ours is not only a valuable acquisition to us, but a just censure of the critical impertinence of those French scribblers who have taken pains to make little cavils and exceptions to lessen the reputation of this great man, whom nature hath made too big to confine him to the exactness of a studied style. He let his mind have its full flight, and showeth, by a generous kind of negligence, that he did not write for praise, but to give the world a true picture of himself and of mankind. He scorned affected periods, or to please the mistaken reader with an empty chime of words. He hath no affection to set himself out, and dependeth wholly upon the natural force of what is his own, and the excellent application of what he borroweth.

" You see, sir, I have kindness enough for Monsieur de Montaigne to be your rival; but nobody can now pretend to be in equal competition with you: I do willingly yield it is no small matter for a man to do to a more prosperous lover; and if you will repay this piece of justice with another, pray believe that he who can translate such an author without doing him wrong, must not only make me glad but proud of being his very humble servant, HALIFAX."

Mr. Cotton prefaces his translation in the following terms :—

" My design in attempting this translation was to present my country with a true copy of a very brave original. How far I have succeeded in that design, is left to every one to judge; and I expect to be the more gently censured, for having myself so modest an opinion of my own performance, as to confess that the author has suffered by me as well as the former translator; though I hope, and dare affirm, the misinterpretations I shall be found guilty of are neither so numerous nor so gross. I cannot discern my own errors; it were unpardonable in me if I could, and did not mend them; but I can see his (except when we are both mistaken) and those I have corrected; but I am not so ill-natured as to show where. In truth, both Mr. Florio and I are to be excused, where we miss the sense of the author, whose language is such, in many places, as grammar cannot reconcile, which renders it the hardest book to make a justifiable version of that I ever yet saw in that or any other language I understand; insomuch that, though I do think, and am pretty confident, I understand French as well as any man, I have yet sometimes been forced to grope at his meaning. Peradventure, the greatest critic would, in some place, have found my author abstruse enough. Yet are not these mistakes I speak of either so many or of so great importance, as to cast any scandalous blemish upon the book, but such as few readers can discover, and they that do will, I hope, easily excuse.

" The errors of the press I must in part take upon myself, living at so remote a distance from it, and supplying it with a slubbered copy from an illiterate amanuensis, the last of which is provided against in the quires that must succeed."

With reference to this translation, the Editor of a later edition remarks :—

" Mr. Cotton has, indeed, succeeded to a miracle in his translation of so celebrated a piece, and we are thoroughly persuaded that very few Frenchmen now living, were they to undertake the task, would find themselves capable of turning Montaigne's Essays into modern French with the same spirit and justice to the author ; but still our translator was not altogether infallible : he had certainly one of the most difficult books in the world to struggle with, and he complains of it himself in his preface ; it is no wonder, then, that he fell into such mistakes, which we should not only have fallen into ourselves, but probably have committed a great many more, had he not first trod the rugged way before us."

The same Editor states that he has altered Mr. Cotton's prose in above three thousand places, and changed his language where fifty years had rendered it obsolete or harsh.

In 1776 appeared a new edition of Cotton's translation, " with very considerable amendments and improvements from the most accurate and elegant French edition of Peter Coste." Of this version there was a reprint in 1811. It exhibits, in many places, just corrections of Mr. Cotton, where that gentleman has obviously misapprehended his author ; but it leaves a far greater number of errors untouched ; while its constant " improvements," in the way of modernizing Mr. Cotton's style and language, divest his translation of nearly all its spirit and *naïveté.* I also, no doubt, subject myself, in the opinion of many persons, to the charge of presumption, for having in my turn, ventured to correct Mr. Cotton; and, indeed, I have had it roundly objected, that in any way to alter Cotton is to damage Montaigne. Having, however, read and re-read both the original work and the translation, the careful comparison I have made of the two has shown me that not to alter Cotton, in many places, were gross injustice to Montaigne; and it is solely with this conviction that I have ventured upon the emendations here made. I most readily admit that Cotton's translation is, as a whole, a masterpiece; but then there occur in it, and at no very long intervals, instances of carelessness which greatly detract from the value of the translation, by making it fall short of, and in some cases absurdly misrepresent, the author's meaning. I could easily collect enough of these instances to make a new chapter in the Curiosities of Literature, but this would be as ungracious as it is unnecessary. One or two illustrations will, I conceive, suffice to form my justification. In chapter 55, Montaigne, chatting about smells, remarks, *En la plus espesse barbarie, les femmes Scythes*, &c. " in an age of the darkest barbarism, the Scythian women," &c.; which in Cotton's version assumes the following shape : " in the wildest parts of Barbary, the Scythian women," &c. In chapter 56, Montaigne, after quoting a curious opinion set forth by Margaret de Valois, who speaks of a young man's saying his prayers in a church regularly after visiting another man's wife, as a testimonial of singular devotion, says,—*Mais ce n'est pas par ceste preuve seulement qu'on pourroit vérifier que les femmes ne sont guères propres à traicter les matières de la théologie:* " But this is not the only proof we have that women are not very fit to treat of theological matters," which Cotton thus renders : " But it is by this proof only, that a man may conclude few men very fit to treat of theological affairs ! " Again, in chapter 57, Montaigne observes, *Il me semble que, considérant la foiblesse de nostre vie et à combien d'escueils ordinaires et naturels elle est exposée, on n'en debvroit pas faire si grande part à la naissance à l'oysifveté, et à l'apprentissage,*—" Methinks considering the frailty of life, and the many natural and ordinary wrecks to which it is exposed, we should not give so large a portion of it to idleness, either in childhood or in apprenticeship to the world,"—which Cotton reads,—" For the frailty of life, and the many natural and accidental rubs to which it is obnoxious and daily exposed, birth though noble, ought not to share so large a vacancy, and so tedious a course of education." Book ii. chapter 2, Montaigne says, *Laissons cette autre secte* (the Stoic) *faisant expresse profession de fierté ;*—" Let us leave that other sect, which makes an express profession of haughty superiority ; " which Cotton converts into this sentence :—" Let us leave that other sect, and make a downright profession of fierceness." In another place, Cotton subjects his author to a sad imputation : Montaigne (book ii. chapter 6), speaking of an accident that threw him into a swoon, says that, however, *Je m'advisais de commander qu'on donnast un cheval à ma femme, que je veoyois s'empestrer et se tracasser dans le chemin, qui est montueux et malaysé,* " I had so much sense about me as to order them to give a horse to my wife, who, I saw, was toiling and labouring along the road, which was a steep and uneasy one ; " this Cotton renders, " I had so much sense as to order that a horse I saw trip and falter on the way, which is mountainous and uneasy, should be given to my wife," &c.

I trust that these illustrations will suffice to justify me, even with the warmest admirers of Cotton,—and he has no sincerer admirer than myself,—for the departures which I have made from his translation. They are frequent, it is true, but for the most part, only where absolutely required to restore the author's meaning. The style and spirit of Cotton's version it would be impossible to improve upon ; and I have no hesitation in expressing the opinion that, the inaccuracies in question being now carefully corrected, the present edition of the essays of Montaigne fully comes up to the definition of a good translation suggested by Lord Woodhouselee, viz: "That in which the merit of the original work is so completely transfused into another language as to be as distinctly apprehended, and as strongly felt, by a native of the country to which that language belongs, as it is to those who speak the language of the original work." Here, indeed, as in the case of Ozell's Rabelais, the position might be even more strongly put.

THE LIFE

OF

MICHAEL DE MONTAIGNE.

MICHAEL DE MONTAIGNE was born, as he himself tells us, " betwixt eleven and twelve o'clock in the forenoon, the last of February, 1533." He was the third son of Pierre Eyquem,[1] *Ecuyer*,[2]
a brave and loyal soldier, who had seen service in the wars beyond the mountains, and had brought back with him from Italy
and Spain a cultivated mind. The description which his son gives
of him, is highly interesting: " He spoke little and well, ever
mixing his language with some illustration out of modern authors,
especially Spanish; and amongst them Marcus Aurelius was very
frequent in his mouth. His behaviour was grave, humble, and
modest; he was very solicitous of neatness and decency in his
person and dress, whether a-foot or on horseback. He was exceedingly punctual to his word, and of a conscience and religion
tending rather toward superstition than otherwise. For a man of
little stature, very strong, well proportioned, and well knit; of a
pleasing countenance, inclining to brown, and very adroit in all
noble exercises. I have yet in the house to be seen canes full of
lead, with which, they say, he exercised his arms for throwing the
bar or the stone; and shoes with leaden soles, to make him after-

---

[1] Scaliger, in the *Scaligerana Secunda*, is reported as saying that Montaigne's
father was a seller of herrings,—whether
in gross or detail is not specified,—but the
statement is a mere falsehood. In the
supplement to the *Chronique Bordelaise*,
by Jean Darnal, there is an account of the
various gradations by which Pierre Eyquem, *Seigneur de Montaigne*, ascended

from the office of first jurat of Bordeaux,
in 1530, to that of mayor, in 1538.

[2] Montaigne himself mentions the surname of Eyquem, though it does not appear that he ever made use of it himself.
He says the name was still borne by a
family in England; its English form was
probably Egham.

wards lighter for running or leaping. Of his vaulting he has left
little miracles behind him ; and I have seen him, when past threescore, laugh at our agilities, throw himself in his furred gown into
the saddle, make the tour of a table upon his thumbs, and scarce
ever mount the stairs up to his chamber without taking three or
four steps at a time."

This gentleman, with some instinctive prescience apparently, of
his son Michael's mental superiority, formed a wish to have him
educated in a manner altogether different from the routine then
gone through. Even before his birth, he consulted learned and
clever men on the subject, and on these consultations and his own
admirable judgment, he formed a system, as Mrs. Shelley observes,
such as may in some sort be considered the basis of Rousseau's ;
and which shows that, however we may consider one age more
enlightened than another, the natural reason of men of talent
leads them to the same conclusions, whether living in an age when
warfare, party struggles, and the concomitant ignorance, were
rife, or when philosophers set the fashion of the day ; " the good
father that God gave me," says he, " who has nothing of me but
the acknowledgment of his bounty, but truly 'tis a very hearty one,
sent me from my cradle to be brought up in a poor village of his,
and there continued me all the while I was at nurse, and even
longer, bringing me up to the meanest and most common way of
living. This humour of his yet aimed this end, to make me familiar with those people, and that condition of men, which most
need our assistance ; believing that I should be more holden to
regard them who extended their arms to me, than those who
turned their backs upon me ; and for this reason also it was that
he provided me godfathers of the meanest fortune, to oblige and
bind me to them."

Next came the question of education. The Greek and Latin
tongues, our author's father felt, are an acquisition of great worth ;
but at the same time they were somewhat dearly bought under the
system which, at that period, universally prevailed, and does so
even now, to a great extent. The elder Montaigne's own reading
being confined to works written in the living tongues, he was the
more anxious that his son should be early made acquainted with
the languages of Athens and Rome, and he meditated long on the
received modes of introducing youth into the chief vestibules of
knowledge. He was struck by the time given to, and the an-

noyances a child suffers in, the acquirement of the dead languages, and had thus been exaggerated to him as a cause why the moderns were so inferior to the ancients in greatness of soul and wisdom. But the difficulty which he felt, the expedient he devised to obviate it, and the result of this expedient, cannot be better told than in Montaigne's own words:—

" My late father having made the most precise inquiry that any man can possibly make amongst men of the greatest learning and judgment, of an exact method of education, was by them cautioned of the inconvenience then in use, and informed that the tedious time we applied to the learning of the languages of those people who, themselves, had them for nothing, was the sole cause we could not arrive to the grandeur of soul and perfection of knowledge of the ancient Greeks and Romans ; I do not, however, believe that to be the only cause ; the expedient my father, however, found out for this was that, in my infancy, and before I began to speak, he committed me to the care of a German (who since died a famous physician in France), totally ignorant of our language, but very fluent and a great critic in Latin. This man, whom he had sent for out of his own country, and whom he entertained, at a very great salary, for this only end, had me continually with him. To whom there were also joined two others of the same nation, but of inferior learning, to attend me, and sometimes to relieve him ; who all of them conversed with me in no other language but Latin. As to the rest of his family, it was an inviolable rule that neither himself, nor my mother, nor man, nor maid, should speak any thing, in my company, but such Latin words as every one had learnt to gabble with me. It is not to be imagined how great an advantage this proved to the whole family ; my father and my mother, by this means, learning Latin enough to understand it perfectly well, and to speak it to such a degree as was sufficient for any necessary use ; as also those of the servants did who were most frequently with me. To be short, we did *Latin* it at such a rate that it overflowed to all the neighbouring villages, where there yet remain, and have established themselves by custom, several Latin appellations of artisans and their tools. As for myself, I was above six years of age before I understood either French or Perigordian any more than Arabic, and without art, book, grammar, or precept, whipping, or the expense of a tear, had by that time learned to speak as pure Latin as my master

himself. If, for example, they were to give me a theme, after the
College fashion, they gave it to others in French, but to me they
gave it in the worst Latin, to turn it into that which was pure and
good; and Nicholas Grouchy, who wrote a book *de Comitiis Romanorum;* William Guerente, who has written a Commentary
upon Aristotle; George Buchanan, that great Scotch poet, and
Marc Antony Muret, whom both France and Italy have acknowledged for the best orator of his time, my domestic tutors [at col-
lege], have all of them often told me that I had in my infancy that
language so very fluent and ready that they were afraid to enter
into discourse with me. Buchanan, whom I since saw attending
the late Mareschal de Brissac, then told me that he was about to
write a Treatise of Education, the example of which he intended
to take from mine, for he was then tutor to that Count de Brissac,
who afterwards proved so valiant and so brave a gentleman."

"As to Greek, of which I have but little smattering, my father
also designed to have taught it me by art, but in a new way, and
as a sort of sport; tossing out declensions to and fro, after the
manner of those who, by certain games, at tables and chess, learn
geometry and arithmetic; for he, amongst other rules, had been
advised to make me relish science and duty by an unforced will,
and of my own voluntary motion, and to educate my soul in all
liberty and delight, without any severity or constraint. Which he
was an observer of to such a degree, even of superstition, that
some being of opinion it troubles and disturbs the brains of children suddenly to wake them in the morning, and to snatch them
violently and over-hastily from sleep (wherein they are much more
profoundly involved than we), he caused me to be waked by the
sound of some musical instrument, and was never unprovided of a
musician for that purpose. By which example you may judge of
the rest, this alone being sufficient to recommend both the prudence and affection of so good a father; who, therefore, is not to
be blamed if he did not reap the fruits answerable to so excellent
a culture. Of which, two things were the cause: first, a sterile
and improper soil; for though I was of a strong and healthful constitution, and of a disposition tolerably gentle and tractable, yet I
was, withal, so heavy, idle, and sluggish, that they could not rouse
me even to any exercise of recreation, nor get me out to play.
What I saw, I saw clear enough; and under this lazy complexion
nourished a bold imagination, and opinions above my age. I had

a slothful wit, that would go no faster than it was led, a slow understanding, a languishing invention, and, above all, an incredible defect of memory; so that it is no wonder if, from all these, nothing considerable could be extracted. Secondly, like those who, impatient of a long and steady cure, submit to all sorts of prescriptions and receipts, the good man being extremely timorous of any way failing in a thing he had so wholly set his heart upon, suffered himself, at last, to be overruled by the common opinion, which always follows the lead of what has gone on before, like cranes; and falling in with the method of the time, having no longer about him those persons he had brought out of Italy, and who had given him his first models of education, he sent me, at six years of age, to the College of Guienne, at that time the best and most flourishing in France. And there it was not possible to add any thing to the care he had to provide me the most able tutors, with all other circumstances of education, reserving also several particular rules contrary to the College practice; but so it was that, with all these precautions, it was a College still. My Latin immediately grew corrupt, and by discontinuance, I have since lost all manner of use of it; and so this new plan of education served me to no other end than only, at my first coming, to prefer me to the first forms; for at thirteen years old, that I left the College, I had gone through my whole course, as they call it, and, in truth, without any manner of improvement, that I can honestly brag of, in all this time." The vigorous idiom of Tacitus and Seneca, which had thus become his natural language, had doubtless, through life, an influence in him greatly over the French, which he learned at a later period, as it were a foreign tongue, and which, having only just been nationalized by Francis I., was as yet any thing but a *langage fait*, took the more freely, in an organ still young, the form given it by the earlier impressions. Locke, in his Treatise on Education, seems to have paid great attention to that of Montaigne; so far admitting the plan pursued with our Essayist, that, while he requires that a child should, in the first instance, learn his maternal language, he at the same time lays it strongly down that he should be provided with a master to teach him Latin also, by conversing with him in that tongue.

As a child, though of a gentle and tractable disposition, it was difficult to rouse him from his quiet, even to join in boyish games; but when he once began to play, then all the sports of his youth-

ful companions seemed to him in the light of serious actions; and
he had an entire repugnance to mix up with them any finesse or
trickery, going always the straight way to play as to work, and
keeping to it. Yet his mind, which seemed inactive, did not fail
to form judgments upon the objects which he became acquainted
with, and he digested his thoughts freely and at leisure. "Yet for
all this heavy disposition of mine," says he, "my mind, when retired into itself, was not altogether idle, nor wholly deprived of
solid inquiry, nor of certain and clear judgments about those objects it could comprehend, and could also without any helps digest
them; but, amongst other things, I do really believe it had been
totally impossible to have made it to submit by violence and force.
Shall I here acquaint you," he adds, "with one faculty of my
youth? I had great boldness and assurance of countenance, and
to that a flexibility of voice and gesture to any part I undertook
to act; for before

> Alter ab undecimo tum me vix ceperat annus,

I played the chief parts in the Latin tragedies of Buchanan, Guerente, and Muret, that were acted in our college of Guienne with
very great form; wherein Andreas Goveanus, our principal, as in
all other parts of his undertaking, was, without comparison, the
best of that employment in France, and I was looked upon as one
of his chief actors." The first taste for reading that Montaigne
acquired, arose in the manner which he himself thus relates:
"The first thing that gave me any taste of books was the pleasure
I took in reading the fables of Ovid's Metamorphoses; and with
them I was so taken that, being but seven or eight years old, I
would steal from all other diversions to read them, both by reason
that this was my own natural language, the easiest book that I was
acquainted with, and for the subject the most accommodated to
the capacity of my age; for as for Lancelot of the Lake, Amadis
of Gaul, Huon of Bordeaux, and such trumpery, which children
are most delighted with, I had never so much as heard their
names, no more than I yet know what they contain; so exact was
the discipline wherein I was brought up. This made me think
the less of the other lessons prescribed me; and here it was infinitely to my advantage to have to do with an understanding tutor,
who was wise enough to connive at this and other truantries of the
same nature; for by this means I ran through Virgil's Æneid,

and then Terence, and then Plautus, and some Italian comedies,
allured by the pleasure of the subject; whereas had he been so
foolish as to have taken me off this diversion, I do really believe I
had brought nothing away from the College but a hatred of books,
as almost all our young gentlemen do. But he carried himself
very discreetly in that business, seeming to take no notice, and
heightened my appetite by allowing me only such time for this
reading as I could steal from my regular studies. For the chief
things my father expected from them to whom he had delivered
me for education, was affability of manners and good humour;
and, to say the truth, my temper had no other vice but sloth and
vant of mettle. The fear was not that I should do ill, but that I
should do nothing. Nobody suspected that I should be wicked,
but most thought I should be useless; they foresaw idleness, but
no malice in my nature; and I find it falls out accordingly. There
is nothing," he adds, " like alluring the appetite and affection, otherwise you make nothing but so many asses laden with books, and
by virtue of the lash give them their pocket full of learning to
keep." Montaigne thus grew towards maturity, with an education more like that of our day than of his own. In the management of those first years of life, it is impossible not to see the
source of much that afterwards marked him out from others. The
main principle of teaching him every thing without requiring any
conscious effect, or producing any sense of struggle on his part,
doubtless disinclined him, as such a system always must, to encounter hardships, or engage in conflict; whence partly the indolence, though a busy indolence, of his life; hence, too, in a great
degree, his reluctance to admit any views of man and duty which
required him to regard life as a long battle against ignorance and
weakness, in a word, against evil; and which estimate the highest
and best of our thoughts and feelings as only then pure and active, when consciously toiling against the stream of self-indulgence.
But as his education gave him not only ease, but also knowledge,
and opened to him an inexhaustible source of mental pleasure, no
wonder that he became a literary epicure, and made the gratification of every whim in speculation, and to a great degree in practice, the only aim, if so it can be called, of his existence. Thanks,
however, to the sound structure of mind and body, to the sturdy
manly nature which he partly inherited from his father, partly
owed to his care, to the strong and honest minds and the admir-

able books with which he was early familiarized, there is under
and around all this capricious idleness predominant, clear, homely
sense, and apprehensiveness for truth, accompanied by sincerity
and kindness of will, the natural yoke-fellows of such endowments,
which give both the most sterling value and the most exquisite
charm to his works.

On attaining the age of thirteen, Montaigne's taste for study,
and perhaps his dislike to military discipline and vexation, were
so decided that, although the son of a gentleman and soldier of
the sixteenth century, he preferred the business of a law-court to
that of a camp; and although the same distaste for restraint must
have disinclined him for the study of the mass of custumal juris-
prudence which at that time overwhelmed not only justice, but
law, he went through the requisite preparations, and became, in
the year 1554, one of the counsellors of the Parliament of Bordeaux, to which office he, in all probability, succeeded in place of
his paternal uncle Busaguet, who died young. The functions of
this office he fulfilled until the death of an elder brother gave him
an independent income. He has been accused by Balzac of
allowing his quality of gentleman to make him so ashamed of
having filled this situation, that he never makes mention of it; but
this is a mistake, for even so late as 1563, in writing publicly to
his father, he signs himself, counsellor of Bordeaux. It is true
that, in the course of so egotistical a work as the Essays, he but
very rarely refers to this period of his life; but whatever may
have been his feelings with regard to his own professional career,
it is certain that, while engaged in it, he gained, and through life
retained, a bitter and scornful disgust at the mass of arbitrary
pedantries and cruel wrongs involved in the system which then
regulated all the social interests of his countrymen. Notwithstanding the ordonnance of Francis I., in 1539, by which all
public acts were ordered to be drawn up in French, these acts
continued in Gascony to be written in Latin. Montaigne pro-
tested against this practice: " What can be more strange," he
observes, " than to see a people obliged to obey and pay a reverence to laws they never heard of, and to be bound in all their
affairs, both private and public, as marriages, donations, wills,
sales, and purchases, to rules they cannot possibly know, being
neither writ nor published in their own language, and of which
they have, of necessity, to purchase both the interpretation and

the use? He was, besides, a warm advocate for simplifying the law and making it uniform. He observes, in his Essays, that there are more books to explain law-books than books on any other subject. There is no end, he says, of commentary upon commentary.

During his life as a counsellor at Bordeaux, he seems to have made, probably on business connected with his office, frequent journeys to Paris and to the Court, where his conversational powers obtained for him the favour and patronage of Henry II., by whom he was appointed a gentleman of the king's bed-chamber. From this monarch, also, according to Dom de Vienne, he received the collar of the order of St. Michael, which, when young, he tells us, he had coveted above all things, it being at that time the utmost mark of honour among the French nobles, and rarely bestowed; but at the time Montaigne received it, it had got into discredit. Pasquier, his contemporary and personal friend, tells us, however, that this latter distinction was conferred upon Montaigne by Charles IX. As to his fulfilment of his duties, his close intimacy with the Sieur de Pibrac and Paul de Foix, his countrymen and fellow-counsellors, and above all, his familiar connection with the Chancellor de l'Hospital and de Thou, announce the high degree of confidence with which he was honoured, more especially as a magistrate representing the interests of an important town, at a period full of the most important events. It is quite clear that he was at different times consulted by men of a prominent position in that most troublous and intricate whirl of politics which then agitated France. The result for us is, that Montaigne knew mankind on many sides, and in the most different classes. He was in a station to associate early with the highest ranks, even with kings, and of habits and a temper that smoothed his intercourse even with the lowest. He had learning to make him an apt companion for scholars; practical shrewdness and knowledge to procure him respect from the world; and the secure and easy circumstances which gave him perfect leisure to indulge his tastes and fancies, to speculate upon those of others. But the most important event of his counsellor's life at Bordeaux, was the friendship he there formed with Stephen de la Boëtie, an affection which makes a streak of light in modern biography almost as beautiful as that left us by Lord Brook and Sir Philip Sidney. Our essayist and his friend esteemed, before they saw each other.

La Boëtie had written a little work, entitled *De la Servitude Volontaire*, [1] in which Montaigne recognized sentiments congenial with his own, and which, indeed, bespeak a soul formed in the mould of classic times. Of Montaigne, La Boëtie had also heard accounts, which made him eager to behold him, and at length they met at a large entertainment given by one of the magistrates of Bordeaux. They saw and loved, and were thenceforward all in all to each other. The picture that Montaigne in his Essays draws of this friendship is in the highest degree beautiful and touching; nor does La Boëtie's idea of what is due to this sacred bond betwixt soul and soul, fall short of the grand perception which filled the exalted mind of his friend. In the treatise just named, its youthful author thus expresses himself on the subject: " Friendship is a sacred name; it is a holy thing; it never arises but between good men; exists only by mutual esteem; supports itself not so much by services on either part as by goodness of life. That which makes one friend certain of the other, is the knowledge he has of his integrity. The sureties which he has for him are his good disposition, fidelity, and steadfastness. There cannot be friendship where there is cruelty, where there is disloyalty, where there is injustice." Indeed, judging from the whole of this brief but admirable work, La Boëtie, observes Mrs. Shelley, evidently deserved the high esteem in which Montaigne held him, though apparently very dissimilar from him in character. Boldness and vigour mark the thoughts and style; love of freedom, founded on a generous independence of soul, breathes in every line; the bond between him and Montaigne rested on the integrity and lofty nature of their dispositions, on their talents, on the warmth of heart that distinguished both, and a fervid imagina-

1 This little book, observes a writer in the *Westminster Review*, seems to have been written when the author was only sixteen. It is a declamation against the lawless government of many by one, with much that recalls Tacitus, and something that resembles the political writings of Milton, but having a pervading tone of idle, imitative rhetoric, which is all but inevitable in the work of one so young. Though doubtless in some degree prompted by the miseries of France in that day, it is chiefly a reproduction of the sonorous and statutesque republicanism of the classical writers; the eloquent, headlong, youthful utterance of a sharp, clear brain and glowing heart, to whom the world was yet but a stage for declamation, while almost all the outward facts of life lay concealed from him, behind the scene-curtain. Warmth and reasonableness are finely blended in the book, though weakened by a kind of abstract vagueness, a dateless nowhere-ness of the facts and topics. There is no trace of the wayward, fantastic self-questioning which gives such charm and peculiarity to Montaigne. But probably, at La Boëtie's age, his friend's writings would have shown much less of this than now appears in them. For passionate life and keenness of style, the " Treatise " is more remarkable even than the Essays.

tion, without which the affections seldom rise into enthusiasm. The friendship of Montaigne for this admirable person yielded only in force to his tenderness for his father, if even to that; for while, it is true, he speaks of his father, in several places of his Essays, with the highest veneration and love, to Friendship he dedicates one whole chapter, in which it is observable that his style rises and becomes as energetic as it is full of soul. Nor was this friendship, glowing and enthusiastic as it was, a passing effervescence. Nine years after the death of La Boëtie,—whose calm and considerate last moments, Montaigne, in a letter to his father, has described in the most eloquent and touching manner,—he tells us: " From the day that I lost him, I have only had a sorrowful and languishing life ; and the very pleasures that present themselves to me, instead of administering any thing of consolation, double my affliction for his loss. We were halves throughout, and to that degree that, methinks, by outliving him, I defraud him of his part." Nay, even eighteen years after, during his journey in Italy, in 1580, he tells us that, while writing to the Cardinal d'Ossat, the recollection of his loss came across his mind, and *il se trouva mal, en pensant à son ami.* Montaigne did not regard women as capable of the same high order of friendship, but his physical complexion was such as made him fond of female society, and the character of his mind led him more especially to seek the friendship of those ladies of his time who were distinguished for their wit and imagination, or for their graver powers of mind. It was this that induced him, in the one case, to pay his court to the authoress of the Heptameron, the gay and *spirituelle* Marguerite de Valois, at whose request he wrote one of the longest and most carefully studied chapters of his Essays ; and, in the other, to address to Diana de Foix his chapter On the Education of Children, and to Madame d'Estissac that On the Affection of Fathers to their Children. It is possible that his notion of a perfect tender friendship, which he in vain sought for among his female acquaintance, might have been realized in Mademoiselle de Gournay, had she been born twenty-five years earlier, and, indeed, Madame de Bourdic, in her *Éloge de Montaigne,* describes the lady in question as being in existence at the same time with La Boëtie, and sharing with him the heart of Montaigne ; but this is a mere poetic fiction, the offspring of a wild enthusiasm.

Montaigne married at the age of thirty-three ; but, as he informs us, not of his own wish or choice. "Might I have had my own will," says he, "I would not have married Wisdom herself, if she would have had me : but 'tis to much purpose to evade it, the common custom and use of life will have it so; the most of my actions are guided by example, not choice. And yet I did not go to it of my own voluntary motion ; I was led and drawn to it by extrinsic occasions; and I was persuaded to it when worse prepared and more backward than I am at present, that I have tried what it is. And as great a libertine as I am taken to be," he adds, "I have in truth more strictly observed the laws of marriage than I either promised or expected." His wife, Françoise de la Chassaigne, was the daughter of Joseph de la Chassaigne, one of the most celebrated counsellors of the Parliament of Bordeaux, and sister of Geoffroi de la Chassaigne, Sieur de Pressac, author of several works. She found, in Montaigne, a husband kind and considerate, though not enthusiastically attached. We read, for instance, that on the occasion of an accident of which he gives a picturesque description, the first thing he did on arousing from the swoon into which he had fallen, was to give a horse to his wife, "who he saw was toiling and labouring along the road, which was a steep and uneasy one." Again, when at Paris, he heard of the death of a daughter of theirs, he sent his wife a letter full of sympathy and kindness, accompanying it with Plutarch's Letter of Consolation to his Wife, written under similar circumstances.

It was from the same natural kindness and ready disposition to oblige and please those whom he loved, that at the desire of his father he translated and addressed to him the Natural Theology of Raymond Sebond. The elder Montaigne, animated with the ardour which influenced Francis I. in encouraging literature, had for a long time kept his house open to learned men, though not a learned man himself. Among others, he had received as a guest Peter Bunel, who warmly recommended to him this work of Sebond's as one very useful to read, at a period when the innovations of Luther were beginning to get into credit, and menaced to shake in many places the ancient faith. Montaigne hastened to translate the volume, and presented it, in its French dress, to his father, who was so delighted with its contents that he had it printed and published. It is from proofs drawn from natural reason that Sebond, after the example of Raymond Lully, here undertook, not to explain the mysteries, but simply to oppose to the innovators, in support of the old faith, the same reason with which they sought to combat it. The work had great success, especially with the ladies; and Montaigne, as their champion, and as the vindicator of the book he had translated, afterwards came forward in its defence, both against those who charged the author with unlicensed boldness in his opinions, and those who sneered at his arguments as devoid of strength or foundation.

It was soon after the publication of this translation that Montaigne succeeded to the château and estate [1] of Montaigne, in consequence of the death of his excellent father, who, according to our essayist, was somewhat apprehensive that the inheritance in the hands of his son Michael, would be wasted by his indolence and carelessness; but Montaigne's faults were negative; and he easily brought himself to regard his income as the limit of his expenses, and even kept within it. His hatred of business and trouble, joined to sound common sense, led him to understand that ease could be best attained by limiting his desires to his means; and by the degree of order necessary to know what these means were; and his practice accorded with this conclusion.

One of the first things that engaged our author's attention, on thus becoming entirely master of himself, was the publication of La Boëtie's *Opuscula*, which, together with his library, that beloved friend had bequeathed him, and which he now sent forth to the world, dedicated to the writer's relations. To the volume thus published, Montaigne added his own account, as addressed to his father, of the circumstances of La Boëtie's death; but, probably out of consideration for those of the author's connections who were attached to the court or to the public service, Montaigne did not deem it advisable to reprint on this occasion the Treatise on Voluntary Servitude, which he perhaps thought might be made a sinister use of by party spirit, in a time of fierce faction and civil trouble.

From this period Montaigne seems to have lived chiefly at his château. At the time of his succeeding to this property, he was under thirty-nine, and thenceforth his time was chiefly spent in reading and writing. It is not to be supposed, however, that he loved a wholly sedentary and inactive life. Though he adhered

---

[1] The estate to which he succeeded comprised the château, and eighteen *métairies*, or farms, around it, comprising one or two small villages. The revenue thence accruing was about 2000 crowns of the money of the time.

to no party, and showed no enthusiasm in the maintenance of his opinions, his disposition was inquisitive to eagerness, ardent, and fiery. The troubles that desolated his country throughout his life, fostered the activity of mind of which his writings are so full. He often travelled about France, and, above all, was well acquainted with Paris and the Court. He loved the capital, and calls himself a Frenchman only through his love of Paris, which he names the glory of France, and an ornament of the world. In one of his essays, he says that a chief reason with him for wishing to live longer, is that he may see the completion of the Pont-Neuf, which was then in course of construction. He attended the Court at the same time with the famous Duc de Guise, and the King of Navarre, afterwards Henry IV. He predicted that the death of one or the other of these princes could alone put an end to the civil war, and he even foresaw the likelihood there was that Henry of Navarre would change his religion. At a later period he was at Blois, when the Duc de Guise was assassinated; and he was a contemporary of the massacre of St. Bartholomew, at the particular period of which our philosopher, humane from sentiment, tolerant from reason, kept himself at home, apart altogether from either party, and attached to his king by an affection, as he says, " purely and entirely legitimate and political; neither attached nor repelled by private interest." In the whole course of the fierce contest between the Catholic party and the Huguenot, Montaigne, though a firm Catholic, abstained from mingling in the mortal struggles that were going on. One of his reasons for not attacking the Huguenots may perhaps be found in the circumstance that one of his brothers, M. de Beauregard, had been converted to the reformed religion. So high an opinion, however, was entertained, not only of his knowledge of the events that were passing around, but of his honesty and good faith, that he was requested to draw up the history of them, but he declined. " I am solicited," he says, " to write the affairs of my own time, by some who fancy I look upon them with an eye less blinded with prejudice or partiality than another, and have a clearer insight into them, by reason of the free access fortune has given me to the heads of both factions; but they do not consider that to purchase the glory of Sallust I would not give myself the trouble, sworn enemy as I am to all obligation, assiduity, and perseverance; besides that there is nothing so contrary to my style as a continued and extended narrative, I so often interrupt and cut myself short in my writing only for want of breath."

We have now come to a period in the life of Montaigne, to which the highest interest attaches. It was towards the year 1572 that he commenced, in his retreat, the composition of his Essays. "When I lately retired myself to my own house," says he, "with a resolution, as much as possibly I could, to avoid all manner of concern in affairs, and to spend in privacy and repose the little remainder of time I have to live, I fancied I could not more oblige my mind than to suffer it at full leisure to entertain and divert itself, which I hoped it might now the better be intrusted to do, as being by time and observation become more settled and mature; but I find,

> Variam semper dant otia mentem,

that, quite the contrary, it is like a horse that has broken from his rider, who voluntarily runs into a much wilder career than any horseman would put him to, and creates me so many chimeras and fantastic monsters, one upon another, without order or design, that, the better at leisure to contemplate their strangeness and absurdity, I have begun to commit them to writing, hoping in time to make them ashamed of themselves." "This fagoting-up of so many divers pieces, he adds elsewhere, "is done in this way: I never set pen to paper but when too great idleness becomes troublesome, and never anywhere but at home; so that it is made up at several interruptions and intervals. I never correct my first by my second conceptions; perhaps I may alter a word or so; but it is only to vary the phrase, and not to omit my former meaning." In this particular, however, Montaigne's statement of the matter is not consistent with fact; for the edition of 1588, for example, contains several passages, which the author afterwards altered or entirely omitted, to the advantage certainly of the work. The materials which he possessed for adding to the wealth of his own mind, the stores of classic intellect and experience, were unusually great for that period. His own library was already a good one, when it was considerably enlarged by the collection of books bequeathed him by La Boëtie. In this library he spent the principal portion of his time, reading, meditating, and writing, or dictating. His custom was to walk about as he read and meditated, "for," says he, "my thoughts go to sleep if I sit down." His mode of proceeding appears to have been altogether of a most desultory character. He would turn over the leaves, now of one book, then of another, without order or apparent design; now he noted, then he meditated, and anon dictated, as he walked, what he had thus digested, more or less maturely. He had a memory, rather of ideas, than of words; what remained in his mind he no longer remembered as the property of another. But let us hear his own account of the matter: " I make no doubt but that I often happen to speak of things that are much better, and more truly handled by those who are masters of the trade. You have here purely an essay of my natural, and not acquired, parts; and whoever shall take me tripping in my ignorance, will not in any sort displease me; for I should be very unwilling to become responsible to another for my writings, who am not so to myself, nor satisfied with them. Whoever goes in quest of knowledge, let him fish for it where it is to be found; there is nothing I so little profess. These are fancies of my own, by which I do not pretend to discover things, but to lay open myself. They may, perhaps, one day be known to me, or have formerly been, according as fortune has put me upon a place where they have been explained; but I have forgotten them; and if I am a man of some reading, I am a man of no retention; so that I can promise no certainty, if not to make known to what point the knowledge I now have rises. Therefore let nobody insist upon the matter I write, but my method in writing it; let them observe, in what I borrow, if I have known how to choose what is proper to raise or help the invention, which is always my own; for I make others say for me what, either for want of language or want of sense, I cannot so well myself express. I do not number my borrowings, I weigh them. And, had I designed to raise their value by their number, I had made them twice as many. They are all, or within a very few, so famed and ancient authors, that they seem, methinks, themselves sufficiently to tell who they are, without giving me the trouble. In reasons, comparisons, and arguments, if I transplant any into my own soil, and confound them amongst my own, I purposely conceal the author, to awe the temerity of those forward censurers that fall upon all sorts of writings, particularly the late ones, of men yet living, and in the vulgar tongue, forsooth, which puts, it would seem, every one into a capacity of judging, and which seems to convict the authors themselves of vulgar conception and design.

I would have them give Plutarch a fillip upon my nose, and put themselves in a heat with railing against Seneca, when they think they rail at me. I must shelter my own weakness under these great reputations. I shall love any one that can unplume me, that is, by clearness of understanding and judgment, and by the sole distinction of the force and beauty of reason; for I, who, for want of memory, am at every turn at a loss to pick them out by their national livery, am yet wise enough to know, by the measure of my own abilities, that my soil is incapable of producing any of those rich flowers that I there find set and growing; and that all the fruits of my own growth are not worth any one of them. I have no other officer to put my writings in rank and file, but fortune. As things come into my head I heap them in; sometimes they advance in whole bodies, sometimes in single files. I am content that every one should see my natural and ordinary pace, ill as it is. I let myself jog on at my own rate and ease. Neither are these subjects which a man is not permitted to be ignorant in, or casually, and at a venture, to discourse of. I could wish to have a more perfect knowledge of things, but I will not buy it so dear as it will cost. My design is to pass over easily, and not laboriously, the remainder of my life. There is nothing that I will break my brain about; no, not knowledge, of what price soever."

The extraordinary knowledge that Montaigne displays of man, in all his several relations, and the infinite variety of historical illustrations, ancient and modern, foreign and domestic, that he adds to his own experiences, have induced many persons to suppose that he had travelled beyond the limits of France at the time he composed his work, and M. Villemain, among others, appears to entertain this opinion, but it is certain that Montaigne's journey into Germany, Switzerland, and Italy, was posterior to the publication of the Essays, in March, 1580. That which has deceived some biographers is the circumstance, that several features in the Journey were inserted by Montaigne himself, as early as 1582, in the edition of the Essays which preceded that wherein that work received the last form it assumed under its author's hands. But this circumstance proves nothing; for in every new edition that Montaigne published, he added something or other, by way of *bonus*, to those former purchasers, who might thereby be induced to buy a copy of the new edition. But Montaigne had travelled sufficiently about France, and in sufficiently stirring times, to give him an extensive and varied insight into human character; indeed, for that matter, there is hardly a village so small, wherein a man who understandingly seeks for this sort of information may not learn a great deal, and our philosopher was precisely the person to obtain it. "I observe in my travels this custom," he says, " ever to learn something from the information of those with whom I converse (which is the best school of all others), and to put my company upon those subjects they are the best able to speak of." We have mentioned his frequent visits to Paris, where, indeed, his attendance was required at intervals, by the place he filled of one of the gentlemen of the king's bed-chamber. He was at Bar-le-Duc with Henry II., and he accompanied Charles IX. to Rouen, probably at the time of the declaration of the majority of this prince, to whom, at our author's instance, were presented the South American Indians, of whom he speaks in his chapter *On Cannibals.* The Abbé Talbert, in his *Éloge de Montaigne*, speaks of it as a well-known fact, that Montaigne not only acted as secretary to Catherine de Medici, when she wrote her letter of instructions to Charles IX., but that the letter itself was the composition of our essayist, a statement which some of the recent editors of Montaigne have concurred in.

As Montaigne advanced in life, he lost his health. The stone, which he believed he inherited from his father, and painful nephritic colics that seized him at intervals, put his philosophy to the test. He would not allow his illness to disturb the usual tenor of his life, and, above all, refused medical aid, having also inherited, he tells us, from his father, a contempt for physicians. There was a natural remedy, however, by which he laid great store, one much in favour at all times on the continent,—mineral and thermal springs. The desire to try these, as well as a wish to quit for a time his troubled country, and the misery multiplying around him, caused him to make a journey into Italy. His love of novelty and of seeing strange things sharpened his taste for travelling; and, as a slighter motive, he was glad to throw household cares aside ; for, though the pleasures of command were something, he received perpetual annoyances from the indigence and sufferings of his tenants, or the quarrels of his neighbours ; to travel was to get rid of all this at once.

Of course his mode of proceeding was peculiar : he had a great distaste for coaches or litters; even a boat was not quite to his mind; and he only really liked travelling on horseback. Then he let every whim sway him as to the route; it gave him no annoyance, but rather pleasure, to go out of his way; if the road was bad to the right, he took that to the left; if he felt too unwell to mount his horse, he remained where he was till he got better; if he found he had passed by any thing he wished to see, he turned back. On the present occasion, his mode of travelling was, as usual, regulated by convenience: sumpter-mules or hired vehicles carried the luggage, while he proceeded on horseback. He appears to have been accompanied on this journey by four gentlemen, his brother, the Sieur de Mattecoulon, M. d'Estissac, M. de Caselis, and M. de Hautoy; Montaigne retaining throughout the direction of the journey, and having things apparently all his own way.

Our traveller set off from the Château de Montaigne on the 22d June, 1580, and after stopping for a short time at the camp of the Marshal de Matignon, who was then besieging the town of La Fere; and, after accompanying to Soissons the body of the Count de Grammont, who had been killed at the siege, he went on to Beaumont-sur-Oise, where he arrived on the 5th of September, and where he was joined by M. d'Estissac; the other gentlemen were already, apparently, with him. The party then proceeded through the northeast of France to Plombieres, where Montaigne took the waters; and then went on by Basle, Baden, in the canton of Zurich, to Constance, Augsburg, Munich, and Trent. It is not to be supposed that he went to these places in a right line: he often changed his mind when half-way to a town, and came back; so that at last his zigzag mode of proceeding rendered several of his party restive. They remonstrated; but he replied that, for his own part, he was bound to no place but that in which he was at the time, and that he could not go out of his way, seeing that the only object he had proposed to himself was to wander in places before unknown to him; and so that he never followed the same road twice, nor visited the same place twice, his scheme was accomplished. If, indeed, he had been alone, he tells us, he had rather have gone towards Cracovia, or overland to Greece, instead of at once to Italy; but, he adds, he could not impart the pleasure he took in seeing strange places, which was such as to cause him to forget ill health and suffering, to any other of his party; so that he was obliged to pursue the uneven tenor of his way to Italy; and, after many windings, having visited Venice, which " he had a hunger to see," he at length found himself at Rome, on the last day of November, having the previous morning risen three hours before daylight, in his eagerness to behold the Eternal City. Here he had food in plenty for his inquiring mind; and, getting tired of his guide, rambled about by himself, finding out remarkable objects, making his shrewd remarks, and trying to discover those ancient spots with which his mind was familiar; for Latin being his mother-tongue, and Latin books his primers, he was more familiar with Roman history than with that of France; and the names of the Scipios and the Metelli were less strange to his ear than those of many Frenchmen of his own day. He was well received by the pope, Gregory XIII., who felt almost grateful to any man of talent and rank who would still abide by, and stand up in defence of, the old religion. Montaigne, before he left home, had printed two books of his Essays; a copy of these was taken from him at the custom-house at Rome, and underwent a censorship; several faults were found, which he particularizes in the Diary, but Montaigne took this fault-finding very easily, saying that he had put down the things in question as his real opinions, and did not regard them as errors, and that, in several cases, the censor had altogether mistaken his meaning. The authority to whom the matter was referred was a man of sense, who, readily admitting the explanations offered by our essayist, the censures were not insisted upon; and when Montaigne left Rome, and took leave of the prelate who had discoursed with him on the subject, the latter paid him a high compliment as to the uprightness of his intentions, his affection for the church, and his talents; adding, that the authorities at Rome thought so highly of his candour and conscientiousness, that they left it entirely to him to make what alterations he thought necessary, in another edition; and, finally, our author was earnestly requested to continue to aid the church with his eloquence, and to remain where he was, away from the troubles of his native country. Montaigne's vanity was highly tickled with all these courtesies, though he speaks of them as mere words of course; and his satisfaction was completed by his being invested with the citizenship of Rome, in a papal bull, pompous in seals and golden letters, and most gracious in its expressions. Nothing, he tells us, ever pleased him more than this honour, empty as it might seem; and he had employed to obtain it, he says, all his five senses, for the sake of the ancient glory and present holiness of the city.

The descriptions (observes Mrs. Shelley) which he gives of Rome, of the Pope, and all he saw, are short, but drawn with a master's hand—graphic, original, and just; and such is the unaltered appearance of the Eternal City, that his pages describe it as it now is, with as much fidelity as they did when he saw it in the sixteenth century. Its gardens and pleasure-grounds delighted him; the air seemed to him the most agreeable he had ever felt; and the perpetual excitement of inquiry in which he lived, his visits to antiquities, and to various beautiful and memorable spots, delighted him; and neither at home nor abroad was he once visited by gloom or melancholy, which he calls his death.

On the 19th of April, he left Rome, and, passing by the eastern road and the shores of the Adriatic, he visited Loretto, where he displayed his piety by presenting a silver *ex-voto*, and performing various religious duties, which prove the sincerity of his Catholic faith. In the month of May he arrived at the Baths of Lucca, whither he had repaired for the sake of the waters, and took up his abode at the Bagno della Villa, where, with the exception of a short interval, during which he visited Florence and Pisa, he remained till September. On the 7th of that month, he received letters to inform him that he had been elected mayor of Bordeaux, a circumstance which forced him to hasten his return, though he did not leave Italy without again visiting Rome. His journey home during winter, although rendered painful by physical suffering, was yet tortuous and wandering among the northern Italian towns. He reëntered France by Mont-Cenis, and, visiting Lyons, continued his route through Auvergne and Perigord, and arrived at the Château de Montaigne on the 30th of November, having been absent seventeen months and eight days.

Of the journey thus performed, we have a Diary, written partly in Montaigne's own hand, partly dictated to his valet, who, though he speaks of his master in the third person, evidently wrote only the words dictated. This work, observes Mrs. Shelley, is singularly interesting. It seems to tell us more of Montaigne than the Essays themselves; or rather, it confirms much said in those, by relating many things omitted, and throws a new light on various portions of his character. For instance, we find that the eager curiosity of his mind led him to inquire into the tenets of the Protestants; and that at the Swiss towns he was accustomed, on arriving, to seek out with all speed some theologian, whom he invited to dinner, and from whom he inquired the particular tenets of the various sects. There creeps out, also, an almost unphilosophical dislike of his own country, springing from the miserable state into which civil war had brought it. The work abounds, too, with amusing illustrations of the vanity which formed so prominent a feature in our author's character. He loved to stop at places where, taking him for a noble of high degree, the local authorities waited upon him in state, bearing the portion of wine, accustomed to be offered to the more distinguished of their visitors, and accompanying it with long complimentary harangues, to which he would gravely reply with all corresponding dignity, and at proportionate length.

Montaigne, though, of course, highly flattered by the unsought-for, and, by him, utterly unexpected, election of the citizens of Bordeaux, which he himself affects to attribute solely to their recollection of his father's former good administration of the office, yet, from ill health, and constitutional dislike to public employments, would have excused himself, as he tells us, had not the king interposed with his commands. On his arrival, he represented himself to his electors, such as he conceived himself to be, " a man without memory, without vigilance, without experience, and without vigour; but withal, without hatred, without ambition, without avarice, and without violence." It has been, indeed, insinuated against him, by M. Balzac, who, however, assigns no grounds for the imputation, that he exhibited indolence and indifference in the execution of the duties of his office; while he himself deemed his negative merits deserving praise, at a time when France was distracted by the dissensions of contending factions; and the citizens themselves gave unequivocal proof of their approbation of his administration, by conferring upon him a second election of the two years' mayoralty, an honour so distinguished and rare that it had never occurred but twice before, in the persons, namely, of M. de Lansac, and of Marshal de Matignon, to whom Montaigne succeeded; and proud was he, he tells us, of so noble a fraternity.

For some time after his return home, Montaigne, amidst all the fierce and licentious struggles of the contending parties, was suf-

fered to remain unmolested in his retreat. "Peradventure," he
writes, "the facility of entering my house, amongst other things,
has been a means to preserve it from the violence of our civil
wars; defence allures an enemy, and mistrust provokes him. I
enervated the soldiers' design by depriving the exploit of danger,
and all matter of military glory, which is wont to serve them for
pretence and excuse. Whatever is bravely is ever honourably
done, at a time when justice is dead. I render them the conquest
of my house cowardly and base; it is never shut to any one that
knocks. My gate has no other guard than a porter, and that of
ancient custom and ceremony, who does not so much serve to defend it, as to offer it with more decency and the better grace. I
have no other guard or sentinel than the stars. A gentleman
would play the fool to make a show of defence, if he be not really
in a condition to defend himself. He that lies open on one side is
everywhere so. Our ancestors did not think of building frontier
garrisons. The means of assaulting, I mean without battery or
army, and of surprising our houses, increase every day, above all
the means to guard them; men's wits are generally bent that way;
invasion every one is concerned in; none but the rich in defence.
Mine was strong for the time when it was built; I have added
nothing to it of that kind, and should fear that its strength should
turn against myself; to which we are to consider that a peaceable
time would require it should be dismantled. There is the danger
never to be able to regain it, and it would be very hard to keep it,
for in intestine dissensions your valet may be of the party you
fear; and where religion is the pretext, even a man's nearest relation may be distrusted with a colour of justice. The public
exchequer will not maintain our domestic garrisons; it would be
exhausted; we ourselves have not means to do it without ruin, or,
which is more inconvenient and injurious, without ruining the
people. As to the rest, you there lose all, and even your friends
will be more ready to accuse your want of vigilance and your
improvidence than to pity you, and the ignorance and heedless-
ness of your profession. That so many garrisoned houses have
been lost, whereas this of mine remains, makes me apt to suspect
that they were only lost by being guarded; this gives an enemy
both an invitation and colour of reason; all defence shows a face
of war. Let who will come to me, in God's name; but I shall not
invite them. 'Tis retirement I have chosen, for my repose from

war. I endeavour to withdraw this corner from the public tempest, as I also do another corner in my soul. Our war may put on what forms it will, multiply and diversify itself into new parties; for my own part, I shall not budge. Amongst so many garrisoned houses, I am the only person of my condition, that I know of, who have purely intrusted mine to the protection of Heaven, without removing either plate, deeds, or hangings. I will neither fear nor save myself by halves." His quiet, however, was at length intruded on, and he was made to feel in his own person the disturbances that desolated his country. It is a strange and instructive thing to picture France divided into two parties, belonging to which were men who risked all for the dearest privilege of life, freedom of thought and faith; and were either forced, or fancied that they were forced, to expose life and property to attain it; and to compare these religionists in arms with the tranquil philosopher, who dissected human nature in his study, and sounded the very depths of all our knowledge in freedom and ease, because he abstained from certain watchwords, and had no desire for proselytes or popular favour. "I regard our king," he says, "with a merely legitimate and political affection, neither attached nor repelled by private interest; and in this I am satisfied with myself. In the same way, I am but moderately and tranquilly attached to the general cause, and am not subject to entertain opinions in a deep-felt and enthusiastic manner. Let Montaigne, if it must be so, be swallowed up, in the public ruin; but if there is no necessity for it, I shall be thankful to Fortune to save it. I treat both parties equally; I say nothing to one that I could not say to the other, with the accent only a little changed; and there is no motive of utility that could induce me to lie." It was in 1585 that the factions, excited by their chief, the Duc de Guise, at once against the Navarrese and against the king himself, who had now entirely given himself up to the society of his favourites, began to make onslaughts both against the sincere royalists and against the moderate Catholics.

Montaigne's account of the Reformers, it may be observed, is by no means flattering; he represents them as men who "go towards reformation by the worst of deformations; who advance towards their salvation by the most express causes that we have of most assured damnation; who by overthrowing the government, magistracy, and laws, in whose protection God has placed them, by tearing their mother (the Church) to pieces, and giving the lacerated limbs to her old enemies to gloat over, by inspiring fraternal minds with parricidal animosities, by calling devils and furies to their aid, think they can assist the holy sweetness and justice of the divine laws. Ambition, avarice, cruelty, and revenge, have not sufficient natural impetuosity of their own; let us bait them with the glorious titles of justice and devotion. The common people," he proceeds, "then suffered therein very much, not present damages only, but future too: the living were to suffer, and so were they who were yet unborn; they pillaged them, and consequently me too, even of hope, taking from them all they had laid up in store to live on for many years. . . . Besides this shock, I suffered others; I underwent the inconveniences that moderation brings along with it in such diseases; I was curried on all hands; to the Ghibelline I was a Guelph; to the Guelph a Ghibelline. The situation of my house, and my friendliness to my neighbours, presented me with one face; my life and my actions with another. They did not lay formal accusations against me, for they had no hold. I never slink from the laws, and whoever would have questioned me, would have done himself a greater prejudice than me; they were only mute suspicions that were whispered about, which never want appearance in so confused a mixture, no more than envious or idle heads. I commonly assist the injurious presumptions that fortune scatters abroad against me, by a way I have ever had of evading to justify, excuse, or explain myself, conceiving that it were to compromise my conscience to plead in its behalf: *Perspicuitas enim augmentatione elevatur.....* At what then befell me an ambitious man would have hanged himself, and a covetous one would have done the same. I have no manner of care of getting; but the losses that befell me by the injury of others, whether by theft or violence, go almost as near my heart as they would do to that of the most avaricious man. The offence troubles me, without comparison, more than the loss. A thousand several sorts of mischief fell upon me in the neck of one another; I could better have borne them all at once.....I had already begun considering," he continues, "to whom amongst my friends I might commit a necessitous and degraded old age; and, having turned my eyes quite round, I found myself altogether at a loss. At last I concluded that it was safest for me to trust to myself in my necessity; and if it should fall out that I should be

put upon cold terms in Fortune's favour, I should so much more
recommend me to my own, and so much the closer attach me to
myself."

It was well for him that he had philosophy to bear him up
against all the evils that now assailed him; for, to complete his
misery, and that of his countrymen, a pestilent fever broke out in
1586, and devastated Guyenne. Montaigne's own account of this
horrible visitation runs thus: "But behold another aggravation
of the evil, which befell me in the tail of the rest. Both without
doors and within, I was assaulted with a plague most violent in
comparison of all others; I had to suffer this pleasant condition,
that the sight of my house was frightful to me; whatever I had
there was without guard, and left to the mercy of every one. I
myself, who am of so hospitable a nature, was myself in very great
distress for a retreat for my family; a wild and scattered family,
frightful both to its friends and itself, and filling every place with
horror where it attempted to settle; having to shift abode as soon
as any one's finger began to ache; all diseases are then concluded
to be the plague, and people do not stay to examine what they
are. And the mischief is, that, according to the rules of art, in
every danger that a man comes near, he must undergo a quaran-
tine in the suspense of his infirmity, your imagination all that
while tormenting you at pleasure, and turning even your health
itself into a fever. Yet all this would have gone the less to my
heart, had I not withal been compelled to be sensible of others'
sufferings, and miserably to serve six months together for a guide
to this caravan; for I carry my own antidotes within myself, which
are resolution and patience. Apprehension, which is particularly
to be feared in this disease, does not much trouble me; and if,
being alone, I should have taken it, it had been a more sprightly
and a longer flight: 'tis a kind of death that I do not think of the
worse sort; 'tis usually short, stupid, without pain, and consoled
by the public condition; without ceremony, without mourning,
and without a crowd. But as to the people about us, the hun-
dredth part of them could not be saved. In this place, my greatest revenue is manual: what a hundred men ploughed for me lay
a long time fallow."

In another place he gives a very interesting account of how, on
one occasion, by presence of mind and self-possession, he saved his
castle from pillage; and elsewhere he relates a somewhat similar

anecdote of the manner in which he got out of the clutches of a
party of the gentlemen freebooters, who then perambulated the
country, seeking what they might devour.

Montaigne's family were long-lived ; but he himself attained no
great age, and his latter years were disturbed by great suffering.
Living in constant expectation of death, he was always prepared
for it ; his affairs were arranged, and he was ready to fulfil all the
last duties of his religion, as soon as he felt himself attacked by
any of the frequent fevers that assailed him.   One of the last and
most agreeable events of his life was his friendship with Mademoiselle de Gournay.   In his Third Book he tells us nothing of this
friend, so worthy of the name, who came to console the philosopher, suffering under the public miseries and his own afflictions of
body ; but he makes her the subject of an addition to the 17th
chapter of Book II. ; where, in the enumeration he gives us of the
persons of his own time, possessed of more than ordinary greatness
of mind, he distinguishes his *fille•d'alliance*, Marie de Gournay.
His picture of her is not only delightful as a testimony of her
merits, but a proof of the unfailing enthusiasm and warmth of his
own heart, which even in suffering and decay equally allied itself
to kindred merit.   Mademoiselle de Gournay was afterward esteemed one of the most learned and excellent women of her time,
and was honoured by the abuse of pedants, who attacked her personal appearance and her age, in revenge for her transcending
even their sex in accomplishments and understanding ; while, on
the other hand, she was regarded with respect and friendship by
the first men of the day.[1]   At the time when Montaigne first saw
her, which was during a long visit he made to Paris, after his
mayoralty at Bordeaux was ended, she was very young, but she
had conceived an enthusiastic love and admiration of him from
reading his Essays, and she called upon, and requested and obtained his acquaintance, which soon ripened into earnest friendship.   She afterwards, in company with her mother, visited him
at Montaigne, and he paid them, in return, several visits at their
chateau in Normandy, where he remained, on the whole, three
months.   Another adoption, very agreeable to his vanity, was that

[1] Besides her other works, this lady is the author of a little volume, not mentioned or contained in the editions of her writings, that appeared in 1626, 1634,
and 1641, and unknown to M. Barbier: *Bienvenue de monseigneur le duc d'Anjou*, dédiée à la sérénissime république de Venise, son parrain désigné, par mademoiselle de G. *Paris, Bourriquant*, 1608 This Duke of Anjou was Gaston, duc
d'Orléans, second son of Henry IV.

of his philosophy by Chanon, who became acquainted with him at Bordeaux, in 1589, and with whom he afterwards contracted a warm friendship. The theologian became the pupil of the philosopher, and his Treatise on Wisdom is little more than a development of the maxims and lessons of his master, fully justifying, if it were needed, the title of *Bréviaire des honnêtes gens*, that Cardinal du Perron assigned to Montaigne's Essays. The pupil, however, was much less read than the master, who, very soon after the first publication of his work, was so much in vogue,—notwithstanding Mademoiselle de Gournay's somewhat unaccountable complaint as to the coldness of its reception,—that edition after edition was called for, and the Essays of Montaigne were to be found on the table of every gentleman in France that could read aught beyond his other *breviary*, and, ere long, became known, by the medium of translations, in Italy, England, and other countries.

The disease which more immediately occasioned the death of Montaigne was a quinsy, that brought on a paralysis of the tongue, in which condition he remained three whole days, with all his senses about him, but unable to speak. Even now his presence of mind, his philosophy, and his kind heart did not forsake him. It is related of him, by Bernard Antoine, in his *Commentaire sur la Coutume de Bordeaux*, that Montaigne, "feeling the approach of death, got out of bed in his shirt, and, putting on his dressing-gown, opened the door of his chamber, and, writing word for all his servants and others, to whom he had left legacies, to be called together, paid them the sums he had respectively bequeathed them, foreseeing the difficulty they might have in obtaining the amount from his heirs." Getting worse and worse, he requested his wife, in writing, to send for some gentlemen, his neighbours; and when they were all assembled, he caused mass to be celebrated in his chamber. At the moment of the elevation, he attempted to rise, but could not, and with his hands crossed, fell back fainting, and in this act of devotion expired, on the 13th September, 1592, in the sixtieth year of his age, presenting in his death, says Pasquier, a fine mirror of the interior of his soul. He was buried at Bordeaux, in the church of the Feuillans, where his widow had a monument erected to him, with inscriptions in Latin and Greek, as follow:—

D. O. M. S.

Michaeli Montano Petrocorensi Petri F. Grimundi. N. Remundi Pron.

Equiti torquato, civi Romano, civitatis Biturigum Viviscorum ex-Majori, viro ad naturæ gloriam nato. Quojus morum suavitudo, ingenii acumen, extemporalis facundia, et incomparabile judicium supra humanam sortem æstimata sunt. Qui amicos usus reges maxumos, et terræ Galliæ primores viros, ipsos etiam sequiorum partium præstites, tamen etsi patriarum legum, et sacrorum avitorum retinentissimus, sine quojusquam offensa, sine palpo, aut pipulo, universis populatim gratus, utque antidhac semper advorsus omnes dolorum minacias mœnitam sapientiam labris et libris professus, ita in procinctu fati cum morbo pertinaciter inimico diutim validissime conluctatus, tandem dicta factis exæquando, poleræ vitæ poleram pausam cum Deo volente fecit.

Vixit ann. LIX. mens. VII. dieb. XI. Obiit anno salutis CIↃ IↃ VIIIↃ. idib. Septemb.

Francisca Chassanea ad luctum perpetuum heu relicta marito dolcissimo univira unijugo, et bene merenti mœrens P. C.

'Ηρίον ὅστις ἰδών, ἥδ' οὔνομα τοὐμὸν ἐρωτᾷς,
Μάνθανε Μοντανός· παύεο θαμβοπαθεῖν.
Οὐκ ἐμὰ ταῦτα, δέμας, γένος εὐγενές, ὅλβος ἀνολβος,
Προστασίαι, δυνάμεις, παίγνια θνητὰ τύχης.

Οὐρανόθεν κατέβην, θεῖον φυτόν, εἰς χθόνα Κελτῶν,
Οὐ σοφὸς Ἑλλήνων ὄγδοος, οὔτε τρίτος
Αὐσονίων· ἀλλ' εἰς πάντων ἀντάξιος ἄλλων,
Τῆς τε βάθει σοφίης, ἀνθέσι τ' εὐεπίης.

'Ος καὶ χριστοσεβεῖ ξυνένωσα διδάγματι σκέψιν
Τὴν Πυρρωνείην, 'Ελλάδα δ' εἷλε φθόνος,
Εἷλε καὶ Αὐσονίην, φθονερὴν δ' ἔριν αὐτις ἐπισχών,
Τάξιν ἐπ' Οὐρανίδων, πατρίδα μευ, ἀνέβην.

Thus rendered by M. de la Monnoye:—

Quisquis ades, nomenque rogas, lugere paratus,
    Montani audito nomine, parce metu.
Nil jacet hîc nostri, nec enim titulosque, genusque,
    Fasces, corpus, opes, nostra vocanda puto.
Gallorum ad terras superis demissus ab oris,
    Non alter cecidi Chilo, Catove novus;
Ast omnes æquans unus, quoscumque vetustas
    Enumerat, celebres corde vel ore Sophos.
Solius addictus jurare in dogmata Christi,
    Cætera Pyrrhonis pendere lance sciens,
Jam mihi de sophiâ Latium, jam Græcia certent,
    Ad Cœlum reducem lis nihil ista movet.

Montaigne's adopted daughter and her mother, to whom information of his illness had been immediately forwarded by the

family, hastened from their château in Normandy, by the assistance of passports, to traverse almost the entire of France, disturbed as it was, but arrived only in time to mix their tears and
lamentations with those of the philosopher's widow and daughter.

The only child that Montaigne left was a daughter, Leonora,
who was afterwards twice married ; she had no children by her
first husband, but by her second, Charles, Viscount de Gamaches,
she had a daughter, Marie de Gamaches, who married Louis de
Lur de Saluces, Baron de Fargues, to whom she bore three
daughters. The youngest, Claude Madeleine de Lur, married
Elias Isaac de Ségur, whose son, Jean de Ségur, was grandfather
to M. le Compte de la Roquette, to whom the château of Montaigne duly descended, in accordance with the testamentary ar-
rangements of the philosopher from whom it received its sole
celebrity.

The present may, perhaps, be the most suitable place for insert-
ing a very interesting account of this château, as it appeared, a
few years ago, to the eyes of an intelligent contributor to the
" Westminster Review."

" At Castellan we exchanged our caleche for a small char-a-
banc, with one horse, which took us to Montaigne St. Michael,
along a detestable road, mostly somewhat ascending. We found
the higher ground to be a wide, broken plain, out of sight of the
Dordogne, and studded with small stone windmills, each carrying
a conical roof.

" The first memorial of the days of Montaigne which we discovered was the parish church, a very old building. There is a
massive square tower, covered by a slightly pointed roof, and
having two large openings near its summit, in each side, which
look like windows, but are without shafts, and seem to distinguish
a good deal of the church architecture of the neighbourhood.
There is a round apsis beyond the tower, at the east end, with
only two small loophole windows, and at the west end is raised a
small, curiously complicated wooden superstructure, designed to
contain the bell of a large clock, to which access is obtained by a
rude, external wooden gallery, painted red, and stretching all the
length of the body of the church, close under the eaves. From
this building runs a straight road, perhaps a quarter of a mile
long, to the chateau.

" The part of Montaigne's house which we first reached was the

tower, described by him in his essay ' On the Three Commerces
(iii. 3), as containing his library and study. It is a plain round
structure, at the southeastern corner of the chateau; a dead-wall
runs from it on either side, at right angles, and rises to about half
its height. This is in reality the exterior of ranges of out-buildings,
which form two sides of the court-yard. In this wall, close to the
tower, and facing us as we approached, was a small gate, through
which we found entrance. The chateau itself was now on our
left, running along the western side of the quadrangle. It is a
high building of gray stone, evidently very ancient, and probably
untouched, except for repairs, since the days of Montaigne's father.
There are a considerable number of windows scattered very irreg-
ularly over the front. Near the middle, at either side of the small
unornamented entrance, are two large and high towers, of unlike
architecture; the one with deep machicolations, the other without
them, and both with conical roofs. If erected, as I presume, by
Montaigne's father, the building must be about three hundred
years old; the whole place has now an air of sluttish neglect,
though not at all of decay. It is now inhabited by an old gentleman, formerly a military man, whose civility we should ill repay
by recording any idle accounts of his simple establishment and
very agreeable conversation. The house is only one room deep,
and behind it runs a long and broad terrace, covered with grass,
and with some trees growing upon it, among others, a large horse-
chestnut. It is bordered by a stone balustrade, which rises on the
edge of a steep, wooded bank, and has beyond it a very extensive
prospect over a flat country, with slight eminences on the horizon,
marked towards the north by the village and château of Mont
Peyroux, which in Montaigne's day was a sort of dependence on
his seigneurie, and belonged to his younger brother. Near it, and
still higher against the sky, are the ruins of the château of Gurson,
destroyed in the Revolution, and which seems to have been a castle in our English sense of the word, that is, a feudal abode con-
structed for defence. It was probably the residence of the lady to
whom Montaigne addresses his " Essay on Education," (i. 25.)
The whole prospect is woody and cultivated, but without water or
any remarkable outlines, open, airy, quiet, and sufficiently prosperous. The old gentleman told us that he was possessed of eleven
métairies or farms, with the château, but that Montaigne had held
eighteen. The property had come by marriage to the Ségur

family, who had taken the name of Ségur de Montaigne. They sold the estate to the present owner, who, in turn, was ready to dispose of it, if he could find a purchaser.

" After taking leave of our host, we returned to the corner tower, which we examined throughout, and were much interested by the minute agreement of its present state with every thing recorded in Montaigne's description. This, too, was evidently not a modern and factitious correspondence, but secured by the abstinence of the successive owners from any changes, however slight. The ground-floor retains the appearance of having been once a small chapel, though now dark and dilapidated. The first floor, which was the sleeping apartment of the Gascon philosopher, does not look as if it had been applied since his day to any other purpose. The third and last story is that so particularly described by its occupant, as having contained his library, and study, and his words would answer in most respects as a description of the spot at this hour, though he who wrote them has been dead two hundred and fifty years. The room still overlooks the entrance of the chateau, and from three windows, in different sides of the circuit, commands the garden, the court, the house, and the out-houses. The books, indeed, are gone; but the many small rafters of the roof are inscribed in their lower faces with mottoes and pithy sentences, which recall, as by a living voice, the favourite studies and thoughts of Montaigne. Such are these few hastily transcribed in a note-book : ' 1. *Solum certum nihil esse certi, et homine nihil miserius aut superbius.* 2. Ἄλλοισιν ἄλλου θεῶν τε κἀνθρώπων μέλει. 3. Ταράσσει τοὺς ἀνθρώπους οὐ τὰ γρίμματα, ἀλλὰ τὰ ἔπη κἀνθρώπων δόγματα. 4. *Quid superbis, terra et cinis?*—Eccl. x. 5. *Væ qui sapientes estis in oculis vestris.*—Eccl. v. 6. *Favere jucunde præsentibus. Cætera extra te.* 7. Πάντι λόγῳ λόγος ἴσος ἀντίκειται. 8. *Nostra vagatur in tenebris, nec circa potest mens cernere verum.* 9. *Fecit Deus hominem similem umbræ post solis occasum.*—Eccl. vii.'

" The chapel still shows the recess where stood the altar, and there are the remains of colours and gilding on the defaced coats-of-arms around the walls. The bedroom-floor presents nothing remarkable; but that above, in which are the inscriptions on its rafters, preserves the exact form described by its ancient occupant. The paces of Montaigne must have been of about a foot and a half, for the diameter of the tower inside is about twenty-four feet.

The circle is at one part cut by two straight walls, joining in an angle, being the portion which he speaks of as adapted for his seat and table. The three windows, affording a rich and free prospect, are still unchanged. There is a sort of closet opening off the room, with the traces of painted ornaments on the walls, a fire-place, as he mentions, at one end, and a window, which entitles it to be spoken of as *très plaisamment percé*—having a pleasant window-light—and which, though directly overlooking the court yard, furnishes a view, above the northern line of offices, towards Mont Peyroux and Gurson.

"The whole appearance and position of this apartment seem especially characteristic of Montaigne. The cheerfulness, the airiness, the quiet, the constant though somewhat remote view of natural objects, and of the far-spread and busy occupations of men—all are suitable to him. The ornamenting the joists of his chamber-roof with several scores of moral sentences, was the work of a speculative idler, and their purport is always, so far as I saw, suitable to his skeptical but humane and indulgent temper. The neglect of all elegance and modern convenience in the house, together with its perfect preservation from decay, add to the in-terest, and seem to prove that it is maintained in its old complete-ness, and bareness, not from any notion of use, but out of respect for the memory of its celebrated owner."

Montaigne had five brothers: Captain St. Martin, who was killed at the age of twenty-three, by the blow of a tennis-ball; the Sieur d'Arsac, possessor of an estate in Médoc, that was buried under the sea-sands; the Sieur de la Brousse, not men-tioned by Bouhier in his Life of Montaigne, but referred to in the Essays, ii. 5; the Sieur de Mattecoulon, who accompanied him on his journey through Italy; and the Sieur de Beauregard, who be-came a convert to Protestantism. Montaigne had one sister, named Eleonora, who married the Sieur de Cumain, counsellor to the Parliament of Bordeaux, and of whom mention is made in the will of Charron, in which the grateful disciple leaves the bulk of his property to the family of his master.

We have thus brought together the principal facts connected with the life of our philosopher. It would have been easy to fab-ricate a very long biography, by reprinting in a consecutive form the information which the Essays themselves afford, for these are nearly taken up by narrations of what happened to himself, or

dissertations on his own nature, so that there is scarcely any man
into whose character we have more insight than that of Montaigne.
The reader, however, will find in the Index a complete reference
to all those passages in which our author thus speaks of himself;
and the critical opinions and *éloges* that precede[1] the body of the
work, will afford those who as yet have not read Montaigne, but
have bowed their heads at his name, on the authority of prescription—an authority that empowers so many thousands to look unutterable things, as they repeat of men of whose works they know
nothing—abundant justification for the faith that is in them, and
will lead them on, with a prepared and understanding mind, to
the Essays themselves.

[1] As we have already indicated, in the Editor's Advertisement, all references to and quotations from critical opinions and *Éloges*, will, in this edition, be found in the general Appendix at the end of the last volume.—ED.

THE AUTHOR TO THE READER.

THIS, reader, is a book without guile. It tells thee, at the very outset, that I had no other end in putting it together but what was domeſtic and private. I had no regard therein either to thy service or my glory ; my powers are equal to no such deſign. It was intended for the particular use of my relations and friends, in order that, when they have loſt me, which they muſt soon do, they may here find some traces of my quality and humour, and may thereby nouriſh a more entire and lively recollection of me. Had I proposed to court the favour of the world, I had set myself out in borrowed beauties ; but 'twas my wiſh to be seen in my ſimple, natural, and ordinary garb, without ſtudy or artifice, for 'twas myself I had to paint. My defects will appear to the life, in all their native form, as far as conſiſts with respect to the public. Had I been born among those nations who, 'tis said, ſtill live in the pleasant liberty of the law of nature, I aſſure thee I ſhould readily have depicted myself at full length and quite naked. Thus, reader, thou perceiveſt I am myself the subject of my book ; 'tis not worth thy while to take up thy time longer with such a frivolous matter ; so fare thee well.

From Montaigne ; this 12th of June, 1580.

MONTAIGNE'S ESSAYS.

THE FIRST BOOK.

CHAPTER I.

THAT MEN BY VARIOUS WAYS ARRIVE AT THE SAME END.

THE most usual way of appeasing the indignation of such
as we have any way offended, when we see them in possession of the power of revenge, and find that we absolutely lie
at their mercy, is, by submission, (than which, Different modes of
nothing more flatters the glory of an adver- mollifying the
sary,) to move them to commiseration and hearts of the
offended.
pity: and yet bravery, firmness, and resolution, however
quite contrary means, have sometimes served to produce the
same effect. Edward, Prince of Wales,[1] the same who so
long governed our province of Guienne, a person whose condition and fortunes have in them a great deal of the most
notable parts of grandeur, having, through some misdemean-
ours of theirs, been highly incensed by the Limosins, in the
heat of that resentment, taking their city by assault, was not,
either by the outcries of the people or the prayers and tears
of the women and children abandoned to slaughter, and
prostrate at his feet for mercy, to be stayed from prosecuting
his revenge; till, penetrating farther into the body of the

---

[1] The Black Prince, son of Edward the Third.

town, he took notice of three French gentlemen, who, with
incredible bravery, alone sustained the whole power of his
victorious army.[1] Then it was that consideration and respect
for such remarkable valour first stopped the torrent of his
fury ; and his clemency, beginning in the preservation of
these three cavaliers, was afterwards extended to all the
remaining inhabitants of the city.

Scanderberg, Prince of Epirus, in great wrath, pursuing
one of his soldiers with a resolute purpose to kill him, and
the soldier having in vain tried, by all the ways of humility
and supplication, to appease him, seeing him, notwithstanding,
obstinately bent to his ruin, resolved, as his last resource, to
face about and await him, sword in hand ; which behaviour
of his gave a sudden check to his captain's fury, who, seeing
him assume so noble a resolution, received him to favour.
An example, however, that might suffer another interpretation with such as have not read of the prodigious strength
and valour of that Prince.

The Emperor Conrad III. having besieged Guelph, Duke
of Bavaria,[2] would not be prevailed upon, what mean and
unmanly satisfactions soever were tendered to him, to condescend to milder conditions than that the gentlewomen only,
who were in the town, might go out without violation of their
honour, on foot, and with so much only as they could carry
about them.   Which was no sooner known but that, with
magnanimity of heart, they presently resolved

Conjugal love.   to carry out, upon their shoulders, their husbands and children, and the Duke himself; a sight at which
the Emperor was so pleased that, ravished with the generosity
of the action, he wept for joy, and immediately extinguishing
in his heart the mortal and implacable hatred he had conceived against this Duke, he from that time forward treated
him and his with all humanity and affection.

---

[1] Froissart, vol. i. book iv. part ii. ch.
cccxx. The names of the three gentlemen were John de Villemure, Hugh de la
Roche, and Roger de Beaufort.

[2] Anno 1140, in Welusberg, a town of
Upper Bavaria.

The one, or the other, of these two ways would, with great facility, work upon my nature; for I have a marvellous propensity to mercy and mildness; nay, to such a degree, that I fancy, of the two, I should sooner surrender my anger to compassion than to esteem; and yet pity is reputed a vice amongst the Stoics, who will that we succour the afflicted, but not that we should Pity reputed a vice amongst the Stoics. be so affected with their sufferings as to suffer or sympathize with them. Now, I conceived these examples suited to the question in hand, and the rather because therein we observe these great souls assaulted and tried by these two several ways to resist the one without relenting, and to be shaken and subjected by the other. It is true that to suffer a man's heart to be totally subdued by compassion may be imputed to facility, effeminacy, and over-tenderness; whence it comes to pass that the weakest natures, as those of women, children, and the common sort of people, are the most subject to it; but after having resisted, and disdained the power of sighs and tears, to surrender a man's animosity to the sole reverence of the sacred image of virtue—this can be no other than the effect of a strong and inflexible soul enamoured of, and doing honour to, a masculine and obstinate valour. Nevertheless, astonishment and admiration may, in less generous minds, beget a like effect. Witness the people of Thebes, who, having put two of their generals upon trial for their lives, for having continued in arms beyond the prescribed term of their commission, would hardly pardon Pelopidas, who, bowing under the weight of so dangerous an accusation, made no manner of defence for himself, nor produced other arguments than prayers and supplications to secure his head; whereas, on the contrary, Epaminondas, being brought to the bar, and failing to magnify the exploits he had performed in their service, and, after a haughty and arrogant manner, reproaching them with ingratitude and injustice, they had not the heart to proceed any further in his trial, but broke up the court, and departed, the whole assembly highly commending the courage and confidence of this great man.[1]

Dionysius the Elder, after having, by a tedious siege, and through exceeding great difficulties, taken the city of Rhegium, and in it the governor Phyton, a great and good man, who had made so obstinate a defence, he was resolved to make him a tragical example of his revenge; in order whereunto, and the more sensibly to afflict him, he first told him that he had the day before caused his son and all his kindred to be drowned; to which Phyton returned no other answer but this, that they were then, by one day, happier than he. After which, causing him to be stripped, and delivering him into the hands of the tormentors, he was, by them, dragged through the streets of the town, and most ignominiously and cruelly whipped, and, moreover, vilified with bitter and contumelious language. Yet still, in the fury of all this persecution, he maintained his courage entire all the way, with a strong voice and undaunted countenance, proclaiming the honourable and glorious cause of his death; namely, for that he would not deliver up his country into the hands of a merciless tyrant; at the same time denouncing against him a speedy chastisement from the offended gods. At which the tyrant, rolling his eyes about, and reading in his soldiers' looks that, instead of being incensed at the haughty language of this conquered enemy, to the contempt of him, their captain, and his triumph, they not only seemed struck with admiration of so rare a virtue, but, moreover, inclined to mutiny, and were even ready to rescue the prisoner out of the hangman's hands, he ordered the execution to cease, and, afterwards, privately caused him to be thrown into the sea.[2]

The cruelty of Dionysius the Elder.

Man, in sooth, is a marvellous, vain, fickle, and unstable subject, and on whom it is very hard to form any certain or uniform judgment. For Pom-

Man a variable animal.

---

[1] Plutarch: *How far a man may praise himself.* c. 5.　　[2] Diodorus Siculus, xiv. 29.

pey could pardon the whole city of the Mamertines, though furiously incensed against it, upon the single account of the virtue and magnanimity of one citizen, Zeno, who took the fault of the public wholly upon himself; neither intreated other favour but alone to undergo the punishment for all.[1] And yet Sylla's host having, in the city of Perusia, manifested the same virtue, obtained nothing by it, either for himself or his fellow-citizens.[2] And, directly contrary to my first examples, the bravest of all men, and who was reputed so gracious and kind to all those he overcame, Alexander the Great, having, after many great difficulties, forced the city of Gaza, and, on entering, found Betis, who commanded there, and of whose valour, in the time of this siege, he had most noble and manifest proofs, alone, forsaken by all his soldiers, his armour hacked and hewed to pieces, and his body covered all over with blood and wounds, and yet still fighting in the crowd of a great number of Macedonians, who were laying on him on all sides, he said to him (nettled at so dear-bought a victory, and at two fresh wounds he had newly received in his own person), "Thou shalt not die, Betis, so honourably as thou dost intend, but shalt assuredly suffer all the torments that can be inflicted on a miserable captive." To which menaces the other returning no other answer but only a fierce and disdainful look : "What," says the conqueror (observing his obstinate silence), "Is he <small>Obstinate silence</small> too stiff to bend a knee? Is he too proud to <small>of Betis.</small> utter one suppliant word? I will assuredly conquer this silence ; and, if I cannot force a word from his mouth, I will, at least, extract a groan from his heart." And, thereupon, converting his anger into fury, presently commanded his heels to be bored through, and caused him to be dragged, alive, mangled, and dismembered, at a cart's tail.[3] Was it

<hr />

1 Plutarch calls him Sthenon in his *Instructions for those who manage state affairs*, c. 17 ; Sthennius, in the *Apothegms ;* and Sthenis, in the *Life of Pompey ;* where, however, the anecdote is related of the city of the Himerians not of that of the Mamertines.

2 Plutarch, *Instructions for those who manage state affairs*, c. 17, tells this story of Præneste, a city of Latium ; and not of Perusia, which is in Tuscany.
3 Quintus Curtius, iv. 6

that the height of courage was so natural and familiar to this
conqueror that, no longer holding it in admiration, he had
come not even to respect it? Or was it that he conceived
valour to be a virtue so peculiar to himself that his pride
could not, without envy, endure it in another? Or was it
that the natural impetuosity of his fury brooked not opposition? Certainly had it been capable of any manner of moderation, it is to be believed, that in the sack and desolation of
Thebes, to see so many valiant men, lost and totally destitute
of any farther defence, cruelly massacred before his eyes,
would have appeased it. For there were above six thousand
put to the sword, of whom not one was seen to fly, or heard
to cry out for quarter; but, on the contrary, every one running here and there to seek out and to provoke the victorious
enemy to help them to an honourable end. There was not
one who did not, to his last gasp, endeavour to revenge himself; and, with all the fury of a brave despair, to sweeten his
own death in the death of an enemy. Yet did their valour
create no pity, and the length of one day was not enough to
satiate the conqueror's revenge; but the slaughter continued
to the last drop of blood that was capable of being shed, and
stopped not till it met with none but naked and impotent persons, old men, women, and children, of whom thirty thousand
were carried away slaves.[1]

CHAPTER II.

OF SORROW.[2]

No man living is more free from this passion than I, who
neither like it in myself, nor admire it in others;
and yet, generally, the world is pleased to hon-

A contemptible passion.

---

[1] Diod. Sic. xvii. 4.
[2] *De la Tristesse*, by which Montaigne   would seem to convey a *sullen habit of*   sorrow.

our it with a particular esteem; endeavouring to make us
believe that wisdom, virtue, and conscience, shroud themselves under this grave and affected appearance. Foolish
and sordid guise! The Italians, however, more fitly apply
the term [1] to indicate a clandestine nature, a dangerous and
bad nature. And with good reason, it being a quality always
hurtful, always idle and vain, and so cowardly, mean, and
base, that 'tis by the Stoics expressly and particularly forbidden their sages.

But the story, nevertheless, says, that Psammenitus, King
of Egypt, being defeated and taken prisoner by Cambyses,
King of Persia, seeing his own daughter pass by him, habited as a menial, with a bucket to draw water, though his
friends about him were so concerned as to break out into
tears and lamentations at the miserable sight, yet he himself
remained unmoved, without uttering a word, with his eyes
fixed upon the ground. And seeing, moreover, his son, immediately after, led to execution, still maintained the same
gravity and indifference of countenance; till, spying, at last,
one of his domestics [2] dragged away amongst the captives, he
could then hold no longer, but fell to tearing his hair and
beating his breast, with all the other extravagances of a wild
and desperate sorrow.[3] A story that may very fitly be
coupled with another of the same kind, of a late prince of
our own nation, who, being at Trent, and having news there
brought him of the death of his elder brother, a brother on
whom depended the whole support and honour of his house;
and, soon after, of that of a younger brother, the second hope
of his family; and, having withstood these two assaults with
an exemplary resolution, one of his servants happening, a
few days after, to die, he suffered his constancy to be overcome by this last accident; and, parting with his courage, so

1 *Tristezza.*
2 Herodotus, iii. 14. The word domestic does not here mean a servant, but an
intimate friend, a *domestic* friend, in
which sense the term was still used even
in the reign of Louis XIV. Herodotus,
indeed, mentions that the old man referred to had always had a place at the
king's table.
3 Valerius Maximus, viii. ii. *ext.* 6;
Cicero, *Orator.* c. 22; Pliny, xxxv. 10;
Quintilian, ii. 13.

abandoned himself to sorrow and mourning, that some, thence, were forward to conclude that he was only touched to the quick by this last stroke of fortune ; but, in truth, it was that, being before brimful of grief, the least addition overflowed the bounds of all patience.   Which might also be said of the former example, did not the story proceed to tell us that Cambyses, asking Psammenitus why, not being moved at the calamity of his son and daughter, he should with so great impatience bear the misfortune of his friend ?   " It is," answered he, " because this last affliction was only to be manifested by tears, the first two exceeding all manner of expression."

Extreme sorrow is unutterable.

And, peradventure, something like this might be working in the fancy of the painter of old, who, having, in the sacrifice of Iphigenia, to represent the sorrow of the bystanders, proportionably to the several degrees of interest each had in the death of this fair innocent virgin ; and having, in the other figures, exhausted the utmost power of his art, when he came to that of her father, he drew him with a veil over his face, meaning thereby that no kind of countenance was capable of expressing such a degree of sorrow.   Which is also the reason why the poets feign the miserable mother, Niobe, having first lost seven sons, and then successively as many daughters, overwhelmed with misery, to be at last transformed into a rock,

Diriguisse malis,[1]

" Hardened with woes—a statue of despair."

thereby to express that melancholy, dumb, and deaf stupidity, which benumbs all our faculties when oppressed with misfortunes greater than we are able to bear ; and, indeed, the violence and impression of an excessive grief must, of necessity, astonish the soul, and wholly deprive her of her ordinary functions ; as it happens to every one of us who, upon any sudden alarm of very ill news, find ourselves surprised, stupefied,

[1] Ovid, *Met.* vi. 304.   The text has *diriguitque malis.*

and, in a manner, deprived of all power of motion, till the soul, beginning to vent itself in sighs and tears, seems a little to free and disengage itself from the oppression, and to obtain some room to work itself out at greater liberty.

Et via vix tandem voci laxata dolore est.[1]

" Till sorrow breaks
A passage, and at once he weeps and speaks."

In the war that King Ferdinand made upon the widow of King John of Hungary, in a battle near Buda, a man at arms was particularly taken notice of by every one, for his singularly gallant behaviour in an encounter; and, though unknown, *Great grief deprives us of the use of speech, and sometimes causes death.* was highly commended and lamented when left dead upon the spot; but by none so much as by Raisciac, a German lord, who was infinitely enamoured of so rare a valour. The body being brought off, the Count, with the common curiosity, came to view it; and the armour was no sooner taken off, but he immediately knew him to be his own son. A thing that added a second blow to the compassion of all the beholders; he only, without uttering a word or turning away his eyes, stood fixedly contemplating the body of his son, till the vehemence of sorrow, having overcome his vital spirits, made him sink down, stone dead, to the ground.

Chi può dir com' egli arde, è in picciol fuoco![2]
" He loves but lightly who his love can tell,"

say the inmoratosa when they would represent an insupportable passion.

Misero quod omnes
Eripit sensus mihi: nam, simul te,
Lesbia, aspexi, nihil est super mi
Quod loquar amens:
Lingua sed torpet; tenuis sub artus
Flamma dimanat; sonitu suopte

[1] Virgil. Æneid, ii. 154.   [2] Petrarch, Son. 137

Tinniunt aures; gemina teguntur
Lumina nocte.[1]

" Thou, Lesbia, robb'st my soul of rest,
    And rais'd-t those tumults in my breast;
For while I gazed, in transports tost,
    My breath was gone, my voice was lost.
My bosom glowed, the subtle flame
    Ran quick through all my vital frame;
O'er my dim eyes a darkness hung,
    My ears with hollow murmurs rung."

So that it is not in the height and greatest fury of the fit that
we are in a condition to pour out our complaints and our persuasions, the soul being, at that time, overburthened, and
labouring with profound thoughts, and the body dejected and
languishing with desire.   And thence it is that proceed those
accidental impotences that sometimes so unseasonably surprise the willing lover, and that frigidity which, by the force
of an immoderate ardour, seizes him even in the very lap of
fruition.   All passions that suffer themselves to be relished
and digested are but moderate.

Curæ leves loquuntur, ingentes stupent.[2]

" Light griefs are plaintive, but the great are dumb."

The surprise of unexpected joys often produces the same
effect.

Ut me conspexit venientem; et Troïa circum
Arma amens vidit, magnis exterrita monstris,
Diriguit visu in medio; calor ossa reliquit;
Labitur; et longo vix tandem tempore fatur.[3]

" But when, at nearer distance, she beheld
My Trojan armour and my Trojan shield,
Astonished at the sight, the vital heat
Forsakes her limbs, her veins no longer beat:
She faints, she falls, and, scarce recovering strength
Thus, with a faltering tongue, she speaks at length."

Besides the examples of the Roman lady who died for joy

1 Catullus, ll. 5.   3 Æneid, iii. 306.
2 Seneca, Hipp. ii. 3, 607.

to see her son safe returned from the defeat of Other effects of Cannæ;[1] of Sophocles, and Dionysius the grief. tyrant, who died of joy;[2] and of Talva, who died in Corsica, on reading the news of the honours the Roman senate had decreed him,[3] we have, moreover, one in our own time, of Pope Leo the Tenth, who, upon news of the taking of Milan, a thing he had so ardently desired, was wrapt with so sudden an excess of joy that he immediately fell into a fever and died.[4]　And, for a more notable testimony of the imbecility of human nature, it is recorded, by the ancients,[5] that Diodorus the Dialectician, died on the spot, out of an extreme passion of shame, for not having been able, in his own school, and in the presence of a great auditory, to disengage himself from a nice argument that was propounded to him.　I, for my part, am very little subject to these violent passions; I am naturally of a stubborn apprehension, which, by reason, I every day harden and fortify more and more.

CHAPTER III.

THAT OUR AFFECTIONS CARRY THEMSELVES BEYOND US.

SUCH as accuse mankind of always gaping after future things, and advise us to make the most of the Mankind too curi- good which is present, and to set up our rest ous after futurity. upon that, as having no hold upon that which is to come, even less than that we have upon what is past, have hit upon the most universal of human errors, if that may be called an error to which nature itself has disposed us, who, in order to the subsistence and continuation of her own work, has,

---

[1] Pliny, vii. 54.
[3] Valerius Maximus, ix. 12. The name is not Talva, but Thalna.
[2] Id. ib. 53.
[4] Guicciardini, xiv.
[5] Pliny. *ut supra.*

amongst several others, prepossessed us with this deceiving imagination, as being more jealous of our action than afraid of our knowledge.

We are never present with, but always beyond, ourselves. Fear, desire, and hope, are still pushing us on towards the future, depriving us, in the mean time, of the sense and consideration of that which is, to amuse us with the thought of what shall be, even when we shall be no more. Calamitosus est animus futuri anxius.[1] " 'Tis a great calamity to have a mind anxious about things to come." We find this great precept often repeated in Plato, " Do thine own work, and know thyself." Of which two parts, both the one and the other, generally comprehends our whole duty, and, in like manner, do each of them involve the other. He who will do his own work aright, will find that his first lesson is to know himself, and what is proper for him ; and he who rightly understands himself, will never mistake another man's work for his own, but will love and improve himself above all other things, will refuse superfluous employments, and reject all unprofitable thoughts and propositions. As folly on the one side, though it should enjoy all it can desire, would, notwithstanding, never be content; so, on the other, wisdom ever acquiesces with the present, and is never dissatisfied with its immediate condition ; and that is the reason why Epicurus dispenses his sages from all forecast and care of the future.

Amongst those laws that relate to the dead, I look upon that to be a very sound one, by which the actions of princes are to be examined and sifted after their decease.[2] While

That the conduct of princes should be canvassed after death. living, they are equal with, at least, if not above, the laws, and, therefore, what justice could not inflict upon their persons, it is but reason should be executed upon their reputations and the estates of their successors ; things that we often value above life itself. It is a custom of singular advantage to those coun-

---

[1] Seneca, *Epist.* 98. "La Prevoyance qui nous porte sans cesse au delà de nous, et souvent nous place ou nous n'arrive-rons point, voilà la veritable source de toutes nos misères." Rousseau—*Emile*, ii.
[2] Cicero, *Tusc. Ques.* v. 18.

tries where it is in use, and much to be desired by all good princes who have reason to take it ill, that the memories of the tyrannical and wicked should be treated with the same respect as theirs. We owe, it is true, subjection and obedience to all our kings, whether good or bad, alike, for that has respect unto their office; but, as to affection and esteem, these are only due to their virtue. Let it be granted that, for the sake of political order, we are, with patience, to endure unworthy princes, to conceal their vices, and to assist them in their indifferent actions, whilst their authority stands in need of our support; yet, the relation of prince and subject being once at an end, there is no reason we should deny the expression of our resentment to our own liberty, and to common justice; or, more especially, deprive good subjects of the glory of having submissively and faithfully served a prince whose imperfections were, to them, so well known; this were to rob posterity of a most useful example; and those who, out of respect to some private obligation, iniquitously vindicate the memory of a faulty prince, do a private right at the expense of public justice. Livy very truly says: "That the language of men bred up in courts is always full of vain ostentation and false testimony," [1] every one indifferently magnifying his own master, and stretching his commendation to the utmost extent of virtue and sovereign grandeur. And it is not impossible but some may condemn the magnanimity of those two soldiers, who so roundly answered Nero to his face; the one being asked, by him, Why he bore him ill-will? "I loved thee," answered he, "whilst thou wert worthy of it; but since thou art become a parricide, an incendiary, a player, and a coachman, I hate thee as thou dost deserve." And the other, Why he should attempt to kill him? "Because," said he, "I could think of no other remedy against thy perpetual mischiefs." [2] But the public and universal testimonies that were given against him, after his death, (and will be to all posterity, both against him and

---

[1] Livy, xxxv. 48.　　　　　[2] Tacitus, *Annal.* xv. 67.

against all other wicked princes like him,) of his tyrannies and abominable conduct, who, of a sound judgment can reprove them?

I am scandalized, I confess, that in so sacred a government as that of the Lacedemonians, there should have been mixed that hypocritical ceremony at the death of their kings; where all their confederates and neighbours, and all sorts and degrees of men and women, as well as their slaves, cut and slashed their foreheads in token of sorrow, repeating, in their cries and lamentations, that that king (let him have been as wicked as the devil) was the best that ever they had; thus attributing to his quality the praises that only belong to merit, and that of right are due to desert, though lodged in the lowest and most inferior subject.[1]

Ceremony of the Lacedemonians at the interment of their kings.

Aristotle (who will still have a hand in every thing) makes a query upon the saying of Solon, " That none can be said to be happy until he is dead;" whether, then, any one who has lived and died according to his heart's desire, if he have left an ill repute behind him, and that his posterity be miserable, can be said to be happy?[2] Whilst we have life and motion, we convey ourselves, by fancy and anticipation, whither and to what we please; but once out of being, we have no more any manner of communication with what is in being; and Solon, therefore, had better have said, "That man is never happy at all, since he is never so till after he is no more."

No man is happy till he is dead.

----------Quisquam
Vix radicitus e vita se tollit, et ejicit:
Sed facit esse sui quiddam super inscius ipse.
Nec removet satis à projecto corpore sese, et
Vindicat.[3]

" No dying man can truss his baggage so,
But something of him he must leave below;

---

[1] Herod. vi. 68.
[2] Herod. i. 32. Aristotle, *Ethics*, i. 10.
[3] Lucretius, iii. 890 and 895. Montaigne has slightly altered the text of the author.

Nor from his carcase, that doth prostrate lie,
Himself can clear, or far enough can fly."

Bertrand du Glesquin, dying before the castle of Randon,[1] near unto Puy, in Auvergne, the besieged were afterwards, upon surrender, enjoined to lay down the keys of the place upon the corpse of the dead general.   Bartholomew d'Alviano, the Venetian general, dying in the service of the Republic, in their wars in Brescia, and his corpse being to be carried to Venice, through the territory of Verona, an enemy's country, most of the army were of opinion to demand safe-conduct from the Veronese; but Theodore Trivulsio opposed the motion, rather choosing to make way for the body by force of arms, and to run the hazard of a battle; saying, it was not fit that he, who in his life was never afraid of his enemies, should seem to apprehend them when he was dead.[2]   And, in truth, in cases of the same nature, by the Greek laws, he who made suit to an enemy for a body to give it burial, did, by that act, renounce his victory, and had no longer the right to erect a trophy; and he to whom such suit was made was ever, whatever otherwise the success had been, reputed victor.   By this means it was that Nicias lost the advantage he had visibly obtained over the Corinthians,[3] and that Agesilaus, on the contrary, assured that which he had before very doubtfully gained over the Bœotians.[4]

These things might appear very odd had it not been a general practice in all ages not only to extend the concern of our persons beyond this life, but, moreover, to fancy that the favours of Heaven accompany us to the grave, and continue, even after life, to our ashes.   Of which there are so many examples among the ancients, waiving those of our times, that it is not necessary I should insist upon it.   Edward the First, King of England, having, in the long wars between him and Robert, King of Scotland, had sufficient experience

The dead treated as though alive.

---

[1] July 13, 1380.
[2] Brantome, ii. Guicciard. xii.
[3] Plutarch, *in vitâ*, c ii.
[4] Id. *in vitâ*, c. vi.

of how great importance his own immediate presence was to
the success of his affairs, having ever been victorious in
whatever he undertook in his own person; when he came to
die, bound his son in a solemn oath, that so soon as he should
be dead, he should boil his body till the flesh parted from the
bones, and, having burned the flesh, preserve the bones to
carry continually with him in his army so often as he should
be obliged to go against the Scots; as if destiny had attached
victory even to those miserable remains. John Zisca, the
same who so often, in vindication of Wickliffe's errors, overran Bohemia, left order that they should flay him after his
death, and of his skin make a drum, to carry in the war
against his enemies, fancying this would contribute to the
continuation of the successes he himself had always obtained
in the war against them. In like manner some Indians, in a
battle with the Spaniards, carried with them the bones of one
of their captains, in consideration of the victories they had
formerly obtained under his conduct. And other people, in
the same new world, carry about with them, in their wars,
the relics of valiant men, who have died in battle, to incite
their courage and advance their fortune. Of which examples the first reserve nothing for the tomb but the reputation
they have acquired by their former achievements; while
these assign to these great men, even in the grave, a certain
power of operation.

The last act of the captain Bayard is of a much better
composition; who, finding himself wounded to death with a
harquebuss shot, and, being by his friends importuned to retire out of the fight, made answer, "That he would not begin,
at the last gasp, to turn his back to the enemy," and, accordingly, still fought on, till, feeling himself too faint, and no
longer able to sit his horse, he commanded his steward to set
him down against the root of a tree, but so that he might
die with his face towards the enemy, which he did.[1]

I must yet add another example, equally remarkable, for

1 Mem. of Martin du Bellay, iv.

the present consideration, with any of the former. The Emperor Maximilian, great grandfather to the present King Philip,[1] was a prince endowed with great qualities, and, amongst the rest, with a singular beauty of person; but had, withal, a humour very contrary to that of other princes, who, for the dispatch of their most important affairs, convert their close-stool into a chair of state; which was that he would never permit any of his bedchamber, in what familiar degree of favour soever, to see him in that posture; and would steal aside to make water, as religiously shy as a virgin, not to discover either to his physician, or any other person, those parts that we are accustomed to conceal. And I myself, who have so impudent a way of talking, am, nevertheless, so modest this way that, unless at the great importunity of necessity or pleasure, I very rarely and unwillingly communicate to the sight of any, those parts or actions, that custom orders us to conceal; wherein I suffer more constraint than I conceive is very well becoming a man, especially of my profession. But he nourished this modest humour to such a degree that he gave express orders in his last will that they should put him on drawers so soon as he should be dead; to which, methinks, he would have done well to have added, by way of codicil, that he should be hoodwinked, too, who put them on. The charge that Cyrus left with his children, that neither they nor any other should either see or touch his body after the soul was departed from it,[2] I attribute to some superstitious devotion of his; both his historian and himself, amongst their other great qualities, having strewed the whole course of their lives with a singular attention and respect to religion.

Modesty of Maximilian the Emperor.

Cyrus's reverence to religion.

I was by no means pleased with a story that was told me by a man of great quality, of a relation of mine, one who had given a very good account of himself both in peace and war; that, coming

The foolishness of much funeral pomp.

---

[1] Philip II. of Spain.   [2] Xenophon, *Cyrop.* viii. 7

to die in a very old age, tormented with an excessive pain of the stone, he spent the last hours of his life in an extraordinary solicitude about ordering the pomp and ceremony of his funeral, pressing all the men of condition who came to see him to engage their word to attend him to his grave; importuning this very prince, who came to visit him at his last gasp, with a most earnest supplication, that he would order his family to be assisting there, alleging several reasons and examples to prove that it was a respect due to a man of his condition; and seemed to die content, having obtained this promise, and appointed the method and order of his funeral parade. I have seldom heard of so long-lived a vanity. The contrary solicitude, of which also I do not want domestic example, seems to be somewhat akin to this; that a man shall cudgel his brains, at the last moments of his life, to contrive his obsequies to some particular and unusual a parsimony, to one single servant with a candle and lanthorn; yet I see this humour commended, and the appointment of Marcus Æmilius Lepidus, who forbad his heirs to bestow upon his corpse even the common ceremonies in use upon such occasions.[1] Is it temperance and frugality to avoid expense and pleasure, of which the use and knowledge is imperceptible to us? This were an easy and cheap reformation. If instructions were at all necessary in this case, I should be of opinion that in this, as in all other actions of life, the ceremony and expense should be regulated by the condition of the person deceased; and the philosopher Lycon, prudently ordered his executors to dispose of his body where they should think most fit, and as to his funeral, to order it to be neither too superfluous, nor too mean.[2] For my part, I shall wholly refer the ordering of this ceremony to custom, and leave the whole matter to the discretion of those to whose lot it shall fall to do me that last office. *Totus hic locus est contemnendus in nobis, non negligendus in nostris.*[3]

---

[1] Livy, *Epis.* xlviii.   [3] Cicero, *Tusc. Quæs.*, 45.
[2] Diog. Laert., *in vitâ.*

" The place of our sepulture is wholly to be contemned by us, but not to be neglected by our friends." And it was a holy saying of a saint, *Curatio funeris, conditio sepulturæ, pompa exsequiarum, magis sunt vivorum solatia, quàm, subsidia mortuorum.*[1] " The care of funerals, the place of sepulture, and the pomp of obsequies, are rather consolations to the living than any benefit to the dead." Which made Socrates answer Criton, who, at the hour of his death, asked him, how he would be buried? "How you will," said he.[2] If I were to concern myself farther about this affair, I should be most tempted, as the greatest satisfaction of this kind, to imitate those who in their lifetime entertain themselves with the ceremony of their own obsequies beforehand, and are pleased with viewing their own monument, and beholding their own dead countenance in marble. Happy are they who can gratify their senses by insensibility, and live by their death! I can hardly keep from an implacable hatred against all popular government, though I cannot but think it the most natural and equitable of all others, so often as I call to mind the inhuman injustice of the people of Athens, who, without remission, or once vouchsafing to hear what they had to say for themselves, put to death their brave captains, newly returned triumphant from a naval victory they had obtained over the Lacedemonians near the Arginusian Isles, the most bloody and obstinate engagement that ever the Greeks fought at sea, for no other reason but that they had followed up their blow and pursued the advantages presented to them by the rule of war, instead of staying to gather up and bury their dead; an execution that is yet rendered more odious by the behaviour of Diomedon, one of the condemned, and a man of eminent virtue, both political and military, who, after having heard their sentence, advancing to speak, no audience till then having been allowed, instead of pleading his cause, and representing the evident injustice of so cruel a sentence, only expressed a

[1] St. August. *de Civitate Dei*, 1, 12.　　　　[2] Plato, *Phædo.*

solicitude for his judges' preservation, beseeching the gods to
convert this sentence to their good, and praying that for
neglecting to fulfil those vows which he and his companions
had made (which he also acquainted them with) in acknowledgment of so glorious a success they might not pull down
the indignation of the gods upon them ; and so without more
words went courageously to his death.[1]　But fortune, a few
years after, punished the Athenians in a suitable way.　For
Chabrias, captain-general of their naval forces, having got
the better of Pollis, admiral of Sparta, off the Isle of Naxos,
totally lost the fruits of his victory, of very great importance
to their affairs, in order not to incur the danger of this example, and in his anxiety not to lose a few bodies of his dead
friends that were floating in the sea, gave opportunity to a
world of living enemies to sail away in safety, who afterwards made them pay dear for this unseasonable superstition.

> Quæris, quo jaceas, post obitum, loco?
> Quo non nata jacent.[2]

> "Dost ask where thou shalt lie when dead?
> With those that never being had."—

The other restores the sense of repose to a body without a
soul.

> Neque sepulcrum, quo recipiatur, habeat portum corporis;
> Ubi, remissâ humanâ vitâ, corpus requiescat a malis.[3]

> "Nor with a tomb as with a haven blest,
> Where, after life, the corpse in peace may rest."

Just as nature demonstrates to us that several dead things
retain yet an occult sympathy and relation to life ; wine
changes its flavour and complexion in cellars, according to
the changes and seasons of the vine whence it came ; and
the flesh of venison, 'tis said, alters its condition and taste in
the powdering tub, according to the seasons of the living
flesh of its kind.

[1] Diod. Sic. xiii. 31.
[2] Senec. Troad, Chor. ii. 30.
[3] Ennius, apud Cicer. Tusc. Quæs i. 44.

CHAPTER IV.

THAT THE SOUL DISCHARGES ITS PASSIONS UPON FALSE OBJECTS, WHERE THE TRUE ARE WANTING.

A GENTLEMAN of my country, who was very subject to the gout, being importuned by his physicians totally to abstain from all manner of salt meats, was wont pleasantly to reply, that he must needs have something to quarrel with in the extremity of his pain, and that he fancied that railing at and cursing, one while the Bologna sausages, and at another the dried tongues and the hams, was some mitigation to his torments. And, in good earnest, as one's arm when it is advanced to strike, if it fail of meeting with that upon which it was designed to discharge the blow, and spends itself in vain, does offend the striker himself; and as, also, to make a pleasant prospect, the sight should not be lost and dilated in a vast extent of empty air, but have some bounds to limit and circumscribe it at a reasonable distance—

> Ventus ut amittit vires, nisi robore densæ
> Occurrunt Silvæ, spatio diffusus inani; [1]

> " As winds exhaust their strength, unless withstood
> By some thick grove of strong opposing wood,"

so it appears that the soul, being transported and discomposed, turns its violence upon itself, if not supplied with something to oppose it, and therefore always requires an object at which to aim, and to keep it in action. Plutarch says of those who are delighted with monkeys and lapdogs, that the amorous part which is in us, for want of a legitimate object, rather than be idle, does after that manner forge and create one frivolous and false; [2] and we see that the soul,

1 Lucan, iii. 362.   2 Life of Pericles, at the beginning.

in the exercise of its passions, inclines rather to deceive itself, by creating a false and fantastical subject, even contrary to its own belief, than not to have something to work upon. And after this manner brute beasts direct their fury to fall upon the stone or weapon that has hurt them, and with their teeth, even execute their revenge upon themselves, for the injury they have received from another.

> Pannonis haud aliter post ictum sævior ursa,
> Quum jaculum parva Lybis amentavit habena,
> Se rotat in vulnus, telumque irata receptum
> Impetit, et secum fugientem circuit hastam.[1]

> "So the fierce bear, made fiercer by the smart
> Of the bold Lybian's mortal wounding dart,
> Turns round upon the wound, and the tough spear
> Contorted o'er her breast doth, flying, bear."

What causes of the misadventures that befall us do we not invent? What is it that we do not lay the fault to, right or wrong, that we may have something to quarrel with? 'Tis not those beautiful tresses, young lady, you so liberally tear off, nor is it the whiteness of that delicate bosom you so unmercifully beat, that, with an unlucky bullet, have slain your beloved brother; quarrel with something else. Livy, speaking of the Roman army in Spain, says, that for the loss of the two brothers,[2] their great captains, *Flere omnes repente, et offensare capita.*[3] "They all wept and tore their hair." 'Tis the common practice of affliction. And the philosopher Bion said pleasantly of the king, who by handfulls pulled his hair off his head for sorrow, "Does this man think that baldness is a remedy for grief?"[4] Who has not seen peevish gamesters tear the cards with their teeth, and swallow the dice in revenge for the loss of their money? Xerxes whipped the sea, and wrote a challenge to Mount Athos.[5] Cyrus employed a whole army several days at work, to revenge himself of the river Gnidus, for the fright it had put him into in

---

1 Lucan, vi. 220.
2 Publius and Cneius Scipio.
3 Livy, xxv. 37.
4 Cicero, *Tusc. Quæs.* iii. 26.
5 Herodotus, vii. 24, 35. Plutarch, *on Anger.*

passing over it;[1] and Caligula demolished a very beautiful palace for the discomfort his mother had once had there.[2]

There was a story current, when I was a boy, that one of our neighbouring kings,[3] having received a blow from the hand of God, swore he would be revenged, and, in order to it, made proclamation that, for ten years to come, no one throughout his dominions should pray to him, nor mention him, nor believe in him; by which we are not so much to take measure of the folly, as of the vainglory of the nation of which this tale was told. These are vices that indeed always go together; but such actions as these have in them more of presumption than want of sense. Augustus Cæsar, having been tost with a tempest at sea, fell to defying Neptune, and, in the pomp of the Circensian games, to be revenged of him, deposed his statue from the place it had amongst the other deities.[4] Wherein he was less excusable than the former, and less than he was afterwards, when, having lost a battle under Quintilius Varus in Germany, in rage and despair, he went running his head against the walls, and crying out, "O Varus! give me my men again!"[5] for those exceed all folly, forasmuch as impiety is joined with it, who invade God himself, or at least Fortune, as if she had ears that were subject to our batteries; like the Thracians, who, when it thunders or lightens, fall to shooting against heaven with Titanian fury,[6] as if by flights of arrows they intended to reduce God to reason. The ancient poet as Plutarch tells us,

> We must not quarrel Heaven in our affairs,
> That nothing for a mortal's anger cares.[7]

But we can never enough condemn the senseless and ridiculous sallies of our passions.

---

[1] Herodotus, l. 189, who calls the river Gyndes, not Gnidus, says that Cyrus spent a whole summer on this fine occupation.

[2] She had been imprisoned in it. Seneca, on Anger, iii. 22.

[3] Alphonzo XI. King of Castile; died, 1350.

[4] Suetonius, in Vitâ, c. 16.

[5] Id. ib. c. 23.

[6] Herod. iv. 94.

[7] Plutarch, on Contentment, c. iv.

CHAPTER V.

WHETHER THE GOVERNOR OF A PLACE BESIEGED OUGHT HIMSELF TO GO OUT TO PARLEY.

LUCIUS MARCIUS,[1] the Roman Legate in the war against *Deceit in warfare* Perseus, king of Macedon, to gain time where- *condemned.* in to reinforce his army, set on foot some overtures of accommodation, with which the king being lulled asleep, concluded a cessation for certain days; by this means giving his enemy opportunity and leisure to repair his army, which was afterwards the occasion of his own ruin. The elder sort of senators, notwithstanding, mindful of their forefathers' virtue, were by no means satisfied with this proceeding; but on the contrary condemned it, as degenerating from their ancient practice, which they said was by valour, and not by artifice, surprises, and night encounters, or by pretended flight, ambuscades, and deceitful treaties, to overcome their enemies; never making war till having first denounced it, and very often assigned both the hour and place of battle. Out of this generous principle it was that they delivered up to Pyrrhus his treacherous physician, and to the Phaliscians their disloyal schoolmaster. And this was indeed a procedure truly Roman, and nothing allied to the Grecian subtilty, or Punic cunning, where it was reputed a victory of less glory to overcome by force than by fraud. Deceit may serve for a need, but he only confesses himself overcome who knows he is neither subdued by policy nor misadventure, but by dint of valour, in a fair and manly war. And it very well appears by the discourse of these good old senators, that this fine sentence was not yet received amongst them,

---

1 Livy, xlii. 37, calls him Quintus Marcius.

——Dolus, an virtus, quis in hoste requirat? [1]

" No matter if by valour, or deceit,
We overcome, so we the better get."

The Achaians, says Polybius, abhorred all manner of double-dealing in war, not reputing it a victory unless where the courage of the enemy was fairly subdued. *Eam vir sanctus et sapiens sciet veram esse victoriam, quæ, salva fide et integra dignitate, parabitur.*[2] "An honest and wise man will acknowledge that only to be a true victory which is obtained without violation of faith, or blemish upon honour," says another.

Vosne velit, an me, regnare hera, quidve ferat, fors,
Virtute experiamur.[3]

" If you or I shall rule, let's fairly try,
And force or fortune give the victory."

In the kingdom of Ternate, amongst those nations which we so roundly call barbarian, they have a custom never to commence war till it be first denounced; adding withal, an ample declaration of what they have to carry it on withal, how many men, what supplies, and what arms, both offensive and defensive; but, that being done, if their enemies do not yield, they afterwards deem it lawful to employ this power without reproach, by any means that may best conduce to their own ends.

The ancient Florentines were so far from wishing to obtain any advantage over their enemies by surprise, that they always gave them a month's warning before they drew their army into the field, by the continual tolling of a bell they call Martinella.[4]

As to us, who are not so scrupulous in this matter, who attribute the honour of the war to him who has the better of it, after what manner soever obtained, and who, after Lysander, say, " Where the lion's skin is too short, we must eke it out with the fox's case,"[5] the most usual occasions of surprise are derived from this practice, and we hold that there are no

---

[1] *Æneid,* ii. 390. [2] Florus, i. 12. [4] From the name of St. Martin, derived
[3] Ennius *apud* Cicero *de Officiis,* i. from that of Mars, the god of war.
12. [5] Plutarch, *in Vitâ,* c. 4.

moments wherein a chief ought to be more circumspect, and
to have his eye so much at watch, as those of parleys and
treaties of accommodation ; and it is therefore become a general rule amongst the military men of these latter times that
a governor of a place never ought in a time of siege to go
out himself to parley. It was for this that in our fathers'
days the Seigneurs de Montmord and de l'Assigni, defending
Mousson against the Count de Nassau, were so highly censured ; yet in this case it would be excusable in that govern-
or who, going out for this purpose, should do it in such a
manner that the safety and advantage should be on his side;
as Count Guido de Rangoni did at Reggiq, (if we are to believe du Bellay, for Guicciardin says it was he himself,) when
Monsieur de l'Escut approached to parley ; for he went so
little away from the wall of his fortress that, a disorder happening during the parley, not only Monsieur de l'Escut and
his party, who were advanced with him, found themselves by
much the weaker (insomuch that Alessandro de Trivulcio
was there slain), but he himself was constrained, as the safest
way, to follow the Count, and relying upon his honour to
secure himself from the danger of the shot within the very
walls of the town.[1]

Eumenes, being shut up in the city of Nora, by Antigonus,
and by him importuned to come out to speak with him, as he
sent him word it was fit he should to a better man than himself, who had the advantage over him, returned this noble
answer, "I never shall think any man better than myself,
whilst I have my sword in my hand ;" and would not consent
to come out to him, till first, according to his own demand,
Antigonus had delivered his own nephew Ptolemy in hostage.[2]

And yet some have done well in going out in person to
parley with the assailant on his word of honour ; witness
Henry de Vaux, a cavalier of Champagne, who being besieged by the English in the castle of Courmicy,[3] and Bar-

[1] Mem. of Martin du Bellay, i. Guicciard. xiv.
[2] Plut. in *Vità*, c. v.
[3] Most of the editions have it Com-
mercy.

tholomew de Bruwes,[1] who commanded at the siege, having
so sapped the greatest part of the castle without, that nothing
remained but setting fire to the props to bury the besieged
under the ruins, he required the said Henry to come out to
speak with him for his own good ; which the other accordingly doing, with three more in company with him, and his own
evident ruin being made apparent to him, he conceived himself singularly obliged to his enemy, to whose discretion he
and his garrison then surrendered themselves ; and, fire being presently applied to the mine, the props no sooner began
to fail but the castle was immediately turned topsy-turvy, no
one stone being left upon another.[2]

I could, and do, with great facility, rely upon the faith of
another ; but I should very unwillingly do it in any case
where it might be judged that it was rather an effect of my
despair and want of courage, than voluntarily and out of confidence and security in the faith of him with whom I had
to do.

———————◆———————

CHAPTER VI.

THAT THE HOUR OF PARLEY IS DANGEROUS.

YET I saw, lately at Mussidan,[3] a place not far from my
house, that those who were driven out thence by our army,
and others of their party, highly complained of treachery, for
that, during a treaty of accommodation, and in the very interim that their deputies were treating, they were surprised and
cut to pieces ; a thing that, peradventure, in another age,
might have had some colour of foul play ; but, as I said
before, the practice of arms in these days is quite another
thing, and there is now no confidence in an enemy excus-

---

[1] Or as it is now written Burghersh.   [3] Or Mucidan.
[2] Froissart, i. c. 118.

able till after the last seal of obligation is fixed; and even then the conqueror has enough to do to keep his word; so hazardous a thing it is to intrust the observation of the faith a man has engaged to a town that surrenders upon easy and favourable conditions, to the necessity, avarice, and license of a victorious army, and to give the soldiers free entrance into it in the heat of blood.

Lucius Æmilius Regillus, a Roman Prætor, having lost his time in attempting to take the city of Phocæa by force, by reason of the singular valour wherewith the inhabitants defended themselves against him, conditioned at last to receive them as friends to the people of Rome, and to enter the town, as into a confederate city, without any manner of hostility; of which he gave them all possible assurance; but having, for the greater pomp, brought his whole army in with him, it was no more in his power, with all the endeavour he could use, to command his people; so that, avarice and revenge despising and trampling under foot both his authority and all military discipline, he there at once saw his own faith violated, and a considerable part of the city sacked and ruined before his face.[1]

The faith of military men very uncertain.

Cleomenes was wont to say that, whatever mischief a man could do his enemy in time of war was above justice, and nothing accountable to it in the sight of gods and men. And, according to this principle, having concluded a cessation with those of Argos for seven days, the third night after he fell upon them when they were all buried in security and sleep, and put them to the sword; alleging, for his excuse, that there had no nights been mentioned in the truce. But the gods punished his subtle perfidy.[2] In a time of parley, also, and while the citizens were intent upon their capitulation, the city of Casilinum was taken by surprise,[3] and that even in the age of the justest captains, and the most perfect discipline of the Roman army; for it is not said that it is not lawful

---

[1] Livy, xxxvii. 32.   [2] Plutarch, *Apothegms.*   [3] Livy, xxiv. 19.

for us in time and place to make advantage of our enemies' want of understanding, as well as their want of courage. And doubtless war has naturally a great many privileges that appear reasonable, even to the prejudice of reason. And therefore here the rule fails, *Neminem id agere, ut ex alterius prædetur inscitia.*[1] "No one should prey upon another's folly." But I am astonished at the great liberty allowed by Xenophon in such cases,[2] and that both by precept and the example of several exploits of his complete general; an author of very great authority, I confess, in those affairs, as being in his own person both a great captain and a philosopher of the first form of Socrates's disciples; and yet I cannot consent to such a measure of license as he dispenses in all things and places.

Monsieur d'Aubigny besieging Capua, after having played a furious battery against it, Signior Fabricio Colonna, governor of the town, having from a bastion begun to parley, and his soldiers in the mean time being a little more remiss in their guard, our people took advantage of their security, entered the place at unawares, and put them all to the sword. And of later memory, at Yvoy,[3] Signior Juliano Rommero having played that part of a novice to go out to capitulate with Monsieur the Constable, at his return found his place taken. But, that we might not escape scot free, the Marquis of Pescara having laid siege to Genoa, where Duke Ottavio Fregosa commanded under our protection, and the articles betwixt them being so far advanced that it was looked upon as a done thing, and upon the point to be concluded, the Spaniards, in the mean time, being slipped in under the privilege of the treaty, seized on the gates, and made use of this treachery as an absolute and fair victory.[4] And since, at Ligny in Barrois, where the Count de Brienne commanded, the Emperor having in his own person beleaguered that place, and Bartheville, the said Count's lieutenant, going

---

[1] Cicero, *de Offic.* iii. 17.
[2] In his *Cyropædia.*
[3] Or Carignan, a small town of old

French Luxembourg, on the river Chiers, four leagues from Sedan.
[4] Mem. of Martin du Bellay, ii.

out to parley, while he was capitulating the town was
taken.[1]

> Fù il vincer sempremai laudabil cosa
> Vincasi o per fortuna, o per ingegno.[2]

> " Fame ever doth the victor's praises ring,
>   And conquest aye was deem'd a glorious thing,
>   Which way soe'er the conqu'ror purchas'd it,
>   Whether by valour, fortune, or by wit,"

say they. But the philosopher Chrysippus was of another
opinion, wherein I also concur; for he was used to say that
those who run a race ought to employ all the force they have
in what they are about, and to run as fast as they can; but
that it is by no means fair in them to lay an hand upon their
adversary to stop him, nor to set a leg before him to throw
him down.[3] And still more generous was the answer of
the Great Alexander to Polypercon, who was persuading
him to take the advantage of the night's obscurity to fall
upon Darius; "no," said he, "it is not for such a man as I
to steal a victory:" *malo me fortunæ pæniteat, quam victoriæ
pudeat.*[4] "I had rather have to lament my fortune than be
ashamed of my victory."

> Atque idem fugientem haud est dignatus Oroden
> Sternere, nec jactâ cæcum dare cuspide vulnus,
> Obvius, adversoque occurrit, seque viro vir
> Contulit, haud furto melior, sed fortibus armis.[5]

> " Then with disdain, the haughty victor viewed
>   Orodes flying, nor the wretch pursued;
>   Nor thought the dastard's back deserved a wound,
>   But, hastening to o'ertake him, gained the ground;
>   Then, turning short, he met him face to face,
>   To give his victory the better grace."

1 Mem. of William du Bellay, ix.
2 Ariosto, Cant. xv. 1.
3 Cicer. *de Offic.* iii. 10.
4 Quint. Curt. iv. 13.
5 *Æneid*, x. 732.

CHAPTER VII.

THAT THE INTENTION IS JUDGE OF OUR ACTIONS.

'Tis a saying, that death discharges us of all our obligations. However, I know some who have taken

Whether death discharges us of an obligation.

it in another sense. Henry VII., king of
England, articled with Don Philip, son to
Maximilian the emperor, or, to give him the more honourable
title, father to the Emperor Charles V., that the said Philip
should deliver up into his hands the Duke of Suffolk, of the
White Rose, his mortal enemy, who was fled into the Low
Countries; which Philip (not knowing how to evade it) accordingly promised to do, but upon condition, nevertheless,
that Henry should attempt nothing against the life of the said
duke, which during his own life the king kept to; but, coming to die, in his last will, he commanded his son to put him
to death immediately after his decease.[1] And lately, in the
tragedy that the Duke of Alva presented to us at Brussels, in
the persons of Count Egmont and Horne, there were many
very remarkable passages; and one amongst the rest, that
Count Egmont, upon the security of whose word and faith
Count Horne had come and surrendered himself to the Duke
of Alva, earnestly entreated that he might first mount the
scaffold, to the end that death might disengage him from the
obligation he had passed to the other. In these cases, methinks death did not acquit the king of his promise, and the
Count was freed from his, even though he had not died.
For we cannot be obliged beyond what we are able to perform, by reason that effects and performances are not at all
in our power, and that indeed we are masters of nothing but
the will, in which, by necessity, all the rules and whole duty

[1] Mem. of Martin du Bellay, i.

of mankind are founded and established. And therefore
Count Egmont, holding his soul and will bound and indebted
to his promise, although he had not the power to make it
good, had doubtless been absolved of his obligation, even
though he had outlived the other ; but the king of England,
premeditatedly breaking his faith, was no more to be excused
for deferring the execution of his infidelity till after his death
than Herodotus's mason, who having inviolably, during the
time of his life, kept the secret of the treasure of the king of
Ægypt his master, at his death discovered it to his children.[1]

I have noticed several, in my time, who, plagued by their
consciences for unjustly detaining the goods of another, have
thought to make amends by their will, and after their decease ; but they had as good do nothing as delude themselves
both in taking so much time in so pressing an affair, and in
going about to repair an injury with so little damage to themselves. They owe, over and above, something of their own,
and by how much their payment is more strict and incom-
modious to themselves, by so much is their restitution more
perfect, just, and meritorious ; for penitence requires penance.
But they do yet worse than these, who reserve the declaration of their animosity against their neighbour to the last
gasp, having concealed it all the time of their lives before,
wherein they declare themselves to have little regard for
their own honour, irritating the party offended against their
memory only ; and less for their conscience, not having the
power, even out of respect to death itself, to make their malice die with them ; but extending the life of their hatred even
beyond their own. Unjust judges, who defer judgment to a
time wherein they can have no cognizance of the cause !
For my part I shall take care, if I can, that my death discover nothing that my life has not first declared, and that
openly.

[1] Herod. ii. 121.

CHAPTER VIII.

OF IDLENESS.

As we see ground that has long lain idle and untilled, if it be rich and naturally fertile, abound with innumerable sorts ∫of weeds and unprofitable wild herbs; and that, to make it perform its true office, we must cultivate and prepare it for such seeds as are proper for our service; and as we see women that, without the knowledge of men, do sometimes of themselves bring forth inanimate and formless lumps of flesh, but that, to cause a natural and perfect generation, they are to be husbanded with another kind of seed; even so it is with our minds, which, if not applied to some certain study that may fix and restrain them, run into a thousand extravagances, and are eternally roving here and there in the inextricable labyrinth of restless imagination.

> Sicut aquæ tremulum labris ubi lumen ahenis,
> Sole repercussum, aut radiantis imagine lunæ
> Omnia pervolitat late loca; jamque sub auras
> Erigitur summique ferit laquearia tecti.[1]

> "Like as the quivering reflection
> Of fountain waters, when the morning sun
> Sheds on the basin, or the moon's pale beam
> Gives light and colour to the captive stream,
> Darts with fantastic motion round the place,
> And walls and roof strikes with its trembling rays."

In which wild and irregular agitation, there is no folly, nor idle fancy they do not light upon :—

> Velut ægri somnia, vanæ
> Finguntur species.[2]

> "Like sick men's dreams, that, from a troubled brain,
> Phantasms create, ridiculous and vain."

---

[1] *Æneid*, viii 22.   [2] *Horace, de Arte Poet.* 7.

The soul that has no established limit to circumscribe it, loses itself; for as the Epigrammatist says: He that is everywhere is nowhere.

> Quisquis ubique habitat, Maxime, nusquam habitat. [1]

When I lately retired myself to my own house, with a resolution, as much as possibly I could, to avoid all manner of concern in affairs, and to spend in privacy and repose the little remainder of time I have to live, I fancied I could not more oblige my mind than to suffer it at full leisure to entertain and divert itself, which I hoped it might now the better be intrusted to do, as being by time and observation become more settled and mature ; but I find,

> Variam semper dant otia mentem. [2]
>
> " —— E'en in the most retir'd estate,
> Leisure itself does various thoughts create: "

that, quite the contrary, it is like a horse that has broken from his rider, who voluntarily runs into a much wilder career than any horseman would put him to, and creates me so many chimæras and fantastic monsters, one upon another, without order or design, that, the better at leisure to contemplate their strangeness and absurdity, I have begun to commit them to writing, hoping in time to make them ashamed of themselves.

CHAPTER IX.

OF LIARS.

There is not a man living whom it would so little become
Montaigne's bad   to speak of memory as myself, for I have
memory.   scarcely any at all ; and do not think that the
world has again another so marvellously treacherous as mine.
My other faculties are all very ordinary and mean ; but in
this I think myself so singular, and to have the defect to such

---

[1] Martial, vii. 73.   [2] Lucan, iv. 704.

a degree of excellence, that I deserve, methinks, to be famous for it, and to have more than a common reputation. Besides the natural inconveniences which I experience from this cause, (for, in truth, the use of memory considered, Plato had reason when he called it a great and powerful goddess ;[1]) in my country, when they would describe a man that has no sense, they say, such an one has no memory ; and when I complain of mine,[2] they seem not to believe I am in earnest, and presently reprove me, as though I accused myself for a fool, not discerning the difference betwixt memory and understanding ; wherein they are very wide of my intention, and do me wrong, experience rather daily showing us, on the contrary, that a strong memory is commonly coupled with infirm judgment. And they do me, moreover, who am so perfect in nothing as in friendship, a greater wrong in this, that they make the same words, which accuse my infirmity, represent me for an ungrateful person ; bringing my affection into question, upon the account of my memory, and, from a natural imperfection, unjustly derive a defect of conscience. "He has forgot," says one, "this request, or that promise ; he no longer remembers his friends, he has forgot to say or do, or to conceal, such and such a thing for my sake." And truly, I am apt enough to forget many things, but to neglect any thing my friend has given me in charge, I never do it. And it should be enough, methinks, that I feel the misery and inconvenience of it without being branded with malice, a vice so contrary to my nature.

However, I derive these comforts from my infirmity ; first, that it is an evil from which principally, I have found reason to correct a worse, that would easily enough have grown upon me, namely *The advantages of a defective memory.*

[1] Plato, *Critias.*
[2] He complains of this defect again in the 17th chapter of the second book. Malebranche, and others, charge him with falsehood, in this respect, (see particularly Baudius, *Not. ad Jamb. II.*) and they allege, as a proof of this, his numerous quotations. But besides that these quotations are frequently inexact, and that he occasionally contradicts himself, even when not quoting, persons accustomed to authorship know that it requires no great memory to quote, and this frequently. *A faulte de memoire naturelle,* says the forgetful Montaigne, *j'en forge de papier* (book 3, c. 13), and this is the whole secret.

ambition; this defect being intolerable in those who take
upon them the negotiations of the world. That, as several
like examples in the progress of nature demonstrate to us,
she has fortified me in my other faculties proportionably as
she has left me unfurnished in this; I should otherwise have
been apt, implicitly, to have reposed my understanding and
judgment upon the bare report of other men, without ever
setting them to work for themselves upon any inquisition
whatever, had the inventions and opinions of others been ever
present with me by the benefit of memory. That by this
means I am not so talkative, for the magazine of the memory is ever better furnished with matter than that of the
invention; and had mine been faithful to me, I had, e'er this,
deafened all my friends with my eternal babble, the subjects
themselves rousing and stirring up the little faculty I have of
handling and applying them, and heating and extending my
discourse. 'Tis a great imperfection, and what I have observed in several of my intimate friends who, as their memories supply them with a present and entire review of things,
carry back their narratives so far, and crowd them with so
many irrelevant circumstances, that, though the story be good
in itself, they make a shift to spoil it; and if otherwise, you
are either to curse the strength of their memory, or the weakness of their judgment. And it is a hard thing to close up
a discourse and to cut it short, when you are once in, and
have a great deal more to say. There is nothing wherein
the strength and breeding of a horse is so much seen as in a
round, graceful, and sudden stop. I see some, even among
those who talk pertinently enough, who would, but cannot,
stop short in their career; for whilst they are seeking out a
handsome period to conclude with, they go on talking at ran-
dom, and are so perplexed and entangled in their own eloquence that they know not what they say, but go on stagger-
ing amidst unmeaning sentences, as men stagger and totter
on their feet from weakness. But, above all, old men, who
yet retain the memory of things past, and forget how often

they have told them, are the most dangerous company for this fault; and I have known stories from the mouth of a man of very great quality, otherwise very pleasant in themselves, become very troublesome by being a hundred times repeated over and over again.

The second obligation I have to this infirm memory of mine is that, by this means, I less remember the injuries I have received; insomuch that (as one of the ancients [1] said), I should have a protocol, a register of injuries, or a prompter, like Darius, who, that he might not forget the offence he had received from those of Athens, so often as he sat down to dinner, ordered one of his pages three times to bawl in his ear, "Sir, remember the Athenians." [2] And, besides, the places which I revisit, and the books I read over again, still smile upon me with a fresh novelty.

It is not without good reason said that he who has not a good memory should never take upon him the Liars should have good memories. trade of lying. I know very well that the grammarians distinguish betwixt an untruth and a lie, and say that to tell an untruth is to tell a thing that is false, but which we ourselves believe to be true; [3] but that the definition of the Latin verb, to lie, [4] whence our French verb is taken, signifies the going against our conscience; and that, therefore, this touches only those who speak against their own knowledge; and it is to this last sort of liars only that I now refer. Now, these either wholly contrive and invent the untruths they utter, or so alter and disguise a true story, that it always ends in a lie; and when they disguise and often alter the same story according to their own fancy, 'tis very hard for them at one time or another to escape being trapped, by reason that the real truth of the thing having first taken possession of the memory, and being there lodged, and imprinted by the way of knowledge and fact, it will be ever ready to present itself to the imagination, and to shoulder out any

[1] Cicero, pro Lig. c. 12. "Oblivisci nihil soles, nisi injurias."
[2] Herod. v. 105.
[3] Nigidius, apud Aul. Gell. xi. 2. No nius, v.
[4] Mentiri, quasi, contra mentem ire.

falsehood of their own contriving, which cannot there have so
sure and settled footing as the other ; and the circumstances
of the first true knowledge evermore running in their minds,
will be apt to make them forget those that are illegitimate,
and only forged by their own fancy.   In what they wholly
invent, forasmuch as there is no contrary impression to jostle
their invention, there seems to be less danger of tripping ; and
yet, even this also, by reason it is a vain body, and without
any other foundation than fancy only, is very apt to escape
the memory, if they be not careful to make themselves very
perfect in their tale.   Of which I have often had very pleasant experience at the expense of such as profess only to
form and accommodate their speech to the affair they have in
hand, or to the humour of the personage with whom they
have to do ; for the circumstances to which these men stick
not to enslave their consciences and their faith, being subject
to various changes, their language must vary accordingly.
Whence it happens, that of the same thing they tell one man
that it is this, and another that it is that, giving it several
forms and colours ; but if these several men once come to
compare notes and find out the cheat, what becomes of this
fine art ?   Besides which they must, of necessity, very often
ridiculously trap themselves ; for what memory can be sufficient to retain so many different shapes as they have forged
upon one and the same subject ?   I have known many in my
time very ambitious of the reputation of this fine sort of clev-
erness ; but they do not see that he who has the reputation of
it can do nothing with it.

In plain truth, lying is a hateful and an accursed vice.   We
are not men, we have no other tie upon one another but our
word.   If we did but perceive the horror and ill consequences
of it, we should pursue it with fire and sword, and more justly
than other crimes.   I see that parents commonly, and with
indiscretion enough, correct their children for little innocent
faults, and torment them for wanton childish tricks that have
neither impression, nor tend to any consequence ; whereas, in

my opinion, lying only, and, what is of something a lower form,
wilful obstinacy, are the faults which ought, on all occasions,
to be combated, both in the infancy and progress of these
vices, which will otherwise grow up and increase with them ;
and, after a tongue has once got the knack of lying, 'tis not
to be imagined how impossible almost it is to reclaim it.
Whence it comes to pass that we see some, who are otherwise
very honest men, so subject to this vice. I have a good fellow
for my tailor, who, yet, I never knew guilty of one truth ;
no, not even when it had been to his advantage. If falsehood had, like truth, but one face only, we should be upon
better terms ; for we should then take the contrary to what
the liar says for certain truth ; but the reverse of truth has a
hundred thousand shapes, and a field indefinite, without bound
or limit. The Pythagoreans make *good* to be certain and
finite ; *evil*, infinite and uncertain ; there are a thousand ways
to miss the white, there is only one to hit it. For my own
part, I have this vice in so great horror, that I am not sure I
could prevail with my conscience to secure myself from the
most manifest and extreme danger by an impudent and solemn lie. An ancient father says that a dog we know is better
company than a man whose language we do not understand.
Ut externus alieno non sit hominis vice.[1] And how much
less sociable is false speaking than silence ?

King Francis the First bragged that he had, by this
means, nonplussed Francis Taverna, the ambassador of
Francis Sforza, Duke of Milan, a man very famous for his
eloquence in those days. This gentleman had been sent to
excuse his master to his Majesty about a thing of very great
consequence, which was this : King Francis, to maintain
some correspondence in Italy, out of which he had been
lately driven, and particularly in the duchy of Milan, had
thought it, to that end, convenient to have a gentleman, on
his behalf, reside at the Court of that Duke ; an ambassador

[1] "As a foreigner, to one that under- *Nat. Hist.* vii. where, however, the text is
stands not what he says, cannot be said *pene non sit*, scarcely is, &c.
to supply the place of a man." Pliny,

in effect. but in outward appearance no other than a private
person, who pretended to be there upon the single account of
his own particular affairs ; for the Duke, much more depending upon the Emperor, especially at that time, when he was
in a treaty of a marriage with his niece, daughter to the
King of Denmark, and since Dowager of Lorraine, could
not own any friendship or intelligence with us, but very
much to his own prejudice.   For this commission then, one
Merveille, a Milanese gentleman, and equerry to the King,
being thought very fit, he was accordingly dispatched thither,
with private letters of credence and his instructions of ambassador, and with other letters of recommendation to the
Duke about his own private concerns, the better to colour and
cloak the business ; and he so long continued in that Court
that the Emperor, at last, had some notion of his real employment there, and complained of it to the Duke, which
was the occasion of what followed after, as we suppose ;
which was, that under pretence of a murder by him said to
be committed, his trial was in two days dispatched, and his
head, in the night, struck off in prison.   Signor Francisco
then, being upon this account come to the Court of France,
prepared with a long counterfeit story to excuse a thing of so
dangerous example, (for the King had applied himself to all
the princes of Christendom, as well as to the Duke himself,
to demand satisfaction for this outrage upon the person of his
minister,) had his audience at the morning council, where,
after he had, for the support of his cause, in a long premeditated oration, laid open several plausible justifications of the
fact, he concluded with roundly saying that the Duke, his
master, had never looked upon this Merveille for other than
a private gentleman, and his own subject, who was there
only in order to his own business, and who had lived there
under no other character ; absolutely disowning that he had
ever heard he was one of the King's servants, or that his
Majesty so much as knew him, so far was he from taking
him for an ambassador.   When he had made an end, the

King, pressing him with several objections and assertions, and sifting him on all hands, gravelled him at last by asking, why then the execution was performed by night, and as it were by stealth? At which the poor confounded ambassador, the more handsomely to disengage himself, made answer that the Duke would have been very loth, out of respect to his Majesty, that such an execution should have been performed in the face of the sun. Any one may guess if he was not well schooled when he came home, for having so grossly tripped in the presence of a prince of so delicate a nostril as King Francis.[1]

Pope Julius the Second having sent an ambassador to the King of England, to animate him against King Francis, the ambassador having had his audience, and the King, before he would give a positive answer, insisting upon the difficulties he found in setting on foot so great a preparation as would be necessary to attack so potent a king, and, urging some reasons to that effect, the ambassador very unseasonably replied that he had also himself considered the same difficulties, and had represented as much to the Pope. From which speech of his, so directly opposite to the thing propounded, and the business he came about, which was immediately to incite him to war, the King first derived argument to conceive, which he afterwards found to be true, that this ambassador, in his own private bosom, was a friend to the French; of which, having advertised the Pope, his estate, at his return home, was confiscated, and himself very narrowly escaped the losing his head.[2]

---

[1] Mem. of Martin du Bellay, i. The incident occurred in 1534.

[2] Erasmus, in his *Lingua*, relates this circumstance as having occurred when he was in England.

CHAPTER X.

OF QUICK OR SLOW SPEECH.

Onc ne furent à touts toutes graces données.[1]

" All graces were never yet to all men given,"

as we see in the gift of eloquence, wherein some have such **a**
facility and promptness, and that which we call a present wit,
so easy that they are ever ready upon all occasions, and
never to be surprised; and others, more heavy and slow,
never venture to utter any thing but what they have long
premeditated, and taken great care and pains to fit and prepare. Now, as we teach young ladies those sports and exercises which are the most proper to set out the grace and
beauty of those parts wherein their chief ornament and perfection lie ; so in these two different advantages of eloquence,
of which the lawyers and preachers of our age seem principally to make profession, if I were worthy to advise, the
The different sorts slow speakers, methinks, should be more proper
of eloquence.   for the pulpit, and the other for the bar ; and
this because the employment of the first does naturally allow
him all the leisure he can desire to prepare himself, and,
besides, his career is performed in an even and unintermitted
line, without stop or interruption ; whereas, the pleader's
business and interest compels him to enter the lists upon all
occasions, and the unexpected objections and replies of his
adverse party often jostle him out of his course, and put him,
upon the instant, to pump for new and extempore answers
and defences. Yet, at the interview betwixt Pope Clement
and King Francis, at Marseilles, it happened, quite contrary,
that Monsieur Poyet, a man bred up all his life at the bar,

---

[1] Etienne de la Boetie; in the Collection of *Vers Français* published by Montaigne in 1572. Sonnet, xiv.

and in the highest repute for eloquence, having the charge
of making the harangue to the Pope committed to him, and
having so long meditated on it beforehand, as, it was said, to
have brought it ready along with him from Paris ; the very
day it was to have been pronounced, the Pope, fearing something might be said that might give offence to the other
Prince's ambassadors who were there attending on him, sent
to acquaint the King with the argument which he conceived
most suiting to the time and place, which, by chance, was
quite another thing to that Monsieur Poyet had taken so
much pains about ; so that the fine speech he had prepared
was of no use, and he had, upon the instant, to contrive
another; which, finding himself unable to do, Cardinal du
Bellay was constrained to perform that office.[1] The pleader's
part is, doubtless, much harder than that of the preacher ;
and yet, in my opinion, we see more passable lawyers than
preachers, at least in France. It should seem that the nature
of wit is to have its operation prompt and sudden, and that
of judgment, to have it more deliberate and more slow ; but
he who remains totally silent for want of leisure to prepare
himself to speak well, and he also whom leisure does no
ways benefit to better speaking, are equally unhappy.

'Tis said of Severus Cassius, that he spoke best extempore,
that he stood more obliged to fortune than his own diligence,
that it was an advantage to him to be interrupted in speaking, and that his adversaries were afraid to nettle him, lest
his anger should redouble his eloquence.[2] I know, by experience, a disposition so impatient of a tedious and elaborate
premeditation, that if it do not go frankly and gaily to work,
can do nothing to the purpose. We say of some compositions that they smell of the lamp, by reason of a certain
rough harshness that laborious handling imprints upon those
where it has been employed. But, besides this, the extreme
solicitude of doing well, and the striving and contending of
a mind too far strained and overbent upon its undertaking,

1 Mem. of Martin du Bellay, iv.   2 Senec. Rhetor. Controv. iii.

breaks and hinders itself, like water that, by force of its own
pressing violence and abundance, cannot find a ready issue
through the neck of a bottle, or a narrow sluice.   In this
condition of nature, of which I now speak, there is this also,
that it would not be disordered and stimulated with such a
passion as the fury of Cassius ; for such a motion would be
too violent and rude ; it would not be jostled, but solicited ;
it would be roused and heated by unexpected, sudden, and
accidental occasions.   If it be left to itself, it flags and lan-
guishes ; agitation only gives it grace and vigour.   I am
always worst in my own possession ; and when wholly at my
own disposition, accident has more title to any thing that
comes from me, than I ; occasion, company, and even the
very rising and falling of my own voice, extract more from
my fancy than I can find when I examine and employ it by
myself, so that the things I say are better than those I write,
if either were to be preferred where neither is worth any
thing.   This also befalls me, that I am at a loss when I seek,
and light upon things more by chance than by any inquisition of my own judgment.   I, perhaps, sometimes hit upon a
good point, when I am writing, (I mean that seems so to me,
though it may appear dull and heavy to another—but no
more of these complimentaries—every one says this sort of
thing about himself,) but when I come to read it, afterwards,
I cannot make out what I meant to say, and, in such cases, a
stranger often finds it out before me.   If I were always to
scratch out such parts, I should make clean work of my
book ; but then, some other time, chance shows me the mean
ing as clear as the sun at noonday, and makes me wonder
what I should stick at.

CHAPTER XI.

OF PROGNOSTICATIONS.

As to oracles, it is certain that, long before the coming of Jesus Christ, they began to lose their credit; for we see that Cicero is troubled to find out *Decay of oracles.* the cause of their decay, in these words: *Cur isto modo jam oracula Delphis eduntur, non modo nostrâ ætate, sed jamdiu, ut nihil possit esse contemptius.*[1] "What should be the reason that the oracles at Delphos are so uttered, not only in this age of ours, but for a great while since, that nothing can be more contemptible?" But as to the other prognostics, calculated from the anatomy of beasts at sacrifices, which Plato does, in part, attribute to the natural constitution of the intestines of the beasts themselves, from the scraping of poultry, the flight of birds, (*Aves quasdam, rerum augurandarum causâ natas esse putamus;*[2] "We think some sorts of birds were purposely created for the purposes of augury;") claps of thunder, the winding of rivers, *multa cernunt aruspices, multa augures provident, multa oraculis declarantur, multa vaticinationibus, multa somniis, multa portentis.*[3] "Soothsayers and augurs conjecture and foresee many things, and many things are foretold in oracles, prophecies, dreams, and portents;" and others of the like nature, upon which antiquity founded most of their public and private enterprises, our Christian religion has totally abolished, although there yet remain amongst us some practices of divination from the stars, from spirits, from the shapes and complexions of men, from dreams and the like (a notable proof of the wild curiosity of our nature grasping at, and anticipating, future things, as if we had not enough to do to digest the present).

[1] Cicer. *de Divin.* II. 57. [3] Cic. *de Nat. Deo.* iii. 6.
[2] Cicer. *de Nat. Deorum.* II. 64.

> Cur hanc tibi, rector Olympi,
> Solicitis visum mortalibus addere curam,
> Noscant venturas ut dira per omnia clades?
>
> .   .   .   .   .
>
> Sit subitum quodcunque paras: sit cæca futuri
> Mens hominum fati; liceat sperare timenti.[1]

> " Why, sov'reign ruler of Olympus, why
> To human breasts, which breathe the anxious sigh,
> Add'st thou this care, that men should be so wise
> To know, by omens, future miseries?
>
> .   .   .   .   .   .
>
> Unlook'd for send the ills thou hast design'd;
> Let human eyes to future fate be blind,
> That hope, amidst our fears, some place may find."

*Ne utile quidem est scire quid futurum sit; miserum est
enim nihil proficientem angi.*[2] " It is of no avail to know
what shall come to pass, for it is a miserable thing to be
vexed and tormented to no purpose." Yet are they of much
less authority now than heretofore. Which makes the example of Francis, Marquis of Saluzzo, so much more
remarkable; who, being lieutenant to King Francis the First,
in his army beyond the mountains, infinitely favoured and
esteemed in our Court, and obliged to the king's bounty for
the Marquisate itself, which had been forfeited by his brother;
and, as to the rest, having no manner of provocation given
him to do it, and even his own affection opposing any such
disloyalty; suffered himself to be so terrified, as it was confidently reported, with the fine prognostics that were spread
abroad in favour of the Emperor Charles the Fifth, and, to
our disadvantage, especially in Italy; where these foolish
prophecies were so far believed that, at Rome, great sums of
money were ventured out upon return of greater when they
came to pass, so certain they made themselves of our ruin;
that, having bewailed, to those of his acquaintance who were
most intimate with him, the mischiefs that he saw would inev-
itably fall upon the Crown of France, and the friends he had
in that Court, he revolted and turned to the other side; but

---

to his own misfortune, however, what constellation soever
governed at that time.   But he carried himself in this affair
like a man agitated with divers passions; for, having both
towns and forces in his hands, the enemy's army, under Antonio de Leyva, close by him, and we not at all suspecting
his design, it had been in his power to have done more than
he did ; for we lost no men by this treason of his, nor any
town but Fossan only, and that after a long siege and a
brave defence.[1]

> Prudens futuri temporis exitum
> Caliginosâ nocte premit Deus;
> Ridetque, si mortalis ultra
> Fas trepidat.[2]

" The God of wisdom has, in shades of night,
Future events conceal'd from human sight;
And laughs when he beholds the tim'rous ass
Tremble at what shall never come to pass."

> Ille potens sui,
> Lætusque deget, cui licet in diem
> Dixisse, vixi; cras vel atrâ
> Nube polum, pater, occupato,
> Vel sole puro.[2]

" He's master of himself alone,
He lives, that makes each day his own;
Who for to-morrow takes no care,
Whether the day prove foul or fair."

> Lætus in præsens animus, quod ultra est
> Oderit curare.[3]

" The man that's cheerful in his present state
Is never anxious for his future fate."

And, on the contrary, those who believe this saying are in
the wrong : *Ista sic reciprocantur, ut et, si divinatio sit, dii
sint ; et, si dii sint, sit divinatio.*[4]   " These things have that
mutual relation to one another that, if there be such a thing
as divination, there must be deities ; and if deities, divination."   Much more wisely Pacuvius :—

[1] Anno. 1536. Mem. of William du Bellay, vi.   [2] Horace, iii. 29.   [3] Id. ib. ii. 16.   [4] Cic. *de Divin.* i. 6.

Nam istis, qui linguam avium intelligunt,
Plusque ex alieno jecore sapiunt. quam ex suo,
Magis audiendum quam auscultandum censeo.[1]

" Those who birds' language understand, and who
More from brutes' livers than themselves do know,
Are rather to be heard than hearkened to."

The so celebrated art of divination, amongst the Tuscans,
origin of the art took its beginning thus : a labourer striking
of divination. deep with his coulter into the earth, saw the
Demi-God Tages to ascend with an infantile aspect, but endued with a mature and senile wisdom. Upon the rumour
of which all the people ran to see the sight, by whom his
words and knowledge, containing the principles and means to
attain to this art, were collected and kept for many ages.[2] A
birth suitable to its progress! I for my part, should sooner
regulate my affairs by the chance of a die than by such idle
and vain dreams. And, indeed, in all Republics, a good
share of the government has ever been referred to chance.
Plato,[3] in the system that he models according to his own
fancy, leaves the decision of several things, of very great
importance, wholly to it ; and will, amongst other things, that
marriages, of the better sort, as he reputes, be appointed by
lot, attributing so great virtue and adding so great a privilege
to this accidental choice as to ordain that the children begot
in such wedlock be brought up in the country, as those begot
in any other to be thrust out as spurious and base ; yet so
that if any of those exiles, notwithstanding. should, peradventure, in growing up, give any early hopes of future ability,
they might be recalled, as, on the other hand, those who had
been retained were to be exiled in case they gave little promise of themselves in their greener years.

1 Pacuvius *apud* Cic. *ut supra*, i. 57.
2 Ovid. *Met.* xv. Cicero, *ut supra*, ii.
25.
3 *Republic*, v.; where he requires that
the chiefs of his commonwealth should
so order it that the men of the greatest
excellence should be matched with the
most excellent women; and, on the contrary, that the most contemptible men
should be married to women of their own
low character; but that the thing should
be decided by a sort of lottery, so artfully
managed (κλῆροι ποιήτεω κομψοί)
that the latter may blame fortune for it,
and not their governors.

I see some, who are mightily given to study, pore and comment upon their almanacs, and produce them for authority when any thing has fallen out; and, indeed, it is hardly possible but that, in saying so much, they must sometimes stumble upon some truth amongst an infinite number of lies. *Quis est enim, qui totum diem jaculans, non aliquando collineet?*[1] "For who shoots all day at buts that does not sometimes hit the white?" I think never the better of them for some accidental hits. There would be more certainty in it if there were a rule and a truth in always lying. Besides, nobody records their flim-flams and false prognostics, forasmuch as they are infinite and common; but if they chop upon one truth, that carries a mighty report, as being rare, incredible, and prodigious. So Diagoras, surnamed the Atheist, answered him in Samothrace, who showing him, in the Temple, the several offerings and stories, in painting, of those who had escaped shipwreck, said to him, "Look, you who think the Gods have no care of human things, what do you say to so many persons preserved from death by their especial favour?"[2] "Why, I say," answered he, "that their pictures are not here who were cast away, which were by much the greater number."

Cicero observes that, of all the philosophers who have acknowledged a Deity, only Xenophanes, the Colophonian, has endeavoured to eradicate all manner of divination.[3] Which makes it the less a wonder if we have sometimes seen some of our princes, to their own cost, rely too much upon these fopperies. I had given any thing, that I had, with my own eyes, seen those two great rarities, the book of Joachim, the Calabrian Abbot, which foretold all the future Popes, their names, and figures; and that of the Emperor Leo, which prophesied all the Emperors and Patriarchs of Greece. This I have been an eye-witness of, that, in public confusions, men, astonished at their fortune, have abandoned their

---

[1] Cicero *de Divinat.* ii. 59.
[2] Cicero *de Nat. Deor.* i. 37.
[3] Id. *de Divinat.* i. 3.

own reason, superstitiously to seek out, in the stars, the ancient causes and menaces of their present mishaps, and, in
my time, have been so strangely successful in it as to make
me believe that, as this study is the amusement for men of
leisure and penetration, those who have been versed in this
knack of unfolding and untying riddles are able, in any
writing, to find out what they want to find there. But,
above all, that which gives them the greatest room to play
in is the obscure, ambiguous, and fantastic gibberish of their
prophetic canting, where the authors deliver nothing of clear
sense, but shroud all in riddle, to the end that posterity may
interpret and apply it according to their own fancy.

Socrates's Dæmon, or Familiar, might perhaps be no other
Socrates's Dæ-   but a certain impulsion of the will, which ob-
mon.   truded itself upon him without the advice or
consent of his judgment; and, in a soul so enlightened as his
was, and so prepared by a continual exercise of wisdom and
virtue, 'tis to be supposed those inclinations of his, though
sudden and undigested, were ever very important and worthy to be followed. Every one finds in himself some image
of such agitations, of a prompt, vehement, and fortuitous
opinion; and I must needs allow them some authority who
attribute so little to our own prudence, and who also myself
have had some, weak in reason, but violent in persuasion or
dissuasion (which were most frequent with Socrates),[1] by
which I have suffered myself to be carried away so fortunately, and so much to my own advantage, that they might
have been judged to have had something in them of a divine
inspiration.

1 Plato, *Theages.*

CHAPTER XII.

OF CONSTANCY, OR FIRMNESS.

THE law of resolution and constancy does not imply that we ought not, as much as in us lies, to decline, and to secure ourselves from, the mischiefs and inconveniences that threaten us; nor, consequently, that we shall not fear lest they should surprise us; on the contrary, all decent and honest ways and means of securing ourselves from harm are not only permitted, but moreover commendable, and the business of constancy chiefly is bravely to stand to, and stoutly to suffer those inconveniences which are not to be avoided. There is no motion of body nor any manner of handling arms, how irregular or ungraceful soever, that we condemn, if it serve to defend us from the blow that is made against us.

In what constancy and resolution consists.

Several very warlike nations have made use of a retiring and flying way of fight, as a thing of singular advantage, and, by so doing, have made their backs more dangerous than their faces to their enemies. Of which kind of fighting the Turks yet retain something in their practice of arms to this day; and Socrates, in Plato, laughs at Laches, who had defined fortitude to be standing firm in the ranks against the enemy: "What," says he, "would it then be reputed cowardice to overcome them by giving ground?"[1] urging, at the same time, the authority of Homer, who commends Æneas for his skill in running away. And whereas Laches, considering better of it, admits 'twas the practice of the Scythians, and in general of all cavalry whatever, he again attacks him with the example of the Lacedemonian foot, (a nation, of all others, the most obstinate in maintaining their ground,)

---

[1] Plato, *Laches.*

who, in the battle of Platea, not being able to break into the
Persian phalanx, bethought themselves to disperse and retire,
that, by the enemies' supposing they fled, they might break
and disunite that vast body of men in the pursuit, and, by
that stratagem, obtained the victory.

As for the Scythians, 'tis said of them that, when Darius
went on his expedition to subdue them, he sent, by a herald,
highly to reproach their King that he always retired before
him and declined a battle; to which Indathyrsis,[1] for that
was his name, returned answer, "That it was not for fear of
him or of any man living, that he did so, but that it was the
way of marching in practice with his nation, who had neither
tilled fields, cities, nor houses to defend, or to fear the enemy
should make any advantage of; but that if he had such a
stomach to fight, let him come but to view their ancient place
of sepulture, and there he should have his fill."

Nevertheless, as to what concerns cannon shot, when a
body of men are drawn up in the face of a train of artillery,
as the occasion of war does often require, 'tis unhandsome to
quit their post to avoid the danger, and a foolish thing to
boot, forasmuch as by reason of its force and swiftness we
account it inevitable, and many a one, by ducking, stepping
aside, and such other motions of fear, has, if no worse, got
laughed at by his companions. And yet, in the expedition
that the Emperor Charles the Fifth made against us into
Provence, the Marquis de Guasto, going to reconnoitre the
city of Arles, and venturing to advance out of the shelter of
a windmill, under favour of which he had made his approach, was perceived by the Seigneurs de Bonneval and the
Seneschal d'Agenois, who were walking upon the *Theatre aux
arènes ;* [2] who, having showed him to the Sieur de Villiers,
commissary of the artillery, he traversed a culverine so ad-
mirably well, and levelled it so exactly right at him, that had
not the Marquis, seeing fire put to it, slipped aside, it was

---

[1] Or rather *Idanthyrses.* Her. iv. 127.   [2] A theatre where public shows of riding, fencing, &c. were exhibited.

certainly concluded the shot had taken him full in the body.[1] And, in like manner, some years before, Lorenzo de Medici, Duke of Urbino, and father to the Queen-mother,[2] laying siege to Mondolpho, a place in the territories of the Vicariat, in Italy, seeing the cannoneer give fire to a piece that pointed directly against him, ducked, and it was well for him, for otherwise the shot, that only razed the top of his head, had, doubtless, hit him full in the breast. To say truth, I do not think that these dodgings are at all a matter of judgment or reflection; for how is a man to judge of high or low aim on so sudden an occasion? It is much more easy to believe that fortune favoured their fear, and that the same movement that at one time saves a man, may, at another, make him step into danger. For my own part, I confess, I cannot forbear starting when the rattle of a harquebuse thunders in my ears on a sudden, and, in a place where I am not to expect it, which I have also observed in others, braver fellows than I.

Neither do the Stoics pretend that the soul of their philosopher should be proof against the first visions and fantasies that surprise him; but, as a natural subject, consent that he should tremble at the terrible noise of thunder or the sudden clatter of some falling ruin, and be affrighted even to paleness and convulsion. And so in other passions, provided a man's judgment remains sound and entire, and that the site of his reason suffers no concussion nor alteration, and that he yields no consent to his fright and discomposure. To him who is not a philosopher, a fright is the same in the first part of it, but quite another thing in the second; for the impression of the passions does not only remain superficially in him, but penetrates farther, even to the very seat of reason, and so as to infect and to corrupt it. He judges according to his fear, and conforms his behaviour to it.[3] But in this verse you may see the true state of the wise stoic learnedly and plainly expressed.

Philosophers not blamable for yielding to the first impulses of the passions.

---

[1] Mem. of William du Bellay, vii.
[2] Catherine de Medici.
[3] Arrian, *Life of Epictetus.* Apud. Aul. Gell. xix. 1.

Mens immota manet, lacrymæ volvuntur inanes.[1]
" Ilis humid eye frail, fruitless tear-drops rains,
    But the firm purpose of his mind remains."

The wise Peripatetic is not himself totally free from per-
turbations of mind, but he moderates them by his wisdom.

———◆———

CHAPTER XIII.

THE CEREMONY OF THE INTERVIEW OF PRINCES.

THERE is no subject so frivolous that does not merit a
place in this rhapsody.   According to the common rule of civility, it would be a notable
affront to an equal, and much more to a superior,
to fail of being at home when he has given
you notice he will come to visit you.   Nay, Queen Margaret
of Navarre farther adds, that it would be rudeness in a gentleman to go out to meet any one that is coming to see
him, let him be of what condition soever; and that it is more
respectful and more civil to stay at home to receive him, if
only upon the account of missing of him by the way, and
that it is enough to receive him at the door, and to wait upon
him to his chamber.   For my part, who, as much as I can,
endeavour to reduce the ceremonies of my house, I very
often forget both the one and the other of these vain offices,
and peradventure some one may take offence at it; if he do,
I am sorry, but I cannot find in my heart to help it; it is
much better to offend him once than myself every day, for it
would be a perpetual slavery; and to what end do we avoid
the servile attendance of courts, if we bring the same, or a
greater trouble, home to our own private houses?   It is also

The respect which gentlemen are obliged to pay to a great man who visits them.

———
[1] Æneid, iv. 449.

a common rule in all assemblies that those of less quality are to be first at the place, by reason that it is a state more due to the better sort to make others wait for them.

Nevertheless, at the interview betwixt Pope Clement,[1] and King Francis, at Marseilles, the king, after he had in his own person taken order for the necessary preparations for his reception and entertainment, withdrew out of the town, and gave the pope two or three days' leisure for his entry, and wherein to repose and refresh himself before he came to him. And in like manner, at the meeting of the pope [2] and the emperor at Bologna, the emperor gave the pope opportunity to come thither first, and came himself after; for which the reason then given was this—that, at all the interviews of such princes, the greater ought to be first at the appointed place, especially before the other in whose territories the interview is appointed to be, intimating thereby a kind of deference to the other, and that it appears proper for the less to seek out, and to apply themselves to the greater, and not the greater to them.

The usual ceremony at the interview of princes.

Not every country only, but every city, and so much as every profession, has its particular forms of civility. There was care enough taken in my education, and I have lived in good company enough to know the formalities of our own nation, and am able to give lessons in it. I love also to follow them, but not to be so servilely tied to their observation that my whole life should be enslaved to ceremonies; of which there are some that, provided a man omits them out of discretion, and not for want of breeding, it will be every whit as handsome in him. I have seen some people rude, by being over civil, and troublesome by their courtesy; though, these excesses excepted, the knowledge of courtesy and good manners is a very necessary study. It is, like grace and beauty, that which begets liking and an inclination

Too much nicety in behaviour not desirable.

The advantages of good manners.

---

[1] The Seventh, in 1533.　　[2] Pope Clement VII. and Charles V. in 1532. See Guicciardine, xx.

to love one another at the first sight, and in the very beginning of an acquaintance and familiarity; and, consequently,
that which first opens the door for us to better ourselves by
the example of others, if there be any thing in the society
worth notice.[1]

---◆---

CHAPTER XIV.

THAT MEN ARE JUSTLY PUNISHED FOR BEING OBSTINATE IN THE DEFENCE OF A FORT THAT IS NOT IN REASON TO BE DEFENDED.

VALOUR, as well as other virtues, has its bounds, which
Valour and its limits. once transgressed, the next step is into the territories of vice; so that by having too large a
proportion of this heroic virtue, unless a man be very perfect in its limits, which upon the confines are very hard to
discern, he may very easily unawares run into temerity, obstinacy, and folly. From this consideration it is that we have
derived the custom, in time of war, to punish, even with
Why too obstinate a defence of a place is punished. death, those who are obstinate to defend a
place that is not tenable by the rules of war.
Otherwise, if there were not some examples
made, men would be so confident upon the hopes of impunity
that not a henroost but would resist and stop a royal army.

Monsieur the constable de Montmorency, having at the
siege of Pavia been ordered to pass the Tesino, and to take
up his quarters in the Fauxbourg St. Antonio, being hindered from doing so, by a tower that was at the end of the
bridge, which was so impudent as to stand a battery, hanged

---

[1] In the edition of 1588, Montaigne placed here the chapter "That the relish of good and evil depends on the opinion we have of either," which he afterwards made the fortieth chapter.

every man he found within it for their labour.[1] And again, since, accompanying the Dauphin in his expedition, beyond the Alps, and taking the castle of Villano by assault, and all within it having been put to the sword, the governor and his ensign only excepted, he caused them both to be trussed up for the same reason ;[2] as also did Captain Martin du Bellay, then governor of Turin, the governor of St. Bony, in the same country, all his people being cut in pieces at the taking of the place.[3]

But, forasmuch as the strength or weakness of a fortress is always measured by the estimate and counterpoise of the forces that attack it, (for a man might reasonably enough despise two culverines that would be a madman to abide a battery of thirty pieces of cannon ;) where also the greatness of the prince who is master of the field, his reputation, and the respect that is due unto him, are put into the account, there is always danger that the balance will turn that way ; and thence it is that such people have so great an opinion of themselves and their power that, thinking it unreasonable any place should dare to shut its gates against them, they put all to the sword where they meet with any opposition, whilst their fortune continues ; as is observable in the fierce and arrogant forms of summoning towns and denouncing war, savouring so much of barbarian pride and insolence, in use amongst the oriental princes, and which their successors to this day do yet retain and practice. And in that part of the world where the Portuguese subdued the Indians, they found some states where it was an universal and inviolable law amongst them that every enemy, overcome by the king in person, or by his representative lieutenant, was out of composition both of ransom and mercy.

So that above all things a man should take heed of falling into the hands of a judge who is an enemy, in arms, and victorious.

[1] Mem. of Martin du Bellay, ii.   [3] Id. ib. ix.
[2] Mem. of William du Bellay, viii.

CHAPTER XV.

OF THE PUNISHMENT OF COWARDICE.

I ONCE heard of a prince, and a great captain, who having a narration given him as he sat at table of the proceeding against Monsieur de Vervins, who was sentenced to death for having surrendered Boulogne to the English,[1] openly maintained that a soldier could not justly be put to death for his want of courage. And in truth, a man should make a great difference betwixt faults that merely proceed from infirmity and those that are visibly the effects of treachery and malice ; for, in the last, men wilfully act against the rules of reason that nature has imprinted in us ; whereas in the former it seems as if we might produce the same nature, who left us in such a state of imperfection and defect of courage, for our justification. Insomuch that many have thought we are not justly questionable for any thing but what we commit against the light of our own conscience. And it is partly upon this rule that those ground their opinion who disapprove of capital and sanguinary punishments inflicted upon heretics and infidels ; and theirs also who hold that an advocate or a judge is not accountable for having failed in his commission from ignorance.

How cowardice ought to be punished in a soldier.

But as to cowardice, it is certain that the most usual way of chastising it is by ignominy and disgrace ; and it is supposed that this practice was first brought into use by the legislator Charondas ; and that before his time the laws of Greece punished those with death who fled from a battle ; whereas he ordained only that they should be three days exposed in the public place dressed in women's attire, hoping yet for some service from

The usual mode of punishing cowardice.

[1] To Henry VIII. who besieged it in person. Mem. of Martin du Bellay, x.

them, having awakened their courage by this open shame;[1] *Suffundere malis hominis sanguinem, quam effundere*,[2] "Choosing rather to bring the blood into their cheeks than to let it out of their bodies." It appears, also, that the Roman laws did anciently punish those with death who had run away; for Ammianus Marcellinus says that the emperor Julian commanded ten of his soldiers, who had turned their backs in an encounter against the Parthians, to be first degraded, and afterwards put to death, according, says he, to the ancient laws.[3] Yet, elsewhere for the like offence, he only condemns others to remain amongst the prisoners under the baggage ensign. The severe punishment the people of Rome inflicted upon those who fled from the battle of Cannæ, and in the same war upon those who ran away with Cneius Fulvius, at his defeat, did not extend to death.[4] And yet methinks men should consider what they do in such cases, lest disgrace should make such delinquents desperate, and not only faint friends, but implacable and mortal enemies.

Of late memory, the Seigneur de Frauget, lieutenant to the Mareschal de Chatillon's company, having, by the Mareschal de Chabannes, been put in governor of Fontarabia, in the place of Mon- sieur de Lude, and having surrendered it to the Spaniards, he was for that condemned to be degraded from all nobility, and both himself and his posterity declared ignoble, taxable, and for ever incapable of bearing arms; which hard sentence was executed at Lyons;[5] and since that all the gentlemen who were in Guise when the Count de Nassau entered it, underwent the same punishment, as several others have done since for the like offence. However, in case of such a manifest ignorance or cowardice as exceeds all ordinary example, 'tis but reason to take it for a sufficient proof of treachery and malice, and to punish it accordingly.

How the governor of a place was punished for his cowardice.

---

[1] Diod. Siculus, xii. 4.
[2] Tertullian, *Apolog.* p. 583.
[3] Ammianus Marcellinus, xxiv. 4, and li. xxv. 1.
[4] Livy, xxv. 7, xxvi. 2.
[5] In 1523. Mem. of Martin du Bellay.

CHAPTER XVI.

A PROCEEDING OF SOME AMBASSADORS.

I OBSERVE in my travels this custom, ever to learn something from the information of those with whom
I confer (which is the best school of all others)
and to put my company upon those subjects
they are the best able to speak of :—

*A wise custom
observed by Mon-
taigne.*

> Basti al nocchiero ragionar de' venti,
> Al bifolco dei tori ; et le sue piaghe
> Conti 'l guerrier, conti 'l pastor gli armenti.[1]

> " The seaman best discourses of the winds,
>   Of oxen none so well as lab'ring hinds ;
>   The soldier best can talk of wounds and knocks,
>   And gentle shepherds of their harmless flocks ; "

for it often falls out that, on the contrary, every one will
rather choose to be prating of another man's business than
his own, thinking it so much new reputation acquired ; witness the jeer Archidamus put upon Periander, that he had
quitted the glory of being an excellent physician to gain the
repute of a very bad poet.[2]   And do but observe what a vast
deal of pains Cæsar is at to make us understand his inventions in building bridges, and contriving engines of war,[3] and
how succinct and reserved in comparison, where he speaks of
the rules of his profession, and his own valour, and military
conduct.   His exploits sufficiently prove him a great captain,
and that he knew well enough, but he would be thought a
good engineer to boot ; a quality not to be expected in him.
The elder Dionysius was a very great captain, as it befitted
his fortune he should be ; but he took very great pains to get

---

[1] Propertius, ii. *Eleg.* i. 43, as rendered
by Ariosto.
[2] Plutarch, *Apoth. of the Lacedemonians.*

[3] See, in particular, his description of
the bridge over the Rhine. *De Bell.
Gall.* iv. 17.

a particular reputation by poetry, and yet he never was cut out for a poet. A gentleman of the long robe being not long since brought to see a study furnished with all sorts of books, both of his own and all other faculties, took no occasion to discourse of any of them, but fell very rudely and impertinently to animadvert upon a barricado placed before the study door, a thing that a hundred captains and common soldiers see every day without taking any notice or offence at.

Optat ephippia bos piger, optat arare caballus.[1]

"The lazy ox would saddle have and bit,
The steed a yoke; neither for either fit."

By this course a man shall never improve himself, nor arrive at any perfection in any thing. He must, therefore, make it his business always to put the architect, the painter, the shoemaker, and so on, upon discourse of his own business.

And, to this purpose, in reading histories, which is everybody's subject, I used to consider what kind of men are the authors; if they be persons that profess nothing but mere learning, I, in and from them, principally observe and learn the style and language; if physicians, I upon that account the rather incline to credit what they report of the temperature of the air, of the health and complexions of princes, of wounds, and diseases; if lawyers, we are from them to take notice of the controversies of right and title, the establishment of laws and civil government, and the like; if divines, of the affairs of the church, ecclesiastical censures, marriages, and dispensations; if courtiers, of manners and ceremonies; if soldiers, of the things that belong to their trade, and principally the accounts of such actions and enterprises wherein they were personally engaged; and if ambassadors, we are to observe their negotiations, intelligences, and practices, and the manner how they are to be carried on.

The importance of knowing the profession of the writer of any book.

And this is the reason why that which perhaps I should

[1] Horace, *Epist.* xiv. 1.

have lightly passed over in another, I dwelt upon and maturely considered in the history writ by the Seigneur de
Langey,[1] (a man well versed in, and of very great judgment
in things of that nature,) that is, where after having given a
narrative of the fine oration Charles V. had made in the con-
sistory at Rome, and in the presence of the bishop of Mascon
and the Seigneur du Velly, our ambassadors there, wherein
he had mixed several tart and injurious expressions to the
dishonour of our nation ; and, amongst the rest, that if his
captains and soldiers were not men of another kind of fidelity,
resolution, and sufficiency in the knowledge of arms, than
those of the king, he would immediately go with a rope about
his neck and sue to him for mercy, (and it should seem the
emperor had really this, or a very little better, opinion of our
military men, for he afterwards, twice or thrice in his life,
said the very same thing ;) as also that he challenged the
king to fight him in his shirt with rapier and poniard, in a
boat ; the said Sieur de Langey, pursuing his history, adds
that the forenamed ambassadors, sending a dispatch to the
king of these things, concealed the greatest part, and particularly the last two passages.   At which I could not but
A question wheth- wonder that it should be in the power of an
er a prince's am-
bassador ought to ambassador to dispense with any thing which
conceal any thing
from him of his he ought to signify to his master especially of
own affairs. so great importance as this, coming from the
mouth of such a person, and spoken in so great an assembly ;
and should rather conceive it had been the servant's duty
faithfully to have represented to him the whole and naked
truth as it passed, to the end that the liberty of disposing,
judging, and concluding might have remained in the master ;
for either to conceal, or to disguise the truth, for fear he
should take it otherwise than he ought to do, and lest it
should prompt him to some extravagant resolution, and in
the mean time to leave him ignorant of his affairs, should
seem, methinks, rather to belong to him who is to give the

1 Martin du Bellay, Seigneur de Langey. See his Mem. v.

law, than to him who is only to receive it; to him who is in
supreme command, and best can judge of his own interests,
and not to him who ought to look upon himself as inferior,
not only in authority, but in prudence and good counsel. At
any rate, I for my part would be loth to be so served in my
little concerns.

We do so willingly slip the collar of command, upon any
pretence whatever, and are so ready to usurp
dominion, and every one does so naturally aspire to liberty and power, that no advantage
whatever derived from the wit or valour of those he employs ought to be so dear to a superior as a downright and
implicit obedience. To obey more as a matter of discretion
than subjection is to corrupt the office, and to subvert the
power of command; and P. Crassus, the same whom the
Romans reputed five times happy,[1] at the time when he was
consul in Asia, having sent to a Greek engineer to cause the
greater of two masts of ships, that he had taken notice of at
Athens, to be brought to him, to be employed about some
engine of battery he had a design to make; the other, pre-
suming upon his own science and sufficiency in those affairs,
thought fit to do otherwise than directed, and to bring the
less; as being, according to the rules of his art, more proper
for the use to which it was designed. But Crassus, though
he gave ear to his reasons with great patience, caused him to
be well whipped for his pains, valuing the interest of discipline much more than that of the thing in hand.

Yet we may, on the other side, consider that so precise and
implicit an obedience as this is only due to positive and per-
emptory commands. The functions of an ambassador are
not so fixed and precise but they must, in the various and
unforeseen occurrences and accidents that may fall out in the
management of a negotiation, be wholly left to their own
discretion. They do not simply execute the will of their

Nothing more dear to a superior than implicit obedience.

[1] In that he was very rich, most noble, and the highest in the priesthood.—*Aul.
most eloquent, most skilful in the law, Gell.* i. 13.

master, but by their own wisdom form and model it also; and I have in my time known men of command who have been checked for having rather obeyed the express words of the king's letters than the necessity of the affairs they had in hand. Men of understanding do yet to this day condemn the custom of the kings of Persia, to give their lieutenants and agents so little rein that, upon the least arising difficulties they must evermore have recourse to farther commands; this delay, in so vast an extent of dominion, having often very much prejudiced their affairs. And Crassus, writing to a man whose profession it was best to understand those things, and pre-acquainting him to what use this mast was designed, did he not seem to consult his advice, and in a manner invite him to interpose his judgment?

CHAPTER XVII.

OF FEAR.

Obstupui, steteruntque comæ, et vox faucibus hæsit.[1]

" Aghast, astonished, and struck dumb with fear,
  I stood; like bristles rose my stiffened hair."

I AM not so good a naturalist (as they call it[2]) as to dis-
The strange effects cern by what secret springs fear acts in us;
of fear.   but I am wise enough to know that it is a
strange passion, and such an one that the physicians say
there is no other whatever that sooner dethrones our judgment from its proper seat; which is so true that I myself
have seen very many become frantic through fear; and even
in those of the best settled temper, it is most certain that it

---

[1] *Æneid.* ii. 774.
[2] By this parenthesis, it would appear that the term *naturalist* was but just adopted into the French language.

begets a terrible astonishment and confusion during the fit.
I omit the vulgar sort, to whom it one while represents their
great grandsires risen out of their graves in their shrouds;
another while hobgoblins, weir-wolves, and chimeras; but
even amongst soldiers (a sort of men over whom, of all
others, it ought to have the least power) how often has it
converted flocks of sheep into armed squadrons, reeds and
bulrushes into pikes and lances, friends into enemies, and the
French white into the red crosses of Spain! When Monsieur de Bourbon took the city of Rome,[1] an ensign, who
was on guard at the Bourg St. Pierre, was seized with such
a fright, upon the first alarm, that he threw himself out at a
breach with his colours upon his shoulder, ran directly upon
the enemy, thinking he was retreating toward the inward
defences of the city; and, with much ado, seeing Monsieur
de Bourbon's people, who thought it had been a sally upon
them, draw up to receive him, at last came to himself; and
finding his error, and then facing about, retreated full speed
through the same breach by which he had gone out; but not
until he had first blindly advanced above three hundred
paces into the open field. It did not, however, fall out so
well with Captain Julius's ensign, at the time when St. Pol
was taken from us by the Count de Bures and Monsieur du
Reu; for he, being so scared with fear as to throw himself
and his fellows out at a porthole, was immediately cut to
pieces by the enemy;[2] and in the same siege it was a very
memorable fear that so seized, contracted, and froze up the
heart of a young gentleman, that he sunk down stone dead
in the breach, without any manner of wound or hurt at all.[3]
The like madness sometimes seizes on a whole multitude;
for in one of the encounters that Germanicus had with the
Germans, two great parties were so amazed with fear that
they ran two opposite ways, the one flying to the same place
from which the other set out.[4] Sometimes it adds wings to

---

[1] In 1527. Mem. of Mart. du Bellay, iii. [3] Id. ib.
[2] Mem. of William du Bellay, viii. [4] Tacitus, *Annal.* i. 63.

the heels, as in the first two cases, and sometime snails them
to the ground, and fetters them from moving; as we read of
the Emperor Theophilus, who, in a battle he lost against the
Agarenes, was so astounded and stupefied that he had no
power to fly; *adeò pavor etiam auxilia formida ;*[1] " so much
does fear dread even the means of safety ;" till such time as
Manuel, one of the principal commanders of his army, having jogged and shaken him so as to rouse him out of his
trance, said to him, " Sir, if you will not follow me, I will
kill you ; for it is better you should lose your life than, by
being taken, lose the empire."[2]   But fear does
Fear sometimes incites to desperate valour. then manifest its utmost power and effect when
it throws us upon a valiant despair, having
before deprived us of all sense, both of duty and honour.
In the first pitched battle the Romans lost against Hannibal,
under the Consul Sempronius, a body of ten thousand foot,
that had taken a fright, seeing no other escape for their cowardice, went and threw themselves headlong upon the great
array of the enemy, which, with wonderful force and fury,
they charged through and through, and routed with a very
great slaughter of the Carthaginians ; thus purchasing an
ignominious flight at the same price they might have done a
glorious victory.[3]

The thing in the world I am most afraid of is fear ; and
with good reason, that passion alone, in the trouble of it,
exceeding all other accidents.   What affliction
Fear supersedes every other passion. could be greater or more just than that of
Pompey's followers and friends, who, in his
ship, were spectators of his horrid and inhuman murder?
Yet so it was, that the fear of the Egyptian vessels they saw
coming to board them possessed them with so great a fear
that it is observed, they thought of nothing but calling upon
the mariners to make haste, and, by force of oars, to escape
away ; till being arrived at Tyre, and delivered from the
apprehension of further danger, they then had leisure to turn

[1] Quint. Curt. iii 2.   [2] Zonaras, iii.   [3] Livy, xxi. 56.

their thoughts to the loss of their captain, and to give vent to those tears and lamentations that the other more prevalent passion had till then suspended.[1]

Tum pavor sapientiam omnem mihi ex animo expectorat.[2]

" My mind with great and sudden fear oppress'd,
Was, for the time, of judgment dispossessed."

Such as have been well banged in some skirmish may yet, all wounded and bloody as they are, be brought on again the next day to charge ; but such as have once conceived a good sound fear of the enemy will never be got so much as to look him in the face. Such as are in immediate fear of losing their estates, of banishment, or of slavery, live in perpetual anguish, and lose all appetite and repose ; whereas such as are actually poor, slaves, and exiles, ofttimes live as merrily as men in a better condition. And so, many people who, impatient of the perpetual alarms of fear, have hanged and drowned themselves, and thrown themselves from precipices, give us sufficiently to understand that it is still more importunate and insupportable than death itself.

The Greeks recognize another kind of fear exceeding any we have spoken of yet,—a fear that surprises us without any visible cause, by an impulse from heaven; so that whole armies and nations have been struck with it. Such a one was that which brought so wonderful a desolation upon Carthage, where nothing was to be heard but voices and outcries of fear ; where the inhabitants were seen to sally out of their houses as to an alarm, and there to charge, wound, and kill one another, as if they had been enemies come to surprise their city. All things were in disorder and fury, till with prayers and sacrifices they had appeased their gods. And this is that they call a panic terror.[3]

---

[1] Cicero. *Tuscul. Quæs.* iii. 26.   [3] Diod. Sic. xv. 7; and Plutarch, *on*
[2] Ennius, *apud* Cicero, *Tuscul. Quæs. Isis and Osiris*, c. 8.
iv. 8.

CHAPTER XVIII.

THAT MEN ARE NOT TO JUDGE OF OUR HAPPINESS TILL AFTER DEATH.

> Scilicet ultima semper
> Expectanda dies homini est; dicique beatus
> Ante obitum nemo supremaque funera debet.[1]

> "Till man's last day is come, we should not dare
> Of happiness to say what was his share;
> Since of no man can it be truly said
> That he is happy till he first be dead."

EVERY schoolboy knows the story of King Crœsus, to this purpose;—that, being taken prisoner by Cyrus, and by him condemned to die, as he was going to execution he cried out, "O Solon! Solon!" which, being presently reported to Cyrus, and he sending to inquire of him what it meant, Crœsus gave him to understand that he now found the warning Solon had formerly given him true to his cost; which was, "That men, however fortune may seem to smile upon them, could never be said to be happy till they had been seen to pass over the last day of their lives; by reason of the uncertainty and mutability of human things, which in an instant are subject to be totally changed into a quite contrary condition."[2] And therefore it was that Agesilaus made answer to one that was saying what a happy man the King of Persia was, to come so young to so mighty a kingdom, "True," said he, "but neither was Priam unhappy at his years."[3] In a short space of time kings of Macedon, successors to the mighty Alexander, have become joiners and scriveners at Rome; a tyrant of Sicily a pedant at Corinth; a conqueror of one half of the world, and general of innumerable armies, a miserable suppliant to the rascally officers of a king of Egypt!

---

[1] Ovid, *Met.* iii. 137.
[2] Herod. i. 86.
[3] Plutarch, *Apotheg. of the Lacedemonians.*

So much did the prolongation of five or six months of life cost the great and noble Pompey; and no longer since than our fathers' days, Lodovico Sforza, the tenth duke of Milan, at whose name all Italy had so long trembled, was seen to die a wretched prisoner at Loches,[1] not till he had lived ten years in captivity, which was the worst part of his fortune. The fairest of all queens,[2] widow to the greatest king in Christendom, has she not just come to die by the hand of an executioner? Unworthy and barbarous cruelty! and a thousand more examples there are of the same kind; for it seems that, as storms and tempests have a spite against the proud and towering heights of our lofty castles, there are also spirits above that are envious of the grandeurs here below.

> Usque adeò res humanas vis abdita quædam
> Obterit, et pulchros fasces sævasque secures
> Proculcare, ac ludibrio sibi habere videtur![3]

> "And hence we fancy unseen powers in those
> Whose force and will such strange confusion brings,
> And spurns and overthrows our greatest kings."

And it should seem also that fortune sometimes lies in wait to surprise the last hour of our lives, to show the power she has in a moment to overthrow what she has been so many years in building, making us cry out with Laberius, *Nimirum hac die unâ plus vixi mihi quàm vivendum fuit:*[4] "I have lived longer by this one day than I ought to have done." And in this sense the good advice of Solon may reasonably be taken; but he being a philosopher, with which sort of men the favours and disgraces of fortune stand for nothing, either to the making a man happy or unhappy, and with whom grandeur and power are mere accidents, almost equally indifferent, I am apt to think he had some further aim, and that

---

[1] In Touraine, under Louis XII., who shut him up there in 1500, in an iron cage, which was still to be seen in 1778.

[2] Mary, Queen of Scotland, and mother of James I., King of England, was beheaded in this kingdom, by order of Queen Elizabeth, in 1587. Montaigne surely wrote this long after the passage in the following chapter, where he tells us that the year he wrote in was but 1572; but we do not find this particular in the quarto edition of 1588.

[3] Lucretius, v. 1232.

[4] Macrobius, *Saturnal.* ii. 7.

his meaning was, that the very felicity of life itself, which depends upon the tranquillity and contentment of a well-descended spirit, and the resolution and assurance of a well-ordered soul, ought never to be attributed to any man till he has first been seen to play the last, and doubtless the hardest, act of his part, because there may be disguise and dissimulation in all the rest, where these fine philosophical discourses are only put on, or where accidents not touching us to the quick give us leisure to maintain the same sober gravity; but in this last scene of death and ourselves there is no more counterfeiting, we must speak plain, and must discover what there is of pure and clean in the bottom.

> Nam veræ voces tum demum pectore ab imo
> Ejiciuntur, et eripitur persona, manet res.[1]

> "For then their words will with their thoughts concur,
> And, all the mask pulled off, show what they were."

Wherefore, at this last, all the other actions of our life ought to be tried and sifted. 'Tis the master-day, 'tis the day that is judge of all the rest, "'tis the day," says one of the ancients, "that ought to judge of all my foregone years."[2] To death do I refer the proof of the fruit of all my studies. We shall then see whether my discourse came only from my mouth or from my heart. I have seen many, by their death, give a good or an ill repute to their whole life. Scipio, the father-in-law of Pompey the Great, in dying well, wiped away the ill opinion that, till then, every one had conceived of him.[3] Epaminondas, being asked which of the three he had in greatest esteem, Chabrias, Iphicrates, or himself,

---

1 Lucretius, iii. 57.
2 Seneca, *Epist.* 102.
3 This remark is taken, if I mistake not, from Seneca. It is a pretty long passage, but so curious a one that I cannot help transcribing it here. Seneca, desirous to fortify his friend against the terrors of death, said to him, in the first place, "I should prevail on you with more ease were I to show that 'not only heroes have despised the moment of the soul's departure out of the body, but that even dastards have, in this matter, equalled those of the greatest fortitude

of mind." And, immediately after, he adds, "Even like that Scipio, the father-in-law of Cn. Pompey, who, being driven by contrary winds to the coast of Africa, when he saw his ship detained by the enemy, stabbed himself with his own sword; and, to those who asked him 'where the General was,' said, 'The General is well.' This word equalled him to his superiors, and did not suffer the glory fatal to the Scipios, in Africa, to be interrupted. It was a great task to conquer Carthage, but a harder to conquer death." Seneca, *Epist.* 24.

"You must first see us die," said he, "before that question can be resolved;"[1] and, in truth, he would infinitely wrong that great man who would weigh him without the honour and grandeur of his end. God has ordered these things as it has best pleased him. But I have, in my time, seen three of the most execrable persons that ever I knew in all manner of abominable living, and the most infamous, who all died a very regular death, and, in all circumstances, composed even to perfection. There are brave and fortunate deaths; I have seen death cut the thread of the progress of a prodigious advancement, and in the flower of its increase, of a certain person,[2] with so glorious an end that, in my opinion, his ambitious and generous designs had nothing in them so high and great as was their interruption; and he arrived, without completing his course, at the place to which his ambition pretended, with greater glory and grandeur than he could himself have either hoped or desired, and anticipated by his fall the name and power to which he has aspired by perfecting his career. In the judgment I make of another man's life, I always observed how he carried himself at its close; and the principal concern I have for my own is that I may die handsomely, that is, patiently and without noise.

CHAPTER XIX.

THAT TO STUDY PHILOSOPHY IS TO LEARN TO DIE.

CICERO says that to study philosophy is nothing but to prepare a man's self to die.[3] The reason of which is because study and contemplation do,

What is the study of philosophy.

[1] Plutarch, *Apoth. of the Ancient Kings, &c.*

[2] Montaigne speaks here of his friend, Boetius, at whose death he was present, as appears by a speech which Montaigne caused to be printed at Paris, in 1571, wherein he mentions the most remarkable particulars of Boetius's sickness and death. As this speech does honour to both these eminent friends, and is become very scarce, I shall insert it hereafter.

[3] *Tuscul. Quæs.* l. 31. The passage is a translation from the *Phædo* of Plato.

in some sort, withdraw from us, and deprive us of our soul,
and employ it separately from the body, which is a kind of
discipline of, and a resemblance of, death, or else because all
the wisdom and reasoning in the world does, in the end, conclude in this point, to teach us not to fear to die. And, to
say the truth, either our reason does grossly abuse us, or it
ought to have no other aim but our contentment only, nor to
endeavour any thing but, in sum, to make us live well, and,
as the Holy Scripture says,[1] at our ease. All the opinions
Pleasure the uni- of the world agree in this, that pleasure is our
versal aim.   end, though we make use of divers means to
attain unto it; they would all of them otherwise be rejected
at the first motion; for who would give ear to him that should
propose affliction and misery for his end? The controversies and disputes of the philosophical sects upon this point
are merely verbal; *Transcurramus solertissimas nugas*.[2]
"Let us skip over those learned trifles." There is more in
them of opposition and obstinacy than is consistent with so
sacred a profession; but what kind of person soever man
takes upon him to personate, he ever mixes his own part
with it. Let the philosophers say what they will, the main
thing at which we all aim, even in virtue itself, is pleasure.
It pleases me to rattle in their ears this word, which they so
nauseate to hear; and, if it signify some supreme pleasure
and excessive delight, it is more due to the assistance of virtue than to any other assistance whatever. This delight for
being more gay, more sinewy, more robust, and more manly,
is only more seriously voluptuous, and we ought to give it
the name of pleasure; as that which is more benign, gentle,
and natural, and not that of vigour, from which we have derived it.

The other more mean and sensual part of pleasure, if
it could deserve this fair name, it ought to be upon the
account of concurrence, and not of privilege; I find it less

1 "I know that there is no good in
them, but for a man to rejoice and do
good in this life."—*Ecclesiast.* iii. 12.

2 Senec. *Epist.* 117.

exempt from traverses and inconveniences than virtue itself; and, besides that, the enjoyment is more momentary, fluid, and frail; it has its watchings, fasts, and labours, even to sweat and blood; and, moreover, has, particular to itself, so many several sorts of sharp and wounding passions, and so stupid a satiety attending it, as are equal to the severest penance. And we much mistake to think that difficulties serve it for a spur and a seasoning to its sweetness, as in nature, one contrary is quickened by another; and to say, when we come to virtue, that like consequences and difficulties overwhelm and render it austere and inaccessible; whereas, much more aptly than in voluptuousness, they ennoble, sharpen, and heighten the perfect and divine pleasure they procure us. He renders himself unworthy of it who will counterpoise his expense with the fruit, and does neither understand the blessing nor how to use it. Those who preach to us that the quest of it is craggy, difficult, and painful, but the fruition pleasant and grateful, what do they mean by that, but to tell us that it is always unpleasing? What human means ever attained it? the most perfect have been forced to content themselves to aspire unto it, and to approach it only without ever possessing it. But they are deceived, for of all the pleasures we know, the very pursuit is pleasant. The attempt ever relishes of the quality of the thing to which it is directed, for it is a good part of, and consubstantial with, the effect. The felicity and beatitude that glitters in virtue, shines throughout all her avenues and ways, even to the first entry, and utmost pale and limits.

Now, of all the benefits that virtue confers upon us, the contempt of death is one of the greatest, as The contempt of death one of the the means that accommodates human life with principal benefits a soft and easy tranquillity, and gives us a pure of virtue. and pleasant taste of living, without which all other pleasures would be extinct; which is the reason why all the rules of philosophy centre and concur in this one article.[1] And

---

[1] *Omnis humani incommodi expers* (says **Valerius Maximus**, viii. 13, in *Ex-*

although they all, in like manner, with one consent, endeavour to teach us also to despise grief, poverty, and the
other accidents, to which human life, by its own nature and
constitution, is subjected, it is not, nevertheless, with the
same earnestness, as well by reason these accidents are not
so certain, the greater part of mankind passing over their
whole lives without ever knowing what poverty is; and some
without sorrow or sickness, as Xenophilus, the musician,
who lived a hundred and six years in a perfect and continual
health; as also, because at the worst, death can, whenever
we please, cut short and put an end to all of these inconveniences.   But as to death it is inevitable.

> Omnes eodem cogimur; omnium
> Versata urnâ; serius, ocius,
>   Sors exitura, et nos in æternum
>   Exilium impositura cymbæ.[1]

> " To the same fate we all must yield in turn,
>   Sooner or later, all must to the urn;
>   When Charon calls abroad, we must not stay,
>   But to eternal exile sail away."

And consequently, if it frights us, 'tis a perpetual torment,
and for which there is no consolation nor redress.   There is
no way by which we can possibly avoid it; it commands all
points of the compass; we may continually turn our heads
this way and that, and pry about as in a suspected country;
quæ quasi saxum Tantalo, semper impendet;[2] " But it ever,
like Tantalus's stone, hangs over us."   Our courts of justice
often send back condemned criminals to be executed upon
the place where the fact was committed, but carry them to all
the fine houses by the way and give them the best entertainment they can.

> Non Siculæ dapes
> Dulcem elaborabunt saporem;

---

ternis, sect. 3.) in summo perfectissimæ
splendore doctrinæ extinctus est; i. e.
After having lived free from every human
ailment, he died in the highest reputa-

tion of being perfect master of his science.
[1] Hor. Od. ii. 3. 25.
[2] Cic. de Finib. i. 18.

Non avium citharæque cantus
Somnum reducent.[1]

" Choicest Sicilian dainties cannot please,
Nor yet of birds or harps the harmonies
Once charm asleep, or close their watchful eyes."

Do you think they could relish it? And that the fatal
end of their journey being continually before their eyes
would not alter and deprave their palate from all relish of
these fine things?

Audit iter, numeratque dies, spatioque viarum
Metitur vitam, torquetur peste futurâ.[2]

" He time and space computes by length of ways,
Sums up the number of his few sad days;
And his sad thoughts, full of his fatal doom,
Have room for nothing but the blow to come."

The end of our race is death, 'tis the necessary object of
our aim; if it frights us, how is it possible to advance a step
without a fit of ague? The remedy the vulgar use is not to
think on't; but from what brutish stupidity can they derive
so gross a blindness? He must needs bridle the ass by the
tail:

Qui capite ipse suo instituit vestigia retro.[3]

" He who the order of his steps has laid
To light and natural motion retrograde."

'Tis no wonder if he be often trapped in the pitfall. They
used to fright people with the very mention of death, and
must cross themselves as if it were the name of the devil;
and because the making a man's will is in reference to
dying, not a man will be persuaded to take a pen in hand, to
that purpose, till the physician has passed sentence upon him
and totally given him over; and then, betwixt grief and
terror, God knows in how fit a condition of understanding he
is to do it.

[1] Hor. *Od.* lii. 1, 18.　　　　　[3] Lucret. iv. 474.
[2] Claudian in *Ruf.* ii. 137.

The Romans, by reason that this poor syllable death was observed to be so harsh to the ears of the people, and the sound so ominous, found out a way to soften and spin it out by a periphrasis, and instead of pronouncing bluntly " such a one is dead," to say, " such a one has lived," or " such a one has ceased to live." For, provided there was any mention of life in the case, though 'twas past, it carried yet some sound of consolation. And from them it is that we have borrowed our expression of " the late Monsieur such a one."

The author's birth. Peradventure, as the saying is, the term is worth the money.[1] I was born betwixt eleven and twelve o'clock in the forenoon, the last of February, 1533, according to our present computation, beginning the year the first of January,[2] and it is now just fifteen days since I was complete nine and thirty years old; I may account to live, at least, as many more. In the mean time, to trouble a man's self with the thought of a thing so far off is a senseless foolery. But, after all, young and old die after the very same manner, and no one departs out of life otherwise than as though he had just before entered into it; neither is any so old and decrepid, who has not heard of Methusalem, that does not think he has yet another twenty years of constitution good at least. Fool that thou art, who has assured unto thee the term of thy life? Thou dependest upon physicians, and their old wives' tales, but rather consult fact and experience, and the fragility of human nature. According to the common course of things, 'tis long since that thou livest by extraordinary favour. Thou hast already outlived the ordinary term of life, and, to convince thyself that it is so, reckon up thy acquaintance, how many more have died before they arrived at thy age, than have

---

[1] This proverb is mostly used by such as, having borrowed money for a long term, take no care for the payment, flattering themselves that something will happen, in the mean time, for their benefit or discharge.

[2] By an ordonnance of Charles IX. promulgated in 1563, the beginning of the year was fixed to be on the first of January, instead of on Easter Day, as before. The year 1564, consequently, began on the first of January, 1563. The Parliament, however, did not conform to this ordonnance till two years after.

attained unto it; and of those who have ennobled their lives
by their renown, take but an account, and I dare lay a wager
thou wilt find more who have died before, than after, five and
thirty years of age. It is full both of reason and piety too
to take the example of the human existence of Jesus Christ
himself, who ended his life at three and thirty years. The
greatest man that ever was, who was no more than man,
Alexander, died also at the same age. How many several
ways has death to surprise us !

> Quid quisque vitet, nunquam homini satis
> Cautum est in horas.[1]

> " Man fain would shun, but 'tis not in his power
> T' evade the dangers of each threat'ning hour."

To omit fevers and pleurisies, who would ever have imagined
that a Duke of Brittany should be pressed to death in a
crowd, as that Duke was at the entry of Pope Clement, my
neighbour, into Lyons?[2] Have we not seen one of our
kings killed at a tilting;[3] and did not one of his ancestors die
by the jostle of a hog?[4] Æschylus, being threatened with
the fall of a house, got nothing by going into the fields to
avoid that danger, for there he was knocked on the head by
a tortoise falling out of an eagle's talons.[5] Another was
choked with a grape-stone.[6] An emperor was killed with
the scratch of a comb, in combing his head; Æmilius Lepidus with a stumble at his own threshold;[7] Aufidius, with a
jostle, against the door, as he entered the council-chamber.
And, in the very embrace of women, Cornelius Gallus, the
Prætor; Tigillinus, captain of the watch at Rome; Ludo-
vico, son of Guido de Gonzaga, Marquis of Mantua; and a

---

[1] Horace, *Od.* xiii. 13.

[2] In 1305, in the reign of Philip le Bel. This Duke of Brittany was named John II. The Pope, whom Montaigne mentions as his neighbour, was Bertrand de Got, Archbishop of Bordeaux, who was elected Pope, fifth of June, 1305, and took the title of Clement V.

[3] Henry II. of France, mortally wounded in a tournament by the Count de Montgomery, one of the captains of his guards.

[4] Philip, or as some say, Lewis VII. son of Louis le Gros, who was crowned in the lifetime of his father.

[5] Val. Max. ix. 12.

[6] Anacreon. See Val. Max. ix. 12.

[7] Pliny, *Nat. H.* vii. 33, whence are also taken the following instances.

still worse example, Speusippus, a platonic philosopher;[1]
and one of our Popes. The poor Judge Bibius, in the eight
days' reprieve he had given a criminal, was himself caught
hold of, his own reprieve of life being expired.[2] And Caius
Julius, the physician, while anointing the eyes of a patient,
had death close his own;[3] and if I may bring in an example
of my own blood, a brother of mine, Captain St. Martin, a
young man of three and twenty years old, who had already
given sufficient testimony of his valour, playing a match at
tennis, received a blow of a ball a little above his right ear,
which, though it was without any manner or sign of wound,
or depression of the skull, and though he took no great notice
of it, nor so much as sat down to repose himself, he nevertheless died within five or six hours after, of an apoplexy
occasioned by that blow.

Which so frequent and common examples passing every
day before our eyes, how is it possible a man should disengage himself from the thought of death; or avoid fancying
that it has us every moment by the collar? What matter is
it, you will say, which way it comes to pass, provided a man
does not terrify himself with the expectation? For my
part, I am of this mind, and by whatever means one could
shield one's self from the blow, were it under a calf's skin, I
am not the man to shrink from it; for all I want is to pass
my time pleasantly and at my ease, and the recreations that
most contribute to it I take hold of; as to the rest, as little
glorious and exemplary as you would desire.

> Prætulerim . . . delirus inersque videri,
> Dum mea delectent mala me, vel denique fallant,
> Quam sapere, et ringi.[4]

> "As fool, or sluggard, let me censur'd be,
> Whilst either fault dost please or cozen me,

---

[1] Tertullian mentions this in his *Apol-
ogetics*, c. 46, but without absolutely
affirming it. Diogenes Laertius says, on
the contrary, that being shattered with a
violent palsy, and broken down with the
weight of old age and vexation, Speusippus put an end to his own life.
[2] Pliny, vii. 53.
[3] Id. ib.
[4] Horace, *Epis.* ii. 2, 126.

> Rather than be thought wise, and feel the smart
> Of a perpetual aching anxious heart."

But 'tis folly to think of doing any thing that way. People go and come, and dance and gad about, and not a word of death. All this is very fine while it lasts, but when death does come either to themselves, or their wives, or their children, or their friends, surprising them at unawares, unprepared, then what torments, what outcries, what madness and despair overwhelm them! Did you ever see any thing so subdued, so changed, and so confounded? A man must, therefore, make himself more early ready for it; and this brutish negligence, even could it lodge in the brain of any man of sense, which I think utterly impossible, sells us its merchandise too dear. Were it an enemy that could be avoided, I would then advise to borrow arms, even of cowardice itself, to that effect. But seeing it is not, and that it will catch you as well flying and playing the poltroon, as standing to it, like a man of honour :—

> Mors et fugacem persequitur virum,
>   Nec parcit imbellis juventæ
>   Poplitibus timidoque tergo.[1]

> " No speed of foot can rob death of his prize,
>   He cuts the hamstrings of the man that flies;
>   Nor spares the fearful stripling's back who starts
>   To run beyond the reach of 's mortal darts."

And seeing that no temper of arms is of proof to secure us,—

> Ille licet ferro cautus se condat et ære,
> Mors tamen inclusum protrahet inde caput;[2]

> " Shield thee with steel or brass, advised by dread,
>   Death from the casque will pull thy cautious head; "

let us learn bravely to stand our ground and fight him. And, to begin to deprive him of the greatest advantage he has over us, let us take a way quite contrary to the common course. Let us disarm him of his strangeness; let us converse and be familiar with him, and have nothing so frequent

---

[1] Horace, *Od.* iii. 2, 14.   [2] Propertius, iii 18, 25.

in our thoughts as death; let us, upon all occasions, represent him in all his most dreadful shapes to our imagination. At the stumbling of a horse, at the falling of a tile, at the least prick of a pin, let us presently consider, and say to ourselves, " Well, and what if it had been death itself?" And thereupon let us encourage and fortify ourselves; let us evermore, amidst our jollity and feasting, keep the remembrance of our frail condition before our eyes, never suffering ourselves to be so far transported with our delights but that we have some intervals of reflecting upon, and considering how many several ways this jollity of ours tends to death, and with how many traps it threatens us. The Egyptians were wont to do after this manner, who, in the height of their feasting and mirth, caused a dried skeleton of a man to be brought into the room to serve for a memento to their guests.[1]

> Omnem crede diem tibi diluxisse supremum:
> Grata superveniet, quæ non sperabitur, hora.[2]

" Think every day, soon as the day is past,
Of thy life's date that thou hast lived the last;
The next day's joyful light thine eyes shall see,
As unexpected, will more welcome be."

Where death waits for us is uncertain; let us every where look for him. The premeditation of death is the premeditation of liberty; he who has learnt to die has forgot what it is to be a slave. There is nothing of evil in life for him who rightly comprehends that the loss of life is no evil: to know how to die delivers us from all subjection and constraint. Paulus Æmilius answered him whom the miserable King of Macedon, his prisoner, sent to entreat him that he would not lead him in his triumph, " Let him make that request to himself."[3]

In truth, in all things, if nature do not help a little, it is very hard for art and industry to perform any thing to purpose. I am, in my own nature, not melancholy, but thoughtful; and there is nothing I have more continually

---

[1] Herod. ii. 78.
[2] Horace, *Epist.* i. 4, 13.
[3] Plut. *in Vitâ*, c. 17. Cicero, *Tusc. Quæs.* v. 40.

entertained myself withal than the imaginations of death, even in the gayest and most wanton time of my life :—

Jucundum cùm ætas florida ver ageret.[1]

" When that my youth rolled on in pleasant spring."

In the company of ladies, and in the height of mirth, some have perhaps thought me possessed with some jealousy, or meditating upon the uncertainty of some imagined hope, whilst I was only entertaining myself with the remembrance of some one surprised a few days before with a burning fever, of which he died, returning from an entertainment like this, with his head full of idle fancies of love and jollity, as mine was then, and that, for aught I knew, the same destiny was attending me.

Jam fuerit, neque post unquam revocare licebit.[2]

' He who of late a being had 'mongst men,
Is gone, and ne'er to be recalled again."

Yet did not this thought wrinkle my forehead any more than any other. No doubt it is impossible but we must feel a sting in such imaginations as these, at first; but with often revolving them in a man's mind, and having them frequent in our thoughts, they at last become so familiar as to be no trouble at all. Otherwise I, for my part, should be in perpetual fright and frenzy; for never man was so distrustful of his life, never man so indifferent for its duration. Neither health, which I have hitherto ever enjoyed very strong and vigorous, and very seldom interrupted, prolongs, nor sickness contracts, my hopes. Every minute methinks 'tis about to escape me; and it eternally runs in my mind that what may be done to-morrow may be done to-day. Hazards and dangers do in truth little or nothing hasten our end; and if we consider how many more remain and hang over our heads beside the misfortune that immediately threatens us, we shall find that the sound and the sick, those that are abroad at sea, and those that sit by the fire; those that are in the wars, and

[1] Catullus, lxviii. 16.   [2] Lucret. iii. 928.

those that sit idle at home, are the one as near it as the other : *Nemo altero fragilior est, nemo in crastinum sui certior.*[1] " No man is more frail than another, nor more certain of the morrow." For any thing I have to do before I die, the longest leisure would appear too short, were it but an hour's business I had to do.

A friend of mine, the other day, turning over my table-book, found in it a memorandum of something I would have done after my decease ; whereupon I told him, as was really true, that, though I was no more than a league's distance from my own house, and merry and well, yet when that thing came into my head I made haste to write it down there, because I was not certain to live till I came home. As a man that am eternally brooding over my own thoughts, and who confine them to my own particular concerns, I am at all hours as well prepared as I am ever like to be ; and death, whenever he shall come, can bring nothing along with him I did not expect long before. We should always (as near as we can) be booted and spurred, and ready to go, and, above all things, take care at that time to have no business with any one but one's self.

> Quid brevi fortes jaculamur ævo
> Multa ?[2]

> " Why cut'st thou out such mighty work, vain man?
> Whose life's short date's comprised in one poor span ? "

For we shall then find work enough to do, without any need of addition. One complains, more than of death, that he is thereby prevented of a glorious victory ; another that he must die before he has married his daughter, or settled and educated his children ; a third seems only troubled that he must lose the society of his wife ; a fourth the conversation of his son, as the principal concerns of his being. For my part I am, thanks be to God, at this instant in such a condition that I am ready to dislodge, whenever it shall please him, without any manner of regret. I disengage myself

---

[1] Senec. *Epist.* 91.   [2] Horace, *Od.* ii. 16, 17.

throughout from all worldly relations; my leave is soon taken of all but myself. Never did any one prepare to bid adieu to the world more absolutely and purely, and to shake hands with all manner of interest in it, than I expect to do. The deadest deaths are the best.[1]

> Miser! O miser! (aiunt) omnia ademit
> Una dies infesta mihi tot præmia vitæ.[2]

> " Wretch that I am (they cry), one fatal day
> So many joys of life has snatched away."

And the builder,

> —— manent (says he) opera interrupta, minæque
> Murorum ingentes, æquataque machina cœlo.[8]

> " The mounds, the works, the walls neglected lie,
> Short of their promised height, that seemed to threat the sky."

A man must design nothing that will require so much time to the finishing, or at least with no such passionate desire to see it brought to a conclusion. We are born to action.

> Cùm moriar, medium solvar et inter opus.[4]

> " When death shall come, he me will find
> Engaged on something I've design'd."

I would always have a man to be doing, and as much as in him lies, to extend and spin out the offices of life; and then let death take me planting cabbages, but without any careful thought of him, and much less of my garden's not being finished. I saw one die, who, at his last gasp, seemed to be concerned at nothing so much as that destiny was about to cut the thread of a history he was then compiling, when he was got no farther than the fifteenth or sixteenth of our kings.

> Illud in his rebus non addunt, nec tibi earum
> Jam desiderium rerum super insidet una.[5]

> " They tell us not, that, dying, we've no more
> The same desire of things as heretofore."

---

[1] Death is here considered as the introduction and actual passage to a state of insensibility which puts a period to our life. The more silently and rapidly we arrive to that state the less ought the passage to terrify us. This comes up very near to the import of that bold and enigmatical expression of Montaigne, viz: " That the deadest deaths are the best."
[2] Lucret. iii. 911.
[8] Æneid, iv. 88. The text has *pendent*.
[4] Ovid, *Amor.* ii. 10, 36.
[5] Lucret. iii. 913.

We should discharge ourselves from these vulgar and hurtful humours and concerns. To this purpose it was that men first put the places of sepulture, the dormitories of the dead, near adjoining to the churches, and in the most frequented places of the city, to accustom (says Lycurgus) the common people, women, and children, that they should not be startled at the sight of a dead corpse; and to the end that the continual sight of bones, graves, monuments, and funeral obsequies, should keep us in mind of our frail condition.[1]

> Quin etiam exhilarare viris convivia cæde
> Mos olim, et miscere epulis spectacula dira
> Certantum ferro, sæpè et super ipsa cadentum
> Pocula, respersis non parco sanguine mensis.[2]

> " 'Twas therefore that the ancients at their feasts
>   With tragic slaughter used to treat their guests;
>   Making their fencers, with their utmost spite,
>   Skill, force, and fury in their presence fight;
>   Till streams of blood o'erflow'd the spacious hall,
>   Crims'ning their tables, drinking-cups, and all."

And as the Egyptians after their feasts were wont to present the company with a great image of death, by one that cried out to them, " Drink and be merry, for such shalt thou be when thou art dead;" so it is my custom to have death not only in my imagination, but continually in my mouth. Neither is there any thing of which I am so inquisitive, and delight to inform myself, as the manner of men's deaths, their words, looks, and gestures; nor any places in history I am so intent upon; and it is manifest enough, by my crowding in examples of this kind, that I have a particular fancy for that subject. If I were a writer of books, I would compile a register, with a comment, of the various deaths of men; and it could not but be useful, for he who should teach men to die would at the same time teach them to live. Dicearchus made one, to which he gave some such title; but it was designed for another and less profitable end.[3] Peradventure some one may object, and say that the pain and

---

[1] Plutarch, *in Vitâ.*   [2] Silius Italicus, ii. 51.   [3] Cicero *de Offic.* ii. 5.

terror of dying indeed does so infinitely exceed It is of great advantage to think of death beforehand.
all manner of imagination that the best fencer
will be quite out of his play when it comes to
the push. But, let them say what they will, to premeditate
it is doubtless a very great advantage; and besides, is it
nothing to get so far, at least, without any visible disturbance
or alteration? But moreover Nature herself does assist and
encourage us. If the death be sudden and violent, we have
not leisure to fear; if otherwise, I find that as I engage further in my disease, I naturally enter into a certain loathing
and disdain of life. I find I have much more ado to digest
this resolution of dying when I am well in health than when
sick, languishing of a fever; and by how much I have less to
do with the comforts of life, I even begin to lose the relish
and pleasure of them, and by so much I look upon death
with less terror; which makes me hope that the further I
remove from the first, and the nearer I approach to the latter, I shall sooner strike a bargain, and with less unwilling-
ness exchange the one for the other. And, as I have
experienced in other occurrences what Cæsar says, " That
things often appear greater to us at a distance than near at
hand," [1] I have found that, being well, I have had diseases in
much greater horror than when really afflicted with them.
The vigour wherein I now am, and the jollity and delight
wherein I now live, make the contrary estate appear in so
great a disproportion to my present condition, that by imagination I magnify and make those inconveniences twice
greater than they are, and apprehend them to be much
more troublesome than I find them really to be, when
they lie the most heavy upon me, and I hope to find death
the same.

Let us but observe in the ordinary changes and declinations
our constitutions daily suffer, how nature deprives us of all
sight and sense of our bodily decay. What remains to an
old man of the vigour of his youth and better days?

[1] *De Bello Gallico*, vii. 89.

Heu! senibus vitæ portio quanta manet! [1]

" Alas! how small a part of life's short stage
Remains to travellers advanced in age! "

Cæsar, to an old weather-beaten soldier of his guards, who came
to ask him leave that he might kill himself, taking notice of
his withered body and decrepid motion, pleasantly answered,
" Thou fanciest, then, that thou art yet alive ! " [2] Should a
man fall into the aches and impotences of age from a sprightly
and vigorous youth, on the sudden, I do not think humanity
capable of enduring such a change. But nature, leading us
by the hand an easy, and, as it were, an insensible pace, little
by little, step by step, conducts us gently to that miserable
condition, and by that means makes it familiar to us, so that
we perceive not, nor are sensible of the stroke then, when
our youth dies in us, though it be really a harder death than
the final dissolution of a languishing body, which is only the
death of old age ; forasmuch as the fall is not so great from an
uneasy being to none at all, as it is from a sprightly and florid
being to one that is unwieldy and painful. The body, when
bowed beyond its natural spring of strength, has less force
either to rise with, or support, a burthen ; and it is with the
soul the same, and therefore it is that we are to raise her up
firm and erect against the power of this adversary. For as
it is impossible she should ever be at rest or at peace within
herself whilst she stands in fear of it, so if she once can
assure herself, she may boast (which is a thing, as it were,
above human condition) that it is impossible that disquiet,
anxiety, or fear, or any other disturbance, should inhabit or
have any place in her.

Non vultus instantis tyranni
Mente quatit solidâ; neque Auster
Dux inquieti turbidus Adriæ,
Nec fulminantis magna Jovis manus. [3]

" A soul well settled is not to be shook
With an incensed tyrant's threat'ning look;

[1] Maximian, *Eleg.* i. 16; *Ex. Pseudo-Gallus.*   [2] Seneca, *Epist.* 77.   [3] Horat. *Od.* iii. 3, 3.

> Nor can loud Auster once that heart dismay,
> The ruffling Prince of stormy Adria;
> Nor yet th' uplifted hand of mighty Jove,
> Though charg'd with thunder, such a temper move."

She is then become sovereign of all her lusts and passions, mistress of necessity, shame, poverty, and all the other injuries of fortune. Let us, therefore, as many of us as can, get this advantage, which is the true and sovereign liberty here on earth, and that fortifies us wherewithal to defy violence and injustice, and to contemn prisons and chains.

> In manicis et
> Compedibus, sævo te sub custode tenebo.
> Ipse Deus, simul atque volam, me solvet. Opinor,
> Hoc sentit: moriar. Mors ultima linea rerum est.[1]

> "'With bolts and chains I'll load thy hands and feet,
> And to a surly keeper thee commit.'—
> But let him show his worst of cruelty,
> The gods propitious soon will set me free;
> By death release me, that full comfort brings,
> For death's the utmost term of human things."

Our very religion itself has no surer human foundation than the contempt of death. Not only the argument of reason invites us to it,—for why should we fear to lose a thing which, being lost, can never be missed or lamented?—but, also, seeing that we are threatened by so many sorts of deaths, is it not infinitely worse eternally, to fear them all than once to undergo one of them? And what matter is it when it shall happen, since it is inevitable once? To him that told Socrates, " The thirty tyrants have sentenced thee to death "—" And nature them," said he.[2] What a ridiculous thing it is to trouble and afflict ourselves about taking the only step that is to deliver us from all misery and trouble! As our birth brought us the birth of all things, so in our death is the death of all things included. And therefore to lament and take on that we shall

The contempt of death a certain foundation of religion.

---

[1] Horace, *Epist.* 1. 16, 76.   [2] Diog. Laert. *in Vitâ.* Cicero, *Tusc. Quæs.* i. 40.

not be alive a hundred years hence, is the same folly as to be
sorry we were not alive a hundred years ago.   Death is the
beginning of another life.   So did we weep, and so much it
cost us to enter into this, and so did we put off our former
veil in entering into it.   Nothing can be grievous that is but
once; and is it reasonable so long to fear a thing that will so
soon be dispatched?   A long life and a short are by death
made all one; for there is no long nor short to things that are
no more.   Aristotle tells us that there are certain little beasts
upon the banks of the river Hypanis that never live above a
day; they which die at eight of the clock in the morning die
in their youth, and those that die at five in the evening in
their extremest age.[1]   Which of us would not laugh to see
this moment of continuance put into the consideration of weal
or woe?   Yet the most, and the least of ours, in comparison
of eternity, or even to the duration of mountains, rivers, stars,
trees, nay, of some animals, is no less ridiculous.[2]   But Nature

Death a part of the order of the universe.

compels us to it: "Go out of this world," says
she, "as you entered it; the same passage you
made from death to life, without passion or
fear, the same, after the same manner, repeat from life to
death.   Your death is a part of the order of the universe,
'tis a part of the life of the world.

Inter se mortales mutua vivunt;

.   .   .   .

Et, quasi cursores, vitæ lampada tradunt.[3]

"Among themselves mankind alternate live,
And life's bright torch to the next runner give."

"Shall I change, to please you, so admirable a system?
'Tis the condition of your creation; death is a part of you,
and whilst you endeavour to evade it, you avoid yourselves.
This very being of yours, that you now enjoy, is equally

[1] Cicero, *Tusc. Quæs.* i. 39.
[2] Seneca, *Consol. ad Marc.* c. 20.
[3] Lucretius, ii. 75.   Alluding to the
Athenian games, wherein those that ran
a race carried torches in their hands;
and their race being done, delivered
them into the hands of those that ran
next.

divided betwixt life and death. The day of your birth is
one day's advance towards the grave.

> Prima, quæ vitam dedit, hora carpsit.[1]

> " The hour that first gave life its breath,
> Was a whole hour's advance to death."

> Nascentes morimur; finisque ab origine pendet.[2]

> " As we are born, we die; and our life's end
> Upon our life's beginning doth depend."

" Every day that you live you purloin from life, you live at
the expense of life itself; the perpetual work of your whole
life is but to lay the foundation of death; you are in death
whilst you live, because you still are after death when you
are no more alive. Or if you had rather have it so, you are
dead after life, but dying all the while you live; and death
handles the dying more rudely, and more feelingly, and essen-
tially than the dead. If you have made your profit of life
you have had enough of it, go your way satisfied.

> Cur non ut plenus vitæ convivia recedis? [3]

> " Why should'st not go, like a full gorged guest,
> Sated with life, as he is with a feast?"

If you have not known how to make the best use of it, and
if it was unprofitable to you, what need you care to lose it?
to what end would you desire longer to keep it?

> Cur amplius addere quæris
> Rursum quod pereat male, et ingratum occidat omne.[4]

> " Why wouldst renew thy time? to what intent
> Live o'er again a life that was ill spent?"

" Life in itself is neither good nor evil; it is the scene of good
or evil, as you make it; and if you have lived a long day
you have seen all. One day is equal and like to all other
days; there is no other light, no other night. This very sun,
this moon, these very stars, this very order and revolution of
things, are all the same your ancestors enjoyed, and that
shall also entertain your posterity.

---

1 Seneca, *Hercul. fur.* act iii. chor.
verse, 874.
2 Manilius, *Astronom.* iv. 16.

3 Lucret. iii. 951.
4 Id. ib. 945.

Non alium videre patres, aliumve nepotes
Aspicient.[1]
"Your grandsires saw no other things of old,
  Nor shall your grandsons other things behold."

"And come the worst that can come, the distribution and
variety of all the acts of my comedy is performed in a year.
If you have observed the revolution of four seasons, they
comprehend the infancy, the youth, the virility, and the old
age of the world. The year has played his part, and knows
no other trick than to begin and repeat the same again; it
will always be the same thing.

Versamur ibidem, atque insumus usque.[2]

" We yearly tread but one perpetual round,
  We ne'er strike out, but beat the former ground."

Atque in se sua per vestigia volvitur annus.[3]

" The year rolls on within itself again."

"I have no mind to create you any new recreations.

Nam tibi præterea quod machiner, inveniamque
Quod placeat, nihil est: eadem sunt omnia semper.[4]
"More pleasures than are made time will not frame,
  For to all times all things shall be the same."

" Give place to others, as others have given place to you.
Equality is the soul of equity.[5] Who can complain of being
comprehended in the same destiny wherein all are involved?
Besides, live as long as you can, you shall by that nothing
shorten the time that you are to lie dead; 'tis all to no purpose; you shall be every whit as long in the condition you
so much fear, as though you had died at nurse.

Licet quot vis vivendo vincere sæcla,
  Mors æterna tamen nihilominus illa manebit.[6]

" And, live as many ages as you will,
  Death ne'ertheless shall be eternal still."

"And yet I will place you in such a condition as you shall
have no reason to be displeased :—

1 Manilius, i. 529.   4 Lucret. iii. 957.
2 Lucret. iii. 1093.   5 Senec. *Epist.* 30.
3 Virg. *Georg.* ii. 402.   6 Lucret. iii. 1103.

> In verâ nescis nullum fore morte alium te,
> Qui possit vivus tibi te lugere peremptum,
> Stansque jacentem.[1]

> When dead, a living self thou canst not have,
> Or to lament or trample on thy grave."

" Nor shall you so much as wish for the life you are so concerned about.

> Nec sibi enim quisquam tum se vitamque requirit.
> · · · · · · · ·
> Nec desiderium nostri nos afficit ullum.[2]

> " Life nor ourselves we wish in that estate,
> Nor thoughts of what we were at first create."

" Death were less to be feared than nothing, if there could be any thing less than nothing.

> Multo . . . . mortem minus ad nos esse putandum,
> Si minùs esse potest quàm quod nihil esse videmus.[3]

> " If less than nothing any thing can show,
> Death then would both appear and would be so."

" Neither can it any way concern you whether you are living or dead ; living, by reason that you are still in being ; dead, because you are no more. Moreover, no one dies before his hour ; and the time you leave behind was no more yours than that was lapsed and gone before you came into the world ; nor does it any more concern you.

> Respice enim quàm nil ad nos anteacta vetustas
> Temporis æterni fuerit.[4]

> " Look back, and tho' times past eternal were,
> In those before us, yet had we no share."

" Wherever your life ends, it is all there ; neither does the utility of living consist in the length of days, but in the well husbanding and improving of time ; and a man may have continued in the world longer than the ordinary age of man that has yet lived but a little while. Make use of time while it is present with you. It depends upon your will, and not

---

[1] Lucret. iii. 898.
[2] Id. ib. 932.
[3] Id. ib. 939.
[4] Id. ib. 985.

upon the number of days, to have a sufficient length of life.
Is it possible you can ever imagine you will not arrive at the
place towards which you are continually going? and yet there
is no journey but hath its end.   And, if company will make
it more pleasant or more easy to you, does not all the world
go the self-same way?

> . . . . Omnia te vitâ perfuncta sequuntur.[1]
>
> " When thou dost die, let this thy comfort be,
>   That all the world, by turn, must follow thee."

" Does not all the world dance the same dance that you do?
Is there any thing that does not grow old as well as you?   A
thousand men, a thousand animals, and a thousand other
creatures, die at the same moment that you expire.

> Nam nox nulla diem, neque noctem aurora, sequuta est,
> Quæ non audierit mistos vagitibus ægris
> Ploratus mortis comites et funeris atri.[2]

> "No night succeeds the day, nor morning's light
> Rises to chase the sullen shades of night;
> Wherein there is not heard the dismal groans
> Of dying men mix'd with the woful moans
> Of living friends, and with the mournful cries
> And dirges fitting fun'ral obsequies."

" To what end should you recoil, since you cannot go
back?   You have seen examples enough of those who have
been glad to die, thereby being manifestly delivered from
intolerable miseries; but have you talked with any of those
who found a disadvantage by it?   It must therefore needs be
very foolish to condemn a thing you have neither experienced
in your own person, nor by that of any other.   Why dost thou
complain of me and destiny?   Do we do thee any wrong?
Is it for thee to govern us, or for us to dispose of thee?
Though peradventure thy age may not be accomplished, yet
thy life is.   A man of low stature is a whole man as well as
a giant; neither men nor their lives are measured by the ell.
Chiron refused to be immortal, when he was acquainted with
the conditions under which he was to enjoy it, by the god of

---

[1] Lucret. iii. 98.   [2] Id. ii. 579.

time itself and its duration, his father Saturn. Do but seriously consider how much more insupportable an immortal and painful life would be to man than what I have already designed him.[1] If you had not death to ease you of your pains and cares, you would eternally curse me for having deprived you of the benefit of dying. I have, 'tis true, mixed a little bitterness in it, to the end that, seeing of what conveniency and use it is, you might not too greedily and indiscreetly seek and embrace it; and that you might be so established in this moderation, as neither to nauseate life, nor have any antipathy for dying, which I have decreed you shall once do, I have tempered the one and the other betwixt pleasure and pain. 'Twas I that first taught Thales, the most eminent of all your sages, that to live and die were indifferent; which made him very wisely answer him who asked him, "Why then did he not die?" "Because," said he, "it is indifferent."[2] The elements of water, earth, fire, and air, and the other parts of this creation of mine, are no more the instruments of thy life than they are of thy death. Why dost thou fear thy last day? it contributes no more to thy dissolution than every one of the rest. The last step is not the cause of lassitude; it does but confess it. Every day travels towards death; the last only arrives at it."[3] These are the good lessons our Mother Nature teaches.

I have often considered with myself whence it should proceed that in war the image of death, whether we look upon it as to our own particular danger or that of another, should without comparison appear less dreadful than at home in our own houses (for if it were not so, it would be an army of whining milksops); and that being still in all places the same, there should be, notwithstanding, much more assurance in peasants

Why death appears less dreadful on the field of battle than at home.

[1] "Si nous étions immortels, nous serions des êtres très misérables. Si l'on nous offrait l'immortalité sur la terre qui est-ce qui voudrait accepter ce triste présent?"—Rousseau, Emile, liv. ii.

[2] Diog. Laertius, in Vitâ.
[3] Lucret. iii. 945, &c. Seneca, Epist. 12. Id. on the Shortness of Life.

and the meaner sort of people than in others of better quality
and education ; and I do verily believe that it is those terrible
ceremonies and preparations wherewith we set it out that
more terrify us than the thing itself. An entirely new way
of living, the cries of mothers, wives, and children, the visits
of astonished and afflicted friends, the attendance of pale and
blubbering servants, a dark room set round with burning
tapers, our beds environed with physicians and divines ; in
short, nothing but ghostliness and horror round about us,
render it so formidable that a man almost fancies himself
dead and buried already. Children are afraid even of those
they love best, and are best acquainted with, when disguised
in a vizor, and so are we : the vizor must be removed as well
from things as persons ;[1] which being taken away, we shall
find nothing underneath but the very same death that a mean
servant or a poor chambermaid died a day or two ago, without any manner of apprehension or concern. Happy therefore is the death that deprives us of the leisure for such grand
preparations !

CHAPTER XX.

OF THE FORCE OF IMAGINATION.

Fortis imaginatio generat casum. " A strong imagination
creates what it imagines," say the schoolmen. I am one of
those who are most sensible of the power of imagination :
every one is jostled, but some are quite overthrown by it.
It has a very great impression upon me ; and I make it my
business to avoid, wanting force to resist it. I could live by
the sole help of healthful and jolly company. The very sight
of another's pain greatly pains me ; and I often go entirely

[1] Seneca, *Epist.* 24.

into the feelings of a third person, and share with him in his torment. A perpetual cough in another tickles my lungs and throat. I more unwillingly visit the sick, in whom I am by duty interested, than those I care not for, and to whom I am less bound. I take possession of the disease I look at, and do not at all wonder that fancy should give fevers, and sometimes kill such as allow of too much scope and are too willing to entertain it. Simon Thomas was a great physician of his time ; and I remember that, happening one day at Thoulouse to meet him at a rich old fellow's house, who was troubled with bad lungs, and discoursing with his patient about the method of his cure, he told him that one thing which would be very conducing to it was to give me such occasion to be pleased with his company that I might come often to see him, by which means, and by fixing his eyes upon the freshness of my complexion, and his imagination upon the sprightliness and vigour that glowed in my youth, and possessing all his senses with the flourishing state wherein I then was, his habit of body might, peradventure, be amended ; but he forgot to say that mine at the same time might be made worse. Gallus Vibius so long cudgelled his brains to find out the essence and motions of madness that in the end he went quite out of his wits, and to such a degree that he could never after recover his judgment ; and he might brag that he was become mad by too much wisdom.[1] Some there are who through fear anticipate the hangman ; like him whose eyes being unbound to have his pardon read to him, was found dead upon the scaffold by the stroke of imagination. We start, tremble, turn pale, and blush, as we are variously moved by imagination ; and being covered over head and ears in bed,

Imagination occasions diseases and death.

---

[1] Seneca, the Rhetorician, from whom Montaigne must have taken this story, does not say that Gallus Vibius lost his reason by endeavouring to comprehend the essence of madness, but by too studious an application to imitate its motions. As this Gallus was a rhetorician by profession, he imagined that the transports of madness, well represented in dialogue, would charm his audience: and took so much pains to play the madman in jest, that he became so in earnest. He is the only man I ever knew (says Seneca) that became mad, not by accident, but by an act of judgment.— *Controvers.* ix. 2.

feel our bodies so agitated with its power as even sometimes
to expire. And boiling youth, when fast asleep, grows so
warm with fancy, as in a dream to satisfy its amorous desires :—

> Ut, quasi transactis sæpè omnibus rebus, profundant
> Fluminis ingentes fluctus, vestemque cruentent.[1]

And although it be no new thing to see horns grown in a
night on the forehead of one that had none when he went to
bed, yet what befell Cippus, King of Italy, is very memorable ; who having one day been a very delighted spectator
of a bull-baiting, and having all the night dreamt that he had
horns on his head, did, by the force of imagination, really
cause them to grow there.[2] Passion made the son of Crœsus
to speak, who was born dumb, thus supplying him with that
which Nature had denied him.[3] And Antiochus fell into a
fever, inflamed with the beauty of Stratonice, too deeply imprinted in his soul.[4] Pliny pretends to have
The story of the seen Lucius Cossitius, who from a woman was
goddess Lyra, in Lucian. turned into a man upon her very wedding-day.[5]
Pontanus and others report the like metamorphoses to have
happened in these later days in Italy ; and through the
vehement desire of him and his mother,

> Vota puer solvit, quæ fœmina voverat, Iphis.[6]

> " Iphis, a boy, the vow defray'd
> That he had promis'd when a maid."

Myself passing by Vitry le Francois,[7] a town in Champagne, saw a man the Bishop of Soissons had in confirmation,

---

Lucretius, iv. 1029. Montaigne has
rendered the meaning of the passage in
the preceding sentence.
[2] Pliny, xi. 45, who, however, puts this
story in the same class with that of Ac-
tæon, and supposes both to be fabulous.
Valerius Maximus, v. 6, gives this Cyppus, or Cippus, the title of Prætor, and
says that as he departed from Rome, in
the habit of a general, the accident which
Montaigne speaks of here happening to
him, the diviners declared that Cyppus

would be king if he returned to Rome;
whereupon he voluntarily condemned
himself to perpetual exile, in order to
prevent it. This explains why Montaigne
calls him King of Italy.
[3] Herod. i. 85.
[4] Lucian, on the Syrian Goddess.
[5] Pliny, Nat. Hist. vii. 4.
[6] Ovid, Met. ix. 793.
[7] September, 1580. The circumstance
is further referred to in our author's
Journey through Germany and Italy.

called Germain, whom all the inhabitants of the place had known and seen to be a girl till two and twenty years of age, by the name of Mary. He was, at the time of my being there, very full of beard, old, and not married, and told us that, in straining himself in a leap, his virile appurtenances came out; and the maids of that place have to this day a song wherein they advise one another not to take too great strides for fear of being turned into men, as Mary Germain was. It were no great wonder if this sort of accident frequently happened; for if imagination have any power in such things, it is so continually and vigorously bent upon this subject that, to the end it may not so often relapse into the same thought and violence of desire, it were better, once for all, to give the wenches the thing they long for.

Some stick not to attribute the scars of King Dagobert and St. Francis to the force of imagination; and it is said, that by it bodies will sometimes be moved from their places; and Celsus tells us of a priest whose soul would sometimes be ravished into such an ecstasy that the body would, for a long time, remain without sense or respiration. St. Augustine makes mention of another,[1] who, upon the hearing of any lamentable or doleful cries, would presently fall into a swoon, and be so far out of himself that it was in vain to call, halloo in his ears, pinch, or burn him, till he voluntarily came to himself; and then he would say that he had heard voices but, as it were, afar off, and felt when they pinched and burned him. And that this was no obstinate dissimulation, in defiance of his sense of feeling, was manifest from this, that all the while he had neither pulse nor breathing.

'Tis very probable that visions, enchantments, and all extraordinary effects of that nature, derive their credit principally from the power of imagination, working as they do, and making their chiefest impression upon vulgar and easy souls, whose belief is so full as to think they see what they do not. *Why such credit is given to visions, enchantments, &c.*

---

[1] *Restitutus.* See St. Aug. *de Civit Dei.* xiv. 24.

I am not satisfied, and make a very great question, whether

Whence it is that lovers sometimes find themselves unable to perform their pleasant labours.

those pleasant marriage locks or impediments, with which this age of ours is so fettered that there is hardly any thing else talked of, are not merely the impressions of apprehension and fear ; for I know, by experience, in the case of a particular friend of mine, one for whom I can answer as for myself, and a man that cannot possibly fall under any manner of suspicion of insufficiency, and as little of being enchanted, who having heard a companion of his make a relation of an unusual disability that surprised him at a very unseasonable time, being afterwards himself engaged upon the same occasion, the horror of that story on a sudden so strangely possessed his imagination that he ran the same fortune the other had done ; and from that time forward (the scurvy remembrance of his disaster running in his mind, and tyrannizing over him), was extremely subject to relapse into the same misfortune. He found some remedy, however, for this inconvenience, by himself frankly confessing and declaring beforehand to the lady with whom he was to have to do, the subjection he lay under, and the infirmity he was victim to, by which means the agitation of his soul was in some sort appeased ; and knowing that now some such misbehaviour was expected from him, the obligation he felt under grew less, and weighed less upon his imagination ; and when he had an opportunity at his leisure, at such times as he could be in no such apprehension (his thoughts being then disengaged and free, and his body being in its true and natural estate), by causing this to be communicated to the knowledge of others, he was at last totally freed from that vexatious infirmity. After a man has once done a woman right, he is never after in danger of misbehaving himself with that person, unless upon the account of some physical weakness. Neither is this disaster to be feared, but in adventures where the soul is extended beyond measure with desire or respect, and especially where one's opportunity happens in a sudden

and pressing manner; in those cases, there is no means for a
man always to keep himself from a scrape of this sort. And
yet I have known some, to whom it has been of service to
come to their mistress, with their heat half sated elsewhere,
and having abated thus the ardour of their fury; and others,
who when old, find themselves less impotent by being less
able; and again, I knew one, who found an advantage in
being assured by a friend of his that he had a counter battery of charms that would defend him from this disgrace.
The story itself is not much amiss, and therefore you shall
have it.

A Count of a very great family, and with whom I was
very familiarly intimate, married a very fair
lady, who had formerly been pretended to and
importunately courted by one who was present
at the wedding; all his friends, especially an old lady, his
kinswoman, who had the ordering of the solemnity, and in
whose house it was kept, were in great fear lest his rival
should in revenge, offer foul play, and procure some of these
kind of sorceries, to put a trick upon him; which fear the
old lady communicated to me, who, to comfort her, bid her
not trouble herself, but rely upon my care to prevent or frustrate any such designs. Now I had by chance about me a
certain flat plate of gold, whereon were graven some celestial figures, supposed to be good against headache, when
applied to the suture; and which, that it might the better
remain firm on its place, was sewed to a ribbon, to be tied
under the chin. A piece of quackery, a thing cousin-german
to that of which I am speaking, and which was by Jaques
Pelletier, who lived in my house, presented to me for a singular rarity, and a thing of sovereign virtue. I had a fancy
to make some use of this knack, and therefore privately told
the Count that he might possibly run the same fortune other
bridegrooms had sometimes done; especially some persons
being in the house who no doubt would be glad to play him
such a trick, but let him boldly go to bed, for I would do him

A curious remedy for imaginary insufficiency in love.

the office of a friend, and if need were, would not spare a
miracle that it was in my power to do, provided he would
engage to me, upon his honour, to keep it to himself, and
only when they came to bring him his caudle in the night,[1] if
matters had not gone well with him, to give me such a sign, and
leave the rest to me.   Well, he had had his ears so battered,
and his mind so prepossessed with the eternal tattle of his
business that, when he came to it, he did really find himself
tied with the trouble of his imagination, and accordingly at
the time appointed gave me the sign; whereupon I whispered
him in the ear that he should rise, under pretence of putting
us out of the room, and after a jesting manner pull my night-
gown from my shoulders, (we were nearly of a height,) throw
it over his own, and there keep it till he had performed what
I appointed him to do, which was that when we were all
gone out of the chamber he should withdraw to make water,
should three times repeat such and such words, and as often
do such and such actions ; that at every of the three times he
should tie the ribbon I put into his hand about his middle,
and be sure to place the medal that was fastened to it, the
figures in such a posture, exactly upon his reins, which being
done, and having, the last of the three times, so well girt and
fast tied the ribbon that it could neither untie nor slip from
its place, let him confidently return to his business, and withal
not forget to spread my gown upon the bed, so that it might
be sure to cover them both.   These apes' tricks are the main
of the effect, our fancy being so far seduced as to believe that
such strange and uncouth formalities must of necessity proceed from some abstruse science.   Their very inanity gives
them reverence and weight.   However, certain it is that my
figures proved themselves more venerean than solar, more in
action than in prohibition, and the fair bride had no reason
to complain.   Now I must tell you, it was a sudden whimsey,
mixed with a little curiosity, that made me do a thing so

---

[1] It was formerly a custom in France to bring the bridegroom a caudle in the
middle of his wedding night.

contrary to my nature; for I am an enemy to all tricks and counterfeits, and abominate all manner of finesse, though it be in sport, and of advantage; for though the action may not be wicked in itself, yet 'tis done after a wicked manner.

Amasis, king of Ægypt, having married Laodicea, a marvellously beautiful Greek virgin, though famous for his abilities elsewhere, found himself quite another man with his wife, and could by no means enjoy her; at which he was so enraged that he threatened to kill her, suspecting her to be a witch. As 'tis usually in things that consist in fancy, she put him upon devotion, and, having accordingly made his vows to Venus, he found himself divinely restored the very first night after his oblations and sacrifices.[1] Women are to blame, to entertain us with that disdainful, coy, and angry countenance they commonly do, which extinguishes our vigour, as it kindles our desire. The daughter-in-law of Pythagoras said that the woman who goes to bed with a man must put off her modesty with her petticoat, and put it on again with the same.[2] The soul of the assailant being disturbed with a variety of alarms, is easily dispirited, and soon loses the power of performance; and whoever the imagination has once put this shame upon (and she never does it but at the first acquaintance, by reason men are then more ardent and eager, and that at this first account a man gives of himself he is much more timorous of miscarrying,) having made an ill-beginning, he becomes peevish at the accident, which will on following occasions be apt to stick to him.

As to married people, whose time is all before them, they ought never to compel, or so much as to offer at the affair, if they do not find themselves quite ready; and it is better to fail in the decorum of handselling the nuptial sheets, when a man perceives himself full of agitation and trembling, and to

---

[1] Herod. ii. 181, who, however, says that, not Amasis, but Laodicea, or Ladice, faithfully performed a vow she had made to Venus, by erecting a statue: "which," the author adds, "was still standing in my time."

[2] Montaigne here speaks of Theano, the famous Pythagorean woman, who was the wife, and not the daughter in-law, of Pythagoras. See Diogenes Laertius in the *Life of Pythagoras*, viii. 42. It is M. Menage who has taken notice of this small mistake of Montaigne.

wait for another opportunity at a better and more private
juncture, when his fancy shall be better composed, than to
make himself perpetually miserable, for having misbehaved
himself, and been baffled at the first assault.   Till possession
be taken, a man that knows himself subject to this infirmity,
should leisurely and at intervals make several little trials and
light offers, without obstinately attempting at once to force an
absolute conquest over his own mutinous and indisposed
faculties.   Such as know their members to be naturally
obedient to their desires, need to take no other care but only
to counterplot their fancy.

The indocility of this member is sufficiently remarkable ;
importunate, unruly, and impatient, at such times as we have
nothing for it to do, and unseasonably stupid and disobedient
when we stand most in need of his vigour, so imperiously
contesting the authority of the will, and with so much obstinacy denying all solicitation both of hand and fancy.   And

All our members
are occasionally
disobedient.

yet, though his rebellion is so universally complained of, and that proofs are not wanting to
condemn him, if he had nevertheless fee'd me
to plead his cause, I should peradventure bring the rest of
his fellow members into suspicion of complotting this mischief
against him, out of pure envy at the importance and pleasure
particular to his employment, so as to have, by this confeder-
acy of theirs, armed the whole world against him, by male-
volently charging him alone with their common offence.
For let any one consider whether there is any one part of
our bodies that does not often refuse to perform its office at
the precept of the will, and that does not often exercise its
function in defiance of her command.   They have every one
of them proper passions of their own, that rouse and awake,
stupefy and benumb them, without our leave or consent.
How often do the involuntary motions of the countenance
discover our inward thoughts, and betray our most private
secrets to the knowledge of the standers-by?   The same
cause that animates this member, does also, without our

knowledge, animate the lungs, the pulse, the heart; the sight
of a pleasing object imperceptibly diffusing a flame through
all our parts with a feverish motion. Is there nothing but
these veins and muscles that swell and flag without the consent, not only of the will, but even of our knowledge also?
We do not command our hairs to stand on end, nor our skin
to shiver either with fear or desire. The hands often convey
themselves to parts to which we do not direct them. The
tongue will be interdict, and the voice as it were suffocated,
without the intervention of the will. When we have nothing to eat, and would willingly forbid it, the appetite of eating and drinking does not for all that forbear to stir up the
parts that are subjected to it, no more nor less than the other
appetite we were speaking of, and in like manner does as
unseasonably leave us. The vessels that serve to discharge
the belly have their proper dilatations and compressions,
without and beyond our intelligence, as well as those which
are destined to purge the reins. And that which, to justify
the prerogative of the will, St. Augustine urges, of having
seen a man who could command his back trumpet to sound
as often as he pleased, and which Vives, his commentator,
fortifies with another example in his time of one that could
do this in tune,[1] does not any the more attribute pure obedience to that part; for is any thing commonly more tumul-
tuary or indiscreet? To which let me add that I myself
knew one so rude and ungoverned as for forty years kept its
master at work with one continued and unintermitted hurri-
cane, and 'tis like will do so till he expire that way. And
I could heartily wish that I only knew, by reading, how oft a
man's belly, by the denial of one single puff, brings him to
the very door of an exceeding painful death; and that the
emperor, who gave liberty to let fly in all places, had at the
same time given us power to do so.[2] But for our will, in
whose behalf we have preferred this accusation, with how

[1] August. *de Civit. Dei.* xiv. 24, and the Comment. of Vives, *in loco.*
[2] Suetonius, *Life of Claudius,* c. 32, who, however, merely mentions that this emperor had it in contemplation to au-thorize this freedom.

much greater similitude of truth may we reproach even her
herself with mutiny and sedition for her irregularity and disobedience?   Does she always will what we would have her
to do?   Does she not often will what we forbid her to will,
and that to our manifest prejudice?   Does she suffer herself,
any more than any of the others, to be governed and directed
by the results of our reason?   To conclude, I should urge
in the behalf of the gentleman, my client, it might be considered that in this matter his cause being inseparably conjoined with an accessary, whose share is not distinctly
marked, yet he only is called in question, and that by arguments and accusations, that cannot be charged nor reflect
upon his said accomplice, for the latter, though he sometimes
inopportunely invites, never refuses, and allures after a tacit
and clandestine manner ; and herein, therefore, is the malice
and injustice of his accusers most manifestly apparent.   But,
be it as it may, let the advocates and judges pass what sentence they please, nature will, in the mean time, proceed after
her own way ; who had done but well, if she had endowed
this member with some particular privilege ; the author, as
he is, of the sole immortal work of mortals, a divine work
according to Socrates ; of love, desire of immortality ; and
himself an immortal Dæmon.

One person, perhaps, by such an effect of imagination,
Confidence in one's physician a great step to-wards one's cure. may have had the good luck to leave that
disease behind him here in France which his
companion carries back with him into Spain.
And that you may see why men in such cases require a
mind prepared for the thing they are to do, why do the physicians tamper with, and prepossess beforehand their patients'
credulity with so many false promises of cure, if not to the
end, that the effect of imagination may supply the defect of
their decoctions?   They know, very well, that a great master
of their trade has given it under his hand, that he has known
some with whom the very sight of a potion would do the
work.   And this conceit comes now into my head, by the

remembrance of a story was told me by an apothecary of
my late father's, a blunt honest Swiss, (a nation not much
addicted to vanity or lying,) of a merchant he had long
known at Thoulouse, who being a valetudinarian, and much
afflicted with fits of the stone, had often occasion to take cly-
sters, of which he caused several sorts to be prescribed him
by the physicians, according to the circumstances of his
attack; one of which being one time brought in, and none
of the usual forms, as feeling if it were not too hot, and
the like, being omitted, he was laid down on his bed, the
syringe applied, and all ceremonies performed, injection excepted; after which, the apothecary being gone, and the
patient accommodated as if he had really received a clyster,
he found the same operation and effect that those do who
have taken one indeed; and if at any time the physician did
not find the operation sufficient, he would usually give him
two or three more after the same manner. And the fellow
moreover swore to me that, to save charges, (for he paid as
if he had really taken them,) this sick man's wife having
sometimes made trial of warm water only, the effect discovered the cheat; and finding these would not do, she was fain
to return to the old way. A woman fancying she had swallowed a pin in a piece of bread, complained of A distemper con-
an intolerable pain in her throat, where she tructed by mere
power of imagina-
thought she felt it stick; but an ingenious fel- tion.
low that was brought to her, seeing no outward tumour nor
alteration, supposing it only to be a fancy taken at some
crust of bread that had pricked her as it went down, caused
her to vomit, and unseen threw a crooked pin into the basin,
which the woman no sooner saw, but, believing she had cast
it up, she presently found herself eased of her pain. I myself knew of a gentleman, who having treated a great deal
of good company at his house, three or four days after, said,
in jest, (for there was no such thing,) that he had made them
eat of a cat-pie; at which a young gentlewoman, who had
been at the feast, took such a horror that, falling into a vio-

lent vomiting and a fever, there was no possible means to save her. Even brute beasts are also subject to the force of imagination as well as we; as is observed in dogs who die of grief for the loss of their masters, and are seen to bark, tremble, and start, as horses will kick and neigh in their sleep.

Animals subject to the effects of imagination.

Now all this may be attributed to the affinity and relation betwixt the souls and the bodies of brutes, mutually communicating their feelings; but 'tis quite another thing when the imagination works upon the souls of rational men, and not only to the prejudice of their own particular bodies, but of others also. And as an infected body communicates its malady to those that approach or live near it, as we see in the plague, the smallpox, and sore eyes, that run through whole families and cities :—

> Dum spectant oculi læsos, læduntur et ipsi;
> Multaque corporibus transitione nocent.[1]

> " Viewing sore eyes, eyes to be sore are brought,
>   And many ills are by transition caught."

so the imagination, being vehemently agitated, darts out infection capable of hurting a foreign object. The ancients had an opinion of certain women of Scythia, that, being animated and enraged against any one, they killed them only with a look. Tortoises and ostriches hatch their eggs with only looking on them, which infers that their eyes have in them such ejaculative virtue. And the eyes of witches are said to be dangerous and hurtful;

> Nescio quis teneros oculus mihi fascinat agnos.[2]

> " Some eye unknown hath witched my tender lambs."

though magicians are no very good authority with me. We see, however, by constant experience, that women impart the marks of their fancy to the unborn children within them; witness her that was brought to bed of a Moor. And there

---

[1] Ovid. *Remed. Amor.* 615.   [2] Virg. *Eclog.* iii. 103.

was presented to Charles, King of Bohemia and Emperor, a girl from about Pisa, all over rough and covered *Its effect on women with child;* with hair, whom her mother said had been conceived by reason of a picture of St. John the Baptist, that hung in her bed.

It is the same with beasts; witness Jacob's sheep, and the hares and partridges that the snow turns white *and animals.* upon the mountains. There was at my house a little while ago a cat seen watching a bird upon the top of a tree, who for some time mutually fixing their eyes upon one another, the bird at last let herself fall as dead into the cat's claws, either dazzled and astonished by the force of her own imagination, or drawn by some attractive power in the cat. Such as are addicted to hawking have heard the story of the falconer, who having earnestly fixed his eyes upon a kite in the air, laid a wager that he would bring her down with the sole power of his gaze, and did so, as it was said; for the tales I borrow I charge upon the consciences of those from whom I have them. The arguments are my own, and found themselves upon the proofs of reason, not *Montaigne's use of illustrations.* of experience, to which every one has liberty to add his own examples; and he who has none, (the numbers and varieties of accident considered,) let him not forbear to believe that these I set down are enough; and if I do not apply them well, let some other do it for me. So in the subjects of which I treat, our manners and motions, the testimonies and instances I produce, how fabulous soever, provided they are possible, serve as well as true ones; whether it has really happened or no, at Rome or at Paris, to Peter or John, 'tis still within the verge of possibility and human capacity, which serves me to good use in the things I write. I see and make my advantage of it as well in shadow as in substance; and amongst the various examples I everywhere meet with in history, I cull out the most rare and memorable to fit my own turn. There are some authors whose only end and design it is to give an account of things that have happened;

mine, if I could arrive unto it, should be to talk of what may
come to pass.   There is a just liberty allowed in the schools,
of supposing and contriving similes, when they are at a loss
for them in their own reading; I do not, however, make any
use of that privilege, and in this respect in superstitious religion surpass all historical authority.   In the examples which
I here bring in of what I have heard, read, done, or said, I
have forbid myself to dare to alter even the most light and
indifferent circumstances; my conscience does not falsify one
tittle,—what my ignorance may do I cannot say.

And this it is that makes me sometimes doubt whether a

A doubt whether
either divines or
philosophers
should write his-
tory.

divine or a philosopher, men of so exquisite
and exact wisdom and conscience, ought to
write history; for how can they stake their
reputation upon a popular belief? how be responsible for the opinions of men they do not know? or
with what assurance deliver their conjectures as ready
money?   Of actions performed before their own eyes, wherein several persons were actors, they would be unwilling to
give evidence upon oath before a judge; nor is there any
man with whose heart they are so familiarly and thoroughly
acquainted that they would become absolute surety for his
intentions.   For my part, I think it less hazardous to write
things past than present, by how much the writer is only to
give an account of things every one knows he must of necessity borrow upon trust.

I am solicited to write the affairs of my own time, by

Montaigne solic-
ited to write the
history of his
time, and why he
would not.

some who fancy I look upon them with an eye
less blinded with prejudice or partiality than
another, and have a clearer insight into them,
by reason of the free access fortune has given
me to the heads of both factions; but they do not consider that to purchase the glory of Sallust I would not
give myself the trouble, sworn enemy as I am to all obligation, assiduity, and perseverance: besides that, there is
nothing so contrary to my style as a continued and extended

narrative, I so often interrupt and cut myself short in my writing, only for want of breath. I am good at neither composition nor comment, and am ignorant beyond a child of the phrases, and even the very words, proper to express the most common things; and for that reason it is that I have undertaken to say only what I can say, and have accommodated my subjects to my force. Should I take one to be my guide, peradventure I should not be able to keep pace with him, and in the precipitancy of my career might deliver judgments which, even in my own thought, and according to reason, would be criminal in the highest degree.

Plutarch would readily tell us of what he has delivered to the light, that is the work of others; that his examples are all and everywhere true; that they are useful to posterity, and are presented with a lustre that will light us the way to virtue, which was his design. But it matters not, as in a medicinal drug, whether an old story run so or so.

CHAPTER XXI.[1]

THAT THE PROFIT OF ONE MAN IS THE INCONVENIENCE OF ANOTHER.

DEMADES the Athenian condemned one of his city, whose trade it was to sell the necessaries for funeral ceremonies, upon pretence that he demanded unreasonable profit, and that this profit could not accrue to him but by the death of a great number of people. A judgment that appears to be ill-grounded, forasmuch as no profit whatever can be made but

1 This chapter, which is itself principally taken from Seneca, on *Benefits*, vi. 88, &c. contains (remarks Mr. Hazlitt) the whole substance of Mandeville's *Fable of the Bees:* with this difference, however, that Mandeville presupposes a vicious state of society, and says that man, if he will have great overgrown cities, and false luxuries, must have what they produce; which is a fine useful moral.

at the expense of another, and that by the same rule he should condemn all manner of gain of what kind soever. The tradesman thrives and grows rich by the pride and wastefulness of youth; the husbandman by the dearness of grain; the architect by the ruin of buildings; the lawyers and officers of justice by suits and contentions of men; nay, even the honour and office of divines are derived from our death and vices. A physician takes no pleasure in the health even of his friends, says the ancient comedian; nor a soldier in the peace of his country; and so of the rest.[1] And, which is yet worse, let every one but dive into his own bosom, and he will find his private wishes spring, and his secret hopes grow up, at another's expense. Upon which consideration it comes into my head that Nature does not in this swerve from her general polity; for physicians hold that the birth, nourishment, and increase of every thing, is the dissolution and corruption of another.

> Nam quodcunque suis mutatum finibus exit,
> Continuò hoc mors est illius quod fuit ante.[2]

> "For what from its own confines chang'd doth pass,
> Is straight the death of what before it was."

CHAPTER XXII.

OF CUSTOM, AND THAT WE SHOULD NOT EASILY CHANGE A LAW RECEIVED.

He seems to me to have had a right and true apprehension of the power of custom who first invented the story of a country-woman, who, having accus-

The force of custom.

---

[1] "Le précepte de ne jamais nuire à autrui emporte celui de tenir à société humaine le moins qu'il est possible; car dans l'état social le bien de l'un fuit ne-cessairement le mal de l'autre."—Rousseau, Emile, iii.

[2] Lucretius, ii. 752.

tomed herself to play with, and carry from the hour of its birth, a calf in her arms, and daily continuing to do so as it grew up, obtained this by custom, that when grown to be a great ox, she was still able to bear it.[1] For, in truth, custom is a violent and treacherous schoolmistress. She, by little and little, slyly and unperceived, slips in the foot of her authority, but having by this gentle and humble beginning, with the aid of time, fixed and established it, she then unmasks a furious and tyrannic countenance, against which we have no more the courage nor the power so much as to lift up our eyes. We see it at every turn forcing and violating the rules of nature: *Usus efficacissimus rerum omnium magister*,[2] "Custom is the greatest master of all things." I believe in Plato's cave in his Republic,[3] and the physicians, who so often submit the reasons of their art to the authority of habit; as also the story of that king who by custom brought his stomach to that pass as to live on poison; and the girl that Albertus reports to have lived upon spiders; and in that new world of the Indies there were found great nations, and in very different climates, who lived upon the same diet, made provision of them, and fed them for their tables; as well as grasshoppers, mice, bats, and lizards; and in a time of a scarcity, a toad was sold for six crowns, all which they cook, and dish up with several sauces. There were also others found, to whom our food and the flesh we eat were venomous and mortal. *Consuetudinis magna vis est: pernoctant venatores in nive; in montibus uri se patiuntur: pugiles, cæstibus contusi, ne ingemiscunt quidem.*[4] "The power of custom is very great; huntsmen will one while lie out all night in the snow, and another suffer themselves to be parched with heat on the mountains; and prize-fighters, though beaten almost to a jelly with the cæstus, utter not a groan." These exam-

---

[1] Stobæus, *Serm.* xxix., who takes it from Favorinus. See also Quintilian, i. 9. It is become a kind of proverb, which Petronius has thus expressed,

——— Tollere taurum
Quæ tulerit vitulum, illa potest.

You will also find it among the adages of Erasmus, Chil. 1, Cent. 2, Ad. 51.

[2] Pliny, *Nat. His.* xxvi. 2.
[3] Plato, *Repub.* vii.
[4] Cicero, *Tusc. Quæs.* ii. 17.

ples will not appear so strange, if we consider what we have ordinary experience of, how much custom dulls our senses. We need not go to be satisfied of this to what is reported of the cataracts of the Nile; and to what philosophers believe of the music of the spheres, that the bodies of those circles being solid and smooth, and coming to touch and rub upon one another, cannot fail of creating a wonderful harmony, the changes and cadences of which cause the revolutions and dances of the stars; but that the hearing sense of all creatures here below being universally, like that of the Egyptians, deafened and stupefied with the continual noise, cannot distinguish it, how great soever it be. Smiths, millers, and armourers could never be able to live in the perpetual noise of their own trades, did it strike their ears as it does ours.

My perfumed doublet gratifies my own nose at first, as well as that of others, but after I have worn it three or four days together, I myself no more perceive it; but it is yet more strange that custom, notwithstanding long intermissions and intervals, should yet have the power to unite, and establish the effect of its impressions upon our senses, as is manifest to such as live near belfries. I myself lie at home in a tower, where every morning and evening a very great bell rings out the Ave Maria, the noise of which shakes my very tower, and at first seemed insupportable to me; but in a little while I got so used to it that I hear it without any manner of offence, and often without awaking at it.

Plato reprehending a boy for playing at some childish game—" Thou reprovest me," said the boy, " for a very little thing." " Custom," replied Plato, " is no little thing." [1]

Vices take root in the most tender years, and ought therefore to be corrected instantly.
Our greatest vices derive their first propension from our most tender infancy; our principal education depends upon the nurse. Mothers are mightily amused to see a child twist off the

---

[1] Diog. Laert. in Vitâ. But Laertius does not say that the person whom Plato reprehended was a boy, or that he was playing at some childish game; but that it was a man playing at dice, which makes Plato's rejoinder far more effective.

neck of a chicken, or divert itself with hurting a dog or a cat; and such wise fathers there are in the world who look upon it as a notable presage of a martial spirit when he hears his son miscall or domineer over a poor peasant or lacquey, that dares not reply or turn again; and a great sign of wit when he sees him cheat and overreach his playfellow by some sly trick; yet these are the true seeds and roots of cruelty, tyranny, and treason. They bud and put out there, and afterwards shoot up vigorously in the hands of custom; and it is a very dangerous mistake to excuse these vile inclinations upon account of the tenderness of their age, and the triviality of the subject; first, it is nature that speaks, whose voice is then more sincere, and whose inward thoughts are more undisguised, as it is younger and more shrill; secondly, the deformity of cozenage does not consist in, nor depend upon, the difference betwixt crowns and pins; but merely upon itself, for a cheat is a cheat, be it more or less; which makes me think it more just to conclude thus, "why should he not cozen in crowns since he does it in pins?" than as they do who say, "they only play for pins, he would not do it if it were for crowns." Children should carefully be instructed to abhor vices for themselves, and the natural deformity of those vices ought so to be represented to them that they may not only avoid them in their actions, but so abominate them in their hearts that the very thought should be hateful to them, with what mask soever they may be palliated or disguised.

Children should be taught to abhor vice for itself.

I know very well, for what concerns myself, that from having been brought up in my childhood to a plain and sincere way of dealing, and from then having had an aversion to all manner of juggling and tricking in my childish sports and recreations, (and indeed it is to be noted that the play of children is not really play, but must be judged of as their most serious actions,) there is no game so small, wherein from my own bosom naturally, and without study or endeav-

our, I have not an extreme aversion for deceit. I shuffle and
cut, and make as much ado with the cards, and keep as strict
account for farthings, as if it were for doubloons; when winning or losing against my wife and daughter, it is indifferent
to me, as when I play in good earnest with others for round
sums. At all times, and in all things, my own eyes are sufficient to look to my fingers; I am not so narrowly watched
by any other, neither is there any I more fear to be discovered by, or to offend, than myself.

I saw the other day at my own house, a little fellow, a na-
Curious instance tive of Nantes, born without arms, who has so
of the feet and
neck doing the well taught his feet to perform the services his
office of the hands. hands should have done him, that indeed they
have half forgot their natural office, and the use for which
they were designed; the fellow, indeed, calls them his hands,
and we may allow him so to do, for with them he cuts any
thing, charges and discharges a pistol, threads a needle, sews,
writes, and puts off his hat, combs his head, plays at cards
and dice, and all this with the utmost dexterity; and the
money I·gave him (for he gets his living by exhibiting himself), he carried away in his foot, as we do in our hand. I
have seen another who, though a mere boy, flourished a two-
handed sword, and (if I may so say) handled a halberd with
the mere motions and writhing of his neck and shoulders for
want of hands, tost them into the air, and caught them again,
darted a dagger, and cracked a whip as well as any carter in
France.

But the effects of custom are much more manifest in the
strange impression she makes in our minds, where she meets
with less resistance. What has she not the power to impose
upon our judgments and belief! Is there any so fantastic
opinion (omitting the gross impostures in religion, with which
we see so many populous nations and so many understanding
men so strangely besotted; for this being beyond the reach
of human reason, any error is the more excusable in such as,
through the divine bounty, are not endued with an extraordi-

nary illumination from above), but in other matters, are there any so senseless and extravagant that she has not planted and established for laws in those parts of the world upon which she has been pleased to exercise her power? And therefore that ancient exclamation was exceeding just—*Non pudet physicum, id est speculatorem venatoremque naturæ, ab animis consuetudine imbutis quærere testimonium veritatis?* [1] "Is it not a shame for a natural philosopher, that is, for an observer and hunter of nature, to seek testimony from minds prepossessed with custom?" I do believe that no so absurd or ridiculous fancy can enter into human imagination that does not meet with some example of public practice, and that, consequently, our reason does not ground and support itself upon. There are people amongst whom it is the fashion to turn their backs upon him they salute, and never look upon the man they wish to honour. There is a court where, whenever the king spits, the favourite lady puts out her hand to receive it; and another nation where the most eminent persons about him stood to take up his ordure in a linen cloth. Let us here steal room to insert a story.

A French gentleman of my acquaintance who was always wont to blow his nose with his fingers—a thing very much against our fashion—would justify himself for so doing, and was a man very famous for pleasant repartees, as thus: Upon such an occasion he asked me what privilege this filthy excrement had, that we must carry about with us a fine handkerchief to receive it, and, which was more, afterwards to lap it carefully up, and carry it all day about in our pockets, which, he said, could not be much more nauseous and offensive than to see it thrown away, as we did all other evacuations. It seemed to me that what he said was not altogether without reason, and, being frequently in his company, that slovenly action of his at last grew familiar to me; which, nevertheless, we make a face at when we hear it reported of another country.

[1] Cicero, *de Nat. Deor.* i. 80. The text has *petere*, not *quærere*

Miracles appear to be so, according to our ignorance of nature, and not according to the essence of nature. The continually being accustomed to any thing blinds the eye of our judgment. Barbarians are no more a wonder to us than we are to them; nor with any more reason, as every one would confess if, after having considered those remote examples, men would reflect upon their own, and rightly compare them together. Human reason is a tincture pretty equally infused into all our opinions and manners, of what form soever they are; infinite in matter, infinite in diversity. But I return to my subject.

There are people where, his wife and children excepted, *The odd customs of divers nations.* no one speaks to the king but through a trumpet. In one and the same nation the virgins discover those parts that modesty should persuade them to hide, and the married women carefully cover and conceal them. To which this custom, in another place has some relation, where chastity, except in marriage, is of no esteem, for unmarried women may prostitute themselves to as many as they please, and, being with child, may lawfully take physic, in the sight of every one, to procure abortion. And, in another place, when a tradesman marries, all of the same condition who are invited to the wedding, lie with the bride before him; and the greater number of them there is, the greater is her honour, and the opinion of her ability and strength; if an officer marry, 'tis the same, the same with a nobleman, and so of the rest; except it be a labourer, or one of mean condition, for then it belongs to the lord of the place to perform that office; and yet a strict fidelity during marriage is afterward enjoined. There is a place where brothels of young men are kept for the pleasure of women, as with us there are of women for men; where the wives go to war as well as their husbands, and not only share in the dangers of battle, but, moreover, in the honours of command. Others where they wear rings not only through their noses, lips, cheeks, and on their toes, but also heavy wedges of gold thrust

through their breasts and buttocks; where, in eating, they
wipe their fingers upon their thighs, genitories, and the soles
of their feet; where children are excluded, and brothers and
nephews only inherit; and, elsewhere, nephews only, saving
in the succession of the crown; where, for the regulation of
community in goods and estates observed in the country, certain sovereign magistrates have committed to them the universal charge of cultivating the lands, and distributing the
produce according to the necessity of every one; where they
lament the death of children, and feast at the decease of old
men; [1] where they lie ten or twelve in a bed, men and their
wives together; where women whose husbands come to violent ends may marry again, and others not; where women
are looked upon with such contempt that they kill all the
native females, and buy wives of their neighbours to supply
their use; where husbands may repudiate their wives without showing any cause, but wives cannot part from their husbands for what cause soever; where husbands may sell their
wives in case of sterility; where they boil the bodies of their
dead, and afterwards pound them to a pulp, which they mix
with their wine, and drink it; where the favourite mode of
burial is to be eaten by dogs; [2] and elsewhere by birds;
where they believe the souls of the happy live in all manner
of liberty, in delightful fields, furnished with all sorts of delicacies, and that it is those souls repeating the words we utter,
which we call echo; where they fight in the water, and
shoot their arrows with the most mortal aim, swimming;
where, for a sign of subjection, they lift up their shoulders,
and hang down their heads, and put off their shoes, when
they enter the king's palace; where the eunuchs who have
charge of the religious women have, moreover, their lips and
noses cut off, that they may not be loved; and the priests
put out their own eyes to get acquainted with their demons
and receive their oracles; where every one creates to himself a deity of what he likes best, according to his own fancy

[1] In Thrace. See Herod. v.   [2] **Sextus Empiricus.** *Pyrrh. Hypot.* iii. 24.

—the hunter, of a lion or a fox; the fisher, of some fish, and idols of every human action or passion; where the sun, the moon, and the earth, are the principal deities, and the form of taking an oath is to touch the earth, looking up to heaven, and where both flesh and fish are eaten raw; where the greatest oath they take is to swear by the name of some dead person of reputation, laying their hand upon his tomb;[1] where the new-year's gift the king sends every year to the princes, his subjects, is fire, which, being brought, all the old fire is put out, and the neighbouring people are bound to fetch of the new, every one for themselves, upon pain of treason; where, when the king, to betake himself wholly to devotion, retires from his administration (which often falls out), his next successor is obliged to do the same; by which means the crown devolves to the third in succession; where they vary the form of government according to the seeming necessity of affairs; depose the king when they think good, substituting ancient men to govern in his stead, and sometimes transferring it into the hands of the common people; where men and women are both circumcised and baptized; where the soldier who, in one or several engagements, has been so fortunate as to present seven of the enemies' heads to the king is made noble; where they live in that singular and unsociable opinion of the mortality of the soul; where the women are delivered without pain or fear; where the women wear copper boots upon both their legs, and, if a louse bites them, are bound, in magnanimity, to bite it again, and dare not marry until first they have made their king a tender of their virginity; where the ordinary mode of salutation is by putting a finger down to the earth, and then pointing up towards heaven: where men carry burthens upon their heads, and women on their shoulders; where the women make water standing, and the men squatting down; where they send some of their blood in token of friendship, and offer incense to the men they would honour, like gods; where, not only to

[1] Herod. iv. 318. Nymphsadorus, *Rerum Barbaricarum*, xiii.

the fourth, but to more remote degrees, kindred are not permitted to marry ; where the children are four years at nurse,
and often twelve ; and where it is accounted mortal to give
the child suck the first day after it is born ; where the correction of the male children is assigned to the fathers, and
that of the females to the mothers ; the punishment being to
hang them by the heels in the smoke ; where they eat all
sorts of herbs, excepting only those that have an ill smell ;
where all things are open, the finest furnished houses being
without doors, windows, or chests to lock, a thief being there
punished double to what they are in other places : where
they crack lice with their teeth, like monkeys, and abhor to
see them killed with one's nails ; where, in all their lives
they neither cut their hair nor pair their nails ; and in another place pare those of the right hand only, letting the left
grow for ornament ; where they suffer the hair on the right
side to grow as long as it will, and shave the other ; and in
the neighbouring provinces some let their hair grow long before, and some behind, shaving close the rest ;[1] where
parents let out their children, and husbands their wives, to
their guests to hire ; where a man may get his own mother
with child, and fathers make use of their own daughters, or
their sons, without scandal or offence : where, at their solemn
feasts, they lend their children to one another, without any
consideration of nearness of blood. In one place men feed
upon human flesh, in another 'tis reputed a pious office for a
man to kill his father at a certain age ;[2] and elsewhere the
fathers dispose of their children whilst yet unborn,—some to
be preserved and carefully brought up, and others to be
made away with. Elsewhere the old husbands lend their
wives to young men, and in another place they are in common without offence ; nay, in one place, the women wear, as
marks of honour, as many gay fringed tassels at the bottom
of their petticoats as they have lain with men.[3] Moreover,
has not custom made a republic of women separate by them-

---

[1] Herod. iv.   [2] Sextus Empiricus, *Pyrrh. Hypot.* iii. 24.   [3] Herod. iv.

selves ? Has it not put arms into their hands, made them to raise armies, and fight battles ? And does she not by mere precept instruct the most ignorant vulgar, and make them perfect in things which all the philosophy in the world could never beat into the heads of the wisest men ? For we know entire nations, where death was not only despised, but entertained with the greatest triumph ; where children of seven years old suffered themselves to be whipped to death without changing their countenance ;[1] where riches were in such contempt that the poorest citizen would not have deigned to stoop to take up a purse of crowns ; and we know regions, very fruitful in all manner of provisions, where, notwithstanding, the most ordinary diet, and that they are most pleased with, is only bread, cresses, and water.[2] Did not custom moreover work that miracle in Chios, that in seven hundred years it was never known that ever maid or wife committed any act to the prejudice of her honour ?[3]

In short, there is nothing, in my opinion, that she does not or may not do ; and therefore with very good reason it is that Pindar, as I am told, calls her "the queen and empress of the world."[4] He that was seen to beat his father, and reproved for so doing, made answer, That it was the custom of their family ; that in like manner his father had beaten his grandfather, his grandfather his great-grandfather. "And this," says he, pointing to his son, "when he comes to my age, will beat me." And the father, whose son was dragging and hauling him along the streets, commanded him to stop at a certain door; for he himself, he said, had dragged his father no further, that being the utmost limit of the hereditary insolence the sons used to practice upon the fathers in their family. "It is as much by custom as disorder," says Aristotle, "that women tear their hair, bite their nails, and eat charcoal and earth, and more by custom than nature that men abuse themselves with one another."

[1] At Lacedemon.
[2] *Persia.* See Xenophon, *Cyrop,* i. 8.
[3] Plutarch, in his treatise *on the Virtuous behaviour of Women,* c. 5.
[4] Herod. iii.

The laws of conscience, which we pretend to be derived
from nature, proceed from custom; every one *Custom the parent of the laws of conscience.*
having an inward veneration for the opinions
and manners approved and received amongst
his own people, cannot without very great reluctance depart
from them, nor apply himself to them without applause. In
times past, when those of Crete would curse any one, they
prayed the gods to engage them in some ill custom.[1] But the
principal effect of the power of custom is so to seize and en-
snare us that it is hardly in our power to disengage ourselves
from its gripe; or so to come to ourselves as to consider of
and weigh the things it enjoins. To say the truth, by reason
that we suck it in with our mother's milk, and that the face
of the world presents itself in this posture to our first sight,
it seems as if we were born upon condition to pursue this
practice; and the common fancies that we find in repute
everywhere about us, and infused into our minds with the
seed of our fathers, appear to be universal and genuine.
From whence it comes to pass that whatever is off the
hinges of custom is believed to be also off the hinges of
reason; though how unreasonably, for the most part, God
knows.

If, as we who study ourselves have learned to do, every
one who hears a good sentence would immediately consider
how it does any way touch his own private concerns, every one
would find that it was not so much a good saying as a sound
lash to the ordinary stupidity of his own judgment. But
men receive the precepts and admonitions of truth as directed
to the common sort only, and not to themselves; and instead
of applying them to their own manners, do only very ignorantly and unprofitably commit them to memory, without
suffering themselves to be at all instructed or converted by
them. But let us return to the empire of custom.

Such people as have been bred up to liberty, and subject
to none but themselves, look upon all other forms of gov-

[1] Valer. Max. vii. in ext. sec. 15

Nations attached
to the form of
government which
they have been
used to.

ernment as monstrous and contrary to nature. Those who are used to monarchy do the same; and what opportunity soever fortune presents them with to change, even then, when with the greatest difficulties they have disengaged themselves from one master, that was troublesome and grievous to them, they presently run with the same difficulties to create another; not being able, how roughly dealt with soever, to hate the government they were born under, and the obedience they have so long been accustomed to. 'Tis by the mediation and persuasion of custom that every one is content with the place where he is planted by nature; and the highlanders of Scotland no more pant after the air of Touraine, than the Scythians after the fields of Thessaly. Darius asked certain Greeks what they would take to assume the custom of the Indians, of eating the dead bodies of their fathers, (for that was their practice, believing they could not give them a better or more noble sepulchre than to bury them in their own bodies,) they made answer, That nothing in the world should hire them to do it; but having also tried to persuade the Indians to leave their barbarous custom, and, after the Greek manner, to burn the bodies of their fathers, they conceived a still greater horror at the proposition; and 'tis the same with us all, forasmuch as use veils from us the true aspect of things.

> Nil adeò magnum, nec tam mirabile quicquam
> Principio, quod non minuant mirarier omnes
> Paulatim.[1]

> "Nothing at first so great or strange appears
> But grows familiar in succeeding years."

Taking upon me once to justify some thing in use amongst us, and that was received with absolute authority for a great many leagues round about us, and not content to establish it, as men commonly are, only by force of law and example, but

---

[1] Lucret. ii. 1027.

by inquiring into its original, I found the foundation so weak that I, who had made it my business to confirm others, was very near being dissatisfied myself. 'Tis by this recipe that Plato undertakes to cure the unnatural and preposterous amours of his time—the recipe which he esteems of sovereign virtue; namely, that the public opinion condemns them; that the poets, and all other writers, relate horrible stories of them. A recipe by virtue of which the most beautiful daughters do not allure their fathers' lust, nor brothers of the finest shape and beauty their sisters' desire. The very fables of Thyestes, Œdipus, and Macareus, having, with the harmony of their song, infused this wholesome opinion and belief into tender brains of infants.[1] Chastity is, in truth, a great and the shining virtue, and of which the utility is sufficiently known; but to govern, and prevail with it according to nature, is as hard as 'tis easy to do it according to custom and the laws and precepts of sober practice. The original and universal reasons are of very difficult search, and our masters either lightly pass them over, or, not daring so much as to touch them, precipitate themselves at once into the liberty of custom, in which they pride themselves, and triumph as much as you please. Such as will not suffer themselves to be withdrawn from this original source do yet commit a greater error, and submit themselves to wild opinions. Witness Chrysippus,[2] who, in so many of his writings, has shown the little account he made of incestuous conjunction committed with how near relations soever.

Whoever would disengage himself from this violent prejudice of custom would find several things received with absolute and undoubting opinion that have no other support than the hoary beard and wrinkled face of ancient use; but this mask torn away, and things being referred to the decision of truth and reason, he will find his judgment convinced and overthrown, and yet restored to a much more sure state.

Custom the only foundation of many things authorized in the world.

---

[1] Plato, *Laws*, viii. 6.   [2] Sextus Empiricus, i. 14.

For example, I will ask him what can be more strange than
to see a people obliged to obey and pay a reverence to laws
they never heard of, and to be bound in all their affairs, both
private and public, as marriages, donations, wills, sales, and
purchases, to rules they cannot possibly know, being neither
writ nor published in their own language, and of which they
have, of necessity, to purchase both the interpretation and
the use? Not according to the ingenious opinion of Iso-
rates, who counselled his king to make the traffics and negotiations of his subjects free, open, and of profit to them, and
their quarrels and disputes burdensome, and laden with heavy
penalties; but, by a monstrous notion, to make sale of reason
itself, and to allow the law to be made a matter of traffic. I
think myself obliged to fortune that, as our historians report,
it was a Gascon gentleman, a countryman of mine, who first
opposed Charlemagne when he attempted to impose upon us
Latin and imperial laws.

What can be more outrageous than to see a nation where,
by lawful custom, the office of a judge is to be
The office of Judge a matter of purchase. bought and sold, where judgments are paid for
with ready money, and where justice may le-
gally be denied to him that has not wherewithal to pay;[1]
where this merchandise is in so great repute, as in our government, to furnish a fourth estate of wrangling lawyers, to
add to the three ancient ones of the church, nobility, and
people; which fourth estate, having the laws in their hands,
and sovereign power over men's lives and fortunes, make a
body separate from the nobility. From whence it comes to
pass that there are double laws, those of honour, and those
of justice, in many things positively opposite to one another;
the nobles as rigorously condemning a lie taken, as the others
do a lie revenged. By the law of arms he shall be degraded
from all nobility and honour who puts up with an affront;
and, by the civil law, he who vindicates his reputation incurs

[1] France, where this custom was introduced by the Chancellor du Prat, under
Francis I.

a capital punishment; he who applies himself to the law for reparation of an offence done to his honour is disgraced; and he who does not is punished by the law. Yet, of these two so different parties, both of them referring to one head, the one has the charge of peace, the other of war; those have the profit, these the honour; those the wisdom, these the virtue; those the word, these the action; those justice, these valour; those reason, these force; those the long robe, these the short, divided betwixt them.

For what concerns indifferent things, as clothes, who is there that would think of bringing them back to their true and real use, the body's service and convenience, and upon which their original grace and decency depend; yet what more fantastic than our fashions? I will instance, amongst others, our square caps, that long tail of velvet that hangs down from our women's heads with its whimsical trinkets, and that idle and absurd model of a member we cannot, in modesty, so much as name, which, nevertheless, we make a parade of in public. These considerations, notwithstanding, will not prevail upon any understanding man to decline the common mode; but, on the contrary, methinks *Men of sense* all singular and particular fashions are rather *should conform* marks of folly and vain affectation than of *their time as to* sound reason; and a wise man ought within to *externals.* withdraw and retire his soul from the crowd, and there keep it at liberty, and in power to judge freely of things; but, as to this outward garb and appearance, absolutely follow and conform himself to the fashion of the time. Public society has nothing to do with our thoughts, but for the rest, as our actions, our labours, our fortunes, and our lives, we should lend and abandon them to the common opinion and public service, as did that good and great Socrates, who refused to preserve his life by a disobedience to the magistrate, though a very wicked and unjust one; for it is the rule of rules, and the general law of laws, that every one observe those of the place wherein he lives.

Νόμοις ἔπεσθαι τοῖσιν ἐγχωρίοις καλόν.[1]

"The country's custom to observe,
    Is proper, and doth praise deserve."

Let us take another view of the subject; it is a very great
doubt whether any so manifest an advantage
can accrue from the alteration of a law or
custom received, let it be what it will, as there
is danger and inconvenience in doing it; forasmuch as government is a structure composed
of several parts and members joined and united together,
with so strict affinity and union that it is impossible to stir
so much as one brick or stone but the whole body will be
sensible of it. The legislator of the Thurians[2] ordained that
whosoever proposed either to abolish old laws, or to establish
new, should present himself, with a halter about his neck, to
the people; to the end that, if the innovation he would introduce should not be approved by every one, he might immediately be hanged; and that of the Lacedemonians[3] made it
the business of his whole life to obtain from his citizens a
faithful promise that none of his laws should be violated.
The Ephorus, who so rudely cut the two strings that Phry-
nis had added to music,[4] never stood to examine whether that
addition made better harmony, or that by that means the
instrument was more full and complete; it was enough for
him to condemn the invention, that it was a novelty, and an
alteration of the old fashion. Which also is the meaning of
the old rusty sword carried before the magistracy of Marseilles.

For my own part I have myself a very great aversion for
novelty, what face, or what pretence soever it may carry
along with it, and have reason, having been an eye-witness
of the great mischiefs produced. One cannot, I confess,
exactly say that the miseries which, for so many years,[5] have

(margin note:) Whether the actual inconvenience of changing received laws is not greater than the possible advantage.

---

1 *Excerpta ex trag. Græc. Hugo Grot.*
interp. p. 937.
2 *Charondas.* See Diod. Sic. xii. 24.
3 *Lycurgus.* See his Life by Plutarch,
c. 21.
4 Plutarch, in his *Apothegms of the
Lacedemonians,* calls this Ephorus, *Eme-
repea.* See also Val. Max. ii. 6.
5 The edition of 1588 reads, "which
for twenty five or thirty years."

lain so heavy upon the kingdom of France, are wholly occasioned by it; but one may say, and with colour enough, that it has accidentally produced and begot the mischief and ruin that have since continued both without and against it, and it is principally what we have to accuse for these disorders.

Heu! patior telis vulnera facta meis.[1]

"Alas! the wounds I now endure
Which my own weapons did procure."

They who give the first shock to a state are voluntarily the first overwhelmed in its ruin; the fruits of public commotion are seldom enjoyed by him who was the first mover; he only beats the water for another's net. The unity and contexture of this monarchy, this great structure, having been, in her old age, broken and torn by this thing, called innovation, has laid open a breach, and given sufficient admittance to the like injuries in these latter times. The regal majesty falls less easily from the summit to the middle, than from the middle to the base. But, if the inventors did the greater mischief, the imitators are more vicious, to follow examples of which they have felt and punished both the horror and the offence. And if there can be any degree of horror in ill-doing, these last are indebted to the other for the glory of contriving, and the courage of making the first attempt. All sorts of new disorders easily draw, from this primitive and overflowing fountain, examples and precedents to trouble and discompose our government. We read in our very laws, made for the remedy of this first evil, the beginning and pretences of all sorts of bad enterprises; and what Thucydides says[2] of the civil wars of his time is applicable to us, that, to smooth over public vices, we give them new and more plausible names, sweetening and disguising their true titles; all that is done is done, forsooth, to reform and improve our faith! *Honesta oratio est;*[3] but the best pretence for inno-

---

[1] Ovid. *Epist. Phillid. Demop.* 48. [3] Terence, *And.* i. 114.
[2] Thucyd. iii. 52.

vation is of very dangerous consequence ; *Adeò nihil motum ex antiquo, probabile est.*[1] And, freely to speak my thoughts, it argues, methinks, a strange self-love and great presumption in a man to set so much value on his own opinions that public peace must be overthrown to establish them, and so many inevitable mischiefs introduced into his own country, and so dreadful a corruption of manners, as a civil war, and the mutations of state consequent to it, always brings in its train. Can there be worse management than to set up so many certain and palpable vices, against errors that are only contested, and disputable, whether they be such or no? And are there any worse sort of vices than those which shock a man's own conscience, and the natural light of his own reason? The senate, upon the dispute betwixt it and the people about the administration of their religion, was bold enough to return this evasion for current pay : *Ad Deos id magis, quàm ad se, pertinere ; ipsos visuros, ne sacra sua polluantur :*[2] "That it more belonged to the gods to determine than to them; let them, therefore, have a care their sacred mysteries were not profaned." As the oracle answered those of Delphos, who, fearing to be invaded by the Persians, in the Median war, inquired of Apollo how they should dispose of the holy treasure of his temple, whether they should hide, or remove it to some other place? He returned them answer, that they should stir nothing thence, but only take care of themselves, for he himself was sufficient to look to what belonged to him.[3] The Christian religion has all the marks of the utmost utility and justice : but none more manifest than the severe injunction it lays indifferently upon all to yield absolute obedience to the civil magistrate, and to maintain and defend the laws; of which what a wonderful example has the divine wisdom left us, who, to work and establish the salvation of mankind, and to conduct his glorious victory over death and sin, would do it after no other

1 Livy, xxxiv. 54.
2 Livy, x. 6, whose words, however, do not at all bear out the application that Montaigne here makes of them.
3 Herod. viii. 36.

way but at the mercy of our ordinary forms of justice, submitting the progress and issue of so high and so salutiferous
an effect to the blindness and injustice of our customs and
observances, suffering the innocent blood of so many of his
elect, and so long a loss of years to the maturing of this inestimable fruit! There is a vast difference betwixt the case
of one that follows the forms and laws of his country, and
another that will undertake to regulate and change them;
the first pleads simplicity, obedience, and precedent, for his
excuse; whatever he may do cannot be imputed to malice,
'tis at the worst but misfortune. *Quis est enim, quem non
moveat clarissimis monumentis testata, consignataque antiqui-
tas?*[1] " For who is it that antiquity, sealed and attested with
so many glorious monuments, cannot move?" Besides what
Isocrates says, that defect is nearer allied to moderation than
excess. The other is a much more ruffling gamester;[2] for
whosoever shall take upon him to choose and alter, usurps
the authority of judging, and ought to look well about him,
and make it his business to discover the defect of what he
would abolish, and the virtue of what he is about to introduce.

This vulgar consideration is that which settled me in my
station, and kept even my most ungoverned youth under the
rein, so as not to burthen my shoulders with so great a weight
as to render myself responsible for a science of that importance; or in this to dare, what in my better and more mature
judgment I durst not do in the most easy and indifferent
things I had learned, and wherein temerity of judging is of
no consequence; it seeming to me very wrong to wish to
subject public and established customs and institutions to the
weakness and instability of a private and particular fancy,
(for private reason is but a private jurisdiction,) and to

---

[1] Cicer. *de Divin.* i. 40.
[2] All that follows from the words, " for
whosoever," to the passage from Cicero
inclusively, ending thus, " not by Zeno,
Cleanthes, or Chrysippus," is not to be
found in the folio edition by Abel Ange-
lier, printed at Paris in 1595, three years
after the death of our author; nor in
another folio edition printed at Paris, by
Michael Blageaut in 1640

attempt that upon the divine, which no government will
endure a man should do upon the civil, laws.   With which,
though human reason has much more commerce than with
the other, yet are they sovereignly judged by their own
proper judges, and the utmost sufficiency serves only to
expound and set forth the law and custom received, but
neither to divest it, nor to introduce any thing of innovation.
And if sometimes the divine providence has gone beyond the
rules to which it has necessarily bound and obliged us, it is
not to give us any dispensation to do the same; those are
only master-strokes of the divine hand, which we are not to
imitate, but only admire ; and extraordinary examples pur-
posed, and particular testimonies of the nature of miracles,
presented before us for manifestations of its almighty power,
equally above both our rules and our strength, which it would
be folly and impiety to attempt to represent and imitate ; and
which we ought not to follow, but to contemplate with the
greatest reverence and astonishment, as arts peculiar to his
person and not to us.   Cotta very opportunely declares,
*Quum de religione agitur, T. Coruncanium, P. Scipionem,
P. Scævolam, pontifices maximos, non Zenonem, aut Clean-
them, aut Chrysippum, sequor.*[1]   "When matters of religion
are in question, I will be governed by T. Coruncanus, P.
Scipio, P. Scævola, the High-Priests, and not by Zeno, Cleanthes, or Chrysippus."   God knows, in our present quarrel,
where there are a hundred articles to dash out and put in,
and those of great consideration, too, how many there are
who can truly boast they have exactly and perfectly weighed
and understood the grounds and reasons of the one and the
other party.   'Tis a number, if it make any number, that
would give us very little disturbance ; but what becomes of
all the rest ?   Under what ensigns do they march ?   In
what quarter do they lie ?   Theirs have the same effect with
other weak and ill-applied medicines, they have only set the
humours they would purge more violently working, stirred

[1] Cic. *de Nat. Deor.* iii. 2.

and exasperated them by the conflict, and left them still behind. The decoction was too weak to purge, but strong enough to weaken us ; so that it does not leave us, but we keep it still in our bodies, and reap nothing from the operation but intestine gripes and long-enduring pain. Yet fortune still reserving her authority above and beyond our reason, does sometimes present us with a necessity so urgent that 'tis requisite the laws should a little yield and give way ; and when one opposes the increase of an innovation that thus intrudes itself by violence, to keep a man's self in so doing in all places, and in all things, within bounds and rules, against those who have the power, and to whom all things are lawful that may any way serve to advance their design, who have no other law nor rule but what serves best to their own purpose, is a dangerous obligation, and an intolerable inequality.

Old laws, however, must in some cases yield to new.

Aditum nocendi perfido praestat fides.[1]

"So simple truth doth her fair breast disarm,
And gives to treachery a power to harm."

The ordinary discipline of a healthful state does not provide against these extraordinary accidents, presupposing a body that supports itself in its principal members and offices, and a common consent to its obedience and observation. To act in conformity with the laws is a cold, heavy, and constrained affair, and not fit to make way against a headstrong and unbridled will. 'Tis to this day a reproach against those two great men, Octavius and Cato, in the two civil wars of Sylla and Cæsar, that they would rather suffer their country to undergo the last extremities than to relieve their fellow-citizens at the expense of its laws, or to be guilty of any innovation ; for, in truth, in these last necessities, where there is no other remedy, it would peradventure be more discreet to stoop, and yield a little before the blow, than by mere wilful opposition, without possibility of doing any good, to

[1] Seneca, *Œdip.* lii. 1, 686.

give occasion to violence to trample all under foot; 'tis better to make the laws do what they can, when they cannot do what they would. After this manner did he who suspended them for four and twenty hours,[1] and he who for once shifted a day in the calendar, and that other who of the month of June made a second May.[2] The Lacedemonians, themselves, who were such religious observers of the laws of their country, being straitened by one of their own edicts, by which it was expressly forbidden to choose the same man to be admiral twice; and on the other hand, their affairs necessarily requiring that Lysander should again take upon him that command, they made one Aracus admiral, 'tis true, but Lysander superintendent of the navy.[3] And, by the same subtilty and equivocation, one of their ambassadors being sent to the Athenians to obtain the revocation of some decree, and Pericles remonstrating to him that it was forbidden to take away the tablet wherein a law had once been engrossed, he advised him to turn it, that not being prohibited;[4] and Plutarch[5] commends Philopœmen, that, being born to command, he knew how to do it, not only according to the laws, but also to overrule even the laws themselves, when the public necessity so required.

CHAPTER XXIII.

VARIOUS EVENTS FROM THE SAME COUNSEL.

JAQUES AMIOT,[6] Grand Almoner of France, one day related to me this story, much to the honour of a prince of ours, (and ours he was upon several very good accounts, though

[1] *Agesilaus.* Plutarch, *in Vitâ*
[2] *Alexander the Great.* Plutarch, *in Vitâ.* c. 5.
[3] Plutarch, *in Vitâ Lysand.* c. 4.
[4] Plutarch, *in Vitâ Pericl.* c. 18.
[5] In the *Parallel between T. Q. Flaminius and Philopœmen*, towards the end.
[6] The celebrated translator of Plutarch.

originally of foreign extraction),[1] that in the time of our first commotions, at the siege of Rouen,[2] this prince, having been advertised by the queen-mother of a conspiracy against his life, and in her letters particular information being given him of the person who was to execute the business, who was a gentleman of Anjou, or of Mayne, and who for this purpose frequented this prince's house, discovered not the least syllable of this intelligence to any one whatever, but going the next day to St. Katherine's Mount, from whence our battery played against the town (for it was during the siege), and having in company with him the said Lord Grand Almoner, and another bishop, he was presently aware of this gentleman, who had been denoted to him, and presently caused him to be called into his presence; to whom, being The clemency of come before him, seeing him pale, and trem- the Duke of Guise. bling with the conscience of his guilt, he thus said : " Monsieur such a one, you already guess what I have to say to you ; your countenance discovers it ; you have nothing hidden from me ; I am so well informed of your business that it will but make worse for you to attempt to deny it ; you know very well such and such things (the most secret circumstances of his conspiracy), and therefore be sure, as you value your life, to confess to me the whole of your design." The poor man, seeing himself thus detected (for the whole business had been discovered to the queen by one of the accomplices), was in so great a confusion he knew not what to do ; but, joining his hands to beg for mercy, he was about to throw himself at the prince's feet, but he, taking him up, proceeded to say : " Come, sir, tell me, have I at any time heretofore done you any injury? or have I, through any private difference, offended any kinsman or friend of yours ? It is not above three weeks that I have known you ; what then could move you to attempt my death?" To which the gentleman, with a trembling voice, replied, " that it was no particular grudge he had to his per-

[1] The Duke of Guise, surnamed *Le Balafré*, of the house of Lorraine.   [2] In 1562.

son, but the general interest and concern of his party, and
that he had been put upon it by some who had persuaded him
it would be a meritorious act, by any means to extirpate so
great and so powerful an enemy of their religion." " Well,"
said the prince, " I will now let you see how much more
charitable the religion is that I hold, than that which you
profess; yours has counselled you to kill me, without a hearing, and without my ever having given you any cause of
offence; and mine commands me to forgive you, convicted,
as you are, by your own confession, of a design to murder
me without reason. Get you gone, and let me see you no
more; and if you are wise, choose henceforward honest men
for your counsellors in your designs." [1]

The Emperor Augustus, being in Gaul, had certain infor-
The clemency of mation of a conspiracy L. Cinna was contriving
Augustus. against him, and thereupon resolved to make
him an example; to that end he sent to summon his friends
to meet the next morning in council; but the night between
he passed in great disquiet of mind, considering that he was
going to put to death a young man, of an illustrious family,
and nephew to the great Pompey, which made him break
out into various ejaculations: "What then," said he, " shall
I live in perpetual anxiety and alarm, and suffer my assassin
in the mean time to walk abroad at his ease? Shall he go
unpunished, after having conspired against my life, a life I
have hitherto preserved in so many civil wars, and so many
battles, both by land and sea? And after I have settled the
universal peace of the world, shall this man be pardoned,
who has conspired not only to murder, but to sacrifice me?"
For the conspiracy was to kill him at sacrifice. After which,
remaining for some time silent, he began again louder, and
exclaiming against himself, said, " Why livest thou, if it be
for the good of many that thou shouldst die? Must there be
no end of thy revenge and cruelty? Is thy life of so great
value that so many mischiefs must be done to preserve it?"

[1] Dampmartin, *La Fortune de la Cour.* ii.

His wife Livia, seeing him in this perplexity, "Will you take a woman's counsel?" said she. "Do as the physicians do, who, when the ordinary recipes will do no good, make trial of the contrary. By severity you have hitherto prevailed nothing; Lepidus has followed Salvidienus; Murena, Lepidus; Cæpio, Murena; and Egnatius, Cæpio. Begin now and try how gentleness and clemency will succeed. Cinna is guilty, forgive him; he will never henceforth have the heart to hurt thee, and it will add to thy glory." Augustus was glad that he had met with an advocate of his own humour; wherefore having thanked his wife, and in the morning countermanded the friends he had summoned to council, he commanded Cinna all alone to be brought to him; who, being come, and a chair by his appointment set him,[1] and having commanded every one else out of the room, he spoke to him after this manner: "In the first place, Cinna, I demand of thee patient audience; do not interrupt me in what I am about to say, and I will afterwards give thee full time and leisure to answer. Thou knowest, Cinna, that having taken thee prisoner in the enemy's camp, and though thou then wert thyself mine enemy, and born so, I gave thee thy life, restored thee thy estate, and by degrees put thee in so good a position that the victorious envied the conquered. The sacerdotal office, which thou madest suit to me for, I conferred upon thee, after having denied it to others, whose fathers have ever borne arms in my service. Having done all this for thee, thou hast undertaken to kill me." At which Cinna crying out that he was far from entertaining so wicked a thought: "Thou dost not keep thy promise, Cinna," continued Augustus, "that thou wouldst not interrupt me. Yes, thou hast undertaken to murder me in such a place, such a

---

1 This circumstance, expressly noted by Seneca, is not immaterial, because it shows us the manners of that age; and therefore I think that the celebrated Corneille did well to make use of it in his tragedy of Cinna. A king who should think it derogatory to his royalty ever to see his subjects sitting in his presence would have but a very diminutive idea of grandeur, which does not depend on distinctions of this kind. A king, truly respectable, may freely dispense with this liberty, without risking the loss of any thing any more than Augustus, Trajan, or Marcus Aurelius.—*Coste.*

day, in such and such company, and in such a manner." **At**
which words seeing Cinna astonished and silent, not upon the
account of his promise so to be, but interdict with the conscience of his crime: " Why," proceeded Augustus, " to what
end wouldst thou do it? Is it to be emperor? Believe me
the republic is in a very bad condition, if I am the only man
betwixt thee and the empire. Thou art not able so much as
to defend thy own house, and but the other day was baffled
in a suit by the opposed interest of a manumitted slave.
What, hast thou neither means nor power in any other thing,
but only to attempt against Cæsar? I will resign the empire, if there is no other but I to obstruct thy hopes; but
canst thou believe that Paulus, that Fabius, that the Cassii
and the Servilii, and so many noble Romans, not only so in
title, but who by their virtue honour their nobility, would
endure thee?" After this, and a great deal more that he
said to him (for he was more than two hours speaking),
" Go, Cinna, go thy way," said he, " I again give thee that
life as a traitor and a parricide which I once before gave
thee as an enemy. Let friendship from this time forward
begin betwixt us, and let us try to make it appear whether I
have given, or thou hast received, thy life with the better
faith;" and so departed from him. Some time after he
raised him to the consular dignity, complaining that he had
not had the confidence to demand it; had him ever after for
his very great friend, and was at last made by him sole heir
to his estates.[1] Now from the time of this affair, which befell
Augustus in the fortieth year of his age, he never had any
conspiracy or attempt against him, and therein reaped the
due reward of this his exemplary clemency. But it did not
so well succeed with our prince;[2] his lenity did not secure
him from afterwards falling into the toils of the like treason;
so vain and frivolous a thing is human prudence; and, in
spite of all our projects, counsels, and precautions, fortune

---

[1] Seneca *de Clementiâ*, i. 9.
[2] The Duke of Guise, before mentioned. He was assassinated at the siege of Or- leans, in 1563, by a gentleman of Angou- mois, named Poltrot.

will still be mistress of events. We repute physicians fortunate when they hit upon a lucky cure, as if there was no other art but theirs that could not stand upon its own legs, and whose foundations are too weak to support itself upon its basis, and as if no other art stood in need of Montaigne's fortune's hand to assist in its operations. For opinion of physic. my part, I think of physic as much good or ill as any one would have me; for, thanks be to God, we have no traffic together. I am of a quite contrary humour to other men, for I always despise it; and when I am sick, instead of recanting, or entering into composition with it, I begin yet more to hate and fear it, telling those who importune me to take physic that they must at least give me time to recover my strength and health, that I may be the better able to support and encounter the violence and danger of the potion. I let nature work, supposing her to be sufficiently armed with teeth and claws to defend herself when attacked, and to uphold that contexture, the dissolution of which she flies and abhors. For I am afraid lest, instead of assisting her when grappled and struggling with the disease, I should assist her adversary, and give her more work to do.

Now, I say, that not in physic only, but in several other more certain arts, fortune has a great share. Fortune, or The poetic sallies that ravish and transport the chance, has sometimes much to do author out of himself, why should we not at- in successful sallies of poetry; tribute them to his good fortune, since the poet himself confesses they exceed his capacity, and acknowledges them to proceed from something else than himself, and that he has them no more in his power than the orators say they have those extraordinary motions and agitations that sometimes push them beyond their design. It is the same in painting, where touches shall sometimes slip and of painting. from the hand of the painter, so surpassing both his fancy and his art as to beget his own admiration and astonishment. Fortune does yet more clearly manifest the share she has in all things of this kind, in the graces and

elegances which are found in them, not only beyond the intention, but even without the knowledge of the artist.   An
intelligent reader does often find out in other men's writings
other perfections, and invest them with a better sense and
higher construction, and more quaint expression, than the
author himself either intended or perceived.

And, as to military enterprises, every one sees how great
a hand fortune has in them all.   Even in our counsels and
deliberations there must certainly be something of chance
and good luck mixed with human prudence, for all that our
wisdom can do alone is no great matter ; the more piercing,
quick, and apprehensive it is, the weaker it finds itself, and is
by so much more apt to mistrust its own virtue.   I am of
Sylla's opinion,[1] and when I more strictly and nearer hand
examine the most glorious exploits of war, I perceive, methinks, that those who carry them on make use of counsel
and debate only for custom's sake, and leave the best part of
the enterprise to fortune ; and, relying upon her favour and
assistance, transgress at every turn the bounds of military
conduct, and the rules of war.   There happen sometimes
accidental alacrities and strange furies in their deliberations,
that, for the most part prompt them to follow the worst and
worst grounded counsels, and that swell their courage beyond
the limits of reason ; whence it has fallen out that many
great captains of antiquity, to justify their rash determina-
tions, have been forced to tell their soldiers that they were
by some inspiration and good omen encouraged and invited
to such attempts.[2]

Wherefore, in this doubt and uncertainty that the short-
sightedness of human wisdom to see and choose
the best, (by reason of the difficulties that the
various accidents and circumstances of things
bring along with them,) does perplex us withal,
the surest way, in my opinion, even did no other considera-

*The course which
must be taken in
cases the event of
which is uncer-
tain.*

---

[1] Plutarch, " *How far a Man may
praise himself.*"   [2] Montluc, *Commentaries.*

tion invite us to it, were to pitch upon the course wherein is
the greatest appearance of honesty and justice, and, not being
certain which is the shortest, to go the straightest and most
direct way; as in the two examples I have just mentioned,
there is no question but that it was more noble and generous
in him who had received the offence to pardon it than to do
otherwise; and if the former miscarried in it, it was not the
fault of his good intention; neither does any one know if he
had proceeded otherwise, whether by that means he had
avoided the end his destiny had appointed for him; and he
had only lost the glory of so generous an act.

You will find in history many who have been under this
fear, and who for the most part have taken the Whether it is
course to meet and prevent conspiracies by of advantage
to seek to prevent
punishment and vengeance; but I find very conspiracies by
sanguinary meas-
few who have reaped any advantage by this ures.
proceeding; witness so many Roman emperors. Whoever
finds himself in this danger, need not expect much, either
from his vigilance or his power; for how hard a thing is it
for a man to secure himself from an enemy who lies concealed under the countenance of the most officious friend we
have, and to discover the secret designs and inward thoughts
of those who are continually doing us service? It is to no
purpose to have a guard of foreigners about a man's person,
or to be always fenced about with a pale of armed men;
whosoever despises his own life is always master of that of
another man.[1] And, moreover, this continual suspicion, that
makes a prince jealous of everybody, must, of necessity, be
a marvellous torment to him. And, therefore, it was that
Dion, being advertised that Callippus watched an opportunity to take away his life, had never the heart to inquire
more particularly into it, saying that he had Mistrust a sad
rather die than live in that misery that he condition.
must continually stand upon his guard, not only against his
enemies but his friends also;[2] which Alexander much more

1 Senec. *Epist.* 4.   2 Plutarch, *Apoth. of the Ancient Kings.*

spiritedly and effectively manifested when, having notice by
a letter from Parmenio, that Philip, his most beloved physician, was, by Darius's money, corrupted to poison him, at the
same time that he gave the letter to Philip to read, drank off
the potion he had brought him.[1] Was not this resolution to
express that if his friends had a mind to dispatch him out of
the world he was willing to give them opportunity to do it?
This prince is indeed the sovereign precedent of all daring
actions ; but I do not know whether there is another passage
in his life, wherein there is so much firmness as in this, nor
so illustrious an image of greatness of mind.

Those who preach to princes so circumspect and vigilant a
jealousy and distrust, under colour of security, preach to them
ruin and dishonour. Nothing noble can ever be effected
without danger. I know a person, naturally of great daring
and courage, whose good fortune is continually marred by
such persuasions as these, " that he must keep close amongst
his own people, and keep those he knows are his friends continually about him ; that he must not hearken to any reconciliation with his old enemies, that he must stand clear off,
and not trust his person in hands stronger than his own, what
promises or offers soever they make him, or what advantages
soever he may see before him." And I know another who
has unexpectedly secured his fortune by following quite the
contrary advice.

Courage, the reputation and glory of which men seek with
so greedy an appetite, represents and sets itself out, when
need requires, as magnificently in a doublet as in a coat of
mail ; in a closet as well as in a camp ; with the arm pendent
as with the arm upraised ; this over-circumspect and wary
prudence is a mortal enemy to all high and generous exploits.

Instances of the good effects of showing confidence in disaffected troops.

Scipio, to sound the intentions of Syphax, leaving his army and abandoning Spain, not yet
secure nor well settled in his new conquest,
passed over into Africa, in two small vessels,

[1] Quint. Curt. iii. 6.

to commit himself, in an enemy's country, to the power of a barbarian king, to a faith untried and unknown, without obligation, without hostage, under the sole security of the greatness of his courage, his good fortune, and the promise of his high hopes.[1] *Habita fides ipsam plerumque fidem obligat.*[2] "Confidence generally inspires confidence." In a life of ambition and eclât, 'tis necessary to keep suspicion in check. Fear and diffidence invite and attract injury and offence. The most distrustful of all our kings[3] established his affairs principally by voluntarily trusting his life and liberty into his enemy's hands, seeming to have an absolute confidence in them, to the end they might repose as great an assurance in him. Cæsar only opposed the authority of his countenance and the sharpness of his rebukes to his mutinous legions, armed against him, having that implicit confidence in himself and his fortune, that he feared not to commit and abandon himself to a seditious and rebellious army.

> Stetit aggere fultus
> Cespitis, intrepidus vultu; meruitque timeri,
> Nil metuens.[4]

> "Upon a parapet of turf he stood,
>   His manly face with resolution shone;
> And froze the mutineers' rebellious blood,
>   Challenging fear from all, by fearing none."

But it is true, withal, that this undaunted assurance is not to be represented in its perfect and genuine form but by those whom the imagination of death, and the worst that can happen, does not affright; for to present it a pretended resolution, with a pale and doubtful countenance, doubting, uncertain, and trembling, for the service of an important reconciliation, will affect nothing to the purpose. 'Tis an excellent way to gain the heart and good-will of another, to intrust one's self frankly to him, provided it be done without the constraint of necessity, and in such a way

[1] Livy, xxviii. 17.
[2] Livy, xxii. 22.
[3] Louis XI. See *Mem. of Comines*, ii.
[4] Lucan, v. 316.

that one manifestly does it out of a pure and entire confi-

Confidence must
be in reality, or
appearance, void
of fear.

dence in the party, at least, with a countenance clear from any cloud of suspicion. When I was a boy I saw a gentleman, who was governor of a great town, upon occasion of a popular commotion, not knowing what other course to take, go out of a place of very great strength and security, and commit himself to the mercy of a seditious rabble, in hopes, by that means, to appease the tumult before it grew to a head; but it was ill for him that he did so, for he was there miserably slain. But, nevertheless, I am not of opinion that he committed so great an error in going out as men commonly reproach his memory with, as he did in choosing a gentle and submissive way for effecting his purpose, and in endeavouring to quiet the storm rather by obeying than commanding, and by entreaty rather than remonstrance. I am rather inclined to believe that a gracious severity, with a soldierlike way of commanding, full of security, and confidence suitable to the quality of his person and the dignity of his charge, would have succeeded better with him; at least, he had perished with greater decency and reputation. There is nothing so little to be hoped for from that many-headed monster, the mob, when stirred up, as humanity and good nature; it is much more capable of reverence and fear. I should also reproach him that, having taken a resolution which, in my judgment, was rather brave than rash, to expose himself, weak and defenceless, in this tempestuous sea of men; he ought to have carried out bolder, what he had begun, to the last; whereas, coming to discover his danger nearer hand, and his nose happening to bleed, the submissive and fawning countenance he had at first put on changed into another of fear and amazement, and showing, both by his voice and eyes, his alarm and agitation; and endeavouring to withdraw and secure his person, this deportment more inflamed their fury, and soon brought the effects of it upon him.

Upon a certain occasion, I remember, it was determined

there should be a general muster of several bodies of troops in arms (a very proper scene of secret revenge, for there is no place where such can be executed with greater safety), and there were public and manifest appearances that there was no safe coming for some, whose principal and necessary office it was to review the troops. Whereupon a consultation was called, and several counsels were proposed, as in a case that was not very nice and of important consequence. Mine was that they should, by all means, avoid giving any sign of suspicion, but that the officers who were most in danger should boldly go, and, with open and erect countenances, ride boldly and confidently through the files and divisions, and that, instead of sparing fire (which the advice of the major part tended to), they should desire the captains to command the soldiers to give round and full volleys in honour of the spectators, and not to save their powder. Which was accordingly done, and had so good an effect as to please and gratify the suspected troops, and thenceforth to beget a mutual and salutary confidence and intelligence amongst them.

I look upon Julius Cæsar's way of gaining men's affections to him as the best that can possibly be put in practice. First, he tried by clemency to make himself beloved even by his enemies, contenting himself, in detected conspiracies, only publicly to declare that he was acquainted with them ; which being done, he took a noble resolution to await, without solicitude or fear, whatever might be the event, wholly resigning himself up to the protection of the gods and fortune ; and, questionless, this was the state he was in at the time when he was killed.

A stranger having publicly said that he could teach Dionysius, the tyrant of Syracuse, an infallible way to find out and discover all the conspiracies his subjects should contrive against him, if he would give him a good sum of money for his pains, Dionysius, hearing of it, caused the man to be brought to him that he might

Advice to a tyrant how to proceed against plots

learn an art so necessary to his preservation ; and, having asked him by what art he might make such discoveries, the fellow made answer that all the art he knew was that he should give him a talent, and afterwards boast that he had obtained a singular secret from him. Dionysius liked the idea, and accordingly caused six hundred crowns to be counted out to him.[1] It was not likely he should give so great a sum to a person unknown, but as a reward for some extraordinary and very useful discovery, and the belief of this served to keep his enemies in awe. Princes, however, do very wisely to publish the informations they receive of all the practices against their lives, to possess men with an opinion that they have such good intelligence, and so many spies abroad, that nothing can be plotted against them but they have immediate notice of it. The Duke of Athens did a great many ridiculous things in establishing his new tyranny over Florence ; but this, especially, was remarkable, that, having received the first intimation of the conspiracies the people were hatching against him, from Matteo di Moroso, one of the conspirators, he presently put him to death to stifle that rumour, that it might not be thought any of the city disliked his government.

I remember to have read a story of some Roman, of great quality, who, flying the tyranny of the triumvirate, had a thousand times, by the subtilty of as many inventions, escaped from falling into the hands of those that pursued him. It happened one day that a troop of horse, which was sent out to take him, passed close by a brake where he lay hid, and missed very narrowly of spying him ; but he considering, upon the instant, the pains and difficulties wherein he had so long continued, to evade the strict and continual searches which were every day made for him, the little pleasure he could hope for in such a kind of life, and how much better it was for him to die once for all, than to be perpetually at this pass, he himself called them back, showed them his hiding-

---

[1] Plutarch, *Apothegms.*

place, and voluntarily delivered himself up to their cruelty, in order to free both himself and them from farther trouble.[1] To invite a man's enemies to come and cut his throat was a resolution that appears a little extravagant and odd; and yet I think he did better to take that course than to live in a constant fever and apprehension of that for which there was no cure. But seeing all the precautions a man can take full of unquietness and uncertainty, 'tis better with a manly courage to prepare one's self for the worst that can happen, and to extract some consolation from this, that we are not certain the thing we fear will ever come to pass.

CHAPTER XXIV.

OF PEDANTRY.

I was often, when a boy, wonderfully concerned to see in the Italian farces, a pedant always brought in for the fool of the play, and that the title of *Magister* was in no greater reverence amongst us; for, being delivered up to their tuition, what could I do less than to be jealous of their honour and reputation? I sought, I confess, to excuse them by the natural incompatibility betwixt the vulgar sort and men of a finer thread, both in judgment and knowledge, forasmuch as they go quite a contrary way to one another; but in this the thing I most stumbled at was that the bravest men were those who most despised them; witness our famous Du Bellay,

Mais ie hay par sur tout un sçavoir pedantesque.[2]

And they used to do so in former times; for Plutarch says

Pedants obnoxious to men of mind.

---

[1] Applan, *H. of the Civil Wars*, iv

[2] "But of all sorts of learning, I most hate that of the pedant"

that *Grecian* and *Scholar* were names of reproach and contempt among the Romans.[1]   And since, with the better experience of age, I find they were much in the right on't, and
that *magis magnos clericos non sunt magis magnos sapientes.*[2]
" The greatest clerks are not the wisest men."   But whence
it should come to pass that a mind enriched with the knowledge of so many things should not become more quick and
sprightly, and that a gross and vulgar understanding should
yet inhabit there without correcting and improving itself,
where all the reasoning and judgments of the greatest minds
the world ever had are collected and stored up, I am yet to
seek.   To admit into one's own brain such large portions of
the brains of others, such great and high fancies (a young
lady, one of our greatest princesses, said once to me, speaking of a certain person), one's own must necessarily be
crowded and squeezed together into a less compass to make
room for the others.   I should be apt to conclude that as
plants are suffocated and drowned with too much moisture,
and lamps with too much oil, so is the active part of the
understanding with too much study and matter, which, being
embarrassed and confounded with the diversity of things, is
deprived of the force and power to disengage itself; and by
the pressure of this weight is bowed, subjected, and rendered
of no use.   But it is quite otherwise, for a soul stretches and
dilates itself the more it fills.   And thus, in the examples of
elder times, we see men excellent at public business, great
captains, and great statesmen, very learned withal ; whereas
the mere philosophers, a sort of men retired from all public
affairs, have been often laughed at by the comic
Mere philosophers
ridiculed by the   writers of their own times ; their opinions and
comic writers.   singularity of manners making them appear, to
men of another method of living, ridiculous and absurd.

And, in truth, would you make them judges of a lawsuit,
or of the actions of a man, they are ready to take it upon
them ; and straight begin to examine if he has life, if he has

---

[1] Plutarch, *Life of Cicero*, c. 2.   [2] Rabelais, i. 39.

motion, if man be any other than an ox; what it is to do and
to suffer, and what animals law and justice are? Do they
speak of the magistrate or to him? 'Tis with a rude, irreverent, and indecent liberty. Do they hear a prince or a king
commended for his virtue? They make no more of him than
of a shepherd or neatherd, a lazy Corydon, that busies himself only about milking and shearing his herds and flocks;
and this after a ruder manner than even the shepherd himself would. Do you repute any man the greater for being
lord of two thousand acres of land? They laugh at such a
pitiful pittance, laying claim themselves to the whole world
for their possession. Do you boast of your nobility and
blood, being descended from seven rich successive ancestors?
They will look upon you with an eye of contempt, as men
who have not a right idea of the universal image of Nature,
and that do not consider how many predecessors every one
of us has had, rich, poor, kings, slaves, Greeks, and barbarians. And though you were the fiftieth descent from
Hercules, they look upon it as a great vanity so highly to
value this, which is only a gift of fortune. And therefore
did the vulgar sort nauseate them, as men ignorant of first
principles, as presumptuous and insolent.[1]

But this Platonic picture is far different from that these
pedants are presented by; for those were en- The distinction
between the old
vied for raising themselves above the common philosophers and
the modern ped-
sort of men, for despising the ordinary actions ants.
and offices of life, for having assumed a particular and inimitable way of living, and for using a certain bombast and
obsolete language quite different from the ordinary way of
speaking. But these are contemned for being as much below
the usual form, as incapable of public employment; for leading the life, and conforming themselves to the mean and

---

[1] Plato, *Theœtetus*. Montaigne, however, has greatly mistaken Plato's sentiment, who says here no more than this:
that the philosopher is so ignorant of
what his neighbour does that he scarce
knows whether he is a man or some other
animal: τὸν τοιοῦτον ὁ μὲν πλησίον
καὶ ὁ γείτων λέληθεν, οὐ μόνον ὃ τι
πράττει, ἀλλ' ὀλίγου καὶ εἰ ἄνθρωπός
ἐστιν, ἤ τι ἄλλο θρέμμα.

vile manners, of the vulgar. *Odi homines ignavâ operâ,
philosophâ sententiâ.*[1] "I hate men who talk like philosophers, but do nothing."

The true philosophers, if they were great in science, were
yet much greater in action. And, as it is said of the geom-
etrician of Syracuse,[2] who having been disturbed from his
contemplation, to put some of his skill in practice for the
defence of his country, that he suddenly set on foot dreadful
and prodigious engines, that wrought effects beyond all human
expectation; himself notwithstanding disdained all this me-
chanical work, thinking in this he had violated the dignity of
his art, of which these performances of his he accounted but
trivial experiments;—so they, whenever they have been put
upon the proof of action, have been seen to fly to so high a
pitch as made it very well appear their souls were strangely
elevated and enriched with the knowledge of things. But
some of them, seeing the reins of government in the hands
of ignorant and unskilful men, have avoided all places and
interest in the management of affairs; and he who demanded
of Crates, how long it was necessary to philosophize, received
this answer: "Till our armies are no more commanded by
fools."[3] Heraclitus resigned the royalty[4] to his brother;
and to the Ephesians, who reproached him that he spent his
time in playing with children before the temple: "Is it not
better," said he, "to do so than to sit at the helm of affairs in
your company?" Others, having their imagination advanced
above the thoughts of the world and fortune, have looked
upon the tribunals of justice, and even the thrones of kings,
with an eye of contempt and scorn; insomuch that Empedocles refused the royalty that the Agrigentines offered him.[5]
Thales, once inveighing against the pains men put themselves

---

[1] Pacuvius, *apud* Aulum Gellium, xiii. 8.

[2] *Archimedes.* Plutarch, *Life of Marcellus*, c. 6.

[3] Diog. Laert. *in Vitâ.*

[4] Diogenes Laertius, in the *Life of He-
-raclitus*, lib. ix. sect. 6. By Βασιλεία

is to be understood, according to Menage, not royalty in the proper sense of
the word, but a particular office which
was so styled at Ephesus, as well as at
Athens and Rome, after their renuncia-
tion of a monarchical government.

[5] Diogenes Laertius, *in Vitâ.*

to to become rich, was answered by one in the company that he did like the fox, who found fault with what he could not obtain. Whereupon he had a mind, for the jest's sake, to show them the contrary; and having, upon this occasion, for once made a muster of all his learning and capacity, wholly to employ them in the service of profit, he set a traffic on foot which in one year brought him as great riches as the most experienced in that trade could, with all their industry, have raked together in the whole course of their lives.[1] That which Aristotle reports of some who said of him, of Anaxagoras, and others of their profession, that they were wise, but not prudent, in not applying their study to more profitable things, besides that I do not well digest this nice distinction, will not serve to excuse my pedants; for to see the low and necessitous fortune wherewith they are content, we have rather reason to pronounce that they are neither wise nor prudent.

But, letting this first reason alone, I think it better to say that this inconvenience proceeds from their applying themselves the wrong way to the study of sciences; and that, after the manner we are instructed, it is no wonder if neither the scholars nor the masters become, though more learned, ever the wiser or more fit for business. In plain truth, the cares and expense our parents are at in our education point at nothing but to furnish our heads with knowledge; but not a word of judgment and virtue. Cry out to the people of one that passes by, "O! what a learned!" and of another, "O! what a good man goes there," they will not fail to turn their eyes, and address their respect to the former.[2] There should then be a third crier, "O the blockheads!" Men are apt to inquire, "Does such a one understand Greek and Latin? Is he a poet? or does he write prose?" But whether he be better

A pedantic mode of learning objected to.

---

[1] Diogenes Laertius, *in Vitâ*. Cicero, *de Divinatione*, i. 49; who mentions that the speculation by which our philosopher got so much money was buying up all the olive-trees in the Milesian field before they were in bloom.
[2] Seneca, *Epist.* 88.

or more discreet, which ought to be the main point, is inquired into last; we should rather examine who is better learned, than who is more learned.

We only toil and labour to stuff the memory, and in the mean time leave the conscience and the understanding unfurnished and void. And, like birds who fly abroad to forage for grain, and bring it home in their beak, without tasting it themselves, to feed their young; so our pedants go picking knowledge here and there out of several authors, and hold it at the tongue's end, only to distribute it amongst their pupils. And here I cannot but smile to think how I have paid off myself in showing the foppery of this kind of learning, who myself am so manifest an example; for do I not the same thing throughout almost this whole book? I go here and there, culling out of several books the sentences that best please me, not to keep them, (for I have no memory to retain them in,) but to transplant them into this; where, to say the truth, they are no more mine than in their first places. We are, I conceive, knowing only in present knowledge, and not at all in what is past, no more than in that which is to come. But the worst

Pedants only aim at making a vain display of their learning.

of it is, their scholars and pupils are no better nourished by it than themselves; it makes no deeper impression upon them than on the other, but passes from hand to hand, only to make a show, to be tolerable company, and to tell pretty stories; like a counterfeit coin, of no other use or value but as counters to reckon with, or set up at cards. *Apud alios loqui didicerunt, non ipsi secum.*[1] "They have learned to speak from others, not with themselves." *Non est loquendum, sed gubernandum.*[2] "The thing is not to talk, but to govern." Nature, to show that there is nothing barbarous where she has the sole command, does oftentimes, in nations where art has the least to do, cause productions of wit, such as may rival the greatest effects of art whatever. In relation to what I am now speaking of, the Gascon proverb, derived from a

---

[1] Cicero, *Tuscul. Quæs.* v. 36.   [2] Seneca, *Epist.* 108.

reed-pipe, is very quaint and subtle : *Bouha prou bouha, mas à remuda lous dits qu'em.* " You may blow till your eyes start out ; but if once you offer to stir your fingers, you will be at the end of your lesson." We can say, Cicero says thus ; These were the manners of Plato ; These are the very words of Aristotle. But what do we say ourselves that is our own ? What do we do ?—what do we judge ? A parrot could say as much as that.

This kind of talking puts me in mind of that rich gentleman of Rome, who had been solicitous with very great expense, to procure men that were excellent in all sorts of science, whom he had always attending his person, to the end that when, amongst his friends, any occasion fell out *The stupidity of a Roman, who fancied himself a man of learning, because he had learned men in his pay.* of speaking on any subject whatsoever, they might supply his place, and be ready to prompt him, one with a sentence of Seneca, another with a verse of Homer, and so forth, every one according to his talent ; and he fancied this knowledge to be his own, because 'twas in the heads of those who lived upon his bounty.[1] As they also do whose learning consists in having noble libraries. I know one who, when I question him about his learning, he presently calls for a book to show me, and would not venture to tell me so much as that he had the piles in his posteriors, till first he had consulted his dictionary what piles and posteriors are.

We take other men's knowledge and opinions upon truth, and that's all, wherein we should make them our own. We are in this very like him who, having need of fire, went to a neighbour's house to fetch it ; and, finding a very good one there, sat *No learning of use but that which we make our own.*

---

[1] *Calvisius Sabinus.* He lived in the time of Seneca, who, besides what Montaigne here says of him, reports stories that are even more ridiculous of this rich impertinent. His memory was so bad that he every now and then forgot the names of Ulysses, Achilles, and Priam, though he had known them as well as we know our pedagogues ; yet he had a mind to be thought learned, and invented this compendious method, viz: he bought slaves at a great price, one who was master of Homer, another of Hesiod, and nine of lyric poetry, to whom he every now and then had recourse for verses, which in rehearsing he often stopped in the middle of a verse, yet he thought he knew as much as any one in the house did. Seneca, *Epist.* 27.

down to warm himself, without remembering to carry any with him home.[1] What good does it do us to have the stomach full of meat, if it does not digest and be incorporated with us; if it does not nourish and support us? Can we imagine that Lucullus, whom letters, without any experience,[2] made so great a leader, learned to be so after this perfunctory manner? We suffer ourselves to lean and rely so very strongly upon the arm of another, that we prejudice our own strength and vigour. Would I fortify myself against the fear of death? It must be at the expense of Seneca. Would I extract consolation for myself or my friend? I borrow it from Cicero; whereas I might have found it in myself, had I been trained up to make use of my own reason. I have no taste for this relative and mendicant understanding; for though we could become learned by other men's reading, a man can never be wise but by his own wisdom.

> Μισῶ σοφιστὴν ὅστις οὐχ' αὑτῷ σοφός.[3]

> "Who, in his own concern's not wise,
> I that man's wisdom do despise."

From whence Ennius, *Nequidquam sapere sapientem, qui ipse sibi prodesse non quiret.*[4] "That wise man knows nothing who cannot profit himself by his wisdom." *Non enim paranda nobis solum, sed fruenda sapientia est.*[5] "For wisdom is not only to be acquired, but to be made use of."

> Si cupidus, si
> Vanus, et Euganeâ quantumvis mollior agnâ.[6]

> "If he be greedy, lying, or effeminate."

Dionysius laughed at the grammarians, who cudgelled their brains to inquire into the miseries of Ulysses, and were ignorant of their own; at musicians, who were so exact in tuning their instruments, and never tuned their manners; and

---

1 Plutarch, *on Hearing.*
2 Cicero, *Acad.* ii.
3 Euripides, *apud* Cicer. *Epist. ad Famil.* xiii. 15.
4 *Apud* Cicer. *Offic.* iii. 15.
5 Cic. *de Finib.* i. 1.
6 Juvenal, viii. 14.

at orators, who studied to declare what was justice, but never took care to do it.[1] If the mind be not better disposed, if the judgment be no better settled, I had much rather my scholar had spent his time at tennis, for at least his body would by that means be in better exercise and breath. Do but observe him when he comes back from school, after fifteen or sixteen years that he has been there; there is nothing so awkward and maladroit, so unfit for company or employment; and all that you shall find he has got is that his Latin and Greek have only made him a greater and more conceited blockhead than when he went from home. He should bring back his mind replete with sound literature, and he brings it only swelled and puffed up with vain and empty shreds and snatches of learning, and really nothing more in him than he had before.

These pedants of ours, as Plato says of the Sophists, their cousin-germans, are, of all men living they who most pretend to be useful to mankind, and who alone of all men not only do not *The character of pretenders to learning.* better and improve what is committed to them, as a carpenter or a mason would do, but make them much worse, and make them pay for being made so, to boot. If the rule which Protagoras proposed to his pupils were followed, either that they should give him his own demand, or declare upon oath in the temple how much they valued the profit they had received under his tuition, and satisfy him accordingly;[2] our pedagogues would find themselves sadly gravelled, especially if they were to be judged by the testimony of my experience. Our vulgar Perigordian patois does pleasantly call these pretenders to learning "lettre-ferits," letter-marked, men on whom letters have stamped and stunned by the blow of a mallet, as 'twere; and, in truth, for the most part, they appear to have a soft place in their skulls, and to be deprived

---

[1] In all the editions of Montaigne, except that of Coste, Dionysius is mentioned; yet the wise reflections which Montaigne here ascribes to Dionysius were made by Diogenes the Cynic, as may be seen in that philosopher's life, written by Diogenes Laertius.

[2] Plato, *Protagoras.*

even of common sense. For you see the husbandman and the cobbler go simply and plainly about their business, speaking only of what they know and understand; whereas these fellows, in seeking to make a parade and a flourish with this ridiculous knowledge of theirs, that swims and floats in the superficies of the brain, are perpetually perplexing and entangling themselves in their own nonsense. They speak fine words sometimes, 'tis true, but leave somebody that is wiser to apply them. They are wonderfully well acquainted with Galen, but not at all with the disease of the patient; they stun you with a long ribble-row of laws, but understand nothing of the case in hand; they have the theories of all things, but 'tis some one else must put them in practice.

I have set by when a friend of mine, in my own house, for sport's sake, has with one of these fellows run on a heap of nonsensical galimatias, patched up of all sorts of disjointed pieces, without head or tail, saving that he now and then interlarded here and there some terms that had relation to their dispute, and held the blockhead in play a whole afternoon together, who all the while thought he had answered pertinently and learnedly to all his objections. And yet this was a man of letters and reputation, and nothing less than one of the long robe.

> Vos, O patricius sanguis, quos vivere fas est
> Occipiti cæco, posticæ occurrite sannæ.[1]

> " But you, patrician youths! whose skulls are blind,
> Watch well your jeering friends, and look behind."

Whosoever shall narrowly pry into and thoroughly sift this sort of people wherewith the world is so pestered, will, as I have done, find that, for the most part, they neither understand others nor themselves; and that their memories are full enough, 'tis true, but the judgment totally void and empty; some excepted, whose own nature has of itself formed them into better fashion. As I have observed, for

---

[1] Persius, i. 62.

example, in Adrian Turnebus, who, having never made other profession than that of mere learning only, in which he was, in my opinion, the greatest man that has been these thousand years, had nothing at all in him of the pedant, but the wearing of his gown, and a little exterior behaviour, that could not be civilized to the garb, which are nothing; and I hate our people, who can worse endure an ill-cut robe than an ill-fashioned mind, and by the bow a man makes, by his behaviour, and even by the shape of his boots, will pretend to tell what sort of man he is. For within all this there was not a more refined and polished soul living upon earth. I have often purposely put him upon arguments quite wide of his profession, wherein I found he had so clear an insight, so quick an apprehension, and so solid a judgment, that a man would have thought he had never practised any other thing but arms, or been all his life employed in affairs of state. 'Tis these are great and vigorous natures:

> Queis arte benignâ
> Et meliore luto finxit præcordia Titan; [1]

> " Formed of superior clay,
> And animated by a purer ray; "

that can keep themselves upright in spite of a pedantic education. But it is not enough that our education does not spoil us; it should alter us for the better.

Some of our parliaments when they are to admit officers, examine them only as to their learning, to which some others also add a trial of their under- standing, by asking their judgment of some cases in law, of which the latter, methinks, proceeds with the better method; for although both are necessary, and that it is very requisite the men should be defective in neither; yet, in truth, knowledge is not so absolutely necessary as judgment, and the last may make shift without the other, but

---

[1] Juvenal, xiv. 34.

the other never without this.   For as the Greek verse
says,

'Ως οὐδὲν ἡ μάθησις, ἦν μὴ νοῦς παρῇ.[1]

" *To what use serves learning, if the understanding be
away?*"   Would to God that, for the sake of justice, our
courts of judicature were as well furnished with understanding and conscience as they are with knowledge.   *Non vitæ,
sed scholæ discimus.*[2]   "We do not study how to live, but how
to dispute."   Whereas we are not to tie learning to the soul,
but to work and incorporate them together ; not to tincture
it therewith only, but to give it a thorough and perfect dye ;
and if it will not take colour, and meliorate its imperfect
state, it were, without doubt, much better to let it alone.   It
is a dangerous weapon, and very likely to wound its master,
if put into an awkward and unskilful hand.   *Ut fuerit melius
non didicisse.*[3]   "So that it were better never to have
learned at all."

And this, perhaps, is the reason why neither we, nor indeed the Christian religion, require much learning in women ;
and that Francis, Duke of Brittany, son of John the Fifth,
to one that was talking with him about his marriage with
Isabella, the daughter of Scotland, and added that she was
homely bred, and without any manner of learning, made answer, " That he liked her the better, and that a woman was
wise enough if she could distinguish between her husband's
shirt and his doublet."

So that it is no so great a wonder, as they make of it,
that our ancestors had letters in no greater esteem, and that even to this day they are but
rarely met with in the privy councils of our
princes ; and if this end and design of acquiring riches,
which is the only thing we propose to ourselves, by the means
of law, physic, pedantry, and even divinity itself, did not uphold and keep them in credit, you would, without doubt, see

Whether learning
be absolutely nec-
essary.

---

[1] And Stobæus. *Serm.* iii. p. 37.   [3] Cicero, *Tusc. Ques.* ii. 4.
[2] Senec. *Epist.* 106.

them as poor and unregarded as ever. And what loss either, if they neither instruct us to think well, nor to do well! *Postquam docti prodierunt, boni desunt.*[1] "After once they become learned, they cease to be good." All other knowledge is hurtful to him who has not the science of honesty and goodness.

But the reason I glanced upon but now, may it not also proceed hence, that our studies in France having almost no other aim but profit, few of those who by nature would seem born to offices and employments, rather of glory than gain, addict- *Letters in France but little studied, except by those who sought to live by them.* ing themselves to letters; or for so little a while, being taken from their studies before they can come to have any taste of them, to a profession that has nothing to do with books, that there commonly remain no other to apply themselves wholly to learning but people of mean condition, who seek a livelihood thereby; and by such people whose souls are, both by nature and education, and domestic example, of the basest metal, the fruits of knowledge are immaturely gathered, and ill digested. For it is not the proper business of knowledge to enlighten a soul that is dark of itself; nor to make a blind man to see. Her business is not to find a man eyes, but to guide, govern, and direct his steps, provided he has sound feet and straight legs to go upon. Knowledge is an excellent drug, but no drug has virtue enough to preserve itself from corruption and decay, if the vessel be tainted and impure wherein it is put to keep. Such a one may have a sight clear and good enough, who yet looks asquint, and consequently sees what is good, but does not follow it, and sees knowledge, but makes no use of it. Plato's principal institution, in his Republic, is to fit his citizens with employments suitable to their nature. Nature can do all, and does all. Cripples are very unfit for exercises of the body, and lame souls for exercises of the mind. Degenerate and vulgar souls are unworthy of philosophy. If we see a shoemaker

[1] Senec. *Epist.* 95.

with his shoes out at the toes, we say, " It is no wonder ; for, commonly, none go worse shod than they." In like manner, experience doth often present us a physician worse physicked, a divine worse reformed, and most frequently a scholar of less sufficiency, than another.

Aristo of Chios had reason to say that philosophers did their auditors harm, forasmuch as most of those that heard them were not capable of making any benefit of their instructions, and if they did not apply them to good, would certainly apply them to ill: *ἀσώτους ex Aristippi, acerbos ex Zenonis scholâ exire.*[1] " They proceeded debauchees from the school of Aristippus, and sour churls from that of Zeno."

In that excellent institution that Zenophon attributes to Education of the Persians, we find that they taught their Persians; children virtue, as other nations do letters. Plato tells us[2] that the eldest son in their royal succession was thus brought up ; as soon as he was born he was delivered, not to women, but to eunuchs of the greatest authority about their kings for their virtue, whose charge it was to keep his body healthful and in good plight ; and after he came to seven years of age, to teach him to ride, and to go a hunting ; when he arrived at fourteen, he was transferred into the hands of four men, the most noted in the kingdom for wisdom, justice, temperance, and valour ; of whom the first was to instruct him in religion, the second to be always upright and sincere, the third to subdue his appetites and desires, and the fourth to despise all danger. It is a thing worthy of very great consideration that, in that excellent, and of the Lacede- and, in truth, for its perfection, prodigious form monians. of civil government set down by Lycurgus, though solicitous of the education of children, as a thing of the greatest concern, and even in the very seat of the Muses, he should make so little mention of learning ; as if their generous youths disdaining all other subjection, but that of virtue only, ought to be supplied, instead of tutors to read to

---

[1] Cicero, *de Nat. Deor.* iii. 31.   [2] In the first Alcibiades.

them arts and sciences, with such masters only as should instruct them in valour, prudence, and justice; an example that Plato has followed in his laws. The manner of their discipline was to propound to them questions upon their judgment of men, and of their actions; and if they commended or condemned this or that person, or fact, they were to give a reason for so doing. By which means they at once sharpened their understanding, and learned what was right and lawful. Astyages, in Xenophon, asking her son Cyrus to give her an account of his last lesson, he made answer thus: "A great boy in the school, having a short cassock, by force took a longer from another that was not so tall as he, and gave him his own in exchange: whereupon I being appointed judge of the controversy, gave judgment that I thought it best each should keep the coat he had, for that they were both better fitted now than they were before. Upon which my master told me I had done ill, in that I had only considered the fitness of the garments, whereas I ought to have considered the justice of the thing, which required that no one should have any thing forcibly taken from him that is his own."[1] And Cyrus added that he was whipped for his pains, as we are in our villages for forgetting the first aorist of τύπτω. My pedant must make me a very learned oration, indeed, *in genere demonstrativo*, before he can persuade me that his school is as good as that. They know how to go the readiest way to work; and seeing that the sciences, when most rightly applied and best understood, can but teach us prudence, moral honesty, and resolution, they thought fit to initiate their children at once with the knowledge of effects, and to instruct them, not by hearsay and by rote, but by the experiment of action, in forming and moulding them; not only by words and precepts, but chiefly by works and examples; to the end it might not be a knowledge of the mind only, but a complexion and a habit; not an acquisition, but a natural possession. One asking, to this purpose, Agesilaus,

[1] *Cyrop.* 1. 8.

what he thought most proper for boys to learn? "What they ought to do when they come to be men," said he.[1] It is no wonder if such an institution produced such admirable effects.

They used to go, it is said, to the other cities of Greece for The difference be-twixt the instruc-tion given to the children of Sparta, and to those of Athens. rhetoricians, painters, and music-masters; but to Lacedemon for legislators, magistrates, and generals of armies. At Athens they learned to speak well, and here to do well; there to disengage themselves from a sophistical argument, and to unravel ensnaring syllogisms; here to evade the baits and allurements of pleasure, and with a noble courage and resolution to confute and conquer the menaces of fortune and death; those cudgelled their brains about words, these made it their business to inquire into things; there was an eternal babble of the tongue, here a continual exercise of the soul. And therefore it is nothing strange if, when Antipater demanded of them fifty children for hostages, they made answer, quite contrary to what we should do, that they would rather give him twice as many full grown men, so much did they value the loss of their country's education.[2] When Agesilaus invited Xenophon to send his children to Sparta to be bred, "It is not," said he, "there to learn logic or rhetoric, but to be instructed in the noblest of all sciences, namely, the science to obey and to command.[3] It is very How Socrates bantered a sophist who had got noth-ing at Sparta. pleasant to see Socrates, after his manner rallying Hippias, who recounts to him what a world of money he had got, especially in certain little villages of Sicily, by teaching school, while he got never a penny at Sparta: "What a sottish and stupid people," says Socrates, "are they, without sense or understanding, who know neither mensuration nor numeration, and make no account either of grammar or poetry, and only busy themselves in studying the genealogies and successions of

[1] Plutarch, *Apoth. of* the Lacedemo-nians.
[2] Id. *ib.*
[3] Id. *Life of Agesilaus*, c. 7

their kings, the foundation, rise, and declension of states, and such old wives' tales." [1] After which, having made Hippias acknowledge the excellency of their form of public administration, and the felicity and virtue of their private life, he leaves him to guess at the conclusion he makes of the inutility of his pedantic arts.

Examples have demonstrated unto us that, both in that military government, and all others of the like nature, the study of the sciences does more soften and enervate the courage of men than fortify and incite it.

The study of the sciences enervates courage.

The most potent empire that at this day appears to be in the whole world, is that of the Turks, a people equally remarkable for their estimation of arms, and the contempt of letters. Rome was more valiant before she grew so learned; and the most warlike nations of our time are the most ignorant; of which the Scythians, Parthians, and the great Tamerlane may serve for sufficient proof. When the Goths overran Greece, the only thing that preserved all the libraries from the fire was that some one possessed them with an opinion that they should do well to leave this kind of furniture entire to the enemy, as being most proper to divert them from the exercise of arms, and to fix them to a lazy and sedentary life. [2] When our King Charles the Eighth, almost without striking a blow, saw himself possessed of the kingdom of Naples, and a considerable part of Tuscany, the nobility about him attributed this unexpected facility of conquest to this, that the princes and nobles of Italy more studied to render themselves ingenious and learned, than vigorous and warlike.

[1] Plato, *Hippias Major*.　　[2] Philip Camerarius, *Medit. Hist. Cent.* iii 51.

CHAPTER XXV.

OF THE EDUCATION OF CHILDREN.

To Madame Diana de Foix, Countess of Gurson.

I NEVER yet saw that father who, let his son be never so
decrepit or scald-pated, would not own him;
not but that, unless he were totally besotted
and blinded with his paternal affection, he does
not well enough discern his defects; but because, notwithstanding all faults, he is still his. Just so it is with me. I
see better than any other that these things I write are but
the idle whimsies of a man that has only nibbled upon the
outward crust of learning in his nonage, and only retained a
general and formless image of it, a little snatch of every
thing, and nothing of the whole *à la Françoise;* for I know,
in general, that there is a science of physic, a science of law,
four parts in mathematics, and I have a general notion what
all these aim at; and, peradventure, I know too what the
sciences in general pretend unto, in order to the service of
human life; but to dive farther than that, and to have cudgelled my brains in the study of Aristotle, the monarch of all
our modern learning, or particularly addicted myself to any
one science, I have never done it; neither is there any one
art of which I am able to draw the first lineaments; insomuch that there is not a boy of the lowest form in a school
that may not pretend to be wiser than I, who am not able to
pose him in his first lesson, which, if I am at any time forced
upon, I am necessitated in my own defence to ask him some
universal questions, such as may serve to try his natural understanding; a lesson as strange and unknown to him as his
is to me.

(margin note: Montaigne's account of what he knew.)

I never seriously settled myself to the reading of any book
L of solid learning, but Plutarch and Seneca ; Plutarch and Sen-
and there, like the Danaides, I eternally fill, eca the favourite
books of Mon-
and it as constantly runs out ; something of taigne.
which drops upon this paper, but very little or nothing stays
L behind with me.   History is my delight, as to reading, or
else poetry, for which I have, I confess, a particular kindness
and esteem ; for, as Cleanthes said, as the voice, forced
through the narrow passage of a trumpet, comes out more
forcible and shrill ; so, methinks, a sentence couched in the
harmony of verse, darts more briskly upon the understanding, and strikes[1] both my ear and apprehension with a
smarter and more pleasing power.   As to the natural parts
I have, of which this is the specimen, I find them to bow under the burthen ; my fancy and judgment do but grope in the
dark, tripping and stumbling in their way, and when I have
gone as far as I can, I am in no degree satisfied, for I discover still a new and greater extent of land before me, but
with troubled and imperfect sight, and wrapt up in clouds
that I am not able to penetrate.   And taking upon me to
write indifferently of whatever comes into my head, and
therein making use of nothing but my own proper and natural means, if I happened, as I often do, accidentally to meet
in any good author the same heads and common places upon
which I have attempted to write (as I did but lately in Plutarch's Discourse of the Force of the Imagination), to see myself so weak and miserable, so heavy and sleepy, in comparison
with those better writers, I at once pity and despise myself.
Yet do I flatter and please myself with this, that my opinions have often the honour and good fortune to tally with
theirs, and that I follow in the same paths, though at a very
great distance, saying, they are quite right ; I am farther satisfied to find that I have a quality, which every one is not

---

[1] Montaigne's expression is, *me fiert*,
and Rousseau, among his other obligations to our author in this and the preceding chapter, owes to the occurrence
of this word—from the Latin *ferit*—his
discovery of the meaning of the motto
of the Solar Family ; *tel fiert que ne tue
pas.* See the *Confessions*, part i. book 8.

blest withal, which is to discern the vast difference betwixt them and me ; and notwithstanding all that, suffer my own ideas, poor as they are, to run on in their career, without mending or plastering up the defects that this comparison has laid open to my own view.   And in truth a man had need of a good strong back to keep pace with these people.   The indiscreet scribblers of our time, who, amongst their laborious noth-

Modern writers discover the poverty of their genius, by pillaging the ancients.

ings, insert whole sections, paragraphs, and pages, out of ancient authors, with a design by that means to do honour to their own writings, do quite contrary ; for the infinite dissimilitude of ornaments renders the complexions of their own compositions so pale, sallow, and deformed, that they lose much more than they get.

The philosophers, Chrysippus and Epicurus, were, in this, of two quite contrary humours ; for the first did not only in his books mix the passages and sayings of other authors, but entire pieces, and in one, the whole Medea of Euripides ; which gave Apollodorus occasion to say " that should a man pick out of his writings all that was none of his, he would leave nothing but blank paper ; "[1] whereas, Epicurus, quite contrary, in three hundred volumes that he left behind him, has not so much as one quotation.[2]

A case in point occurred the other day : I was reading a French book, where, after I had a long time been dragging over a great many words, so dull, so insipid, so void of all wit or common sense that, indeed, they were only words, after a long and tedious travel I came, at last, to meet with a piece that was lofty, rich, and elevated to the very clouds.   Now had I found either the declivity easy, or the ascent more sloping, there had been some excuse ; but it was so perpendicular a precipice, and so wholly cut off from the rest of the work, that by the first words I found myself flying into the other world, and thence discovered the vale whence I came, so deep and low that I had never since the heart to descend

<hr>

[1] Laertius, *Life of Chrysippus*   [2] Id. *Life of Epicurus.*

into it any more. If I should set out my discourses with such rich spoils as these, the plagiarism would too manifestly discover the imperfection of my own writing. To reprehend the fault in others that I am guilty of myself, appears to me no more unreasonable than to condemn, as I often do, those of others in myself. They are to be every where reproved, and ought to have no sanctuary allowed them. I know very well how impudently I myself, at every turn, attempt to equal myself to my thefts, and go hand in hand with them, not without a daring hope of deceiving the eyes of my reader from discerning the difference; but, withal, it is as much by the benefit of my application that I hope to do it as by that of my invention, or any force of my own. Besides, I do not offer to contend with the whole body of these old champions, nor hand to hand with any one of them; 'tis only by flights and little light skirmishes that I engage them; I do not grapple with them, but try their strength only, and never engage so far as I make a show to do. If I could hold them in play I were a brave fellow; for I never attack them but where they are strongest. To cover a man's self, as I have seen some do, with another man's armour, so as not to discover so much as their fingers' ends; to carry on his design, as it is not hard for a man that has any thing of a scholar in him, in an ordinary subject, to do, under old inventions, patched up here and there; and then to endeavour to conceal the theft, and to make it pass for his own, is, first, injustice and meanness of spirit in whoever does it; who, having nothing in them of their own fit to procure them a reputation, endeavour to do it by attempting to impose things upon the world in their own name, which they have really no manner of title to; and then a ridiculous folly to content themselves with acquiring the ignorant approbation of the vulgar by such a pitiful cheat, at the price, at the same time, of discovering their insufficiency to men of understanding, the only persons whose praise is worth any thing, who will soon smell out and trace them under their borrowed crust. For my own part there is nothing I would not sooner do than that; I quote others only in order the better to express myself. In this I do not, in the least, glance at the composers of centos, who declare themselves for such; of which sort of writers I have, in my time, seen many very ingenious, particularly one, under the name of Capilupus,[1] besides the ancients.[2] These are really men of wit, and that make it appear they are so, both by that and other ways of writing; as, for example, Lipsius, in that learned and laborious contexture of his politics.

But be this how it will, and how inconsiderable soever these essays of mine may be, I will ingenuously confess I never intended to conceal them, any more than my old, bald, grizzled portrait before them, where the painter has presented you not with a perfect face, but with the resemblance of mine. For these are my own particular opinions and fancies, and I deliver them for no other but only what I myself believe, and not what others are to believe, neither have I any other end in this writing but only to discover myself, who shall, peradventure, be another thing to-morrow, if I chance to meet any book or friend to convince me in the mean time. I have no authority to be believed, neither do I desire it, being too conscious of my own incrudition to be able to instruct others.

Montaigne's opinion as to his Essays.

A friend of mine then, having read the preceding chapter, the other day, told me that I should have enlarged a little more upon the education of children. Now, madam, were my abilities equal to the subject, I could not possibly employ them better than in presenting them to the little gentleman that threatens you shortly with a happy birth, and your friends are in daily

Montaigne's opinion concerning education.

---

[1] Lelius Capilupus, a native of Mantua, who flourished in the sixteenth century, was famous for compositions of this kind, as may be seen under his name in Bayle's Dictionary, who says that the Cento, which he wrote against the monks, is inimitable; it is to be found at the end of the Regnum Papisticum of Neogeorgus. He wrote one also against the women, which Mr. Bayle also mentions as a very ingenious piece, but too satirical. It was inserted in a collection, entitled *Bandii Amores*, printed at Leyden, in 1638. This Lelius had a nephew, named Julius Capilupus, who signalized himself by Centos, and even had a talent for it superior to his uncle, if we may believe Possevin. *Poet. Select. Lib.* xvii. 24.

[2] At the Centos of Ausonius, composed wholly out of the verses of Virgil.

hopes of (you are too generous to begin otherwise than with a male) ; for having had so great a hand in your marriage, I have a sort of right and interest in the greatness and prosperity of all that shall proceed from it ; besides, as you have been so long in possession of a title to the best of my services, I am obliged to desire the honour and advantage of every thing that concerns you. But, in truth, all I understand, as to this particular, is only this, that the greatest and most important difficulty of human science is the nurture and education of children. For, as in agriculture, all that precedes planting, as also planting itself, is certain, plain, and easy ; but, after that which is planted takes life and shoots up, there is a great deal more to be done, and much more difficulty to be got over to cultivate and bring it to perfection ; so it is with men ; it is no hard matter to plant them, but after they are born then begins the trouble, solicitude, and care, to train and bring them up.[1] The symptoms of their inclinations at that tender age are so slight and obscure, and the promises so uncertain and fallacious, that it is very hard *The difficulty of guessing by the first actions of children what they will be hereafter.* to establish any solid judgment or conjecture upon them. Look at Cimon, for example, and Themistocles, and a thousand others, whose manhood has given the lie to the ill-promise of their early youth. Bears' cubs and puppies discover their natural inclination ; but men, so soon as they are grown up, immediately applying themselves to certain habits, engaging themselves in certain opinions, and conforming themselves to particular laws and customs, do easily change, or, at least, disguise, their true and real disposition. And yet it is hard to force the propensity of nature ; whence it comes to pass that, for not having chosen the right course, a man throws away very great pains, and consumes great part of his time in training up children to things for which, by their natural

---

[1] This sentiment is taken from one of Plato's Dialogues, entitled *Theages*. where a father applying, with his son, to Socrates, to consult him to whom he should put his son for education, made the very same remark as Montaigne has in this place.

aversion, they are totally unfit. In this difficulty, nevertheless, I am clearly of opinion that they ought to be clemented
in the best and most advantageous studies, without taking too
much notice of, or being too superstitious in, those light prognostics we too often conceive of them in their tender years;
to which Plato, in his republic, gives, methinks, too much
authority.

But, madam, learning is doubtless a very great ornament,
The great utility and a thing of marvellous use, especially to
of sound learning. persons raised to that degree of fortune in
which you are placed; and, in truth, in persons of mean and
low condition, it cannot perform its true and genuine office,
being naturally more prompt to assist in the conduct of war,
in the government of a people, and in negotiating leagues
with princes and foreign nations, than in forming a syllogism
in logic, in pleading a process in law, or in prescribing a dose
of pills in physic. Wherefore, madam, believing you will
not omit this so necessary embellishment in the training of
your posterity, yourself having tasted the delights of it, and
being of a learned extraction (for we yet have the writings
of the ancient Counts of Foix, from whom my lord, your
husband, and yourself are both descended, and Monsieur
Francis de Candale, your uncle, does, every day, oblige the
world with others, which will extend the knowledge of this
quality in your family to many succeeding ages,) I will, upon
this occasion, presume to acquaint you with one particular
fancy of my own, contrary to the common method, which is
all I am able to contribute to your service in this matter.

The charge of the tutor you shall provide for your son,
upon the choice of whom depends the whole success of his
education, has several other great branches
How much de- which, however, I shall not touch upon, as
pends on the
choice of a tutor. being unable to add any thing of moment to
the common rules; and also in this, wherein I take upon me
to advise, he may follow it so far only as it shall appear
rational and conducing to the end in view. For a boy of

quality then, who pretends to letters, not upon the account of profit (for so mean an object as that is unworthy of the grace and favour of the muses ; and, moreover, has reference to others), nor so much for outward ornament, as for his own proper and peculiar use, and to furnish and enrich himself within, having rather a desire to come out an accomplished gentleman than a mere learned man ; for such a one, I say, I would have his friends solicitous to find him out a tutor who has rather an elegant than a learned head, though both, if such a person can be found ; but, however, to prefer manners and judgment before reading, and that this man should pursue the exercise of his charge after a new method.

'Tis the custom of schoolmasters to be eternally thundering in their pupils' ears, as they were pouring *The tutor of a lad* into a funnel, whilst the business of these is *ought to make him speak some-* only to repeat what the others have said be- *times before, and sometimes after,* fore. Now I would have a tutor to correct *him.* this error ; and that, at the very first outset, he should, according to the capacity he has to deal with, put it to the test, permitting his pupil himself to taste and relish things, and of himself to choose and discern them, sometimes opening the way to him, and sometimes making him break the ice himself ; that is, I would not have him alone to invent and speak, but that he should also hear his pupil speak in turn. Socrates, and, since him, Arcesilaus, made first their scholars speak, and then spoke to them.[1] *Obest plerumque iis qui discere volunt auctoritas eorum qui docent.*[2] "The authority of those who teach is very often an impediment to those who desire to learn." The tutor should make his pupil, like a young horse, trot before him, that he may judge of his going, and how much he is to abate of his own speed to accommodate himself to the vigour and capacity of the other. For want of which due proportion we spoil all ; yet to know how to adjust it, and to keep within an exact and due measure, is one of the hardest things I know, and 'tis

---

[1] Laertius, *in Vitâ.*   [2] Cicero, *de Nat. Deor.* i. 5.

the effect of a strong and well-tempered mind to know how to condescend to his puerile motions and to govern and direct them. I walk firmer and more secure up hill than down.

Such as, according to our common way of teaching, undertake, with one and the same lesson, and the same measure of direction, to instruct several boys of so differing and unequal capacities, need not wonder if, in a multitude of scholars, there are not found above two or three who bring away any good account of their time and discipline. Let the master not only examine him about the bare words of his lesson, but also as to the sense and meaning of them, and let him judge of the profit he has made, not by the testimony of his memory, but by that of his understanding. Let him make him put what he hath learned into a hundred several forms, and accommodate it to so many several subjects, to see if he yet rightly comprehend it, and has made it his own; taking instruction by his progress from the institutions of Plato. 'Tis a sign of crudity and indigestion to throw up what we have eaten in the same condition it was swallowed down; the stomach has not performed its office unless it hath altered the form and condition of what was committed to it to concoct. Our minds work only upon trust, being bound and compelled to follow the appetite of another's fancy; enslaved and captive under the authority of another's instruction, we have been so subjected to the trammels that we have no free nor natural pace of our own, our own vigour and liberty is extinct and gone. *Nunquam tutelæ suæ fiunt.*[1] "They are never out of wardship."

I was privately at Pisa carried to see a very honest man, but so great an Aristotelian that his invariable dogma was "That the touchstone and square of all solid imagination and all truth was an absolute conformity to Aristotle's doctrine, and that all besides was nothing but inanity and chimera; for that he had seen all and said all." A position that having been a little too broadly and maliciously interpreted, brought him into and long kept him in great trouble in the Inquisition at Rome.

Let the tutor make his pupil examine and thoroughly sift every-thing he reads, and lodge nothing in his head upon simple authority and upon trust. Let Aristotle's Principles be no more principles to him than those of Epicurus and the Stoics; let the diversity of opinions be propounded to, and laid before, him, he will himself choose, if he be able; if not, he will remain in doubt.

> Che non men che saper, dubbiar m' aggrada.[1]
>
> "I love sometimes to doubt as well as know."

For if he embrace the opinions of Xenophon and Plato, by the exercise of his reason they will no more be theirs, but become his own. Who follows another, follows nothing, finds nothing, nay, seeks nothing. *Non sumus sub rege; sibi quisque se vindicet.*[2] "We are not under a king; let every one dispose of himself." Let him, at least, know that he does know. 'Tis for him to imbibe their knowledge, but not to adopt their dogmas; and no matter if he forgets where he had his learning, provided he knows how to apply it to his own use; truth and reason are common to every one, and are no more his who spoke them first than his who spake them after. 'Tis no more according to Plato than according to me, since both he and I equally see and understand in the same manner. Bees cull their several sweets from this flower and that blossom, here and there where they find them, but themselves after make the honey which is all and purely their own, and no longer thyme and marjoram; so the several fragments the pupil borrows from others he will transform and blend together to compile a work that shall be absolutely his own; that is to say, his judgment, which his instruction, labour, and study should alone tend to form. He is not obliged to discover whence he had his materials, but only to produce what he has done with them. Men that live

---

[1] Dante, *Inferno*, 1. 93.   [2] Senec. *Epist*. 33.

upon rapine and borrowing, readily parade their purchases and buildings to every one, but do not proclaim how they came by the money. We do not see the fees and perquisites of a gentleman of the long robe; but we see the noble alliances wherewith he fortifies himself and his family, and the titles and honours he has obtained for him and his. No man accounts to the public for his revenue; but every one makes a show of his purchases, and is content the world should know his good condition.

The advantages of our study are to become better and wiser. 'Tis, says Epicharmus, the understand-
What the advantages of study are. ing that sees and hears, the understanding that improves every thing, that orders every thing, and that acts, rules, and reigns.[1] All other faculties are blind and deaf, and without soul; and certainly we render it timorous and servile in not allowing it the liberty and privilege to do any thing of itself. Who ever asked his pupil what he thought of grammar and rhetoric, or of such and such a sentence of Cicero? Our pedagogues stick them full feathered in our memories, and there establish them like oracles, of which the very letters and syllables are the substance of the thing. To know by rote is no knowledge, 'tis no more than only to retain what one has intrusted to his memory. That which a man rightly knows and understands he is the free disposer of at his own full liberty, without any regard to the author from whom he had it, or fumbling over the leaves of his book. A mere bookish learning is a poor stock to go upon; though it may serve for some
What true philosophy is, according to Plato. kind of ornament, there is yet no foundation for any superstructure to be built upon it, according to the opinion of Plato, who says that constancy, faith, and sincerity, are the true philosophy; and the other sciences, that are directed to other ends, are but cozenage. I could wish to know whether Le Paluel or Pompey, famous dancing-masters of my time, could have taught us to cut capers by

[1] Clement. Alex. *Stromat.* ii.

only seeing them do it, without stirring from our places, as these men pretend to inform our understandings, without ever setting them to work; or whether we could learn to ride, handle a pike, touch a lute, or sing, without practice, as these attempt to make us judge and speak well, without exercising us in judging or speaking. Now while we are in our apprenticeship to learning, whatsoever presents itself before us is a book worth attending to. An arch trick of a page, a blunder of a servant, or a jest at a table, are so many new subjects.

And for this very reason acquaintance with the world is of very great use, and travel into foreign countries of singular advantage; not to bring back (as most of our young Monsieurs do) an account only of how many paces Santa Rotonda[1] is in circuit; or of the richness of Signiora Livia's attire; or, as some others, how much Nero's face, in a statue in such an old ruin, is longer and broader than that made for him in such an old medal; but to be able to give an account of the humours, manners, customs, and laws of those nations where he has been. And, that we may whet and sharpen our wits, by rubbing them upon those of others, I would that a boy should be sent abroad very young, and, in order to kill two birds with one stone, into those neighbouring nations whose language differs most from our own, and to which, if it be not formed betimes, the tongue will be grown too stiff to bend.

'Tis the general opinion of all, that children should not be brought up in their parents' lap. Their natural affection is apt to make the most discreet of them all so over-fond that they can neither find in their hearts to give them due correction for the faults they commit, nor suffer them to be brought up in those hardships and hazards they ought to be. They would not endure to see them return all dust and sweat from their exercise, to drink cold water when they are hot, or see them mount

The utility of travelling young.

Fondness of parents pernicious to education.

---

[1] The Pantheon.

an unruly horse, or take a foil in hand against a rough fencer, or so much as to discharge a carbine. And yet there is no remedy ; whoever will have a boy to be good for any thing when he comes to be a man, must by no means spare him when young, and must very often transgress the rules of physic :—

> Vitamque sub dio et trepidis agat
> In rebus.[1]

> " He must sharp cold and scorching heat despise,
>   And most tempt danger where most danger lies."

It is not enough to fortify his soul, you are also to make his sinews strong ; for the soul will be oppressed, if not assisted by the body, and would have too hard a task to discharge two offices alone. I know very well how much mine groans under the disadvantage of a body so tender and delicate that eternally leans and presses upon her ; and often in my reading perceive that our masters, in their writings, make examples pass for magnanimity and fortitude of mind, which really have more to do with toughness of skin and hardness of bones.

I have seen men, women, and children, born of so hard and insensible a constitution of body that a sound cudgelling has been less to them than a flirt with a finger would have been to me, and that would neither cry out, nor wince at a good swinging beating ; when wrestlers counterfeit the philosophers in patience, it is rather strength of nerves than stoutness of heart. Now to be inured to labour is to be able to endure pain. *Labor callum obducit dolori.*[2] " Labour supplies pain with a certain callosity that hardens it to the blow." A boy must be broken in by the pain and hardship of severe exercise, to inure him to the pain and hardship of dislocations, colics, cauteries, and even of imprisonment and the rack itself, for he may come by misfortune, to be reduced to the worst of these, which (as this world goes) sometimes befall the good as well as the bad. As for proof, in our present

---

[1] Horace, *Od.* ii. 3, 5.   [2] Cicero, *Tusc. Quæs.* ii. 14.

civil war, whoever draws his sword against the laws threatens all honest men with the whip and the halter.

And, moreover, by living at home, the authority of this tutor, which ought to be sovereign over the boy he has received into his charge, is often checked, interrupted, and hindered by the presence of parents; to which may also be added, that the respect the whole family pay him, as their master's son, and the knowledge he has of the estate and greatness he is heir to, are, in my opinion, no small inconveniences at these tender years.

In one's converse with the world, I have often observed this vice, that instead of gathering observations from others, we make it our whole business to give them our own, and are more concerned *That a retired modesty is greatly desirable in youth.* how to expose and set out our own commodities than how to acquire new. Silence and modesty are very advantageous qualities in conversation, and one should therefore train up the boy to be sparing, and a good husband of what he knows, when once acquired; and to forbear taking exceptions at, or reproving every idle saying, or ridiculous story, spoken or told in his presence; for it is a great rudeness to controvert every thing that is not agreeable to our own palate. Let him be satisfied with correcting himself, and not seem to condemn every thing in another he would not do himself, nor dispute against common customs. *Licet sapere sine pompâ, sine invidiâ.*[1] "Let him be wise without assumption and without envy." Let him avoid this pedagoguish and uncivil fashion, this childish ambition of coveting to appear something better and greater than other people, proving himself in reality something less; and as though finding fault were a proof of genius, seeking to found a special reputation thereon. For, as it becomes none but great poets to make use of the poetic license, so it is intolerable that any but men of great and illustrious souls should be privileged above the authority of custom. *Si quid Socrates et Aristippus contra morem et*

[1] Seneca, *Epist.* 103.

consuetudinem fecerunt, idem sibi ne arbitretur licere : mag-
nis enim illi et divinis bonis hanc licentiam assequebantur.[1]
" If Socrates and Aristippus have transgressed the rules of
custom, let him not imagine that he is licensed to do the same;
for it was by great and sovereign virtues that they obtained
this privilege." Let him be instructed not to engage in discourse, or dispute but with a champion worthy of him, and
even there, not to make use of all the little subtleties that
may serve his purpose; but only such as may best serve him
upon that occasion. Let him be taught to be nice in the
choice of his reasons, to see they are pertinent, and to affect
brevity ; above all, let him be lessoned to acquiesce and submit to truth as soon as ever he shall discover it, whether in
his opponent's argument, or upon better consideration of his
own ; for he should never be preferred to the chair for a
mere clatter of words and syllogisms, nor be engaged to any
argument whatever, than as he shall in his own judgment
approve it ; nor be bound to that trade, where the liberty of
recantation, and getting off upon better thoughts, are to be
sold for ready money. *Neque, ut omnia quæ præscripta et
imperata sint defendat, necessitate ullâ cogitur.*[2] " Neither is
there any necessity or obligation upon him at all, that he
should defend all things that are recommended to and enjoined him."

If his tutor be of my humour, he will form his will to be a
very good and loyal subject to his prince, very affectionate to
his person, and very stout in his quarrel ; but withal, he will
cool in him the desire of having any other tie to his service
than public duty ; because, besides several other inconveniences, that are inconsistent with the liberty every honest
man ought to have, a man's judgment being bribed and prepossessed by these particular obligations and favours, is either
blinded and less free to exercise its function, or shall be
Dependence upon blemished either with ingratitude or indiscre-
princes.   tion.   A man that is purely a courtier can

[1] Cic. *de Offic.* l. 41.   [2] Cicero, *Acad. Quæs.* iv. 8.

neither have power nor wit to speak or think otherwise than favourably of a master, who, amongst so many thousands of other subjects, has picked out him with his own hand, to nourish and advance him. This favour, and the profit flowing from it, must needs, and not without some show of reason, corrupt his freedom of speaking, and dazzle him. And we commonly see these people speak in another kind of phrase than is ordinarily spoken by the rest of the nation, and are not much to be believed in such matters.

Let conscience and virtue be eminently manifest in his speech, and have only reason for their guide. Sincerity to be Make him understand that to acknowledge the cultivated. error he shall discover in his own argument, though only found out by himself, it is an effect of judgment and sincerity, which are the principal things he is to seek after. That obstinacy and contention are common qualities, most appearing in and best becoming a mean soul. That to recollect and correct himself, and to forsake a bad argument in the height and heat of dispute, are great and rare philosophical qualities. Let him be directed, being in company, to have He must be admonished when in his eye and ear in every corner of the room; company, to be attentive to every for I find that the places of greatest honour thing said or done. are commonly possessed by men that have least in them, and that the greatest fortunes are not always accompanied with the ablest parts. I have been present, when, whilst they at the upper end of the table have been only commending the beauty of the arras, or the flavour of the wine, many fine things have been lost or thrown away at the lower end of the table. Let him examine every man's talent; a peasant, a bricklayer, or any casual passenger, a man may learn something from every one of these in their several capacities, and something will be picked out of their discourse, whereof some use may be made at one time or another; nay, even the folly and weakness of others will contribute to his instruction. By observing the graces and manners of all he sees, he will create to himself an emulation of the good, and a contempt of the bad.

Let an honest curiosity be planted in him to inquire after
every thing, and whatever there is of singular and rare near
the place where he shall reside, let him go and see it; a fine
house, a fountain, an eminent man, the place where a battle
was anciently fought, the passage of Cæsar or of Charle-
maigne,

> Quæ tellus sit lenta gelu, quæ putris ab æstu,
> Ventus in Italiam quis bene vela ferat.[1]

> " What lands are frozen, what are parched, explore,
>   And what wind bears us to the Italian shore."

Let him inquire into the manners, revenues, and alliances
of princes, things in themselves very pleasant to learn and
History a profita- very useful to know. In thus conversing with
ble study.   men, I mean, and principally, those who only
live in the records of history; let him, by reading those
books, converse with the great and heroic souls of better ages.
It is an idle study, I confess, to those who choose to make it
so, by doing it after a negligent manner; but to those also
who choose to make it so, by care and observation, it is a
study of inestimable fruit and value; and the only one, as
Plato reports, the Lacedemonians reserved to themselves.[2]
What profit shall he not reap, as to the business of men, by
reading the lives of Plutarch? But, withal, let my tutor remember to what end his instructions are principally directed,
and that he do not so much imprint in his pupil's memory
the date of the ruin of Carthage, as the manners of Hannibal
and Scipio; nor so much where Marcellus died as why it was
unworthy of his duty that he died there. Let him read history, not as an amusing narrative, but as a discipline of the
judgment. 'Tis this study to which, in my opinion, of all
others, we apply ourselves with the most differing and uncertain measures. I have read an hundred things in Livy, that
another has not, or not taken notice of, at least; and Plutarch
has read a hundred more than ever I could find, or than peradventure the author ever writ. To some it is merely a

---

[1] Propertius, iv. 3. 39.   [2] Plato, *Hippias Major*.

grammar-study; to others, the very anatomy of philosophy, by which the most secret and abstruse parts of our human nature are penetrated into. There are in Plutarch many long discourses very worthy to be carefully read and observed, for he is, in my opinion, of all other, the greatest master in that kind of writing; but withal, there are a thousand others which he has only touched and glanced upon, where he only points with his finger to direct us which way we may go if we will, and contents himself sometimes with only giving one brisk hit in the nicest article of the question, whence we are to grope out the rest; as, for example, where he says, "That the inhabitants of Asia came to be vassals to one only, for not having been able to pronounce one syllable, which is *no*."[1] Which saying of his gave perhaps matter and occasion to Boetius to write his "Voluntary Servitude."[2] Even this, but to see him pick out a light action in a man's life, or a word that does not seem to be of any such importance, is itself a whole discourse. It is a pity that men of understanding should so immoderately affect brevity; no doubt but their reputation is the better for it; but in the mean time we are the worse. Plutarch had rather we should applaud his judgment than commend his knowledge, and had rather leave us with an appetite to read more, than glutted with that we have already read. He knew very well that a man may say too much even upon the best subjects, and that Alexandrides did justly reproach him who made very elegant, bu' too long, speeches to the Ephori, when he said, "O stranger! thou speakest the things thou oughtest to speak, but not after

[1] Plutarch, in his Treatise *on False Shame*.

[2] This was Montaigne's friend, of whom I shall have occasion to say more elsewhere. His name was Stephen Boetius, and he composed that book of *Voluntary Servitude*, which is here mentioned by Montaigne, and of which we shall find him discoursing more particularly in the 27th chapter of this book, under the article of Friendship. One thing very surprising is that, in almost all the editions which I have consulted, instead of Boe- tius we read Bœotia, a country of Greece, and that in those which have short marginal lemmas of what is contained in the pages, we are told, upon account of this passage in Plutarch, that this country of Greece voluntarily submitted to slavery; a fatal accident, which care has been taken to point out in the margin, by these words, which are by no means equivocal. "The voluntary slavery of the Bœotians." Thus a very material confusion has arisen from a small error in typography.

the manner thou shouldest speak them."[1] Such as have
lean and spare bodies stuff themselves out with clothes; so
they who are defective in matter endeavour to make amends
with words.

Human understanding is marvellously enlightened by daily
conversation with men, for we are otherwise in
ourselves stupid and dull, and have our sight
limited to the length of our own noses. One
asking Socrates of what country he was, he did not make
answer, "Of Athens," but, "Of the world;"[2] having an
imagination rich and expansive, he embraced the whole
world for his country, and extended his society, his friendship, and his knowledge, to all mankind; not as we do, who
look no farther than our feet. When the vines of our village are nipped with the frost, the parish-priest presently
concludes that the indignation of· God is gone out against all
the human race, and that the cannibals have already got the
pip. Who is it that, seeing these civil wars of ours, does
not cry out, That the machine of the whole world is upset-
ting, and that the day of judgment is at hand! without considering that many worse things have been seen, and that, in
the mean time, people are very merry in ten thousand other
parts of the earth, notwithstanding. For my part, considering the license and impunity that always attend such commotions, I wonder they are so moderate, and that there is
no more mischief done. To him that feels the hailstones
patter about his ears, the whole hemisphere appears to be in
storm and tempest; like the ridiculous Savoyard, who said
very gravely, "That if that simple king of France had managed well he might in time have come to be steward of the
household to the duke his master." The fellow could not, in
his shallow imagination, conceive that there could be any
thing greater than a Duke of Savoy. And, in truth, we are
all of us insensibly in this error, an error of very pernicious
consequence. But whoever shall represent to his fancy, as

Conversation with the world greatly assists the understanding.

---

[1] Id. *Apothegms.*   [2] Id. *On Banishment.* Cicero. *Tusc. Quæs.* v. 37.

in a picture, that great image of our mother nature, portrayed in her full majesty and lustre ; whoever in her face shall read so general and so constant a variety, whoever shall observe himself in that figure, and not himself but a whole kingdom, no bigger than the least touch of a pencil, in comparison of the whole, that man alone is able to value things according to their true estimate and grandeur.

This great world, which some do yet multiply as several species under one genus, is the mirror wherein we are to behold ourselves, to be able to know ourselves as we ought to do. In short, I would *The world a mirror in which all should look.* have this to be the book my young gentleman should study with the most attention ; for so many humours, so many sects, so many judgments, opinions, laws, and customs, teach us to judge aright of our own, and inform our understanding to discover its imperfection and natural infirmity, which is no trivial lesson. So many mutations of states and kingdoms, and so many turns and revolutions of public fortune, will make us wise enough to make no great wonder of our own. So many great names, so many famous victories and conquests drowned and swallowed in oblivion, render our hopes ridiculous of eternizing our names by the taking of half a score light horse, or a paltry turret, which only derives its memory from its ruin. The pride and arrogance of so many foreign pomps and ceremonies, the inflated majesty of so many courts and grandeurs, accustom and fortify our sight, without winking, to behold and endure the lustre of our own. So many millions of men buried before us, encourage us not to fear to go seek such good company in the other world, and so of all the rest. Pythagoras was wont to say, that our life resembled the great and populous assembly of the Olympic Games : some exercise the body for glory, others carry merchandise to sell for profit ; there are also some, and those none of the worst sort, who pursue no other advantage than only to look on, and to consider how and why every thing is done, and to be inactive spectators of the lives

of other men, thereby the better to judge of and regulate
their own.

As examples, all the instruction couched in philosophical
discourses may be taken, to which all human actions, as to
their best rule, ought to be especially directed; where a man
shall be taught to know,

> Quid fas optare; quid asper
> Utile nummus habet; patriæ charisque propinquis
> Quantum elargiri deceat; quem te Deus esse
> Jussit, et humanâ quâ parte locatus es in re;
> Quid sumus, aut quidnam victuri gignimur.[1]

> " Think what we are, and for what ends design'd;
> How we may best through life's long mazes wind;
> What we should wish for—how we may discern
> The bounds of wealth, and its true uses learn;
> How fix the portion which we ought to give
> To friends, relations, country—how to live
> As fits our station; and how best pursue
> What God has placed us in this world to do; "

what it is to know, and what to be ignorant; what ought to
be the end and design of study; what valour, temperance,
and justice are; the difference betwixt ambition and avarice,
servitude and subjection; licentiousness and liberty; by what
token a man may know true and solid content; how far death,
pain, and disgrace are to be feared,

> Et quo quemque modo fugiatque feratque laborem.[2]

> " And what thou may'st avoid, and what must undergo."

By what secret springs we move, and the reason of our various irresolutions. For, methinks, the first doctrine with
which one should season his understanding ought to be that
which regulates his manners and his sense; that teaches him
to know himself, and how both well to die and well to live.
Amongst the liberal sciences, let us begin with that which
makes us free;[3] not that they do not all serve in some
measure, to the instruction and use of life, as all other things
in some sort, also do; but let us make choice of that which

---

1 Persius, iii. 67.   3 Seneca, *Epist.* 88.
2 *Æneid,* iii. 459.

directly and professedly serves to that end. If we were once able to restrain the offices of human life within their just and natural limits, we should find that most of the sciences in use are of no great use to us, and, even in those that are, that there are many very unnecessary cavities and dilatations which we had better let alone, and, following Socrates's direction, limit the course of our studies to those of real utility :[1]

> Sapere aude:
> Incipe. Vivendi recte qui prorogat horam,
> Rusticus expectat dum defluat amnis; at ille
> Labitur et labetur in omne volubilis ævum.[2]

> " Dare to be wise; and now
> Begin: the man who has it in his power
> To practise virtue, and puts off the hour,
> Waits, like the clown, to see the brook run low
> Which onward flows, and will for ever flow."

'Tis a great foolery to teach our children

> Quid moveant Pisces, animosaque signa Leonis,
> Lotus et Hesperiâ quid Capricornus aquâ.[3]

> " What influence Pisces and fierce Leo have,
> Or Capricornus in the Hesperian wave."

The knowledge of the stars and the motion of the eighth sphere before their own.

> Τί πλειαδέσσι καμοί;
> Τί δ' ἀστράσιν βοώτεω;[4]

> " How swift the seven sisters' motions are,
> Or the dull churls how slow, what need I care."

Anaximenes, writing to Pythagoras, " To what purpose," said he, " should I trouble myself in searching out the secrets of the stars, having death or slavery continually before my eyes? " (For the kings of Persia were at that time preparing to invade his country.) Every one ought to say the

---

[1] Diogenes Laertius, in the Life of Socrates. *Socrates primus philosophiam devocavit e cœlo et coegit de vitâ et moribus rebusque bonis et malis quærere.* " Socrates first called down philosophy from the heavens, and made life and manners, and good and evil, the objects of its inquiry."—Cicero, *Tusc. Quæst.* v. 4.
[2] Horace, *Epist.* i. 2, 40.
[3] Propert. iv. 1, 85.
[4] Anac. xvii. 10.

same: " Being assailed, as I am, by ambition, avarice, temerity, and superstition, and having within so many other enemies of life, shall I go cudgel my brains about the world's revolutions?"[1]

After having taught our pupil what will make him more wise and good, you may then show him the ele-

In what way the sciences should be taught. ments of logic, physic, geometry, and rhetoric; and the science which he shall then himself most incline to, his judgment being, beforehand, formed and fit to choose, he will quickly make his own. The way of instructing him ought to be, sometimes by discourse, and sometimes by reading; sometimes his governor shall put the author himself, which he shall think most proper for him, into his hands, and sometimes only the marrow and substance of it; and if the governor himself be not conversant enough in books to turn to all the fine discourses the book contains, there may some man of letters be joined to him, that, upon every occasion shall supply him with what he desires and stands in need of, to recommend to his pupil. And who can doubt but that this way of teaching is much more easy and natural than that of Gaza?[2] In which the precepts are so intricate, and so harsh, and the words so vain, empty, and insignificant, that there is no hold on them; nothing that quickens and elevates the wit and fancy; whereas, here the mind has what to feed upon and to digest. This fruit, therefore, is not only, without comparison, much finer, but will also be much more early ripe.

'Tis a thousand pities that matters should be at such a pass, in this age of ours, that philosophy, even with men of understanding, should be looked upon as a vain and fantastic name, a thing of no use, no value, either in opinion or effect; and I think 'tis these miserable ergotisms, by taking possession of the avenues unto it, are the cause. People are much to blame to represent it to children as a thing of so difficult access,

[1] Laertius, *in Vitâ.*
[2] A literary man of the fifteenth century, born at Thessalonica, who took up his residence in Italy. He is the author of an indifferent Greek grammar, very obscure and complicated in its rules.

and with such a frowning, grim, and formidable aspect. Who
is it has disguised it thus with this false, pale, and hideous
countenance? There is nothing more airy, more gay, more
frolic, I had like to have said, more wanton. She preaches
nothing but feasting and jollity; a melancholy, thoughtful,
look, shows that she does not inhabit there. Demetrius, the
grammarian, finding in the Temple of Delphos, a knot of
philosophers set chattering together, said to them, " Either I
am much deceived, or, by your cheerful and pleasant countenance, you are engaged in no very deep discourse." To
which one of them, Heracleon, the Megarean, replied, " 'Tis
for such as puzzle their brains about inquiring whether the
future tense of the verb βάλλω be spelt with a double λ, or
that hunt after the derivation of the comparatives χείρον,
βέλτιον, and the superlatives χείριστον, βέλτιστον, to knit their
brows whilst discoursing of their science; but as to philosophical discourses they always amuse and cheer up those that
treat of them, and never deject them, or make them sad." [1]

> Deprendas animi tormenta latentis in ægro
> Corpore, deprendas et gaudia; sumit utrumque
> Inde habitum facies.[2]

> ———" For still we find
> The face the unerring index of the mind,
> And as this feels or fancies joys or woes,
> That pales with anguish, or with rapture glows."

The soul that entertains philosophy ought by its necessarily
healthy condition, to render the body healthful *Philosophy*
too; she ought to make her tranquillity and sat- *soothes the body*
isfaction shine, so as to appear without, and her *mind.* *as well as the*
contentment ought to fashion the outward behaviour to her
own mould, and consequently to fortify it with a graceful
confidence, an active and joyous carriage, and a serene and
contented countenance. The most certain sign of wisdom is
a continual cheerfulness; her state is like that *Cheerfulness a*
of things in the regions above the moon, always *sign of wisdom.*

---

[1] Plutarch, *Of oracles that have ceased.*   [2] Juvenal, ix. 18.

clear and serene. 'Tis *Baroco* and *Baralipton*[1] that render
their disciples so dirty and ill-favoured, and not she ; they do
not so much as know her but by hearsay. 'Tis she that
calms and appeases the storms and tempests of the soul, and
who teaches famine and fevers to laugh and sing ; and this
not by certain imaginary epicycles, but by natural and manifest reasons. She has virtue for her end ; which is not, as
the schoolmen say, situate upon the summit of a steep, rugged, and inaccessible precipice. Such as have approached
her find it, quite the contrary, to be seated in a fair, fruitful,
and flourishing plain, whence she easily discovers all things
below her ; but to which any one may arrive if he know the
way, through shady, green, and sweet-scented walks and avenues, by a pleasant, easy, and smooth descent, like that of
the celestial arches. 'Tis for not having frequented this supreme, this beautiful, triumphant, and amiable, this equally
delicious and courageous virtue, this so professed and implacable enemy to anxiety, sorrow, fear, and constraint, who,
having nature for her guide, has fortune and pleasure for her
companions, that they have gone according to their own weak
imagination, and created this ridiculous, this sorrowful, queru-
lous, despiteful, threatening, terrible image of it, and placed
it upon a solitary rock amongst thorns and brambles, and
made of it a hobgoblin to frighten people from daring to approach it.

But the tutor that I would have, knowing it to be his duty

Virtue ought to be represented to youth as a thou-sand times more amiable than vice. to possess his pupil with as much or more affection, than reverence, to virtue, will be able to
inform him that the poets[2] have evermore accommodated themselves to the public humour,
and make him sensible that the gods have planted far more

1 Two of the terms of ancient scholastic logic. The whole of the nineteen fic-
titious words which expressed the nineteen forms of syllogism were these :

Barbara, celarent, daril, ferio, baralipton,
Celantes, dabitis, fapesmo, frisosomorum,

Cesare, camestres, festino, baroco, da-
rapti,
Felapton, disamis, datisi, bocardo, feri-
son.

2 Hesiod, 'Εργ. καὶ 'Ημ. 27.

toil in the avenues of the cabinets of Venus, than in those of Minerva. And when he shall once find him begin to apprehend he shall represent to him a Bradamante or an Angelica for a mistress;[1] a natural, active, generous, not masculine, but manly beauty, in comparison of soft, delicate, artificial, simpering, and affected charms; the one in the habit of an heroic youth with a glittering helmet on her brow; the other tricked up in curls and ribbons, like a silly minx; he will then judge his love to be brave and manly, if he finds him choose quite contrary to that effeminate shepherd of Phrygia.

Such a tutor will make a pupil to digest this new lesson, that the height and value of true virtue consists in the facility, utility, and pleasure of its exercise; so far from difficulty that boys as well as men, and the innocent as well as the subtle, may make it their own; and 'tis by order and good conduct, not by force, that it is to be acquired. Socrates, her first favourite, is so averse to all manner of violence as totally to throw it aside, to slip into the more natural facility of her own progress. 'Tis the nursing-mother of all human pleasures, who, in rendering them just, renders them also pure and permanent; in moderating them, keeps them in breath and appetite; in interdicting those which she herself refuses, whets our desire to those which she allows; and, like a kind and liberal mother, abundantly allows all that nature requires, even to satiety, if not to lassitude; unless we choose to say that the regimen that stops the toper's hand before he has drunk himself drunk, the glutton's before he has eaten to a surfeit, and the wencher's career before he needs a surgeon, is an enemy to pleasure. If the ordinary fortune fail her, she does without her, or frames another, wholly her own, not so fickle and unsteady. She can be rich, potent, and wise, and knows how to lie upon a soft and perfumed couch. She loves life, beauty, glory, and health; but her proper and peculiar office is to know how regularly to make

[1] Two heroines in Ariosto.

use of all these good things, and how to part with them without concern; an office much more noble than troublesome, and without which the whole course of life is unnatural, turbulent, and deformed; and there it is indeed that men may justly represent those monsters upon rocks and precipices. If this pupil shall happen to be of so cross and contrary a disposition that he had rather hear an idle tale than the true narrative of some noble expedition or some wise and learned discourse; who at the beat of a drum, that excites the youthful ardour of his companions, leaves that to follow another that calls to a morrice-dance or the bears; and who would not wish nor find it more delightful to return all over dust victorious from a battle than from tennis or a ball, with the prize of those exercises; I see no other remedy[1] but that he be bound apprentice in some good town to learn to make minced-pies, though he were the son of a duke; according to Plato's precept, "That children are to be placed out in life, not according to the condition of the father, but according to their own capacities."

Since philosophy is that which instructs us to live, and that

Philosophy ought to be taught to children

infancy has there its lessons as well as other ages, why is it not communicated to children betimes?

> Udum et molle lutum est; nunc, nunc properandus, et acri
> Fingendus sine fine rotâ.[2]

> "The clay is moist and soft; now, now make haste,
> And form the vessel, for the wheel turns fast."

They begin to teach us to live when we have almost done living. A hundred students have got the pox before they have come to read Aristotle's Lecture on Temperance. Cic-

---

[1] In M. Naigeon's edition the passage stands thus; "That his tutor in good time strangle him, if he is without witnesses: or that he be put," &c. "This *remarkable* passage," observes M. Naigeon, "is not found in any edition of the Essays, but it is in the handwriting of Montaigne, in the copy which he corrected. The remedy pointed out by this philosopher is one of those acts of rigour which the public interest or reasons of state sometimes command, and always justify." If this passage does not appear in any of the editions of Montaigne, it is doubtless because his enlightened mind recognized, upon reflection, the horrible abuses to which the introduction of such a *remedy* would lead.

[2] Persius, iii. 23.

ero said that, though he should live two men's ages, he should never find leisure to study the lyric poets ; and I find the Sophists yet more deplorably unprofitable. The boy we would train has a great deal less time to spare ; he owes but the first fifteen or sixteen years of his life to his tutor, the remainder is due to action ; therefore let us employ that short time in necessary instruction. Away with your crabbed logical subtleties ; they are abuses, things by which our lives can never be amended. Take me the plain discourses of philosophy, learn first how rightly to choose, and then rightly to apply them ; they are more easy to be understood than one of Boccaccio's novels ; a child from nurse is much more capable of them than of learning to read or to write. Philosophy has discourses equally proper for childhood as for old age.

I am of Plutarch's mind, that Aristotle did not so much trouble his great disciple with the knack of forming syllogisms, or with the elements of geometry, as with infusing into him good precepts concerning valour, prowess, magnanimity, temperance, and the contempt of fear ; and with this ammunition sent him, whilst yet a boy, with no more than 30,000 foot, 4,000 horse, and but 42,000 crowns, to subjugate the empire of the whole earth. As for the other arts and sciences, Alexander, he says, highly indeed commended their excellence, and had them in very great honour and esteem, but was not ravished with them to that degree as to be tempted to effect the practice of them in his own person.

Aristotle's method of instructing Alexander the Great.

Petite hinc, juvenesque senesque,
Finem animo certum, miserisque viatica canis.[1]

"Seek then, both old and young, from truths like these,
That certain aim which life's last cares may ease."

Epicurus, in the beginning of his letter to Meniceus, says that neither the youngest should refuse to philosophize, nor the eldest grow weary of it.[2] And who does otherwise seem tacitly to imply that either the time of living happily is not

[1] Persius, v. 64.   [2] Laertius, in Vitâ.

yet come, or that it is already past. Yet, for all that, I would not have this pupil of ours imprisoned and made a slave to his book ; nor would I have him given up to the morose and melancholic humour of a sour, ill-natured pedant. I would not have his spirit cowed and subdued by applying him to the rack and tormenting him, as some do, fourteen or fifteen hours a day, and so make a packhorse of him. Neither should I think it good when, by reason of a solitary and melancholy complexion, he is discovered to be too much addicted to his book, to nourish that humour in him, for that renders him unfit for civil conversation, and diverts him from better employments. And how many have I seen in my time totally brutified by an immoderate thirst after knowledge ! Carneades was so besotted with it that he would not find time so much as to comb his head or pare his nails.[1] Neither would I have his generous temper spoiled and corrupted by the incivility and barbarity of that of another French wisdom was anciently turned into a proverb, " Early, but of no continuance ; " and in truth we yet see that nothing can be more ingenuous and pretty than the children of France ; but they ordinarily deceive the hope and expectation that have been conceived of them, and, grown up to be men, have nothing extraordinary or worth taking notice of. I have heard men of good understanding say these colleges of ours, to which we send our young people (and of which we have but too many), make them such animals as they are.

But to our young friend, a closet, a garden, the table, his bed, solitude, and company, morning and evening, all hours Philosophy, the shall be the same, and all places to him a study ; formatrix of man- for philosophy, who, as the formatrix of judg- ners, is nowhere inactive. ment and manners, shall be his principal lesson, has that privilege to have a hand in every thing. The orator Isocrates being at a feast entreated to speak of his art, all the company were satisfied with and commended his answer.

[1] Laertius, *in Vitâ.*

"It is not now a time," said he, "to do what I can do; and that which it is now time to do I cannot do." [1] For to make orations and rhetorical disputes in a company met together to laugh and make good cheer had been very unseasonable and improper, and as much might be said of all the other sciences. But as to philosophy, that part of it at least that treats of man, and of his offices and duties, it has been the joint opinion of all wise men that, out of respect to the sweetness of her conversation, she is ever to be admitted in all sports and entertainments.[2] And Plato having invited her to his feast, we see after how gentle and obliging a manner, accommodated both to time and place, she entertained the company, though in a discourse of the sublimest and most salutary nature.

> Æquè pauperibus prodest, locupletibus æquè,
> Et, neglecta, æquè pueris senibusque nocebit.[3]

> "It profits poor and rich alike; and when
> Neglected, t' old and young is hurtful then."

By which method of instruction, my young pupil will be much more and better employed than those of the college are. But as the steps we take in walking to and fro in a gallery, though three times as many, do not tire a man so much as those we employ in a formal journey; so our lesson, occurring as it were accidentally, without any set obligation of time or place, and falling naturally in with every action, will insinuate insensibly itself. Our very exercises and recreations, running, wrestling, music, dancing, hunting, riding, and fencing, will prove to be a good part of our study. I would have his outward behaviour and mien, and the disposition of his limbs, formed at the same time with his mind. It is not a soul, it is not a body, that we are training up; it is a man, and we ought not to divide him into two parts; and, as Plato says, we are not to fashion one without the other, but make them draw together like two horses harnessed to a coach.[4]

---

[1] Plutarch, *Table-Talk.*
[2] Id. *Table-Talk.*
[3] Horace, *Epist.* i. 25.

[4] Plutarch, *on the Preservation of Health.*

By which saying of his, does he not seem to allow more time for, and to take more care of, exercises for the body, and to believe that the mind in a good proportion does her business at the same time too?

As to the rest, this method of education ought to be carried on with a firm gentleness, quite contrary to the practice of our pedants, who instead of tempting and alluring children to letters, present nothing before them but rods and ferules, horror and cruelty. Away with this violence! away with this compulsion! than which, I certainly believe nothing more dulls and degenerates a well-born nature. If you would have him fear shame and chastisement, do not harden him to them. Inure him to heat and cold, to wind and sun, and to dangers that he ought to despise. Wean him from all effeminacy in clothes and lodging, eating and drinking; accustom him to every thing, that he may not be a Sir Paris, a carpet-knight, but a sinewy, hardy, and vigorous young man. I have ever, from a child to the age wherein I now am, been of this opinion, and am still constant to it. But, amongst other things, the strict government of most of our colleges has always displeased me, and peradventure they might have erred less perniciously on the indulgent side. They are mere jails, where imprisoned youths are taught to be debauched, by being punished for it before they are so. Do but come in when they are about their lesson, and you shall hear nothing but the outcries of boys under execution, and the thundering of pedagogues, drunk with fury. A very pretty way this to tempt these tender and timorous souls to love their book! leading them on with a furious countenance, and a rod in hand! a wretched and pernicious way! besides what Quintilian has very well observed, that this insolent authority is often attended by very dangerous consequences, and particularly our way of chastising.[1] How much more decent would it be to see their classes strewed with leaves and flowers, than with bloody

Severity an enemy to education. (marginal note)

---

[1] *Instit. Orat.* i. 3.

stumps of birch! Were it left to my ordering, I should paint the school with pictures of joy and gladness, Flora and the Graces, as the philosopher Speusippus did his;[1] that where their profit is they might there have their pleasure too. Such viands as are proper and wholesome for children should be seasoned with sugar, and such as are dangerous to them with gall. It is admirable to see how solicitous Plato is in his laws for the gayety and diversion of the youth of his city, and how he enlarges upon their races, sports, songs, leaps, and dances; of which he says that antiquity has given the ordering and patronage to the gods themselves, to Apollo, Minerva, and the Muses. He insists upon a thousand precepts for exercise; but as to the lettered sciences says very little, and only seems particularly to recommend poetry upon the account of music.

All singularity in our manners and condition should be avoided, as obnoxious to society. Who is not astonished at so strange a constitution as that *Singularity of manners to be avoided.* of Demophoon, steward to Alexander the Great, who sweated in the shade, and shivered in the sun?[2] I have seen those who have run from the smell of an apple with greater precipitation than from a harquebuss shot; others are afraid of a mouse; others vomit at the sight of cream; others at seeing a bed shaken; and there was Germanicus, who could neither endure the sight nor the crowing of a cock.[3] There may, peradventure, be some occult cause for these aversions in these cases; but certainly, in my opinion, a man might conquer them, if he took them in time. Precept has in this wrought so effectually upon me, though not without some endeavour on my part, I confess, that, beer excepted, my appetite accommodates itself indifferently to all sorts of diet.

Young bodies are supple; one should therefore in that age bend and ply them to all fashions and customs;

---

[1] Laertius, *in Vitâ.*   [3] Plutarch, *On Tastes and Distastes.*
[2] Sextus Empiricus, *Pyrrh. Hypot.* l.
14.

Young men should be habituated to all customs, so as to be able to comply with them to excess, if need be.

and, provided a man can restrain the appetite and the will within limits, let a young man be rendered fit for all nations and all companies, even to debauchery and excess, if occasion be, that is, where he shall do it out of complaisance to the customs of a place. Let him be able to do every thing, but love to do nothing but what is good. The philosophers themselves do not justify Calisthenes for forfeiting the favour of his master, Alexander the Great, by refusing to pledge him a cup of wine. Let him laugh, carouse, and debauch with his prince; nay, I would have him, even in his debauches, excel his companions in ability and vigour, so that he may not give over doing it either through defect of power or knowledge how to do it, but for want of will. *Multum interest, utrum peccare aliquis nolit, aut nesciat.*[1] "There is a vast difference betwixt forbearing to sin, and not knowing how to sin." I thought I passed a compliment upon a Lord, as free from these excesses as any man in France, by asking him, before a great deal of good company, how many times in his life he had got drunk in Germany, in the time of his being there about his majesty's affairs; which he also took as it was intended, and made answer, three times; and withal, told us the whole story of his bouts. I know some who, for want of this faculty, have been put to great inconvenience in negotiating with that nation. I have often with great admiration reflected upon the wonderful constitution of Alcibiades, who so easily could transform himself to so various fashions, without any prejudice to his health;[2] one while outdoing the Persian pomp and luxury, and another the Lacedemonian austerity and frugality; as temperate in Sparta as voluptuous in Ionia.

> Omnis Aristippum decuit color, et status, et res.[3]

> "Old Aristippus every dress became,
> In every state and circumstance the same."

I would have my pupil to be such a one,

---

[1] Senec. *Epist.* 90.　　[2] Plutarch, *in Vitâ.*　　[3] Horace, *Epist* i. 17, 23.

Quem duplici panno patientia velat,
Mirabor, vitæ via si conversa decebit,
Personamque feret non inconcinnus utramque.[1]

" But that a man whom patience taught to wear
A coat that's patched, should ever learn to bear
A changed life with decency and grace,
May justly, I confess, our wonder raise."

These are my lessons, and he who puts them in practice shall reap more advantage than he who has had them read to him only, and only knows them. If you see him, you hear him; if you hear him, you see him. "The gods forbid," says one in Plato, " that to philosophize should be only to read a great many books, and to learn the arts."[2] *Hanc amplissimam omnium artium bene vivendi disciplinam vitâ magis quam litteris persequuti sunt.*[3] "They have more illustrated and improved this discipline of living well, which of all arts is the greatest, by their lives, than by their reading." Leo, prince of the Phlasians, asking Heraclides Ponticus of what art or science he made profession; "I know," said he, " neither art nor science, but I am a philosopher."[4] One reproaching Diogenes that, being ignorant, he should pretend to philosophy; " I, therefore," answered he, " pretend to it with so much the more reason."[5] Hegesias entreated that he would read a certain book to him. " You are an amusing person," said he, "you who choose those figs that are true and natural, and not those that are painted, why do you not also choose exercises which are natural and true, rather than those written ? "[6]

A man should not so much repeat his lesson as practise it; let him repeat it in his actions. We shall discover if there be in him prudence, by his undertakings; if goodness and justice, by his deportment; if grace and judgment, by his speaking; if

The progress a young man makes ought to be judged of by his actions.

[1] Horace, *Epist.* i. 25.
[2] In the *Rivals*.
[3] Cicero, *Tusc. Quæs.* iv. 3.
[4] It was not Heraclides, but Pythagoras, who returned this answer to Leo; but it is from a book of Heraclides, a dis-

ciple of Plato, that Cicero quotes this passage, in his *Tusc. Quæs.* v. 3. Plato was not born till above one hundred years after Pythagoras.
[5] Laertius, *in Vitâ.*
[6] Id. *ib.*

firmness, by his sickness; if modesty, by his recreations; temperance, by his pleasures; order, by the management of his affairs; and indifference, by his palate, whether what he eats or drinks be flesh or fish, wine or water. *Qui disciplinam suam non ostentationem scientiæ, sed legem vitæ putet; quique obtemperet ipse sibi, et decretis pareat.*[1] "Who considers his own discipline, not as a vain ostentation of science, but as a law and rule of life; and who obeys his own decrees, and observes that regimen he has prescribed to himself." The conduct of our lives is the true mirror of our doctrine. Zeuzidamus, to one who asked him why the Lacedemonians did not commit their constitutions of chivalry to writing, and deliver them to their young men to read, made answer that it was because they would inure them to action and not to words.[2] With such a one compare, after fifteen or sixteen years' study, one of our college Latinists, who has thrown away so much time in nothing but learning to speak. The world is nothing but babble; and I never yet saw that man who did not rather prate too much than speak too little; and yet half of our lives is lost this way. We are kept four or five years to learn words only, and to tack them together into phrases; as many more to put larger masses of these into four or five parts; and other five years, at least, to learn succinctly to mix and interweave them after some subtle and intricate manner. Let us leave such work to those who make it their trade.

Going one day to Orleans, I met, in the plain, on this side Clery, two pedants travelling to Bourdeaux,

The story of two pedagogues going to Bourdeaux.

about fifty paces distant from one another; and, a good way farther behind them, I saw a troop of horse with a gentleman at the head of them, the late Monsieur le Compte de la Rouchefoucault. One of my people inquired of the foremost of these Domines who that gentleman was that came after him; he, not having seen the train that followed after, and thinking my man meant his

---

[1] Cicero, *Tusc. Quæst.* ii. 4.   [2] Plutarch, *Apothegms.*

companion, pleasantly answered, " He is not a gentleman; he is a grammarian, and I am a logician." Now we, on the contrary, who do not here seek to breed a grammarian or a logician, but a gentleman, let us leave them to throw away their time at their own fancy; our business lies elsewhere. Let but our pupil be well furnished with things, words will follow but too fast; he will pull them after him, if they do not come voluntarily. *A youth of a good family ought to be more carefully instructed in the knowledge of things than of words.* I have observed some to make excuses that they cannot express themselves, and pretend to have their fancies full of a great many very fine things, which yet, for want of eloquence, they cannot bring out; a mere shift and nothing else. Will you know what I think of it? I think they are nothing but shadows of some imperfect images and conceptions that they know not what to make of within, nor consequently how to bring out; they do not yet themselves understand what they would be at, and if you but observe how they haggle and stammer upon the point of parturition, you will soon conclude that their labour is not in delivery, but in conception, and that they are but licking their formless embryo. For my part I hold, and Socrates is positive in it, that whoever has in his mind a vivid and clear idea, will express it well enough in one way or other; and if he be dumb, by signs.

Verbaque prævisam rem non invita sequentur.[1]

" When once a thing conceiv'd is in the wit,
Words soon present themselves to utter it."

And as another, as poetically, says in prose, *Cum res animum occupavere, verba ambiunt.*[2] " When things are once formed in the fancy, words offer themselves." And this other, *Ipsæ res verba rapiunt.*[3] " The things themselves force words to express them." He knows nothing of ablative, conjunctive, substantive, or grammar, no more than his

[1] Horace, *de Arte Poet.* 311.
[2] Seneca, *Controv.* iii.
[3] Cicero, *de Finib.* iii. 5.

lackey or a fishwife of the Petit-Pont; and these yet will give you your fill of talk, if you will hear them, and, peradventure, shall trip as little in their language as the best masters of art in France. He knows no rhetoric, nor how, in a preface, to bribe the benevolence of the courteous reader; neither does he care, nor is it very necessary he should know it. Indeed all this fine sort of painting is easily obscured by the lustre of a simple truth; these fine ingenious flourishes serve only to amuse the vulgar, of themselves incapable of more solid and nutritive diet, as Aper does very evidently demonstrate in Tacitus.[1] The ambassadors of Samos, prepared with a long elegant oration, came to Cleomenes, King of Sparta, to incite him to the war against the tyrant Polycrates; he, after he had heard their harangue with great gravity and patience, gave them this short answer: "As to the exordium I remember it not, nor consequently the middle of your speech, and as to your conclusion, I will not do what you desire."[2] A very pretty answer this, methinks, and a pack of learned orators no doubt finely gravelled! And what did this other say? The Athenians were to choose one of two architects for a great building they designed; the first, a pert affected fellow, offered his service in a long premeditated discourse upon the subject, and by his oratory inclined the voices of the people in his favour; but the other had his say in three words, "Lords of Athens, what this man hath said, I will do."[3] When Cicero was in the height and heat of his eloquence, many were struck with admiration; but Cato did only laugh at it, saying, "We have a pleasant Consul."[4] Let it go before, or come after, a good sentence,

1 *De Causis Corruptæ Eloquentiæ.*
2 Plutarch, *Apothegms.*
3 Plutarch, *Instructions to those who manage state affairs.*
4 Montaigne gives too general a latitude to Cato's reflections, though, perhaps, he did so for the purpose. Cato did not ridicule Cicero's eloquence in the general, but only his abuse of it while he was consul. When he was pleading one day for Murena against Cato, he fell to ridi-

culing the gravest principles of the stoic philosophy in too comic a manner, and, consequently not becoming the august station he then was in. This is what drew Cato's answer above mentioned, which was more stinging than all the invectives which Cicero had so lately cast at this great man, who was much more a stoic by his manners than by his discourses. Plutarch, *Life of Cato.*

a thing well said is always in season; if it neither suit well with what went before, nor has any very close coherence with what follows after, it is good in itself. I am none of those who think that good rhyme makes a good poem. Let the writer make short long, and long short, if he will, 'tis no great matter; if there be invention, and that the wit and judgment have well performed their office, I will say, here's a good poet, but an ill rhymer.

Emunctæ naris, durus componere versus.[1]

"He rallied with a gay and easy air,
But rude his numbers, and his style severe."

Let a man, says Horace, divest his work of all measures:

Tempora certa modosque, et, quod prius ordine verbum est,
Posterius facias, præponens ultima primis . . .
Invenias etiam disjecti membra poetæ.[2]

"Let tense and mood, and words be all misplaced,
Those last that should be first, those first the last;
Though all things be thus shuffled out of frame,
You'll find the poet's fragments not to blame."

He will never the more forfeit his praise; the pieces will be fine by themselves. Menander's answer _Invention the great test of true poetry._ had this meaning, who, being reproved by a friend, the time drawing on at which he had promised a comedy, that he had not yet put his hand to it, "It is ready," said he, "all but the verses."[3] Having contrived the subject and disposed the scenes in his head, he took little care for the rest. Since Ronsard and Du Bellay have given reputation to our French poetry, every little dabbler swells his words as high, and makes his cadences very near as harmonious, as they. _Plus sonat, quam valet._[4] "More sound than sense." There were never so many poetasters as now; but though they find it no hard matter to rhyme nearly as well as their masters, they yet fall altogether short of the

1 Horace, _Sat._ 4, i. 8.
2 Id. _ib._ 58.

3 Plutarch, _Whether the Athenians were more eminent in arms than in letters._
4 Seneca, _Epist._ 4.

rich descriptions of the one, and the delicate invention of the other.

But what will become of our young gentleman if he be Sophistical subtleties condemned. attacked with the sophistic subtilty of some syllogism? "A Westphalia ham makes a man drink, drink quenches thirst, therefore a Westphalia ham quenches thirst." Why, let him laugh at it, and it will be more discretion to do so than to go about to answer it,[1] or let him borrow this pleasant evasion from Aristippus; why should I trouble myself to untie that which, bound as it is, gives me so much trouble? A person offering at this dialectic juggling against Cleanthes, Chrysippus took him short, saying, "Reserve these baubles to play with children, and do not by such fooleries divert the serious thoughts of a man of years." [2] If these ridiculous subtleties, *Contorta et aculeata sophismata*,[3] "Perplexed and crabbed sophisms," are designed to possess him with an untruth, they are then dangerous; but if they remain without effect and only make him laugh, I do not see why a man need to be fortified against them. There are some so ridiculous as to go a mile out of their way to hook in a fine word. *Aut qui non verba rebus aptant, sed res extrinsecùs arcessunt quibus verba conveniant.*[4] "Who do not fit words to the subject, but seek out things quite from the purpose to fit those words they are so enamoured of." And, as another says, *Qui alicujus verbi decore placentis, vocentur ad id quod non proposuerant scribere.*[5] "Who, by their fondness of some fine sounding word, are tempted to something they had no intention to treat of." I, for my part, rather bring in a fine sentence by head and shoulders to fit my purpose than divert my designs to hunt after a sentence. 'Tis for words to serve and to follow us; and let Gascon come in play where French will not do.[6] I would have

1 Seneca, *Epist.* 49.
2 Laertius, *in Vitâ.*
3 Cicero, *Acad.* iv. 24.
4 Quintilian, viii. 3.
5 Seneca, *Epist.* 59.
6 Rousseau also says, somewhere, "Toutes les fois qu'à l'aide d'un solécisme je pourrai me faire mieux entendre, ne pensez pas que j'hésite." He made himself, however, very well understood without the help of any solecisms, and his declaration, therefore, seems unnecessary; but it shows, at least, that he was as little a slave to purism as our Gascon.

things so possess the imagination of him that hears that he should have something else to do than to think of words. The way of speaking that I love is natural and plain, as well in writing as speaking, and a sinewy and significant way of expressing one's self, short and pithy, and not so elegant and artificial as prompt and vehement.

> Hæc demum sapiet dictio, quæ feriet.[1]
>
> "The language which strikes the mind will please it."

Rather hard than harsh, free from affectation; irregular, incontinuous, and bold, where every piece makes up an entire body; not like a pedant, a preacher, or a pleader, but rather a soldierlike style, as Suetonius calls that of Julius Cæsar; and yet I see no reason why he should call it so.[2]

I have been ready enough to imitate the negligent garb which is observable among the young men of our time, to wear my cloak on one shoulder, my bonnet on one side, and one stocking in something more disorder than the other, which seems to express a kind of manly disdain of those exotic ornaments, and a contempt of art; but I find that negligence of even greater use in the form of speaking. All affectation, particularly in the French gayety and freedom, is ungraceful in a courtier, and in a monarchy every gentleman ought to be fashioned according to the court model; for which reason an easy and natural negligence does well. I like not a piece of stuff where the knots and seams are to be seen, and as little do I like, in a fine proportioned man, to be able to tell all the bones and veins. *Quæ veritati operam dat oratio, incomposita sit et simplex. Quis accuratè loquitur, nisi qui vult putidè loqui?*[3] "Let the language that is dedicated to truth be plain and unaffected. For who studies to speak quaintly and accurately that does

Affectation unbecoming a courtier.

---

[1] Lucan, *apud* Fabricius, *Biblioth. Lat.* li. 16.

[2] The expression is in Suetonius's *Life of Cæsar*, near the beginning. Montaigne, however, was misled by the common edition, which reads, "Eloquentia militari; qua re aut æquavit." &c.; whereas the later and better editions run thus, "Eloquentia, militarique re, aut æquavit," which removes Montaigne's objection to the passage.

[3] Seneca. *Epist.* 40, 75.

not, at the same time, design to perplex his auditory?" That eloquence prejudices the subject it would advance which wholly attracts us to itself. And as, in our outward habit, 'tis a ridiculous effeminacy to distinguish ourselves by a particular and unpractised garb or fashion ; so, in language, to study new phrases, and to affect words that are not of current use, proceeds from a childish and scholastic ambition. As for me, may I never use any other language than what is understood in the markets of Paris! Aristophanes, the grammarian, was quite out, when he reprehended Epicurus for this plain way of delivering himself, and that the end and design of his oratory was only perspicuity of speech.[1] The imitation of words by its own facility, immediately disperses itself through a whole people. But the imitation of invention and judgment in applying those words is of a slower progress. The generality of readers, when they find a like robe, very mistakingly imagine they have the same body inside it, but force and sinews are not to be borrowed, though the attire may. Most of those I converse with speak the same language I here write ; but whether they think the same thoughts I cannot say. The Athenians, says Plato, study length and elegance of speaking; the Lacedemonians affect brevity ; and those of Crete aim more at fecundity of conception than fertility of speech, and these are the best.[2] Zenon used to say that he had two sorts of disciples, one that he called φιλολόγως, curious to learn things, and these were his favourites ; the other, λογοφίλως, that cared for nothing but words.[3] Not but that proper speaking is a very good and commendable quality ; but 'tis not so excellent and so necessary as some would make it ; and I am scandalized that our whole life should be spent in nothing else. I would first understand my own language and that of my neighbours, with whom most of my business and conversation lies.

No doubt but Greek and Latin are very great ornaments

---

[1] Laertius, *Life of Epicurus*, x. sec. 13.   [3] Stobœus, *Serm.* 34.
[2] *Laws*, i.

and of great use, but we buy them too dear. I will here mention one way which also has been experimented in my own person, by which they

The mode in which Montaigne learned Latin;

are to be had cheaper than in the usual mode, and such may make use of it as will. My late father having made the most precise inquiry that any man can possibly make amongst men of the greatest learning and judgment, of an exact method of education, was by them cautioned of the inconvenience then in use, and informed that the tedious time we applied to the learning of the languages of those people who, themselves had them for nothing, was the sole cause we could not arrive to the grandeur of soul and perfection of knowledge of the ancient Greeks and Romans : I do not, however, believe that to be the only cause ; the expedient my father, however, found out for this was that, in my infancy, and before I began to speak, he committed me to the care of a German (who since died a famous physician in France), totally ignorant of our language, but very fluent and a great critic in Latin. This man, whom he had sent for out of his own country, and whom he entertained, at a very great salary, for this only end, had me continually with him. To whom there were also joined two others of the same nation, but of inferior learning, to attend me, and sometimes to relieve him ; who all of them conversed with me in no other language but Latin. As to the rest of his family, it was an inviolable rule that neither himself, nor my mother, nor man, nor maid, should speak any thing, in my company, but such Latin words as every one had learnt to gabble with me. It is not to be imagined how great an advantage this proved to the whole family ; my father and my mother, by this means, learning Latin enough to understand it perfectly well, and to speak it to such a degree as was sufficient for any necessary use ; as also those of the servants did who were most frequently with me. To be short, we did *Latin* it at such a rate that it overflowed to all the neighbouring villages, where there yet remain, and have established themselves by custom, several Latin appellations of artisans and their tools. As for myself, I was above six years of age before I understood either French or Perigordin any more than Arabic, and without art, book, grammar, or precept, whipping, or the expense of a tear, had by that time learned to speak as pure Latin as my master himself. If, for example, they were to give me a theme after the College fashion, they gave it to others in French, but to me they gave it in the worst Latin, to turn it into that which was pure and good; and Nicholas Grouchy, who wrote a book *de Comitiis Romanorum;* William Guerente, who has written a Commentary upon Aristotle; George Buchanan, that great Scotch Poet, and Marc Antony Muret, whom both France and Italy have acknowledged for the best orator of his time, my domestic tutors, have all of them often told me that I had in my infancy that language so very fluent and ready that they were afraid to enter into discourse with me. Buchanan, whom I since saw attending the late Mareschal de Brissac, then told me that he was about to write a Treatise of Education, the example of which he intended to take from mine, for he was then tutor to that Count de Brissac, who afterwards proved so valiant and so brave a gentleman.

As to Greek, of which I have but little smattering, my
and Greek.   father also designed to have taught it me by
art, but in a new way, and as a sort of sport; tossing out declensions to and fro, after the manner of those who, by certain games, at tables and chess, learn geometry and arithmetic; for he, amongst other rules, had been advised to make me relish science and duty by an unforced will, and of my own voluntary motion, and to educate my soul in all liberty and delight, without any severity or constraint. Which he was an observer of to such a degree, even of superstition, that some being of opinion it troubles and disturbs the brains of children suddenly to wake them in the morning, and to snatch them violently and over-hastily from

sleep (wherein they are much more profoundly involved than we), he only caused me to be waked by the sound of some musical instrument, and was never unprovided of a musician for that purpose. By which example you may judge of the rest, this alone being sufficient to recommend both the prudence and affection of so good a father; who, therefore, is not to be blamed if he did not reap the fruits answerable to so excellent a culture. Of which, two things were the cause: first, a sterile and improper soil; for though I was of a strong and healthful constitution, and of a disposition tolerably gentle and . tractable, yet I was, withal, so heavy, idle, and sluggish, that they could not rouse me even to any exercise of recreation, nor get me out to play. What I saw, I saw clear enough, and under this lazy complexion, nourished a bold imagination, and opinions above my age. I had a slothful wit, that would go no faster than it was led, a slow understanding, a languishing invention, and, above all, an incredible defect of memory; so that it is no wonder if, from all these, nothing considerable could be extracted. Secondly, like those who, impatient of a long and steady cure, submit to all sorts of prescriptions and receipts, the good man being extremely timorous of any way failing in a thing he had so wholly set his heart upon, suffered himself, at last, to be overruled by the common opinion, which always follows the lead of what has gone on before, like cranes; and falling in with the method of the time, having no longer about him those persons he had brought out of Italy, and who had given him his first models of education about him, he sent me, at six years of age, to the College of Guienne, at that time, the best and most flourishing in France. And there it was not possible to add any thing to the care he had to provide me the most able tutors, with all other circumstances of education, reserving also several particular rules contrary to the college practice; but so it was that, with all these precautions, it was a college still. My Latin immediately grew corrupt, and, by discontinuance, I have since lost all manner of use of it;

and so this new plan of education served me to no other end than only, at my first coming, to prefer me to the first forms; for at thirteen years old, that I left the college, I had gone through my whole course, as they call it, and, in truth, without any manner of improvement, that I can honestly brag of, in all this time.

The first thing that gave me any taste of books was the pleasure I took in reading the fables of Ovid's Metamorphoses; and with them I was so taken that, being but seven or eight years old, I would steal from all other diversions to read them, both by reason that this was my own natural language, the easiest book that I was acquainted with, and for the subject the most accommodated to the capacity of my age; for as for Lancelot du Lake, Amadis de Gaul, Huon of Bourdeaux, and such trumpery, which children are most delighted with, I had never so much as heard their names, no more than I yet know what they contain; so exact was the discipline wherein I was brought up. This made me think the less of the other lessons prescribed me; and here it was infinitely to my advantage to have to do with an understanding tutor, who was wise enough to connive at this and other truantries of the same nature; for by this means I ran through Virgil's Æneids, and then Terence, and then Plautus, and some Italian comedies, allured by the pleasure of the subject; whereas had he been so foolish as to have taken me off this diversion, I do really believe I had brought nothing away from the college but a hatred of books, as almost all our young gentlemen do. But he carried himself very discreetly in that business, seeming to take no notice, and heightened my appetite by allowing me only such time for this reading as I could steal from my regular studies. For the chief things my father expected from them to whom he had delivered me for education was affability of manners and good humour; and, to say the truth, my temper had no other vice but sloth and want of mettle. The fear was not that

Montaigne's first taste for reading.

I should do ill, but that I should do nothing. Nobody suspected that I should be wicked, but most thought I should be useless; they foresaw idleness, but no malice in my nature; and I find it falls out accordingly. The complaints I hear of myself are these: "He is idle, cold in the offices of friendship and relationship, and remiss in those of the public; he is too particular, he is too proud." The most injurious do not say, "Why has he taken such a thing?—why has he not paid such a one?" But "Why does he part with nothing?—why does he not give?" And I should take it for a favour that men would expect from me no greater effects of supererogation than these. But they are unjust to exact from me what I do not owe, far more rigorously than they exact from others that which they do owe; and in condemning me to it they efface the gratification of the act, and deprive me of the gratitude that would be due to me upon such a bounty; whereas the active benefit ought to be of so much the greater value from my hands, by how much I am not passive that way at all. I can the more freely dispose of my fortune the more it is mine, and of myself the more I am my own. Nevertheless, if I were good at setting out my own actions, I could peradventure very well repel these reproaches, and could give some to understand that they are not so much offended that I do not enough, as that I am able to do a great deal more than I do.

Yet for all this heavy disposition of mine, my mind, when retired into itself, was not altogether idle nor wholly deprived of solid inquiry nor of certain and clear judgments about those objects it could comprehend, and could also without any helps digest them; but, amongst other things, I do really believe it had been totally impossible to have made it to submit by violence and force. Shall I here acquaint you with one faculty of my youth? I had great boldness and assurance of countenance, and to that a flexibility of voice and gesture to any part I undertook to act; for before

Alter ab undecimo tum me vix ceperat annus,[1]

"I had hardly entered on my twelfth year,"

I played the chief parts in the Latin tragedies of Buchanan, Guerente, and Muret, that were acted in our college of Guienne with very great form; wherein Andreas Goveanus, our principal, as in all other parts of his undertaking, was, without comparison, the best of that employment in France, and I was looked upon as one of his chief actors. 'Tis an exercise that I do not disapprove in young people of condition, and I have since seen our princes, after the example of the ancients, perform such parts in person well and commendably; and it was moreover allowed to persons of the greatest quality to profess and make a trade of it in Greece. *Aristoni tragico actori rem aperit: huic et genus et fortuna honesta erant; nec ars, quia nihil tale apud Græcos pudori est, ea deformabat.*[2] "He imparted this affair to Aristo the tragedian, a man of a good family and fortune, which nevertheless did neither of them receive any blemish by that profession, nothing of that kind being reputed a disparagement in Greece." I have always taxed those with impertinence who condemn these entertainments, and those with injustice who refuse to admit such comedians as are worth seeing into our towns, and grudge the people that public diversion. A sensible plan of government takes care to assemble its citizens not only to the solemn duties of devotion, but also to sports and spectacles. They find society and friendship augmented by it; and besides, can there possibly be afforded a more orderly diversion than what is performed in the sight of every one, and very often in the presence of the supreme magistrate himself? I, for my part, think it desirable that the prince should sometimes gratify his people at his own expense, with paternal kindness as it were, and that in great and popular cities there should be theatres erected for such entertainments, if but to divert them from worse and more private actions.

[1] Virgil, *Eclog.* viii. 39.   [2] Livy, xxiv. 24.

To return to my subject; there is nothing like alluring the appetite and affection, otherwise you make' nothing but so many asses laden with books, and by virtue of the lash give them their pocket full of learning to keep; whereas, to do well, you should not only lodge it with them, but make them espouse it.

CHAPTER XXVI.

THAT IT IS FOLLY TO MEASURE TRUTH AND ERROR BY OUR OWN CAPACITY.

'Tis not perhaps without reason that we attribute facility of belief and easiness of persuasion to simplicity and ignorance, for I have heard belief compared to an impression stamped upon the soul, which, by how much softer and of less resistance it is, is the more easily imposed. *Ut necesse est lancem in librâ ponderibus impositis deprimi, sic animum perspicuis cedere.*[1] "As the scale of the balance must give way to the weight that presses it down, so the mind must of necessity yield to demonstration." By how much the soul is more empty and without counterpoise, with so much greater facility it yields under the weight of the first persuasion. This is the reason that children, the common people, women, and sick folks, are most apt to be led by the ears. But then, on the other hand, 'tis a very great presumption to slight and condemn all things for false that do not appear to us likely to be true; which is the ordinary vice of such as fancy themselves wiser than their neighbours. I was myself once one of these; and if I heard talk of dead folks walking, of prophecies, enchantments, witchcrafts, or any other story, I had no mind to believe,

[1] Cicero, *Acad. Quæs.* iv. 12.

Somnia, terrores magicos, miracula, sagas,
Nocturnos lemures, portentaque Thessala.[1]

" Can you in earnest laugh at all the schemes
  Of magic terrors, visionary dreams,
  Portentous prodigies, and imps of hell,
  The nightly goblins and enchanting spell? "

I presently pitied the poor people that were abused by these
follies; whereas I now find that I myself was to be pitied as
much, at least, as they; not that experience has taught me
any thing to supersede my former opinion, though my curiosity has endeavoured that way; but reason has instructed
me that thus resolutely to condemn any thing for false and
impossible, is to circumscribe and limit the will of God and
the power of nature within the bounds of my own capacity,
than which no folly can be greater. If we give the names
of monster and miracle to every thing our reason cannot comprehend, how many such are continually presented before
our eyes! Let us but consider through what clouds, and, as
it were, groping through what darkness, our teachers lead us
to the knowledge of most of the things we apply our studies
to, and we shall find that it is rather custom than knowledge
that takes away the wonder, and renders them easy and
familiar to us.

Jam nemo, fessus saturusque videndi, .
Suspicere in cœli dignatur lucida templa.[2]

" Already glutted with the sight, now none
  Heaven's lucid temples deigns to look upon."

And that if those things were now newly presented to us we
should think them as strange and incredible, if not more so,
than any others.

Si nunc primum mortalibus adsint
Ex improviso, ceu sint objecta repentè,
Nil magis his rebus poterat mirabile dici,
Aut minus ante quod auderent fore credere gentes.[3]

1 Horace, *Epist.* ii. 2, 208.   2 Lucretius, ii. 1037. The text has
3 Lucretius, ii. 1034.   *satiate videndi.*

" Were those things suddenly and by surprise
Just now presented, new to mortal eyes,
At nothing could they be astonish'd more,
Nor could have formed a thought of them before."

He that had never seen a river imagined the first he met
with to be the sea ; and the greatest things that have fallen
within our knowledge we conclude the extremes that nature
makes of the kind.

Scilicet, et fluvius qui non est maximus, ei est
Qui non ante aliquem majorem vidit; et ingens
Arbor, homoque videtur; et omnia de genere omni
Maxima quæ vidit quisque, hæc ingentia fingit.[1]

" A little river unto him does seem,
That bigger never saw, a mighty stream;
A tree, a man, all things seem to his view
O' th' kind the greatest that ne'er greater knew."

Consuetudine oculorum assuescunt animi, neque admiran-
tur, neque requirunt rationes earum rerum quas semper vident.[2]
" Things grow familiar to men's minds by being often seen ;
so that they neither admire nor are inquisitive into things
they daily see." The novelty, rather than the greatness of
things tempts us to inquire into their causes. But we are to
judge with more reverence, and with greater acknowledgment of our own ignorance and infirmity, of the infinite power
of nature. How many unlikely things are there testified by
people of very good repute, which if we cannot persuade
ourselves absolutely to believe, we ought at least to leave
them in suspense ! For to condemn them as impossible is
by a temerarious presumption to pretend to know the utmost
bounds of possibility. Did we rightly understand the difference betwixt the impossible and the unusual, and what is contrary to the order and course of nature and against the
common opinion of men, in not believing rashly, and on the
other hand in being not too incredulous, we should then
observe the rule of *Ne quid nimis,* enjoined by Chilo.[3]

[1] Lucretius, vi. 674.
[2] Cicero, *de Natura Deor.* ii. 38.
[3] Μηδέν ἄγαν, Aristotle in his *Rheto-*
ric, and Pliny (*Nat. Hist.* vii. 32), ascribe this maxim to Chilo, as does Diogenes
Laertius in the Life of Thales; but he
afterwards ascribes it to Solon in his Life
of Solon. It has been also attributed to
others. See Menage's Observations on
Diogenes Laertius in the Life of Thales.

When we find in Froissard that the Count de Foix knew in Bearn the defeat of John, King of Castile, at Juberoth, the next day after, and the means by which he tells us he came to do so, we may be allowed to be a little merry at it, as also at what our annals report, that Pope Honorius, the same day that King Philip Augustus died at Mante, performed his public obsequies at Rome, and commanded the like throughout Italy; the testimony of these authors not being perhaps of authority enough to restrain us. But if Plutarch, besides several examples that he produces out of antiquity, tells us, of his certain knowledge, that in the time of Domitian the news of the battle lost by Antony in Germany was published at Rome many days' journey thence,[1] and dispersed throughout the whole world the same day it was fought; and if Cæsar was of opinion that it has often happened that the report has preceded the event, shall we say that, forsooth, these simple people have suffered themselves to be deceived with the vulgar, not having been so clear-sighted as we? Is there any thing more delicate, more clear, more sprightly than Pliny's judgment, when he is pleased to set it to work?—any thing more remote from vanity? Setting aside his great learning, of which I make less account, in which of these two do any of us excel him? Yet there is no schoolboy that does not convict him of lying, and that pretends not to instruct him in the progress of the works of nature.

When we read in Bouchet the miracles of St. Hilary's relics, never heed them; his authority is not sufficient to take from us the liberty of contradicting him; but generally to condemn in a lump all such stories seems to me a singular impudence. The great St. Augustine tells us he himself saw a blind child recover sight upon the relic of St. Gervaise and St. Protasius at Milan;[2] a woman at Carthage cured of a cancer by the sign of the cross made upon her by a woman newly baptized; Hesperius, a familiar

---

[1] Above 840 leagues, says Plutarch, in his *Life of Paulus Æmilius*, but the real distance is only 250 leagues.

[2] *De Civit. Dei*, xxii. 8.

friend of his, to drive away the spirits that haunted his house with a little earth of the sepulchre of our Lord;[1] and this earth being transported thence into the church, a paralytic to have there been suddenly cured by it; a woman in a procession, having touched St. Stephen's shrine with a nosegay, and after rubbing her eyes with it to have recovered her sight lost many years before; with several other miracles, of which he professes himself to have been an eyewitness. Of what shall we accuse him and the two holy bishops Aurelius and Maximinus, both of whom he attests to the truth of these things? Shall it be of ignorance, simplicity, and facility, or of knavery or imposture? Is any man now living so impudent as to think himself comparable to them either in virtue, piety, learning, judgment, or capacity? *Qui, ut rationem nullam afferrent, ipsâ auctoritate me frangerent?*[2] "Who, though they should give me no reason for what they affirm, would yet convince me with their authority?" 'Tis a presumption of great danger and consequence, besides the absurd temerity it draws after it, to contemn what we do not comprehend. For after that, according to your fine understanding, you have established the limits of truth and error, and that afterwards there appears a necessity upon you of believing stranger things than those you have contradicted, you are already obliged to quit your hold and to acquiesce. That which seems to me so much to disorder our consciences, in the commotions we are now in concerning religion, is the Catholics dispensing so much with their belief. They fancy they appear moderate and wise when they give up to the Huguenots some of the articles in question; but besides that they do not discern what advan-

---

[1] St. Austin, however, does not ascribe this expulsion of the evil spirits to that small quantity of the earth of our Lord's sepulchre, which Hesperius had in his house; for, according to St. Austin, one of his priests having repaired to his house and offered the sacrifice of the body of Christ, and having prayed earnestly to God to put a stop to this disturbance, God did so at the very instant. As to the earth taken from the holy sepulchre, Hesperius kept it suspended in his own bedchamber, to secure him from the insults of the devils, who had been very mischievous to his slaves and cattle; for though he was protected against the evil spirits of the earth, yet this influence did not extend to the rest of his family.

[2] Cicero, *Tusc. Quæs.* i. 21.

tage it is to those with whom we contend for us to begin to give ground and to retire, and how much this animates the enemy to follow up his blow, the articles which they select as the most indifferent are sometimes of very great importance. We are either wholly and absolutely to submit ourselves to the authority of our ecclesiastical polity, or totally throw off all obedience to it; 'tis not for us to determine what and how much obedience we owe to it. And this I can say, having myself made trial of it, and having formerly taken the liberty of my own swing and fancy, and neglected certain of the observations of our church which seemed to me vain and unmeaning, that, coming afterwards to discourse the matter with learned men, I have found those very things to be built upon very good and solid foundation; and that nothing but dulness and ignorance make us receive them with less reverence than the rest. Why do we not consider what contradictions we find in our own judgments, how many things were yesterday articles of our faith that to-day appear mere fables? Glory and curiosity are the scourges of the soul; of which the last prompts us to thrust our noses into every thing, and the other forbids us to leave any thing doubtful and undecided.

CHAPTER XXVII.

OF FRIENDSHIP.

HAVING observed the method of a painter I have, that serves me, I had a mind to imitate his way. He chooses the best place, the middle of a panel, wherein to draw a picture, which he finishes with his utmost care and art, and the empty space he fills with grotesque, odd, fantastic figures, without any grace but what they derive from their variety

and the extravagance of their shapes. And, in truth, what
are these things I scribble, other than grotesques, monstrous
pieces of patchwork, without any certain figure, or any other
than accidental order, coherence, or proportion ?

Desinit in piscem mulier formosa supernè.[1]
" That a fair woman's face above doth show,
But in a fish's tail doth end below."

In this second part I go hand in hand with my painter,
but fall very short of him in the first, and the better ; my
power of handling not being such that I dare to offer as a
fine piece richly painted and set off according to art. I have
therefore thought best to borrow one of Estienne de la Boetie,[2] and such a one as will honour and adorn all the rest of
my work ; namely, a discourse that he called Voluntary Servitude, which others have since further baptized Le Contre-
Un,[3] a piece written in his younger years, by way of essay,
in honour of liberty against tyrants, and which has since been
in the hands of several men of great learning and judgment,
not without singular and merited commendation, for it is
finely written and as full as any thing can possibly be. Yet
I may confidently say it is far short of what he is able to do ;
and if in that more mature age wherein I knew him, he had
taken a design like this of mine, to commit his thoughts to
writing, we should have seen a great many rare things, and
such as would have gone very near to have rivalled the best
writings of antiquity ; for in natural parts, especially, I know
no man comparable to him. But he has left nothing behind
him save this treatise only (and that too by chance, for I
believe he never saw it after it first went out of his hands),
and some observations upon that edict of January,[4] made

[1] Horace, de Arte Poet. 4.
[2] Yet it is not here; and why Montaigne has not inserted it he tells us at the end of the chapter.
[3] Meaning a discourse against mon-archy, or government by one person alone, agreeably to what Montaigne says at the end of this chapter, " That if Boe-

tius could have made his option. he would rather have been born at Venice than at Sarlac."
[4] Promulgated in 1562, in the reign of Charles IX., then a minor. This edict permitted to the Huguenots the public exercise of their religion. The parliament at first refused to register it, saying,

famous by our civil wars, which also shall elsewhere, peradventure, find a place. These were all I could recover of his
remains; I, to whom, with so affectionate a remembrance,
upon his death-bed, he by his last will bequeathed his library
and papers, the little book of his works only excepted, which
I committed to the press.[1] And this particular obligation I
have to this treatise of his, that it was the occasion of my
first coming acquainted with him; for it was showed to me
long before I saw him, and gave me the first knowledge of
his name; proving so the first cause and foundation of a
friendship which we afterwards improved and maintained so
long as God was pleased to continue us together, so perfect,
inviolate, and entire, that certainly the like is hardly to be
found in story, and amongst the men of this age there is no
sign nor trace of any such thing. So many concurrents are
required to the building of such a one, that 'tis much if fortune bring it but once to pass in three ages.

There is nothing to which nature seems so much to have
inclined us as to society; and Aristotle says[2] that good legislators had more respect to friendship than to justice. Now

Perfect friendship, what it is. the most supreme point of its perfection is this:
for generally all those that pleasure, profit,
public or private interest, create and nourish, are so much

Friendship does not tally properly with the four sorts of connection dis-tinguished by the ancients. the less noble and generous, and so much the
less friendships, by how much they mix up
another cause and design than friendship itself.
Neither do the four ancient kinds, natural, sociable, hospitable, and venerean, either separately or jointly,
make up a true and perfect friendship.

That of children to parents is rather respect; friendship
being nourished by communication, which cannot, by reason
of the great disparity, be betwixt them; but would rather

"Nec possumus, nec debemus;" but
they consented, after receiving two positive orders from the king on the subject.
The edict contains a rule of conduct for
the Protestants, which, among other
things, directs that "they shall advance

nothing against the Council of Nicea,
against the symbol, or against the Old
and New Testament."

[1] It was published at Paris, in 1571, by
Frederick Morel.
[2] *Ethics,* viii. 1.

perhaps violate the duties of nature; for neither are all the secret thoughts of fathers fit to be communicated to children, lest it beget an indecent familiarity betwixt them; nor can the advices and reproofs, which is one of the principal offices of friendship, be properly performed by the son to the father. There are some countries where 'tis the custom for children to kill their fathers; and others where the fathers kill their children, to prevent their being sometimes an impediment to one another in their designs; and moreover, the expectation of the one does naturally depend upon the ruin of the other. There have been great philosophers who have made nothing of this tie of nature; as Aristippus for one, who, being pressed home about the affection he owed to his children, as being come from him, presently fell to spit, saying that also came from him, and that we did also breed worms and lice; [1] and that other, that Plutarch endeavoured to reconcile to his brother, "I make never the more account of him," said he, "for coming out of the same place." [2] This name of brother does indeed carry with it an amiable and affectionate sound, and for that reason he and I called one another brothers." [3] But the complication of interests, the division of estates, the raising of the one at the undoing of the other, does strangely weaken and slacken the fraternal tie; and brothers pursuing their fortune and advancement by the same path, 'tis hardly possible but they must of necessity often jostle and hinder one another. Besides, why should the correspondence of manners, parts, and inclinations, which beget true and perfect friendships, always meet and concur in these relations? The father and the son may be of quite contrary humours, and brothers be without any manner of sympathy in their natures. He is my son, he is my father; but he is passionate, ill-natured, or a fool. And moreover, by how much these are

[1] Laertius, *in Vitâ.*
[2] Plutarch, *on Brotherly Love.*
[3] That is to say that, according to the usage established in Montaigne's time, they gave one another the style of brothers, as it was to be the token and pledge of the friendship which they had contracted. And upon the same principle Mademoiselle de Gournay styled herself Montaigne's daughter, and not because Montaigne married her mother, as I have heard it affirmed.

friendships that the law and natural obligation impose upon
us, so much less is there of our own choice and freewill,
which freewill of ours has no creation properly its own than
through affection and friendship.   Not that I have not in my
own person experienced all that can possibly be expected of
that kind, having had the best and most indulgent father, even
to an extreme old age, that ever was, and who was himself
descended from a family for many generations famous and
exemplary for brotherly concord : —

> Et ipse
> Notus in fratres animi paterni.[1]
> " And he himself noted the rest above
> Towards his brothers for paternal love."

We are not here to bring the love we bear to women,
though it be an act of our own choice, into comparison ; nor
rank it with the others.   Its fire, I confess,

> Neque enim est Dea nescia nostri
> Quæ dulcem curis miscet amaritiem ;[2]
> " Nor is my goddess ign'rant what I am,
> Who pleasing sorrows mixes with my flame ;"

is more active, more eager, and more sharp ; but, withal, 'tis
more precipitous, fickle, moving, and inconstant ; a fever subject to intermission and paroxysms, that has hold but on one
part of us ; whereas, in friendship, 'tis a general and universal fire, but temperate and equal, a constant and steady heat,
all easy and smooth, without poignancy or roughness.   Moreover, in love, 'tis no other than a frantic desire for that which
flies from us :

> Come segue la lepre il cacciatore
> Al fredo, al caldo, alla montagna, al lito ;
> Ne più la stima poi che presa vede,
> E sol dietro a chi fugge affretta il piede :[3]
> " Like hunters that the flying hare pursue
> O'er hill and dale, through heat and morning dew,
> Which being ta'en, the quarry they despise,
> Being only pleased in following that which flies."

So soon as ever it enters into the terms of friendship, that

---

[1] Horace, *Od.* ii. 2, 6.　　　[2] Catul. *Epist.* lxvii. 17.　　　[3] Ariosto, x. Stanza 7.

is to say, into a concurrence of desires, it vanishes and is gone, fruition destroys it, as having only a fleshly end, subject to satiety. Friendship, on the contrary, is enjoyed proportionably as it is desired, and only grows up, is nourished and improves by enjoyment, as being spiritual, and the soul growing still more perfect by use. Under this perfect friendship I cannot deny but that the other vain affections have, in my younger years, found some place in my thoughts, to say nothing of him, who himself confesses it but too much in his verses; so that I had both these passions, but always so that I could myself well enough distinguish them, and never in any degree of comparison with one another; the first maintaining its flight at so lofty a height as with disdain to look down and see the other flying at a far humbler pitch below.

As to marriage, besides that it is a covenant the making of which is only free, but the continuance in it forced and compelled, having another dependence than that of our own freewill, and a bargain, moreover, commonly contracted to other ends, there happen a thousand intricacies in it to unravel, enough to break the thread, and to divert the current, of a lively affection; whereas, friendship has no manner of business or traffic with any thing but itself. Moreover, to say truth, the ordinary talent of women is not such as is sufficient to maintain the conference and communication required to the support of this sacred tie; nor do they appear to be endued with firmness of mind to endure the constraint of so hard and durable a knot. Doubtless if there could be such a free and voluntary familiarity contracted, where not only the souls might have this entire fruition, but the bodies also might share in the alliance, and the whole man be engaged in it, the friendship would certainly be more full and perfect; but there is no example that this sex ever arrived at such perfection, and, by the ancient schools, is wholly rejected. That other, the Grecian license, justly abhorred by our manners, from having, according to their practice, a so necessary dis- Friendship against nature very much in use among the Greeks. Montaigne's opinion of it.

parity of age and difference of offices betwixt the lovers, answers as little to the perfect union and harmony of the lovers
that we here require.   *Quis est enim iste amor amicitiæ ?*
*Cur neque deformem adolescentem quisquam amat, neque for-
mosum senem ?* [1] " For what is the love of friendship ? Why
does no one love a deformed youth or a comely old man ? "
The very picture that the Academy presents of it will not, as
I conceive, contradict me when I say that the first fury inspired by the son of Venus, in the heart of the lover, upon
the sight of blooming youth, to which they allow all the
insolent and passionate efforts that an immoderate ardour can
produce, was simply founded upon an external beauty, the
false image of corporal generation ; for upon the soul it could
not ground this love, the sight of which, as yet, lay concealed,
was but now springing up, and not of maturity to blossom.
Which fury, if it seized upon a mean spirit, the means by
which he preferred his suit were rich presents, advancement
to dignities, and other such trumpery, which they by no
means approve ; if on a more generous soul the pursuit was
suitably generous, by philosophical instructions, precepts to
revere religion, to obey the laws, to die for the good of his
country ; by examples of valour, prudence, and justice, the
lover studying to render himself acceptable by the grace and
beauty of his soul, that of his body being long since faded
and decayed, hoping by this mental society to establish a
more firm and lasting contract.   When this courtship came
to its effect, in due season, for that which they do not require
in the lover, namely, leisure and discretion in his pursuit, they
strictly require in the person loved ; forasmuch as he is to
judge of an internal beauty, of difficult knowledge, and
obscure discovery, then there sprung in the person loved,
the desire of a spiritual conception by the mediation of a
spiritual beauty.   This was the principal, the corporeal
but an accidental and secondary part, all contrary to the
lover.   For this reason they prefer the person beloved,

---

[1] Cicero, *Tusc. Quæs.* iv. 33.

maintaining that the gods, in like manner, prefer him too, and very much blame the poet Æschylus for having, in the loves of Achilles and Patroclus, given the lover's part to Achilles, who was in the first flower and pubescency of his youth, and the handsomest of all the Greeks. After this general familiarity and mutual community of thoughts, is once settled, supposing the sovereign and most worthy part to govern and to perform its proper offices, they say that thence great utility was derived, both to private and public concerns, that the power of countries received its beginning thence, and that it was the chief security of liberty and justice. Of which the salutary loves of Harmodius and Aristogiton is an instance; and, therefore, it is that they called it sacred and divine, and conceived that nothing but the violence of tyrants and the baseness of the common people was inimical to it. In short, all that can be said in favour of the Academy is that it was a love which ended in friendship; which well enough agrees with the stoical definition of love: *Amorem conatum esse amicitiæ faciendæ ex pulchritudinis specie.*[1] "That love is a desire of contracting friendship from the beauty of the object."

I return to my own more just and true description. *Omninò amicitiæ, corroboratis jam confirmatisque et ingeniis et ætatibus, judicandæ sunt.*[2] "Those are only to be reputed friendships that are fortified and confirmed by judgment and length of time." For the rest, what we commonly call friends and friendships are nothing but an acquaintance and connection, contracted either by accident or upon some design, by means of which there happens some little intercourse betwixt our souls; but, in the friendship I speak of, they mingle and melt into one piece, with so universal a mixture that there is left no more sign of the seam by which they were first conjoined. If any one should importune me to give a reason why I loved him, I feel it could no otherwise be expressed than by making answer, " Because it was he ; be-

---

[1] Cic. *Tusc. Quæs.* iv. 34.   [2] Id. *de Amicitiâ,* c. 20.

cause it was I." There is beyond what I am able to say,
I know not what inexplicable and inevitable power that
brought on this union. We sought one another long before
we met, and from the characters we heard of one another,
which wrought more upon our affections than in reason mere
reports should do, and, as I think, by some secret appointment of heaven ; we embraced each other in our names ; and
at our first meeting, which was accidentally at a great city
entertainment, we found ourselves so mutually pleased with
one another, we became, at once, mutually so endeared, that
thenceforward nothing was so near to us as one another.
He wrote an excellent Latin satire, which is printed,[1] wherein
he excuses and explains the precipitateness of our intimacy,
so suddenly come to perfection. Having so short a time to
continue, as being begun so late, for we were both full grown
men, and he some years the older, there was no time to lose ;
nor was it tied to conform itself to the example of those slow
and regular friendships that require so many precautions of a
long preliminary conversation. This has no other idea than
that of itself, and can have no relation but to itself. 'Tis no
one particular consideration, nor two, nor three, nor four, nor
a thousand. 'Tis I know not what quintes-
sence of all this mixture which, seizing my
whole will, carried it to plunge and lose itself in his ; and
that having seized his whole will, brought it, with equal concurrence and appetite, to plunge and lose itself in mine. I
may truly say lose, reserving nothing to ourselves that was
either his or mine.

The quintessence of true friendship.

When Lælius, in the presence of the Roman Consuls, who,
after they had sentenced Tiberius Gracchus, prosecuted all
those who had any familiarity with him also, came to ask

[1] In the collection, before mentioned.
—Paris, 1571. The following are some
of the verses spoken of by Montaigne

Prudentum bona pars vulgo male credula
    nulli
Fidit amicitiæ, nisi quam exploraverit
    ætas,
Et vario casus luctantem exercuit usu.

At nos jungit amor paullo magis annuus,
    et qui
Nil tamen ad summum reliqui sibi fecit
    amorem . . .
Te, Montane, mihi casus sociavit in
    omnes
Et natura potens, et amoris gratior illex,
Virtus .   .   .

Caius Blosius, who was his chief friend and confidant, how much he would have done for him? he made answer, "All things." "How! All things!" said Lælius. "And what if he had commanded you to fire our temples?" "He would never have commanded me that," replied Blosius. "But what if he had?" said Lælius. "I would have obeyed him," said the other.[1] If he was so perfect a friend to Gracchus as the histories report him to have been, there was yet no necessity of offending the consuls by such a bold confession, though he might still have retained the assurance he had of Gracchus's disposition. Still, those who accuse this answer as seditious, do not well understand the mystery; nor presuppose, as was the fact, that he had Gracchus's will in his sleeve, both by the power of a friend and the perfect knowledge he had of the man. They were more friends than citizens, and more friends to one another than either friends or enemies to their country, or than friends to ambition and innovation. Having absolutely given up themselves to one another, each held absolutely the reins of the other's inclination, which they governed by virtue, and guided by the conduct of reason; which, without these, it is not possible to do, and, therefore, Blosius's answer was such as it ought to have been. If their actions flew out of the handle, they were neither, according to my notion, friends to one another nor to themselves. As to the rest, this answer carries no worse sound than mine would do to one that should ask me, "If your will should command you to kill your daughter, would you do it?" And that I should make answer that I would; for this expresses no consent to such an act, forasmuch as I do not, in the least, suspect my own will, and as little should I that of such a friend. 'Tis not in the power of all the eloquence in the world to dispossess me of the certainty I have of the intentions and resolutions of mine; nay, no one action of his, what face soever it might bear, could be presented to me, of which I could not presently, and at first sight, find

---

[1] Plut. *Lives of the Gracchi*, c. 5. Cic. *De Amicit.* c. 2.

out the moving cause. Our souls have drawn so unitedly together, and we have, with so mutual a confidence, laid open the very bottom of our hearts to one another's view, that I not only knew his as well as my own, but should, certainly, in any concern of mine, have trusted my interest much more willingly with him than with myself. Let no one, therefore, rank common friendship with such a one as this. I have

The idea of common friendship.

had as much experience of these as another, and of the most perfect of their kind ; but I do not advise that any should confound the rules of the one and the other ; for they would find themselves much deceived. In ordinary friendships you must walk bridle in hand, with prudence and circumspection, for in them the knot is not so sure that a man may not fully depend upon its not slipping. " Love him," said Chilo, " so as if you were one day to hate him ; and hate him so as you were one day to love him." [1] A precept that, though abominable in the sovereign and perfect friendship which I speak of, is, nevertheless, very sound as to ordinary cases, and to which the saying that Aristotle had so frequently in his mouth, " O my friends, there is no friend," [2] may very fitly be applied. In this glorious com-

Amongst friends all things are common.

merce, the good offices, and benefits, by which other friendships are supported and maintained, do not deserve so much as to be mentioned, and are, by this concurrence of our wills, rendered of no use. As the kindness I have for myself receives no increase, for any thing I relieve myself withal, in time of need, whatever the Stoics say, and as I do not find myself obliged to myself for any service I do myself, so the union of such friends, being really perfect, deprives them of all idea of acknowledgment of such duties, and makes them loathe and banish from

---

[1] Aulus Gellius, i. 3. Diogenes Laertius, *In the Life of Bias,* attributes this saying to that wise man, i. 87, as Aristotle had done before, in his *Rhetoric,* ii. 13, where we read the second article, viz : " That a man should be hated as if some day hereafter he should be loved ; " which is not in Diogenes Laertius. As to the first article, " That a man should only be loved as if he were some day to be hated," Cicero says that he cannot imagine such an expression came from Bias, one of the seven wise men. *De Amicitiâ,* 16.

[2] Laertius, *in Vitâ,* v. 21.

their conversation these words implying a difference and distinction, benefit, obligation, entreaty, thanks, and the like.
All things, wills, thoughts, opinions, goods, wives, children,
honour, and life, being, in effect, common betwixt them, and
their condition being no other than one soul in two bodies,
according to the very proper definition of Aristotle,[1] they
can neither lend nor give any thing to one another. This is
the reason why the lawgivers, to honour marriage with some
imaginary resemblance of this divine alliance, interdict all
gifts betwixt man and wife ; inferring by that that all should
belong to each of them, and that they have nothing to divide
between or to give one another. If, in the friendship of
which I speak, one could give to the other, the *In perfect friend-*
receiver of the benefit would be the man that *ship the giver is*
obliged to the
obliged his friend ; for each of them, above all *receiver.*
things, studying how to be useful to the other, he that affords
the occasion is the generous man, in giving his friend the
satisfaction of doing that which, above all things, he does
most desire. When the philosopher, Diogenes, wanted
money, he used to say that he re-demanded it of his
friends, not that he demanded it ;[2] and to let you see the
practice of this, I will here produce an ancient and singular
example : Eudamidas, a Corinthian, had two friends, Charixenus, a Syconian, and Aretheus, a Corinthian ; this man
coming to die, being poor, and his two friends being rich, he
made his will, after this manner : " I bequeathe to Aretheus
the maintenance of my mother, to support and provide for
her in her old age ; and to Charixenus I bequeathe the care
of marrying my daughter, and to give her as good a portion
as he is able ; and in case one of these chances to die, I here-
by substitute the survivor in his place."[3] They who first
saw this will made themselves very merry at the contents ;
but the heirs being made acquainted with it, accepted the
legacies with very great content ; and one of them, Charixenus, dying within five days after, and Aretheus having thus

1 Laertius, *in Vità*, v. 20.   2 Id. *ib.*   3 Lucian, *Tozaris*, c. 22.

the charge of both devolved solely to him, he nourished the
old woman with very great care and tenderness, and, of five
talents he had, gave two and a half in marriage with an only
daughter he had of his own, and two and a half in marriage
with the daughter of Eudamidas, and in one and the same
day solemnized both their nuptials. This example is very
full to the point, if one thing were not to be
objected, namely, the multitude of friends; for
the perfect friendship I speak of is indivisible; each one
gives himself so entirely to his friend that he has nothing left
to distribute to others; nay, is sorry that he is not double,
treble, or quadruple, and that he has not many souls and
many wills to confer them all upon this one
object. Common friendships will admit of division, one may love the beauty of this, the
good humour of that person, the liberality of a third, the
paternal affection of a fourth, the fraternal love of a fifth,
and so on. But this friendship that possesses the whole soul,
and there rules and sways with an absolute sovereignty, can
admit of no rival. If two, at the same time, should call to
you for succour, to which of them would you run? Should
they require of you contrary offices, how could you serve
them both? Should one commit a thing to your secrecy that
it were of importance to the other to know, how would you
disengage yourself? The one particular friendship disunites and dissolves all other obligations
whatsoever. The secret I have sworn not to
reveal to any other I may, without perjury, communicate to
him who is not another, but myself. 'Tis miracle enough,
certainly, for a man to double himself, but they that talk of
tripling, talk they know not of what. Nothing is extreme
that has its like; and whoso shall suppose that, of two, I
love one as much as the other, that they love one another
too, and love me as much as I love them, does multiply into
a society that which is the most single and *one* of all things,
and wherein, moreover, one only is the hardest thing in the

*Perfect friendship
is indivisible.*

*The ordinary
friendships may
be shared by
many persons.*

*A singular and
prime friendship
dissolves all other
obligations.*

world to find. The remaining part of this story suits **very** well with what I said before; for Eudamidas, as a bounty and favour, bequeathes to his friends a legacy of employing themselves in his service; he leaves them heirs to this liberality of his, which consists in giving them the opportunity of conferring a benefit upon him, and, doubtless, the force of friendship is more eminently apparent in this act of his than in that of Aretheus. In short, there are effects not to be imagined nor comprehended by such as have no experience of them, and which make me infinitely honour and admire the answer of that young soldier to Cyrus, by whom, being asked how much he would take for a horse, with which he had won the prize of a race, and whether he would exchange him for a kingdom? " No, truly, sir," said he, " but I would give him with all my heart for a true friend, could I find a man worthy of that relation." [1] He did well in saying, *could I find*, for though a man may almost everywhere meet with men sufficiently qualified for a superficial acquaintance, yet, in this, where a man is to deal from the very bottom of his heart, without any manner of reservation, it will be requisite that all the wards and springs be true and plain, and perfectly sure. In leagues that hold but by What is necessary one end, we have only to provide against the in confederacies and in domestic imperfections that particularly concern that acquaintance. end. It can be of no importance to me of what religion my physician or my lawyer is, provided the one be a good lawyer, and the other a good physician; this consideration has nothing in common with the offices of friendship, and I am of the same indifferency in the domestic acquaintance my servants must necessarily contract with me; I never inquire, when I take a footman, if he be chaste, but if he be diligent; and am not solicitous if my chairman be given to gaming, so he be strong and able, or if my cook be a swearer, so he be a good cook. I do not, however, take upon me to direct what other men should do in such matters—there are those

[1] *Cyropædia*, viii. 3, sect. 11, 12.

that meddle enough with that—but only give an account of
what I do myself.

> Mihi sic usus est: tibi, ut opus est facto, face.[1]
>
> " This has my practice been: but thou may'st do
> What thy affairs or fancy prompt thee to."

At table, I prefer the witty before the grave; in bed,
beauty before goodness; and in common discourse, eloquence,
whether or no there be sincerity in the case. And as he[2]
that was found astride upon a stick, playing with his children,
entreated the person who had surprised him in that posture
to say nothing of it till he himself came to be a father, supposing that the fondness that would then possess his own soul
would render him a more equal judge of such an action, so I
also could wish to speak to such as have had experience of
what I say; though, knowing how remote a thing such a
friendship is from the common practice, and how rarely such
is to be found, I despair of meeting with any one qualified
to be a judge. For even the discourses left us by antiquity
upon this subject seem to me flat and low, in comparison of
the sense I have of it, and in this particular the effects surpass the very precepts of philosophy.

> Nil ego contulerim jucundo sanus amico.[3]
>
> " I know no pleasure that can health attend,
> Like the delight of an amusing friend."

Menander of old declared him to be happy that had the
good fortune to meet with but the shadow of a friend;[4] and
doubtless he had good reason to say so, especially if he spoke
by experience; for, in good earnest, if I compare all the rest
of my life,—though, thanks be to God, I have always passed
my time pleasantly enough and at my ease, and, the loss of
such a friend excepted, free from any grievous affliction, and
in great tranquillity of mind, having been contented with my

---

[1] Terence, *Heautont.* i. sc. 1, 28.   [3] Horace, *Sat.* i. 5, 44.
[2] *Agesilaus.* Plutarch, *in Vitâ.*   [4] Plutarch, *on Brotherly Love.*

natural and original conveniences and advantages, without being solicitous after others,—If I should compare it all, I say, with the four years I had the happiness to enjoy the sweet society of this excellent man, 'tis nothing but smoke, but an obscure and tedious night. From the day that I lost him,

> Quem semper acerbum,
> Semper honoratum (sic Dî voluistis!) habebo,[1]

> " Which, since 'tis Heaven's decree, though too severe,
> I shall lament, but ever shall revere,"

I have only led a sorrowful and languishing life ; and the very pleasures that present themselves to me, instead of administering any thing of consolation, double my affliction for his loss. We were halves throughout, and to that degree that, methinks, by outliving him I defraud him of his part.

> Nec fas esse ullâ me voluptate hic frui
> Decrevi, tantisper dum ille abest meus particeps.[2]

> " No pleasing thought shall e'er my soul employ
> While he is absent who was all my joy."

I was so accustomed to be always his second in all places, and in all things, that, methinks, I am no more than half a man, and have but half a being.

> Illam meæ si partem animæ tulit
> Maturior vis, quod moror altera?
>   Nec carus æquè, nec superstes
>   Integer. Ille dies utramque
> Duxit ruinam.[3]

> " For, since that half my soul was snatched away
> By riper age, why does the other stay?
> Which now's not dear, nor truly does survive
> That day our double ruin did contrive."

There is no act or imagining of mine wherein I do not miss him. For as he surpassed me by infinite degrees in virtue and all other accomplishments, so he also did in all offices of friendship.

[1] *Æneid*, v. 49.
[2] Terence, *Heautont.* i. 97. Montaigne has here made some little variation in Terence's words, for the sake of applying them to his subject.
[3] Horace, *Od.* ii. 17, 5.

Quis desiderio sit pudor, aut modus
Tam cari capitis?[1]

"Why should we stop the flowing tear?
Why blush to weep for one so dear?"

O misero frater adempte mihi!
Omnia tecum una perierunt gaudia nostra,
Quæ tuus in vitâ dulcis alebat amor.
Tu mea, tu moriens, fregisti commoda, frater;
Tecum una tota est nostra sepulta anima:
Cujus ego interitu totâ de mente fugavi
Hæc studia, atque omnes delicias animi.

Alloquar? audiero nunquam tua verba loquentem?
Nunquam ego te, vitâ frater amabilior,
Aspiciam posthac? at certè semper amabo.[2]

"Ah! brother, what a life did I commence,
From that sad day when thou wert snatched from hence!
Those joys are vanished which my heart once knew,
When in sweet converse all our moments flew:
With thee departing, my good fortune fled,
And all my soul is' lifeless since thou'rt dead.
The Muses at thy fun'ral I forsook,
And of all joy my leave for ever took.
Dearer than life! am I so wretched then,
Never to hear or speak to thee again?
Nor see those lips, now frozen up by death?
Yet I will love thee to my latest breath!"

But let us hear a boy of sixteen speak:—In this place I had intended to have inserted his Memoirs upon the famous edict of January; but as I have since found that they are already printed,[3] and with a malicious design, by some who make it their business to molest and endeavour to subvert the state of our government, not caring whether they mend and reform it or no; and that they have mixed up this writing Apology of Estienne de Boëtie. of his with others of their own leaven, I desist from that purpose. But that the memory of the author may not suffer with such as were not acquainted

---

[1] Horace, *Od.* i. 24, 1.
[2] Catullus, lxvii. 20, lxix. 9.
[3] Stephen de la Boëtie's *Traité de la Servitude Volontaire* was printed for the first time in 1578, in the third volume of the *Mémoires de l' Estat de la France* *sous Charles IX.* The second title of this work, *Le Contr'un* (translated by De Thou, *Ant-Henoticon*), is rendered by Vernier, in his *Notice sur les Essais de Montaigne,* "*Les Quatres Contre un,*"—a curious blunder.

with his principles, I here give them to understand that it was written by him in his very early years, and that by way of exercise only, as a common theme that has been tumbled and tossed about by a thousand writers. I make no question but that he himself believed what he wrote, being so conscientious that way that he would not so much as lie in jest; and I moreover know that, could it have been in his own choice, he would rather have been born at Venice than at Sarlac, and he had reason; but he had another maxim sovereignly imprinted in his soul, religiously to obey and submit to the laws under which he was born. There never was a better citizen, nor more anxious for his country's peace; neither was there ever a greater enemy to all the commotions and innovations of his time; so that he would, without doubt, much rather have employed his talent to the extinguishing of those civil flames than have added any fuel to them; for he had a mind framed to the model of better ages. But in exchange of this serious piece, I will present you with another of a more gay and frolic air from the same hand, and writ at the same age.

CHAPTER XXVIII.

NINE AND TWENTY SONNETS OF ESTIENNE DE LA BOËTIE

To Madame de Grammont, Countess of Guissen.

MADAM, I offer you nothing of mine, either because it is already yours, or because I find nothing in my writings worthy of you. But I have a great desire that these verses, into what part of the world soever they may travel, may carry your name in the front, for the honour will accrue to them, by having the great Corisande d'Andoins for their safe conduct.[1] I conceive this present, madam, so much the more proper for you, both by reason there are few ladies in France who are so good judges of poetry and make so good use of it as you do ; as also that there is none who can give it the spirit and life you can, by that incomparable voice nature has added to your other perfections. These verses, madam, deserve your esteem, and you will concur with me in this, that Gascony never yielded any with more invention, finer expression, or that more evidently show themselves to have flowed from a master-hand. And be not jealous then that you have but the remainder of what I published some years since, under the name of Monsieur de Foix, your worthy kinsman ; for certainly these have something in them more sprightly and luxuriant, as being written in a greener youth, when he was inflamed with a certain noble ardour, madam, of which I will tell you in your ear. The others were written since, when he was a suitor, in honour of his wife, and already smack somewhat of matrimonial coldness. And, for my part, I am of the same opinion with those who hold that poetry appears nowhere so gay as in a wanton and irregular subject.

[*These nine-and-twenty sonnets that were inserted here, are since printed with Boëtie's other works. They are very indifferent compositions, being little else than amorous complaints, expressed in a rough style, exhibiting the follies and outrages of a restless passion, overgorged as it were, with jealousies, fears, and suspicions. Indeed, Montaigne himself, in the editions subsequent to that of 1588, omits them, observing, " These verses are to be found elsewhere."*]

---

[1] Diana, Viscountess of Louvigni, surnamed the *Fair Corisande* of Andouins, married in 1567 Philibert, Count of Grammont and Guiche, who died at the siege of La Fère, in 1580. Andouins, or Andoins, was a Barony of Bearn, three leagues from Pau. The King of Navarre, afterwards Henry IV., fell in love with the fair widow, and at one time had even an idea of marrying her. Count Hamilton, in his *Epistle to Count Grammont*, thus reminds him of his illustrious ancestors :—

" Honneur des rives éloignées
    Où Corisande vit le jour," &c.

CHAPTER XXIX.

OF MODERATION

As though we had an infectious touch, we, by our manner of handling, corrupt things that in themselves _{Whether virtue} are laudable and good. We may grasp virtue _{can be too vehemently sought after.} so hard that it becomes vice, if we embrace it ^{ter.} too eagerly and with too violent a desire. Those who say there is never any excess in virtue, forasmuch as it is no virtue when it once becomes excess, only play upon words.

> Insani sapiens nomen ferat, æquus iniqui,
> Ultra quàm satis est, virtutem si petat ipsam,[1]

> " Mad grow the wise, the just unjust are found,
> When e'en to virtue they prescribe no bound.'

This is a subtle consideration in philosophy. A man may both be too much in love with virtue and be excessive in a just action. Holy Writ agrees with this : " Be not wiser than you should, but be soberly wise." [2] I have known a great man prejudice the opinion men had of his religion, by pretending to be devout beyond all examples of others of his condition.[3] I love temperate and moderate nature. An immoderate zeal, even for that which is good, though it does not offend, does astonish me, _{An immoderate zeal for that which is good.} and puts me to study what name to give it. Neither the mother of Pausanias,[4] who was the first sug-

---

[1] Horace, *Epist.* i. 6–15.
[2] *Romans*, xii. 3.
[3] It is likely that Montaigne means Henry III. of France. The Cardinal d'Ossat, writing to Louisa, his queen dowager, told her, in his frank manner, that he had lived as much or more like a monk than a monarch. (*Letter* xxiii.)—And Sextus Quintus, speaking of that prince one day to the Cardinal de Joyeuse, protector of the affairs of France, said to him pleasantly, " There is nothing that

your king hath not done, and does not do still, to be a monk, nor any thing that I have not done not to be a monk." See the note by Amelot de la Houssaye upon the words of the Cardinal d'Ossat, just now mentioned, p. 74, tom. i. of the Cardinal d'Ossat's *Letters*, Paris, 1698.
[4] Montaigne would here give us to understand, upon the authority of Diodorus of Sicily, that Pausanias's mother gave the first hint of the punishment that was to be inflicted on her son.

gester of her son's death, and lay the first stone towards it ; nor Posthumius, the dictator, who put his son to death, whom the ardour of youth had pushed upon the enemy a little before the rest of his squadron ;[1] appear to me so just as strange ; and I should neither advise, nor like to follow, a virtue so savage in itself, and that costs so dear. The archer that shoots over the mark misses as much as he that falls short ; and 'tis equally troublesome to my eyes to look up at a great light as to look down into a dark abyss. Callicles, in Plato,[2] says that the extremity of philosophy is hurtful, and advises not to dive into it beyond the limits of profit ; that taken moderately it is pleasant and useful, but that in the extreme it renders a man brutish and vicious ; a contemner of religion and the common laws ; an enemy to civil conversation and all human pleasures ; incapable of all public administration ; unfit either to assist others or to relieve himself ; and a fit object to be injured and affronted without remedy. He says true, for in its excess it enslaves our natural freedom, and by an impertinent subtlety leads us out of the fair and beaten way that nature has traced out for us.

Love to wives restrained by divinity.

The love we bear to our wives is very lawful, and yet theology thinks fit to curb and restrain it. As I remember, I have read one place of

---

" Pausanias," says this historian, " perceiving that the Ephori and some other Lacedemonians aimed at apprehending him, got the start of them, and went and took sanctuary in Minerva's temple ; and the Lacedemonians being doubtful whether they ought to take him thence in violation of the franchise there, it is said that his own mother came herself to the temple, but spoke nothing, nor did any thing, more than lay a piece of brick, which she brought with her, on the threshold of the temple, which, when she had done, she returned home. The Lacedemonians, taking the hint from the mother, caused the gate of the temple to be walled up, and by this means starved Pausanias, so that he died with hunger, &c." The name of Pausanias's mother was Alcithea, as we are informed by Thucydides's scholiast, who only says that it was reported that when they set about walling up the gates of the chapel in which Pausanias had taken refuge, his mother Alcithea laid the first stone

[1] Opinions differ as to the truth of this matter. Livy thinks he has good authority for rejecting it, because it does not appear in history that Posthumius was branded with it, as T. Manlius was, about 100 years after his time ; for Manlius, having put his son to death for the like cause, obtained the odious name of Imperiosus, and since that time Manliana Imperia has been used as a term to signify orders that are too severe. " Manliana Imperia," says Livy, " were not only horrible for the time present, but of a bad example to posterity." And this historian makes no doubt but such commands would have been actually styled Posthumiana Imperia if Posthumius had been the first who set so barbarous an example. (T. Livius, iv. 29, and viii. 7.)—But, however, Montaigne has Valerius Maximus on his side, who says expressly that Posthumius caused his son to be put to death, ii. 76 ; and Diodorus of Sicily, xii. 19.

[2] In the Gorgias.

St. Thomas of Aquin, where he condemns marriage within
any of the forbidden degrees,—for this reason, amongst others, that there is danger lest the friendship a man bears to
such a woman should be immoderate; for if the conjugal
affection be full and perfect betwixt them, as it ought to be,
and that it be over and above surcharged with that of kindred too, there is no doubt but such an addition will carry the
husband beyond the bounds of reason.[1]

Those sciences that regulate the manners of men, divinity
and philosophy, will have a say in every thing. Divinity and phi-
There is no action so private that can escape losophy dictate in
every thing.
their inspection and jurisdiction. They are
best skilled who themselves can regulate and control their
liberty; and not be like women who are ready enough to
expose their persons for an amorous embrace, though they
are too shy, forsooth, to do so to the physician, however great
the need. Let me, therefore, in behalf of these sciences,
teach those husbands, if such there be, who are too sensual,
this lesson—that the very pleasures they enjoy in their converse with their wives are reproachable, if immoderate; and
that a licentious and riotous abuse of them is a fault, as
much as an illicit embrace. Those immodest tricks and pos-
tures that the first ardour suggests to us in this affair are not
only indecently but prejudicially practised upon our wives.
Let them at least learn impudence from another hand; they
are always apt enough for our business, and I, for my part,
always went the plain way to work.

Marriage is a solemn and religious connection, and therefore
the pleasure we extract thence should be sober and serious,
and mixed with a certain degree of gravity; it should be a kind
of discreet and conscientious pleasure. And the chief end of
it being generation, some make a question whether, when men
have not that object in view, as when their wives are super-
annuated or already with child, it be lawful to embrace them.
'Tis homicide, according to Plato;[2] and certain nations (the

---

[1] St. Thomas Aquinas, *Secunda Secundæ*, quæs. 154, art. 9.   [2] *Laws*, viii.

Mahometan amongst others) abominate all conjunction with women with child, and so do others with women in their courses. Zenobia would never admit her husband for more than one encounter, after which she left him to his own swing for the whole time of her conception, and not till after that would again receive him. A noble and worthy example of conjugal continency.[1] It was doubtless from some lascivious poet, and one that himself was in great distress for a little of this sport, that Plato borrowed this story;[2] that Jupiter was one day so hot upon his wife that, not having so much patience as till she could get to the couch, he threw her upon the floor, where the vehemence of pleasure made him forget the great and important resolutions he had but newly taken with the rest of the gods in his celestial council, and to boast that he had had as good a bout as when he got her maidenhead unknown to her parents.

The kings of Persia were wont to invite their wives to the beginning of their festivals; but when the wine began to work in good earnest, and that they were to give the reins to pleasure, they sent them back to their private apartment, that they might not participate of their immoderate lust, sending for other women in their stead, with whom they were not obliged to so great a decorum and respect. All pleasures, and all sorts of gratifications, are not properly and fitly conferred upon all sorts of persons. Epaminondas had imprisoned a young man for certain debauches; Pelopidas requested he might be set at liberty, which Epaminondas denied to him, but granted it at the first word to a wench of his, who made the same intercession; saying, "That it was a gratification due to such a one as she, but not to a captain."[3] Sophocles being joint praetor with Pericles, seeing a fine boy pass by, "Oh! what a

Marginal note: Wives of the kings of Persia, how received at their festivals.

---

1 Trebellius Pollio, *Trigint. Tyrann.* c. 30.

2 Montaigne here laughs at Homer without thinking of it, for this fiction is taken from the *Iliad*, xiv. 194. See Plato's *Republic*, iii. 433. If Montaigne had looked into Homer he would not have been so mistaken as he has been in some circumstances of this affair.

3 Plutarch, *Instruct. to those who manage State Affairs.*

handsome boy is that," said he. "It would be well enough for any other than a prætor," answered Pericles, "who ought not only to have his hands, but his eyes chaste."[1] Ælius Verus, the Emperor, answered his wife, who *Conjugal love ought to be accompanied with respect.* reproached him for his amours with other women, that he did it upon a conscientious account, inasmuch as marriage was a state of honour and dignity, not of wanton and lascivious desire.[2] And our ecclesiastical history preserves the memory of that woman in great veneration who parted from her husband because she would not comply with his indecent and inordinate desire. In fine, there is no so just and lawful pleasure wherein intemperance and excess is not to be condemned.

But, in truth, is not man a most miserable creature the while? It is scarce, by his natural condition, *Man a miserable creature.* in his power to taste one pleasure pure and entire; and yet he must be contriving doctrines and precepts to curtail that little he has. He is not yet wretched enough, unless by art and study he augments his own misery.

> Fortunæ miseras auximus arte vias.[3]
>
> "We with misfortune 'gainst ourselves take part
> And our own miseries increase by art."

Human wisdom makes as ill use of her talent, when she exercises it in lessening the number and sweetness of those pleasures that are naturally our due, as she employs it favourably and well in artificially disguising and tricking out the ills of life, to alleviate the sense of them. Had I ruled the roast, I should have taken another and more natural course, which, to say the truth, is both convenient and sacred, and should, peradventure, have been able to have limited it, too; notwithstanding that both our spiritual and corporal physicians, as by compact betwixt themselves, can find no other way to cure, nor other remedy for the infirmities of the body and the soul, than what is ofttimes worse than the dis-

[1] Cicero, *Offic.* l. 40.　[2] Ælian. Spart. *in Vitâ.*　[3] Propertius, iii 7, 32.

ease, by tormenting us more, and by adding to our misery and pain. To this end watchings, fastings, hair-shirts, remote and solitary banishments, perpetual imprisonments, whips, and other afflictions, have been introduced amongst men; but so that they should carry a sting with them, and be real afflictions indeed; and not fall out so as it once did to one Gallio, who, having been sent an exile to the Isle of Lesbos, news was not long after brought to Rome that he there lived as merry as the day was long; and that what had been enjoined him for a penance, turned to his greatest pleasure and satisfaction. Whereupon the Senate thought fit to recall him home to his wife and family, and confine him to his own house, to accommodate their punishment to his feeling and apprehension.[1] For to him whom fasting would make more healthful and more sprightly, and to him to whose palate fish was more acceptable than flesh, these would be no proper nor salutary recipe; no more than in the other sort of physic, where the drugs have no effect upon him who swallows them with appetite and pleasure. The bitterness of the potion, and the abhorrence of the patient, are necessary circumstances to the operation. The nature that would eat rhubarb like buttered turnips, would frustrate the use and virtue of it; it must be something to trouble and disturb the stomach that must purge and cure it. And here the common rule, that things are cured by their contraries, fails; for in this, one ill is cured by another.

This notion somewhat resembles the ancient one, of thinking to gratify the gods and nature by massacre and murder; an opinion once universally received in all religions, even in the time of our fathers. Amurath, at the taking of the Isthmus, immolated six hundred young Greeks to his father's soul, as a propitiatory sacrifice for the sins of the deceased. And in the new countries discovered in this age of ours, which are pure, and virgins yet, in comparison of ours, this

The sacrifice of human flesh a practice formerly in almost all religions.

practice is in some measure everywhere received. All their idols reek with human blood, not without various examples of horrid cruelty. Some they burn alive, and half-broiled take them off the coals to tear out their hearts and entrails; others, even women, they flay alive, and with their bloody skins clothe and disguise others. Neither are we without great examples of constancy and resolution in this affair. The poor souls that are to be sacrificed, old men, women, and children, go about some days before to beg alms for the offering of their sacrifice, and present themselves, singing and dancing about with the spectators, to the slaughter. *How practised in the new world.* *Wonderful firmness of those who are sacrificed there.*

The ambassadors of the king of Mexico, setting forth to Fernando Cortez the power and greatness of their master, after having told him that he had thirty vassals, of whom each was able to raise an hundred thousand fighting men, and that he kept his court in the fairest and best fortified city under the sun, added at last, that he yearly offered to the gods fifty thousand men. Indeed, they affirmed that he maintained a continual war with some potent neighbouring nations, not only to keep the young men in exercise, but principally to have wherewithal to furnish his sacrifices with his prisoners of war. At a certain town in another place, for the welcome of the said Cortez, they sacrificed fifty men at once. I will tell you this one tale more, and I have done. *The prodigious number sacrificed by the king of Mexico.* *Compliment paid by the Americans to Fernando Cortez.* Some of these people being beaten by him, sent to acknowledge him, and to treat with him of a peace, whose messengers carried him three sorts of presents, which they presented in these terms: " Behold, lord, here are five slaves; if thou art a furious god, that feedest upon flesh and blood, eat these, and we will bring thee more; if thou art an affable god, behold here incense and feathers; if thou art a man, take these fowls and these fruits that we have brought thee."

CHAPTER XXX.

OF CANNIBALS.

WHEN Pyrrhus, king of Epirus, invaded Italy, having viewed and considered the order of the army the Romans sent out to meet him,—" I know not," said he, " what kind of barbarians (for so the Greeks called all other nations) these may be; but the disposition of this army that I see has nothing of the barbarian in it."[1] As much said the Greeks of that which Flaminius brought into their country;[2] and Philip, beholding from an eminence, the order and disposition of the Roman camp, led into his kingdom by Publius Sulpitius Galba, spoke to the same effect.[3] By which it appears how cautious men ought to be of taking things upon trust from vulgar opinion, and that we are to judge by the eye of reason, and not from common report. I have long had a

Reflections on the discovery of the new world. man in my house that lived ten or twelve years in the new world discovered in these latter days, and in that part of it where Villegaignon landed, which he called Antartic France.[4] This discovery of so vast a country seems to be of very great consideration; and we are not sure that hereafter there may not be another found, so many wiser men than we having been deceived in this. I am afraid our eyes are bigger than our bellies, and that we have more curiosity than capacity; for we grasp at all, but catch nothing but air.

The island of Atlantis. Plato[5] brings in Solon, relating that he had heard from the priests of Sais, in Egypt, that of old, and before the deluge, there was a great island, called Atlantis, situate directly at the mouth of the Strait of

[1] Plutarch, *in Vitâ,* c. 8.
[2] Id. *Life of Flaminius,* c. 3.
[3] Livy, xxxi. 34.
[4] Brazil, where he arrived in 1557.
[5] In the *Timæus.*

Gibraltar, which contained more ground than both Africa and Asia put together; that the kings of that country, who not only possessed that isle, but extended their dominion so far into the continent that they had a country as large as Africa to Egypt, and as long as Europe to Tuscany, had attempted to encroach even upon Asia, and to subjugate all the nations that border upon the Mediterranean Sea, as far as the Great Gulf;[1] and to that effect had overrun all Spain, the Gauls, and Italy, as far as Greece, where the Athenians stopped the torrent of their arms; but some time after both the Athenians, they, and their island, were swallowed by the flood. It is very likely that this violent eruption and inundation of water made strange alterations in the habitable parts of the earth; as 'tis said, for instance, that the sea then cut off Sicily from Italy; *Deluges the cause of great alterations in the habitable world.*

> Hæc loca, vi quondam et vastâ convulsa ruinâ,
>
> .   .   .   .
>
> Dissiluisse ferunt, cum protenus utraque tellus
> Una foret.[2]

> "'Tis said those places by the o'erbearing flood,
> Too great and violent to be withstood,
> Split, and were thus from one another rent,
> Which were before one solid continent."

Cyprus from Syria; the isle of Negropont from the Continent of Bœotia; and elsewhere, united lands that were separate before, by filling up the channel betwixt them with sand and mud;

> Sterilisque diù palus, aptaque remis,
> Vicinas urbes alit, et grave sentit aratrum.[3]

> "Where once bare remigable marshes, now
> Feed neighb'ring cities and admit the plough."

But there is no great appearance that this isle was this new world so lately discovered; for that almost touched upon Spain,[4] and it were an incredible effect of an inundation to

<hr/>

[1] The Black Sea.
[2] *Æneid*, lii. 414.
[3] Horace, *de Art. Poet.* 65.

[4] Plato does not say any thing of the sort. The reader will observe in the following passages several geographical

have carried so prodigious a mass above twelve hundred leagues; besides that our modern navigators have already almost discovered it to be no island, but firm land and continent, with the East Indies on the one side, and the land under the two poles on the other; or, if it be separated from them, 'tis by so narrow a strait that it never more deserves the name of an island for that. It should seem that, in this great body, there are two sorts of motions, the one natural, and the other febrific, as there are in ours. When I consider the impression that my own river, Dordoigne, has made, in my time, on the right bank of its descent, and that, in twenty years, it has gained so much, and undermined the foundation of so many houses, I perceive it to be an extraordinary agitation; for, had it always gone on at this rate, or were hereafter to do it, the aspect of the world would be totally changed. But rivers alter in this respect, sometimes spreading out against the one side, and sometimes against the other, and sometimes quietly keeping the channel. I do not speak of sudden inundations, the causes of which every body understands. In Medoc, by the sea-shore, the Sieur d'Arsac, my brother, had an estate, he had there, buried under the sands which the sea vomits before it; the tops of some houses are yet to be seen, but his good land is converted into pitiful barren pasturage. The inhabitants of the place affirm that, of late years, the sea has driven so vehemently upon them that they have lost four leagues of land. These sands are her harbingers; and we now see great heaps of moving sand that march half a league before her, and take possession of the land.

The other testimony from antiquity, to which some would apply this discovery of the new world, is in Aristotle; at least, if that little book of unheard-of miracles be his. He there tells us that certain Carthaginians, having crossed the Atlantic sea, without the Straits of Gibraltar, and sailed a

blunders, which were, doubtless, spread abroad by the first travellers in America.

very long time, discovered, at last, a great and fruitful island, all covered over with wood, and watered with several broad and deep rivers, far remote from any continent, and that they, and others, after them, allured by the pleasantness and fertility of the soil, went thither, with their wives and children, and began to plant a colony. But the senate of Carthage, perceiving their people, by little and little, to grow thin, issued out an express prohibition, that no one, upon pain of death, should transport themselves thither; and also drove out the new inhabitants, fearing, 'tis said, lest, in process of time, they should so multiply as to supplant themselves and ruin their state. But this relation of Aristotle's does no more agree with our new found lands than the other. This man that I have is a plain ignorant fellow, and, therefore, the more likely to tell truth; for though your better-bred sort of men are much more curious in their observation, and discover a great deal more, *The qualities requisite in an historian.* they gloss upon it, and, to give the greater weight to what they deliver, and allure your belief, they cannot forbear a little to alter the story. They never represent things to you simply as they are, but rather as they appeared to them, or as they would have them appear to you, and, to gain the reputation of men of judgment, and the better to induce your faith, are willing to help out the business with something more than is really true, of their own invention. Now, in this case, we should either have a man of irreproachable veracity, or so simple that he has not wherewithal to contrive and to give a colour of truth to false relations, and that can have no ends in forging an untruth. Such a one is mine; and, besides the little suspicion the man lies under, he has divers times brought me several seamen and merchants that, at the same time, went the same voyage. I shall, therefore, content myself with his information, without inquiring what the cosmographers say to the business. We need topographers to trace out to us the particular places where they have been; but for having had this advantage over us, to have seen the Holy Land, they would have the privilege, forsooth,

Authors should write no more on a subject than what they know of it. to tell us stories of all the other parts of the world besides. I would have every one write what he knows, and as much as he knows, but no more; and that not in this only, but in all other subjects; for such a person may have some particular knowledge and experience of the nature of such a river, or such a fountain, that as to other things knows no more than what everybody does, and yet, to keep a clutter with this little pittance of his, will undertake to write the whole body of physics; a vice whence many great inconveniences derive their original.

Now, to return to my subject, I find that there is nothing

Barbarism, what it is taken for. barbarous and savage in this nation, by any thing that I can gather, excepting that every one gives the title of barbarism to every thing that is not in use in his own country; as, indeed, we have no other level of truth and reason than the example and idea of the opinions and customs of the place wherein we live. There is always the perfect religion, there the perfect government, there the perfect every thing. This nation are savages, in the same way that we say fruits are wild, which nature produces of herself, and by her own ordinary progress; whereas, in truth, we ought rather to call those wild whose natures we have changed by our artifice, and diverted from the common order. In those, the genuine, most useful, and natural virtues and properties, are vigorous and active, which we have degenerated in these, by accommodating them to the pleasure of our own corrupted palate. And yet, for all this, our taste confesses a flavour and delicacy, excellent even to emulation of the best of ours, in several fruits those countries abound with, without art or culture; nor is it reasonable that art should gain the point over our great and powerful mother, Nature. We have so oppressed her beauty and the richness of her works, by our inventions, that we have almost smothered her; but, where she shines in her own purity and proper lustre, she marvellously baffles and disgraces all our vain and frivolous attempts.

> Et veniunt hederæ sponte suâ meliùs,
> Surgit et in solis formosior arbutus antris;
>
> .   .   .   .   .   .
>
> Et volucres nullâ dulcius arte canunt.[1]

> " Best thrives the ivy when no culture spoils,
> The strawb'ry most delights in shaded soils;
> Birds, in wild notes, their throats harmonious stretch
> With greater art than art itself can teach."

Our utmost endeavours cannot arrive at so much as to imitate the nest of the least of birds, its contexture, its elegance, its convenience; not so much as the web of a contemptible spider. "All things," says Plato, "are produced either by nature, or by fortune, or by art; the greatest and most beautiful by the one or the other of the former, the least and the most imperfect by the last." [2]

These nations then seem to me to be so far barbarous, as having received but very little form and fashion from art and human invention, and being consequently not much remote from their original simplicity. *In what sense the American savages are barbarians.* The laws of nature govern them still, not as yet much vitiated with any mixture of ours; nay, in such purity that I am sometimes troubled we were no sooner acquainted with these people, and that they were not discovered in those better times, when there were men much more able to judge of them than we are. I am sorry that Lycurgus and Plato had no knowledge of them; for, to my apprehension, what we now see in those natives does not only surpass all the images with which the poets have adorned the golden age, and all their inventions in feigning a happy state of man, but moreover the fancy, and even the wish and desire of philosophy itself. So native and so pure a simplicity as we by experience see to be in them, could never enter into their imagination, nor could they ever believe that human society could have been maintained with so little artifice. Should I

---

[1] Propertius, i. 2, 10.   [2] *On Laws*, x.

The excellency of their polity. tell Plato that it is a nation wherein there is **no** manner of traffic, no knowledge of letters, **no** science of numbers, no name of magistrate, nor political superiority; no use of service, riches or poverty; no contracts, no successions, no dividends, no properties, no employments, but those of leisure; no respect of kindred, but in common; no clothing, no agriculture, no metal, no use of corn or wine; and where so much as the very words that signify lying, treachery, dissimulation, avarice, envy, detraction, and pardon, were never heard of—how much would he find his imaginary republic short of this perfection? *Viri a diis recentes.*[1] "Fresh from the hands of the gods."

Hos natura modos primum dedit.[2]

"These were the manners first by nature taught."

As to the rest, they live in a country beautiful and pleasant, and so temperate, as my intelligence informs me, that 'tis very rare to hear of a sick person there; and they moreover assure me that they never saw any of the natives either paralytic, blear-eyed, toothless, or crooked with age. The situation of their country is along the sea-shore, and inclosed on the side towards the land with great and high mountains, having about an hundred leagues in breadth between. They have great store of fish and flesh meat that have no resemblance to ours, which they eat without any other cookery than plain boiling, roasting, or broiling. The first that carried a horse thither, though in several other voyages he had contracted an acquaintance and familiarity with them, put them into so terrible a fright at his appearance so mounted, that they killed him with their arrows before they could come to discover who he was. Their buildings, which are very long, and of capacity to hold two or three hundred people, are made of the barks of tall trees, reared with one end upon

The nature of their climate.

Their meals, their drink, and their bread.

---

[1] Seneca. *Epist.* 90. This quotation whence was printed M. Naigeon's edition, only appears in the copy of the *Essays.* Montaigne omitted it elsewhere, probably on account of the quotation which immediately follows.
[2] Virg. *Georg.* ii. 20.

the ground, and leaning against and supporting one another
at the top, like some of our barns, of which the covering
hangs down to the very ground, and serves for the side
walls. They have wood so hard that they cleave it into
swords, and make grills of it to broil their meat. Their beds
are of cotton, hung swinging from the roof, like our seamen's
hammocks; for every one, the wives lying apart from their
husbands. They rise with the sun, and so soon as they are
up eat for all day; for they have no more meals but that.
They do not drink then (as Suidas reports of some other
people of the east, that never drink at their meals), but drink
very often in the day, and sometimes a great deal. Their
liquor is made of a certain root, and is as red as our claret ·
and this they never drink but lukewarm. It will keep only
two or three days, has a sharp taste, is nothing heady, but
very wholesome to the stomach, laxative for strangers, and a
very pleasant beverage to such as are used to it. Instead of
bread they make use of a certain white matter, like coriander
comfits; I have tasted of it, the taste is sweet, but somewhat
insipid. The whole day is spent in dancing. Their pastimes.
The young men go a hunting after wild beasts
with bows and arrows, and one part of their women are employed in preparing their drink the while, which is their
chief employment. Some of their old men in the morning,
before they fall to eating, preach to the whole family, walking to and fro from the one end of the house to the other,
several times repeating the same sentence, till they have finished their round (for their houses are at least a hundred
yards long); enjoining valour towards their enemies and love
towards their wives are the two heads of his discourse, never
failing, as a burden, to put them in mind that 'tis to their
wives they are obliged for providing them their drink warm
and relishing. The fashion of their beds, ropes, swords, and
the wooden bracelets, which they tie about their wrists when
they go to fight, and of their great canes, bored hollow at one
end, by the sound of which they keep the cadence of their

dances, is to be seen in several places, and amongst others at my house. They shave all over, and much more closely than we, without any other razor than one of wood or of stone.

They believe the immortality of the soul. They believe the immortality of the soul, and that those who have merited well of the gods are lodged in that part of heaven where the sun rises, and the accursed in the west. They have a kind

Their priests and prophets, their morality, and how they are treated, if their prophecies prove false. of priests and prophets that rarely present themselves to the people, having their abode in the mountains. At their arrival there is a great feast and solemn assembly of many villages made, that is, all the neighbouring families, for every house, as I have described it, makes a village, and are about a French league distant from one another. This prophet declaims to them in public, exhorting them to virtue and their duty; but all their ethics consist in these two articles— resolution in war and affection to their wives. He also prophesies to them events to come, and the issues they are to expect from their enterprises, prompts them to, or diverts them from, war. But let him look to't; for if he fail in his divination, and any thing happen otherwise than he has foretold, he is cut into a thousand pieces, if he be caught, and condemned for a false prophet; and for that reason, if any of them finds himself mistaken, he is no more to be heard of. Divination is a gift of God, and therefore to abuse it ought to be a punishable imposture. Amongst the Scythians, when

False prophets burnt by the Scythians. their diviners failed in the promised effect, they were laid, bound hand and foot, upon carts laden with firewood, and drawn with oxen, on which they were burnt to death.[1] Such as only meddle with things subject to the conduct of human capacity are excusable in doing the best they can; but those other sort of people that come to delude us with assurances of an extraordinary faculty beyond our understanding, ought they not to be punished for the temerity of their imposture, when they do not make good the effect of their promise?

1 *Herod.* iv. 69.

They have wars with the nations that live farther within
the main land, beyond their mountains, to which they go
naked, and without other arms than their bows and wooden
swords, pointed at one end like the head of a javelin.   The
obstinacy of their battles is wonderful ; they never end without great effusion of blood ; for as to running away, or fear,
they know not what it is.   Every one for a trophy brings
home the head of an enemy he has killed, which he fixes
over the door of his house.   After having a long time treated
their prisoners very well, and given them all _{They eat their}
the luxuries they can think of, he to whom the _{prisoners, and why.}
prisoner belongs invites a great assembly of his
kindred and friends, who being come, he ties a rope to one
of the arms of the prisoner, of which at a distance, out of his
reach, he holds the one end himself, and gives to the friend
he loves best the other arm, to hold after the same manner ;
which being done, they two, in the presence of all the
assembly, dispatch him with their swords.   After that they
roast him, eat him amongst them, and send some chops to
their absent friends ; which nevertheless they do not do, as
some think, for nourishment, as the Scythians anciently did,
but as a representation of an extreme revenge, as will immediately appear.   Having observed the Portuguese, who were
in league with their enemies, to inflict another sort of death
upon any of them they took prisoners, which was to set them
up to the girdle in the earth, to shoot at the remaining part
till it was stuck full of arrows, and then to hang them ; they
who thought those people of the other world (as men who
had sown the knowledge of a great many vices amongst their
neighbours, and were much greater masters in all kind of
malignity than they), did not exercise this sort of revenge
without reason, and that it must needs be more painful than
theirs, began to leave their old way and to follow this.   I am
not sorry that we should here take notice of the barbarous
horror of so cruel an act, but that, seeing so clearly into their
faults, we should be so blind to our own.   I conceive there is

more barbarity in eating a man alive than when he is dead;
in tearing a body that is yet perfectly sentient, limb from
limb, by racks and torments, in roasting it by degrees, causing it to be bit and worried by dogs and swine (as we have
not only read, but lately seen, not amongst inveterate and
mortal enemies, but amongst neighbours and fellow-citizens,
and, what is worse, under colour of piety and religion), than
to roast and eat him after he is dead.

Chrysippus [1] and Zeno, chiefs of the Stoic sect, were of
opinion that there was no harm in making use of our dead
carcasses, in what kind soever, for our necessity, and in
feeding upon them too; as our ancestors, who, being besieged by Cæsar in the city of Alexia, resolved to sus-
tain the famine of the siege with the bodies of their old men,
women, and other persons, who were incapable of bearing
arms.

> Vascones (fama est) alimentis talibus usi,
> Produxere animas.[2]

> " The Gascons once, the story yet is rife,
>   With such dire aliment sustained their life."

And the physicians made no scruple of employing it to all
sorts of use, either to apply it outwardly, or to give it in-
wardly for the health of the patient. But there never was
any opinion so irregular as to excuse treachery, disloyalty,
tyranny, and cruelty, which are our familiar vices. We may,
then, well call these people barbarous, in respect to the rules
of reason; but not in respect to ourselves, who, in all sorts
of barbarity, exceed them. Their wars are
throughout noble and generous, and carry as
much excuse and fair pretence as this human
malady is capable of; having with them no other foundation
than the sole jealousy of valour. Their disputes are not for
the conquests of new lands, those they already possess being
so fruitful by nature as to supply them, without labour or concern, with all things necessary, in such abundance that they

The savages of America make war after a very noble manner.

---

[1] Laertius, *in Vitâ.*   [2] Juvenal, xv. 93.

have no need to enlarge their borders. And they are moreover happy in this, that they only covet so Their moderation.
much as their natural necessities require; all
beyond that is superfluous to them. Men of the same age
generally call one another brothers, those who are younger,
sons and daughters, and the old men are fathers Their cordiality to one another.
to all. These leave to their heirs in common
this full possession of goods, without any manner of division,
or other title than what nature bestows upon her creatures in
bringing them into the world. If their neighbours pass the
mountains, and come to attack them, and obtain a victory, all
the victors gain by it is glory only, and the ad-
vantage of having proved themselves the better All that they get is glory by any victory over their neighbours.
in valour and virtue; for they never meddle
with the goods of the conquered, but presently
return into their own country, where they have no want of
any necessary; nor of this greatest of all goods, to know how
to enjoy their condition happily, and to be content. And
these in turn do the same. They demand of their prisoners
no other ransom than acknowledgment that they are overcome. But there is not one found in an age that will not
rather choose to die than make such a concession; or either
by word or look recede from the grandeur of an invincible
courage. There is not a man amongst them who had not
rather be killed and eaten, than so much as to open his mouth
to entreat he may not. They use them with all liberality
and freedom, to the end their lives may be so much the
dearer to them; but frequently entertain them withal with
menaces of their approaching death, of the torments they are
to suffer, of the preparations that are making in order to it,
of the mangling their limbs, and of the feast that is to be
made, where their carcass is to be the only dish. All which
they do to no other end but only to extort some gentle or
submissive word from them, or to frighten them so as to
make them run away; so that they may obtain this advantage, that they had terrified them, and that their constancy

was shaken. And indeed, if rightly taken, it is in this **point** only that a true victory consists.

> Victoria nulla est
> Quàm quæ confessos animo quoque subjugat hostes.[1]

> "No victory's so true and so complete,
> As when the vanquish'd own their just defeat."

The Hungarians, a very warlike people, never pursued their point farther than to reduce the enemy to their discretion; for, having forced this confession from them, they let them go without injury or ransom, excepting, at the most, to make them engage their word never to bear arms against them again. We get several advantages over our enemies that are borrowed, and not truly our own: 'tis the quality of a porter, and no effect of valour, to have stronger arms and legs; 'tis a dead and spiritless quality to draw up well; 'tis a stroke of fortune to make our enemy stumble, or to dazzle him with the light of the sun; 'tis a trick of science and art, which may happen in any cowardly blockhead, to be a good fencer. The estimation and value of a man *What constitutes the true merit of a man, and his superiority over his fellow-creatures.* consist in the heart and in the will; there his true honour lives. Valour is stability, not of legs and arms, but of the courage and the soul; it does not lie in the goodness of our horse, or of our arms, but in ourselves. He that falls, firm in his courage,—*Si succiderit, de genu pugnat;*[2] "If his legs fail him, fights upon his knees;" he, who, despite the danger of death near at hand, abates nothing of his assurance; who, dying, does yet dart at his enemy a fierce and disdainful look, is overcome, not by us, but by fortune; he is killed, not conquered; the most valiant[3] are sometimes the most unfortunate. There are some defeats more triumphant than victories. *Defeats that are more meritorious than the greatest victories.* Those four sister-victories, the fairest the sun ever beheld, of Salamis, Platea, Mycale, and Sicily, never opposed all

---

[1] Claudian, *De Sexto Consul. Honorii*, 248.

[2] Seneca, *de Provid.* c. 2. The text has *etiam si cederit.*

[3] Seneca, *De Const. Sap.* c. 6.

their united glories to the single glory of the discomfiture of King Leonidas and his heroes at the Pass of Thermopylæ. Who ever ran with a more glorious desire and greater ambition to the winning, than the Captain Ischolas to the certain loss of a battle? Who ever set about with more ingenuity and eagerness to secure his safety than he did to assure his ruin? He was ordered to defend a certain pass of Peloponnesus against the Arcadians, which, from the nature of the place and the inequality of forces, finding it utterly impossible for him to do, and seeing clearly that all who presented themselves to the enemy must certainly be left upon the place; and, on the other hand, reputing it unworthy of his own virtue and magnanimity, and of the Lacedemonian name, to fail in his duty, he chose a mean betwixt these two extremes, after this manner: the youngest and most active of his men he preserved for the service and defence of their country, and therefore sent them back; and with the rest, whose loss would be of less consideration, he resolved to make good the pass, and, with the death of them, to make the enemy buy their entry as dear as possibly he could. And so it fell out; for, being presently encompassed on all sides by the Arcadians, after having made a great slaughter of the enemy, he and his men were all cut in pieces.[1] Is there any trophy dedicated to conquerors which is not much more due to those who were thus overcome? The part that true conquering has to play lies in the encounter, not in the coming off; the honour of valour consists in fighting, not in subduing.

But to return to my story. These prisoners are so far from discovering the least weakness for all the terrors can be represented to them, that on the contrary, during the two or three months that they are kept, they always appear with a cheerful countenance; importune their masters to make haste to *The constancy of those savages that are taken prisoners.*

---

[1] Diodorus Sic. xv. 7; where the action of Ischolas is compared to that of King Leonidas, which Montaigne extols above the most celebrated victories.

bring them to the test; defy, rail at them, and reproach them with cowardice, and the number of battles they have lost against those of their country. I have a song

The martial song of one of the savage prisoners.

made by one of these prisoners, wherein he bids them come all and dine upon him, and welcome, for they shall withal eat their own fathers and grandfathers, whose flesh has served to feed and nourish him. "These muscles," says he, "this flesh, and these veins, are your own. Poor fools that you are, you little think that the substance of your ancestors' limbs is here yet; taste it well, and you will find in it the relish of your own flesh." In which song there is to be observed an invention that smacks nothing of the barbarian. These that paint these people dying after this manner, represent the prisoner spitting in the face of his executioners, and making at them a wry mouth. And 'tis most certain that, to the very last gasp, they never cease to brave and defy them both in word and gesture. In plain truth, these men are very savage in comparison of us, for, of necessity, they must either be absolutely so, or else we are savages; for there is a vast difference betwixt their manners and ours.

The men there have several wives, and so much the greater number by how much they have the

The wives of the Cannibals. The nature of their jealousy.

greater reputation for valour; and it is one very remarkable virtue their women have, that the same endeavours our wives' jealousy use to hinder and divert us from the friendship and familiarity of other women, these employ to acquire it for their husbands; being, above all things, solicitous of their husband's honour, 'tis their chiefest care to procure for him the most companions in his affections they can, forasmuch as it is a testimony of their husbands' valour. Ours will cry out that 'tis monstrous: it is not so; 'tis a truly matrimonial virtue, though of the highest form. In the Bible, Sarah, Leah, and Rachel, and the wives of Jacob, gave the most beautiful of their handmaids to their husbands; Livia promoted the appetites

of Augustus to her own prejudice; and Stratonice, the wife
of King Dejotarus, not only gave up a fair young maid that
served her, to her husband's embraces, but, moreover, carefully brought up the children he had by her, and assisted
them in the succession to their father's crown.[1]

And, that it may not be supposed that all this is done by a
simple and servile observance of their common practice, or
by any authoritative impression of their ancient custom, without judgment or reason, or, from having a soul so stupid that
it cannot contrive what else to do, I must here give you some
touches of their sufficiency in point of understanding. Besides what I repeated to you before, which was one of their
songs of war, I have another, a love-song, that A love-song of
begins thus: "Stay, adder, stay, that, by thy theirs.
pattern, my sister may draw the fashion and work of a rich
belt I would present to my beloved; so may thy beauty and
the excellent order of thy scales be for ever preferred before
all other serpents." The first couplet is the burden of the
song. Now I have conversed enough with poetry to judge
thus much; that not only there is nothing barbarous in this
composition, but, moreover, that it is perfectly anacreontic.
Indeed, their language is soft, of a pleasing accent, and something bordering upon the Greek terminations. What some of the
Three of these people, not foreseeing how dear savages who came
to France thought
their knowledge of the corruptions of this part of our manners.
of the world will, one day, cost their happiness and repose,
and that the effect of this commerce will be their ruin;
which, I suppose, is in a very fair way (miserable men, to
suffer themselves to be deluded with desire of novelty, and
to have left the serenity of their own heaven to come so far
to gaze at ours!), went to Rouen, at the time that the late
King Charles the Ninth was there. The king himself talked
to them a good while, and they were made to see our fashions, our pomp, and the form of a great city; after which
some one asked their opinion, and would know of them, what

[1] Plutarch, *Virtuous deeds of women.*

of all the things they had seen they found most to be admired? To which they made answer, three things, of which I have forgot the third, and am vexed at it, but two I yet remember. They said that, in the first place, they thought it very strange that so many tall men wearing beards, strong and well armed, who were about the king ('tis like, they meant the Swiss of the guard), should submit to obey a child, and that they did not rather choose out one amongst themselves to command; secondly, (they have a way of speaking in their language, to call men the half of one another,) that they had observed that there were, amongst us, men full and crammed with all manner of luxuries, whilst, in the mean time, their halves were begging at their doors, lean and half-starved with hunger and poverty; and thought it strange that these necessitous halves were able to suffer so great an inequality and injustice, and that they did not take the others by the throats, or set fire to their houses. I talked to one of them a long while, but I had an interpreter, who followed so ill, and whose stupidity kept him from understanding my questions so almost entirely that I could get

Answer of one of the savages to Montaigne.

nothing out of him of any moment. Asking him what advantage he reaped from the superiority he had amongst his own people—for he was a captain, and our mariners called him king,—he told me, to march at the head of them to war; and demanding of him, farther, how many men he had to follow him? he showed me a space of ground, to signify as many as could march in such a compass; which might be four or five thousand men; and, putting the question to him, whether or no his authority expired with the war? he told me this remained; that when he went to visit the villages in his dependency, they cleared him paths through the thick of their woods, through which he might pass at his ease. All this does not sound very ill, but then, forsooth, they wear no breeches.

CHAPTER XXXI.

THAT A MAN IS SOBERLY TO JUDGE OF DIVINE ORDINANCES.

THINGS unknown are the principal and true field of imposture, forasmuch as, in the first place, their very strangeness lends them credit ; and, moreover, by not being subjected to our ordinary reason, they deprive us of the means to question and dispute them. On which account, says Plato,[1] it is much more easy to satisfy the hearers, when speaking of the nature of the gods, than of the nature of men, because the ignorance of the auditory affords a fair and large career, and all manner of liberty in the handling of recondite things; and thence it comes to pass that nothing is so firmly believed as what we least know; nor any people so confident as those who entertain us with fables, such as your alchemists, judicial astrologers, fortune-tellers, physicians, and *id genus omne.* To whom I could, willingly, if I durst, join a set of people that take upon them to interpret and control the designs of God himself, making a business of finding out the cause of every accident, and of prying into the secrets of the divine will, there to discover the incomprehensible motives of his work. And although the variety and the continual discordance of events throw them from corner to corner, and toss them from east to west, yet do they still persist in their vain inquisition, and, with the same pencil, paint black and white. In a nation of the Indies, there is this commendable custom, that when any thing befalls them amiss in any encounter or battle, they publicly ask pardon of the sun, who is their God, as having committed an unjust action, always imputing their good or

The subjects of imposture.

---

[1] *Critias.*

evil fortune to the divine justice, and to that submitting their
No authority can be ascribed to our religion from events. own judgment and reason. 'Tis enough for a Christian to believe that all things come from God, to receive them with acknowledgment of his divine and inscrutable wisdom, and thankfully to accept and receive them with what face soever they may present themselves. But I do not approve of what I see in use, that is, to seek to conform and support our religion by the prosperity of our enterprises. Our belief has other foundation enough without going about to authorize it by events; for the people, being accustomed to such arguments as these, so plausible, and so fitted to their own taste, it is to be feared lest, when they fail of success, they should also stagger in their faith. As in the war, wherein we are now engaged, upon the account of religion, those who had the better in the affair of Rochelabeille,[1] making great brags of that success, as an infallible approbation of their cause, when they came afterwards to, excuse their misfortunes of Jarnac and Moncontour,[2] 'twas by saying they were fatherly scourges and corrections; if they have not a people wholly at their mercy, they make it manifestly enough to appear what it is to take two sorts of grist out of the same sack, and with the same mouth to blow hot and cold. It were better to possess the vulgar with the solid and real foundations of truth. 'Twas a brave naval battle that was gained a few months since, against the Turks, under the command of Don Juan of Austria;[3] but it has also pleased God, at other times, to let us see as great victories at our own expense. In fine, 'tis a hard matter to reduce divine things to our balance without losing a great deal of the weight. And he that would take upon him to give a reason why Arius and his Pope Leo, the principal heads of that heresy, should die at different times, of such similar and such strange deaths (for being withdrawn

---

[1] A great skirmish that had like to have caused a general battle betwixt the troops of the Admiral de Coligny, and those of the Duke of Anjou, in May, 1569

[2] These battles were won by the Duke of Anjou, the first in March, and the last in October, 1569.

[3] In the Gulf of Lepanto, 7th October, 1571.

from the disputation by a disorder of the bowels, they both
of them suddenly gave up the ghost upon the close-stool [1]),
and would aggravate this divine vengeance by the circumstances of the place; might as well add the death of Helio-
gabalus, who was also slain in a house of office.[2] But what
then? Irenæus was involved in the same for-
tune; God being pleased to show us that the
good have something else to hope for; and the
wicked something else to fear, than the fortunes
The good or bad
success of men no
proof either of
their merit or
demerit.
and misfortunes of this world; he manages and applies pleasure, and deprives us of the means foolishly to make our own
profit. And those people both abuse themselves and us who
will pretend to dive into these mysteries by the strength of
human reason. They never give one hit that they do not
receive two for it; of which St. Augustin gives a very great
proof upon his adversaries. 'Tis a conflict that is more decided by strength of memory than the force of reason. We
are to content ourselves with the light it pleases the sun to
communicate to us by his rays, and he who will lift up his
eyes to take in a greater, let him not think it strange if, for
the reward of his presumption, he there lose his sight. *Quis
hominum potest scire consilium Dei? Aut quis poterit cogi-
tare quid velit Dominus?*[3] "Who amongst men can know
the counsel of God? Or who can think what the will of the
Lord is?"

[1] Athanasius, *Epist. ad Serapion.* [3] *Wisdom,* ix. 18.
[2] Ælian. Lamp. *in Vitâ.*

CHAPTER XXXII.

THAT WE ARE TO AVOID PLEASURES EVEN AT THE EXPENSE OF LIFE.

I HAVE, long ago, observed most of the opinions of the ancients to concur in this, that it is high time to die when there is more ill than good in living, and that to preserve life, to our own torment and inconvenience, is contrary to the very laws of nature, as these old lines instruct us :—

> Ἡ ζῆν ἀλύπως, ἢ θανεῖν εὐδαιμόνως.
> Καλὸν τὸ θνήσκειν οἷς ὕβριν τὸ ζῆν φέρει.
> Κρεῖσσον τὸ μὴ ζῆν ἐστὶν, ἢ ζῆν ἀθλίως.[1]

> "Adieu! want, care, with misery's various train,
> Death then is happy, when to live is pain."

But to push this contempt of death so far as to employ it to the removing our thoughts from the coveting of honours, riches, dignities, and other favours, and goods of fortune, as we call them, as if reason had not sufficient to do to persuade us to avoid them without adding this new charge, I had never seen it either enjoined or practised, till this passage of Seneca fell into my hands ; who, advising Lucilius, a man of great power and authority about the Emperor, to alter his voluptuous and magnificent way of living, and to retire himself from this worldly vanity and ambition, to some solitary, quiet, and philosophical life, and the other alleging some difficulties : "I am of opinion," says he,[2] "either that you leave that life or life itself; but I would advise thee to the gentler way, and to untie, rather than to break, the knot thou hast ill knit, provided that, if it be not otherwise to be untied, thou resolutely break it. There is no man so great a coward that had not rather once fall than be always falling." I should have found

[1] Stobæus, *Serm.* 20.   [2] *Epist.* 22.

this counsel conformable enough to the stoical roughness; but it appears the more strange for being borrowed from Epicurus, who writes the same thing upon the like occasion to Idomeneus. And I think I have observed something like it, but with Christian moderation, amongst our own people. St. Hilary, Bishop of Poictiers, that famous enemy of the Arian heresy, being in Syria, had intelligence thither sent him that Abra, his only daughter, whom he left at home under the eye and tuition of her mother, was sought in marriage by the greatest nobleman of the country, as being a virgin virtuously brought up, fair, rich, and in the flower of her age. Whereupon he writ to her (as it appears upon record) that she should remove her affection from all the pleasures and advantages proposed unto her; for he had in his travels found out a much greater and more worthy fortune for her, a husband of much greater power and magnificence, that would present her with robes and jewels of inestimable value; wherein his design was to dispossess her of the appetite and use of worldly delights, to join her wholly to God. But the nearest and most certain way to this being, as he conceived, the death of his daughter, he never ceased, by vows, prayers, and orisons, to beg of the Almighty that he would please to call her out of this world, and to take her to himself; as accordingly it came to pass; for soon after his return she died, at which he expressed a singular joy. This seems to outdo the others, forasmuch as he applies himself to this means in the first instance, which they only take subsidiarily, and, besides, it was towards his only daughter. But I will not omit the latter end of this story, though it be from my purpose. St. Hilary's wife, having understood from him how the death of their daughter was brought about by his desire and design, and how much happier she was, to be removed out of this world than to have stayed in it, conceived so lively an apprehension of the eternal and heavenly beatitude that she begged of her husband with the extremest importunity to do as much for her; and God, at their joint request, shortly after calling her to him, it was a death embraced on both sides with singular content.

CHAPTER XXXIII.

THAT FORTUNE[1] IS OFTENTIMES OBSERVED TO ACT BY THE RULE OF REASON.

THE inconstancy of the various motions of fortune may reasonably make us expect she should present us with all sorts of faces. Can there be a more express act of justice than this? The Duke of Valentinois, having resolved to poison Cardinal Adrian Corneto, with whom his father, Pope Alexander the Sixth, and himself, were to sup in the Vatican, sent before a bottle of poisoned wine, with strict order to the butler to keep it very safe. The Pope being come before his son, and calling for drink, the butler, supposing this wine had only been so strictly recommended to his care upon the account of its excellence, presented it immediately to the Pope, and the Duke himself, coming in presently after, and being

---

[1] The word *fortune*, so often used by Montaigne, and sometimes in passages where he might have employed the word *providence*, was censured by the *docteurs moines*, who examined the Essays during the author's stay in Rome, in 1581. (See his Journey in Italy.) In countries subject to the Inquisition, at Rome especially, it was forbidden to say *fatum* or *fata*. An author having occasion to use the word, printed it *facta*, but in the *errata* put "for *facta*, read *fata*." And similar stratagems were more than once resorted to. Thus the Protestant Daniel Heinsius, sending forth in that city a work in which he spoke of Pope Urban VIII., called him in the text, *Ecclesiæ Caput*, but, in the *errata*, *Ecclesiæ Romanæ Caput*. It would seem that the censorship of books was not always exercised by persons of much ability. La Mothe le Vayer says, that Naudæus himself told him that in a work which he wished to print at Rome, and which contained these words, *Virgo fata est*, the Inquisitor noted in the margin, *Propositio hæretica; nam non datur* FATUM. The prohibition was so closely carried in force that Addison, in his Travels in Italy, tells us he was much amused at reading, at the head of an opera-bill, the following: " PROTESTA. *Le Voci, Fato, Deità, Destino, e simili*, che per entro questo dramma troverai, son messe per ischerzo poetico, è non per sentimento vero, credendo sempre in tutto quello, che crede et comanda santa madre Chiesa." Montaigne justifies himself, in chap. lvi. of this work, for having used some of these prohibited words, *verba indisciplinata*, as he calls them; it would seem, from the old editions, that he did not put forth this sort of apology till after his return from Rome.

confident that they had not meddled with his bottle, took also his cup; so that the father died immediately upon the spot, and the son, after having been long tormented with sickness, was reserved to another and a worse fortune.[1]   Sometimes she seems to play upon us just in the nick of an affair.   Monsieur d'Estrée, at that time stand-ard-bearer to Monsieur de Vendosme, and Mon-sieur de Liques, lieutenant to the Duke of Ascot's troop, being both suitors to the Sieur de Founguesselles's sister,[2] though of different parties (as it oft falls out amongst frontier neigh-bours), the Sieur de Liques carried her; but on the same day he was married, and, which was worse, before he went to bed to his wife, the bridegroom having a mind to break a lance in honour of his new bride, went out to skirmish near St. Omers, where the Sieur d'Estrée proving the stronger, took him prisoner; and the more to illustrate his victory, the lady herself was fain

Fortune seems sometimes to sport with us.

> Conjugis antè coacta novi dimittere collum
> Quàm veniens una atque altera rursùs hyems
> Noctibus in longis avidum saturasset amorem,[3]

> "Of her fair arms, the am'rous ring to break,
> Which clung so fast to her new spouse's neck,
> Ere of two winters many a friendly night
> Had sated her love's greedy appetite,"

to request him of courtesy to deliver up his prisoner to her, as he accordingly did; the gentlemen of France never deny-ing any thing to the ladies.   Does this not seem a master-stroke; Constantine, the son of Helen, founded the empire of Constantinople; and so many ages after, Constantine, the son of Helen, put an end to it.

Sometimes she is pleased to emulate our miracles.   We are told that King Clovis besieging Angouleme, the walls fell down of themselves by divine favour.   And Bouchet has it from some author, that King Robert, having sat down

---

[1] In 1503. Guicciardini, vi.
[2] Or rather *Fouquerolles*. See Mem. of   [3] Catullus, lxvi. 81.
Mart. du Bellay, ii.

before a city, and being stolen away from the siege to keep
the feast of Saint Aignan at Orleans; as he was in devotion
at a certain point of the mass, the walls of the beleaguered
city, without any effort of the besiegers, fell down in ruins.
But she did quite contrary in our Milan war; for Captain
Rense, laying siege to the city of Arona,[1] and having carried
a mine under a great parcel of the wall, the mine being
sprung, the wall was lifted from its base, but dropped down
again nevertheless whole and entire, and so exactly upon its
foundation that the besieged suffered no inconvenience by
that attempt.

Sometimes she plays the doctor. Jason of Phereus, being

*Fortune some-
times turns
doctor.*

given over by the physicians, by reason of a
desperate imposthume in his breast, having a
mind to rid himself of his pain, by death at
least, in a battle threw himself desperately into the thickest
of the enemy, where he was so fortunately wounded quite
through the body that the imposthume broke, and he was

*Sometimes she is
superior to art;*

perfectly cured.[2] Did she not also excel the
painter Protogenes in his art? who having
finished the picture of a dog, quite tired and out of breath,
in all the other parts excellently well to his own liking, but
not being able to express as he would the slaver and foam
that should come out of his mouth, vexed and angry at his
work, he took his sponge, which by cleansing his brushes had
imbibed several sorts of colours, and threw it in a rage against
the picture, with an intent utterly to efface it; when fortune
guiding the sponge to hit just upon the mouth of the dog, it

*and sometimes
she corrects our
counsels.*

there performed what all his art was not able
to do.[3] Does she not sometimes direct our
counsels and correct them? Isabella, Queen
of England, being to sail from Zealand into her own king-

---

[1] On the Lago Maggiore. Mem. of Mart.
du Bellay, ii.
[2] Pliny, *Nat. Hist.* vii. 50. Valerius
Maximus, who mentions this accident, i.
9, in Externis, represents the fact in a
manner still more miraculous; for he
says that Jason received this important
service from an assassin. Seneca ascribes
this accident to the same cause. *De
Benef.* ii. 19.
[3] Pliny, *Nat. Hist.* xxxv. 10.

dom,[1] with an army in favour of her son against her husband, had been lost had she come into the port she intended, being there laid wait for by the enemy; but fortune, against her will, threw her into another haven, where she landed in safety. And he of old who, throwing a stone at a dog, hit and killed his mother-in-law, had he not reason to pronounce this verse :—

Ταυτόματον ἡμῶν καλλίω βουλεύεται.[2]

" fortune has more judgment than we."

Icetes[3] had engaged with two soldiers to kill Timoleon at Adrano in Sicily. These chose their time to do it, when he was assisting at a sacrifice, and, thrusting into the crowd, as they were making signs to one another, that now was a fit time to do their business, in steps a third, who with a sword takes one of them full drive on the head, lays him dead upon the place, and runs away. Which the other seeing, and concluding himself discovered and lost, he runs to the altar and begs for mercy, promising to discover the whole truth, which as he was doing, and laying open the whole conspiracy, behold the third man, who, being apprehended, was as a murderer thrust and hauled by the people through the crowd towards Timoleon and other the most eminent persons of the assembly, before whom being brought he cried out for pardon, pleaded that he had justly slain his father's murderer; which he also proved upon the place, by sufficient witnesses, whom his good fortune very opportunely supplied him withal, that his father was really killed in the city of the Leontines by that very man on whom he had taken his revenge; he was presently awarded ten attic minæ, for having had the good fortune, in designing to revenge the death of his father, to preserve the life of the common father of Sicily. Thus fortune, in her conduct, surpasses all the rules of human prudence. But, to conclude, is

She surpasses the rules of human prudence.

---

[1] In 1326. Mem. of Froissart.
[2] Menander.
[3] He was a Sicilian, born at Syracuse, that aimed to oppress the liberty of his country, of which Timoleon was the protector. Plutarch, *Life of Timoleon*, 9.

there not a direct application of her favour, bounty, and piety,

A father and son proscribed, die together by a special favour of fortune. manifestly discovered in this action? Ignatius the father and Ignatius the son being proscribed by the triumviri of Rome, resolved upon this generous act of mutual kindness, to fall by the hands of one another, and by that means to frustrate and defeat the cruelty of the tyrants; and accordingly, with their swords drawn, ran full drive one upon another, where fortune so guided the points that they made two equally mortal wounds, affording withal so much honour to so brave a friendship, as to leave them just strength enough to draw out their bloody swords, that they might have liberty to embrace one another in this dying condition, with so close an embrace that the executioners cut off both their heads at once, leaving the bodies still fast linked together in this noble knot, and their wounds joined, affectionately sucking in the last blood and remainder of the lives of one another.[1]

CHAPTER XXXIV.

OF ONE DEFECT IN OUR GOVERNMENT.

My late father, who, for a man that had no other advantages than experience only, and his own natural parts, was **The project of an office of agency.** of a very clear judgment, formerly told me that he once had thoughts of endeavouring to introduce this practice, that there might be in every town a certain place assigned, to which such as stood in need of any thing might repair, and have their business entered by an officer appointed for that purpose. As, for example, I want to sell pearls; I want to buy pearls; such a one wants company

[1] Appian, *de Bell. Civil*, iv.

to go to Paris; such a one inquires for a servant of such a quality; such a one for a master; such a one for such an artificer; some for one thing, some for another, every one according to what he wants. And it seems to me that these mutual advertisements would be of no contemptible advantage to the public business; for there are, every day, conditions that seek after one another, and for want of knowing one another's occasions, leave men in very great necessity. I hear, to the great shame of the age we live in, that in our very sight two most excellent men for learning died so poor that they had scarce bread to put in their mouths, Lilius Gregorius Giraldus,[1] in Italy, and Sebastianus Castalio,[2] in Germany. And I believe there are a thousand men would have invited them into their families, on advantageous conditions, or have relieved them where they were, had they known their wants. The world is not so generally corrupted but that I know a man that would heartily wish the estate his ancestors have left him might be employed, so long as it shall please fortune to give him leave to enjoy it, to secure remarkable persons of any kind, whom misfortune sometimes persecutes to the last degree, from the danger of necessity; and, at least, place them in such a condition that they must be very hard to please if they were not contented. My father, in his domestic government, had this order (which I know how to commend but by no means imitate), that besides the daybook or register of the household affairs, where the small accounts, payments, and disbursements, which do not require a special hand, were entered, and which a bailiff always had in custody; he ordered him whom he kept to write for him, to keep a journal, and in it to set down all the remarkable occurrences, and, day by day, the memoirs of the affairs of his house;

The miserable deaths of Giraldus and Castalio.

The laudable regulations observed by Montaigne's father.

---

[1] Born at Ferrara, 1489, died there 1552. His works, of which the principal are a History of the Gods, and Dialogues on the Poets, were published by Jensius, at Leyden, 1696.

[2] A native of Dauphiny, born 1515, died 1563. He is principally known by his Latin version of the Bible, in which he affects to use only the Ciceronian style of language.

very pleasant to look over when time begins to wear things
out of memory, and very useful sometimes to put us out of
doubt, when such a thing was begun, when ended, what
courses were debated on, what concluded; our voyages, ab-
sences, marriages, and deaths, the reception of good or ill
news, the change of principal servants, and the like. An
ancient custom which I think it would not be amiss for every
one to revive in his own house; and I did very foolishly in
neglecting it.

———————◆———————

CHAPTER XXXV.

OF THE CUSTOM OF WEARING CLOTHES.

WHATEVER I shall say upon this subject, I must, of neces-
What gave rise to sity, invade some of the bounds of custom, so
the custom of
some nations to go careful has she been to shut up all the avenues.
stark naked.   I was discussing with myself, in this shivering
season, whether the fashion of going naked, in those nations
lately discovered, is imposed upon them by the hot temperature of the air, as we say of the Moors and Indians, or
whether it was the original fashion of mankind. Men of understanding, forasmuch as all things under the sun, as Holy
Writ declares, are subject to the same laws, have been wont,
in such considerations as these, where we are to distinguish
the natural laws from those of man's invention, to have
recourse to the general polity of the world, where there can
be nothing counterfeited. Now, all other creatures being
sufficiently furnished with all things necessary for the support of their being, without needle and thread, it is not to be
imagined that we only should be brought into the world in a
defective and indigent condition, and in such a state as cannot
subsist without foreign assistance; and therefore it is that I

believe that, as plants, trees, and animals, and all things that have life, are seen to be, by nature, sufficiently clothed and covered to defend them from the injuries of weather,

> Proptereaque ferè res omnes, aut corio sunt,
> Aut setâ, aut conchis, aut callo, aut cortice tectæ.[1]

> "And, therefore, shells, or rinds, or films, inclose,
> Or skin, or hair, on ev'ry body grows."

so were we; but as those who, by artificial light, put out that of the day, so we, by borrowed forms and fashions, have destroyed our own. And 'tis plain enough to be seen that 'tis custom only which renders that impossible that otherwise is nothing so; for, of those nations who have no manner of knowledge of clothing, some are situated under the same temperature that we are, and some in much colder climates. And, besides, our most tender parts are always exposed to the air, as the eyes, mouth, nose, and ears; and our country fellows, like our ancestors, go with their breasts open. Had we been born with a necessity upon us of wearing petticoats and breeches, there is no doubt but nature would have fortified those parts she intended should be exposed to the fury of the seasons with a thicker skin, as she has done the fingers' ends and the soles of the feet. And why should this seem hard to believe? I observe much greater distance betwixt my mode of dress and that of one of our country peasants, than betwixt his and a man that has no other covering but his skin. How many men, especially in Turkey, go naked merely upon account of devotion? Somebody, I forget who, asked a beggar, whom he saw in his shirt, in the depth of winter, as brisk and frolic as he who goes muffled up to the ears in furs, how he was able to endure to go so? " Sir," said the fellow, " you go with your face bare; I am all face." The Italians have a story of the Duke of Florence's fool, whom his master asking how, being so thin clad, he was able to support the cold, when he, himself, warm wrapt up as he was, was hardly able to do it? " Why,"

[1] Lucretius, iv. 933.

replied the fool, " use my receipt ; put on all the clothes you
have at once, as I do, and you'll feel no more cold than I."
King Massinissa, to an extreme old age, could never be prevailed upon to go with his head covered, how cold, stormy,
or rainy soever the weather might be.[1] Which also is
reported of the Emperor Severus. Herodotus tells us [2] that,
in the battles fought betwixt the Egyptians and the Persians,
it was observed, both by himself and others, that of those
who were left dead upon the place, the heads of the Egyptians were found to be, without comparison, harder than those
of the Persians, by reason that the last had gone with their
heads always covered from their infancy, first, with biggins,
and then with turbans, and the others always shaved and
bare.   And King Agesilaus continued to a decrepit age, to
wear always the same clothes in winter that he did in summer.[3]   Cæsar, says Suetonius, marched always at the head
of his army, for the most part on foot, with his head bare,
whether it was rain or sunshine, and as much is said of Hannibal,

> Tum vertice nudo,
> Excipere insanos imbres, cœlique ruinam.[4]

> " Exposing his bare head to furious show'rs,
> While hail or rain in torrents on it pours."

A Venetian, who has long lived in Pegu, and is lately
returned thence, writes, that the men and women of that
kingdom, though they cover the rest of their persons, go
always barefoot, and ride so too. And Plato does very earnestly advise, for the health of the whole body, to give the
head and the feet no other clothing than what nature has
bestowed.   He whom the Poles have elected for their king,[5]
since ours left them, who is indeed one of the greatest princes
of this age, never wears any gloves, and for winter, or whatever weather may come, never wears any other cap abroad
than the same he wears at home.   Whereas, I cannot endure

[1] Cicero, *De Senect.* c. 10.
[2] Book iii.
[3] Plutarch, *in Vitâ.*
[4] Silius, Italicus, i. 250.
[5] Stephen Bathory.

to go unbuttoned or loose, our neighbouring labourers would
think themselves in chains if they were so braced. Varro is
of opinion that when it was ordained we should be bare in
the presence of the gods, and before the magistrate, it was
rather so ordered upon the score of health, and to inure us to
the injuries of weather, than upon the account of reverence.[1]
And since we are now talking of cold, and are Frenchmen,
used to trick ourselves out in many colours, (not I myself, for
I seldom wear other than black or white, in imitation of my
father,) let us add another story of Captain Martin du Bellay, who affirms, that in the journey through Luxemburg, he
saw such a great frost that the munition-wine was cut with
hatchets and wedges, delivered out to the soldiers by weight,
and carried away in baskets ; [2] and Ovid,

> Nudaque consistunt formam servantia testæ
> Vina, nec hausta meri, sed data frusta, bibunt.[3]

> " The wine
> Stript of its cask, retains the figure still,
> Nor do they draughts, but crusts of Bacchus, swill."

At the mouth of the Lake Mœotis, the frosts are so severe
that in the very same place where Mithridates's lieutenant
had fought the enemy dry-foot, and given them a defeat, the
summer following he also obtained over them a naval victory.[4]
The Romans fought at a very great disadvantage in the engagement they had with the Carthaginians near Placentia,
by reason that they went to the charge with their blood con-
gealed, and their limbs numbed with cold,[5] whereas Hannibal
had caused great fires to be made through his camp to warm
his soldiers, and oil to be distributed amongst them, to the
end that, anointing themselves, they might render their
nerves more supple and active, and fortify the pores against
the violence of the air, and freezing wind that then raged.

---

[1] Pliny, *Nat. Hist.* xxviii. 6.
[2] In 1543. *Mem. de Mart. du Bellay.*
x.—Philip de Comines, speaking of such
cold weather in his time (1469,) in the
principality of Liege, says, that the wine
was in like manner frozen in their pipes,
and that it was dug out, and cut into the
form of wedges, and so carried off by gentlemen in hats or baskets, ii. 14.
[3] Ovid, *Trist.* iii. 10, 23.
[4] Strabo, vii.
[5] Livy, xx. 54

The retreat the Greeks made from Babylon into their own country is famous for the difficulties and calamities they had *Terrible ravages* to overcome. Of which this was one, that be-*made by snow, in* ing encountered in the mountains of Armenia *the mountains of* *Armenia.* with a horrible storm of snow, they lost all knowledge of the country, and of the ways, and being shut up, were a day and a night without eating or drinking, most of their cattle dead, many of themselves starved dead, several struck blind with the driving and glittering of the snow, many of them maimed in their fingers and toes, and many stiff and motionless with the extremity of the cold, who yet *Fruit-trees buried* had their understanding entire.[1] Alexander *in the winter.* saw a nation where they bury the fruit-trees in winter, to defend them from the frost,[2] and we also may see *How often the* the same. But concerning clothes, the King *King of Mexico* of Mexico changed his apparel four times a *changed his* *clothes in a day.* day, and never put them on more, employing those he left off, in his continual liberalities and rewards; nor was either pot, dish, or other utensil of his kitchen or table ever served up to him twice.

CHAPTER XXXVI.

OF CATO THE YOUNGER.

I AM not guilty of the common error of judging another by myself. I easily believe that in another's humour which is contrary to my own; and though I find myself engaged to one certain form, I do not oblige others to it, as many do, but believe and apprehend a thousand different ways of living; and, contrary to most men, more easily admit of differences

[1] Xenophon, *Expedition of Cyrus*, iv. 5.   [2] Quintus Curtius, vii. 8.

than uniformity amongst us. I, as frankly as any one would have me, discharge a man from my humours and principles, and consider him simply as he is, without reference to myself, taking him according to his own particular model. Though I am not continent myself, I nevertheless sincerely approve of the continency of the Feuillans and the Capuchins, and highly commend their way of living. I insinuate myself very well by imagination into their place, and love and honour them the more for being other than I am myself. I very much desire that we may be judged every man by himself, and would not be drawn into the consequences of common examples. My weakness does nothing alter the esteem I ought to have of the force and vigour of those who deserve it. *Sunt qui nihil suadent quàm quod se imitari posse confidunt.*[1] "There are those who persuade nothing but what they believe they can imitate themselves." Crawling upon the slime of the earth, I do not, for all that, the less observe in the clouds the inimitable height of some heroic souls. 'Tis a great deal for me to have my judgment regular and right, even though the effects cannot be so, and to maintain this sovereign power at least free from corruption; 'tis something to have my will right and good when my legs fail me. This age wherein we live, in our part of the world at least, is grown so stupid that not only the exercise, but the very imagination of virtue is defective, and seems to be nothing but college jargon.

> Virtutem verba putant; ut
> Lucum ligna.[2]

> " Words finely couch'd these men for virtue take,
> As if each wood a sacred grove could make."

Quam vereri deberent, etiam si percipere non possent.[3] "Which they ought to reverence, though they cannot comprehend." 'Tis a mere gewgaw to hang in a cabinet, or at the end of the tongue as on the tip of the ear, for ornament

---

[1] Cicero. *De Orat.* c. 7.
[2] Horace, *Epist.* i. 6, 81.
[3] Cicero, *Tusc. Quæs.* v. 2. Montaigne applies to virtue what Cicero here says of philosophy, and of those who presume to find fault with it.

only. There are no more virtuous actions

Vicious motives destroy the essence of virtue.

extant, and those actions that carry a show of
virtue have yet nothing of its essence ; for 'tis
profit, glory, fear, and custom, and other such-like foreign
causes, are the incentives to produce them. Our justice also,
our valour and good offices, may be called so too in respect
to others, and according to the face they appear with to the
public ; but in the doer it can by no means be virtue, because
there is another end proposed, another moving cause. Now,
Virtue owns nothing to be hers but what is done by herself,
and for herself alone. In that great battle of Platæa, which
the Greeks, under the command of Pausanias,

Why the Spartans refused the reward of valour to a person who signalized himself the most in a battle.

obtained against Mardonius and the Persians,
the conquerors, according to their custom, coming to divide amongst them the glory of the exploit, they assigned to the Spartan nation the
preëminence of valour in this engagement. The Spartans,
great judges of bravery, when they came to determine to
what particular man of their nation the honour was due of
having best behaved himself upon this occasion, found that
Aristodemus had, of all others, hazarded his person with the
greatest courage ; but they did not, however, allow him any
prize or reward, by reason that his valour had been incited
by a desire to clear his reputation from the reproach of his
miscarriage at the affair of Thermopylæ, and, with a desire
to die bravely, to wipe off that former blemish.[1] Our judgments are yet sick, and obey the humour of our depraved

Many people study to depreciate the noblest deeds of the ancients.

manners. I observe most of the wits of these
times exercise their ingenuity in endeavouring to
blemish and darken the glory of the greatest and
most generous actions of former ages, putting
one vile interpretation or another upon them all, and forging
and supposing vain causes and motives for them. A mighty
fine subtlety indeed! Give me the greatest and purest
action that ever the day beheld, and I will furnish a hundred

[1] Nepos, *Life of Pausanias.* Herod. ix.

plausible vicious motives to obscure it. God knows, whoever will stretch them out to the full, what diversity of images our internal wills suffer under; they do not play the
censurers so maliciously as they do it ignorantly and rudely.
The same pains and license that others take to bespatter these
illustrious names, I would willingly undergo to Montaigne acts
lend them a shoulder to raise them higher. quite contrary,
and why.
These rare images, that are culled out by the
consent of the wisest men of all ages for the world's example,
I should endeavour to honour anew, as far as my invention
would permit, in all the circumstances of favourable interpretation. And we may well believe that the force of our
invention is infinitely short of their merit. 'Tis the duty of
good men to draw virtue as beautiful as they can, and there
would be no impropriety in the case should our passion a
little transport us in favour of so sacred a form. What these
people do to the contrary they either do out of malice, or by
the vice of confining their belief to their own capacity, as
I have said before; or, which I am more inclined to think,
from not having their sight strong, clear, and elevated enough
to conceive the splendour of virtue in her native purity. As
Plutarch complains that, in his time, some attributed the
cause of the younger Cato's death to his fear Various opinions
of Cæsar, at which he is very angry, and with of the death of
the younger Cat.
good reason, by that a man may guess how
much more he would have been offended with those who
have attributed it to ambition. Senseless people! He
would have performed a just and generous action, even
though he were to have had ignominy for his reward instead
of glory. That man was, in truth, a pattern that nature
chose out to show to what height human virtue
and constancy could arrive. But I am not Choice passages
out of five poets
capable of handling so noble an argument, and in praise of Cato,
compared and
shall therefore only set five Latin poets to- estimated by
Montaigne.
gether by the ears, to see who has done best
in the praise of Cato; and, inclusively, for their own too.

Now, a man well read in poetry will think the two first, in comparison of the others, a little languishing; the third, more vigorous, but overthrown by the extravagance of his own force. He will then think that there will be yet room for one or two gradations of invention to come to the fourth; but, coming to mount the pitch of that, he will lift up his hands for admiration; the last, the first by some space (but a space that he will swear is not to be filled up by any human wit), he will be astonished, he will not know where he is. These are wonders. We have more poets than judges and inter-

Excellent poetry above rules. preters of poetry. It is easier to write an indifferent poem than to understand a good one. There is, indeed, a certain low and moderate sort of poetry that a man may well enough judge by certain rules of art; but the true, supreme, and divine poesy is above all the rules of reason. Whoever discerns the beauty of it, with the most assured and most steady sight, sees no more than the quick reflection of a flash of lightning. This is a sort of poetry that does not exercise, but ravishes and overwhelms, our judgment. The fury that possesses him who is able to penetrate into it, wounds yet a third man by hearing him repeat it. It is like a loadstone, that not only attracts the needle, but also infuses into it the virtue to attract others. And this is more evidently seen at our theatres, where the sacred inspiration of the muses, having first stirred up the poet to anger, sorrow, hatred, and out of himself, to whatever it will, does moreover by the poet possess the actor, and by the actor, consecutively, all the spectators,—showing how much our passions hang and depend upon one another.[1] Poetry has

What sort of poetry Montaigne preferred. ever had that power over me, from a child, to transpierce and transport me. But this quick sense of it, that is natural to me, has been variously handled by variety of forms, not so much higher and lower (for they were ever the highest of every kind), as differing in colour. First, a gay and sprightly fluency,

[1] Plato, *Ion*.

afterwards a lofty and penetrating subtlety; and, lastly, a mature and constant force. Their names will better express them: Ovid, Lucan, Virgil. But our poets are beginning their career :—

> Sit Cato, dum vivit, sanè vel Cæsare major.[1]

> "Let Cato's fame,
> Whilst he shall live, eclipse great Cæsar's name,"

says one.

> Et invictum devictâ morte Catonem,[2]

> "And Cato fell, invincible in death,"

says the second. And the third, speaking of the civil wars betwixt Cæsar and Pompey, says,

> Victrix causa diis placuit, sed victa Catoni.[3]

> "Heaven approves
> "The conquering cause the conquer'd Cato loves."

The fourth, upon the praises of Cæsar, writes,

> Et cuncta terrarum subacta,
> Præter atrocem animum Catonis.[4]

> "And conquer'd all, where'er his eagle flew,
> But Cato's mind, that nothing could subdue."

And the master of the choir, after having set forth all the names of the greatest Romans, ends thus :—

> . . . . his dantem jura Catonem.[5]

> "And Cato giving laws to all the rest."

CHAPTER XXXVII.

THAT WE LAUGH AND CRY FOR THE SAME THING.

WHEN we read in history that Antigonus was very much displeased with his son, for presenting him the head of King

[1] Martial, vi 32.
[2] Manlius, *Astron.* iv. 87.
[3] Lucan, i. 128.
[4] Horace, *Od.* ii. 1, 23.
[5] *Æneid,* viii. 670.

The vanquished bewailed by the victors.

Pyrrhus, his enemy, newly slain, fighting against him, and that seeing it he wept;[1] that René, Duke of Lorraine, also lamented the death of Charles, Duke of Burgundy,[2] whom he had himself defeated, and appeared in mourning at his funeral; and that in the battle of Auroy,[3] which Count de Montfort obtained over Charles de Blois, his competitor for the duchy of Brittany, the conqueror, meeting the dead body of his enemy, was very much afflicted at his death;—we must not presently cry out,

> E così avven, che l'animo ciascuna
> Sua passion sotto 'l contrario manto
> Ricopre, con la vista or' chiara, or' bruna [4]

> " That every one, whether of joy or woe,
> The passion of his mind can govern so
> As when most griev'd to show a visage clear,
> And melancholy when best pleased appear."

When Pompey's head was presented to Cæsar, the histories tell us that he turned away his face, as from a sad and unpleasing object.[5] There had been so long an intelligence and companionship betwixt them in the management of the public affairs, such a community of fortunes, so many mutual offices, and so near an alliance, that this countenance he wore ought not to suffer under any misinterpretation, or to be suspected for either false or counterfeit, as this other seems to believe:—

> Tutumque putavit
> Jam bonus esse socer; lachrymas non sponte cadentes
> Effudit, gemitusque expressit pectore læto,
> Non aliter manifesta putans abscondere mentis
> Gaudia, quam lachrymas." [6]

> " And now he saw
> 'Twas safe to be a pious father-in-law,
> He shed forc'd tears, and from a joyful breast
> Fetch'd sighs and groans, conceiving tears would best
> Conceal his inward joy."

---

[1] Plutarch, *Life of Pyrrhus*.
[2] In 1477, before Nancy.
[3] Or Auray, near Vannes. The battle was fought under Charles V., 29th Sept. 1364.
[4] Petrarch, edit. 1545, p. 25.
[5] Plutarch, *Life of Cæsar*, c. 18.
[6] Lucretius, ix. 1037.

For though it be true that the greatest part of our actions are no other than vizor and disguise, and that it may sometimes be real and true that

Hœredis fletus sub personâ risus est,[1]

"The heir's dissembled tears, behind the screen
Could one but peep, would joyful smiles be seen,"

yet, in judging of these matters, we should con- Mankind subject to different passions. sider how much our souls are oftentimes agitated with divers passions. And as they say that in our bodies there is a congregation of divers humours, of which that is the sovereign which, according to the complexion we are of, is commonly most predominant in us ; so, though the soul has in it divers motions to agitate it, yet must there of necessity be one to overrule all the rest, though not with so necessary and absolute a dominion but that through the flexibility and inconstancy of the soul those of less authority may, upon occasion, reassume their place and make a little sally in turn. Thence it is that we see not only children, who innocently obey and follow nature, often laugh and cry at the same thing ; but none of us can boast, what journey soever he may have in hand that he has the most set his heart upon, but when he comes to part with his family and friends he will find something that troubles him within ; and though he restrain his tears, yet he puts his foot in the stirrup with a sad and cloudy countenance. And what gentle flame soever may have warmed the heart of modest and well-born virgins, yet have they to be forced from about their mothers' necks to be put to bed to their husbands, whatever this boon companion is pleased to say :—

Estne novis nuptis odio Venus? anne parentum
Frustrantur falsis gaudia lachrymulis,
Ubertim thalami quas intra limina fundunt?
Non, ita me divi, vera gemunt, juverint.[2]

"Does the fair bride the sport so greatly dread
That she takes on so when she's put to bed?

[1] Aulus Gellius, xvii. 14. [2] Catullus, de Comâ Ber. lxv. 15.

> Her parents' joys t' allay with a feign'd tear.
> She does not cry in earnest, I dare swear."

Neither is it strange to lament a person dead whom a man would by no means wish to be alive. When I rattle my servant I do it with all my mettle, and load him with no feigned, but downright, real curses; but the heat being over, if he should stand in need of me, I should be very ready to do him good; for I instantly turn the leaf. When I call him calf and coxcomb I do not pretend to entail those titles upon him for ever; neither do I think I give myself the lie in calling him an honest fellow presently after. No one quality possesses us solely and universally. Were it not like a fool to talk to one's self, there would hardly be a day or an hour wherein I might not be heard to mutter to myself and against myself, " Fool, blockhead ! " and yet I do not think that to be my character. Who, for seeing me one while cold, and presently very kind to my wife, believes the one or other to be counterfeit, is an ass. Nero, taking leave of his mother, whom he sent to be drowned, was nevertheless sensible of some emotion at the farewell, and was struck with horror and pity. 'Tis said that the light of the sun is not one continuous thing, but that he darts new rays so thick one upon another, that we cannot perceive the intermission :—

> Largus enim liquidi fons luminis, æthereus Sol
> Irrigat assiduè cœlum candore recenti,
> Suppeditatque novo confestim lumine lumen.[1]

> " For the æthereal sun that shines so bright,
> Being a fountain large of liquid light,
> With fresh rays sprinkles still the cheerful sky,
> And with new light the light does still supply."

Just so the soul variously and imperceptibly darts out her passions. Artabanus, surprising once his nephew Xerxes, chid him for the sudden alteration of his countenance. He was considering the immeasurable greatness of his forces passing over the Hellespont for the Grecian expedition, and

---

[1] Lucret. v. 282.

was first seized with a palpitation of joy to see so many
thousands of men at his command, and this appeared in the
gayety of his looks; but his thoughts at the same instant sug-
gesting to him that of so many lives there would not be one
left in a century, at most, he presently knit his brows and
grew sad, even to tears.[1] We have resolutely pursued the
revenge of an injury received, and been sensible of a singular satisfaction at our victory; but we weep notwithstanding.
Yet 'tis not for the victory that we weep; there The soul does not
is no alteration as to that. But the soul looks look upon things
with one and the
upon the thing with another eye, and repre- same eye, nor with
one and the same
sents it to itself with another kind of face; for bias.
every thing has many faces and several aspects, like a ball.
Relations, old acquaintance, and friendships, possess our imaginations, and make them tender for the time; but the turn
is so quick that it escapes us in a moment.

> Nil adeò fieri celeri ratione videtur,
> Quàm si mens fieri proponit, et inchoat ipsa.
> Ociùs ergo animus, quàm res se perciet ulla,
> Ante oculos quarum in promptu natura videtur.[2]

> " As no one action seems so swiftly done
> As what the mind has plann'd and once begun;
> This observation evidently proves
> The mind than other things more swiftly moves."

And, therefore, while we would make one continued thing of
all this succession of passion, we deceive ourselves. When
Timoleon[3] laments the murder he had committed upon so
mature and generous deliberation, he does not lament the
liberty restored to his country, he does not lament the tyrant,
but he laments his brother. One part of his duty is performed, let us give him leave to perform the other.

[1] Herod. vii. Pliny, *Epist.* iii. 7. Val.   [3] Cornelius Nepos, xx. 1. Diod. Sic.
Max. ix. 13.   xvi. 65.
[2] Lucret. iii 183.

CHAPTER XXXVIII.

OF SOLITUDE.

LET us pass over that old comparison betwixt the active and the solitary life; and as for the fine saying in which ambition and avarice cloak themselves, "That we are not born for ourselves, but for the public,"[1] let us boldly appeal to those who are in the thick of public affairs, and let them lay their hands upon their hearts and then say whether, on the contrary, they do not rather aspire to titles and offices, and the tumult of the world, to make their private advantage at the public expense. But we need not ask them the question; for the corrupt ways by which men push on towards the height at which their ambitions aspire, do manifestly enough declare that their ends cannot be very good. Let us then tell ambition that it is she herself that gives us a taste of solitude; for what does she so much avoid as society? What does she so much seek as elbow-room? A man may do well or ill everywhere; but if what Bias says be true, that the greatest part is the worse,[2] or what the preacher says, that there is not one good in a thousand,

> Rari quippe boni; numero vix sunt totidem, quot
> Thebarum portæ, vel divitis ostia Nili.[3]

> "How few good men are numbered on this soil!
> Scarce more than gates of Thebes or mouths of Nile."

The contagion is very dangerous in the crowd. A man must either imitate the vicious or hate them. Both are dangerous, either to resemble them, because they are many, or to hate many, because they are unresembling.[4] And merchants that go to sea are in the right, when they are cautious that those

---

[1] Lucan's Eulogy on Cato of Utica.
Nec sibi, sed toti gentium se credere mundo.
Luc. ii. 380.

[2] Laertius, in Vitâ.
[3] Juvenal, xiii. 26.
[4] Seneca, Epist. 7.

who embark with them in the same ship be neither dissolute blasphemers nor vicious otherways; looking upon such society as unfortunate. And therefore it was that Bias pleasantly said to some who, being with him in a dangerous storm, implored the assistance of the gods, " Peace! speak softly," said he, " that they may not know you are here in my company."[1] And a more forcible example : Albuquerque, viceroy in the Indies for Emanuel, King of Portugal, in an extreme peril of shipwreck, took a young boy upon his shoulders, for this only end, that in the society of their common danger his innocency might serve to protect him and to recommend him to the divine favour, that they might get safe to shore. 'Tis not that a wise man may not live everywhere content, and be alone in the crowd of a palace, but if it be left to his own choice he, according to the school, will fly the very sight of it. He can endure that, if need be ; but if it be referred to him, he will choose this. He cannot think himself sufficiently rid of vice if he must yet contend with it in other men. Charondas punished as bad men those who were convicted of keeping bad company.[2] There is nothing so unsociable and sociable as man ; the one by his vice, the other by his nature. And Antisthenes, in my opinion, did not give him a satisfactory answer, who reproached him with frequenting bad company, by saying, " That physicians live well amongst the sick."[3] For if they contribute to the health of the sick, no doubt but by the contagion, continual sight of, and familiarity with, diseases, they must of necessity impair their own. Now the end I suppose is all one, to live at more leisure and at greater ease. But men do not always choose the right way ; for they often think they have totally taken leave of all business, when they have only exchanged one employment for another. There is little less trouble in governing a private family than a whole kingdom. Wherever the mind is perplexed it is in an entire disorder, and domestic employments are not less troublesome for being less

1 Laertius, *in Vitâ.*   2 Diod. Sic. xii. 12.   3 Laertius, *in Vitâ.*

important. Moreover, for having shaken off the court and
the exchange, we have not taken leave of the principal vexa-
tions of life :—

> Ratio et prudentia curas,
> Non locus effusi latè maris arbiter, aufert.[1]

> " Reason and prudence our affections ease,
> Not the bold site that wide commands the seas."

Solitude does not free us from our vices Our ambition, avarice, irresolution, fear, and
inordinate desires, do not leave us with change
of place :—

> Et
> Post equitem sedet atra Cura.[2]

> " And when he rides, black Care sits close behind."

They often follow us even to the cloisters and to the philosophical schools ; nor deserts, nor caves, hair-shirts, nor fasts,
can disengage us from them.

> Hæret lateri lethalis arundo.[3]

> " The fatal shaft sticks to the wounded side."

One telling Socrates that such a one was nothing improved
by his travels : " I very well believe it," said he, " for he
took himself along with him." [4]

> Quid terras alio calentes
> Sole mutamus ? Patriæ quis exul
> Se quoque fugit ? [5]

> " To change our native soil why should we run,
> And seek one warmed by a fiercer sun ?
> For who in exile ever yet could find
> He went abroad and left himself behind ? "

If a man do not first discharge both himself and his mind of
the burden with which he finds himself oppressed, motion
will but make it press the harder and sit the heavier, as the
lading of a ship is of less incumbrance when fast stowed in a
settled posture. You do a sick man more harm than good in
removing him from place to place ; you fix and establish the

[1] Horace, *Epist.* i. 11, 25.   [4] Seneca, *Epist.* 104.
[2] Hor. iii. i. 40.   [5] Horace, *Od.* ii. 16, 18.
[3] *Æneid*, iv. 73.

disease by motion, as stakes go deeper and more fixedly into the earth by being moved up and down in the place where they are designed to stand. And therefore it is not enough to get remote from the public; 'tis not enough to shift one's self,—a man must fly from the popular dispositions that have taken possession of his soul—he must sequester and tear himself from himself.

> Rupi jam vincula, dicas:
> Nam luctata canis nodum arripit; attamen illi,
> Cum fugit, a collo trahitur pars longa catenæ.[1]

> " Thou'lt say, perhaps, that thou hast broke the chain;
> Why, so the dog has gnaw'd the knot in twain
> That tied him there; but, as he flies, he feels
> The ponderous chain still rattling at his heels."

We still carry our fetters along with us; 'tis not an absolute liberty; we yet cast back a kind look upon what we have left behind us; the fancy is still full of our old way of living:—

> Nisi purgatum est pectus, quæ prælia nobis
> Atque pericula tunc ingratis insinuandum?
> Quantæ conscindunt hominem cupidinis acres
> Solicitum curæ? quantique perinde timores?
> Quidve superbia, spurcitia, ac petulantia, quantas,
> Efficiunt clades? quid luxus, desidiesque? [2]

> " Unless the mind be purged, what conflicts dire,
> And dangers will not ev'ry thought inspire!
> Th' ungrateful man, how many bitter cares
> Incessant gall, and then how many fears!
> What horrid massacres from pride ensue,
> From sloth, lust, petulance, and from luxury, too!

The mind itself is the disease, and cannot escape from itself; *In what true solitude consists.*

> In culpâ est animus, qui se non effugit unquam,[3]

> " Still, in the mind the fault doth lie,
> That never from itself can fly,"

and therefore it should be called home, and be confined within itself; that is the true solitude, which may be enjoyed in

---

[1] Persius, v. 158.
[2] Lucretius, v. 44.
[3] Horace, *Epist.* i. 14, 13

populous cities and in the courts of kings, though more com-
modiously apart.

Now, since we will attempt to live alone, and to waive all
conversation amongst men, let us so order it that our content
may depend wholly upon ourselves; let us dissolve all obligations that ally us to others. Let us obtain this from ourselves, that we may live alone in good earnest,
and live at our ease too. Stilpo, having escaped
from the fire that consumed the city where he
lived, and where he had his wife, children, goods, and every
thing he was master of destroyed by the flames, Demetrius
Poliorcetes seeing him, amidst so great a ruin, appear with a
serene and undisturbed countenance, asked him if he had
received no loss? To which he made answer: No; and
that, thanks be to God, nothing was lost of his.[1] The philosopher Antisthenes pleasantly said, that men should only
furnish themselves with such things as would swim, and might
with the owner escape the storm;[2] and certainly a wise man
never loses any thing, if he has himself. When the city of
Nola was ruined by the Barbarians, Paulinus, who was
bishop of that place, having there lost all he had, and being
himself a prisoner, prayed after this manner: "O Lord,
keep me from being sensible of this loss; for thou knowest
they have yet touched nothing of that which is mine."[3] The
riches that made him rich, and the goods that made him good,
were still entire. This it is to make choice of treasures
that can secure themselves from plunder and violence,
and to hide them in a place into which no one can enter,
and which no one can betray but ourselves. Wives, children, goods, must be had, and especially health, by him that
can get it; but we are not so to set our heart upon them
that our happiness must have its dependence upon any
of them; we must reserve a withdrawing-room, wholly our
own, and entirely free wherein to settle our true liberty, our

Constancy in the midst of misfor- tunes.

---

[1] Seneca, *Epist.* ix.
[2] Laertius, *in Vitâ*
[3] August. *de Civit. Dei.* i. 10.

principal solitude and retreat. And in this we must, for the most part, entertain ourselves with ourselves, and so privately that no knowledge or communication of any foreign concern be admitted there; there to laugh and to talk, as if without wife, children, goods, train, or attendance; to the end that, when it shall so fall out that we must lose any or all of these, it may be no new thing to be without them. We have a mind that can turn to itself, that can be its own company; that has wherewithal to attack and to defend, to receive and to give. Let us not then fear, in this solitude, to languish in an uncomfortable vacancy of thought.

> In solis sis tibi turba locis.[1]

> "In solitary places be
> Unto thyself good company."

Virtue is satisfied with herself, without discipline, without words, without effects. In our ordinary actions there is not one of a thousand that concerns ourselves. He that thou seest scrambling up that battered wall, furious and transported, *[Men put themselves into a hurry for a thousand things that don't concern them.]* against whom so many musket-shots are levelled; and that other, all over scars, pale, and fainting with hunger, yet resolved rather to die than to open the gate to him, dost thou think that these men are there upon their own account? No, peradventure in the behalf of one whom they never saw, and that never concerns himself for their pains and danger, but lies wallowing the while in sloth and pleasure. And this other snivelling, weak-eyed, slovenly fellow, that thou seest come out of his study after midnight, dost thou think he has been tumbling over books to learn how to become a better man, wiser and more content? No such matter, he will there end his days, but he will teach posterity the measure of Plautus's verses, and the true orthography of some Latin word. Who is there that does not voluntarily exchange health, repose, and life itself, for reputation and glory, the

---

[1] Tibullus, iv. 13, 12.

most useless, frivolous, and false coin that passes current
amongst us? As though our own death were not sufficient
to terrify and trouble us, we charge ourselves, in addition,
with those of our wives, children, and family ; as though our
own affairs did not afford us anxiety enough, we take upon
us to annoy ourselves and disturb our brains, with those of
our neighbours and friends :—

> Vah! quemquamne hominem in animum instituere, aut
> Parare, quod sit carius quam ipse est sibi ? [1]

> " Alas! what mortal will be so unwise
> Any thing dearer than himself to prize ? "

Solitude seems to me to have the best pretence in such as
have already employed most their active and
flourishing age in the world's service ; as for
example, Thales. We have lived enough for others, let us
at least live out the small remnant of life for ourselves ; let
us now call in our thoughts and intentions to ourselves, and to
our own ease and repose. 'Tis no light thing to make a sure
retreat ; it will be enough to do, without mixing up with it
other enterprises and designs. Since God gives us leisure to
prepare for, and to order our removal, let us make ready,
pack up our baggage, take leave betimes of the company, and
disentangle ourselves from those strong ties that engage us
elsewhere, and separate us from ourselves. We must break
the knot of our obligations, how powerful soever, and hereafter love this, or that, but espouse nothing but ourselves.
That is to say, let the remainder be our own, yet not so
joined and so riveted as not to be forced away without flay-
ing us, or tearing away a part of the whole
piece. The greatest thing in the world is for
a man to know how to be his own ; 'tis time
to wean ourselves from society when we can no
more add any thing to it ; he who is not in a condition to
lend must forbid himself to borrow. Our forces begin to fail
us ; let us call them in, and lock them up at home. He that

In whom solitude is most becoming.

*Of what impor-
tance it is for a
man to know that
he is his own mas-
ter.*

---

[1] Terence, *Adelph.* I. 1, 13.

can convert and resolve into himself the offices of so many friendships, and of society, let him do it. In this decay of nature, which renders him useless, burdensome, and troublesome to others, let him take care not to be useless, burdensome and troublesome to himself. Let him soothe and caress himself, and above all things be sure to govern himself with reverence to his reason and conscience to that degree as to be ashamed to make a false step in their presence. *Rarum est enim ut satis se quisque vereatur.*[1] " For 'tis rarely that men have respect and reverence enough for themselves." Socrates says, that boys should cause themselves to be instructed, men exercise themselves in well doing, and old men retire from all. civil and military employments, living at their own discretion, without the obligation to any office.[2] There are some complexions more proper for these precepts of retirement, than others. Such as are of a soft and faint apprehension, and of a delicate will, and affection which is not easily subdued to em-

> The constitutions most fitted for retirement.

ployment, which is my own case, will sooner incline to this advice than active and busy souls who embrace all, engage in all, and are hot upon every thing, who offer, present, and give themselves up to every occasion. We should avail ourselves of these accidental and extraneous things, so far as they are pleasant to us, but by no means lay our principal foundation thereon, for it is no true one ; neither nature nor reason can allow it so to be ; and why, then, should we, contrary to their laws, enslave our own content by giving it into the power of another? So, to anticipate also the accidents of fortune, and to deprive ourselves of the advantages we have in our own power, as several have done upon the account of devotion, and some philosophers upon a principle of reason, for a man to be his own servant, to lie hard, to put out his own eyes, throw wealth into the river, and seek out grief, as some do, that by the misery of this life they may

---

[1] Quint. x. 7.

[2] Montaigne assigns this maxim of the Pythagoreans to Socrates, because, in the work whence he took it, (Stobæus, *Serm.* xli.) it is immediately preceded by a saying of that philosopher.

pretend to bliss in another; and others, that by laying themselves on the ground they may avoid the danger of falling,
are acts of an excessive virtue. The stoutest and firmest
natures render even their retirement glorious and exemplary.

> Tuta et parvula laudo,
> Cum res deficiunt, satis inter vilia fortis;
> Verum, ubi quid melius contingit et unctius, idem
> Hos sapere, et solos aio bene vivere, quorum
> Conspicitur nitidis fundata pecunia villis.[1]

> " Thus I, when better entertainment fail,
>   Bravely commend a plain and frugal meal;
>   On cheaper suppers show myself full wise;
>   But if some dainties more luxurious rise,
>   I call those wise and blest, and only those,
>   Whose large estates their splendid mansion shows.'"

A great deal less would serve my turn well enough. 'Tis
enough for me, while in Fortune's favour, to prepare myself
for her disgrace, and being at my ease to represent to myself,
as far as my imagination can stretch, the ill to come; just as
we practise at jousts and tiltings, where we counterfeit war in
the greatest calm of peace. I do not think Arcesilaus, the
philosopher, the less a philosopher for knowing that he made
use of gold and silver vessels,[2] as the condition of his fortune
allowed him to do; and, indeed, have a better opinion of him

The limits of nat- than if he had denied himself what he used
ural necessities. with liberality and moderation. I see the utmost limits of natural necessity, and considering a poor man
begging at my door often more jocund and more healthy than
I myself am, I put myself into his place, and attempt to dress
my mind after his fashion. And running in like manner
over other examples, though I fancy death, poverty, contempt, and sickness treading on my heels, I easily resolve
not to be affrighted, forasmuch as a less than I am takes them
with so much patience; I am not willing to believe that a
weak understanding can do more than a strong one; or that
the effects of reason cannot be as great as those of custom.

[1] Hor. *Epist.* i. 15, 42.   [2] Laertius, *in Vitâ*

And knowing how slight and uncertain these accidental conveniences are, I never forget, in the height of these enjoyments, to make it my chief prayer to God that he will please to render me content with myself, and the condition wherein he has placed me. I see young men, gay, merry fellows, who nevertheless keep a provision of pills in their trunks at home, to take when they catch a cold, which they fear so much the less because they think they have the remedy at hand. We should all take the example, and, if we find ourselves subject to some more violent disease, should furnish ourselves with such medicines as may numb and stupefy the part affected. The employ-

What occupation suits a solitary life.

ment a man should choose for a solitary life ought neither to be a laborious, nor an unpleasing one, otherwise 'tis to no purpose at all to be retired. And this depends upon every one's liking and humour; mine has no turn for household matters, and such as love this occupation ought to apply themselves to it with moderation;

> Conentur sibi res, non se submittere rebus:[1]

> " A man should to himself his business fit,
> And not himself to 's business submit."

otherwise 'tis a very servile employment, as Sallust tells us;[2] though some parts of it are more colourable than others, as the care of gardens, which Xenophon gives to Cyrus;[3] a mean may be found out betwixt that low and sordid application, so full of perpetual solicitude, which is seen in men who make it their entire business and study, and that stupid and extreme negligence, letting all things go to rack, which we see in others.

> Democriti pecus edit agellos
> Cultaque, dum peregrè est animus sine corpore velox.[4]

> " Democritus's cattle spoils his corn,
> Whilst he aloft on Fancy's wings is borne."

[1] Hor. *Epist.* 1. 1, 19.
[2] *Catiline*, iv.
[3] Œconom. iv. 20. Cicero, *On Old Age*, c. 17.
[4] Hor. *Epist.* i. 12, 12.

But let us hear what advice the younger Pliny gives his
With what view Pliny and Cicero advised retirement. friend, Cornelius Rufus, upon the subject of solitude : " I advise thee, in the pleasant retirement wherein thou art, to leave to thy servants that base and abject care of thy domestic matters, and to addict thyself to the study of letters, to extract thence something that may be entirely and absolutely thine own." [1]   By which he means reputation ; like Cicero, who says that he wishes to employ his solitude and retirement from public affairs, to acquire by his writings an immortal life. [2]

> Usque adeone
> Scire tuum nihil est, nisi te scire hoc sciat alter. [3]

> " Is knowledge nothing worth, unless you show
> To others all that you pretend to know ? "

It appears to be reason, when a man talks of retiring from the world, that he should look quite out of himself. Those do it but by halves. They design well enough for themselves, 'tis true, when they shall be no more in it ; but still they pretend to extract the fruits of their design from the world, when absent from it, by a ridiculous contradiction.

The imagination of those who seek solitude upon the account of devotion, filling up their courage with the certainty of the divine promises in the other life, is much more rationally founded. They propose to themselves God, an infinite object in goodness and power. The soul has there where-
What is to be thought of the solitude which is courted for the sake of devotion. withal, at full liberty, to satiate her desires. Afflictions and sufferings turn to their advantage, being undergone for the acquisition of an eternal health and everlasting joys. Death is to be wished and longed for, where it is the passage to so perfect a condition. And the severe rules they impose upon themselves are immediately softened down by custom, and all their carnal appetites baffled and subdued, by refusing to humour and feed them : they being only supported by use

---

[1] *Epist.* i. 3. It is *Caninius*, and not Cornelius Rufus, whom Pliny addresses.

[2] Cicero, *Orat.* c. 43.
[3] Pers. i. 23.

and exercise. This sole end, therefore, of another happy and immortal life, is that which really merits that we should abandon the pleasures and conveniences of this. And he who can really and constantly enflame his soul with the ardour of this lively faith and hope, does erect for himself in his solitude a more voluptuous and delicious life than any other sort of life. Neither the end, then, nor the means, of this advice of Pliny pleases me, The defect of Pliny's and Cicero's advice. for we often fall out of the frying-pan into the fire. This book-employment is as painful as any other, and as great an enemy to health, which ought to be the first thing in every man's thoughts; neither ought a man to be allured with the pleasure of it, which is the same that destroys the wary, avaricious, voluptuous, and ambitious men. The sages give us caution enough to beware of the treachery of our appetites, and to distinguish true and entire pleasures from such as are mixed and complicated with pain. For the greatest part of pleasures (say they) tickle and caress only to strangle us like those thieves whom the Egyptians called Philetas.[1] If headache came before drunkenness, we should have a care of drinking too much; but pleasure to deceive us marches before, and conceals her train. Books are pleasant, but if by their use we impair our health, and spoil our good humour, the best things we have, let us give them over. I, for my part, am one of those who think that no fruit derived from them can recompense so great a loss. As men who feel themselves weakened by a long series of indisposition give themselves up at last to the mercy of medicine, and submit to certain rules of living, which they are for the future never to transgress; so he who retires, weary of, and disgusted with, the common way of living, ought to model this new one he enters into by the rules of reason, and to institute and arrange it by premeditation, and after the best method he can contrive. He ought to have taken leave of all sorts of labour, what face soever it bears; and generally to have

---

[1] Seneca, *Epist.* 51.

shaken off all those passions which disturb the tranquillity of
body and soul, and then choose the way that best suits his
own humour :

> Unusquisque suâ noverit ire viâ.[1]

> " We each best know to what we are inclined."

In attending to domestic matters, in study, hunting, and all
other exercises, we should go to the utmost limits of pleasure ;
but must take heed of proceeding farther, or trouble begins
to mix in it. We are to reserve so much employment only
as is necessary to keep us in breath ; and to defend us from
the inconveniences that the other extreme, of a dull and
Certain sciences stupid laziness, bring along with it. There are
with which the some sterile, knotty sciences, and chiefly ham-
mind must not
be embarrassed. mered out for the crowd ; let such be left to
them who are engaged in the service of the world. I for my
part care for no other books but either such as are pleasant
and easy, to tickle my fancy, or those that comfort and instruct me how to regulate my life and death.

> Tacitum sylvas inter reptare salubres,
> Curantem quidquid dignum sapiente bonoque est.[2]

> " Silently meditating in the groves,
> What best a wise and honest man behoves."

Wiser men may propose to themselves a repose wholly spiritual, as having great force and vigour of mind ; but for me,
who am but ordinarily furnished that way, I find it necessary
to support myself with bodily conveniences ; and age having
of late deprived me of those pleasures that were most acceptable to me, I instruct and whet my appetite to those that
remain, and are more suitable to this new season of my life.
We ought to hold fast, tooth and nail, of the use of the pleasures of life, that our years, one after another, snatch away
from us.

> Carpamus dulcia ; nostrum est
> Quod vivis ; cinis et manes et fabula fies.[3]

---

1 Propertius, ii 25, 39.   3 Persius, v. 151.
2 Horace, *Epist.* i. 4, 7

> " And our time employ
> In pleasures which alone give life its zest;
> You'll be a tale and ashes like the rest."

Now, as to the end that Pliny and Cicero propose to us of glory, 'tis infinitely wide of my account; ambition is, of all others, the most contrary humour to solitude. Glory and repose are so inconsistent that they cannot possibly inhabit in one and the same place ; and, as far as I understand, those who seek the two have only their arms and legs disengaged from the crowd ; their mind and wishes remain engaged behind more than ever.

Glory and tranquillity incompatible.

> Tun', vetule, auriculis alienis colligis escas?[1]
> " Old as you are, will you the food supply
> For other ears ? "

They are only retired to take a better leap, and by a stronger motion to give a brisker charge into the crowd. Will you see how they shoot short ? Let us put into the balance the advice of two philosophers, of two very different sects,[2] writing the one to Idomeneus, the other to Lucilius, their friends, to retire into solitude from worldly honours and the administration of public affairs. " You have," say they, " hitherto lived swimming and floating ; come now to die in the harbour. You have given the first part of your life to the light, give what remains to the shade. It is impossible to give over business if you do not also quit the fruit, and therefore disengage yourselves from all the concerns of name and glory. 'Tis to be feared the lustre of your former actions will give you but too much light, and follow you into your most private retreat. Quit with other pleasures that which proceeds from the approbation of the world. And as to your knowledge and parts, never concern yourselves, they will not lose their effect if yourselves be ever the better for them.[3] Remember

---

1 Persius, i. 19.
2 Epicurus and Seneca. See Seneca *Epist.* 21), who quotes a passage of Epicurus's Letter to Idomeneus, very different from that preserved by Laertius.

3 " Cur ego, inquis, ista didici? Non est quod timeas ne operam perdideris: tibi didicisti."—Seneca, *Epist.* 7.

him who, being asked Why he took so much pains in an art that could come to the knowledge of but few persons?[1] 'A few are enough for me,' replied he; 'I have enough with one, I have enough with never a one.' He said true; yourself and a companion are theatre enough to one another, or you to yourself.[2] Let us be to you the whole people, and the whole people to you but one.[3] 'Tis a low ambition, to think to derive glory from a man's sloth and privacy. You should do like the beasts of chase, who efface the track at the entrance into their den.[4] You are to concern yourselves no more how the world talks of you, but how you are to talk to yourselves. Retire yourself into yourself, but first prepare yourself there to receive yourself.[5] It were a folly to trust yourself in your own hands, if you cannot govern yourself.[6] A man may miscarry alone as well as in company; till you have rendered yourself one before whom you dare not trip, and till you have a bashfulness and respect for yourself; *obversentur species honestæ animo*.[7] (Let just and honest things be still represented to the mind.) Present continually to your imagination Cato, Phocion, and Aristides, in whose presence fools themselves will hide their faults, and make them controllers of all your intentions. Should these deviate from virtue, your respect to those will again set you right; they will keep you in the way of being contented with yourself, to borrow nothing of any other but yourself; to restrain and fix your soul in certain and limited thoughts, wherein she may please herself, and, having comprehended the true and real good which men the more enjoy the more they understand, to rest satisfied, without desire of prolongation of life or

1 Seneca, *Epist.* 7.

2 " Satis magnum alter alteri theatrum sumus." This is what Epicurus wrote to one of his friends.

3 Seneca ascribes this saying to Democritus. *Ep.* 7.

4 Senec. *Epist.* 68.

5 Id. *ib.*

6 " Prodest sine dubio custodem sibi imposuisse, et habere quem respicias, quem interesse tuis cogitationibus ju-

dices. Omnia nobis mala solitudo persuadet. Cum jam profeceris ut sit tibi etiam tui reverentia, licebit dimittas paedagogum. Interim te aliquorum auctoritate custodi. Aut Cato ille sit, aut Scipio, aut Lælius, aut cujus interventa perditi quoque homines vitia supprimerent, dum te efficis coram quo peccare non audit."—Seneca, *Epist.* 25.

7 Cicero, *Tusc. Quæs.* ii. c. 21.

memory." These are the precepts of the true and natural philosophy, not of a boasting and prating philosophy, such as that of the two former.[1]

CHAPTER XXXIX.

A CONSIDERATION UPON CICERO.

ONE word more by way of comparison betwixt these two. There are to be gathered out of the writings of Cicero and the younger Pliny (who, in my opinion, but little resembles his uncle in his humour), infinite testimonies of a nature boundlessly ambitious ; and, amongst others, this for one, that they both, in the sight of all the world, solicit the historians of their time not to forget them in their memoirs ;[2] and fortune, as it were in spite, has made the vanity of these requests live upon record down to this age of ours, while she has long since buried the histories of themselves in oblivion. But this exceeds all meanness of spirit in persons of such quality as they were to think to derive any glory from babbling and prating ; even to the making use of their private letters to their friends, and so withal that, though some of them were never sent, the opportunity being lost, they nevertheless published them with this worthy excuse, that they were unwilling to lose their labour and have their lucubrations thrown away.[3] Was it not well

The ambition of Cicero and Pliny.

---

1 Pliny the Younger and Cicero.
2 Cicero writing to Luccelus (*Epist.*v.12), and Pliny to Tacitus (vil. 33), with this most remarkable difference, however, that the first earnestly desires his friend not to attach himself scrupulously to the rules of, but boldly to leap the barriers of, truth in his favour. "Te plané etiam, atque etiam rogo, ut et ornes ea ; vehementius etiam quam fortasse sentis, et in eo leges historiæ negligas ; " whereas Pliny declares expressly that he does not desire Tacitus to give the least offence to the truth :—" Quamquam non exigo ut excedas rei actæ modum. Nam nec historia debet egredi veritatem, et honeste factis veritas sufficit." One would have thought that Montaigne should, in justice to Pliny, have distinguished him from Cicero in this particular.
3 Montaigne is mistaken in supposing that the Letters of Cicero were written

becoming two consuls of Rome, sovereign magistrates of the
republic that commanded the world, to spend their time in
patching up elegant missives, in order to gain the reputation
of being well versed in their own mother-tongue?   What
could a pitiful schoolmaster have done worse, who by it got

Why Xenophon
and Cæsar wrote
their own histo-
ries.

his living?   If the acts of Xenophon and Cæsar had not far transcended their eloquence, I
don't believe they would ever have taken the
pains to write them.   They made it their business to recommend not their saying, but their doing.   And could the perfection of eloquence have added any lustre proportionable to
the merit of a great person, certainly Scipio and Lælius had
never resigned the honour of their comedies, with all the
luxuriances and delicacies of the Latin tongue, to an African
slave ; for that the work was theirs its beauty and excellency
sufficiently prove ; besides, Terence himself confesses as
much,[1] and I should take it ill in any one that would dispossess me of that belief.   'Tis an injurious mockery and imper-

Qualities, which
are not suitable to
a man's rank in
the world, cannot
do him honour.

tinence to extol a man for qualities misbecoming
his condition, though otherwise commendable
in themselves, and for such as ought not to be
his chief talent ; as if a man should commend
a king for being a good painter, a good architect, a good
marksman, or a good runner at the ring.   Commendations
that add no honour unless in combination with, and in addition to. those that are befitting him, namely, justice and the
knowledge how to govern his people both in peace and war.
'Tis in this way only that agriculture was an honour to Cyrus, and eloquence and the knowledge of letters to Charlemagne.   I have, indeed, in my time, known some who, by a
knack of writing, have got both title and fortune, yet disown
their apprenticeship, purposely corrupt their style, and affect

---

for the public. Cicero himself had only
preserved seventy of them (ad Attic.
xvi.); the rest were collected by Tiron.
It is only necessary to read the letters of
Atticus to be convinced that they were
addressed to him alone. What Montaigne says applies only to Pliny the
Younger.
[1] He does not confess it exactly, but
he does not deny it very forcibly.

ignorance of so vulgar a quality (which also our nation observes to be rarely seen in very learned hands), carefully seeking a reputation by better qualities.

The companions of Demosthenes in the embassy to Philip, extolling that prince as handsome, eloquent, and a stout drinker, Demosthenes said, "That those were commendations more proper for a woman, an advocate, or a sponge, than for a king." [1]

Great men are not to be praised for common things.

> Imperet bellante prior, jacentem
> Lenis in hostem. [2]

> " First let his empire from his valour flow,
> And then from mercy on a prostrate foe."

'Tis not his profession to know either how to hunt or to dance well :—

> Orabunt causas alii, cœlique meatus
> Describent radio, et fulgentia sidera dicent;
> Hic regere imperio populos sciat. [3]

> " Let others
> Plead better at the bar, describe the skies,
> And when the stars descend, and when they rise,
> But, Rome! 'tis thine alone, with awful sway,
> To rule mankind, and make the world obey."

Plutarch says moreover, that to appear so excellent in these less necessary qualities is to produce witness against a man's self, that he has spent his time, and applied his study ill, which ought to have been employed in the acquisition of more necessary and more useful things. Thus, Philip, King of Macedon, having heard the great Alexander, his son, sing at a feast, to the wonder and envy of the best musicians there : "Art thou not ashamed," said he to him, "to sing so well?" [4] And to the same Philip, a musician with whom he was disputing about something concerning his art, said, "Heaven forbid, sir, that so great a misfortune should ever befall you as to understand these things better than I." [5] A king should be able to an-

Great men should not excel in things not altogether necessary.

1 Plutarch, *in Vitâ.*
2 Hor. *Carmen Secul.* 51.
3 *Æneid,* vi. 849.
4 Plutarch, *Life of Pericles.*
5 Id. *How to distinguish a flatterer.*

---

swer, as Iphicrates did the orator, who pressed upon him in his invective after this manner: "And who art thou, that thou bravest it at this rate? Art thou a man-at-arms? Art thou an archer? Art thou a pikeman?" "I am none of all this, but I know how to command all these."[1] And Antisthenes took it for an argument of little valour in Ismenias that he was commended for playing excellently well upon a flute.[2] I know very well that when I hear any one insist upon the language of these Essays, I had rather a great deal he would say nothing. 'Tis not so much to elevate the style as to depress the sense, and so much the more offensively as they do it obliquely. I am much deceived if many other writers deliver more worth noting as to the matter; and, how well or ill soever, if any other writer has strewed them either with much more material, or thicker upon his paper, than myself. To bring the more in, I only put in the heads; were I to annex the sequels, I should vastly multiply this volume. And how many stories have I scattered up and down here that I only touch upon, which, should any one more curiously search into, they would find matter enough to produce infinite Essays. Neither these stories, nor my allegations, do always serve simply for example, authority, or ornament; I do not only regard them for the use I make of them; they carry sometimes, besides what I apply them to, the seed of a richer and a bolder matter, and sometimes, collaterally, a more delicate sound, both to me myself, who will say no more about it in this place, and to others who shall happen to be of my fancy.

But returning to the speaking virtue; I find no great choice betwixt not knowing to speak any thing but ill, and not knowing any thing but speaking well. *Non est ornamentum virile, concinnitas.*[3] "Neatness of style is no manly ornament." The sages tell us that, as to what concerns knowledge, there is nothing but philosophy; and to what

---

1 Plutarch, *On Fortune.*
2 Id. *Life of Pericles.*
3 Seneca, *Epist.* cxv.

concerns effects, nothing but virtue, that is generally proper to all degrees, and to all orders. There is Epicurus and Seneca set in opposition to Pliny and Cicero. something like this in these two other philosophers, for they also promise eternity to the letters they write to their friends; but 'tis after another manner, and by accommodating themselves for a good end, to the vanity of another; for they write to them, that if the concern of making themselves known to future ages, and the thirst of glory, do yet detain them in the management of public affairs, and make them fear the solitude and retirement to which they would persuade them; let them never trouble themselves more about it, forasmuch as they shall have credit enough with posterity to assure them that, were there nothing else but the very letters thus writ to them, those letters will render their names as known and famous as their own public actions themselves could do.[1] And besides this difference, these are not idle and empty letters, that contain nothing but a fine gingle of well-chosen words, and fine couched phrases, but replete and abounding with grave and learned discourses, by which a man may render himself not more eloquent, but more wise; and that instruct us not to speak, but to do well. Away with that eloquence that so enchants us with its harmony that we should more study it than things; unless you will affirm that of Cicero to be of so supreme a perfection as to form a complete body of itself. And of him I shall farther add one story we read of him to this purpose, wherein his nature will much more manifestly be laid open to us. He was to make an oration in public, and found himself a little straitened in time, to fit his words to his mouth, as he had a mind to do; when Eros, one of his slaves, brought him word that the audience was

---

[1] When Epicurus wrote to Idomeneus, then the slave of rigid power, and who had great affairs in his hands, to persuade him from a gay life, to the pursuit of true and solid glory. "If," said he, "you are fond of glory, my epistles will make you more celebrated than all things that you admire, and for which you are admired." Seneca, (*Epist.* xxi.) who, in the same epistle, says to his friend, Lucilius, "The very thing which Epicurus could promise to his friend, I promise to you, Lucilius; I shall be in the favour of posterity; it is in my power to bring out names that shall be lasting."

deferred till the next day, at which he was so ravished with joy that he enfranchised him for the good news.[1]

Upon this subject of letters, I will add, that it is a kind of writing wherein my friends think I can do something; and, I am willing to confess, I should rather have chosen to publish my whimsies that way than any other, had I had to whom to write; but I wanted such a settled correspondent as I once had, to attract me to it, to raise my fancy, and keep me to it. For to traffic with the wind, as some others have done, and to forge vain names to direct my letters to, in a serious subject, I could never do it but in a dream, being a sworn enemy to all manner of falsification. I should have been more diligent, and more confident, had I had a judicious and indulgent friend to whom to address, than thus to expose myself to various judgments of a whole people; and I am deceived if I had not succeeded better. I have naturally a comic and familiar style; but it is peculiar to myself, and not proper for public business, but, like the language I speak, too compact, irregular, abrupt, and singular. And as to letters of ceremony, that have no other substance than a fine contexture of courteous words, I am wholly to seek; I have no faculty nor relish for those tedious offers of service and affection; I don't much believe in them, and should not forgive myself, should I say more than I meant, which is very remote from the present practice; for there never was so abject and servile a prostitution of tenders of life, soul, of devotion, adoration, vassal, slave, and I know not what, as now; all which expressions are so common, and so indifferently used to and fro by every one, and to every one, that, when they would profess a greater and more respectful inclination upon more just occasions, they have not wherewithal to express it.

I mortally hate all air of flattery, which is the cause that I naturally fall into a dry, rough, and crude way of speaking,

Montaigne's account of himself as a letter-writer.

---

[1] Plutarch, *Apothegms.*

which, to such as do not know me, may seem a little to smack of disdain. I honour those most to whom I show the least honour; and where my soul moves with the greatest cheerfulness, I easily forget the ceremonies of look and gesture; I offer myself faintly and bluntly to them whose I effectually am, tendering myself the least to him to whom I am the most devoted. Methinks they should read it in my heart, and that my expression would but injure the love I have conceived within. To welcome, take leave, give thanks, accost, offer service, and such verbal formalities as the laws of our modern civility enjoin, I know no man so stupidly unprovided of language as myself. And I have never been employed in writing letters of favour and recommendation but he in whose behalf it was did not think my mediation cold and imperfect. The Italians are great printers of letters. I do believe I have at least a hundred several volumes of them, of all which, those of Annibal Caro[1] seem to me to be the best.

If all the paper I have scribbled to the ladies at the time when my hand was really prompted by my passion were now in being, there might, peradventure, be found a page worthy to be communicated to our young inamoratos that are besotted that way. I always write my letters post-haste, and so precipitately that, though I write an intolerable bad hand,[2] I rather choose to do it myself than to employ another; for I can find none able to follow me, and I never transcribe. I have accustomed the great folks that know me to endure my blots and dashes, and paper without fold or margin. Those that cost me the most pains are the worst; when I once begin to draw them on, 'tis a sign my mind's not there.

---

[1] The celebrated translator of the *Æneid*, born 1507, at Citta-Nuova, in the Marches of Ancona; died at Rome, 1566. The first part of his Letters appeared in 1572, and the second in 1574. They are reckoned among the models of Italian prose writing.

[2] Montaigne must not be believed altogether, when he talks of his bad handwriting. I have seen the copy of his Essays, corrected by his own hand, from which Naigeon's edition was printed, and I can affirm that his handwriting is very legible, straight, and, which is remarkable, exhibits but slight traces of the extreme vivacity of his character. — A. DUVAL.

I fall to without premeditation or design, the first paragraph begets the second, and so to the end of the chapter. The letters of this age consist more in margin and prefaces than matter; whereas, just as I had rather write two letters than fold up one, and always assign that employment to another person, so, when the business of my letter is dispatched, I would, with all my heart, transfer it to another hand, to add those long harangues, offers, and prayers that we place at the bottom, and should be glad that some new custom would discharge us of that trouble altogether; as also superscribing them with a long ribble-row of qualities and titles, for fear of making mistakes in which I have several times omitted writing, and especially to men of the long robe and of finance. There are so many new offices, that 'tis hard to place so many titles of honour in their proper and due order, though, being so dearly bought, they are neither to be mistaken nor omitted without offence. I find the same fault likewise with loading the fronts and title-pages of the books we commit to the press with such a clutter of titles.

CHAPTER XL.

THAT THE RELISH OF GOOD AND EVIL IN A GREAT MEAS-URE DEPENDS UPON THE OPINION WE HAVE OF THEM.

MEN (says an ancient Greek sentence[1]) are tormented with the opinions they have of things, and not by the things themselves. It would be a great victory obtained for the relief of our miserable human condition, could this proposition be established for certain and true throughout. For

[1] Epictetus, *Manual*, c. 10.

if evils have no admission into us but by the judgment we ourselves make of them, it should seem that it is then in our own power to despise them or to turn them to good. If things surrender themselves to our mercy, why do we not convert and accommodate them to our advantage? If what we call evil and torment is neither evil nor torment in itself, but only that our fancy gives it that quality, and makes it so, it lies in us to change and alter it; and it being in our own choice, if there be no constraint upon us, we must certainly be very strange fools to take arms for that side which is most offensive to us, and to give sickness, want, and contempt, a nauseous taste, if it be in our power to give them a more grateful relish, and if, fortune simply providing the matter, 'tis our business to give it its form. Now what we call evil is not so of itself, or at least that, be it what it may, it depends upon us to give it another taste or complexion (for all comes to one), let us examine how this can be maintained. If the original being of those things we fear had power to lodge itself in us by its own authority, it would then lodge itself alike and in like manner in all; for men are all of the same kind, and, saving in greater and less proportions, are all provided with the same utensils and instruments to conceive and to judge; but the diversity of opinions we have of those things does clearly evince that they only enter us by composition. One particular person, peradventure, admits them in their true being; but a thousand others give them a new and contrary being in them. We hold death, poverty, and grief, to be our principal enemies; now this death, which some repute the most dreadful of all dreadful things, who knows but that others call it the only secure harbour from the storms and tempests of life; the sovereign good of nature; the sole support of liberty; and the common and ready remedy for all evils? And, as the one expects it with fear and trembling, the others support it with greater ease than life. This fellow complains of its facility :—

What evil is, and how it concerns us.

The different ideas of death.

Mors, utinam pavidos vitæ subducere nolles,
Sed virtus te sola daret! [1]

"O death! I wish thou would⸱t the coward spare,
That of thy gift the brave alone might share."

But let us leave this vaunting courage. Theodorus answered
Lysimachus, who threatened to kill him, "Thou wilt do a
brave feat," said he, "to arrive at the force of a cantha-
rides." [2] The greatest portion of philosophers are observed
to have either purposely anticipated, or hastened and assisted,
their own death. How many ordinary people do we see led
to execution, and that not to a simple death, but mixed with
shame, and sometimes with grievous torments, who yet appear with such assurance, some through obstinacy, some from
natural simplicity, that one can discover no change from their
ordinary condition; settling their domestic affairs, commending themselves to their friends, singing, preaching, and talking with the people; nay, sometimes passing jokes to make
the bystanders laugh, and drinking to their companions, just
as well as Socrates. One that they were lead-
ing to the gallows, told them they must not
carry him through such a street, lest a merchant that lived there should arrest him by the way for an
old debt. Another told the hangman he must not touch his
neck, for fear of making him laugh, he was so ticklish;
another answered his confessor, who promised him that he
should that day sup with our Lord, "Do you go then," said
he, "in my room; for I for my part keep fast to-day."
Another having called for drink, and the hangman, having
drunk first, said he would not drink after him, for fear of
catching the pox. Everybody has heard the tale of the
Picard, to whom, being upon the ladder, they presented a
girl of the town, telling him (as our law does sometimes
permit) that if he would marry her they would save his life;
he having a while considered her, and perceiving that she
halted, "Tie up, tie up," said he, "she limps." And they

Merry jokes of some persons led to execution.

1 Lucret. iv. 580.   2 Cicero, Tus. Quæs. v. 40.

tell another story of the same kind, of a fellow in Denmark, who, being condemned to lose his head, and the like condition being proposed to him upon the scaffold, refused it, by reason the girl they offered him had hollow cheeks and too sharp a nose. A servant at Thoulouse, being accused of heresy, for the sole ground of his belief, referred himself to that of his master, a young student, prisoner with him, and chose rather to die than suffer himself to be persuaded that his master could err. We read of the inhabitants of Arras, when Louis the Eleventh took that city, that a great many let themselves be hanged, rather than they would say, "God save the king." And amongst that mean-souled race of men, the buffoons, there have been some who would not leave their fooling at the very moment of death. He that the hangman turned off the ladder cried, "Launch the galley," a slang saying of his; and another, who at the point of death was laid upon a pallet before the fire, the physician asking him where his pain lay, "Betwixt the bench and the fire," said he; and the priest, to give him extreme unction, groping for his feet, which his pain had made him pull up to him, "You will find them," said he, "at the end of my legs." To one that being present exhorted him to recommend himself to God, "Why? who's going there?" said he. And the other replying, "It will presently be yourself if it be his good pleasure."— "Would I were sure to be there by to-morrow night," said he. "Do but recommend yourself to him," said the other, "and you will soon be there." "I were best then," said he, "to carry my recommendations myself."

In the kingdom of Narsingua to this day the wives of their priests are buried alive with the bodies of their husbands; all other wives are burnt at their husband's funerals, which they not only firmly, but cheerfully, undergo.[1] At the death of their

Women that bury or burn themselves alive with the dead bodies of their husbands.

[1] In the Indies (says Cicero), where it is the custom for a man to have several wives, when the husband dies the women dispute who was his greatest favourite; and she who carries the question is over- joyed, and burnt on the same pile with her husband. (*Tus. Quæs.* v. 27.) The same custom was observed by a people of Thrace, according to Herodotus, v., and is still kept up in Indostan.

king his wives and concubines, his favourites, all his officers and domestic servants, who make up a great number of people, present themselves so cheerfully to the fire where his body is burnt that they seem to take it for a singular honour to accompany their master in death. During our late war

Death fondly coveted. of Milan, where there happened so many takings and retakings of towns, the people, impatient of so many various changes of fortune, took such a resolution to die that I have heard my father say he there saw a list taken of five and twenty masters of families that made themselves away in one week's time. A misfortune somewhat resembling that of the Zanthians, who being besieged by Brutus precipitated themselves, men, women, and children, into such a furious appetite of dying that nothing can be done to evade death which these did not put in practice to avoid life; insomuch that Brutus, with all his endeavours, could save but a very small number.[1]

Even opinion is of force enough to make itself to be

Opinions espoused at the expense of life. espoused at the expense of life. The first article of that valiant oath that Greece took and observed, in the Median war, was that every one should sooner exchange life for death than their own laws for those of Persia.[2] What a world of people do we see, in the wars betwixt the Turks and the Greeks, rather embrace a cruel death than to uncircumcise themselves to admit of baptism! An example of which no sort of religion

Cruel treatment of Jews by the King of Castile. is incapable. The kings of Castile, having banished the Jews out of their dominions, John, king of Portugal, in consideration of eight crowns a-head, sold them a retirement into his for a certain limited time, he undertaking to furnish them with shipping to transport them into Africa. The limited day being come, which, once lapsed, they were given to understand that such as were afterwards found in the kingdom should remain

---

[1] Fifty only, who were saved against their will.—Plutarch, *Life of Marcus Brutus*, c. 8.

[2] Diod. Sic. v. 29.

slaves, vessels were very slenderly provided, and those who embarked in them were rudely and villanously used by the seamen, who, besides other indignities, kept them cruising upon the sea, one while forwards, and another backwards, till they had consumed all their provisions, and were constrained to buy of them at so dear a rate, and for so long a time, that they set them not on shore till they were all stripped to their very shirts. The news of this inhuman usage being brought to those who remained behind, the greater part of them resolved upon slavery, and soon made a show of changing their religion. Emanuel, the successor of John, being come to the crown, first set them at liberty; and afterwards, altering his mind, ordered them to depart his country, assigning three ports for their departure;—hoping (says the Bishop Osorius, no contemptible Latin historian of these latter times), that the favour of the liberty he had given them having failed of converting them to Christianity, yet the aversion to commit themselves to the outrages of the mariners, and to abandon a country they were now habituated to, and were grown very rich in, to go and expose themselves in strange and unknown regions, would certainly do it. But, finding himself deceived in his expectation, and that they were all resolved upon the voyage, he cut off two of the ports he had promised them, to the end that the length and incommodity of the passage might reduce some; or that he might have opportunity, by crowding them all into one place, the more conveniently to execute what he had designed; which was to force all the children under fourteen years of age from the arms of their fathers and mothers, to transport them from their sight and conversation into a place where they Jews, that out of might be instructed and brought up in our re- zeal for their relig-
ligion.[1] He says that this produced a most selves and chil-
dren.

---

[1] Mariana, the celebrated Jesuit, says, in his history of Spain, tom. ii. xxvi. 13, that, by an edict of this prince, those children were baptized by force: a cruel edict, says the good Jesuit, altogether contrary to the Christian laws and insti- tutes. What! he adds, shall violence be used to force men to embrace Christianity, and, in the most important affair of the world, to rob those whom God has been pleased to leave to their own discretion, of that heavenly present, LIBERTY!

horrid spectacle; the natural affections betwixt the parents and their children, and, above all, their zeal to their ancient belief, contending against this violent decree, fathers and mothers were commonly seen making themselves away, and, by a still sadder and sterner example, precipitating, out of love and compassion, their young children into wells, to avoid the severity of this law. As to the remainder of them, the time that had been prefixed being expired, for want of means to transport them, they again returned into slavery. Some turned Christians, upon whose faith, or rather that of their posterity, even to this day, which is a hundred years after, few Portuguese rely, or believe them to be real converts; though custom, and length of time, are much more powerful counsellors in such changes than any constraint whatever. In the town of Castlenau-Darry,

Albigenses heretics chose rather to be burnt than recant their opinions. fifty heretics, Albigenses, at one time suffered themselves to be burnt alive in one fire, rather than they would renounce their opinions. *Quoties non modò ductores nostri* (says Cicero), *sed universi etiam exercitus, ad non dubiam mortem concurrerunt?* [1] " How oft have not only our leaders, but whole armies, run to certain death ! " I have seen an intimate friend of mine, with a real affection that was rooted in his heart by divers plausible arguments, which I could never dispossess him of, ardently seek death, and, upon the first honourable occasion that offered itself, precipitate himself into it ; and that, too, without any manner of visible reason, with an obstinate and ardent desire of dying. We have several examples in our own times of those, even among little children, who, for fear of a whipping, or some such little thing, have dispatched themselves. And what shall we not fear (says one of the ancients), if we

To proceed so far is a horrible crime, as well as to force children with this view from the arms of their parents. The Portuguese nation, however, committed sin in these two points, having dragged the children to baptism by force, and without the consent of their parents, and having engaged those more advanced in years to make profession of Christianity, by loading them with reproaches and injuries, and especially by fraudulently depriving them of the means of retiring elsewhere, which they had expressly obliged themselves to grant them.

[1] *Tusc. Quæs.* l. 37.

dread that which cowardice itself has chosen for its refuge ?[1]

To produce here a catalogue of those of all sexes, and conditions, and sects, even in the most happy ages, who have either with great constancy looked death in the face, or voluntarily sought it ; and sought it not only to avoid the evils of this life, but some purely to avoid the satiety of living, and others, for the hope of a better condition elsewhere ; I should never have done. Nay, the number is so infinite that in truth I should have a better bargain on't to reckon up those who have feared it. This one, therefore, shall serve for all. Pyrrho, the philosopher, being one day in a boat, in a very great tempest, showed to those he saw the most affrighted about him, and encouraged them by the example of, a hog that was there, nothing at all concerned at the storm.[2] Shall we then dare to say that this advantage of reason, of which we so much boast, and upon the account of which we think ourselves masters and emperors over all other creatures, was given us *To what use the knowledge of things should be applied.* for a torment? To what end serves the knowledge of things, if it renders us more unmanly; if, with it, we lose the tranquillity and repose we should enjoy without it, and if it puts us into a worse condition than Pyrrho's hog? Shall we employ the understanding that was conferred upon us for our greatest good to our own ruin ; setting ourselves against the design of nature, and the universal order of things, which intend that every one should make use of the faculties, members, and means he has, to his own best advantage ? But it may peradventure be objected against me:—Your rule is true enough as to what concerns death ; but what will you say of indigence ? What will you say of pain, which Aristippus, Hieronymus, and almost all the wise men, have reputed the worst of evils ? And those who have denied it by word of mouth have confessed it in effects. Possidonius, being extremely tormented with a sharp and painful disease, Pom-

[1] Seneca, *Epist.* 70.　　　　[2] Laertius, *in Vitâ.*

peius came to visit him, excusing himself that he had taken so unseasonable a time to come to hear him discourse of philosophy : " The gods forbid," said Possidonius, " that pain should ever have the power to hinder me from talking of it ; " and thereupon fell immediately upon a discourse of the contempt of pain. But, in the mean time, pain was playing its part, and plagued him incessantly ; on which he cried out, " Do thy worst, pain, thou shalt never make me say thou art an evil." [1] This story, that they make such a clutter about, what is there in it of the contempt of pain ? It only fights it with words, and in the mean time, if its shootings did not move him, why did he let it interrupt his discourse ? Why did he fancy he did so great a thing in refusing to call it an evil ? All does not here consist in the imagination ; our fancies may work upon other things. But this is a certain knowledge that is playing its part, and of which our senses themselves are judges.

> Qui nisi sunt veri, ratio quoque falsa sit omnis. [2]

> " Which, if not true, even reason itself must be false."

Shall we persuade our skins that the lashes of a whip tickle us ? Or our palates, that a potion of aloes is *vin de Grave ?* Pyrrho's hog is here in the same predicament with us ; he is not afraid of death, 'tis true, but if you beat him, he will cry out to some purpose. Shall we force the general law of nature, which in every living creature under heaven is seen to tremble under pain ? The very trees seem to groan under the blows they receive. Death is only felt by reason, forasmuch as it is but the movement of an instant :—

> Aut fuit, aut veniet ; nihil est præsentis in illâ ;
> Morsque minus pœnæ, quam mora mortis, habet. [3]

> " Still past or future, here no present tense
> Submits the fleeting object to our sense ;

[1] Cicero, *Tusc. Quæs.* ii. 25.
[2] Luc. iv. 487.
[3] The first verse of this distich is taken from a satirical composition which Montaigne's friend, Boëtius, addressed to him, and of which I quoted the beginning in chap. 27, *Of Friendship.* The second is from Ovid's Epistle, *Ariadne to Theseus,* ver. 84.

Death cuts so quick the thread of life in twain,
The thought is far more dreadful than the pain."

A thousand beasts, a thousand men, are dead ere they are threatened. That also which we principally pretend to fear in death is pain, the ordinary forerunner of it; yet, if we may believe a holy father, *Malum mortem non facit, nisi quod sequitur mortem.*[1] "Nothing makes death evil but what follows it." And I should say, yet more probably, that neither that which goes before, nor that which follows after, are at all the appurtenances of death. We excuse ourselves falsely, and I find, by experience, that it is rather our impatience at the imagination of death that makes us impatient of pain; and that we find it doubly grievous, as it threatens us with death. But reason, accusing our cowardice for fearing a thing so sudden, so unavoidable, and so insensible, we take the other as the more excusable pretext. All ills that carry no other danger along with them, but simply the evils themselves, we despise as things of no danger. The toothache, or the gout, painful as they are, being yet not reputed mortal, who reckons them in the catalogue of diseases?

Now let us suppose that in death we principally regard the pain; so, also, there is nothing to be feared in poverty but the miseries it brings along with it, thirst, hunger, cold, heat, watching, and the other inconveniences it makes us suffer; here, still, we have nothing to do but with pain. Pain the worst accident of our being, how it may be mitigated. I will grant, and very willingly, that it is the worst misfortune of our being; (for I am the man upon earth that the most hates and avoids it, considering that hitherto, I thank God, I have had so little to do with it;) but still, it lies in us, if not to annihilate, at least to lessen it by patience; and, though the body should mutiny, to maintain the soul and reason, nevertheless, in good temper. And were it not so, who would ever have given any reputation to virtue, valour, strength, magnanimity, and resolution? Where were their parts to be played, if there were no pain

[1] St. August. *de Civit. Dei*, l. 11.

to be defied? *Avida est periculi virtus.*[1] "Virtue is greedy
of danger." Were there no lying upon the ground, no enduring, armed at all points, the meridian heat, no feeding
upon the flesh of horses and asses, no seeing ourselves hacked
and hewed to pieces, no having a bullet pulled out from
amongst the shattered bones, no stitching up, cauterizing, and
searching of wounds, by what means were the advantage we
covet to have over the vulgar to be acquired? 'Tis very far
from flying evil and pain, what the sages say, that of actions
equally good, a man should most covet to perform that wherein there is greatest labour and pain. *Non enim hilaritate, nec
lasciviâ, nec risu, aut joco, comite levitatis, sed sæpè etiam tris-
tes firmitate et constantiâ, sunt beati.*[2] "For men are not
always happy by mirth and wantonness, nor by laughter and
jesting, the companions of levity, but very often the graver
and more melancholy sort of men reap felicity from their
steadiness and constancy." And for this reason it ever was
impossible to persuade our forefathers but that the victories
obtained by dint of force, and the hazard of war, were still
more honourable than those gained in security, by stratagem
or wiles.

> Lætius est, quoties magno sibi constat honestum.[3]

> "A noble act more noble does appear
> By how much more it costs the doer dear."

Besides, this ought to be our comfort, that naturally, *Si
gravis, brevis; si longus, levis.*[4] "If the pain be violent, 'tis
short; and if long, not violent." Thou wilt not feel it long,
if thou feelest it much, it will either put an end to itself, or
to thee, which comes to the same thing; if thou canst not
support it, it will export thee. *Memineris maximos morte
finiri; parvos multa habere intervalla requietis; mediocrium
nos esse dominos: Ut si tolerabiles sint, feramus; sin minùs,
e vitâ, quum ea non placeat, tanquam e theatro, exeamus.*[5]
"Remember that great pains are terminated by death, that

1 Senec. *De Provid.* iv.
2 Cicero. *de Finibus,* ii. 20.
3 Luc. ix. 404.
4 Cicero, *ut supra,* ii. 29.
5 Cicero. Id. *ib.* i. 15.

small ones have many intermissions of repose, and that we
are masters of the moderate sort; so that, if tolerable, we
may bear them, if not, we can go out of life as from a theatre, where the entertainment does not please us." That
which makes us suffer pain with so much impatience is the
not being accustomed to repose our chiefest contentment in
the soul, that we do not enough rely upon her who is the sole
and sovereign mistress of our condition. The body, saving
in greater or less proportion, has but one and the same bent
and bias; whereas, the soul is variable into all sorts of forms,
and subjects to herself, and to her own empire, all things
whatsoever; both the senses of the body, and all other accidents. And therefore it is that we ought to study her, to
inquire into her, and to rouse up all her powerful faculties.
There is neither reason, form, nor prescription, that can
any thing prevail against her inclination and choice. Of so
many thousands of biasses that she has at her disposal, let
us give her one proper to our repose and conversation, and
then we shall not only be sheltered and secured from all manner of injury and offence, but moreover gratified and obliged,
if she will it, with evils and offences. She makes her profit
indifferently of all things. Error and dreams serve her to
good use, as lawful matter, to lodge us in safety and contentment. 'Tis plain enough to be seen that 'tis the sharpness of
our mind that gives the edge to our pains and pleasures.
Beasts, that have no such things, leave to their bodies their
own free and natural sentiments, and are consequently, in
every kind, very near the same, as appears by the resembling application of their motions. If we should not disturb,
in our members, the jurisdiction that appertains to them in
this, 'tis to be believed it would be the better for us, and that
nature has given them a just and moderate temper, both to
pleasure and pain; neither can it fail of being just, being
equal and common. But seeing we have enfranchised ourselves from her rules, to give ourselves up to the rambling
liberty of our own fancies, let us, at least, help to incline

them to the most agreeable side.   Plato[1] fears our too vehemently engaging ourselves with grief and pleasure, forasmuch
as these too much knit and ally the soul to the body; whereas I rather, on the contrary, by reason it too much separates
and disunites them.   As an enemy is made more fierce by
our flight, so pain grows proud to see us truckle under her.
She will surrender upon much better terms to them who
make head against her; a man must oppose, and stoutly set
himself against her.   In retiring and giving ground, we invite, and pull upon ourselves, the ruin that threatens us.   As
the body is more firm in an encounter, the more stiffly and
obstinately it applies itself to it; so it is with the soul.   But
let us come to examples, which are the proper commodity for
fellows of such feeble reins as myself; where shall we find
that it is with pain, as with stones, that receive a brighter or
duller lustre, according to the foil they are set upon, that it
has no more room in us than we are pleased to allow it;
Tantùm doluerunt, quantùm doloribus se inseruerunt.[2]   "The
more they give way to pain, the more it pained them."   We
are more sensible of one little touch of a surgeon's lancet
than of twenty sword-cuts in the heat of fight.
The pains of child-bearing supported with ease.   The pains of child-bearing, said by the physician, and even by God himself,[3] to be very
great, and which our women keep so great a clutter about,
there are whole nations that make nothing of them.   To say
nothing of the Lacedemonian women, what alteration can you
see in the Swiss wives of our foot soldiers, saving, as they
trot after their husbands, you see them to-day with the child
hanging at their backs that they carried yesterday in their
bellies?   And the counterfeit gypsies we have amongst us,
go themselves to wash their infants as soon as they come into
the world, in the first river they meet.   Besides the many
wenches that daily steal their children out of their womb, as
before they stole them in; that fair and noble wife of Sabi-

---

[1] In the *Phæd.*   [3] Genesis, iii. 16.
[2] St. August. *de Civit. Dei.* i. 10.

nus, a patrician of Rome, for another's interest alone, without
help, without crying out, or so much as a groan, endured the
bearing of twins.[1] A poor simple boy of Lacedemon, having stolen a fox (for they more feared the shame of bung-
ling in a theft, than we do the punishment of our knavery),
and having got him under his coat, chose rather to endure the
beast's tearing out his bowels than he would discover his
theft.[2] And another, offering incense at a sacrifice, suffered
himself to be burnt to the bone by a coal that fell into his
sleeve, rather than disturb the ceremony.[3] And there have
been a great number who, only for a trial of virtue, following their institutions, have at seven years old endured to be
whipped to death, without changing their countenance. And
Cicero has seen them fight in parties, with fists, feet, and
teeth, till they have fainted and sunk down, rather than confess themselves overcome. *Nunquam naturam mos vinceret;
est enim ea semper invicta; sed nos umbris, deliciis, otio, lan-
guore, desidiâ, animum infecimus; opinionibus maloque more
delinitum mollivimus.*[4] " Custom would never conquer Nature, for she is ever invincible, but we have infected the mind
with shadows, delights, wantonness, negligence, and sloth;
and with vain opinions, and corrupt manners, rendered it
effeminate and mean." Every one knows the story of Scævola, who, having slipped into the enemies' camp to kill their
general, and missing his blow, to repair his fault by a more
strange invention, and to deliver his country, boldly confessed
to Porsenna (who was the king he had an intent to kill), not
only his design, but moreover added that there were then in
his camp a great number of Romans, his accomplices in the
enterprise, as good men as he, and, to show what he himself
was, having caused a pan of burning coals to be brought, he
saw and endured his arm to broil and roast, till the king himself, conceiving horror at the sight, commanded the pan to be
taken away.[5] What would you say of him that would not

1 Plutarch, *On Love*, c. 84.　　4 Cicero, *Tusc. Quæs.* v. 27.
2 Id. *Life of Lycurgus*.　　5 Liv. ii. 9.
3 Val. Max. ii. 32.

vouchsafe to respite his reading of a book, whilst he was
under incision?[1] And of the other that.persisted to mock
and laugh, in contempt of the pains inflicted upon him; so
that the irritated cruelty of the executioners that had him in
handling, and all the inventions of tortures redoubled upon
him, one after another, spent in vain, only added to his
triumph?[2] A gladiator of Cæsar's endured, laughing all the
while, his wounds to be probed and laid open. *Quis medi-*
ocris gladiator ingemuit? Quis vultum mutavit unquam?
Quis non modò stetit, verùm etiam decubuit, turpiter? Quis,
cum decubuisset, ferrum recipere jussus, collum contraxit?[3]
" What common gladiator ever so much as gave a groan?
Which of them ever so much as changed his countenance?
Which of them, standing or falling, did either with shame?
Which of them, when he was down, and commanded to receive the stroke of the sword, ever shrunk in his neck?"
Let us bring in the women, too. Who has not heard, at
Paris, of her who caused her face to be fleaed, merely for the
sake of getting the fresher complexion of a new skin? There
are some who have drawn good and sound teeth to make
their voices more soft and sweet, or to range the rest in better order. How many examples of the contempt of pain
have we in that sex? What can they not do? What do
they fear to do, for never so little hopes of an addition to
their beauty?

> Vellere queis cura est albos à stirpe capillos,
> Et faciem, dempta pelle, referre novam.[4]

> " Who by the roots pluck their gray hairs, and try
> With a new skin an old face to supply."

I have seen some of them swallow sand, ashes, and do their
utmost to destroy their stomachs, to get pale complexions.
To make a fine Spanish, slender waist, what racks will they
not endure in tightening and bracing, till they have notches
in their sides, cut to the quick, aye, sometimes to death? It

---

[1] Seneca, *Epist.* 78.					[3] Cicero, *Tusc. Ques.* II. 16.
[2] *Anaxarchus.* See Laertius, *in Vitâ.*		[4] Tibullus, i. 8, 45.

is an ordinary thing with several nations at this day to wound themselves in good earnest, to gain credit to what they profess; of which our king relates notable examples of what he has seen in Poland and had done towards himself.[1] But besides this, which I know to have been imitated by some in France, when I came from that famous Assembly of the Estates at Blois, I had a little before seen a girl in Picardy who, to manifest the sincerity of her promises, and also her constancy, gave herself, with a bodkin she wore in her hair, four or five good stabs in the arm, till the blood gushed out to some purpose. The Turks make on themselves great scars in honour of their mistresses, and, to the end they may the longer remain, they presently clap fire to the wound, where they hold it an incredible time, to stop the wound and form the cicatrice. People that have been eye-witnesses of it have both writ and sworn it to me. But for ten aspers[2] there are there every day fellows to be found that will give themselves a good deep slash in the arms or thighs. I am willing, however, to have the testimonies nearest to us, where we have most to do with them, for Christendom furnishes us enough. And, after the example of our blessed Guide, there have been many who, from devotion, would bear the cross. We learn by testimony very worthy of belief, that King St. Louis wore a hair shirt, till in his old age his confessor gave him a dispensation to leave it off; and that every Friday he caused his shoulders to be drubbed by his priest with five small chains of iron, which were always carried about amongst his night accoutrements for that purpose. William, our late Duke of Guienne, the father of that Eleanor who transmitted this duchy into the houses of France and England, continually, for ten or twelve years before he

---

[1] M. de Thou says expressly that, when this prince came away privately from Poland, the great chamberlain of the kingdom, who followed and with much ado overtook him on the frontier of Austria, having in vain persuaded him to return back to Poland, quitted him at last, after having promised inviolable fidelity to him, by piercing his arm with a dagger and then sucking the blood, to the great astonishment of the king, to whom he meant thereby to testify his devotion. De Thou's *Hist.* lib. lviii. at the year 1574.

[2] An asper is worth about a halfpenny.

died, wore a suit of armour under a religious habit, by way
of penance. Fulk, Count of Anjou, went as far as Jerusa-
lem, to cause himself to be whipped there by two of his servants, with a rope about his neck, before the sepulchre of our
Lord. But do we not, moreover, every Good Friday, in
several places, see great numbers of men and women beat
and whip themselves till they lacerate and cut the flesh to
the very bones? I have often seen this, and without any
enchantment in the matter; and it was said there were some
amongst them (for they go disguised), who for money undertook by this means to save harmless the religion of others;
showing herein a contempt of pain so much the greater, as
the incentives of devotion are more effectual than those of
avarice. Q. Maximus buried his son when he was a consul,
and M. Cato his when prætor elect; and L. Paulus both his,
within a few days one after the other, with such countenances
as expressed no manner of grief. I said once merrily of a
certain person that he had disappointed the divine justice; for
the violent death of three grown-up children of his being one
day sent him for a severe scourge as it is to be supposed, he
was so far from being afflicted that he rather took it for a
particular grace and favour of heaven. I do not follow these
monstrous humours, though I lost two or three at nurse, if
not without grief, at least without repining; and yet there is
hardly any misfortune that pierces nearer to the quick. I
see a great many other occasions of sorrow that, should they
happen to me, I should hardly feel; and have despised some,
when they have befallen me, to which the world has given so
terrible a figure that I should blush to boast to people of my
firmness therein. *Ex quo intelligitur, non in naturâ, sed in
opinione, esse ægritudinem.*[1] "By which it is understood that
the grievance is not in nature, but opinion." Opinion is a
powerful body, bold and without measure. Who ever so
greedily hunted after security and repose as Alexander and
Cæsar did after disquiet and difficulties? Terez, the father

---

[1] Cicero, *Tusc. Quæs.* iii. 28.

of Sitalces, was wont to say that when he had no war in hand he fancied there was no difference betwixt him and his groom.[1] Cato, when consul, to secure some cities of Spain from revolt, merely interdicting the inhabitants from wearing arms, a great many killed themselves. *Ferox gens, nullam vitam rati sine armis esse.*[2] "A fierce people, who thought there was no life without war." How many do we know who have forsaken the calm and sweetness of a quiet life, at home amongst their acquaintance, to seek out the horror of uninhabitable deserts; and, having precipitated themselves into so abject a condition as to become the scorn and contempt of the world, have hugged themselves with the conceit, even to affectation. Cardinal Borromeo,[3] who died lately at Milan, in the midst of all the jollity that the air of Italy, his youth, birth, and great riches invited him to, kept himself in so austere a way of living, that the same robe he wore in summer served him for winter, too; he had only straw for his bed, and his hours of vacation from the affairs of his charge he continually spent in study upon his knees, having a little bread and water set by his book, which was all the provision for his repast, and all the time he spent in eating. I know some who consentingly have acquired both profit and advancement from their own cuckoldom, of which the bare name affrights so many people.

If the sight be not the most necessary of all our senses, 'tis at least the most pleasant. But, at once, the most pleasant and the most useful of all our members, seem to be those of generation; and yet a great many people have conceived a mortal hatred against them only for this, that they were too delightful; and have deprived themselves of them only for their value. As much thought he of his eyes that put them out. The generality and most solid sort of men look upon abundance of children as a great blessing; I, and some others, think it as great a benefit to be without them. And

---

[1] Diod. Sic. xii. 15.
[2] Livy, xxxiv. 17.
[3] Archbishop of Milan, born 1538, died 1584, canonized as St. Charles. His works were collected in 5 vols. folio, 1747.

when you ask Thales why he does not marry, he tells you because he has no mind to leave any posterity behind him.[1]

That our opinion gives the value to things is very manifest in the great number of those which we do not so much regard for themselves, but on our own account; never considering either their virtues or their use, but only how dear they cost us, as though that were a part of their substance, and reputing for value in them, not what they bring to us, but what we add to them. By which I understand that we are great managers of our expense. As it weighs, it serves for so much as it weighs; our opinion will never suffer it to want of its value. The price gives value to the diamond, difficulty to virtue, suffering to devotion, and griping to physic. One man,[2] to be poor, threw his money into the same sea which so many others, in all parts of the world, rummage and rifle for riches. Epicurus says that to be rich is no advantage, but only an alteration of affairs.[3] In plain truth it is not want, but rather abundance, that creates avarice. Let me give my own experience in this matter.

I have, since my childhood, lived in three sorts of condi-

Montaigne's account of three conditions in whih he had lived.

tions: the first, which continued for nearly twenty years, I passed over without any other means but what were accidental, and depending upon the allowance and assistance of others, without stint, but without certain revenue. I then spent my money so much the more cheerfully, and with so much the less care how it went, as it wholly depended upon my confidence in fortune; and I never lived more at my ease. I never found the purse of any of my friends shut against me, having enjoined myself this necessity above all other necessities whatever, by no means to fail of payment at the appointed time; which they have a thousand times respited, seeing how anxious I was to satisfy them; so that I made my good faith both a matter of thrift, and, withal, a kind of allure-

---

[1] Laertius, *in Vitâ*.　　　　　[3] Seneca, *Epist.* 17.
[2] *Aristippus.* See Laertius, *in Vitâ.*

ment. I naturally feel a kind of pleasure in paying, as if I eased my shoulders of a troublesome weight and an image of slavery; besides that, I have a great satisfaction in pleasing another and doing a just action. I except that kind of payment where reckoning and roundabout settlements are required; and in such cases where I can meet with nobody to ease me of that hateful torment, I avoid them, how scandalously and injuriously soever, all I possibly can, for fear of any altercation, for which both my humour and way of speaking are so totally unfit. There is nothing I hate so much as driving a bargain; 'tis a mere traffic of cozenage and impudence; where, after an hour's cheapening and dodging, both parties abandon their word and oath for five halfpence advance or abatement. And yet I always borrowed at great disadvantage, for, wanting the confidence to speak to the person myself, I committed my request to the persuasion of a letter, which usually is no very successful advocate, and gives very great opportunity to him who has a mind to deny. I, in those days, more jocundly and freely referred the conduct of my affairs to the stars than I have since done to my own providence and judgment. Most good managers look upon it as a horrible thing to live always thus in uncertainty; not considering, in the first place, that the greatest part of the world live so, and how many worthy men have wholly slighted and abandoned the certainty of their own estates, and still daily do it, to trust to the inconstant favour of princes and fortune. Cæsar ran in debt above a million of gold more than he was worth, to become Cæsar; and how many merchants have begun their traffic by the sale of their farms, which they sent to the Indies?

> Tot per impotentia freta? [1]

> "Over so many stormy seas."

In so great a dearth of devotion as we see in these days, we have a thousand and a thousand convents, that go on

[1] Catull. 4.

comfortably enough, expecting every day their dinner from
the liberality of heaven.   Secondly, they do not take notice
that this certitude, upon which they so much rely, is not
much less uncertain and hazardous than hazard itself.   I see
misery as near, beyond two thousand crowns a-year, as if
it stood close by me; for, besides that it is in the power of
chance to make a hundred breaches to poverty through the
greatest strength of our riches, there being very often no
mean betwixt the highest and the lowest fortune,

Fortuna vitrea est: tum, quum splendet, frangitur;[1]

" Fortune is glass, the brighter it doth shine
More frail; and soonest broken when most fine; "

and to turn all our barricades and bulwarks topsy-turvy, I
find that, by divers causes, indigence is as frequently seen to
inhabit with those who have property as with those that have
none; and, peradventure, it is then far less grievous, when
alone, than when accompanied with riches; which flow more
from good management than income.   *Faber est suæ quisque
fortunæ.*[2]   " Every one is the maker of his own fortune; "
and an uneasy, necessitous, busy man, seems to me more
miserable than he that is simply poor.   *In divitiis inopes,
quod genus egestatis gravissimum est.*   " Poor in the midst of
riches, which is the most insupportable kind of poverty." [3]
The greatest and most wealthy princes are by poverty and
want driven to the most extreme necessity; for can there be
any more extreme than to become tyrants and unjust usurp-
ers of their subjects' goods and estates ?

My second condition of life was to have money of my
own; wherein I so ordered the matter that I had soon
laid up a notable sum out of so mean a fortune; considering
with myself that that only was to be reputed having which
a man reserved from his ordinary expense, that a man
could not absolutely rely upon revenue to be received, how
clear soever his estate might be.   For what, said I, if I

[1] Ex Mimis Publii Syri.
[2] Sallust. *De Republ. Ordin.* i. 1.
[3] Seneca, *Epist.* 74. At the beginning,

Montaigne has transposed Seneca's words
to apply them to his subject.

should be surprised by such or such an accident; and after
suchlike vain and vicious imaginations would very learnedly,
by this hoarding of money, provide against all inconveniences;
and could moreover answer such as objected to me that the
number of them was too infinite, that if I could not lay up
for all, I could do it at least for some and for many. Yet
was not this done without a great deal of solicitude and
anxiety of mind. I kept it very close, and though I dare
talk so boldly of myself, never spoke of my money but falsely,
as others do who, being rich, pretend to be poor, and being
poor, pretend to be rich, dispensing their consciences from
ever telling sincerely what they have. A ridiculous and
shameful prudence. Was I going a journey? methought I
was never enough provided; and the more I loaded myself
with money, the more also was I loaded with fear, one while
of the danger of the roads, another of the fidelity of him who
had the charge of my baggage, of whom, as of some others
that I know, I never felt secure, if I had him not always in
my eye. Did I leave my box behind me—what suspicions
and anxiety of mind did I enter into? and, which was worse,
without daring to acquaint anybody with it. My mind was
eternally taken up with such things, so that, all considered,
there is more trouble in keeping money than in getting it.
And if I did not altogether so much as I say, or was not
effectually so scandalously solicitous of my money as I have
made myself out, yet it cost me something at least to govern
myself from being so. I reaped little or no advantage by
what I had, and my expenses seemed nothing less to me for
having the more to spend; for, as Bion said, "hairy men
are as angry as the bald to be pulled;"[1] and after you are
once accustomed to it, and have once set your heart upon
your heap, it is no more at your service; you cannot find in
your heart to break it; 'tis a building that you fancy must
of necessity all tumble down in ruins, if you stir but the least
pebble. Necessity must first take you by the throat, before

1 Seneca, *De Tranquillité*, c. 8.

you can prevail upon yourself to touch it; and I would have pawned any thing I had, or sold a horse, with much less constraint upon myself than have made the least breach in that beloved purse I had laid by.   But the danger was that a man cannot easily prescribe certain limits to this desire (they are hard to find in things that a man conceives to be good), and to stint economy so that it may not degenerate into avarice.   Men are still intent upon adding to the heap, and increasing the stock from sum to sum, till at last they vilely deprive themselves of the enjoyment of their own proper goods, deriving their whole gratification from hoarding their treasures, without making any use of them at all. According to this rule, they are the richest people in the world who have charge of the gates and walls of a wealthy city.   All moneyed men I take to be covetous.   Plato places corporal or human riches in this order; health, beauty, strength, wealth; and wealth, says he, is not blind, but very clear-sighted when illuminated by prudence.[1]   Dionysius the son [2] did a very sensible thing upon this subject.   He was informed that one of the Syracusans had hid a treasure in the earth, and thereupon sent to the man to bring it to him, which he accordingly did, privately reserving a small part of it only to himself, with which he went to another city, where, being cured of his appetite of hoarding, he began to live at a more liberal rate; which Dionysius hearing, caused the rest of his treasure to be restored to him, saying that, since he had learnt how to use it, he very willingly returned it back to him.

I continued some years in this hoarding humour, when I

How Montaigne regulated his expenses.   know not what good genius fortunately put me out of it, as he did the Syracusan, and made me throw abroad all my reserve.   The pleasure of a certain voyage I took at very great expense [3] having made me spurn this absurd fancy under foot, by

---

[1] On Laws, 1.
[2] Or rather the father, according to Plutarch in his *Apothegms of Kings*, &c.
[3] Probably that into Italy in 1580 and 1581.

which means I am now fallen into a third way of living
(I speak what I think of it), doubtless much more pleasant
and better regulated, which is that my expenses run level
with my revenue; sometimes, indeed, the one, sometimes the
other, may perhaps exceed, but 'tis very little that they differ
at all.   I live from hand to mouth, and content myself in
having sufficient for my present and ordinary expense; for
as to extraordinary occasions, all the laying up in the world
would never suffice; and 'tis the greatest folly imaginable to
expect that fortune should ever sufficiently arm us against
herself.   'Tis with our own arms that we are to fight her,
accidental ones will betray us in the pinch of the business.
If I lay up, 'tis for some near and designed expense, and not
to purchase lands, of which I have no need, but to purchase
pleasure.   *Non esse cupidum, pecunia est; non esse emacem,
vectigal est.*[1]   "Not to be covetous is money; not to be a
purchaser is a revenue."   I neither am in any great apprehension of wanting, nor in any desire of getting more;
Divitiarum fructus est in copiâ; copiam declarat satietas.[2]
"The fruits of riches lie in abundance; satiety declares abundance."   And I am very well pleased with myself, that this
reformation in me has fallen out in an age naturally inclined
to avarice, and that I see myself freed of a folly so common
to old men, and the most ridiculous of all human follies.

Feraulez, a man who had run through both fortunes, and
found that the increase of substance was no   A fine instance of
increase of appetite, either to eating or drink-   the contempt of
riches.
ing, sleeping, or the enjoyment of his wife;
and who, on the other hand, felt the care of his economy lie
heavy upon his shoulders, as it does on mine; was resolved
to please a poor young man, his faithful friend, who panted
after riches, by making him a gift of all his, which were ex-
cessively great, and moreover of all he was in the daily way
of getting by the liberality of Cyrus, his good master, and by
war; conditionally that he should take care handsomely to

[1] Cicero, *Paradox.* vi. 3.   [2] Id. *ib.* 2.

maintain and to entertain him as his guest and friend, and they afterwards lived very happily together, both of them equally content with the change of their condition.[1]

An example that I could imitate with all my heart, and I very much approve the fortune of an ancient prelate, whom I see to have so absolutely stripped himself of his purse, his revenue, and expenditure, committing them one while to one trusty servant, and another while to another, that he has spun out a long succession of years, as ignorant by this means of his domestic affairs as a mere stranger. The confidence in another man's virtue is no light evidence of a man's own, and God is pleased to favour such a confidence. As to him of whom I am speaking, I see nowhere a better governed family, nor a house more nobly and uniformly maintained than his; happy in this, to have regulated his affairs to so just a proportion that his estate is sufficient to do it without his care or trouble, and without any hindrance, either in the spending or laying it up, to other more suitable and quiet employments, and more to his liking.

Another instance to the same purpose.

Plenty then and indigence depend upon the opinion every one has of them; and riches, no more than glory or health, have no more either beauty or pleasure than he is pleased to invest them with by whom they are possessed. Every one is well or ill at ease, according as he finds himself; not he whom the world believes, but he who believes himself to be so, is content; and therein alone belief gives itself being and reality. Fortune does us neither good nor hurt; she only presents us the matter and the seed, which our soul, more powerfully than she, turns and applies as she best pleases, being the sole cause and sovereign mistress of her own happy or unhappy condition. All external accessions receive taste and colour from the internal constitution, as clothes warm us not with their heat, but our own, which they are adapted to cover and keep

What renders a man contented or indigent.

[1] Xenophou, *Cyrop.* viii. 8.

in; and who would cover a cold body would do the same service for the cold, for so snow and ice are preserved. And after the same manner that study is a torment to a sluggard, abstinence from wine to a drunkard, frugality to the spendthrift, and exercise to a lazy, tender-bred fellow, so it is of all the rest. The things are not so painful and difficult of themselves, but our weakness or cowardice makes them so.[1] To judge of great and high matters requires a suitable soul, otherwise we attribute the vice to them which is really our own. A straight oar seems crooked in the water; it does not only import that we see a thing, but how and after what manner we see it.

But, after all this, why amongst so many discourses, that by so many arguments persuade men to despise death and endure pain, can we not find out one that makes for us? And of so many sorts of imaginations as have prevailed upon others, why does not every one apply some one to himself, the most suitable to his own humour? If he cannot digest a strong working drug to eradicate the evil, let him at least take a lenitive to ease it. *Opinio est quædam effeminata ac levis, nec in dolore magis, quam eadem in voluptate; quâ, quum liquescimus fluimusque mollitiâ, apis aculeum sine clamore ferre non possumus. Totum in eo est, ut tibi imperes!"* [2] " There is a certain frivolous and effeminate opinion, and that not more in pain than it is even in pleasure itself, by which, whilst we wallow in ease and wantonness, we cannot endure so much as the sting of a bee without crying out. The whole secret is this, to command thyself." For the rest, a man does not escape philosophy by permitting the acrimony of pains and human frailty to prevail beyond measure; for they constrain it to these invincible replies: " If it be ill to live in necessity, at least there is no necessity to live in necessity." [3] " No man continues in discomfort long, but by his own fault." He who has neither the courage to die, nor the heart to live, who will neither resist nor fly what should one do with him?

The notion of pain, on what it is founded.

---

[1] Seneca, *Epist.* 81.　　[2] Cicero, *Tusc. Quæs.* ii 21.　　[3] Senec. *Epist.* 12.

CHAPTER XLI.

NOT TO COMMUNICATE A MAN'S HONOUR OR GLORY.

OF all the foolish dreams of the world, that which is most universally received is the solicitude of reputa-

The vanity of a passion for honour. tion and glory, which we are fond of to that degree as to abandon riches, peace, life, and health, which are effectual and substantial good, to pursue this vain phantom and empty word, that has neither body nor hold to be taken of it.

> La fama, ch' invaghisce a un dolce suono
> Gli superbi mortali, et par sì bella,
> É un' eco, un sogno, anzi d'un sogno un' ombra
> Ch' ad ogni vento si dilegua et sgombra.[1]

> "Glory, whose sweet and captivating sound
> Enchants proud mortals all the world around,
> Is but an echo, dream, or phantom fair,
> Mov'd and dispers'd by ev'ry breath of air."

And of all the irrational humours of men, it should seem that the philosophers themselves have the most ado, and do the least disengage themselves from this the most restive and obstinate of all follies.[2] *Quia etiam bene proficientes animos tentare non cessat.*[3] "Because it ceases not to tempt the wisest minds." There is not any one vice of which reason does so clearly accuse the vanity as that; but it is so deeply rooted in us that I doubt whether any one ever clearly freed himself from it or no. After you have said all, and believed all that has been said to its prejudice, it creates so intestine an inclination in opposition to your best arguments that you have little power and firmness to resist it; for, as Cicero says,[4] even those who controvert it would yet that the books

1 Tasso. *Gierusal.* xiv 63.
2 This idea seems borrowed from Tacitus, *Hist.* iv. 6: *Etiam sapientibus, cupido gloriæ novis. ima exuitur.* "The

desire of glory is the last passion of which even wise men can divest themselves."
3 St. August. *de Civit. Dei.* v. 14.
4 "Ipsi illi philosophi, etiam illis libel-

they write should appear before the world with their names in the title-page, and seek to derive glory from seeming to despise it. All other things are communicable and fall into commerce; we lend our goods and stake our lives for the necessity and service of our friends; but to communicate one's honour, and to robe another with one's own glory, is very rarely seen.

And yet we have some examples of that kind. Catulus Luctatius, in the Cymbrian war, having done all that in him lay to make his flying soldiers face about upon the enemy, ran himself at last away with the rest, and counterfeited the coward, to the end his men might rather seem to follow their captain than to fly from the enemy;[1] which was to abandon his own reputation to palliate the shame of others. When Charles the Fifth came into Provence, in the year 1537, 'tis said that Antonio de Leva, seeing the emperor positively resolved upon this expedition, and believing it would redound very much to his honour, did nevertheless very stiffly oppose it in the council, to the end that the entire glory of that resolution should be attributed to his master; and that it might be said his wisdom and foresight had been such as that, contrary to the opinion of all, he had brought about so great an enterprise; which was to do him honour at his own expense.[2]

The Thracian ambassadors, coming to comfort Archielonida, the mother of Brasidas, upon the death of her son, and commending him to that height as to say he had not left his like behind him, she rejected this private and particular commendation to attribute it to the public: "Tell me not that," said she; "I know the city of Sparta has several citizens greater and more valiant than he."[3] In the battle of Crecy, the Prince

Private or particular praise refused.

lis quos de contemnendâ gloriâ scribunt, nomen suum inscribunt; in eo ipso in quo prædicationem nobilitatemque despiciunt, prædicari de se ac nominari volunt."—*Orat. pro Archiâ Poetâ*, cap. 11.

1 Plutarch, *Life of Marius*, c. 8.
2 *Mem. of William du Bellay;* and Brantome. *Lives of Illustrious Men*, at the article Antonio de Leva.
3 Plutarch, *Apothegms*.

of Wales, being then very young, had the van-
guard committed to him; the main stress of
the battle happened to be in that place, and the
lords that were with him, finding themselves
wellnigh overmatched, sent to King Edward to advance to
their relief; who thereupon inquiring what condition his son
was in, and being answered that he was living and on horseback, " I should then do him wrong," said the king, " now to
go and deprive him of the honour of winning this battle he
has so long and so bravely disputed; what hazard soever he
runs, it shall be entirely his own." And accordingly would
neither go nor send, knowing that, if he went, it would be
said all had been lost without his succour, and that the honour
of the victory would be wholly attributed to him : [1] *Semper
enim quod postremum adjectum est, id rem totam videtur trax-
isse.*[2] " For the last stroke to a business seems always to
draw along with it the merit of the performance of the whole
action." Many at Rome thought, and 'twas commonly said,
that the greatest of Scipio's acts were, in part, due to Lelius,
whose constant practice it was still to advance and promote
Scipio's grandeur and renown, without any care of his own.[3]
And Theopompus, king of Sparta, to him who told him the
republic could not miscarry, since he knew so well how to
command, " 'Tis rather," answered he, " because the people
know so well how to obey."

As women succeeding to peerages had, notwithstanding
their sex, the right to assist, and give their votes in the
causes that appertained to the jurisdiction of peers, so the
ecclesiastical peers, notwithstanding their profession, were
obliged to assist our kings in their wars, not only with their
friends and servants, but in their own persons. A Bishop of
Beauvais did so, who being with Philip Augus-
tus at the battle of Bouvines,[4] took a gallant
share in that action, but did not think it fit for

Side notes:
Edward III. chooses to leave all the honour of the victory to his son.

Conduct of a bish-op at the battle of Bouvines.

1 Froissart, vol. l.
2 Livv. xxvii. 45.   4 Fought 1214, between Lille and Tour-
3 Plutarch. *Instructions for those who* nay.
manage State Affairs.

him to participate in the fruit and glory of that violent and bloody trade. He with his own hand reduced several of the enemy that day to his mercy, whom he delivered to the first gentleman he met, either to kill, or to receive them to quarter, referring this part to another hand. As also did William, Earl of Salisbury, to Messire John de Nesle. With a like subtlety of conscience to the other, he would kill, but not wound him, and for that reason, fought only with a mace. And a certain person in my time, being reproached by the king that he had laid hands on a priest, stiffly and positively denied it. The case was, he had cudgelled and kicked him.

----◆----

CHAPTER XLII.

OF THE INEQUALITY AMONGST US.

PLUTARCH says somewhere [1] that he does not find so great a difference betwixt beast and beast, as he does betwixt man and man ; which is said in reference to the internal qualities, and the perfection of the soul. And, in truth, I find, according to my poor judgment, so vast a distance betwixt Epaminondas and some that I know, who are yet men of common sense, that I would willingly enhance upon Plutarch, and say that there is more difference betwixt such and such a man than there is betwixt such a man and such a beast :—

Hem, vir viro quid præstat ! [2]

"How much, alas,
One man another doth surpass ! "

and that there are as many and as innumerable degrees of mind, as there are cubits betwixt this and heaven. But

[1] In his treatise, *That Beasts have the use of Reason*, towards the end.

[2] Terence, *Eunuch.* ii. 8, 1.

touching the estimate of men, 'tis strange that, ourselves excepted, no other creature is esteemed beyond its proper qualities.   We commend a horse for his strength and sureness of
foot,

> Volucrem
> Sic laudamus equum, facili cui plurima palma
> Fervet, et exultat rauco victoria circo; [1]

> " 'Tis thus we praise the horse that mocks our eyes,
> While to the goal with lightning's speed he flies;
> Whom many a well-earn'd palm and trophy grace,
> And the circle hails, unrivalled in the race;"

and not for his rich caparisons ; a greyhound for his speed,
not for his fine collar ; a hawk for her wing, not for her jesses
and bells.   Why, in like manner, do we not

*A man to be val-
ued for what he
has in him, and
not what he has
about him.*

value a man for what is properly his own?
He has a great train, a beautiful palace, so
much credit, so many thousand pounds a year ;
all these are about him, not in him.   You will not buy a pig
in a poke.   If you cheapen a horse you will see him stripped
of his housing clothes, you will see him naked and open to
your eye ; or if he be clothed, as they anciently were wont
to present them to princes to sell, 'tis only on the less important parts, that you may not so much consider the beauty of
his colour, or the breadth of his crupper, as principally to
examine his limbs, eyes, and feet, which are the members of
greatest use : —

> Regibus hic mos est: ubi equos mercantur, opertos
> Inspiciunt; ne, si facies, ut sæpe, decora
> Molli fulta pede est, emptorem inducat hiantem
> Quod pulchræ clunes, breve quod caput, ardua cervix.[2]

> " When kings steeds clothed, as 'tis their manner, buy,
> They straight examine very curiously,
> Lest a short head, a thin and well-raised crest,
> A broad spread buttock, and an ample chest,
> Should all be propt with an old beaten hoof,
> To gull the buyer when they come to proof."

Why, in giving your estimate of a man, do you value him

---

[1] Juvenal, viii. 57.   [2] Horace, *Sat.* i. 2, 86.

wrapt and muffled up in clothes? He then discovers nothing to you but such parts as are not in the least his own; and conceals those by which alone one may rightly judge of his worth. 'Tis the price of the blade that you inquire into, and not of the scabbard. You would not, peradventure, bid a farthing for him if you saw him stripped. You are to judge him by himself, and not by what he wears. And as one of the ancients very pleasantly said, "Do you know why you repute him tall? You reckon withal the height of his clogs," whereas the pedestal is no part of the statue. Measure him without his stilts, let him lay aside his revenues and his titles, let him present himself in his shirt; then examine if his body be sound and sprightly, active, and disposed to perform its functions. What soul has he? Is she beautiful, capable, and happily provided with all her faculties? Is she rich of what is her own, or of what she has borrowed? Has fortune no hand in the affair? Can she, without winking, stand drawn swords? Is she indifferent whether her life expire by the mouth or through the throat? Is she settled, even, and content? This is what is to be examined, and by that you are to judge of the vast differences betwixt man and man. Is he

Sapiens, sibique imperiosus;
Quem neque pauperies, neque mors, neque vincula terrent;
Responsare cupidinibus, contemnere honores,
Fortis; et in seipso totus, teres atque rotundus,
Externi ne quid valeat per læve morari;
In quem manca ruit semper fortuna? [1]

"The wise, who well maintains
An empire o'er himself; whom neither chains,
Nor want, nor death, with slavish fear inspire,
Who boldly answers to his warm desire,
Who can ambition's vainest gifts despise,
Firm in himself who on himself relies,
Polish'd and sound who runs his proper course,
And breaks misfortune with superior force."

Such a man is raised five hundred fathoms above kingdoms and duchies; he is an absolute monarch in and to himself.

[1] Horace, *Sat.* ii. 7, 83.

> Sapiens . . . pol! ipse fingit fortunam sibi.[1]
> "The wise man his own fortune makes."

What remains for him to desire?

> "Nonne videmus,
> Nil aliud sibi naturam latrare, nisi ut quoi
> Corpore sejunctus dolor absit, mente fruatur
> Jucundo sensu, curâ semotu, metuque?[2]

> "We see that nature only seeks for ease,
> A body free from pains, free from disease,
> A mind from cares and jealousies at peace."

Compare with such a one the common rabble of mankind, stupid, mean-spirited, servile, instable, and continually floating with the tempest of various passions, that tosses and tumbles them to and fro, all depending upon others, and you will find a greater distance than betwixt heaven and earth; and yet the blindness of common usage is such that we make little or no account of it. Whereas, if we consider a peasant and a king, a nobleman and a clown, a magistrate and a private man, a rich man and a poor, there appears a vast disparity, though they differ no more (as a man may say) than in their breeches.

In Thrace the king was distinguished from his people after a very pleasant and rare manner. He had a religion by himself, a god of his own, whom his subjects might not presume to adore, which was Mercury, whilst on the other hand, he disdained to have any thing to do with theirs, Mars, Bacchus, and Diana.[3] And yet they are no other than pictures, that make no essential dissimilitude; for as you see actors in a play representing a duke or an emperor upon the stage, and immediately after, in the tiring-room, return to their true and original condition; so the emperor, whose pomp so dazzles you in public.

Wherein the kings of Thrace distinguished themselves from their subjects.

---

[1] Plautus. *Trinummus*, li. 2, 84.
[2] Lucret. li. 16.
[3] Herodotus, indeed, says (lib. v.) that the Thracian kings worshipped Mercury above all other gods; that they swore by him alone, and pretended to be descended from him; but he does not say that they despised Mars, Bacchus, and Diana, the only deities of their subjects.

Scilicet et grandes viridi cum luce smaragdi
Auro includuntur, teriturque Thalassina vestis.
Assidue, et Veneris sudorem exercita potat.[1]

" Great emeralds richly are in gold enchast,
To dart green lustre; and the sea-green vest
Continually is worn and rubb'd to frets,
While it imbibes the juice that Venus sweats."

Do but peep behind the curtain, and you'll see nothing but an ordinary man, and peradventure more con- Kings subject to temptible than the meanest of his subjects. the same passions and accidents as men. *Ille beatus introrsum est ; istius bracteata felici-* *tas est.*[2] " True happiness lies within, the other is but a counterfeit felicity." Cowardice, irresolution, ambition, spite, and envy, work in him as in another.

Non enim gazæ, neque consularis
Summovet lictor miseros tumultus
Mentis, et curas laqueata circum
        Tecta volantes.[3]

" For neither wealth, honours, nor offices,
Can the wild tumults of the mind appease,
Nor chase those cares that, with unwearied wings,
Hover about the palaces of kings."

Cares and fears attack him even in the centre of his armies.

Re verâque metus hominum, curæque sequaces,
Nec metuunt sonitus armorum, nec fera tela;
Audacterque inter reges, rerumque potentes,
Versantur, neque fulgorem reverentur ab auro.[4]

" For fears and cares warring with human hearts,
Fear not the clash of arms, nor points of darts;
But with great kings and potentates make bold,
Maugre their purple and their glitt'ring gold."

Do fever, headache, and the gout, spare them any more than one of us? When old age hangs heavy upon a prince's shoulders, can the archers of the guard ease him of the burden? When he is transfixed with the apprehension of death, can the gentlemen of his bedchamber reassure him? When jealousy, or any other caprice, swims in his brain, can

1 Lucretius, iv. 1119   3 Horace, *Od.* ii. 16, 9.
2 Seneca, *Epist.* 115.   4 Lucret. ii. 46.

our compliments and ceremonies restore him to his good humour? The canopy embroidered with pearl and gold he lies under has no virtue against a violent fit of the stone or cholic.

> Nec calidæ citius decedunt corpore febres,
> Textilibus si in picturis, ostroque rubenti
> Jactaris, quàm si plebeia in veste cubandum est.[1]

> "Nor sooner will a bed superb assuage
> The dreadful symptoms of a fever's rage,
> Than if the homely couch were meanly spread
> With poorest blankets of the coarsest thread."

The flatterers of Alexander the Great possessed him that he was the son of Jupiter; being one day wounded, and looking at the blood streaming from his wound—"What say you now!" exclaimed he. "Is not this blood of a crimson colour, and purely human? This is not of the complexion with that which Homer makes to issue from the wounded gods!"[2] The poet Hermodorus had writ a poem in honour of Antigonus, wherein he called him the son of the Sun. "He that has the emptying of my close-stool," said Antigonus, "will find 'tis no such thing."[3] He is but a man at best, and if he be deformed, or ill qualified from his birth, the empire of the universe can neither mend his shape nor his nature;

Alexander and Antigonus scorn their flatterers.

> Puellæ
> Hunc rapiant, quicquid calcaverit hic, rosa fiat.[4]

> "Though virgins rush the favoured youth to greet,
> And roses spring where'er he sets his feet,"

what of all that, if he be a fool? Even pleasure and good fortune are not relished without vigour and understanding.

In what sense the favours of fortune are a good.

> Hæc perinde sunt, ut illius animus, qui ea possidet,
> Qui uti scit ei bona; illi qui non utitur recte, mala.[5]

> "Things to the souls of their possessors square,
> Goods, if well us'd, if ill, they evils are."

[1] Lucret. ii. 34.
[2] Plutarch, *Apothegms*.
[3] Id. *ib.*
[4] Persius, ii. 38.
[5] Terence, *Heaut.* i. 3, 21.

Whatever the benefits of fortune are, they require a palate fit to relish them. 'Tis enjoyment, and not possession, that renders us happy.

> Non domus et fundus, non æris acervus et auri,
> Ægroto domini deduxit corpore febres,
> Non animo curas. Valeat possessor oportet,
> Qui comportatis rebus bene cogitat uti;
> Qui cupit aut metuit, juvat illum sic domus aut res,
> Ut lippum pictæ tabulæ, fomenta podagram.[1]

> " Nor house, nor lands, nor heaps of laboured ore
> Can give their fev'rish lord one moment's rest,
> Or drive one sorrow from his anxious breast.
> The fond possessor must be blest with health
> Who rightly means to use his hoarded wealth.
> Houses and riches gratify the breast
> For lucre lusting, or with fear depress'd,
> As pictures glowing with a vivid light,
> With painful pleasure charm a blemish'd sight,
> As chafing soothes the gout."

Is he a sot, his taste palled and flat?—he no more enjoys what he has than one that has a cold relishes the flavour of Canary; or than a horse is sensible of his rich caparison. Plato is in the right when he tells us that health, beauty, vigour, and riches, and all the other things called goods, are equally evil to the unjust, as good to the just; and the evil on the contrary the same.[2] And, therefore, where either the body or the mind are in disorder, to what use serve these external conveniences? seeing that the least prick with a pin, or the least passion of the soul, is sufficient to deprive us of the pleasure of being sole monarch of the world. At the first twitch of the gout, it signifies much, truly, to be called " sire," and " your majesty; "

> Totus et argento conflatus, totus et auro,[3]

> " Altho' his chests are cramm'd, whilst they will hold,
> With untold sums of silver coin and gold,"

does he not forget his palaces and grandeurs? If he be angry, can his being a prince keep him from looking red, and

---

[1] Horace, *Epist.* i. 2, 47.   [2] *Laws*, ii.   [3] Tibullus, i. 71.

looking pale, and grinding his teeth like a madman? If he
be a man of parts, and well born, royalty adds very little to
his happiness :—

> Si ventri bene, si lateri est, pedibusque tuis, nil
> Divitiæ poterunt regales addere majus.[1]

> " If thou art well and sound from head to foot,
>   A king's revenue can add nothing to't."

He discerns 'tis nothing but counterfeit and gullery. Nay,
perhaps he would be of King Seleucus's opinion, " That he
that knew the weight of a sceptre would not deign to stoop
to take it up, though he saw it lying on the ground ; "[2] which
he said in reference to the great and painful duty incumbent
upon a good king. Assuredly it can be no easy task to rule
others, when we find it so hard a matter to govern ourselves.
And as to the thing, command, that seems so sweet and
charming, considering the imbecility of human judgment, and
the difficulty of choice in things that are new and doubtful to
us, I am very much of opinion that it is far more pleasant to
follow than to lead ; and that it is a great settlement and
satisfaction of mind to have one path to walk in, that's traced
out for us, and to have none to answer for but one's self ;

> Ut satius multo jam sit parere quietum,
> Quam regere imperio res velle.[3]

> " So that 'tis better calmly to obey,
>   Than in the storms of state a sceptre sway."

To which we may add that saying of Cyrus, That no man
Kings not in such ought to rule but he who, in his own worth, was
a condition to
taste pleasures as better than all those he has to govern. But
private men.   King Hiero, in Xenophon,[4] says farther, that
in the enjoyment even of pleasure itself, they are in a worse
condition than private men ; forasmuch as the facility they
have of commanding those things at will takes off from the
delight, which we, who find the matter more difficult, experience in fruition.

---

1 Horace, *Epist.* l. 12, 5.   3 Lucret. v. 1126.
2 Plutarch, *Whether a wise man should*   4 In the treatise entitled, *Hiero, or*
meddle with state affairs.   *the Condition of Kings.*

Pinguis amor, nimiumque potens, in tædia nobis
Vertitur, et, stomacho dulcis ut esca, nocet.[1]

" Excessive love in loathing ever ends,
As highest sauce the stomach most offends."

Can we think that the singing-boys of the choir take any great delight in their own music? The satiety does rather render it troublesome and tedious to them. Feasts, balls, masquerades, tiltings, delight such as rarely see, and who have long desired to see them; but having been frequently at such entertainments, the relish of them grows flat and insipid; nor do women so much delight those who make a common practice of the sport. He who will not give himself leisure to be thirsty can never find the true pleasure of drinking. Farces and tumbling tricks are pleasant to the spectators, but mere drudgery to those by whom they are performed. And that this is so we see that princes divert themselves sometimes in disguising their qualities, awhile to depose themselves, and to stoop to the poor and ordinary mode of life of the meanest of their people.

Plerumque gratæ principibus vices,
Mundæque parvo sub lare pauperum
Cœnæ, sine aulæis et ostro,
Sollicitam explicuere frontem.[2]

" Changes have often pleased the great;
And in a cell a homely treat
Of healthy food and cleanly dress'd,
Though no rich hangings grace the rooms,
Or purple wrought in Tyrian looms,
Have smooth'd a wrinkled brow and calmed a ruffled breast."

Nothing is so distasteful and disappointing as abundance. What appetite would not be checked to see three hundred women at its command, as the Grand Seignior has in his seraglio? And what enjoyment of the sport did that ancestor of the Turks reserve to himself, who never went a hawking without seven thousand falconers? And besides this, I fancy that this lustre of grandeur brings with it no little dis-

[1] Ovid. *Amor.* ii. 19, 25. [2] Horace, *Od.* iii. 29, 13.

Why great men ought to be more careful of concealing their faults than others. turbance and uneasiness upon the enjoyment of the most charming pleasures; they are too conspicuous, and lie too open to every one's view.

Neither do I know to what end they should any more than us be required to conceal their faults, since what is only reputed indiscretion in us, the people brand with the names of tyranny and contempt of the laws in them; and besides their proclivity to vice, it would seem they held it as a heightening pleasure to insult over the laws and to trample upon public observances. Plato, indeed, in his Gorgias, defines a tyrant to be one who in a city has license to do whatever his own will leads him to. And by reason of his impunity, the publication of their vices does ofttimes more mischief by its example than the vice itself.[1] Every one fears to be pryed into and overseen; but princes are so, e'en to their very gestures, looks, and thoughts, the people conceiving they have right and title to censure and be judges of them; besides, that faults appear greater, according to the eminency and lustre of the place where they are seated; as a mole or a wart appears greater on the forehead than a wide gash elsewhere. And this is the reason why the poets feign the amours of Jupiter to be performed in the disguises of so many borrowed shapes; and amongst the many amorous practices they lay to his charge there is only one, as I conceive, where he appears in his own majesty and grandeur.

But let us return to Hiero, who further complains of the **Kings confined in the limits of their own country.** inconveniences he found in his royalty, in that he could not go abroad and travel the world at liberty, being, as it were, a prisoner to the bounds and limits of his own dominion, and that in all his actions he was evermore surrounded with a troublesome crowd. And, in truth, to see our kings sit all alone at table, environed with so many people prating about them, and so many strangers staring upon them, as there always are, I have often been moved rather to pity than to envy their condition.

---

[1] Plusque exemplo, quam peccato, nocent.—Cicero, de Legib. iii. 41.

King Alphonsus was wont to say that in this asses were in a better condition than kings, their masters permitting them to feed at their own case and pleasure; a favour that kings cannot obtain of their servants; and it would never come into my head that it could be of any great advantage in the life of a man of sense to have twenty people about him when he is at stool; or that the services of a man of ten thousand livres a year, or that has taken Casal or defended Sienna, should be either more commodious or more acceptable to him than those of a good groom of the chamber that understands his business. The advantages of sovereignty are little better than imaginary. Every degree of fortune has in it some image of principality. Cæsar calls all the lords of France, having jurisdiction within their own demesnes, *kinglets*.[1] And, in truth, the title of sire excepted, they go pretty far towards kingship; for do but look into the provinces remote from court, as Brittany, for example, take notice of the train, the vassals, the officers, the employments, service, ceremony, and state of a lord that lives retired amidst his own estates and his own tenants, and observe withal the flight of his imagination, there is nothing more royal; he hears talk of his master once a year as of the king of Persia, and only recognizes him from some remote cousinship his secretary keeps note of in some musty record. And, to speak the truth, our laws are easy enough, so easy that a gentleman of France scarce feels the weight of sovereignty pinch his shoulders above twice in his life. Real and effectual subjection only concerns such amongst us as voluntarily thrust their necks under the yoke, and who design to get wealth and honour by such services. Any man that loves his own fireside, and can govern his house

The condition of country gentlemen in France in Montaigne's time.

---

[1] As Cæsar does not say any thing of the sort respecting the Gauls, M. Coste imagines that our author, by inadvertence, applied to the Gauls what Cæsar wrote of the Germans, *Bello Gall.* vi. 23, where he says: "In pace, nullus est communis et magistratus: sed principes regionum atque pagorum inter suos jus dicunt, controversiasque minuunt." Montaigne, however, may have had in his mind that passage of a letter of Cæsar's which Cicero has preserved (*Epist. Fam.* vii. 5), where the great general says: "M. Orfium, quem mihi commendas, vel *regem* Gallice factam, vel hunc septæ delega."

without falling by the ears with his neighbours, or engaging in suits of law, is as free as the Duke of Venice. *Paucos servitus, plures servitutem tenent.*[1] "Servitude seizes on few, but many seize on her."

But that which Hiero is most concerned at is that he finds himself stripped of all friendship and deprived of all mutual society, wherein the true and most perfect fruition of human life consists. For what testimony of affection and good will can I extract from him that owes me, whether he will or no, all that he is able to do? Can I form any assurance of his real respect to me from his humble way of speaking and submissive behaviour, which, when they are ceremonies, it is not in his choice to deny? The honour we receive from those that fear us is not honour; those respects are paid to my royalty, and not to me.

> Maximum hoc regni bonum est,
> Quod facta domini cogitur populus sui
> Quam ferre, tam laudare.[2]

> "'Tis the great benefit of kings that they
> Who are by law subjected to their sway
> Are bound, in all their princes say or do,
> Not only to submit, but praise it too."

Do I not see that the wicked and the good king, he that is hated and he that is beloved, has the one as much reverence paid him as the other? My predecessor was, and my successor shall be, served with the same ceremony and state. If my subjects do me no offence, 'tis no evidence of any good affection; why should I look upon it as such, seeing it is not in their power if they would? No one follows me, or obeys my commands, upon the account of any friendship betwixt him and me; there can be no contracting of friendship where there is so little relation and correspondence. My own height has put me out of the familiarity of, and intelligence with, men; there is too great disparity and disproportion betwixt us. They follow me upon the account of appearance and custom;

---

[1] Seneca, *Epist.* 22.   [2] Seneca, *Thyestes*, ii. 1, 30.

or rather my fortune and me, to increase their own. All they say to me, or do for me, is forced and dissembled, their liberty being on all parts restrained by the great power and authority I have over them. I see nothing about me but what is dissembled and disguised.

The Emperor Julian, being one day applauded by his courtiers for his exact justice, "I should be proud of these praises," said he, "did they come from persons that durst condemn or disapprove the contrary, in case I should do it." [1] All the real advantages of princes are common to them with men of moderate condition ('tis for the gods to mount winged horses and feed upon ambrosia); they have no other sleep nor other appetite than we; the steel they arm themselves withal is of no better temper than that we also use; their crowns do neither defend them from the rain nor sun.

Diocletian, who wore a crown so fortunate and revered, resigned it to retire himself to the felicity of a private life. And some time after, the necessity of public affairs requiring that he should reassume his charge, he made answer to those who came to solicit him to it: "You would not offer to persuade me to this, had you seen the fine condition of the trees I have planted in my orchard, and the fair melons I have sowed in my garden." [2]

In the opinion of Anacharsis, the happiest state of government would be where, all other things being equal, precedency should be regulated to the virtues, and repulses to the vices of men.

When King Pyrrhus prepared for his expedition into Italy, his wise counsellor Cyneas, to make him sensible of the vanity of his ambition: "Well, sir," said he, "to The vain ambition what end do you make all this mighty prepara- of Pyrrhus. tion?" "To make myself master of Italy," replied the king. "And what after that is done?" said Cyneas. "I will pass over into Gaul and Spain," said the other. "And

---

[1] Ammianus Marcellinus, xxii. 10.　　[2] Aurelius Victor in the article *Diocletian.*

what then?" "I will then go to subdue Africa; and lastly, when I have brought the whole world to my subjection, I will sit down and live content at my ease." "For God's sake, sir!" replied Cyneas, "tell me what hinders you, if you please, from being now in the condition you speak of? Why do you not now at this instant settle yourself in the state you say you aim at, and spare the labour and hazard you interpose?"[1]

> Nimirum, quia non bene norat quæ esset habendi
> Finis, et omnino quoad crescat vera voluptas.[2]

> "The end of being rich he did not know,
> Nor to what height felicity should grow."

I will conclude with an old versicle that I think very pat to the purpose.

> Mores cuique sui fingunt fortunam.[3]

> "Himself, not fortune, ev'ry one must blame,
> Since men's own manners do their fortune frame."

CHAPTER XLIII.

OF SUMPTUARY LAWS.

The way by which our laws attempt to regulate idle and vain expenses in meat and clothes, seems to be quite contrary to the end designed. The true way would be to beget in men a contempt of silks and gold, as vain, frivolous, and useless; whereas, we augment to them the honours, and enhance the value of such things, which is a very absurd mode of creating a disgust. For to enact that none but princes shall eat turbot, shall

Gold and silver more to be despised by a prince than the subjects.

---

[1] Plutarch, *Life of Pyrrhus*, c. 7.   [3] Nepos, *Life of Atticus*, 11.
[2] Lucret. v. 1431.

wear velvet, or gold lace, and to interdict these things to the people, what is it but to bring them into a greater esteem, and to set every man more agog to eat and wear them? Let kings leave off these ensigns of grandeur, they have others enough besides; these excesses are more excusable in any other than a prince. We may learn, by the example of several nations, many better ways of exterior distinction of quality (which, truly, I conceive to be very requisite in a state), without fostering up for this purpose this corruption and inconvenience. 'Tis strange how suddenly, and with how much ease, custom, in these indifferent things, establishes itself, and becomes authority. We had scarce When silk clothes worn cloth a year, at court, for the mourning of first began to be despised in Henry the Second, but that silks were already France. grown into such contempt with every one that a man so clad was presently concluded a cit. Silks were left in share betwixt the physicians and surgeons, and though all other people almost went dressed alike, there was, notwithstanding, in one thing or other, sufficient distinction of the calling and condition of men. How suddenly do greasy chamois doublets become the fashion in our armies, whilst all neatness and richness of habit fall into reproach and contempt? Let kings but take the lead, and begin to leave off this expense, and in a month the business will be done throughout the kingdom without edict or ordinance; we shall all follow. It should be rather proclaimed, on the contrary, that no one should wear scarlet, or goldsmith's work, but whores and tumblers.

Zeleucus, with such an invention, reclaimed the corrupted manners of the Locrians. His laws were, The laws of That no free woman should be allowed more Zeleucus. than one maid to follow her, unless she was drunk; nor was to stir out of the city by night, wear jewels of gold about her, or go in an embroidered robe, unless she was a professed public woman. That, panders excepted, no man was to wear a gold ring, nor be habited in fine cloth, such as that wove in the city of Miletum.[1]   By which ignominious exceptions he ingeniously diverted his citizens from superfluities and pernicious pleasures; it was a most useful mode of attracting men by honour and ambition, to their duty and obedience.

Our kings can do what they please in such external reformations; their own inclinations stand in this case for a law; *Quicquid principes faciunt, præcipere videntur.*[2] "What princes themselves do, they seem to enjoin others to do." Whatever is done at court passes for a rule through the rest of France. Let the courtiers but fall out with these abominable breeches, that discover so much of those parts which should be concealed; these unwieldy doublets, that make us look like I know not what; and are so unfit to admit of the use of arms; these long effeminate tresses of hair; this foolish custom of kissing what we present to our equals, and our hands in saluting them; a ceremony in former times only due to princes; and that a gentleman shall appear in a place where he owes respect, without his sword, unbuttoned and untrussed, as though he came from the house-of-office; and that, contrary to the custom of our forefathers, and the particular privilege of the noblesse of this kingdom, we shall stand a long time bareheaded before our princes, in what place soever, and the same to a hundred others, so many tiercelets and quartelets of kings have we got now-a-days; and so with other like degenerate innovations; they will see them all presently vanished and cried down. These are, 'tis true, but superficial errors, but still, of ill consequence; 'tis enough to inform us that the fabric itself is crazy and tottering, when we see the rough-cast of our walls to cleave and split.

The court practice is a rule for the French nation.

Plato, in his laws,[3] esteems nothing of more pestiferous consequence to his city than to give young men the liberty of introducing any change in their habits, gestures, dances, songs, and exercises, from one form to another; shifting from this to that, hunting after nov-

New fashions fatal to youth.

elties, and applauding the inventors; by which means manners are corrupted, and old institutions come to be nauseated and despised. In all things, saving only in those that are evil, a change is to be feared; even the change of seasons, winds, viands, and humours. And no laws are in their true credit, but such to which God has given so long a continuance that no one knows their beginning, or that there ever was any other.

CHAPTER XLIV.

OF SLEEP.

REASON directs that we should always go the same way, but not always the same pace. And consequently, though a wise man ought not to give the reins to human passions, so as to let them deviate him from the right path; he may, notwithstanding, without prejudice to his duty, leave it to them to hasten or to slacken his speed, and not fix himself like a motionless and insensible Colossus. Could virtue itself put on flesh and blood, I believe the pulse would beat faster going on to an assault than in going to dinner; that is to say, there is a necessity she should beat, and be moved. I have taken notice, as of an extraordinary thing, of some great men who, in the highest enterprises and greatest dangers, have kept themselves in so settled a calm as not at all to hinder their usual serenity, or break their sleep. Alexander the Great, on the day assigned for that furious battle betwixt him and Darius, slept so profoundly, and so late in the morning, that Parmenio was fain to enter his chamber, and, coming to his bedside, to call him several times by name, the time to go

The profound sleep of some great personages in their most important affairs.

to fight being come.[1] The Emperor Otho, having put on a
resolution to kill himself, the same night, after having settled
his domestic affairs, divided his money amongst his servants,
and set a good edge upon a sword he had made choice of for
the purpose, and now staying only to be satisfied whether all
his friends were retired in safety, he fell into so sound a sleep
that the gentlemen of his chamber heard him snore.[2] The
death of this emperor has in it many circumstances resembling that of the great Cato, and particularly this; for Cato
being ready to dispatch himself, whilst he only stayed his
hand in expectation of the return of a messenger he had sent,
to bring him news whether the senators he had sent away
were put out from the port of Utica, he fell into so sound a
sleep that they heard him snore in the next room; and he
whom he had sent to the port, having awaked him to let him
know that the tempestuous weather had hindered the senators
from putting to sea; he dispatched another messenger, and,
composing himself again in the bed, settled again to sleep,
and did so till, by the return of the last messenger, he had
certain intelligence they were gone.[3] We may
here further compare him with Alexander, too,
in that great and dangerous storm that threatened him by the sedition of the tribune, Metellus, who, wishing to renew the decree for the calling in of Pompey with
his army into the city, at the time of Catiline's conspiracy,
was only, and that stoutly, opposed by Cato, so that very
sharp language, and bitter menaces, passed between them in
the senate about that affair; but it was the next day, in the
great square, that the matter was to be decided; where Metellus, besides the favour of the people, and of Cæsar (at
that time of Pompey's faction), was to appear, accompanied
with a rabble of foreign slavers and fencers; and Cato, only
fortified with his own courage and firmness; so that his rela-

Cato's tranquillity just before a popular commotion.

[1] Plutarch, *Life of Alexander.* 'Twas
the same with the great Condé on the
eve of the Battle of Rocroi: "Le lende-
main, à l'heure marquée il fallut réveil-
ler d'un profond sommeil cet autre Alex-
andre."—Bossuet, *Ora. Funeb. de Condé*
[2] Plutarch, *in Vitâ*, c. 8.
[3] Id. *ib.* c. 19.

tions, domestics, and many good people were in great apprehension for him, and to that degree that some there were who
passed over the whole night without sleep, eating, or drinking, for the manifest danger they saw him running into; at
which his wife and sisters did nothing but weep and torment
themselves in his house; whereas he, on the contrary, comforted every one, and, having supped after his usual manner,
went to bed, and slept so profoundly till morning that one of
his fellow tribunes roused him to go to the encounter.[1] The
knowledge we have of the greatness of this man's courage
by the rest of his life, may warrant us surely to judge that
his indifference proceeded from a soul so much elevated
above such accidents that he disdained to let it take any
more hold of his imagination than any other ordinary affair.

In the naval engagement which Augustus won against
Sextus Pompeius in Sicily, just as they were
to begin the fight he was so fast asleep that
his friends were compelled to wake him to give
the signal of battle.[2] And this it was that gave Mark Antony
afterwards occasion to reproach him that he had not the
courage so much as with open eyes to behold the order of
his own squadrons, and that he had not dared to present
himself before the soldiers till first Agrippa had brought him
news of the victory obtained.   But, as to the business of
young Marius, who did much worse (for the day of his last
battle against Sylla, after he had ordered his army, and given
the word and signal of battle, he laid him down under the
shade of a tree to repose himself, and fell so fast asleep, that
the rout and flight of his men could hardly awake him, having
seen nothing of the fight), he is said to have been at that time
so extremely spent and worn out with labour and want of
sleep that nature could hold out no longer.[3] Upon this matter the physicians may determine whether sleep be so necessary that our lives depend upon it; for we read that they

Profound sleep of Augustus just before a battle.

1 Plutarch, *in Vità*, c. 8.   3 Plutarch, *Life of Sylla*, c. 18.
2 Suetonius, *in Vità*, c. 16.

killed King Perseus of Macedon, a prisoner at Rome, **by**
keeping him from sleep; but Pliny instances some who have
lived long without sleep.[1]   Herodotus speaks of nations where
the men sleep and wake by half years;[2] and they who write
the life of the sage Epimenides affirm that he slept seven and
fifty years together.[8]

CHAPTER XLV.

OF THE BATTLE OF DREUX.

OUR battle of Dreux[4] was full of extraordinary accidents;
but such men as have no great kindness for M. de Guise, nor
much favour his reputation, are willing to have him thought
to blame, and say that his making a halt, and delaying time
with the forces he commanded, whilst Monsieur the Constable,
who was general of the army, was raked through and through
with the enemies' artillery, is not to be excused; and that he
had much better have run the hazard of charging the enemy
in flank than staying for the advantage of falling in upon the
rear, to suffer so great a loss.   But, besides what the event
demonstrated, he who will consider it without
passion or prejudice will easily be induced to
confess that the aim and design not of a captain
only, but of every private soldier, ought to look at the victory
in general; and that no particular occurrences, how nearly
soever they may concern his own interest, should divert him
from that pursuit.   Philopœmen, in an encounter with
Machanidas, having sent before a good strong party of his
archers to begin the skirmish, the enemy having routed these,

Victory the principal aim of the general and every soldier.

---

1 Pliny mentions but one instance that
I find, which is of Mæcenas, who he says
for the last three years of his life had not
one moment's sleep. *Nat. Hist.* vii. 52.
   2 Herodotus speaks of this only by hearsay, and positively declares he did not
believe it. Book iv.
   3 Laertius. *in Vitâ.* Pliny, vii. 52.
   4 Fought 1562, in the reign of Charles
IX.

pursued them post haste in the heat of victory, and in that pursuit passing by the place where Philopœmen was, though his soldiers were impatient to fall on, yet he did not think fit to stir from his post, nor to present himself to the enemy to relieve his men, but, having suffered them to be chased about the field, and cut in pieces before his face, charged in upon their body of foot, when he saw them left naked by their horse ; and, notwithstanding that they were Lacedemonians, yet taking them in the nick, when, thinking themselves secure of the victory, they began to disorder their ranks, he did his business with great facility, and then put himself in pursuit of Machanidas.[1] Which case is very like that of Monsieur de Guise.

In that fierce battle betwixt Agesilaus and the Bœotians, which Xenophon, who was present at it, reports to be the roughest he had ever seen, Agesilaus waived the advantage that fortune presented to him, to let the Bœotians' battalion pass by, and then to charge them in the rear, how certain soever he made himself of the victory, judging it would rather be an effect of conduct than valour to proceed that way. And therefore, to show his prowess, rather chose, with a wonderful ardour of courage, to charge them in the front; but he was well beaten, and wounded for his pains, and constrained at last to disengage himself and to take the course he had at first neglected, opening his battalion to give way to this torrent of Bœotians, and being past by, taking notice that they marched in disorder, like men that thought themselves out of danger, he then pursued and charged them in flank, yet could not prevail so far as to bring it to so general a rout, but that they leisurely retreated, still facing about upon him, till they were retired into safety.[2]

Battle of Agesilaus with the Bœotians.

---

[1] Plutarch, *in Vitâ.*　　　　[2] Id. *Life of Agesilaus.*

CHAPTER XLVI.

OF NAMES.

WHAT variety of herbs soever are put together in the dish, yet the whole is called by the one name of a salad. In like manner, under the consideration of names, I will here make a hodge-podge of different articles.

Every nation has certain names that, I know not why, are taken in no good part: as with us John, William,[1] and Bene-

Some names disliked; others fatally affected in the genealogies of some princes. dict. *Item,* in the genealogy of princes, also, there seem to be certain names fatally affected, as the Ptolemies of Egypt, the Henrys of England, the Charleses of France, the Baldwins of Flanders, and the Williams of our ancient Aquitaine, from whence 'tis said the name of Guienne has its derivation; which would seem far-fetched, were there not as crude derivations in Plato himself.[2]

Item, 'tis a frivolous thing in itself, but nevertheless worthy

Nobility placed at different tables at a feast, by a resemblance of names. to be recorded for the strangeness of it, which is writ by an eye-witness, that Henry, Duke of Normandy, son of Henry the Second, King of England, making a great feast in France, the concourse of nobility and gentry was so great that being, for sport's sake, divided into troops, according to their names, in the first troop, which consisted of Williams, there were found an hundred and ten knights sitting at the table of that name, without reckoning the simple gentlemen and their servants.

It is as pleasant to distribute the tables by the names of

---

[1] *William,* says the Dictionary of Trevoux, was once applied by way of contempt to persons who were thought slightingly of.

[2] The name of *Guienne* derives not from *Guillaume,* but from *Aquitania, Aquitaine,* whence, first, *Aquienne,* then *Guienne.*

the guests as it was in the Emperor Geta to Dishes of meat served up according to the order of the alphabet. distribute the several courses of his meat by the first letters of the meats themselves, where those that began with *b* were served up together, as brawn, beef, bream, bustards, and beccaficos, and so of others.[1]

Item, there is a saying that it is a good thing to have a good name, that is to say, credit and a good repute. But besides this, it is convenient to have a well-sounding name, such as is at the same time easy of pronunci- It is good to have a name easy to be pronounced. ation, and easy to be remembered, by reason that kings and other great persons do by that means the more easily know and the more hardly forget us ; and, indeed, of our own servants, we more frequently call and employ those whose names are most ready upon the tongue. I myself have seen that Henry the Second could not for his heart hit of a gentleman's name of our country of Gascony ; and moreover was fain to call one of the queen's maids of honour by the general name of her family, her own being so difficult to pronounce or remember. And Socrates thinks it worthy a father's care to give fine names to his children.

Item, 'tis said that the foundation of Notre Dame la Grande, at Poictiers, took its original hence : that a de- The origin of the foundation of Notre Dame la Grande, at Poictiers. bauched young fellow, formerly living in that place, having picked up a wench, and, at her first coming in, asking her name, and being answered that it was Mary, he felt himself so suddenly darted through with the awe of religion, and the reverence to that sacred name of the blessed Virgin, that he not only immediately sent the girl away, but became a reformed man, and so continued the remainder of his life. And that, in consideration of this miracle, there was erected upon the place where this young man's house stood, first a chapel dedicated to our Lady, and afterwards the church that we now see standing there. This auricular reproof wrought upon the conscience,

---

[1] Spartian, *Life of Geta*, c. 5.

and that right into the soul. This that follows insinuated itself merely by the senses. Pythagoras, being in company with some wild young fellows, and perceiving that, heated with the feast, they complotted to go violate an honest house, commanded the singing-wench to alter her wanton airs ; and by a solemn, grave, and spondaic music, gently enchanted and laid asleep their ardour.[1]

Item, will not posterity say that our modern reformation has been wonderfully exact, in having not only scuffled with and overcome errors and vice, and filled the world with devotion, humility, obedience, peace, and all sorts of virtue ; but to have proceeded so far as to quarrel with the ancient baptismal names of Charles, Louis, and Francis, to fill the world with Methusalems, Ezekiels, and Malachis, of a far more spiritual sound ? A gentleman, a neighbour of mine, a great admirer of antiquity, and who was always preferring the excellency of preceding times in comparison with this present age of ours, did not (amongst the rest) forget to magnify the lofty and magnificent sound of the gentlemen's names of those days, Don Grumedan, Quadregan, Agesilan, &c. which but to hear named he conceived to be other kind of men than Pierre, Guillot, and Michel.

Superb and magnificent names of the ancient noblesse.

Item, I am mightily pleased with Jaques Amiot for leaving, throughout a whole French oration, the Latin names entire, without varying and dissecting them, to give them a French termination. It seemed a little harsh and rough at first ; but already custom, by the authority of his Plutarch, has overcome that novelty. I have often wished that such as write chronicles in Latin would leave our names as they find them, for in making of Vaudemont *Vallemontanus*, and metamorphosing names to dress them out in Greek or Latin, we know not where we are, and with the persons of the men lose the benefit of the story.

To conclude, 'tis a scurvy custom, and of very ill conse-

---

[1] Sextus Empiricus, *adversus Mathem*, vi.

quence, which we have in our kingdom of A custom in France for gentlemen to go by the name of their estates; why blamable? France, to call every man by the name of his manor or seigneury; 'tis the thing in the world that does the most confound families and descents. A younger brother of a good family, having a manor left him by his father, by the name of which he has been known and honoured, cannot handsomely leave it; ten years after his decease it falls into the hand of a stranger, who does the same. Do but judge whereabouts we shall be concerning the knowledge of these men. We need look no farther for examples than our own royal family, where every partition creates a new surname, whilst in the mean time the original of the family is totally lost. There is so great a liberty taken in these mutations that I have not in my time The obscurest families most liable to be falsified. seen any one advanced by fortune to any extraordinary grandeur, who has not presently had genealogical titles added to him, new, and unknown to his father, and who has not been engrafted upon some illustrious stem; and, by good luck, the obscurest families are the most proper for falsification. How many gentlemen have we in France, who, by their own talk, are of royal extraction? More, I think, than of those that will confess they are not.

Was not this a pleasant passage of a friend of mine? There were a great many gentlemen assembled together about the dispute of one seigneur with another; which other had, in truth, some preëminence of titles and alliances above the ordinary run of nobility. Upon the debate of this priority, every one standing up for himself, to make himself equal to him, alleged, one one extraction, another another; one the near resemblance of name; another of arms; another an old worm-eaten patent; and the least of them made himself out great-grandchild to some foreign king. When they came to sit down to dinner, my friend, instead of taking his place amongst them, retiring with the most profound congees, entreated the company to excuse him for having hitherto

lived with them at the saucy rate of a companion ; but, being now better informed of their quality, he would begin to
pay them the respect due to their birth and grandeur, saying
it would ill become him to sit down among so many princes.
After jesting with them for some time, he made them a thousand reproaches : " Let us, in God's name, satisfy ourselves
with what our fathers were contented with, and with what we
are.   We are great enough, if we rightly understand how to
maintain it.   Let us not disown the fortune and condition of
our ancestors, but lay aside these ridiculous imaginations, that
can never be wanting to any one that has the impudence to
allege them."

Arms offer no more security than surnames.   I bear
The uncertainty   *Azur semé de trefles d'or, à une patte de lyon de*
of coats of arms.   *même, armée de gueules, mise en fasce.*   What
privilege has this to continue particularly in my house and
name ?   A son-in-law will transport it into another family ;
or some paltry purchaser will make them his first arms.
There is nothing wherein there is more change and confusion.

But this consideration leads me perforce into another
subject.   Let us look a little narrowly into, and, in God's
name, examine upon what foundation we erect this glory
and reputation, for which the world is turned topsy-turvy.
Wherein do we place this renown that we hunt after with
such infinite anxiety and trouble ?   It is, in the end, Peter or
William that bears it, takes it into his possession, and whom
it only concerns.   O, what a valiant faculty is hope, that in a
mortal subject, and in a moment, makes nothing of usurping
infinity, immensity, eternity, and of supplying her master's
indigence, at her pleasure, with all things he can imagine or
desire !   Nature has here given us a pretty toy to play
withal.   And this Peter or William, what is it but a sound,
when all is done ?   Or three or four dashes with a pen, so
easy to be varied that I would fain know to whom is to be
attributed the glory of so many victories, to Guesquin, to

Glesquin, or to Gueaquin ?[1]   And yet there would be something more in the case than in Lucian, that Sigma should
serve Tau with a process ;[2] for

> Non levia aut ludicra petuntur
> Praemia;[3]
> " He seeks no mean rewards: "

the quest is here in good earnest.   The point is, which of
these letters is to be rewarded for so many sieges, battles,
wounds, imprisonments, and services done to the crown of
France by this famous constable.

Nicholas Denisot[4] never concerned himself further than
the letters of his name, of which he has altered the whole
contexture to build up by anagram the Count d'Alsinois,
whom he has endowed with the glory of his poetry and
painting.   And the historian Suetonius looked only to the
meaning of his ; and so cashiering his father's surname, *Le-
nis*, left *Tranquillus* successor to the reputation of his writings.   Who would believe that the Captain Bayard should
have no honour but what he derives from the great deeds of
Peter Terrail ;[5] and that Antonio Escalin should suffer himself to his face to be robbed of the honour of so many navi-
gations and commands at sea and land by Captain Poulin
and the Baron de la Garde ![6]

Secondly, these are dashes of the pen, common to a thousand people.   How many are there in every race of the same

1 In Froissart's History, where we find
all the most memorable actions of this
great man, both before and after his advancement to the dignity of constable,
and to his death, he is not named Guesquin, nor Glesquin, nor Gueaquin, but
Guesclin.   It is true that the same Froissart, (tom. ii. book 3.) long after, having
mentioned his death, tells us that having
called him by the name of Glesquin, in
presence of William d'Ancenis, a gentleman of Britanny, that gentleman said to
him, "That Glay Aquin was the right surname of this famous constable," which
he proved to him by a very pleasant story, which has, however, all the air of ro-
mance.   Ménage, however, mentions no
fewer than fourteen different ways of
spelling the name.

2 Referring to Lucian's *Judgment of the
Vowels*.
3 *Aeneid*, xii. 764.
4 Painter and poet, born at Mans, 1515.
5 Bayard's name.
6 Antonio Escalin (the real name) was
named Poulin, from Poulin, in the Albi-
geois, where he was born.   He took the
name of De la Garde from a corporal of
that name, who, passing one day through
Poulin, with a company of foot soldiers,
took a fancy to him, and carried him off
with him to make him his boy.   He distinguished himself by his wit, valour, and
conduct, in the several employments
which he had, as general of the galleys,
ambassador to the Porte, and to England,
&c., in the reigns of Francis I. and his
successors, down to Charles IX. — See
Brantome, *Illustrious Men*.

name and surname? And how many in several races, ages, and countries? History tells us of three Socrateses, five Platos, eight Aristotles, seven Xenophons, twenty Demetriuses, twenty Theodores; and how many more she was not acquainted with, we may imagine. Who hinders my groom from calling himself Pompey the Great? But, after all, what virtue, what springs are there that convey to my deceased groom, or the other Pompey, who had his head cut off in Egypt, this glorious renown, and these so much honoured flourishes of the pen so as to be of any advantage to them?

> Id cinerem et manes credis curare sepultos.[1]
> " Can we believe the dead regard such things? "

What sense have the two companions in the greatest esteem of men,—Epaminondas, of this glorious verse, that has been so many ages current in his praise;

> Consiliis nostris laus est attrita Laconum;[2]
> " One Sparta by my counsels is o'erthrown; "

and Africanus, of this other,

> A sole exoriente, supra Mæoti' Paludes,
> Nemo est qui factis me æquiparare queat.[3]

> " From early dawn unto the setting sun,
> There's none can match the deeds that I have done."

The survivors, indeed, tickle themselves with these praises, and, by them incited to jealousy or desire, inconsiderately and according to their own fancy, attribute to the dead this their own feeling; vainly flattering themselves that they shall one day in turn be capable of the same. God knows, however,

> Ad hæc se
> Romanus, Grajusque, et Barbarus induperator
> Erexit; causas discriminis atque laboris
> Inde habuit; tanto major famæ sitis est, quam
> Virtutis![4]

[1] *Æneid*, iv. 34.
[2] This verse, translated from the Greek, by Cicero, (*Tusc. Quæs.* v. 17,) is the first of the four elegiac verses that were engraved on the base of the statue of Epam-inondas (Pausanias, ix. 15). In Cicero, however, you find *Attonsa*, not *Attrita*.
[3] Cicero, *Tusc. Quæs.* v. 17.
[4] Juvenal, x. 137.

" Fir'd with the love of these, what countless swarms
Barbarians, Romans, Greeks, have rush'd to arms,
All danger slighted, and all toil defied,
And madly conquer'd, or as madly died!
So much the raging thirst of fame exceeds
The generous warmth which prompts to worthy deeds."

CHAPTER XLVII.

OF THE UNCERTAINTY OF OUR JUDGMENT.

It was well said by the poet,

'Επέων δὲ πολὺς νόμος ἔνθα καὶ ἔνθα.[1]

" There is every where liberty of talking enough, and
enough to be said on both sides."

Whether a conquered enemy should be pursued to extremity. Reasons for and against it.

For example :—

Vince Hannibal, et non seppe usar poi
Ben la vittoriosa sua ventura.[2]

" The Carthaginian, though renown'd in fight,
Improv'd not all his victories as he might."

Such as would take this side, and condemn the oversight of
our leaders, in not pushing home the victory at Moncontour ;
or accuse the King of Spain [3] of not knowing how to make
his best use of the advantage he had against us at St.
Quentin, may conclude these oversights to proceed from a
soul drunk with success, or from a courage which, being full
and overgorged with this beginning of good fortune, had lost
the appetite of adding to it, having already enough to do to
digest what it had taken in ; he has his arms full, and can
embrace no more. Unworthy of the benefit fortune had put
into his hands ; for what utility does he reap from it if, notwith-

---

[1] Homer, *Iliad*, xx. 249.
[2] Petrarch, *Son.* 83.
[3] Philip II., who defeated the French
near St. Quentin, the 20th of August,
1556, being St. Lawrence's day.

standing, he gives his enemy time to rally? What hope is there that he will dare at another time to attack an enemy reunited and recomposed, and armed anew with despite and revenge, who did not dare to pursue him when routed and unmanned by fear?

Dum fortuna calet, dum conficit omnia terror.[1]

" Whilst Fortune's in a heat, and terror throws
A dismal gloom, confounding all their foes."

But, withal, what better opportunity can he expect than that he has lost? 'Tis not here, as in fencing, where the most hits win ; for so long as the enemy is on foot, the game is new to begin; that is not to be called a victory that does not put an end to the war. In the encounter where Cæsar had the worse, near the city of Oricum, he reproached Pompey's soldiers that he had been lost, had their general known how to overcome ;[2] and afterwards showed him a very different trick, when he beat him in his turn.

But why may not a man also argue on the contrary, that it is the effect of a precipitous and insatiate spirit not to know how to restrain its ardour; that it is to abuse the favour of God to exceed the measure he has prescribed them ; and that again to throw a man's self into danger, after a victory is obtained, is again to expose himself to the mercy of fortune ; and that it is one of the highest rules in the art of war not to drive an enemy to despair? Sylla and Marius, in the social war, having defeated the Marsians, seeing yet a body of reserve that, prompted by despair, was coming on like furious beasts to charge in upon them, thought it not convenient to await them. Had not Monsieur De Foix's ardour transported him so precipitously to pursue the remains of the victory of Ravenna, he had not obscured it by his own death. And yet the recent memory of his example served to preserve Monsieur d'Anguien from the same misfortune at the battle of Serisoles. 'Tis dangerous to attack a man you have deprived of all means to escape but by his arms; for necessity teaches violent resolutions; *Gravissimi sunt morsus irritatæ necessitatis.*[1] "Enraged necessity bites deep."

Vincitur haud gratis, jugulo qui provocat hostem.[2]

"The foe that meets the sword sells his life dear."

This it was that made Pharax withhold the King of Lace-demon, who had won a battle of the Mantineans, from going to charge a thousand Argians, who were escaped in an entire body from the defeat; but rather let them steal off at liberty, that he might not encounter valour whetted and enraged by mischance.[3] Clodomir, King of Aquitaine, after a victory pursuing Gondemar, King of Burgundy, beaten and flying, compelled him to face about, and make head; and his obstinacy deprived him of the fruit of his conquest, for he there lost his life.

In like manner, if a man were to choose whether he would have his soldiers richly accoutred and armed, or armed only for necessary defence; this argument would step in in favour of the first (of which opinion were Sertorius, Philopœmen, Brutus, Cæsar, and others), that it is to a soldier an enflaming of courage, and a spur to glory, to see himself bravely apparalled, and withal, affords occasion to be more obstinate in fight, having his arms, which are in a manner his estate and inheritance, to defend; which is the reason, says Xenophon, why those of Asia carried their wives, concubines, with their choicest jewels and greatest wealth, along with them to the wars.[4] But then these arguments would offer on the other side; that a general ought rather to lessen than increase, in his soldiers, their solicitude of preserving themselves; that by this means they will be in a double fear of hazarding their persons; as also that it will be a double temptation to the enemy to fight for a victory where so rich spoils are to be obtained. And this very thing has been observed, in former times,

Whether soldiers should be richly armed.

1 *Declamat. Porc. Latro. apud* Sallust.   3 Diod. Sic. xii. 25.
2 Lucan, iv. 275.   4 *Cyropædia*, iv. 4.

notably to encourage the Romans against the Samnites. Antiochus, showing Hannibal the army he had raised, wonderfully splendid, and rich in all sorts of equipage, asked him —" Will the Romans be satisfied with that army ? " " Satisfied ! " replied the other ; " yes, doubtless, were their avarice never so great." [1]   Lycurgus not only forbad his soldiers all manner of sumptuousness in their equipage, but moreover to strip their conquered enemies, because, he said, he would have poverty and frugality shine with the rest of the battle.[2]

At sieges, and elsewhere, where occasion draws us near to

Whether soldiers should be suffered to brave and insult the enemy. the enemy, we readily suffer our men to brave, rate, and affront the enemy with all sorts of injurious language ; and not without some colour of reason ; for it is of no little consequence to take from them all hopes of mercy and composition, in representing to them that there is no fair quarter to be expected from an enemy they have incensed to that degree, nor other remedy remaining, but in victory.   And yet Vitellius found himself out in this way of proceeding ; for having to do with Otho, weaker in respect of his soldiers, long unaccustomed to war, and effeminated with the delights of the city ; he so nettled them at last, with stinging language, reproaching them with cowardice, and the regret of the mistresses and entertainments they had left behind at Rome, that by this means he inspired them with such resolution as no exhortation would have had the power to have done ; and himself made them fall upon him, with whom their own captains before could by no means prevail.   And, indeed, when they are injuries that touch to the quick, it may very well fall out that he who went but sluggishly to work in the behalf of his prince will fall to it with another sort of mettle, when the quarrel is his own.

Considering of how great importance is the preservation

Whether generals ought to disguise themselves before a battle. of the general of an army, and that the universal aim of an enemy is levelled directly at the head upon which all others depend ; the advice

---

[1] Aulus Gellius, v. 5.   [2] Plutarch, *Apoth. of the Lacedemonians*

seems to admit of no dispute, which we know has been taken by many great captains, of changing their dress, and disguising their persons, upon the point of going to engage. Nevertheless, the inconvenience a man, by so doing, runs into, is not less than that he thinks to avoid; for the captain, by this means, being concealed from the knowledge of his own men, the courage they should derive from his presence and example comes by degrees to cool and to decay; and not seeing the wonted marks and ensigns of their leader,[1] they presently conclude him either dead, or that, despairing of the business, he is gone to shift for himself. Experience shows us that both these ways have been both successful and otherwise. What befèll Pyrrhus in the battle he fought against the consul Levinus, in Italy, will serve us to both purposes; for though, by shrouding his person under the arms of Megacles, and making the latter wear his, he undoubtedly preserved his own life, yet by that very means he was withal very near running into the other mischief of losing the battle. Alexander, Cæsar, and Lucullus, loved to make themselves known in battle, by rich accoutrements and arms of a particular lustre and colour. Agis, Agesilaus, and that great Gilippus,[2] on the contrary, used to fight obscurely armed, and without any imperial attendance or distinction.

Amongst other oversights Pompey is charged withal, at the battle of Pharsalia, he is condemned for making his army stand still to receive the enemy's charge;[3] "by reason that" (I shall here steal Plutarch's own words, that are better than mine),

Whether it is best to fall upon an enemy, or to wait for an attack.

---

[1] As at the battle of Ivry, in the person of Henry the Great.

[2] It is my opinion, observes M. Coste, that one who has been forced to fly his country from a sentence of death, for having robbed the public, can never deserve the title of a great man. As to the infamous robbery committed by this Gilippus, see Diodorus of Sicily. His father, whose name was Clearchus, was in the same scrape. Being cast for his life, he fled, says Diodorus, before the sentence. Thus, adds the historian, did these two personages, who in other respects were both reputed excellent men, throw a scandal upon the rest of their lives and actions, by suffering themselves to be corrupted with sordid avarice.

[3] It is Cæsar himself that lays this blame on Pompey.—*De Bello Civili*, lii. 17.

" he, by so doing, deprived himself of the violent impression
the motion of running adds to the first shock of arms, and
hindered the impetus of the combatants, which was wont to
give great impetuosity and fury to the first encounter;
especially when they come to rush in with their utmost vigour, their courages increasing by the shouts and the career:
thereby rendering his soldiers' animosity and ardour, as a
man may say, more reserved and cold." This is what Plutarch says;[1] but if Cæsar had come by the worse, why
might it not as well have been urged that, on the contrary,
the strongest and most steady posture of fighting is that
wherein a man stands planted firm, without motion; and
they who make a halt upon their march, closing up, and
reserving their force within themselves for the push of the
business, have a great advantage against those who are disordered, and who have already spent half their breath in
running on precipitously to the charge. Besides, that an
army, being a body made up of so many members, it is
impossible for it to move in this fury with so exact a motion
as not to break the order of battle, and that the readiest are
engaged before their fellows can come up to relieve them.
In that disgraceful battle betwixt the two Persian brothers,
the Lacedemonian, Clearchus, who commanded the Greeks
of Cyrus's party, led them on gently, and without precipitation, to the charge; but coming within fifty paces, put them
to full speed, hoping, in so short a career, both to preserve their
order, to husband their breath, and, at the same time, to give
the advantage of impetuosity both to their persons and their
missive arms.[2] Others have regulated this question in charging, thus: " if your enemy come running upon you, stand
firm to receive him; if he stand to receive you, run full
drive upon him." [3]

In the expedition of the Emperor, Charles the Fifth, into
Provence, King Francis was put to choose whether to

---

[1] *Life of Pompey*, c. 19.   [2] Plutarch, *Precepts of Marriage*.
[3] Xenophon, *Anabasis*, i. 8.

go meet him in Italy, or to await him in his Whether it is best for a prince to wait for his enemy in his own territory, or to go and attack him upon his. own dominions; and though he well considered of how great advantage it was to preserve his own territories entire, and clear from the troubles of war, to the end that, being unexhausted of her stores, it might continually supply men and money at need; that the necessity of war requires at every turn to spoil and lay waste the country before them, which cannot very well be done upon one's own; besides which, the country people do not so easily digest such havoc by those of their own party as from an enemy, so that seditions and commotions might by such means be kindled amongst us; that the license of pillage and plunder, which is not to be tolerated at home, is a great ease and refreshment against the fatigues and sufferings of war; and that he who has no other prospect of gain than his bare pay, will hardly be kept from running home, being but two steps from his wife and his own house; that he who lays the cloth is ever at the charge of the feast; that there is more alacrity in assaulting than defending; and that the shock of the loss of a battle in our own bowels is so violent as to endanger the disjointing of the whole body, there being no passion so contagious as that of fear, that is so easily believed, or that so suddenly diffuses itself; and that the cities that should hear the rattle of this tempest, that should take in their captains and soldiers, still trembling and out of breath, would be in danger, in this heat and hurry, to precipitate themselves upon some untoward resolution; notwithstanding all this, he chose to recall the forces he had beyond the mountains, and to suffer the enemy to come to him.

For he might, on the other hand, imagine that, being at home, and amongst his friends, he could not fail of plenty of all manner of conveniences; the rivers and passes he had at his devotion would bring him in both provisions and money in all security, and without the trouble of convoy; that he should find his subjects by so much the more affectionate to him, by how much their danger was more near and pressing; that having so many cities and barriers to secure him, it would be in his power to give battle at his own opportunity and best advantage; and, if it pleased him to delay the time, that under covert, and at his own ease, he might see his enemy founder and defeat himself with the difficulties he was certain to encounter, being engaged in an enemy's country, where before, behind, and on every side, war would be upon him; no means to refresh himself, or to enlarge his quarters, should disease infest them, or to lodge his wounded men in safety. No money, no victuals, but all at the point of the lance; no leisure to repose and take breath; no knowledge of the ways or country, to secure him from ambushes and surprises; and, in case of losing a battle, no possible means of saving the remains.[1] Neither is there want of example in both these cases.

Scipio thought it much better to go and attack his enemy's territories in Africa than to stay at home to defend his own, and fight him in Italy, where he then was; and it succeeded well with him. But, on the contrary, Hannibal, in the same war, ruined himself, by abandoning the conquest of a strange country, to go and defend his own. The Athenians, having left the enemy in their own dominions, to go over into Sicily, were not favoured by fortune in their design; but Agathocles, King of Syracuse, found her favourable to him, when he went over into Africa, and left the war at home.

Thus we are wont to conclude, and with reason, that events, especially in war, do for the most part depend upon fortune, who will not be governed by, nor submit unto, human reason or prudence, according to the poet,

Et malè consultis pretium est; prudentia fallax;
Nec fortuna probat causas, sequiturque merentes,
Sed vaga per cunctos nullo discrimine fertur.
Scilicet est aliud quod nos cogatque regatque
Majus, et in proprias ducat mortalia leges.[2]

[1] The whole of this reasoning is taken, word for word, from a speech made by Francis I. in council, and preserved by William du Bellay, in his *Memoirs* Book vi.

[2] Manilius, iv. 95.

" Prudence deceitful and uncertain is,
　Ill counsels sometimes hit, where good one's miss;
　Though Fortune sometimes the best cause approves,
　Adverse and wildly she as often roves.
　To that some greater and more constant cause
　Rules and subjects all mortals to its laws."

But, to take the thing right, it should seem that our counsels and deliberations depend as much upon fortune as any thing we do, and that she engages our very reason in her uncertainty and confusion. "We argue rashly and adventurously," says Timæus in Plato, "because, as well as ourselves, our reason has a great share in the temerity of chance."

———◆———

CHAPTER XLVIII.

OF DESTRIERS.

HERE am I become a grammarian—I, who never learned any language but by rote, and who do not yet know adjective, conjunctive, or ablative. I think I have read that the Romans had a sort of horses, by them called *Funales*, or *Dextrarios*,[1] which were either led-horses, or relay-horses, to be taken fresh upon occasions; and thence it is that we call our horses of service *Destriers*; and our romances commonly use the phrase of *Adestrer* for *Accompagner*, to accompany. They also called those horses *Desultorios Equos*, which were taught to run full speed side by side, without bridle or saddle, so as that the Roman gentlemen, armed at all points, would shift and throw themselves from the one to the other. The Numidian men-at-arms had always a led-horse in one hand, besides that they

Horses to change in the height of speed.

---

[1] Suetonius (Life of Tiberius), and Statius (Thebaid. vi. 461), have employed the term *funalis* in this sense; but *dextrarius* is a barbarism used only by the authors of the middle ages.

rode upon, to change in the heat of battle. *Quibus, desulto-rum in modum, binos trahentibus equos, inter acerrimam sæpe pugnam in recentem equum, ex fesso, armatis transsultare mos erat ; tanta velocitas ipsis, tamque docile equorum genus.*[1] "Whose custom it was, leading along two horses, after the manner of the Desultorii, armed as they were, in the heat of fight, to vault from a tired horse to a fresh one ; so active were the men, and the horses so docile." There are many horses trained to help their riders, so as to run upon any one that presents a drawn sword, to fall both teeth and heels upon any that front or oppose them. But it often falls out that they do more harm to their friends than their enemies ; besides that you cannot reduce them again into order, when they are once engaged and grappled ; so that you remain at the mercy of their quarrel. It happened very unfortunately to Artybius, general of the Persian army, fighting man to man with Onesilus, King of Salamis, to be mounted upon a horse taught in this school ; for it was the occasion of his death ; the squire of Onesilus cleaving him down with a scythe betwixt the shoulders, as the horse was reared up upon his master.[2] And what the Italians report, that, in the battle of Fornuova, King Charles's horse, with kicks and plunges, disengaged his master from the enemy that pressed upon him, without which he had been slain, seems a strange effect of chance, if it be true.[3] The Mamelukes make their boast that they have the most adroit horses of any cavalry in the world ; that by nature and custom they are taught to know and distinguish the enemy, whom they are to fall foul upon with mouth and

The horses of the Mamelukes very dexterous.

[1] Livy, xxiii. 29.
[2] Herodot. v. 111.
[3] In the narrative which Philip de Comines has given of this battle (viii. 6), in which he himself was present, he tells us of wonderful performances by the horse on which the king was mounted. The name of the horse was Savoy, and it was the most beautiful horse he had ever seen. During the battle the king was personally attacked, when he had nobody near him but a valet de chambre, a little fellow, and not well armed. "The king," says Philip de Comines, "had the best horse under him in the world, and therewith he stood his ground bravely, till a number of his men, not a great way from him, arrived at the critical minute, when the Italians ran away." This does not seem very contradictory to what the Italians say, that had it not been for his horse, King Charles would have been lost.

heels, according to a word or sign given; as also to gather up, with their teeth, darts and lances scattered upon the field, and present them to their riders, according as he orders. 'Tis said of Cæsar, and also of the great Pom- *Cæsar and Pompey good horsemen* pey, that, amongst their other excellent quali- ties, they were both excellent horsemen, and particularly of Cæsar, that, in his youth, being mounted on the bare back of a horse, without saddle or bridle, he could make him run, stop, and turn, with his hands behind him.[1] As Nature designed to make of this personage, and of Alexander, two miracles of military art, you may say she did her utmost to arm them after an extraordinary manner. For every one knows that Alexander's horse, Bucephalus, had a head inclining to the shape of a bull, that he *Alexander's horse.* would suffer himself to be mounted nor accoutred by none but his master, and that he was so honoured after his death as to have a city erected to his name. Cæsar had also another, that had fore feet like the *Cæsar's horse.* hands of a man, his hoof being divided in the form of fingers, which likewise was not to be ridden by any but Cæsar himself; who, after his death, dedicated his statue to the goddess Venus.[2]

I do not willingly alight when I am once on horseback; for it is the place where, whether well or sick, I find myself most at ease. Plato recommends *Riding a very wholesome exercise.* it for health,[3] and also Pliny says it is good for the stomach and the joints.[4] Let us pursue the matter a little further, since we have entered upon it.

We read, in Xenophon, a law forbidding any one, who was master of a horse, to travel on foot.[5] Trogus and Justin say,[6] that the Parthians were wont to perform all offices and ceremonies, not only in war, but also all affairs, *The Parthians almost always on horseback.* whether public or private, make bargains, confer, entertain, take the air, and all on horse-

1 Plutarch, *Life of Cæsar*, c. 5. 4 Book xxviii. 24.
2 Suetonius, *Life of Cæsar*, c. 61 5 *Cyropædia*, iv. 3.
3 *Laws*, vii. 6 Justin, xli.

back; and that the greatest distinction betwixt freemen and
slaves amongst them was that the one rode on horseback and
the other went on foot; an institution of which King Cyrus
was the founder.

There are several examples in the Roman History (and
Suetonius more particularly remarks it in Cæsar [1]) of captains who, in pressing occasions, commanded their cavalry to
alight, both by that means to take from them all hopes of flight,
as also for the advantage they hoped for in this sort of fight.
Quo, haud dubie, superat Romanus: "Wherein the Romans
did, questionless, excel;" says Livy.[2] The first thing they
did to prevent insurrections in the nations of new conquest
was to take from them their arms and horses; and therefore
it is that we so often meet in Cæsar: *Arma proferri, jumenta
produci, obsides dari jubet.*[3] "He commanded the arms to
be produced, the horses brought out, and hostages to be
given." The Grand Seignior, to this day, suffers not a Christian or a Jew to keep a horse of his own throughout his
empire.

Our ancestors, particularly at the time they had war with the
English, in all their greatest engagements and
pitched battles, fought for the most part on foot,
that they might have nothing but their own
strength and courage to trust to in a quarrel of so great concern
as life and honour. You stake (whatever Chrysanthes in Xenophon says to the contrary) your valour and your fortune
upon that of your horse; his wound or death brings you into
the same danger; his fear or fury shall make you rash or
cowardly; if he have an ill mouth, or will not answer to the
spur, your honour must answer it.[4] And, therefore, I do not
think it strange that those battles were more firm and furious
than those that are fought on horseback :—

Inconvenience of fighting on horse-back.

Cedebant pariter, pariterque ruebant
Victores victique; neque his fuga nota, neque illis; [5]

---

[1] Suetonius, *Life of Cæsar*, c. 60.   [4] *Cyropædia,* iv. 8, 8.
[2] Livy, ix. 22.   [5] *Æneid,* x. 756.
[3] *De Bell. Gall.* vii. 11.

> " By turns they quit their ground, by turns advance,
> Victors and vanquished, in the various field,
> Nor wholly overcome, nor wholly yield : "

their battles were much better contested ; now-a-days there are nothing but routs ;—*Primus clamor atque impetus rem decernit.*[1] " The first shout, or the first charge, settles the business." And the arms we make use of in so great a hazard should be as much as possible at our own command ; wherefore I should advise to choose them of the shortest, and such of which we are able to give the best account. A man may repose more confidence in a sword he holds in his hand than in a bullet he discharges out of a pistol, wherein there must be a concurrence of several executions to make it perform its office, the powder, the stone, and the wheel, if any of which fail, it endangers your fortune. The blow a man strikes himself, is much surer than that which the air carries for him : —

> Et, quo ferre velint, permittere vulnera ventis;
> Ensis habet vires; et gens quæcunque virorum est,
> Bella gerit gladiis." [2]

> " Far off with bows
> They shoot, and where it lists the wind bestows
> Their wounds ; but the sword-fight does strength require ;
> All manly nations the sword-fight desire."

But of that weapon I shall speak more fully when I come to compare the arms of the ancients with our own ; the astonishment of the ear excepted, which every one grows familiar with in a little time, I look upon it as a weapon of very little execution, and hope we shall one day lay it aside. That missile weapon which the Italians formerly made use of, both with fire and without, was much more terrible. They called a certain kind of javelin, armed at the point The use of the with an iron three feet long, that it might phalarica, a weapon of the ancient pierce through and through an armed man, Italians. *phalarica*, which they sometimes in the field threw by hand, sometimes from engines, for the defence of beleaguered places; the shaft whereof being rolled round with flax, wax, rosin, oil, and other combustible matter, took fire in its flight, and, lighting upon the body of a man, or his target, took away all the use of arms and limbs. And yet, coming to close fight, I should think they would also endamage the assailant, and that the field, being covered with these flaming truncheons, would produce a common inconvenience to the whole crowd : —

> Magnum stridens contorta phalarica venit,
> Fulminis acta modo.[1]

> " A knotted lance, large, heavy, strong,
> Which roared like thunder as it whirled along."

They had, moreover, other devices which custom made them perfect in, but which seem incredible to us who have not used them, by which they produced the effects of our powder and shot. They darted their heavy spears with so great force as ofttimes transfixed two targets, and two armed men at once, and pinned them together. Neither was the effect of their slings less certain or speedy. *Saxis globosis . . . fundâ, mare apertum incessentes . . . coronas modici circuli, magno ex intervallo loci, assueti trajicere ; non capita modo hostium vulnerabant, sed quem locum destinassent.*[2] " Culling round stones from the shore for their slings, and with them practising at a great distance to throw through a circle of very small circumference, they would not only wound an enemy in the head, but hit any other part at pleasure." Their pieces of battery had not only the execution, but the thunder of our cannon :—*Ad ictus mœnium cum terribili sonitu editos, pavor et trepidatio cepit.*[3] " At the battering of the walls, which is performed with a dreadful noise, the defenders began to fear and tremble." The Gauls, our kinsmen, in Asia, abominated these treacherous missile arms, it being their use to fight with greater bravery, hand to hand. *Non tam patentibus plagis moventur. . . . Ubi latior quam altior plaga est, etiam gloriosius se pugnare putant : iidem, quum aculeus sagittæ aut glandis abditæ introrsus tenui vulnere in speciem urit ... tum, in rabiem et pudorem, tam parvæ perimentis pestis versi, prosternunt corpora humi.*[1] "They are not so much concerned at large wounds; when a wound is wider than deep, they think they have fought with greater glory; but when they find themselves tormented with a slight wound with the point of a dart, or some concealed glandulous body, then, transported with fury and shame, to perish by so mean a messenger of death, they fall to the ground;" a representation something very like a musket-shot. The ten thousand Greeks, in their long and famous retreat, met with a nation who very much galled them with great and strong bows, carrying arrows so long that, taking them up, one might return them back like a dart, and with them pierce a buckler and an armed man through and through.[2] The engines that Dionysius invented at Syracuse, to shoot vast massy darts, and stones of a prodigious size, with impetuosity,[3] and at a great distance, came very near to our modern inventions.

But don't let us forget the pleasant posture of one Maistre Pierre Pol, a doctor of divinity, whom Monstrelet reports always to have rode through the streets of Paris, aside upon his mule, like a woman. He says also, elsewhere, that the Gascons had terrible horses that would wheel in their full speed, which the French, Picards, Flemings, and Brabanters looked upon as a miracle, "having never seen the like before;" these are his very words.[4] Cæsar, speaking of the Suabians,[5] "in the charges they made on horseback," says he, "they often throw themselves off to fight on foot, having taught their horses not to stir in the mean time from the place, to which they presently run again upon occasion; and, ac-

---

[1] Livy, xxviii. 21.

[2] Xenophon, *Anab.* v. ii.

[3] The *Catapulta*, which Ælian, in his *Various Histories*, vi. 12, assigns the invention of to Dionysius himself. Diodorus Siculus, xiv. 12, merely says that it was invented at Syracuse in the time of Dionysius the Elder. Pliny, vii. 56, states that this engine was first used by the Syro-Phœnicians.

[4] Monstrelet, vol. i. c. 66, who to the Gascons adds the Lombards, whom Montaigne forgot, or purposely omitted.

[5] All the editions, up to Coste's, have it, *Swedes*, which must be an error of the press. Cæsar's expression is *Suevorum gens*. Sweden was not known to the Romans in Cæsar's time, which Montaigne must have known very well.

cording to their custom, nothing is so unmanly and so base as
to use saddles or pads, and they despise such as make use of
them ; insomuch that, though but a very few in number, they
fear not to attack a great many." That which
I have formerly wondered at, to see a horse
made to perform all his airs with a switch only,
and the reins upon his neck, was common with
the Massilians, who rode their horses without saddle or bridle.

*The Massilians, a
people of Africa,
ride on horses
without saddle or
bridle.*

> Et gens quæ nudo residens Massylia dorso,
> Ora levi flectit, frænorum nescia, virgâ.[1]
>
> Et Numidæ infræni cingunt.[2]
>
> " Massilians, who unsaddled horses ride,
>   And with a switch, not knowing bridles, guide
>   The rapid steed; and fierce Numidians, too,
>   That use no rein, begirt us round."

*Equi sine frænis ; deformis ipse cursus, rigidâ cervice, et extento
capite currentium.*[3] " The career of a horse without a bridle
must needs be ungraceful, his neck being extended stiff, and
his nose thrust out."

King Alphonso,[4] he who first instituted the order of the
Chevaliers de la Bande, or, *de l'Escharpe,*
amongst other rules of the order, gave them
thus, That they should never ride mule or
mulet, upon a penalty of a mark of silver, which I read
lately in Guevara's letters, of which, whoever gave them the
title of Golden Epistles, had another kind of opinion than I
have. " The Courtier "[5] says that, till his time, it was a
disgrace to a gentleman to ride one of those creatures. But
the Abyssinians, on the contrary, as they are nearer advanced
to the person of Prester John, their prince, affect to ride
large mules for the greater dignity and grandeur.

*To ride on mules
honourable or dis-
honourable in dif-
ferent countries.*

Xenophon tells us[6] that the Assyrians were fain to keep

1 Lucan, iv. 682.
2 Æneid, iv. 41.
3 Livy, xxxv. 11.
4 Alphonso XI. of Leon and Castile died
1850.

5 Il Cortigiano, by Balthasar Castiglino,
published 1528. This passage cited by
Montaigne, is at the beginning of the second book.
6 Cyropædia, iii. 3.

their horses fettered in the stable, they were so fierce and vicious; and that it required so much time to loose and harness them that, to avoid any disorder this tedious preparation might bring upon them, in case of surprise, they never sat down in their camp till it was first well fortified with ditches and ramparts. His Cyrus, who was so great a master of equestrian exercises, made his horses pay their shot, and never suffered them to have any thing till first they had earned it by the sweat of some kind of work. The Scythians, when in the field, and in scarcity of provisions, used to let their horses' blood, which they drank, and sustained themselves by that diet:— *The blood and urine of horses serve for nourishment in case of need.*

> Venit et epoto Sarmata pastus equo.[1]

> "Hither the Scythian also steers his course,
> Gorged with the juices of his bleeding horse."

Those of Crete, being besieged by Metellus, were in so great necessity for drink that they were fain to quench their thirst with their horses' urine.[2]

And to show how much cheaper the Turkish armies support themselves than ours do, 'tis said that, besides that the soldiers drink nothing but water and eat nothing but rice and salt flesh pulverized (of which every one may easily carry about with him a month's provision) they can feed upon the blood of their horses as well as the Muscovites and Tartars, and salt it for their use. *How the Turkish armies subsist.*

These new discovered Indians, when the Spaniards first landed amongst them, had so great an opinion both of the men and horses, that they looked upon them equally as gods, or at least animals ennobled above their own nature; insomuch that some of them, after they were subdued, coming to the soldiers to sue for peace and pardon, and to bring them gold and provisions, failed not to offer the same to the horses, with the same kind of harangue to them which they had made to *Horses as much esteemed by the Americans as by the Spaniards themselves.*

---

[1] Martial, *Spectac.* lib. iii. 4.   [2] Val. Max. vii. 6. *Ext.* i.

the men, interpreting their neighing for a language of truce
and friendship.

In the other Indies, to ride upon an elephant was anciently
the highest honour; the second to ride in a coach with four
horses; the third to ride upon a camel, and the last and
lowest to be carried or drawn by one horse only.[1] One of
our late writers tell us that he has been in a country in those
parts where they ride upon oxen with pads, stirrups, and
bridles, and that he found this equipage very much to his
ease.

Quintus Fabius Maximus Rutilianus,[2] in a battle with the
Samnites, seeing his cavalry, after three or four charges, had
failed of breaking into the enemies' main body, took this
course—to make them unbridle all their horses, and spur
their horses with all their might, so that, having nothing to
check their career, they might, through weapons and men,
open the way for his foot, who by that means gave them a
bloody defeat. The same command was given by Quintus
Fulvius Flaccus against the Celtiberians: *Id cum majore vi
equorum facietis, si effrænatos in hostes equos immittitis;
quod sæpè Romanos equites cum laude fecisse suâ memoriæ
proditum est. . . . . . Detractisque frænis, bis ultro citroque
cum magna strage hostium, infractis omnibus hastis, transcur-
rerunt.*[3] "You will do your business with greater advantage
of your horses' strength if you spur them unbridled upon the
enemy, as it is recorded the Roman horse to their great glory
have often done. . . . . . And their bits being pulled off
without breaking a lance, they charged through and through
with great slaughter of the enemy."

The Duke of Muscovy was anciently obliged to pay this
reverence to the Tartars, that when they sent
any embassy to him he went out to meet the
ambassadors on foot, and presented them with a
goblet of mare's milk (a beverage of greatest esteem among

Mare's milk the
delight of the Tar-
tars.

[1] Arrian, *Hist. Ind.* c. 17.   [3] Livy, xl. 40.
[2] Or rather *Rullianus.* See Livy, vii.
30.

them); and if, in drinking, a drop fell by chance upon the horse's mane, he was bound to lick it off with his tongue.[1] The army that Bajazet had sent into Russia was overwhelmed with so dreadful a tempest of snow that, to shelter and preserve themselves from freezing, many ripped up and embowelled their horses, to creep into their bellies and enjoy the benefit of that vital heat. Bajazet, after that furious battle wherein he was overthrown by Tamerlane,[2] was in a hopeful way of securing his own person by the fleetness of an Arabian mare he had under him, had he not been constrained to let her drink her fill at the ford of a river in his way, which rendered her so heavy and indisposed that he was afterwards easily overtaken by those that pursued him. They say, indeed, that to let a horse stale takes him off his mettle; but I should rather have thought that drinking would have refreshed her and revived her spirits.

Crœsus, marching his army over a common near Sardis, met with an infinite number of serpents, which the horses devoured with great appetite, and which Herodotus says[3] was a bad omen to his affairs.

We call a horse *cheval entier* that has his mane and ears entire, and no other will pass muster. The Lacedemonians, having defeated the Athenians in Sicily, returning triumphant from the victory into the city of Syracusa, amongst other bravadoes caused all the horses they had taken to be shorn and led in triumph.[4] Alexander fought with a nation called Dahæ; a people whose discipline it was to march two and two together, armed and on horseback, to the war; but being in fight, one always alighted, and so they fought one while on horseback and another on foot, one after another, by turns.[5]

Horses clipped to be led in triumph.

I do not think that for good and graceful riding any nation

---

1 See the *Chronicle of Muscovy*, by Peter Petrejus, a Swede, printed in Iligh Dutch, at Leipsic, in 1620, in 4to. part ii. p. 159. This species of slavery began about the middle of the thirteenth century, and lasted near 260 years.

2 In 1401.
3 Book 1. c. 78.
4 Plutarch, *Life of Nicias*, c. 10
5 Quintus Curtius, vii. 7.

excels the French, though a good horseman, according to our way of speaking, seems rather to respect the courage of the man than his horsemanship and address in riding. The most knowing in that art that ever I knew, that had the best seat and the best method in taming a horse, was Monsieur de Carnavalet, who served our King Henry the Second in this

Instances of the wonderful dexterity of riders. respect. I have seen a man ride with both his feet upon the saddle, take off the saddle, and at his return take it up again, refit and remount it, riding all the while full speed; having galloped over a cap, make at it very good shots backward with his bow, take up any thing from the ground, setting one foot down and the other in the stirrup, with twenty other apes' tricks, which he got his living by.

There has been seen in my time at Constantinople two men upon a horse, who, in the height of his speed, would throw themselves off and into the saddle again by turn; and one who bridled and saddled his horse with nothing but his teeth. Another, who betwixt two horses, one foot upon one saddle and another upon the other, carrying another man upon his shoulders, would ride full career; the other standing bolt upright upon him, making excellent shots with his bow. Several, who would ride full speed with their heels upwards and their heads upon the saddle, betwixt the rows of scimitars fixed in the harness. When I was a boy, the Prince of Sulmona, riding a rough horse at Naples, to all his airs, held reals under his knees and toes as if they had been nailed there, to show the firmness of his seat.

CHAPTER XLIX.

OF ANCIENT CUSTOMS.

I SHOULD willingly pardon our people for admitting no other pattern or rule of perfection than their own peculiar manners and customs, it being a common vice not of the vulgar only, but almost of all men, to look upon their own country's fashions as the best. I am content when they see Fabricius or Lœlius, that they look upon their countenance and behaviour as barbarous, seeing they are neither clothed nor fashioned according to our mode. But I find fault with their especial indiscretion in suffering themselves to be so imposed upon and blinded by the authority of the present custom, as every month to alter their opinion, if custom so require, and that they should so vary their judgment in their own particular concern. When they wore the belly-pieces of their doublets as high as their breast, they stiffly maintained that they were in their proper place. Some years after they were slipped down between their thighs, and then they laughed at the former fashion as uneasy and intolerable. The new fashion in use makes them absolutely condemn the old with so great a warmth, and so universal a contempt, that a man would think there was a kind of madness crept in amongst them, that infatuates their understandings to this strange degree. Now seeing that our change of fashions is so prompt and sudden that the inventions of all the tailors in the world cannot furnish out new whim-whams enough, there will often be a necessity that the old despised ones must again come in vogue, and again fall into contempt; and that the same judgment must, in the space of fifteen or twenty years, take up not only different, but contrary, opinions, with an incredible

The French very changeable in their dress.

lightness and inconstancy.   There is not any of us so discreet that suffers not himself to be gulled with this contradiction, and both in external and internal sight to be insensibly blinded.

I will here muster up some old customs that I have in memory ; some of them the same with ours, others different, to the end that, bearing in mind this continual variation of human things, we may have our judgments clearer and more firmly settled.

The use amongst us of fighting with rapier and cloak, was in practice amongst the Romans also : *Sinistras* *sagis involvunt, gladiosque distringunt,*[1] " They wrapped their cloaks round the left arm, and wielded the sword with the right," says Cæsar ; and he mentions an old vicious custom of our nation, which continues yet amongst us, which is to stop passengers we meet upon the road, to compel them to give an account who they are, and to take it for an injury and just cause of quarrel if they refuse to do it.[2]

The practice of the ancient Romans to fight with rapier and cloak.

At the bath, which the ancients made use of every day before they went to dinner, and, indeed, as frequently as we wash our hands, they at first only bathed their arms and legs,[3] but afterwards, and by a custom that has continued for many ages in most nations of the world, they bathed stark naked in mixed and perfumed water, so that it became a mark of great simplicity of life to bathe in pure water.   The most delicate and affected perfumed themselves all over three or four times a day.   They often caused all their hair to be pulled out, as the women of France have some time since taken up a fancy to do their foreheads,

The ancients bathed every day before dinner.

> Quod pectus, quod crura tibi, quod brachia vellis,[4]

> " How dost thou twitch thy breast, thy arms and thighs,"

though they had ointments proper for that purpose.

---

[1] Cæsar, *De Bello Civili*, i. 75.
[2] Id. *De Bello Gallico*, iv. 5.
[3] Seneca, *Epist.* 86
[4] Mart. ii. 62, 1.

Psilotro nitet, aut acidâ latet oblita cretâ.[1]

"This in wild-vine shines; or else doth calk
Her rank pores up in a dry crust of chalk."

They delighted to lie soft, and allowed it for a great testimony of hardiness, to lie upon a mattrass;[2] they all lying
upon beds, much after the manner of the Turks in this age.

Inde toro pater Æneas sic orsus ab alto.[3]

"Then thus Æneis from his bed of state."

And 'tis said of the younger Cato, that, after the battle of
Pharsalia, being entered into a melancholic disposition at the
ill posture of the public affairs, he took his food always
sitting, assuming a strict and austere course of life.[4]   It
was also their custom to kiss the hands of great persons by
way of honouring and caressing them; and meeting with
their equals, they always kissed in salutation, as do the Vene-
tians :—

Gratatusque darem cum dulcibus oscula verbis;[5]

"And kindest words I would with kisses mix."

In petitioning or saluting any great man, they used to lay their
hands upon his knees.   Pasicles, the philosopher, brother of
Crates, instead of laying his hand upon the knee, laid it upon
the private parts, and, being roughly repulsed by him to
whom he addressed himself, "What," said he; "is not that
part your own, as well as the other?"[6]   They used to eat
their fruit as we do, after dinner.   They cleaned themselves
after stool with a sponge, which is the reason that *spongia* is
a smutty word in Latin; which sponge was also fastened to
the end of a stick, as appears by the story of him who, as he
was led along to be thrown to the wild beasts in the sight of
the people, asked leave to do his business, and, having no
other way to dispatch himself, forced the sponge and stick

---

[1] Mart. vi. 93, 9.
[2] "Laudare solebat Attalus culcitam quæ resisteret corpori. Tali utor etiam senex," says Seneca, *Epist.* 108.
[3] *Æneid*, ii. 2.
[4] Plutarch, *Life of Cato of Utica*, c. 15
[5] Ovid, *De Ponto*, iv. 9, 13.
[6] Diog. Laertius, vi. 89.

down his own throat, and choked himself.[1] They used to
terge, after coition, with perfumed wool :—

> At tibi nil faciam, sed lotâ mentula lanâ.[2]

They placed in the streets of Rome certain vessels and
little tubs for passengers to make water in :—

> Puri sæpe lacum propter, se, ac dolia curta,
> Somno devincti, credunt extollere vestem.[3]

They had collation betwixt meals.   There were in summer
They cooled their wine with snow. persons who made a business of selling snow
to cool the wine; and some there were who
made use of snow in winter, not thinking their
wine cool enough even at that season of the year.   The men
of quality had their cup-bearers and carvers, and their buffoons to make them sport; they had their meat served up in
winter upon a sort of chafing dishes which were set upon the
They had portable kitchens; table, and had portable kitchens (of which I
myself have seen some), wherein all their ser-
vice was carried after them.

> Has vobis epulas habete, lauti;
> Nos offendimur ambulante cœnâ.[4]

> " Those feasts to you may pleasure be,
> But walking suppers suit not me."

In summer they had a contrivance to bring fresh and clear
and fish-pools in their lower rooms. rills through their lower rooms, wherein were
great store of living fish which the guests took
out with their own hands to be dressed, every
man according to his own liking.[5] Fish has ever had this
preëminence, and keeps it still, that even great men pretend
to be cooks in their favour; and, indeed, the taste is more
delicate than that of flesh, at least to me.   But in all sorts

[1] Senec. *Epist.* 70.
[2] Martial, xi. 58, 11.
[3] Lucretius, iv. 1020.
[4] Martial, vii. 48. See also Seneca, *Epist.* 78.
[5] Or, " Every man in his place," ac-

cording to some editions. Beckford, in
his account of a visit to the Convent of
Alcobaca, gives a description of one of
these interior fish-pools that he met with
there.

of magnificence, debauchery, and voluptuous inventions of effeminacy and expense, we do, in truth, all we can to equal them (for our wills are as corrupt as theirs), but we want power to reach them; we are no more able to parallel them in their vicious, than in their virtuous qualities; for both the one and the other proceed from a vigour of soul which was, without comparison, greater in them than in us; and souls by how much the weaker they are, by so much have they less power to do very well, or very ill.

The place of honour amongst them was the middle. The name going before or following after, either in writing or speaking, had no signification of grandeur, as is evident by their writings. They *The most honourable place among the Romans.* as readily said "Oppius and Cæsar," as "Cæsar and Oppius;" and "me and thee" indifferently with "thee and me." This is the reason that made me formerly take notice in the life of Flaminius, in our French translation of Plutarch, of one passage, where it seems as if the author, speaking of the jealousy of glory betwixt the Ætolians and Romans, as to the winning of a battle they had with their joint forces obtained, made it of some importance that in the Greek songs they had put the Ætolians before the Romans; if there be no amphibology in the words of the French version.

The ladies in their baths made no scruple of admitting men amongst them, and moreover made use of their serving-men to rub and anoint them:— *The men and women bathed together.*

> Inguina succinctus nigrâ tibi servus alutâ
> Stat, quoties calidis nuda foveris aquis.[1]

> " Whene'er her body in the bath she laves,
> Her naked limbs are 'nointed by men slaves."

They powdered themselves with a certain powder, to moderate perspiration.

The ancient Gauls, says Sidonius Apollinaris,[2] wore their

---

[1] Martial, vii. 35.   [2] *Carm.* v. 239.

hair long before, and quite short behind, a fashion that begins to be revived by this vicious and effeminate age.

The Romans used to pay the watermen their fare at their first stepping into the boat, which we never do till after landing:—

The Romans paid their watermen at embarking.

> Dum æs exigitur, dum mula ligatur,
> Tota abit hora.[1]

> " Whilst the fare's paying and the mule is tied,
>   A whole hour's time, at least, away doth slide."

The women used to lie on that side the bed next the wall; and for that reason they called Cæsar, *Spondam Regis Nicomedis*.[2]

They took breath in their drinking, and watered their wine :—

> Quis puer ocius
> Restinguet ardentis falerni
> Pocula prætereunte lymphâ?[3]

> " To cool our wine, the boy shall bring
>   Fresh water from the limpid spring."

And the roguish looks and gestures of our lacqueys were also in use amongst them.

> O Jane! a tergo quem nulla ciconia pinsit,
> Nec manus auriculas imitata est mobilis altas,
> Nec linguæ quantum sitiet canis Appula tantum.[4]

> " O Janus! happy in thy double face!
>   Safe and protected from unseen grimace!
>   From pecking finger, and from gibes and sneers,
>   Provok'd by wagging hands, like asses' ears,
>   From lolling tongue, such as the Appulian hound,
>   Panting with thirst, drops almost to the ground."

The Argian and Roman ladies always mourned in white,[5] as ours did formerly; and should do still, were I to govern in this point. But there are whole books might be made on this subject.

[1] Horace, *Sat.* i. 5, 13.
[3] Horace, *Od.* ii. 11, 18.
[4] Persius, i. 58.
[2] Suetonius, *Life of Cæsar*, c. 49. *Sponda* is the Latin word for the inner side of the bed.
[5] Herod. iv. 2, 6.

CHAPTER L.

OF DEMOCRITUS AND HERACLITUS.

THE judgment is an utensil proper for all subjects, and will have an oar in every thing; which is the reason that, in these Essays, I take hold of all occasions.   If I light on a subject I do not very well understand, I try, however, sounding it at a distance ; and, if I find it too deep for my stature, I keep me on the firm shore.   And this knowledge, that a man can proceed no further, is one effect of its virtue ; aye, and one on which it prides itself the most.   Sometimes, in an idle and frivolous subject, I try to find out matter whereof to compose a body, and then to prop and support it.   Another while I employ it in a noble subject, one that has been tossed and tumbled by a thousand hands, wherein a man can hardly possibly introduce any thing of his own, the way being so beaten on every side that he must of necessity walk in the steps of another.   In such a case, 'tis the work of the judgment to take the way that seems best, and, of a thousand paths, to determine that this or that was the best chosen.   I leave the choice of my arguments to Fortune, and take that she first presents me ; they are all alike to me ; I never design to go through any of them ; for I never see all of any thing ; neither do they who so largely promise to show it others.   Of a hundred members and faces that every thing has, I take one—one while to look it over only, another while to ripple up the skin, and sometimes to pinch it to the bones ; I give a stab, not so wide, but as deep as I can ; and most frequently like to take it in hand by some less-used light. Did I know myself less, I might, perhaps, venture to handle something or other to the bottom, and to be deceived in my

The judgment active in every thing.

own inability, but sprinkling here one word, and there
another, patterns cut from several pieces, and scattered without design, and without engaging myself too far, I am not
responsible for them, or obliged to keep close to my subject,
without varying it at my own liberty and pleasure, and giving up myself to doubt and uncertainty, and to my own governing method, ignorance.

All motion discovers us.   The very same soul of Cæsar
that made itself so conspicuous in marshalling and command-
 The mind is ing the battle of Pharsalia, was also seen as
discovered in all solicitous and busy in the softer affairs of love.
its motions.

A man judges of a horse not only by seeing
him caracole and exhibit airs in the riding-school, but by his
walk, nay, and by seeing him stand in the stable.

Amongst the functions of the soul there are some of a
lower and meaner form, and he who does not see her in those
inferior offices, as well as those of nobler note, is never fully
acquainted with her ; and peradventure she is best discovered where she moves her own natural pace.   The winds
of the passions take most hold of her in her highest flights ;
and the rather, by reason that she wholly applies herself to,
and exercises her whole virtue upon, each particular subject,
and never handles more than one thing at a time, and that
not according to it, but according to herself.   Things in
It gives things respect to themselves have peradventure their
what shape and weight, measure, and condition; but when we
colour it pleases. once take them into us, the soul forms them as
she pleases.   Death is terrible to Cicero, coveted by Cato,
and indifferent to Socrates.   Health, conscience, authority,
knowledge, riches, beauty, and their contraries, do all strip
themselves at their entering into us, and receive a new robe,
and of another fashion, from the soul; brown, bright, green,
dark ; sharp, sweet, deep, or superficial, as best pleases each particular soul, for they are not agreed upon any common standard
of forms, rules, or proceedings ; every one is a queen in her
own dominions.   Let us, therefore, no more excuse ourselves

upon the external qualities of things; it belongs to us to give ourselves an account of them. Our good or ill has no other dependence but on ourselves. 'Tis there that our offerings and our vows are due, and not to fortune; she has no power over our manners; on the contrary, they draw and make her follow in her train, and cast her in their own mould. Why should not I judge Alexander, roaring and drinking at the rate he sometimes used to do? Or, if he played at chess, what string of his soul was not touched by this idle and childish game? I hate and avoid it because it is not play enough—that it is too grave and serious a diversion; and I am ashamed to lay out as much thought and study upon that as would serve to much better uses. He did not more pump his brains about his glorious expedition into the Indies; and another, that I will not name, took not more pains to unravel a passage upon which depends the safety of all mankind. To what a degree then does this ridiculous diversion molest the soul, when all her faculties shall be summoned together upon this trivial account? And how fair an opportunity she herein gives every one to know, and to make a right judgment of, himself? I do not more thoroughly sift myself in any other posture than this. What passion are we exempted from in this insignificant game? Anger, spite, malice, impatience, and a vehement desire of getting the better in a matter wherein it were more excusable to be ambitious of being overcome; for to be eminent, and to excel above the common rate in frivolous things is nothing becoming in a man of quality and honour. What I say in this example may be said in all others. Every particle, every employment of man, does exhibit and accuse him equally with any other.

Democritus and Heraclitus were two philosophers, of which the first, thinking human condition ridiculous and vain, never appeared abroad but with a jeering and laughing countenance; whereas

Montaigne's opinion of chess.

The game may help us to know ourselves.

Democritus and Heraclitus, their different humours.

Heraclitus, commiserating that condition of ours, appeared always with a sorrowful look and tears in his eyes.

Alter
Ridebat, quoties a limine moverat unum
Protuleratque pedem; flebat contrarius alter.[1]

"One always, when he o'er his threshold stept,
Laugh'd at the world, the other always wept."

I am clearly for the first humour; not because it is more pleasant to laugh than to weep, but because it is more contemptuous, and expresses more condemnation than the other; for I think we can never be sufficiently despised to our desert. Compassion and bewailing seem to imply some esteem of, and value for, the thing bemoaned; whereas the things we laugh at are by that expressed to be of no moment. I do not think that we are so unhappy as we are vain, or have in us so much malice as folly; we are not so full of mischief as inanity, nor so miserable as we are vile and mean. And therefore Diogenes, who passed away his time in rolling himself in his tub, and made nothing of the great Alexander, esteeming us no better than flies, or bladders puffed up with wind, was a sharper and more penetrating, and consequently,

Diogenes and Timon the Manhater.

in my opinion, a juster judge than Timon, surnamed the Man-hater; for what a man hates he lays to heart. This last was furious against mankind, passionately desired our ruin, and avoided our conversation as dangerous, and proceeding from wicked and depraved natures; the other valued us so little that we could neither trouble nor infect him by our contagion, and left us to herd with one another, not out of fear, but contempt of our society, concluding us as incapable of doing good as ill.

Of the same strain was Statilius's answer when Brutus

Why Statilius would not enter into the conspiracy against Cæsar.

courted him to the conspiracy against Cæsar: "He was satisfied that the enterprise was just, but he did not think mankind so considerable as to deserve a wise man's concern."[2] According to the

---

[1] Juven. 10, 28.　　　　[2] Plutarch, *Life of M. Brutus,* c. 3.

doctrine of Hegesias, who said, "a wise man ought to do nothing but for himself, forasmuch as he only is worthy of it;"[1] and to that of Theodorus, "That it is not reasonable a wise man should hazard himself for his country, and endanger wisdom for a set of fools."[2] Our condition is as ridiculous as risible.

CHAPTER LI.

ON THE VANITY OF WORDS.

A RHETORICIAN of times past said, That his profession was to make little things appear great. This also a shoemaker can do; he can make a great shoe for a little foot.[3] They would, in Sparta, have sent such a fellow to be whipped for making profession of a lying *The art of rhetoric deceitful.* and deceitful art; and I fancy that Archidamus, who was king of that country, was a little surprised at the answer of Thucydides, when inquiring of him which was the better wrestler, Pericles or he, he replied, "That is hard to affirm; for when I have thrown him, he always persuades the spectators that he had no fall, and carries away the prize."[4] They who paint and plaster up women, filling up their wrinkles and deformities, are less to blame, for it is no great loss not to see them in their natural complexion. Whereas these make it their business to deceive not our sight only, but our judgments, and to adulterate and corrupt the very essence of things. The republics that have maintained themselves in a regular and well-modelled government, such as those of Lacedemon and Crete, had orators in no very great esteem.[5]

1 Laertius, *in Vitâ.*
2 Id. *ib.*
3 This is a saying of Agesilaus. See Plutarch, *Apothegms of the Lacedemonians.*
4 Plutarch, *Life of Pericles,* c. 5.
5 Sextus Empiricus, *Advers. Mathem.* ii.

Aristo did wisely define rhetoric to be "a science to persuade the people;"[1] Socrates and Plato[2] "an art to flatter and deceive." And those who deny it in the general description, verify it throughout in their precepts. The Mahometans will not suffer their children to be instructed in it, as being useless; and the Athenians, perceiving how pernicious the practice of it was, it being in their city of universal esteem, ordered the principal part, which is to move affections, to be taken away, with the exordiums and perorations. 'Tis an engine invented to manage and excite a disorderly and tumultuous rabble, and is never made use of but like physic, in a diseased state. In those governments where the vulgar or the ignorant, or both together, have been all-powerful, as in Athens, Rhodes, and Rome, and where the public affairs have been in a continual tempest of commotion, to such places have the orators always flocked. And, in truth, we find few persons in those republics who have pushed their fortunes to any great degree of eminence without the assistance of eloquence. Pompey, Cæsar, Crassus, Lucullus, Lentulus, and Metellus, have therein found their chiefest aid in mounting to that degree of authority to which they did at last arrive; making it of greater use to them than arms, contrary to the opinion of better times; for L. Volumnius, speaking publicly in favour of the election of Q. Fabius and Pub. Decius to the consular dignity: "These are men," said he, "born for war, and great in execution; in the combat of the tongue altogether to seek; spirits truly consular. The subtle, eloquent, and learned are only good for the city to make prætors of, to administer justice."[3]

Eloquence flourished most at Rome, when the public affairs were in the worst condition, and the republic most disquieted with civil wars, as a free and untilled soil bears the worst weeds.

When eloquence was most flourishing at Rome.

By which it would seem that a monarchical government has less need of it than any other; for the stupidity and facility

of the common people, which render them subject to be
turned and twined, and led by the ears by this charming harmony of words, without weighing or considering the truth and
reality of things by the force of reason ;—this facility, I say,
is not easily found in a single person, and it is also more easy,
by good education and advice, to secure him from the impression of this poison. There never was any famous orator
known to come out of Persia or Macedon.

I have entered into this discourse upon the occasion of an
Italian I lately received into my service, who was clerk of
the kitchen to the late Cardinal Caraffa till his death. I put
this fellow upon an account of his office; where *The palate-science*
he fell to discourse of this palate-science with *pleasantly ridi-*
such a settled countenance and magisterial *culed.*
gravity, as if he had been handling some profound point of
divinity. He made a learned distinction of the several sorts
of appetites, of that which a man has before he begins to eat,
and of those after the second and third service ; the means
simply to satisfy the first, and then to raise and quicken the
other two ; the ordering of the sauces, first in general, and
then proceeded to the qualities of the several ingredients and
their effects. The difference of salads, according to their
seasons, which of them ought to be served up hot, and which
cold ; the manner of their garnishment and decoration, to
render them yet more acceptable to the eye. After which he
entered upon the order of the whole service, full of weighty
and important considerations :—

> Nec minimo sane discrimine refert,
> Quo gestu lepores et quo gallina secetur ; [1]

> " Nor with less criticism did observe
> How we a hare, and how a hen, should carve."

And all this set out with lofty and magnificent words, the
very same we make use of when we discourse of the government of an empire ; which learned lecture of my man brought
this of Terence to my memory :—

[1] Juvenal, v. 123.

Hoc salsum est, hoc adustum est, hoc lautum est parum ;
Illud rectè; iterum sic memento: sedulo
Moneo, quæ possum, pro mea sapientiâ.
Postremo, tanquam in speculum, in patinas, Demea,
Inspicere jubeo, et moneo quid facto usus sit.[1]

" This is too salt, this burnt; this is too plain,
That's well, remember to do so again.
Thus do I still advise to have things fit,
According to the talent of my wit.
And then, my Demea, I command my cook,
That into ev'ry dish he pry and look,
As if it were a mirror, and go on
To order all things as they should be done."

And yet even the Greeks themselves did very much admire
and highly applaud the order and disposition that Paulus
Æmilius observed in the feast he made for them at his return
from Macedon.[2] But I do not here speak of effects ; I speak
of words only.

I do not know whether it may have the same operation
The language of upon other men that it has upon me, but when
architects.   I hear our architects thunder out their bombast
words of pilasters, architraves, and cornices, of the Corinthian
and Doric orders, and such like stuff, my imagination is presently possessed with the palace of Apollidonius ;[3] when, after
all, I find them but the paltry pieces of my own kitchen-door.

And to hear men talk of metonymies, metaphors, and alle-
                gories, and other grammar words, would not a
Of grammarians. man think they signified some rare and delicate
and exotic form of speaking? yet these are terms which
apply to the chatter of your chambermaid.

And this other is a gullery of the same stamp, to call the
Too lofty titles giv- offices of our kingdom by the lofty titles of the
en to offices, and   Romans, though they have no similitude of
illustrious sur-
names misapplied function, and still less authority or power. And
to persons of mean
talents.   this, also, which I doubt will one day turn to

1 Terence, Adelphi, iii. 4, 62.
2 Plutarch, Life of Paulus Æmilius,
c. 15.
3 The reader who desires to be acquainted with the marvels of this palace, and
with Apollidonius who built it by magic
art, must read the first chapter of the
second book of Amadis de Gaul, and the
second chapter of the fourth book.

the reproach of our present age, unworthily and indifferently to confer upon any we think fit the most glorious surnames with which antiquity honoured but one or two persons in several ages.

Plato carried away the surname of Divine by so universal a consent that never any one repined at it, or attempted to take it from him. And yet the Italians, who pretend, and with good reason, to more sprightly wits and sounder judgments than the other nations of their time, have lately honoured Aretin with the same title; in whose writings, except it be a tumid phrase set out with some smart periods, ingenious indeed, but far-fetched and fantastic, and some degree of eloquence, I see nothing above the ordinary writers of his time, so far is he from approaching the ancient divinity. And we make nothing of giving the surname of Great to princes that have nothing in them above a popular grandeur.

CHAPTER LII.

OF THE PARSIMONY OF THE ANCIENTS.

ATTILIUS REGULUS, general of the Roman army in Africa, in the height of all his glory and victories over the Carthaginians, wrote to the Republic to acquaint them that a certain peasant, whom he had left in charge of his estate, which was in all but seven acres of land, was run away with all his instruments of husbandry, entreating, therefore, that they would please to call him home, that he might take order in his own affairs, lest his wife and children should suffer. Whereupon the Senate appointed another to manage his business, caused his losses to be made good, and ordered his family to be maintained at the public expense.[1]

[1] Val. Max. iv. 4, 6.

The elder Cato, returning consul from Spain, sold his war-horse, to save the money it would have cost in bringing him back by sea into Italy; and, being governor of Sardinia, made all his visitations on foot, without other attendant than one officer of the republic, to hold up the train of his gown, and carry a censer for sacrifices ; and, for the most part, carried his mail himself.　He bragged that he had never worn a gown that cost above ten crowns, nor had ever sent above tenpence to the market for one day's provisions ; and that, as to his country-houses, he had not one that was rough-cast on the outside.[1]

Scipio Æmilianus, after two triumphs and two consulships, went an embassy with no more than seven servants in his train.[2] 'Tis said that Homer had never more than one, Plato three, and Zeno, founder of the sect of Stoics, none at all.[3] Tiberius Gracchus was allowed but fivepence-halfpenny a day when employed on a mission about the public affairs, and being at that time the greatest man of Rome.[4]

———◆———

CHAPTER LIII.

OF A SAYING OF CÆSAR.

If we would sometimes bestow a little consideration upon ourselves, and employ that time in examining our own abilities which we spend in prying into other men's actions, and discovering things without us, we should soon perceive of how infirm and decaying materials this fabric of ours is composed.

1 Plutarch, *in Vitâ*, c. 3.
2 Val. Max. iv. 3, 13.
3 Seneca, *Consolat. ad Helviam*, c. 12.
4 Plutarch, in the Life of Tiberius Gracchus, cap. 4. But here Montaigne mis-employs this passage, which makes nothing for his purpose; for Plutarch there says, expressly, that this little sum was allowed to Tiberius Gracchus purely to vex and mortify him.

Is it not a singular testimony of imperfection that we cannot establish our satisfaction in any one thing, and that even our own fancy and desire should deprive us of the power to choose what is most proper and useful for us? A very good proof of this is the great dispute that has ever been amongst the philosophers of finding out what is man's sovereign good—a dispute that continues yet, and will eternally continue, without solution or agreement.

> Dum abest quod avemus, id exuperare videtur
> Cætera; post aliud, cum contigit illud, avemus,
> Et sitis æqua tenet.[1]

> " Still with desire through Fancy's regions tost,
> We seek new joys, and prize the absent most."

Whatever it is that falls within our knowledge and possession, we find it satisfies not, and we still pant after things to come, and unknown; and these because the present do not satiate us; not that, in my judgment, they have not in them wherewith to do it, but because we seize them with a weak and ill-regulated hold.

> Nam cum vidit hic, ad victum quæ flagitat usus,
> Omnia jam ferme mortalibus esse parata,
> Et per quæ possent vitam consistere tutam;
> Divitiis homines et honore et laude potentes
> Affluere, atque bonâ natorum excellere famâ;
> Nec minus esse domi cuiquam tamen anxia corda,
> Atque animum infestis cogi servire querelis:
> Intellexit ibi vitium vas efficere ipsum,
> Omniaque, illius vitio, corrumpier intus,
> Quæ collata foris et commoda quæque venirent.[2]

> " For when he saw all things that had regard
> To life's subsistence for mankind prepar'd,
> That men in wealth and honours did abound,
> That with a noble race their joys were crown'd;
> That yet they groan'd, with cares and fears oppress'd,
> Each finding a disturber in his breast;
> He then perceiv'd the fault lay hid in man,
> In whom the bane of his own bliss began."

[1] Lucret. iii. 1095.   [2] Lucret. vi. 9.

Our appetite is irresolute and fickle, it can neither **keep** nor enjoy any thing as it should. Man, concluding it to be the fault of the things he is possessed of, fills himself with, and feeds himself upon, the idea of things he neither knows nor understands, to which he devotes his hopes and his desires, paying them all reverence and honour, according to the saying of Cæsar: *Communi fit vitio naturæ, ut invisis, latitantibus atque incognitis rebus magis confidamus, vehementiùsque exterreamur.*[1] " 'Tis the common vice of nature that we have the most confidence in, and the greatest fear of, things unseen, concealed, and unknown."

CHAPTER LIV.

OF VAIN SUBTLETIES.

THERE are a sort of little knacks and frivolous subtleties from which men sometimes expect to derive reputation and Poetry of an odd applause; as the poets, who compose whole fancy. poems with every line beginning with the same letter. We see the shapes of eggs, globes, wings, and hatchets, cut out by the ancient Greeks by the measure of their verses, making them longer or shorter, to represent such or such a figure. Much in this manner did he spend his time who made it his business to compute into how many several ways the letters of the alphabet might be transposed, and found out that incredible number mentioned in Plutarch. I am mightily pleased with the humour of him who, having a man brought before him that had learned to throw a grain of millet with such dexterity as never to miss the eye of a needle; and being afterwards desired to give something for the reward of so rare an attainment, pleasantly, and in my

[1] *De Bello Civil.* ii. 4.

opinion ingeniously, ordered several bushels of the same grain to be delivered to him, that he might not want wherewithal to exercise so famous an art.[1] 'Tis a strong evidence of a weak judgment when men approve of things for their being rare and new, or where virtue and usefulness are not conjoined to recommend them.

I come just now from playing with my own family at who could find out the most things that were in use only in the two extremes: as *Sire*, which is a title given to the greatest person in the nation, *Instances of things that are kept up by the two extremities.* the king, and also to the vulgar, as peddlers and mechanics, but never to any degree of men between. The women of great quality are all called *Madam*, inferior gentlewomen, *Mademoiselle*, and the meaner sort of women, *Madam*, as the first. The canopy of state over tables is not permitted but in the palaces of princes and in taverns. Democritus said that gods and beasts had sharper senses than men, who are of a middle form.[2] The Romans wore the same habit at funerals and at feasts.

It is certain that extreme fear and extreme ardour of courage do equally trouble and relax the stomach. The nickname of Trembling, with which they surnamed Sancho XII., King of Navarre, informs us that valour will cause a trembling in the limbs as well as fear. Those who were arming him or some other of a like nature, tried to compose him, by representing *The very same effect produced by fear and by extraordinary courage.* as less the danger he was going to engage himself in: "You understand me ill," said he; "for could my flesh know the danger my courage will presently carry it into, it would sink down to the ground." The faintness that surprises us from frigidity or dislike in the exercises of Venus are also occasioned by a too violent desire and an immoderate heat. Extreme cold and extreme heat boil and roast. Aristotle says that sows of lead melt and run with cold in the extremity of

---

[1] *Alexander the Great.* See Quintilian, ii. 20; who, however, mentions small peas, not millet

[2] Plutarch, *de Placitis Philos.* iv. 10.

winter as well as with a vehement heat.[1] Desire and satiety
fill all the gradations above and below pleasure

*Wisdom and igno-
rance attain to the
same ends.*

with pain. Stupidity and wisdom meet at the
same centre of sentiment and resolution in the
suffering of human mishaps; the wise control and triumph
over ill, the others know it not. These last are, as a man
may say, on this side of misfortune, the others are beyond
them; who, after having well weighed and considered their
qualities, measured and judged them what they are, by virtue
of a vigorous soul, leap out of their reach. They disdain and
trample them under foot, having a solid and well fortified
soul, against which the darts of fortune coming to strike, they
must of necessity rebound and blunt themselves, meeting
with a body upon which they can fix no impression; the
ordinary and middle conditions of men are lodged betwixt
these too extremes, consisting of such who perceive evils, feel
them, and are not able to support them. Infancy and de-
crepitude meet in the imbecility of the brain; avarice and
profusion in the same thirst and desire of getting.

A man may say, with some colour of truth, that there is

*Two kinds of
ignorance.*

an abecedarian ignorance that precedes knowledge, and a doctoral ignorance that comes after
it; an ignorance which knowledge creates and begets, as she
dispatches and destroys the first. Of simple understandings,
little inquisitive, and little instructed, are made good Chris-

*The fitness of
plain understand-
ings to Christian-
ity.*

tians, who by reverence and obedience implicitly believe, and are constant in their belief.
In the moderate understandings, and the middle
sort of capacities, error of opinions is forgot. They follow
the appearance of the first sense, and have some colour of
reason on their side, to impute our walking on in the old beaten
path to simplicity and stupidity,—I mean in us who have not

*Men of the great-
est minds the
completest Chris-
tians.*

informed ourselves by study. The higher and
nobler souls, more solid and clear-sighted, make
up another sort of true believers, who by a

---

[1] Aristotle, *de Mirab. Auscul.*, whose expressions, however, do not convey, exactly Montaigne's interpretation of them.

long and religious investigation have obtained a clearer and more penetrating light into the Scriptures, and have discovered the mysterious and divine secret of our ecclesiastical polity.   And yet we see some who have arrived to this last stage in the second, with marvellous fruit and confirmation, as to the utmost limit of Christian intelligence, and enjoying their victory with great spiritual consolation, humble acknowledgment of the divine favour, exemplary reformation of manners, and singular modesty.   I do not intend with these to rank some others, who, to clear themselves from all suspicion of their former errors, and to satisfy us that they are sound and firm to us, render themselves extremely indiscreet and unjust in the carrying on our cause, and by that means blemish it with infinite reproaches of violence and oppression. The simple peasants are good people, and so are the philosophers, or, as we call them now-a-days, men of strong and clear reason, whose souls are enriched with an ample provision of useful science.

The mere peasant and the philosopher good men.

The mongrels, who have disdained the first form of the ignorance of letters, and have not been able to attain the other (sitting betwixt two stools, as I and a great many more of us do), are dangerous, foolish, and troublesome ; these are they that disturb the world.   And therefore it is that I, for my own part, retreat as much as I can towards my first and natural station whence I so vainly attempted to advance.

The vulgar and purely natural poetry has in it certain proprieties and graces, by which she may come into some comparison with the greatest beauty of poetry perfected by art ; as is evident in our

Popular poetry comparable to the most perfect.

Gascon villanelles, and the songs that are brought us from nations that have no knowledge of any manner of science, nor so much as the use of writing.   The indifferent and middle sort of poetry betwixt the two is despised, of no value, honour, or esteem.

But seeing that the ice being once broke, and a path laid

Middling poetry intolerable. open to the fancy, I have found, as it commonly falls out, that what we make choice of for a rare and difficult subject, proves to be nothing so, and that after the invention is once warm it finds out an infinite number of parallel examples. I shall only add this one—that **Montaigne's opinion of his Essays.** were these Essays of mine considerable enough to deserve a criticism, it might then, I think, fall out that they would not much take with common and vulgar capacities, nor be very acceptable to the rarer and more eminent; for the first would not understand them enough, and the last too well; and so they might hover in the middle region.

CHAPTER LV.

OF SMELLS.

It has been reported of others, as well as of Alexander the Great,[1] that their sweat exhaled an odorifer-**Alexander's sweat had an agreeable smell.** ous smell, occasioned by some very uncommon and extraordinary constitution, of which Plutarch and others have been inquisitive into the cause. But the ordinary constitution of human bodies is quite otherwise, and their best condition is to be exempt from smells. Nay, the sweetness even of the purest breaths has nothing in it of greater perfection than to be without any offensive smell, like those of healthful children; which made Plautus say,—

> Mulier tum bene olet, ubi nihil olet.[2]

> " The best odour in a woman is not to smell at all."

Foreign perfumes create a suspicion. And such as make use of exotic perfumes are with good reason to be suspected of some natural imperfection, which they endeavour by these odours

---

[1] Plutarch, *in Vitâ*, c. 1.   [2] *Mostellaria*, i. 3, 116. The text has " *recte* olet."

to conceal.[1] Whence the ancient poets said that to smell well was to stink.

> Rides nos, Coracine, nil olentes:
> Malo, quam bene olere, nil olere.[2]

> "Because thou, Coracinus, still dost go
> With musk and ambergrease perfumed so,
> We under thy contempt, forsooth, must fall;
> I'd, rather than smell sweet, not smell at all."

And elsewhere,

> Posthume, non bene olet, qui bene semper olet.[3]

> "He does not, in reality, smell well
> Who always of perfumes does smell."

I am, nevertheless, a great lover of pleasant smells, and as much abominate the ill ones, which also I reach at a greater distance, I think, than other men :—

> Namque sagacius unus odoror,
> Polypus, an gravis hirsutis cubet hircus in alis,
> Quam canis acer ubi latent sus.[4]

Of smells, the most simple and natural seem to me the most pleasing. And let the ladies look to this, for 'tis chiefly their concern. In an age of the darkest barbarism, the Scythian women, after bathing, were wont to powder and crust the face, and the whole body, with a certain odoriferous drug, growing in their country; which being washed off, when they were about to have familiarity with men, made them perfumed and sleek. 'Tis not to be believed how strangely all sorts of odours cleave to me, and how apt my skin is to imbibe them. He that complains of Nature, that she has not furnished mankind with a vehicle to convey smells to the nose, had no reason; for they convey it themselves; especially in me, for my very mustachios, which are large, perform that office; if I but touch them with my gloves or

---

[1] "Still to be neat, still to be drest,
As you were going to a feast,
Still to be powder'd, still perfum'd,
Lady, it is to be presum'd,
Though art's hid causes are not found,
All is not sweet, all is not sound,"
says Ben Jonson.

[2] Martial, vi. 55, 4.
[3] Ib. ii. 12, 4.
[4] Horace, *Epod.* 12, 4. The meaning of the quotation is expressed generally in the preceding sentence.

handkerchief, the smell will remain a whole day; they show where I have been. The close, luscious, devouring, glowing kisses of youthful ardour left, in my former days, a sweetness upon my lips for several hours after. And yet I have ever found myself very little subject to epidemic diseases, that are caught either by conversing with the sick, or bred by the contagion of the air; I have escaped from those of my time, of which there have been several sorts in our cities and armies. We read of Socrates that, though he never departed from Athens during the frequent plagues that infested that city, he was the only man that was never infected.[1]

Physicians might (I believe), if they would, extract more uses from odours than they do; for I have often observed that they cause an alteration in me, and work upon my spirits according to their several virtues; which makes me approve of what is said, namely, that the use of incense and perfumes

The origin of the use of incense in churches.

in churches, so ancient, and so universally received in all nations and religions, was intended to cheer us, and to rouse and purify the senses, the better to fit us for contemplation.

I could have been glad, the better to judge of it, to have tasted of the culinary art of those cooks who had so rare a

Meat seasoned with odoriferous drugs.

way of seasoning exotic odours with the relish of meats; as it was particularly observed in the service of the King of Tunis,[2] who, in our days, landed at Naples, to have an interview with Charles the emperor. His meats were stuffed with odoriferous drugs, to that degree of expense that the cookery of one peacock and two pheasants amounted to a hundred ducats, to dress them after their fashion. And when the carver came to cut them up, not only the dining-room, but all the apartments of his palace, and the adjoining streets, were filled with a fragrant vapour, which was some time dissipating.

---

1 Laertius, in Vitâ

2 Muley-Hassan, who landed at Naples in 1543, to implore for a second time the aid of Charles V. against his revolted subjects. The emperor, however, was not there. In chap. 8, of the second book, Montaigne, in again referring to this personage, calls him Muleasses.

My chief care in choosing my lodging is always to avoid a thick and stinking air; and those beautiful cities, Venice and Paris, very much lessen the kindness I have for them, the one by the offensive smell of her marshes, and the other of that of her dirt.

———◆———

CHAPTER LVI.

OF PRAYERS.

I PROPOSE formless and undetermined fancies, like those who publish subtle questions to be after disputed upon in the schools, not to establish truth, but to seek it; I submit them to the better judgments of those whose office it is to regulate, not my writings and actions only, but moreover my very thoughts. Let what I here set down meet with correction or applause, it shall be of equal welcome and utility to me, myself beforehand condemning it for absurd and impious, if any thing shall be found, through ignorance or inadvertency, set down in this rhapsody, contrary to the holy resolutions and prescripts of the Apostolical and Roman Catholic Church, in which I was born, and in which I will die.[1] And yet, always submitting to the authority of their censure, who have an absolute power over me, I thus temerariously venture at every thing, as upon this present subject.

I don't know whether I am deceived or not; but since, by a particular favour of the Divine bounty, a *Paternoster a prayer which* certain form of prayer has been prescribed and *Christians ought* dictated to us, word for word, from the mouth *constantly to use.* of God himself, I have ever been of opinion that we ought to have it in more frequent use than we have, and, if I were

---

1 Montaigne, in his lifetime, was ac- ing touched with the heresy of Baius; cused, on account of this chapter, of be- but the Inquisition took no notice of the matter.

worthy to advise, at sitting down to, and rising from, our tables, at our rising and going to bed, and in every particular act wherein prayer is wont to be introduced, I would have Christians always make use of the Lord's prayer; if not that prayer alone, yet, at least, that prayer always. The Church may lengthen or alter prayers according to the necessity of our instruction, for I know very well that it is always the same in substance, and the same thing. But yet such a preference ought to be given to that prayer that the people should have it continually in their mouths; for it is most certain that all necessary petitions are comprehended in it, and that it is infinitely proper for all occasions. 'Tis the only prayer I use in all places and circumstances, and what I still repeat instead of changing; whence it also happens that I have no other by heart but that.

It just now comes into my mind whence we should derive that error of having recourse to God in all our designs and enterprises, to call him to our assistance in all sorts of affairs, and in all places where our weakness stands in need of support, without considering whether the occasion be just, or otherwise; and to invoke his name and power, in what condition soever we are, or action we are engaged in, how vicious soever. He is, indeed, our sole and only protector, and can do all things for us; but, though he is pleased to honour us with his paternal care, he is, notwithstanding, as just as he is good and mighty, and does oftener exercise his justice than his power, and favours us according to that, and not according to our petitions.

Men ought not to call upon God indifferently upon all occasions.

Plato, in his Laws, makes out three sorts of belief injurious to the gods; " that there is none; that they concern not themselves about human affairs; and that they never reject or deny any thing to our vows, offerings, and sacrifices." The first of these errors, according to his opinion, did never continue rooted in any man, from his infancy to his old age; the other two, he confesses, men might be obstinate in.

God's justice and his power are inseparable, and 'tis therefore in vain we invoke his power in an unjust cause. We must have our souls pure and clean, at that *The soul must be quite pure when it prays to God.* moment at least wherein we pray to him, and purified from all vicious passions, otherwise we ourselves present him the rods wherewith to chastise us. Instead of repairing any thing we have done amiss, we double the wickedness and the offence, when we offer to him, to whom we are to sue for pardon, an affection full of irreverence and hatred. Which makes me not very apt to applaud those whom I observe to be so frequent on their knees, if the actions nearest the prayer do not give me some evidence of reformation.

> Si, nocturnus adulter,
> Tempora Santonico velas adoperta cucullo.[1]

> " With night adulteries disgraced and foul,
> Thou shad'st thy guilty forehead with a cowl."

And the practice of a man that mixes devotion with an execrable life seems in some sort even more to be condemned than that of a man conformable to his own propension, and dissolute throughout; and for that reason it is that our church denies admittance to, and communion with, men obstinate and incorrigible in any kind of wickedness. We *Praying to God, only for fashion's sake, blamable.* pray only by custom, and for fashion's sake; or rather, we read and pronounce our prayers aloud, which is no better than a hypocritical show of devotion. And I am scandalized to see a man make the sign of the cross thrice at the benedicite, and as often at another's saying grace (and the more, because it is a sign I have in great veneration and constant use, even when I yawn), and to dedicate all the other hours of the day to acts of malice, avarice, and injustice; one hour to God, the rest to the devil, as if by commutation and consent. 'Tis a wonder to me actions so various in themselves succeed one another with such an uniformity of method as not to interfere nor suffer

[1] Juvenal, viii. 144.

any alteration, even upon the very confines and passes from the one to the other. What a prodigious conscience must that be that can be at quiet within itself, whilst it harbours under the same roof, with so agreeing and so calm a society, both the crime and the judge!

A man whose whole meditation is continually working upon nothing but lechery, which he knows to be so odious to God, what can he say when he comes to speak to him? He reforms, but immediately falls into a relapse. If the object of the divine justice, and the presence of his maker, did, as he pretends, strike and chastise his soul, how short soever the repentance might be, the very fear of offending that infinite majesty would so often present itself to his imagination that he would soon see himself master of those vices that are most natural and habitual in him. But what shall we say of those who settle their whole course of life upon the profit and emolument of sins which they know to be mortal! How many trades and vocations have we admitted and countenanced amongst us, whose very essence is vicious! And he that opening himself to me voluntarily told me that he had all his lifetime professed and practised a religion, in his opinion, damnable and contrary to that which he had in his heart, only to preserve his credit and the honour of his employments, how could his courage suffer so infamous a confession! What can men say to the divine justice upon this subject! Their repentance consisting in a visible and manifest reformation and restitution, they lose the colour of alleging it both to God and man. Are they so impudent as to sue for remission without satisfaction and without penitence? I look upon these as in the same condition with the first; but the obstinacy is not there so easy to be overcome. This contrariety and volubility of opinion, so sudden and violent as they pretend, is a kind of miracle to me. They present us with the state of an indigestible anxiety and doubtfulness of mind.

What we must think of the prayers of those who obstinately persist in vicious habits.

It seemed to me a fantastic and ridiculous imagination in those who, these late years past, used to reproach every man whom they knew to be of any extraordinary parts, and at the same time made profession of the Roman Catholic religion, that it was but outwardly; maintaining, moreover, to do him honour, forsooth, that, whatever he might pretend to the contrary, he could not but in his heart be of their reformed opinion. An untoward disease, that a man should be so rivetted to his own belief as to fancy that no man can believe otherwise than as he does; and yet worse in this, that they should entertain so vicious an opinion of such parts as to think that any man so qualified should prefer any present advantage of fortune before the hope of eternal happiness, or the fear of eternal damnation. They may believe me; could any thing have tempted my youth, the ambition of the danger and difficulties in the late commotions had not been the least motives.

It is not without very good reason, in my opinion, that the church interdicts the promiscuous, indiscreet, *How, and by* and irreverent use of the holy and divine *whom, David's* *Psalms ought to* Psalms, with which the Holy Ghost inspired *be sung.* King David. We ought not to mix God in our actions but with the highest reverence and caution. That poetry is too sacred to be put to no other use than to exercise the lungs and to delight our ears. It ought to come from the soul, and not from the tongue. It is not fit that a 'prentice in his shop, amongst his vain and frivolous thoughts, should be permitted to pass away his time, and divert himself with such sacred things. Neither is it decent to see the Holy Bible, the rule of our worship and belief, tumbled up and down a hall or a kitchen. They were formerly mysteries, but are now become sports and recreations. 'Tis a study too serious and too venerable to be cursorily or slightly turned over. The reading of the Scripture ought to be a temperate and premeditated act, and to which men should always add this devout preface, *sursum corda*, preparing even the body to so humble

and composed a gesture and countenance as shall evidence
their veneration and attention. Neither is it a book for
every one to handle, but the study of select men set apart
for that purpose, and whom Almighty God has been pleased
to call to that office and sacred function; the wicked and
ignorant blemish it. 'Tis not a story to tell, but a history to
reverence, fear, and adore. Are not they then amusing persons who think they have rendered it palpable to the people
by translating it into the people's tongue? Does the understanding of all therein contained only stick at words? Shall
I venture to say, farther, that, by coming so near to understand a little, they are much wider of the whole scope than
before? A total ignorance, and wholly depending upon the
exposition of other and qualified persons, was more instructive and salutary than this vain and verbal knowledge, the
nurse of temerity and presumption.

And I believe, farther, that the liberty every one has
taken to disperse the sacred Writ into so many idioms, carries with it a great deal more of danger than utility. The
Jews, Mahometans, and almost all others, have espoused and
revere the language wherein their laws and mysteries were
first conceived, and have expressly, and not without colour
of reason, forbid the version or alteration of them into any
other. Are we assured that in Biscay and in Brittany there
are competent judges enough of this affair to establish this
translation into their own language? The universal church
has not a more difficult and solemn judgment to make. In
preaching and speaking 'tis different; for here the interpretation is vague, unrestrained, variable, and disconnected.

One of our Greek historians does justly accuse the age he
lived in for that the secrets of the Christian religion were
dispersed into the hands of every mechanic, to expound and
argue upon according to his own fancy; and that we ought
to be much ashamed, we who by God's especial favour enjoy
the purest mysteries of piety, to suffer them to be profaned
by the ignorant rabble; considering that the Gentiles ex-

pressly forbade Socrates, Plato, and the other sages, to inquire into, or so much as to mention, the things committed only to the priests of Delphos; saying moreover that the factions of princes, upon theological subjects, are armed not with zeal, but with fury; that zeal springs from the divine wisdom and justice, and governs itself with prudence and moderation; but degenerates into hatred and envy, producing tares and nettles instead of corn and wine, when conducted by human passions. And it was truly said by another, who, advising the Emperor Theodosius, told him that disputes did not so much rock the schisms of the church asleep as it roused and animated heresies; that therefore all contentions and logical disputations were to be avoided, and men absolutely to acquiesce in the prescripts and formulas of faith established by the ancients. And the Emperor Andronicus,[1] having overheard some great men at high words in his palace with Lapodius, about a point of ours of great importance, rebuked them severely, and even threatened to cause them to be thrown into the river if they did not desist. The very women and children, now-a-days, take upon them to school the oldest and most experienced men about the ecclesiastical laws; whereas the first of those of Plato forbids them to inquire so much as into the reason of civil laws, which were to stand instead of divine ordinances. And allowing the old men to confer amongst themselves, or with the magistrate, about those things, he adds, provided it be not in the presence of young or profane persons.

A bishop [2] has left, in writing, that, at the other end of the

---

[1] *Andronicus Comnena.* See Nicetas, ii. 4, who, however, does not say a word about Lapodius.

[2] Osorius, Bishop of Silves, in Algarves, author of the work entitled *de Rebus gestis Emmanuelis Regis Lusitaniæ.* But it is from the Sieur Goulart, his translator, and not from Osorius himself, that Montaigne has quoted what he tells us about the inhabitants of the island *Dioscorides.* The first edition of the *Essays,* published in 1580, contains nothing upon the subject, for Goulart's translation did not appear till 1581. When our author says that the Dioscoridans "were so chaste that none of them were permitted to have to do with more than one woman in their lives," he misapprehends the meaning of Goulart, who says, conformably to the Latin of Osorius (*unam tantum uxorem ducunt*), that they marry only one wife, simply indicating that polygamy was not permitted among them, they being Christians. The modern name of this island is Socotora (in the Red Sea), a name which retains some vestiges of its ancient appellation. See Bayle's *Dict* in the article *Dioscorides.*

world, there is an island, by the ancients called Dioscorides,
abundantly fertile in all sorts of trees and fruits, and of an
exceeding healthful air, the inhabitants of which are Christians, having churches and altars adorned only with cruci-
fixes, without any other images ; great observers of fasts and
feasts ; exact payers of their tithes to the priest ; and so
chaste that none of them is permitted to have to do with
more than one woman in his life. As to the rest, so content
with their condition that, environed with the sea, they know
nothing of navigation ; and so simple that they understand
not one syllable of the religion they profess, and wherein
they are so devout. A thing incredible to such as do not
know that the pagans, who are so zealous idolaters, know
nothing more of their gods than their bare names and their
statues. The ancient beginning of *Menalippus,* a tragedy
of Euripides, ran thus :—

> Jupiter, for that name alone,
> Of what thou art, to me is known.

I have seen also, in my time, some men's writings found
Theology stands best by itself. fault with for being purely human and philosophical, without any mixture of divinity ; and
yet he would not be without reason on his side who should,
on the contrary, say that divine doctrine, as Queen and
Regent of the rest, better keeps her state apart ; that she
ought to be sovereign throughout, not subsidiary and suffra-
gan ; and that, peradventure, grammatical, rhetorical, and
logical examples may elsewhere be more suitably chosen,
and also the arguments for the stage, and public entertainments, than from so sacred a matter ;[1] that divine reasons
are considered with greater veneration and attention when
by themselves, and in their own proper style, than when
mixed with, and adapted to, human discourses ; that it is a
fault much more often observed, that the divines write too
humanly, than that the humanists write not theologically
enough. Philosophy, says St. Chrysostom, has long been

[1] Plutarch *On Love.*

banished the holy schools as a handmaid altogether useless, and thought unworthy to peep, so much as in passing by the door, into the sanctum of the divine doctrine; the human way of speaking is of a much lower form, and ought not to clothe herself with the dignity, majesty, and authority of divine eloquence. I leave him, *verbis indisciplinatis*,[1] to talk of fortune, destiny, accident, good and evil, the gods, and other such like phrases, according to his own humour; I, for my part, propose fancies merely human and my own simply as human fancies, and separately considered, not as determined by an ordinance from heaven, incapable of doubt or dispute; matter of opinion, not matter of faith; things which I discourse of according to my own capacity, not what I believe according to God; after a laical, not clerical, and yet always a very religious, manner, as children propose their essays, instructable, not instructing.

And it were as rational to affirm that an edict enjoining all people but such as are public professors of divinity to be very reserved in writing of religion, would carry with it a colour of utility and justice; and me, amongst the rest, to hold my prating. I have been told that even those who are not of our church do neverthe-less, amongst themselves, expressly forbid the name of God to be used in common discourse; not so much as by way of interjection, exclamation, assertion of a truth, or comparison; and I think them in the right. And upon what occasion soever we call upon God to accompany and assist us, it ought always to be done with the greatest reverence and devotion.

God's name ought not to be used in common discourse.

There is, as I remember, a passage in Xenophon, where he tells us that we ought so much the more sel-dom to call upon God, by how much it is hard to compose our souls to such a degree of calm-ness, penitency, and devotion as it ought to be in at such a

God ought to be seldom prayed to, and why.

---

[1] "In vulgar and unhallowed terms." St. August., *De Civit. Dei*, x. 29. See note to c. 33.

time, otherwise our prayers are not only vain and fruitless, but vicious in themselves. " Forgive us our trespasses, as we forgive them that trespass against us ;"—what do we mean by this, but that we present him a soul free from all rancour and revenge ? And yet we make nothing of invoking God's assistance in our vices, and inviting him to our unjust designs.

> Quæ, nisi seductis, nequeas committere divis.[1]

> " Which only to the gods apart,
>   Thou hast the daring to impart."

The covetous man prays for the conservation of his vain and superfluous riches ; the ambitious for victory, and the conduct of his fortune ; the thief calls God to his assistance to deliver him from the dangers and difficulties that obstruct his wicked designs, or returns him thanks for the facility he has met with in robbing a poor peasant. At the door of a house they are going to scale, or break into by force of a petard, men fall to prayers for success, having their heads and hopes full of cruelty, avarice, and lust.

> Hoc igitur, quo tu Jovis aurem impellere tentas,
> Dic agedum, Staio; proh Jupiter! ô bone, clamet,
> Jupiter! at sese non clamet Jupiter ipse? [2]

> " This, then, intended for Jove's private ear,
>   Take courage, and let honest Staius hear.
>   Defend us, mighty Jove! will he exclaim,
>   And will not Jove cry out in his own name ? "

Marguerite, Queen of Navarre, tells of a young prince (whom, though she does not name, is easily enough, by his great quality, to be known), who, going upon an amorous assignation to lie with an advocate's wife of Paris, his way thither being through a church, he never passed that holy place, going to, or returning from, this godly exercise, but he always kneeled down to pray. In what he would implore the divine favour, his soul being full of such virtuous

---

[1] Persius, II. 4.　　　　　[2] Ib. II. 21.

meditations, I leave others to judge. Yet this she instances for a testimony of singular devotion.[1] But this is not the only proof we have that women are not altogether fit to treat of theological matters.

A true prayer, and religious reconciling of ourselves to God, cannot enter into an impure soul, subjected at the time to the dominion of Satan. He who calls God to his assistance, whilst in the pursuit of vice, does as if a cut-purse should call a magistrate to help him, or like those who introduce the name of God to the attestation of a lie.

> Tacito mala vota susurro
> Concipimus.[2]

"In whispers oft we guilty prayers do make."

There are few men who durst publish to the world the prayers they make to God : [3]

> Haud cuivis promptum est, murmurque, humilesque susurros
> Tollere de templis, et aperto vivere voto.[4]

"Few are there in the temple's daily crowd
Who scorn such tricks, and think and wish aloud."

And this is the reason why the Pythagoreans would have them always public, to be heard by every one, to the end they might not prefer indecent or unjust petitions, as he did,

> "Clare cum dixit, Apollo!
> Labra movet, metuens audiri: "pulchra Laverna,
> Da mihi fallere, da justum sanctumque videri;
> Noctem peccatis, et fraudibus objice nubem." [5]

> "Who with loud voice pronounc'd Apollo's name;
> But when the following prayers he preferr'd,
> Scarce moves his lips for fear of being heard.
> 'Beauteous Laverna, my petition hear;
> Let me with truth and sanctity appear:
> Oh! give me to deceive, and with a veil
> Of darkness and of night, my crimes conceal!'"

---

1 *Heptameron*, Day 3, Novel 25, where, however, the prince is represented as stopping to pray only on his return; a discriminating devotion.

2 Lucan, v. 104.

3 "How great," says Seneca, (*Epist.* 10) "is the folly of mankind! they whisper the most execrable prayers to the Gods, and if any mortal lend an ear, they are silent for fear men should know what they mutter to the Deity."

4 Persius, ii. 6.

5 Horace, *Ep.* i. 16, 59.

The gods did severely punish the wicked prayers of Œdipus in granting them. He had prayed that his children might amongst themselves determine the succession to his throne by arms; and was so miserable as to see himself taken at his word. We should not pray that all things fall out as our will would have them, but that our will should subserve what is just and right.

We seem in truth to make use of our prayers as a kind of gibberish, and as those do who employ holy words in sorceries and magical operations; and as if we made account the benefit we are to reap from them depended upon the contexture, sound, and jingle of words, or upon the composing of the countenance. For having the soul contaminated with concupiscence, not touched with repentance, or comforted by any late reconciliation with Almighty God, we go to present him such words as the memory suggests to the tongue, and hope thence to obtain the remission of our sins. There is nothing so easy, so gentle, and so favourable, as the divine law; she calls and invites us to her, guilty and abominable as we are; extends her arms, and receives us into her bosom, foul and polluted as we at present are, and are for the future to be. But then, in return, we are to look upon her with a pleased eye, we are to receive this pardon with gratitude and submission, and, for that instant at least wherein we address ourselves to her, to have the soul angry with its faults, and at defiance with those passions that seduced her to offend. Neither the gods nor good men (says Plato[1]) will accept the present of a wicked man.

> Immunis aram si tetigit manus,
> Non sumptuosâ blandior hostiâ,
> Mollivit aversos Penates,
> 　Farre pio, et saliente micâ.[2]

> " The pious off'ring of a piece of bread,
> 　If by pure hands upon the altar laid,
> 　Than costly hecatombs will better please
> 　Th' offended gods, and their just wrath appease."

1 *Laws*, iv.　　　　　　　　2 Horace, *Od.* iii. 23, 17.

CHAPTER LVII.

OF AGE.

I CANNOT approve of the proportion we settle upon our-
selves, and the space we allot to the duration Age of Cato when
he killed himself.
of life; I see that the sages contract it very
much, in comparison of the common opinion. "What," said
the younger Cato to those who would stay his hand from
killing himself, " am I now of an age to be reproached that I
go out of the world too soon?" And yet he was but eight
and forty years old.[1] He thought that to be a mature and
competent age, considering how few arrive to it. And such
as, soothing their thoughts with what they call the course of
nature, promise to themselves some years beyond it, might
have some reason to do so, could they be privileged from the
infinite number of accidents to which they are by natural
subjection exposed, and which may at any moment interrupt
this natural course they look forward to. What an idle conceit it is to expect to die of a decay of strength, which is the
last effect of the extremest age, and to propose to ourselves
no shorter lease of life than that, considering it is a kind of
death of all others the most rare, and very hardly seen?
We call that only a natural death, as if it were contrary to
nature, to see a man break his neck with a fall, be drowned
in shipwreck, or snatched away with a pleurisy or the plague,
and as if our ordinary condition of life did not expose us to
these and many more inconveniences. Let us no more flatter
ourselves with these fine-sounding words; we ought rather
to call that natural which is common and universal.

To die of old age is a death rare, extraordinary, and singular, and therefore so much less natural than the others.

[1] Plutarch, *in Vita*, c. 20.

To die of old age a thing singular and extruordinary. 'Tis the last and extremest sort of dying, and the more remote the less to be hoped for. It is indeed the boundary of life, beyond which we are not to pass; which the law of nature has pitched for a limit not to be exceeded. But to last till then is withal a privilege she is rarely seen to give us. 'Tis a lease she only signs by particular favour, it may be, to one only, in the space of two or three ages; and then with a pass to boot, to carry him through all the traverses and difficulties she has strewed in the way of this long career. And therefore my opinion is that when once forty years old, we should consider it as an age to which very few arrive; for, seeing that men do not usually proceed so far, it is a sign that we are pretty well advanced; and since we have exceeded the ordinary bounds, which make the just measure of life, we ought not to expect to go much farther. Having escaped so many precipices of death, whereinto we have seen so many other men fall, we should acknowledge that so extraordinary a fortune as that which has hitherto rescued us from those imminent perils, and kept us alive beyond the ordinary term of living, is not likely to continue long.

'Tis a fault in our very laws to contain this error, that a The defect of the laws, in making it so late in life before they admit men to the management of their estates. man is not capable of managing his estate till he be five and twenty years old, whereas he will have much ado to manage his life so long. Augustus cut off five years from the ancient Roman standard, and declared that to be thirty years old was sufficient for a judge.[1] Servius Tullius relieved the knights of above seven and forty years of age from the fatigues of war;[2] Augustus dismissed them at forty-five. Though methinks men should hardly be sent to the fireside till five and fifty, or sixty years of age. I should be of opinion that our employment should be as long as possible extended for the public good; I find the fault on the other side, that they do not employ us early enough. This em-

---

[1] Suetonius, *in Vitâ*, c. 12.   [2] Aulus Gellius, x. 28.

peror was arbiter of the whole world at nineteen, and yet would have a man to be thirty before he could decide a dispute about a gutter.

For my part, I believe our souls are adult at twenty as much as they are ever like to be, and as capa- *Souls adult at* ble then as ever. A soul that has not by that *twenty years of* *age.* time given evident earnest of its force and virtue will never after come to proof. Natural parts and excellences produce what they have of vigorous and fine within that term, or never:—

> Si l'espine nou picque quand nai,
> A pene que picque jamai,[1]

as they say in Dauphiny. Of all the great human actions I ever heard or read of, of what sort soever, I *What age is capa-* have observed, both in former ages and our *ble of the finest* *actions.* own, more performed before thirty than after; and ofttimes in the lives of the same men. May I not confidently instance in those of Hannibal, and his great competitor, Scipio? The better half of their lives they lived upon the glory they had acquired in their youth; great men after, 'tis true, in comparison of others, but by no means in comparison of themselves. As to myself, I am certain that since that age both my understanding and my constitution have rather decayed than improved, retired rather than advanced. 'Tis possible that, with those who make the best use of their time, knowledge, and experience, may grow up and increase with their years; but the vivacity, quickness, steadiness, and other qualities, more our own, of much greater importance, and much more essential, languish and decay.

> Ubi jam validis quassatum est viribus ævi
> Corpus, et obtusis ceciderunt viribus artus,
> Claudicat ingenium, delirat linguaque mensque.[2]

> " When once the body's shaken by time's rage,
> The blood and vigour ebbing into age,

---

[1] " If the thorn pricks not when it first shoots, it hardly ever will at all."

[2] Lucret. iii. 452.

No more the mind its former strength displays,
But every sense and faculty decays."

Sometimes the body first submits to age, sometimes the soul;
and I have seen men enough who had got a weakness in
their brains before either in their legs or stomach; and by
how much the more it is a disease of no great pain to the
infected party, and of obscure symptoms, so much greater
the danger is.

And for this reason it is that I complain of our laws; not
that they keep us too long to our work, but that they set us
to work too late. Methinks, considering the frailty of life,
and the many natural and ordinary wrecks to which it is
exposed, we should not give so large a portion of it to idleness, either in childhood or in apprenticeship to the world.

THE SECOND BOOK.

CHAPTER I.

OF THE INCONSISTENCY OF OUR ACTIONS.

THOSE who make it their business to observe human actions, never find themselves so much puzzled in any thing as how to reconcile and set them before the world in a self-consistent light and reputation; for they are generally such strange contradictions in themselves that it seems almost impossible they should proceed from one and the same person. Onewhile we find young Marius, the son of Mars, and another time the son of Venus.[1] Pope Boniface the Eighth, it is said, crept into the papal throne like a fox, reigned like a lion, and died like a dog. And who could believe it to be the same Nero, that perfect image of all cruelty, who, in the beginning of his reign, having the sentence of a condemned man brought to him to sign, cried out, "O, that I had never been taught to write!"[2] So much it went to his heart to condemn a man to death. The history of every nation is so full of such examples, and all men are able to produce so many to themselves, either from their own conduct or observation, that I often wonder to see men of sense *Irresolution the* give themselves the trouble of sorting these *most common* pieces, and endeavouring to reconcile such con- *vice of our nature.* tradictions; especially when irresolution appears to me to be

---

[1] Plutarch, *in Vitâ*.   [2] Seneca, *De Clementiâ*, ii. 1.

the most common and manifest vice of our nature; witness
the famous verse of the comedian Publius :—

Malum consilium est, quod mutari non potest.[1]

"That counsel's bad that will admit no change."

There seems indeed some possibility of forming a judgment
of a man from the habitual features of his life, but, considering the natural instability of our manners and
opinions, I have often thought even the best
authors a little mistaken in so obstinately endeavouring to mould us into any consistent and solid contexture. They choose some general air, and according to
that arrange and interpret all the actions of a man, of which,
if some be so stiff and stubborn that they cannot bend or
turn them to any uniformity to the rest, they then, without
further ceremony, impute them to dissimulation. Augustus
has, nevertheless, escaped those gentlemen; for there was in
him so apparent, so sudden, and so continued a variety of
action, throughout the whole course of his life, that he has
slipt away clear from the boldest judges. For my part, I
am with much more difficulty induced to believe in a man's
consistency than in any other virtue in him; while there is
nothing I so readily believe as his inconsistency; and whoso
will meditate upon the matter closely and abstractedly will
agree with me. Out of all antiquity 'twould be difficult to
produce a dozen men who have formed their lives to one
certain and fixed course, which is the principal design of
wisdom; for, says one of the ancients,[2] to comprise it all in
one word, and to contract all the rules of human life into
one, "It is to *will*, and not to *will*, always the same thing; I
shall not descend," continues he, "to add, provided the *will*
be just, for if it be not so, it is impossible it should be always
one." I have, indeed, formerly learnt that vice is nothing
but irregularity and want of measure, and therefore 'tis im-

The difficulty of
determining the
characters of men
in general.

---

[1] *Ex Publii mimis.*, apud Aul. Gell.
xvii. 14.   [2] Seneca, *Epist.* 20.

possible to fix consistency to it. 'Tis a saying of Demosthenes,[1] "that the beginning of all virtue is consultation and deliberation; the end and perfection, consistency." If, by reason, we were to resolve on any certain course, we should pitch upon the best, but nobody has thought of it :—

> Quod petiit, spernit; repetit quod nuper omisit;
> Æstuat, et vitæ disconvenit ordine toto.[2]

> "He now despises what he late did crave,
> And what he last neglected now would have:
> He fluctuates, and flies from that to this,
> And his whole life a contradiction is."

Our ordinary practice is to follow the inclinations of our appetite, which way soever they guide us, whether to the right or to the left, upwards or downwards, just *The inconsistency* according as we are wafted by the breath of *of our conduct, on what founded.* occasion. We never meditate what we would have till the instant we have a mind to it; and change like that little creature which takes its colour from what it is laid upon. What we but just now proposed to ourselves, we immediately alter, and presently return to it again; 'tis nothing but shifting and inconstancy :—

> Ducimur, ut nervis alienis mobile lignum.[3]
> "Like tops with leathern thongs we're whipped about."

We do not go, we are driven; like things that float, now leisurely, then with violence, according to the gentleness **or** fierceness of the current;

> Nonne videmus,
> Quid sibi quisque velit nescire, et quærere semper;
> Commutare locum, quasi onus deponere possit?[4]

> "Day after day we see men toil to find
> Some secret solace to an anxious mind,
> Shifting from place to place, if here or there
> They might set down the burthen of their care."

Every day produces a new whim, and our humours keep motion with time :—

---

[1] In the Funeral Oration, attributed to Demosthenes, on the warriors slain at Cheronœa.

[2] Horace, *Epist.* l. 1, 98.
[3] Ib. *Sat.* ii. 7, 82.
[4] Lucretius, lii. 1070.

MONTAIGNE'S ESSAYS.

Tales sunt hominum mentes, quali pater ipse
Jupiter auctifero lustravit lumine terras.[1]

> " Such are the motions of the inconstant soul,
> As are the days and weather fair or foul."

We fluctuate betwixt various notions; we will nothing freely, nothing absolutely, nothing constantly.[2] In any one that has prescribed and laid down determinate rules and laws to himself for his own conduct, we should perceive an equality of manners, an order, and an infallible relation of one thing or action to another, shine through his whole life (Empedocles [3] observed this contradiction in the Agregentines, that gave themselves up to delights as if every day was to be their last, and built as if they were to live for ever) ; and a judgment would not then be hard to make. And this is shown in the younger Cato ; he who has touched one note, has touched all. 'Tis a harmony of very agreeing sounds, that cannot jar. But with us 'tis quite contrary, every particular action requires a particular judgment. The surest way, in my opinion, would be to take our measures from the nearest allied circumstances, without engaging in a longer inquisition, or without concluding any other consequence.

I was told, in the civil disorders of our unhappy kingdom, that a maid-servant, hard by the place where I then was, had thrown herself out of a window to avoid being forced by a ragamuffin soldier that was quartered in the house. She was not killed by the fall, and therefore, redoubling her attempt, would have cut her own throat, but was hindered ; though not before she had wounded herself dangerously. She herself confessed that the soldier had not as yet importuned her otherwise than by courtship, solicitation, and presents ; but that she was afraid that in the end he would have proceeded to violence ; all which she delivered with such a countenance

[1] These two verses, preserved by St. Augustin, (de Civit. Dei. v. 8,) are a translation by Cicero from the Odyssey, xviii. 135. He is supposed to have quoted them in his Academics, in reference to what Aristotle says of the Human Soul, by which author also these verses are quoted in his treatise On the Soul, iii. 3.
[2] Seneca, Epist. 52.
[3] Diog. Laertius, in Vitâ. Ælian attributes the remark to Plato, Var. Hist. xii. 29.

and language, and withal embrued in her own blood, the testimony of her virtue, that she appeared quite another Lucretia; and yet I have since been well assured that, both before and after she was no very difficult piece. As in the tale,—— "Be as handsome a man, and as fine a gentleman as you will, never build too much upon your mistress's inviolable chastity; for, having been repulsed by her, you do not know but she may have a much better stomach for your groom." [1]

Antigonus, having taken one of his soldiers into a degree of favour and esteem for his virtue and valour, gave his physicians strict charge to cure him of an inward distemper which had a long time tormented him; and observing that after his cure he went much more coldly to work than before, he asked him what had so altered and cowed him? "You, yourself, sir," replied the other, "by having eased me of the pains that made me weary of my life." [2] One of Lucullus's soldiers having been rifled by the enemy, performed a brave exploit against him by way of revenge, by which he recovered his loss and more. Lucullus, who from that action had conceived a very advantageous opinion of the man, endeavoured, with all the persuasions and fine promises he could think of,

Verbis, quæ timido quoque possent addere mentem.[3]
"With words that might a coward's heart inspire,"

to engage him in an enterprise of danger; but "No," said the fellow; "employ some miserable devil that has lost all his money."

Quantumvis rusticus, ibit,
Ibit eo, quo vis, qui zonam perdidit, inquit.[4]

"An't please you, captain, let another trudge it,
The man may venture who has lost his budget,"

and flatly refused to go.

When we read that Mahomet having furiously reprimanded Chasan, Aga of the Janisaries, who seeing the Hungarians

---

1 The Host's tale, in Ariosto.
2 Plutarch, *Life of Pelopidas*, c. 1.
3 Horace, *Epist.* ii. 2, 36.
4 Ib. *id.* ii. 2, 39.

break into his battalion, had behaved himself very ill in the business, and that Chasan, instead of any other answer, rushed furiously, alone, with his scimitar in his hand, into the first body of the enemy, where he was presently cut to pieces, we are not to look upon this as so much a generous design to vindicate himself from the reproach of cowardice as a change of mind; not so much natural valour as sudden vexation. The man you see to-day so adventurous and brave, you must not think it strange to find him as great a poltroon to-morrow; anger, necessity, company, wine, or the sound of the trumpet may have roused his spirits; this is no valour formed and established by meditation; but accidentally created by those circumstances, and therefore it is no wonder, if by contrary circumstances, it appears quite another thing. These supple variations and contradictions in us have given some people occasion to believe that man has two souls; others two distinct powers which always accompany and incline us, one towards good, and the other towards evil, according to its own nature and propension; so sudden a variety of inclination not being to be imagined to flow from one and the same fountain.

For my part, I must own that the puff of every accident not only carries me along with it, according to its own proclivity, but that moreover I discompose and trouble myself by the instability of my own posture; and whoever will look narrowly into his own breast will hardly find himself twice in the same condition. I give my soul sometimes one face, and sometimes another, according to the side I turn her to. If I speak variously of myself, it is because I consider myself variously. All contrarieties are there to be found in one corner or another, or after one manner or another. Bashful, insolent; chaste, lustful; talkative, silent; laborious, delicate; ingenious, heavy; melancholic, pleasant; lying, sincere; learned, ignorant; liberal, covetous, and prodigal; I find all this in myself, more or less, according as I turn myself about; and whoever will sift himself to the bottom will be conscious, even by his own judgment, of this volubility and discordance. I have nothing to say of myself entirely, simply, and solidly, without mixture and confusion, nor, in a word; *distinguo* is the universal part of my logic.

Though I always intend to speak well of the good, and rather interpret in a good sense such things as may be so, yet such is the strangeness of our condition that we are sometimes pushed on to A good action to be judged of by the intention only. do well, even by vice itself, if well doing were not judged by the intention only. One gallant action, therefore, ought not to conclude a man valiant; if a man was brave, indeed, he would be always so, and upon all occasions. If it were a habit of virtue, and not a sally, it would render a man equally resolute in all accidents; the same alone as in company, the same in lists as in battles; for, let people say what they please, there is not one valour for the street, and another for the field. He would bear a sickness in his bed as bravely as a wound in the trenches, and no more fear death in his own house than at an assault. We should not then see the same man charge into a breach with a brave assurance, and afterwards torment himself, or whine like a woman, for the loss of a lawsuit, or the death of a child. When being a coward in arms, he is firm under poverty; when he starts at the sight of a barber's razor, but rushes fearless among the swords of the enemy, the action is commendable, not the man. Many of the Greeks, says Cicero, cannot endure the sight of an enemy, and yet are courageous in sickness; the Cimbrians and Celtiberians quite the contrary. *Nihil enim potest esse æquabile, quod non a certâ ratione proficiscatur.*[1] "Nothing can be uniform that does not proceed from solid reason." No valour could be more extreme in its kind than that of Alexander; but it was but one kind; nor was that kind full enough throughout, or universal. As peerless as it was, it had yet some blemishes; and of this his being so often at his wits' end upon every light suspicion of his cap-

[1] *Tusc. Quæs.* ii. 27.

tains conspiring against his life, and the behaving himself in such inquiries with so much vehemency and injustice, and with a fear that subverted his natural reason, is one striking instance. The superstition also with which he was so much tainted carries along with it some image of pusillanimity; and the excess of his penitence for the murder of Clytus is likewise another testimony of the unevenness of his courage. All we do is a mere cento, as a man may say, of odds and ends,[1] and we would acquire honour by a false title. Virtue will not be followed but for herself; and, if we sometimes borrow her mask for some other occasion, she presently pulls it off again. 'Tis a strong and lively tincture, which, when the soul has once thoroughly imbibed it, will not out again but with the piece. And therefore to make a right judgment of a man, we are long and very observingly to follow his trace. If consistency does not there stand firm upon her own proper base, *Cui vivendi via considerata atque provisa est;*[2] " If the course of life is not plainly marked out;" if the variety of occurrences makes him to alter his pace (his path I mean, for the pace may be faster or slower), let him go; such a one runs before the wind, *a vau le vent*, as the Talbot motto has it.

Virtue only to be courted for its own sake.

'Tis no wonder, says one of the ancients,[3] that chance has so great a dominion over us, since it is by chance we live. It is not possible for any one who has not designed his life for some certain end to dispose of particular actions. It is not possible for any one to fit the pieces together who has not the whole form already contrived in his imagination. To what use are colours to him, or to what end should he provide them, that knows not what he is to paint? No one lays down a certain plan of life; we only deliberate it by pieces. The archer ought first to know at what he is to aim, and then accommodate his arm, bow, string, shaft, and motion to it. Our

---

[1] In the edition of 1588, corrected by the Author, the following passage is inserted: " Voluptatem contemnunt; in dolore sunt molles; gloriam negligunt; franguntur infamiâ."

[2] Cicero, *Paradox.* v. i.

[3] Senec. *Epist.* 71.

opinions deviate and wander, because not levelled to any determinate end. No wind serves him who has no destined port. I cannot acquiesce in the judgment given by one in the behalf of Sophocles,[1] who concluded him capable of the management of domestic affairs, against the accusation of his son, from having seen one of his tragedies.

Neither do I think the conjecture of the Parians, sent to regulate the Milesians, sufficient for such a consequence as they drew from it. Coming to visit the island, they took notice of such grounds as were best cultivated, and such country houses as were best governed; and having taken the names of the owners, when they had assembled the citizens, they appointed those farmers for the new governors and magistrates, concluding that they who had been so provident in their own private concerns would be so of the public too.[2] We are all unformed lumps, and of so various a contexture that every moment every piece plays its own game, and there is as much difference betwixt us and ourselves as betwixt us and others. *Magnam rem puta, unum hominem agere*.[3]—" 'Tis a great matter to be always the same man." Since ambition can teach men valour, temperance, and liberality, and even justice; seeing that avarice can inspire a shopboy, bred and nursed up in obscurity and ease, with courage enough to expose himself, far from the fireside, to the mercy of the angry waves, in a frail boat; that, further she can teach discretion and prudence; and that even Venus can infuse boldness and resolution into boys under the discipline of the rod, and inflame the hearts of tender virgins not out of leading-strings, with masculine courage;

> Hac duce, custodes furtim transgressa jacentes,
> Ad juvenem tenebris sola puella venit; [4]

> " With Venus' aid, while sleep the guard disarms,
> She stole by night to her young lover's arms; "

'tis not sound understanding to judge us simply by our out-

[1] Cicero, *De Senectute*, c. 7.   [3] Senec. *Epist.* 120.
[2] Herod. vi.   [4] Tibullus, ii. 1, 75.

ward action ; we must penetrate the very soul, and there discover by what springs the motion is guided ; but that being a high and hazardous undertaking, I could wish that fewer would attempt it.

CHAPTER II.

OF DRUNKENNESS.

THE world is nothing but variety and disproportion ; vices are all alike, as they are vices, and 'tis thus,

There are some vices more enormous than others. perhaps, the Stoics understand it ; but, though they are equally vices, yet they are not all equal vices ; and that he who has transgressed the bounds by a hundred paces,

> Quos ultra, citraque, nequit consistere rectum,[1]

> " Whence we cannot deviate without going wrong,"

should not be in a worse condition than he who has transgressed them but ten, is not to be believed ; or that sacrilege is not worse than stealing a cabbage :—

> Nec vincet ratio, tantumdem ut peccet, idemque,
> Qui teneros caules alieni fregerit horti,
> Et qui nocturnus divum sacra legerit. . . .[2]

> " Nor seems it reason he as much should sin
> That steals a cabbage plant, as he who in
> The dead of night a temple breaks, and brings
> Away from thence the consecrated things."

There is in this as great diversity as in any thing whatever. The confounding of the order and measure of

The confounding of sins is a dangerous thing. sins is dangerous ; murderers, traitors, and tyrants gain too much therein ; it is not reasonable they should solace their consciences, because another

---

[1] Horace, i. 1, 107.   [2] Id. *ib.* 3, 115.

man is idle or lascivious, or less assiduous at his devotion than he ought to be. Every one lays weight upon the sins of his companions, and lightens his own. In my opinion, our very instructors themselves range them very ill. As Socrates said, that the principal office of wisdom was to distinguish good from evil, we, the best of whom are always vicious, ought also to say of knowledge that it is to distinguish betwixt vice and vice, without which, and that very exactly performed too, the virtuous and the wicked will remain confounded and undistinguishable.

Now among the rest, drunkenness seems to me to be a gross and brutish vice. The soul has more to do in all the rest, and there are some vices that have something, if a man may say so, of the high and generous in them. *Drunkenness a stupid, brutish vice.* There are vices wherein there is a mixture of knowledge, diligence, valour, prudence, dexterity, and cunning; this is totally corporeal and earthly. The thickest-skulled nation this day in Europe is that where it is the most in fashion. Other vices discompose the understanding; this totally overthrows it, and stuns the body.

> Cum vini vis penetravit, . . .
> Consequitur gravitas membrorum, præpediuntur
> Crura vacillanti, tardescit lingua, madet mens,
> Nant oculi; clamor, singultus, jurgia, gliscunt.[1]

> " When fumes or wine have fill'd the swelling veins,
> Unusual weight throughout the body reigns;
> The legs, so nimble in the race before,
> Can now exert their wonted pow'r no more;
> Falters the tongue, tears gush into the eyes,
> And hiccoughs, noise, and jarring tumults rise."

The worst condition of a man is that wherein he loses the knowledge and government of himself. And 'tis said, amongst other things upon that subject, that as the must, fermenting in a vessel, works up to the top whatever it has in the bottom, so wine, in those who have drunk beyond the measure, vents the most inward secrets.

[1] Lucret. iii. 475.

Tu sapientium
Curas, et arcanum jocoso
Consilium retegis Lyæo.[1]

"And, sportive, strip from grave disguise
The cares and secret counsels of the wise."

Josephus tells us[2] that, by giving an ambassador, whom the enemy had sent to him, his full dose of liquor, he wormed out his secrets. And yet Augustus, committing the most inward secrets of his affairs to Lucius Piso, who conquered Thrace, never found him guilty of blabbing in the least; no more than Tiberius did Cossus, with whom he intrusted his whole counsels, though we know they were both so given to drink that they have often been carried home, both one and the other, drunk out of the senate-house.[3]

Hesterno inflatum venas, de more, Lyæo.[4]

"And swollen their veins, as wont, with wine of yesterday."

And the design of killing Cæsar was as safely communicated to Cimber, though he was often drunk, as to Cassius, who drank nothing but water; and upon this, Cimber once said merrily, "Shall I, who cannot bear wine, bear with a tyrant?"[5] We see our Germans, though never so drunk, know their post, remember the word, and perform their duty :—

Nec facilis victoria de madidis, et
Blæsis, atque mero titubantibus.[6]

"Nor find it easy victory to command
O'er men so drunk they scarce can speak or stand."

I could not have believed there had been so profound, senseless and dead a degree of drunkenness, had I not read in history that Attalus, having, in order to put a notable affront upon Pausanias, who for this cause afterwards killed

[1] Horace, *Od.* iii. 21, 14.
[2] In his *Life*, p. 1016.
[3] Senec. *Epist.* 83.
[4] Virgil, *Eclog.* vi. 15. The text has it, "Inflatum hesterno venas ut semper, Iaccho."
[5] Senec. *Epist.* 83. The words in this author are, "Ego *quemquam feram, qui vinum ferre non possum?*" But he has spoiled Cimber's jest for not having had the courage to give Cæsar the name of a tyrant, as Montaigne does.
[6] Juvenal, xv. 47.

Philip, King of Macedon, who, by his excellent qualities, gave sufficient testimony of his education in the house and company of Epaminondas, invited him to supper, and made him drink to such a pitch that he could dispose of his body as that of a common prostitute to the grooms and meanest servants of the house. And I have been told by a lady whom I highly honour and esteem, that near Bordeaux, towards Castres, where she lives, a country-woman, a widow of excellent character, perceiving in herself the first symptoms of breeding, innocently told her neighbours that, if she had a husband, she should think herself with child ; but the causes of suspicion every day more and more increasing, and at last growing up to a manifest proof, the poor woman was reduced to the necessity of causing it to be proclaimed at her parish church that whoever had done that deed and would frankly confess it, she did not only promise to forgive, but moreover to marry him, if he liked the offer ; upon which a young fellow that served her in the quality of a labourer, encouraged by this proclamation, declared, that one holy-day he found her, having taken too much of the bottle, so fast asleep in the chimney-corner, and in so indecent a posture, that he made use of her without waking her ; they still live together man and wife.

It is certain that antiquity has not much decried this vice ; the writings of several philosophers speak very tenderly of it ; and even amongst the Stoics there are some who advise to give one's self sometimes the liberty to drink to a debauch, to recreate and refresh the soul.

Drunkenness not much declaimed against by the ancients.

> Hoc quoque virtutum quondam certamine, magnum
> Socratem palmam promeruisse ferunt.[1]

> "And Socrates the wise, they say of yore,
> Amongst boon-blades the palm of drinking bore."

That censor and reprover of others, Cato, was reproached with being a toper :—

[1] Corn. Gallus, i. 47.

Narratur et prisci Catonis
　　Sæpe mero caluisse virtus.[1]

"——— of old
Cato's virtue, we are told,
Often with a bumper glowed."

Cyrus, that so renowned king, among his other qualities, by
which he claimed to be preferred before his brother Artaxerxes, urged this excellency, that he could drink a great deal

Drinking to a debauch in use amongst the best governed nations. more than he.[2] And in the best governed nations this trial of skill in drinking was very
much in use. I have heard Silvius, an excel-
lent physician of Paris, say that, lest the digestive faculties
of the stomach should grow idle, it were not amiss once a
month to rouse and spur them on by this excess, lest they
should grow dull and resty; and 'tis written that when the
Persians were to consult upon any important affair they first
warmed themselves well with wine.[3]

My taste and constitution are greater enemies to this vice

Drunkenness a vice not so bad as some others. than I am; for, besides that I easily submit my
belief to the authority of ancient opinions, I
look upon it as a mean and stupid vice, but
less malicious and hurtful than the others, almost every one
of which more directly jostles public society. And if we
cannot please ourselves but it must cost us something, as
they hold, I conceive this vice costs a man's conscience less
than any of the rest; besides, it is of no difficult preparation,
nor is what we look for hard to be found; a consideration
not altogether to be despised. A man well advanced both in
dignity and age, among three principal comforts, which he
said still remained to him of life, told me this of drinking
was one; and where would a man more justly find it than
among the natural conveniences? But he did not take it

Delicacy to be avoided in wine. right; for delicacy and a curious choice in
wines is therein to be avoided. If you ground

---

[1] Horace, *Od.* iii. 21, 11.　　　　　　　[3] Herod. i. 133.
[2] Plutarch, *Life of Artaxerxes*, c. 2.

your pleasure upon drinking the best, you condemn yourself
to the penance of drinking the worst.

Your taste must be more indifferent and free; a delicate
palate does not suit a good toper. The Germans drink
almost indifferently of all wines with delight; their business
is to pour down, and not to taste; and 'tis so much the better
for them, their pleasure is so much the more constant and
nearer at hand. On the other hand, not to drink after the
French fashion, but at meals, and then very moderately too,
is too much to restrict the bounty of the god of wine; there
is more time and constancy required than so. The ancients
spent whole nights in this exercise, and ofttimes added the
day following to piece it out; we ought therefore to take
greater liberty than we do, and stick closer to our work. I
have seen a great lord of my time, a man of high enterprise
and famous success, who without setting himself to it, and
after his ordinary rate of drinking at meals, swallowed down
not much less than five quarts of wine, and at his going away
appeared but too wise and discreet, to the detriment of our
affairs. The pleasure we design an esteem for during the
course of our lives, ought to have a greater share of our time
dedicated to it. We should, like journeymen and labourers,
refuse no occasion, and omit no opportunity, of drinking, and
always have it in our minds. But methinks we every day
abridge and curtail the use of wine; and the breakfast, drinking, and collations, I used to see in my father's house when I
was a boy, were in those days more usual and frequent than
at present. Is it that we pretend to reformation? Truly
no; but it may be we are more addicted to Venus than
our fathers were. They are two exercises that hinder one
another in their vigour. Lechery has weakened our stomach on the one side, and on the other sobriety renders us
more amorous and vigorous for the exercise of love.

'Tis not to be imagined what strange stories I have heard
my father tell of the chastity of that age where- A character of the
in he lived. He might very well talk so, author's father.

being both by art and nature cut out and finished for the
service of ladies. He spoke little and well, ever mixing
his language with some illustration out of modern authors,
especially Spanish; and amongst them Marcus Aurelius was
very frequent in his mouth.[1] His behaviour was grave,
humble, and modest; he was very solicitous of neatness and
decency in his person and dress, whether a-foot or on horseback. He was exceedingly punctual to his word, and of a
conscience and religion tending rather towards superstition
than otherwise. For a man of little stature, very strong,
well proportioned, and well knit; of a pleasing countenance,
inclining to brown, and very adroit in all noble exercises. I
have yet in the house to be seen canes full of lead, with which,
they say, he exercised his arms for throwing the bar or the
stone; and shoes with leaden soles, to make him afterwards
lighter for running or leaping. Of his vaulting he has left
little miracles behind him; and I have seen him, when past
threescore, laugh at our agilities, throw himself in his furred
gown into the saddle, make the tour of a table upon his
thumbs, and scarce ever mount the stairs up to his chamber
without taking three or four steps at a time. But as to what
Marvellous chas- I was speaking of before, he said there was
tity of the age scarce one woman of quality of ill fame in a
wherein the au-
thor's father lived. whole province; would tell of strange privacies,
and some of them his own, with virtuous women, without any
manner of suspicion. And, for his own part, solemnly swore
he was a virgin at his marriage; and yet it was after a long
practice of arms beyond the mountains, of which war he has
left us a written journal under his own hand, wherein he has
given a precise account, from point to point, of all passages,

---

1 Mery Causaubon, who mentions this
book, in a short advertisement prefixed
to his English translation of the genuine
work of the Emperor Marcus Aurelius,
tells us this book was writ originally in
Spanish, and translated into Italian,
French, English, &c. "The author,"
he adds, "would fain have his work pass
for a faithful translation of the treatise
of Marcus Aurelius; but there is nothing
in the whole book which shows that the
learned Spaniard who composed it had
seen the treatise of this wise emperor."
This Spaniard is Guevara, who does not
deserve the title of *learned*, which is
here given him by Mery Causaubon.
The reader may see the character of his
wit and works in Bayle's *Dictionary*,
under the title of *Guevara*.

both relating to the public and to himself. And he was married moreover at a well advanced maturity, in the year 1528, the three and thirtieth year of his age, upon his way home from Italy. But let us return to our bottle.

The incommodities of old age, which stand in need of some refreshment and support, might with rea- Drinking the last son beget in me a desire of this faculty, it pleasure which man is capable of being, as it were, almost the last pleasure enjoying. which the course of years deprives us of. The natural heat, say the good fellows, first seats itself in the feet, that concerns infancy; from thence it mounts to the middle region, where it makes a long abode, and produces, in my opinion, the only true pleasures of corporal life; all other pleasures sleep in comparison. Towards the end, like a vapour that still mounts upwards, as it exhales, it arrives at the throat, where it makes its last stop. I cannot nevertheless understand how men come to extend the pleasure of drinking beyond thirst, and to forge in the imagination an appetite artificial and against nature. My stomach would not proceed so far; it has enough to do with what it takes for necessity. My constitution is not to care to drink, but as it follows eating, and to wash down my meat, and for that reason my last draught is always the greatest. And as in old age we have our palates furred with phlegms, or depraved by some other ill constitution, the wine does not taste so well till the pores are washed and laid open; at least, I seldom relish the first glass much. Anacharsis[1] wondered that the Greeks drank in greater glasses toward the end of a meal than at the beginning; which was, I suppose, for the same reason. The Germans do the same, who then begin the battle.

Plato[2] forbids children to drink wine till eighteen years of age, or to get drunk till forty; but after forty The use of wine gives them leave to please themselves, and to denied to children, mix somewhat liberally in their feasts the influ- grown men. ence of Dionysius,[3] that good deity, who restores young men

---

[1] Laertius, *in Vitâ*.   [2] *Laws*, ii.   [3] One of the names of Bacchus

their good humour, and old men their youth, who mollifies
the passions of the soul, as iron is softened by fire; and in
his laws allows such merry meetings, provided they have a
discreet chief to govern and keep them in order, as good and
useful; drunkenness being, says he, a true and certain trial
of every one's nature, and withal fit to inspire old men with
mettle to divert themselves in dancing and music; things of
great use, but which they dare not attempt when sober. He
moreover says that wine is able to supply the soul with temperance and the body with health. Neverthe-

Restrictions re-
quired in the use
of wine.
less these restrictions, in part borrowed from
the Carthaginians, please him; that they use it
sparingly in expeditions of war;[1] that every judge and
magistrate abstain from it when engaged in the duties of his
post or in the consultation on the public affairs;[2] that such
part of the day is not to be embezzled with it, as is due to
other employments; nor that night in which a man intends
to get a child.

'Tis said that the philosopher Stilpo, when oppressed with

Pure wine an
enemy to old age.
age, purposely hastened his end, by drinking
pure wine.[3] The same thing, but not of his
own design, dispatched also the philosopher Arcesilaus,[4] weakened by years.

But 'tis an old and pleasant question, whether the soul of
a man can be overcome by the strength of wine?

Si munitæ adhibet vim sapientiæ?[5]

"And each grave thought for frolic airs resign?"

The most regular
souls liable to be
disordered by
various accidents.
To what vanity does the good opinion we
have of ourselves push us! The most regular and most perfect soul in the world has but

---

[1] This construction of "using sparingly" does not convey Plato's meaning.
What he says is, "that he approves the
Carthaginian law, which orders that no
sort of wine be drunk in the camp, nor
any thing but water." *Laws*, towards
the end.

[2] Or, as it is said, more properly, in

Plato, during the year of their magistracy.

[3] Laertius, *in Vitâ.*

[4] Id. *in Vitâ.*

[5] Hor. *Od.* iii. 28, 4. Montaigne, however, has given rather a parody on the
text than a quotation. The original
stands,

Munitæque adhibe vim sapientiæ.

too much to do to keep itself upright, from being overthrown by its own weakness. There is not one of a thousand that is right and settled so much as one minute in his
life; and it may very well be doubted whether, according to
her natural condition, it can ever be otherwise. But to join
consistency to it is her utmost perfection; I mean though
nothing should jostle and discompose her, which a thousand
accidents may do. 'Tis to much purpose, indeed, that the
great poet Lucretius keeps such a clutter with his philosophy,
when behold he is ruined with a love-draught. Is it to be
imagined that an apoplexy will not knock down Socrates as
well as a porter? Some have forgotten their own names by
the violence of a disease, and a slight wound has turned the
judgment of others topsy-turvy. Let a man be as wise as he
will, he is still a man; and than that, what is there more
frail, more a mere nothing? Wisdom does not force our
natural dispositions :—

> Sudores itaque et pallorem existere toto
> Corpore, et infringi linguam, vocemque aboriri,
> Caligare oculos, sonere aures, succidere artus,
> Denique concidere, ex animi terrore, videmus: [1]

> " Paleness and sweat the countenance confounds,
> The tongue's delivered of abortive sounds;
> The eyes grow dim, ears deaf, the knees grow lame,
> And do refuse to prop the trembling frame;
> And lastly, out of fear of mind, we all
> Things see into a dissolution fall: "

he must shut his eyes against the blow that threatens him;
he must tremble upon the brink of a precipice, like a child;
nature having reserved these light works of her authority,
not to be forced by our reason and stoical virtue, to teach
man his mortality and little power. He turns pale with fear,
red with shame, and groans with the cholic, if not very loud
and despairingly, at least with a hoarse and broken voice :—

> Humani a se nihil alienum putet.[2]

> " Let him not think he's free from human ties."

---

[1] Lucret. iii. 155.
[2] Terence, *Heautont.* i. 1, 25. Mon- taigne has altered the text, to adapt it to his sentence.

The poets, that feign all things at pleasure, dare not acquit their greatest heroes of tears :—

> Sic fatur lacrymans, classique immittit habenas.[1]
> " He said, and wept, then spread his sails."

'Tis sufficient for a man to curb and moderate his inclinations; for totally to suppress them is not in him to do. Even our Plutarch, that excellent and perfect judge of human actions, when he sees Brutus and Torquatus kill their own children, begins to doubt whether virtue could proceed so far, and to question whether these persons had not rather been stimulated by some other passion.[2] All actions exceeding the ordinary bounds are liable to sinister interpretation; forasmuch as our taste does no more affect what is above than what is below it.

Let us leave that other sect, which makes an express profession of haughty superiority;[3] but when, even in that sect,[4] reputed the most quiet and gentle, we hear these rhodomontades of Metrodorus: *Occupavi te, Fortuna, atque cepi; omnesque aditus tuos interclusi, ut ad me adspirare non posses;*[5] " Fortune, I have forestalled thee, and so fast shut up all the avenues thou canst not come at me;" when Anaxarchus, by the command of Nicocreon, tyrant of Cyprus, was put into a stone mortar and pounded with iron mallets, ceases not to say, " Strike, batter, 'tis not Anaxarchus, 'tis but his sheath that you pound;[6] when we hear our martyrs cry out to the tyrant in the middle of the flame, " This side is roasted, fall to and eat; it is enough done, begin to cook the other;"[7] when we hear the child in Josephus, torn piecemeal with biting pincers, defying Antiochus, and crying out with a firm and assured voice, " Tyrant, thou losest thy labour, I am still at ease; where is the pain, where are the torments with which thou didst so threaten me? Is this all thou canst do?

---

[1] *Æneid,* vi. 1.
[2] Plut. *Life of Publicola.*
[3] That of the Stoics, or of Zeno, its founder.
[4] That of Epicurus.
[5] Cicero, *Tusc. Quæs.* v. 9.
[6] Diog. Laert. *in Vitâ.*
[7] This is what Prudentius makes St. Laurence say, in his book entitled περὶ στεφάνων, concerning crowns. *Hymn* ii ver. 401, &c.

My constancy torments thee more than thy cruelty does me. O pitiful coward! thou faintest, and I grow stronger; make me complain, make me bend, make me yield, if thou canst; encourage thy satellites, cheer up thy executioners; see, see, they faint and can do no more; arm them, flesh them anew, spur them up;"[1] really a man must confess that there is some excitement and fury, how holy soever, that does at that time possess those souls. When we come to these stoical sallies, "I had rather be furious than voluptuous," Μανείην μᾶλλον, ἢ ἡσθείην, a saying of Antisthenes; when Sextius tells us, "He had rather be fettered with affliction than pleasure;" when Epicurus takes upon him to play with his gout, and, refusing health and ease, with gayety of heart defies torment, and despising the lesser pains, as disdaining to contend with them, covets and calls out for sharper, more violent, and more worthy of him;[2]

> Spumantemque dari, pecora inter inertia, votis
> Optat aprum, aut fulvum descendere monte leonem;[3]

> "Impatiently he views the feeble prey,
> Wishing some nobler beast to cross his way,
> And rather would the tusky boar attend,
> Or see the tawny lion downward bend;"

who can but conclude that these are sallies of a courage that has broken loose from its place? Our soul cannot from her own seat reach so high; 'tis necessary she must leave it, raise herself up, and, taking her bridle in her teeth, transport her man so far that he shall afterwards himself be astonished at what he has done. As in war the heat of battle sometimes pushes the gallant soldiers to perform things of so infinite danger as, after having recollected themselves, they themselves are the first to wonder at; as poets, too, are often struck with admiration of their own writings, and know not the track through which they made so fine a career; this is in them called ardour, fury. Plato says—"'Tis to no pur-

---

[1] *De Maccab.* c. 8.   [3] *Æneid,* iv. 158.
[2] Seneca, 66 and 92.

pose for a sober man to knock at the door of the Muses;"[1] and Aristotle says—"That no excellent soul is exempt from a mixture of folly;"[2] and he has reason to call all transports, how commendable soever, folly, when they surpass our own judgment and understanding; because wisdom is a regular government of the soul, which is carried on with measure and proportion, and for which she is answerable to herself. Plato argues thus, "That the faculty of prophecy is above us; that we must be out of ourselves when we meddle with it, and our prudence must either be obstructed by sleep, or sickness, or lifted from her place by some celestial rapture.[8]

[1] Seneca, *de Tranquillitate Animi,* c. 15.
[2] *Problem,* sec. 30. Cicero, *Tusc. Quæs.* i. 33. Seneca, *ut supra.*
[8] In the *Timæus.*